D0389395

Susan

THE WHEEL

Howatch

OF FORTUNE

Volume 1

SIMON AND SCHUSTER • NEW YORK

Copyright © 1984 by Leaftree Limited
All rights reserved
including the right of reproduction
in whole or in part in any form
Published by Simon and Schuster
A Division of Simon & Schuster, Inc.
Simon & Schuster Building
Rockefeller Center
1230 Avenue of the Americas
New York, New York 10020
SIMON AND SCHUSTER and colophon are registered trademarks
of Simon & Schuster, Inc.

Manufactured in the United States of America

The author is grateful for permission to reprint lyrics from "Walk Right Back" by Sonny
Curtis, copyright © 1960 by Warner-Tamerlane Publishing Corp. All rights reserved.

In memory of my uncle, Jack Watney, 1916–1983

Contents

PART ONE

ROBERT

1913

I know the many disguises of that monster, Fortune, and the extent to which she seduces with friendship the very people she is striving to cheat, until she overwhelms them with unbearable grief at the suddenness of her desertion. . . .
—Boethius
The Consolation of Philosophy

1

I

How SEDUCTIVE are the memories of one's youth! My cousin Ginevra once said she would never forget dancing with me beneath the chandeliers at Oxmoon while the orchestra played "The Blue Danube." Women are such incurable romantics. I was a romantic myself once but I recovered. A rational disposition must necessarily preclude a romantic outlook on life, and only the failures of this world can afford to dispense with a rational disposition.

No one could have called me a failure. I have always recoiled from the second-rate; whenever I compete I have to come first, and every time I come first I take another step away from that disaster I can never forget, that catastrophe which followed my dance with Ginevra, my own Ginette, beneath the chandeliers at Oxmoon while the orchestra played "The Blue Danube."

However as a rational man I could hardly mourn an adolescent tragedy like a lovesick swain sighing for some lost Arcadia. I admit I still had my maudlin moments, but they seldom survived sunrise, breakfast and the leading article in *The Times*. Recovering from an ill-starred romance is, after all, to anyone of sufficient willpower and self-respect, purely an attitude of mind.

I reminded myself of this proven fact when I opened *The Times* on that May morning in 1913, perused the leading article on the Marconi scandal and then found I could not remember a word I had read. To skim uncomprehendingly through an article on financial machinations is pardonable; nothing can be more boring than high finance at its most convoluted. But to skim uncomprehendingly through an article on the idiotic financial machinations of Isaacs and Lloyd George suggested an absence of mind amounting almost to derangement. I was involved in politics, particularly in Liberal politics. I greatly admired Asquith, the Prime Minister, but Lloyd George, his Chancellor of the Exchequer, was the Welshman in whom I felt a special interest. To find my attention now wandering from the latest headlines in his history was disturbing in the extreme, and after making a mental note to find a new mistress without delay I applied myself to reading the article again. A prolonged abstinence from carnal satisfaction—never a desirable state of affairs—had evidently resulted in a depression which was affecting my powers of concentration, and remedial measures had to be taken without delay.

At this point my man Bennett glided into the room with the morning's post. I sighed with relief. Now I could postpone asking myself why I had lost interest in carnal matters; now I could avoid examining the shining surface of my well-ordered private life for blemishes which logic dictated could not and should not exist. With alacrity I cast aside *The Times*, picked up the paper knife and slit open the envelopes which lay waiting to divert me.

I divided the contents into four piles; invitations, personal notes, bills and rubbish; all business correspondence was delivered to my chambers downstairs. The invitations were wearisome but most of them would have to be accepted. A rising young barrister with unlimited ambition must seize every opportunity to meet the people who matter, but how much more entertaining life would be if the people who mattered had more to recommend them! However, boredom on social occasions is an inescapable hazard for the overeducated, and for the overambitious it must be endured with what my mother would no doubt have called Christian resignation.

So much for the invitations. The personal letters included a typically dreary offering from my mother herself—my mother was a good woman but with a provincial cast of mind—an obsequious scrawl from one of my numerous tiresome siblings, but still nothing from my father. That was a pity but evidently he was too busy to escape to London for one of his "little sprees." The remainder of my correspondence, I saw as I unfolded writing paper of varying degrees of opulence, consisted of *billets-doux*. If I had been vain I would have found such attentions flattering but I knew well enough that these society women saw me only as a myth in my barrister's wig and gown. No woman had ever seen me as I really was, no woman except my cousin Ginevra long ago in that lost paradise we had shared at Oxmoon.

So much for the personal letters. I turned to the bills and found them unpleasant but not unreasonable. I was not given to wild extravagances which I considered to be the mark of an inferior intellect. I neither gambled nor showered overpriced gems on music-hall girls. Even when I was not living like a monk I never kept a mistress; my mistresses were kept, usually in great style, by their complaisant husbands. Soon, I knew, I would have to marry in order to further the political career I intended to have, but since I naturally intended to marry money my bank account would hardly suffer when I made the required trip to the altar. I intended to marry into the aristocracy too, but not the impoverished aristocracy, no matter how charming its feminine representatives might be. Man cannot live on charm alone, and an ambitious man cannot live on anything less than wealth, good social connections and substantial political influence. One must be rational about such matters, and being rational need not mean being cold. I had every intention of being fond of my future wife, whoever she might be, and I had every confidence that we would do tolerably well together. Marrying for love might be romantic but I considered it the hallmark of an undisciplined private life. Romance is the opiate of the dissatisfied; it anesthetizes them from the pain of their disordered second-rate lives. I was neither disordered nor second-rate and so I had no need of opiates, just as I no longer had any need of my cousin Ginevra, my own Ginette, now fifteen years married and still living happily ever after in New York.

So much for the bills. Turning to the rubbish I discovered not only circulars and begging letters but also passionate outpourings from disturbed females who apparently thought I wanted to wreck my future political career by making a speech in favor of women's suffrage. I consigned all these effusions to the wastepaper basket, filed the invitations, bills and personal letters in the appropriate pigeonholes of my desk and took a deep breath. My day was about to begin. My life was in perfect order. I was healthy, wealthy and supremely successful and if I were not happy I was a fool.

I was not a fool, therefore I had to be happy.

I *was* happy. Life was exciting, glittering, a perpetually coruscating challenge. First I had to go downstairs to consult my clerk, talk to my fellow attorneys, glance through the new briefs that had arrived. Then I would take a cab to the Old Bailey where I was in the midst of defending a most charming woman who had promised me tearfully that it had been sheer coincidence that she had bought arsenic three days before her husband had died such an unpleasant death; I could not believe this but the jury would—by the time I had finished with them. Later I would dine out. The McKennas were giving a political dinner party and I had heard Lloyd George was to be present; my young hostess Pamela would make much of me and to repay her I would be debonair and charming, stifling my yawns as the ladies rattled on interminably about the wedding of Princess Victoria Louise. But after the ladies had withdrawn and the port was circulating the real business of the evening would begin.

We would talk of politics; I would keep respectfully silent as Lloyd George discussed Welsh Disestablishment—but if he were to ask me for my opinion I would, of course, have a few well-chosen words prepared. Then no doubt someone would say what a bore the suffragettes were and someone else would say what a bore most women were anyway, and Lloyd George and I would look at each other, two Welshmen in the land of our masters, and wonder how English gentlemen ever summoned the effort to reproduce themselves.

Then the port would go round again and we would talk of Turkey and

Bulgaria and the Kaiser and the Dreadnoughts until propriety forced us to join the ladies in the drawing room and talk of Caruso, Melba and the rising price of pre-Raphaelite paintings. However I would escape before eleven; someone was sure to invite me to Brooks's or some other club, but I would have to retire to my chambers and burn the midnight oil in order to ensure that I won my case on the morrow. By the time I went to bed I would be exhausted, too exhausted to lie awake and think maudlin thoughts, but when I awoke at six another enthralling day would be waiting for me—for I was so lucky, always fortune's favorite, and I had everything I had ever wanted, everything but the life I longed to lead with the woman I could never have, but what did such sentimental aspirations matter when I was so happy, success personified, forever coming first and winning all the way along the line?

I told myself I could not be unhappy because it was logically impossible. But then I remembered those Greek philosophers, all eminently sane and rational, arguing with inexorable logic towards a truth which turned out to be not a truth but an absurdity. Zeno had proved everything in the world was fixed and unchanging, Heraclitus had proved everything in the world was changing continuously, and both men had provided impeccable arguments to support their points of view. But reality, as Democritus had later tried to show, had all the time lain elsewhere.

I saw a chaotic world of infinite complexity where reason was impotent, and instinctively I recoiled from it. I had long since decided that a successful life was like a well-ordered game governed, as all games were, by rules. One grew up, learned the rules, played one's chosen game and won. That was what life was all about. Any fool knew that.

But what was the nature of my chosen game? And how had I wound up in this particular game in the first place? And suppose it was the wrong game? And if it was the wrong game then what was the point of winning it? And if winning was meaningless what was my life all about? And if I had no idea what my life was all about, did this mean my life was in a mess and if my life was in a mess did this mean I was a failure? And what exactly had I failed to do and how could I repair the omission when I had no idea what I had left undone?

The telephone rang in the hall.

"I'm not in!" I shouted to Bennett as he emerged from the pantry.

The ringing ceased as Bennett addressed himself to the instrument. Presently I heard him say, "One moment, Mr. Godwin, I thought he'd left but it's possible—"

I sprang to my feet and sped to the hall.

"Papa?" I said into the mouthpiece as Bennett yielded his place to me. "Is something wrong?" There was no telephone at Oxmoon, and I thought such an unexpected communication might herald news of a family disaster, but I was worrying unnecessarily. My father's letter telling me of his imminent visit to London for a "little spree" had gone astray; he had arrived late on the previous evening at his club, and finding no note from me awaiting him there he was now telephoning to ask when we could meet.

"—and I've got the most extraordinary news, Robert—"

For one aghast moment I wondered if my mother was pregnant. My parents had an obsession with reproducing themselves and were the only couple I knew who had celebrated their silver wedding anniversary with such undisciplined zest that an infant had arrived nine months later to mark the occasion.

"—and I wonder if I should tell you over the telephone or whether I should wait till I see you—"

"My God, it's not Mama, is it?"

"What? Oh no, she's fine, in capital form, sent you her love and so on—"

"Then what is it? What's happened?"

"Well, it's about Ginevra. She—hullo? Robert?"

"Yes, I'm still here. Go on."

"What?"

"What's the news about Ginette?"

"Well, there's no need to shout, Robert! I may be on the wrong side of fifty now but I'm not deaf!"

"God Almighty, I swear I shall go mad in a moment. My dear Papa, could you kindly tell me with as much speed as possible—"

"It's Ginevra's husband. He's dead, Robert. She's coming home."

II

In my dreams I always said to her, "Take me back to Oxmoon, the Oxmoon of our childhood. Take me back to Oxmoon and make it live again."

How seductive indeed were the memories of my youth, and the older I grew the more alluring they became to me until they assumed the gilded quality of myth. If romance is the opiate of the dissatisfied, then surely nostalgia is the opiate of the disillusioned, for those who see all their dreams come true and find themselves living in a nightmare. The present may be ungovernable, crammed with questions that have no answers, and the future may be unimaginable, obscured by doubt and bewilderment, but the past thrives with increasing clarity, not dead at all but running parallel to the present and often seeming, in my memory, more real than the reality of my daily life in 1913.

At the beginning of my life there were my parents, who were hardly more than children themselves, and at Oxmoon with my parents was this grubby little girl who talked to me, pinched me, played with me, slapped me, helped me to walk and generally made herself useful. She was somewhat stout and vain as a peacock; she was always standing on tiptoe to examine her ringlets in the looking glass. For the first few years of my life I found her full name impossible to pronounce, but she was gracious and permitted me to use an abbreviation, a favor that was never granted to anyone else.

I seem always to have known she was not my sister. "You're not my sister, are you?" I said to her once, just to make sure, and she exclaimed, "Heavens, no—what an idea!" and was most offended. She knew I disliked sisters. Later she explained to me, "I'm Bobby's cousin," although when I asked her how that could be possible when my father was so much older than she was, she snapped, "Ask no questions and you'll be told no lies," which meant she had no idea.

I thought that if this story was true she should call my father "Cousin Bobby" but in truth my father, still resurrecting his bankrupt estate from the grave, hardly had the time to concern himself with a minor detail of family etiquette. Later when my mother had recovered from the nightmare of her first years at Oxmoon she became more strict about what she called "doing the done thing," but even then Ginette usually forgot to address her guardian as "Cousin" so the exact nature of the relationship between us was never stressed.

Eventually I discovered that her father and my grandfather had been half-brothers; her father, the child of a second marriage, had been the younger by twenty years, a circumstance that meant he belonged more to the generation of his nephew, my father, than to the generation of his half-brother, my grandfather. He had spent his early childhood at Oxmoon and in later life long after he had removed to the English Midlands, he and my father had remained good friends. My father had even borrowed money from him when the reconstruction of the Oxmoon estate was begun, so presumably the ties of affection which united them had remained strong; that those ties survived unimpaired despite the borrowing of money was demonstrated when my great-uncle drew up a will in which he named my father the guardian of the infant Ginevra. Within a month he had died of typhoid, and his young widow, who must have been a tiresome creature, went into a decline and eventually managed to starve herself to death on the nearest picturesque chaise longue.

I was nine months old when Ginette came to live with us, and Oxmoon was barely habitable at the time. My parents pretended to occupy the entire house but in fact lived in three rooms on the ground floor. However despite my parents' straitened circumstances it never crossed their minds that they might make some other provision for Ginette and they always treated her as if she were their daughter. No doubt my father's affection for her father made any other course of action unthinkable to him, while my mother too would have felt bound by an absolute moral duty.

"Poor little me!" said Ginette later when she reflected on her predicament. "But never mind, all the best heroines are beautiful orphans, abandoned to their fate, and the one thing that's certain about my situation is that I'm going to be a heroine when I grow up."

"Can I be a hero?"

"Well, I suppose you can try. But you'll have to try very hard."

I can remember that moment clearly. My parents had by that time reoccupied the whole house, but we had left the nurseries to escape from the smell of boiled milk and wet nappies and were heading for the kitchen garden to rifle the strawberry beds. Ginette wore a white pinafore with an egg stain on it, and there were holes in both her stockings. She must have been about eight years old.

"I don't think you're at all likely to be a heroine," I said, aggrieved by her pessimism on the subject of my heroic potential.

"Why, what impertinence! Here I am, being constantly noble by devoting all my time to you even though you're two years younger and a boy and do nothing but drive me wild! The truth is that if I wasn't a heroine I wouldn't do it. I think I'm wonderful."

We gorged ourselves on the strawberries in silence, but eventually I said, "Heroes have to marry heroines, don't they."

"Of course. But actually I don't believe I'll marry anyone. Think of all the nasty smelly babies one would have to have!"

We shuddered.

"Friendship's best," I said, "and friendship's forever because no baby can come along to spoil it." And when I grabbed her hand she laughed and we ran off down the path together to our secret camp in the woods.

We had decided while my sister Celia was an infant that babies were undesirable. Unfortunately in our family a new baby arrived every eighteen months but to our relief they all, apart from Celia, failed to survive. Charlotte lived a year but succumbed to measles. William breathed his last within a week of his birth and Pamela faded away at the age of six months. Only Celia flourished like a weed, whining around our ankles and trying to follow us everywhere, but I took no notice of her. I was the male firstborn and I came first. That was a fact of nursery life, as immutable as a law of nature.

"First is best, isn't it?" I said to my father as we walked hand in hand through the woods past the ruined Norman tower, and he smiled as he answered, "Sometimes!"—which, as I knew very well at the age of eight, meant "Yes, always."

"First is best, isn't it?" I said to my mother in the housekeeper's room after my eighth birthday when she decided to increase my pocket money by a ha'penny a week. In the affable atmosphere generated by this gesture I had decided the time was ripe to seek reaffirmation of my privileged status.

"What, dear?"

"I said first is best, isn't it?"

"Well, that depends," said my mother. "I was the second in my family and I always thought *I* was the best—but then my father spoiled me abominably and gave me ideas quite above my station. In fact I think that for a time I was a very horrid little girl indeed."

That was when I first realized the most disconcerting difference between my parents: my father told me what I wanted to hear and my mother told me what she felt I ought to hear. Resentment simmered. I sulked. When Lion was born a month later I knew straight away that I was outraged.

I waited for him to die but soon I realized that this was not the kind of baby who would oblige me by fading away into the churchyard at Penhale. I tried to ignore him but found he was not the kind of baby, like Celia, who could be ignored. He was huge and imperious. He roared for everyone's attention and got it. My mother began in my opinion to behave very foolishly indeed. I felt more outraged than ever.

"Robert dearest," said my mother after overhearing my declaration to Olwen the nursemaid that I had no intention of attending the christening, "I think it's time you and I had a little talk together."

My mother was famous for her "little talks." Her little talks with servants were conducted in the housekeeper's room and her little talks with children were conducted upstairs in the large bedroom that belonged by tradition to the master and mistress of the house. My mother had a table there where she did her sewing, but when she had an arduous interview to conduct she always sat at her dressing table and pretended to busy herself with rearranging the pots, jars and boxes lined up below the triple looking glass. My mother seldom glanced directly at her victims while she spoke, but watched them constantly in the cunningly angled reflections.

"Now, Robert dearest," she said, emptying a jar of pins and beginning to stick them with mathematical precision into a new pincushion, "I know quite well you think of yourself as a little prince in a fairy tale, but because I love you and want the best for you"—a quick glance in the mirror—"I think it's time someone told you a few home truths. The first truth is that you're not a prince, and the second truth," said my mother, turning to look at me directly, "is that this is no fairy tale, Robert."

She paused to let me digest this. I contented myself with assuming my most mutinous expression but I took care to remain silent.

"I thought life was a fairy tale once," said my mother, resuming her transformation of the pincushion. "I thought that until I was sixteen and came to Oxmoon—and then, when I found myself face to face with what really went on in the world, I felt angry with my parents for failing to prepare me for it.

However," said my mother, glancing into the far mirror, "now is hardly the time for me to talk to you about the ordeal your father and I endured at the hands of his mother and Mr. Bryn-Davies. You're too young. Suffice it to say that the world is a very wicked place and that one has to be very resolute to lead a decent orderly life—and you do want to lead a decent orderly life, don't you, Robert? People who have no self-discipline, who are perpetual slaves to all their weaknesses, are inevitably very unhappy indeed. In fact I would go so far as to say," said my mother, pinning away busily, "that tragedy inevitably lies waiting for Those Who Fail to Draw the Line."

"Yes, Mama." It took a great deal to cow me but I was cowed—not by this familiar reference to drawing the moral line but by the mention of the Great Unmentionable, my grandmother and Mr. Bryn-Davies. Even though I was only eight years old I knew that Oxmoon had not always been a pastoral paradise where little children wandered happily around the kitchen garden and feasted at the strawberry beds.

"So we must always reject morally unacceptable behavior," said my mother, tipping the rest of the pins from the jar and aligning them between two scent bottles, "and one kind of behavior that is morally unacceptable, Robert, is jealousy. Jealousy is a very wicked emotion. It destroys people. And I won't have it, not in this house—because *here I have my standards,*" said my mother, facing me again, *"and here I Draw the Line."*

I opened my mouth to say, "I'm not jealous!" but no words came out. I stared down at my shoes.

"There, there!" said my mother kindly, seeing I had fully absorbed her homily. "I know you're a good intelligent boy and I now have every confidence that you'll behave well towards Lionel—and towards Celia—in the future."

I retired in a rage. When I found my father I said, "Mama's been very rude to me, and if you please, sir, I'd be obliged if you'd tell her not to be so horrid in future." But my father said abruptly, "I won't hear one word against your mother. Pull yourself together and stop behaving like a spoiled child."

I ran away and hid in a basket in the wet laundry. I realized that my father, who normally never said a cross word to me, had been suborned into sternness by my mother, while my mother, normally affectionate enough, had been rendered hostile by her irrational desire to place the infant on an equal footing with me. I felt I was being subjected to a monstrous injustice. Vengeance should be mine; I decided to repay.

Leaving the wet laundry, I prowled around the house to the terrace and found two of the estate laborers installing a new pane of glass in the dining-room window. The previous pane had been cracked when a sea gull had flown into it in an indecent haste to return to the coast which lay a mile away beyond Rhossili Downs. When the laborers had retired I remained, eying the new pane meditatively. Then I extracted a croquet ball from the summer-house, returned to the terrace and took a quick look around. No one appeared to be in sight but unfortunately the new pane was reflecting the light so that I could not see the maid who was setting the table in the room beyond. When the croquet ball crashed through the window she dropped six plates and ran screaming to my mother.

My mother went to my father and my father lost his temper. This was a great shock to me because I had not realized he had a temper to lose. Then he beat me. That was an even greater shock because he had never laid a finger on me before; he always said he had a horror of violence. Finally he summoned my mother and when he told her it was high time I was sent away to school, my mother agreed with him.

I cried. I said they wanted to get rid of me so that Lion could be first and best. I told them they were making a very big mistake and that they would both live to regret it.

"What rubbish!" said my father, still in a towering rage, but my mother, whom I had thought so implacable, knelt beside me and said, "There, there! You always knew you'd be going off to Briarwood when you were eight—you can't pretend now that you're being sent away to make room for Lion!"

But I recoiled from her. She was responsible for Lion and Lion was responsible for my humiliation. I turned to my father, and then miraculously the violent stranger vanished as he swung me off my feet into his arms. All he said was, "Don't you worry about Lion," and that was when I knew first was still best in his eyes despite all my iniquity; that was when I knew nothing mattered except coming first and staying first, over and over again.

"I'll be the best pupil Briarwood's ever had," I said to him, "and you'll be prouder of me than you could ever be of anyone else"—and thus I was committed to the compulsive pursuit of excellence and set squarely on the road to disaster.

III

"It's Ginevra's husband. He's dead, Robert. She's coming home," said my father twenty-three years later, and my immediate reaction was This time I shall come first. This time I'm going to win.

"What an amazing piece of information! Well, I daresay it'll be rather amusing to see the old girl again." I was almost unconscious with emotion. I had to lean against the wall to ensure that I remained upright. "When does she arrive?"

"I don't know. I'll show you her wire when we meet tonight. . . ." My father went on talking but I barely heard him. I was only just aware that I was arranging to meet him at the Savile after my dinner party. When the conversation ended silence descended on the hall, but in my memory I could hear the orchestra playing in the ballroom at Oxmoon and see the candles shimmering on the chandeliers.

I thought of my mother saying long ago, "This is no fairy tale, Robert." But who was to say now that my own private fairy tale could never come true? If I got what I wanted—and I usually did—then I would go home at last to Oxmoon, the Oxmoon of my childhood, and Ginette would share my life once more in that lost paradise of my dreams.

The prospect stimulated such a powerful wave of euphoria that I almost wondered if I should become a romantic again, but fortunately my common sense intervened and I restrained myself. This was a situation that called for care, calculation and a cool head. The jilted hero who still yearned passionately for his lost love might possibly seem attractive in a French farce but it was quite definitely a role which I had no wish to play in public.

Thinking of roles reminded me of the living I had to earn, and an hour later, masked by my barrister's wig and gown, I had slipped back into my familiar role as the hero of the Old Bailey.

But all the time I was thinking of Ginette.

IV

I survived a day that would normally have reduced me to exhaustion and arrived, clear-eyed and fresh, at my father's club soon after eleven that night. The idea of a widowed Ginette was a powerful stimulant. I felt taut with nostalgia, prurient curiosity, sexual desire and impatience. It was a lethal mixture, and as I drifted through the rooms in search of my father I half-feared that I might be vibrating with excitement like some wayward electrical device, but fortunately all my acquaintances who accosted me assumed I was merely excited by the result of the trial.

When I finally reached the corner where my father was waiting I found he had Lion with him. I assumed a benign expression and prayed for tolerance.

"I hear you won your case, Robert!" my father was saying with enthusiasm. "Very many congratulations!"

"Thank you. Hullo, Lion."

"Hullo, Robert—I can't tell you how proud I am to be related to you! Why, I'm famous at the bank just because I'm your brother!" He sighed with childlike admiration, a huge brainless good-natured youth towards whom I occasionally contrived to feel a mild affection. It seemed preposterous to think that I could ever have wasted energy being jealous of him. Graciously I held out my hand so that he could shake it.

"Well, Lion," said my father mildly when further banalities had been exchanged, "I won't detain you—as you tell me you have such trouble getting to work on time in the mornings I'm sure you'll want to be in bed before midnight."

But Lion wanted to hear more about the trial and ten minutes passed before he consented to being dispatched.

"Stunning news about Ginevra, isn't it!" he remembered to add over his shoulder as he ambled off. "Won't it be wonderful to see her again!"

I smiled politely and refrained from comment, but seconds later I was saying to my father in the most casual voice I could muster, "Let's see this wire she sent."

The missive was almost criminally verbose. I have come to believe women should be banned from sending cables; they are constitutionally incapable of being succinct in a situation that demands austerity.

DARLINGS, gushed this deplorable communication, SOMETHING TOO DREADFUL HAS HAPPENED I HARDLY KNOW HOW TO PUT IT INTO WORDS BUT CONOR IS DEAD I STILL CAN'T BELIEVE IT ALTHOUGH I SAW IT HAPPEN HE MUST BE BURIED IN IRELAND SO I AM TAKING HIM THERE AT ONCE I CAN'T STAY HERE ANYWAY IT'S NOT POSSIBLE I'LL WRITE FROM DUBLIN ALL I WANT IS TO COME HOME TO OXMOON LONGING TO SEE YOU ALL DEEPEST LOVE GINEVRA.

"Typical," I said. "She squanders a fortune on a wire but still manages to omit all the relevant details of her predicament. She seems to assume we'll know by telepathic intuition when she plans to arrive in Wales."

"My dear Robert, don't be so severe! The poor girl's obviously distraught!"

"To be distracted is pardonable. To be incoherent is simply unobliging. However I suppose in due course we'll get a letter. What was Mama's response to the news?"

"Well, naturally," said my father, "her first thought—and mine—was for you."

I took a sip from my glass of brandy before saying in what I hoped was my most charming voice, "I assume my mother sent you to London to find out exactly what was going on in my mind. Perhaps when you return you could be so kind as to remind her that I'm thirty-one years old and I take a poor view of my mother trespassing on my privacy."

My father stiffened. I immediately regretted what I had said but he gave me no chance to retract those words spoken in self-defense. With a courtesy that put me to shame, he said, "I'm sorry you should find our concern for you offensive, Robert. I'm sure neither of us would wish to pry into your private life."

"Forgive me—I expressed myself badly—I've had such an exhausting day—"

"Bearing the past in mind we can't help but be concerned. And of course, as you must know, we've been increasingly anxious about you for some time."

"My dear Papa, just because I'm taking my time about marrying and settling down—"

"I wasn't criticizing you, Robert. I wish you wouldn't be so ready to take offense."

"I'm not taking offense! But the thought of you and Mama worrying about me when I'm having this dazzling career and enjoying life to the full is somehow more than I can tolerate with equanimity!"

"Your mother and I both feel that if only you could come back to Oxmoon—"

"Please—I know this is a painful subject—"

"It's as if you've got lost. Sometimes I think it don't do for a man to be too educated—or too successful. It cuts him off from his roots."

"I'm not cut off. Oxmoon's my home and always will be, but for the moment I must be in London. I have my living to earn at the bar and soon I'll have a political career to pursue—and it was you, don't forget, who wanted me to go into politics!"

"I just wanted you to be the local M.P. More fool me. I should have listened to Margaret when she said you'd never be satisfied until you'd wound up as Prime Minister."

"What's wrong with being Prime Minister?"

"Success on that scale don't make for happiness. Look at Asquith. Why does he drink? I wouldn't want you to end up a drunkard like that."

"Asquith's not a drunkard. He's a heavy drinker. There's a difference."

"Not to me," said my father, looking at his untouched glass of brandy, "and not to your mother either."

We were silent. There was nothing I could say. My father was the son of a drunkard and had endured a horrifying childhood about which he could never bring himself to speak. No rational debate on drink was possible for him.

At last I said neutrally, "We seem to have wandered rather far from the subject of Ginette."

"No, it's all one, we're still discussing your obsessions. Robert," said my father urgently, leaning forward in his chair, "you mustn't think that I don't understand what it is to be haunted by the past, but you must fight to overcome it, just as I've fought to overcome the memory of my parents and Owain Bryn-Davies—"

"Quite, but aren't we wandering from the point again? Let me try and end this Welsh circumlocution by exhibiting a little Anglo-Saxon bluntness! You and Mama, it seems, are worried in case I now resurrect my adolescent passion for Ginette and embark on some romantic course which you can only regard as disastrous. Very well. Then let me set your mind at rest by assuring you that I'm not planning to conquer Ginette as soon as she sets foot again on Welsh soil."

"And afterwards?"

"Papa, I'm not a prophet, I'm a lawyer. I don't waste time speculating about the future on the basis of insufficient evidence."

"Of course not, but—"

"The one inescapable fact here is that Ginette is now a stranger to me. Who knows what I shall think of her when we meet again? Nobody knows, it's unknowable, and so in my opinion any attempt to answer such a question can only be futile."

"That's true. But all the same—"

"Go home and tell Mama," I said, "that I no longer believe in fairy tales—and tell her too," I concluded strongly, "that despite the somewhat dramatic nature of these circumstances I have every intention of behaving like a mature and intelligent man."

Yet all the while I was speaking in this commendably sensible manner I was listening to the voice in my mind whispering to Ginette as it had whispered so often in my dreams: "Take me back to Oxmoon, the Oxmoon of our childhood. Take me back to Oxmoon and make it live again."

V

"Friendship's forever!" said the child Ginette in that lost paradise of Oxmoon when I had no rival for her affections. "I wonder if you can possibly realize how lucky you are to have a friend like me?"

I did realize. During my first term at school I had spent many a homesick night imagining her playing with Gwen de Bracy or Angela Stourham and forgetting my existence. When one is eight and has a friend of ten one is perpetually worrying for fear one may be dismissed in favor of more sophisticated contemporaries.

"No matter how long I'm away at school I'll always come first with you, won't I?" I said, anxious to quash any lingering insecurity generated by my absence.

"Always. Here, lend me a penny, would you? I want to buy some of those boiled sweets."

We were in the village of Penhale, two miles from Oxmoon, and enjoying one of our regular excursions to the village shop. I remember thinking as I stood in the dark cozy interior and gazed at the tall jars of sweets that perfect happiness consisted of returning home from school and finding everything unchanged, Ginette still with the holes in her stockings and the stains on her pinafore, the jars in the village shop still waiting to gratify our greed.

"I wish it could be like this forever," I said as we walked home munching our purchases.

"I don't. I'm becoming partial to the idea of growing up and getting married, like Bobby and Margaret. They're always laughing and behaving as if marriage was rather a lark."

"But think of all the babies!"

"Maybe they'd be rather a lark too."

I was silent. My dislike of infants had remained unchanged, although I now took care to conceal this from my parents. I was aloof but polite to Celia. I feigned an Olympian interest in Lion. But I was still quite unable to imagine myself responding to a sibling with genuine enthusiasm.

Then, two years after Lion was born, John arrived in the world.

Lion was livid. That automatically pleased me, and from the beginning I patted John's head when I made my regular visits to the nursery to inspect him. This delighted my mother but Lion was enraged and tried to block my path to the cradle by flailing his little fists at my knees. My mother became cross with him. Their discord was most gratifying.

Finally, much to my surprise, I realized I was becoming genuinely interested in the infant. He was acute. He talked at an early age, a fact that made communication less of an effort. Although we lived in an English-speaking area of Wales Welsh was my father's first language, and because he wanted his children to grow up bilingual my mother had followed a policy of employing Welsh-speaking nursemaids. However for some reason although we all grew up with a rudimentary knowledge of Welsh colloquialisms, John was the only one who became bilingual. This impressed me. After Celia and Lion, who were both stupid, I had not anticipated the advent of an intelligent brother. Later, as an intellectual experiment, I taught him a letter or two and found him keen to learn, but before we could advance further into the world of literacy I was obliged to depart for my first term at public school and the lessons fell into abeyance. However when I returned from Harrow for the Christmas holidays, there was John, waiting for me on the doorstep, eyes shining with hero worship.

Here was someone who had realized, even at a tender age, that first was best. My private opinion of siblings underwent a small but telling revision.

"I think that child might turn out reasonably well," I remarked to Ginette as he waited on us hand and foot in the holidays.

"Isn't he a poppet? So different from ghastly Lion. Honestly, I can't think what Margaret sees in that monster. If ever I give birth to something so plain and stupid, I hope I'd have the sense to drown it."

She was fifteen. I was thirteen. The gap in our ages was widening but I was unaware of it. As far as I was concerned she was still my own Ginette and paradise was still coming home to Oxmoon and finding her waiting to welcome me back; paradise was still riding with her over the Downs or walking to the sea or scrambling across the tidal causeway called the Shipway where long ago Mr. Owain Bryn-Davies had drowned and my grandmother had gone mad and my father had witnessed all manner of horrors which were now enshrined in local myth; paradise was laughing over such distant melodrama and saying how droll it was that dotty old Grandmama should ever have played the role of the tragic heroine. We laughed, how we laughed, and paradise was laughing with Ginette at Oxmoon while we played croquet on the lawn and paradise was suppressing laughter in church as I tried to make her giggle at the wrong moment and paradise was laughing at her latest three-decker novel which she found so romantic and laughing as she tried to box my ears and laughing as we rode to hounds with the West Gower hunt, laughing, laughing, laughing from Llangennith to Porteynon, from Penrice to Oxwich, from Penhale to Rhossili, from Llanmodoc Hill to Cefn Bryn, and paradise was the Gower Peninsula, sixteen miles of heaven on earth stretching westwards into the sea beyond the industrial wasteland of Swansea, and the glory of Gower was Oxmoon and the glory of Oxmoon was Ginette.

It remained so clear in my mind, that paradise lost, the blue skies, the corn stubble, the lush stillness of the bluebell woods, the purple of the heather on the Downs, the brilliant sea, the shimmering sands. I remember even the golden shade of the lichen on the dry-stone walls and the streaks of pink in the rocks on the summit of Rhossili Downs and the coarseness of the grass in the sand burrows of Llangennith. I remember the cattle being driven to market along the dusty white roads and the sheep being herded across the Downs; I can hear the larks singing and the Penhale church clock celebrating a cloudless high noon. It all seemed so immutable. I thought nothing would ever change. And then in the June of 1896, shortly after I had celebrated my fourteenth birthday, my father wrote to me at Harrow.

My dear Robert, I read, *this is just a quick line to let you know we've had a spot of trouble with Ginevra. To put the matter in a nutshell, I can only tell you that she tried to elope with a cousin of the Kinsellas but he's gone away now and Ginevra's staying with the Applebys while she recovers. I'm afraid she's cross with us at the moment, but I'm sure it won't last so don't distress yourself—it was really just a little storm in a teacup and no harm's been done. I remain as always your very affectionate father,* R.G.

At first I was so stunned by this communication that I was incapable of action. I merely sat and stared at the letter. I had, of course, been aware that Ginette was growing up in various ways which were all too visible but I had long since decided it would be kindest to take no notice; I felt genuinely sorry for anyone who had to grow up into a woman. But the thought that she might now be old enough to take a carnal interest in the opposite sex had never occurred to me. I found the notion both horrifying and repellent, but far more horrifying and repellent was the knowledge that she could have cared deeply about someone other than myself. I had thought myself safe till she was eighteen and put her hair up—by which time I would be sixteen and, puberty permitting, fit to present myself as a future husband without arousing either her laughter or her incredulity. But now I was so young that I could hardly stake a claim without looking ridiculous. My voice had not finished breaking. I was too lanky. None of my clothes seemed to fit me. I had decided that surviving adolescence was purely an attitude of mind but now when I contemplated the utterly unfinished nature of my physique I was in despair. How could I ever compete with a full-grown male who displayed predatory intentions? The entire future had become a nightmare.

In agony I reread the letter in the vain hope that I had misinterpreted it, and this time the news seemed so preposterous that I seriously wondered if my father had gone mad. The theory seemed all too plausible. I remembered my grandmother, locked up in a Swansea lunatic asylum and allowed home only once a year, and the next moment before I could stop myself I was writing urgently to my mother for reassurance.

My dearest Mama, I began, determined to conceal my panic behind a civil, rational epistolary style, *I have just had the most extraordinary letter from Papa. In it he appears to state that Ginette has left Oxmoon and is staying at All-Hallows Court. Is there perhaps some misunderstanding here? Ginette thinks Sir William Appleby an old bore and Lady Appleby dry as dust, and as for that lily-livered Timothy, Ginette and I both agree that you could put him through a mangle and wring out enough water to fill a well. How can she choose to live with such people? I suspect someone is not being quite honest with me about this.*

Have you and Papa thrown her out of Oxmoon because you suspect she's lost her virtue? If so please accept my respectful assurance that you must be mistaken: she would never lose it. The heroines of those dreary novels she reads always preserve themselves most conscientiously, and Ginette is well aware that Fallen Women are inevitably doomed to a tragic fate. (Please excuse any indelicacy here and kindly attribute any unwitting coarseness to my inexperience in writing on such subjects.) Anyway, how could any cousin of the Kinsellas' be less than sixty years old? I didn't even know they had any relatives except for some bizarre Irish connection which they do their best to conceal.

Dearest Mama, please believe me: even if Ginette were partial to gross behavior, for her to lose her virtue to a man over sixty must surely be physically impossible, and for her to lose her virtue to an Irishman of any age is mentally inconceivable. Please, I beseech you, write and tell me what's really going on. Ever your affectionate and devoted son, ROBERT.

I then wrote Ginette a fevered note in which I begged her to solve the mystery at once, but it was my mother who answered by return of post; Ginette failed to reply. My mother wrote with calm fluency: *My dearest Robert, I am so sorry that you should have been so distressed. I know that was* the last thing your father desired when he wrote to you, but your father, though acting with the best will in the world, finds it hard to adopt a blunt, or one might almost say an Anglo-Saxon, approach to unpalatable facts. This is neither a fault nor a virtue but merely a racial difference which one must recognize and accept. However let me do what I can to clarify the situation.

First of all let me assure you that nothing bizarre has occurred. Alas, I fear such incidents happen only too frequently when a young girl is as beautiful as Ginevra and is heiress to a fortune of thirty thousand pounds. Second, let me quash your notion that the elopement was some extraordinary fiction. The man was, as you surmised, one of the Kinsellas' Irish connections, but you were wrong in assuming he had to be over sixty. He was twenty-four, tall, dark and handsome, but having said that I must add that he was quite definitely not a gentleman by English standards, and I have no doubt that he had only one purpose in coming to our obscure corner of Wales and paying his respects to these aging, distant but wealthy relatives of his. He had the mark of the adventurer upon him, and of course it wouldn't have taken him long, in our small community, to find out that Ginevra is an heiress.

We met him at the Mowbrays' house, but if it hadn't been there it would have been somewhere else—indeed even Lady de Bracy might have received him at Penhale Manor out of courtesy to his relatives who are so thoroughly blameless and respectable. When we met him I could see Ginevra was charmed at once, just as I could see that the young man was, as my dear papa used to say, "a wrong 'un." I said afterwards to your father: "That's one young man we don't invite to Oxmoon," and your father agreed with me.

Shortly after this meeting with young Mr. Kinsella a most unfortunate episode occurred. I had to go away—you will remember how I wrote to you recently from Staffordshire after poor Aunt May's baby died. Of course it's most unusual for me to be away as I hate leaving home, but May wrote me such a pathetic letter that I felt I would be failing in my sisterly duty if I refused to visit her for a few days. I should have taken Ginevra with me but I knew May would want no visitors other than myself and besides I thought Miss Sale would be able to supervise Ginevra without trouble. Miss Sale might have had her shortcomings as a governess, but she had always been a conscientious chaperone and I had complete confidence in her.

What can I say except that my confidence was misplaced? There were clandestine meetings on the Downs. I don't blame Ginevra entirely. Young Conor Kinsella is the kind of man who would lead even the devoutest nun astray, but of course when I came back and found out—as I inevitably did— what was going on I was very angry and so was your father. (Being greatly preoccupied with the estate he too had been all too ready to put his trust in Miss Sale's competence.)

Your father and I told Ginevra that we could not permit her to see Mr. Kinsella again, and this edict, I regret to say, led to some most unfortunate words being exchanged between the three of us. This was the night on which Ginevra slipped out of the house and rode all the way to Porteynon to the Kinsellas' house where she proceeded to throw stones against a window which she supposed to belong to her beloved. It belonged, however, to Miss Bridget. More distasteful scenes ensued. It is quite unnecessary for me to chronicle them in detail, so I shall simply say that Ginevra was left feeling so humiliated and miserable that it seemed kindest to suggest she stayed elsewhere for a while. When she received the suggestion gratefully I appealed to Maud Appleby and Ginevra's removal to All-Hallows Court was then arranged with the utmost speed.

Why should she go and live with such people, you ask with such regrettable rudeness. I shall tell you. Looking after Ginevra is going to be an increasingly arduous responsibility and I did not feel Bobby and I had the right to ask for help in any other quarter. As Sir William is her godfather, it is nothing less than his moral duty to help us surmount such a crisis.

Your father saw Mr. Kinsella in order to buy him off, but much to our surprise Mr. Kinsella refused to take a penny. We might have been impressed by this if he hadn't sworn he had never at any time behaved with any impropriety. Of course he was trying to save his skin—no doubt he thought that if he accepted money from us it would rank as a confession of guilt in the eyes of his wealthy relatives—but I fear poor Ginevra must have been quite crushed when she heard he had denied his advances to her. All we can do now is hope and pray she has learned from the experience and will be a little wiser when the next fortune hunter makes his inevitable approach.

So much for Mr. Kinsella. The gossips of Gower, needless to say, are having a fine time exercising their tongues, but believe nothing you hear which does not accord with the above account.

You were perfectly correct in your assumptions regarding Ginevra's virtue; you may be distressed that her reputation has suffered, as it inevitably has, but you may rest assured that she has not been sullied beyond redemption by this squalid but by no means catastrophic experience. (Your remarks on the subject were somewhat singular but I realize you were trying to express yourself with propriety and on the whole, considering your youth, I think you did well. In future, however, you should not allude to the carnal capacities of gentlemen in any letter you may write to a female. This is most definitely not The Done Thing.)

And now I must close this letter. I do hope I have to some extent alleviated any anxiety you may have suffered through being ill-informed, but should there be any further questions you wish to ask about this unfortunate incident, please do write to me at once so that I can set your mind at rest. Meanwhile I send all my love and in adding that I long to see you again I remain, dearest Robert, your most affectionate and devoted MAMA.

VI

I became obsessed with the name Conor Kinsella. I remember writing it down and as I stared at it I thought what a sinister name it was, so foreign, so different, so smooth yet so aggressive, the stress falling on the first syllable of each word so that the hard C and the hard K seemed doubly emphasized, twin bullets of sound followed by the soft ripple of easy consonants and vowels. The Porteynon Kinsellas, an elderly celibate trio of a brother and two sisters, were descended from an Irish pirate, sole survivor of an eighteenth-century shipwreck in Rhossili Bay, and the wild lawless Gower Peninsula of a hundred years ago had been just the place for a wild lawless Irishman to settle down and feel at home.

Remembering the past I at once saw Conor Kinsella as an Irish pirate, invading my home and capturing what was mine by right. Scraping the barrel of my unsophisticated vocabulary I thought of him as a cad and a blackguard, a rip, a rake and a rotter, but all the while I was reducing him to cardboard in this fashion I was aware that somewhere in the world was a flesh-and-blood man ten years my senior who ate and drank and slept and breathed and shaved and cursed and counted his pennies with anxiety and probably gave flowers to his mother on her birthday and perhaps even helped little old ladies over the road on his way to church.

The truth was that I knew nothing of Conor Kinsella. Yet when I finally saw him, I recognized him at once, not merely because he fitted my mother's chilling description but because I sensed he was like Ginette, and in knowing her I knew him.

I am uncertain how I knew that he was going to come back into her life. Perhaps it was because in the beginning she herself was so sure of it.

"He swore he'd come back for me," she said. "He told me he'd go to America and make some money and then he'd come back and sweep me off on horseback into the sunset and we'd get married and live happily ever after."

"I didn't know men ever talked such rot. You didn't believe him, did you?"

"Yes, I did. He meant it."

We were at All-Hallows Court, the Applebys' home, which stood three miles from Oxmoon on the parish boundary of Penhale and Llangennith. The house, which was considerably smaller than Oxmoon, was what we in South Wales call a squarsonage, meaning that it was a cross between the home of a parson and the residence of a country squire, and the unlikely name was said (erroneously no doubt) to be a corruption of "Hail Mary," the last words of a group of Catholics slaughtered during the Reformation by a faction group of Gower wreckers dead drunk on contraband brandy. The Applebys were smugglers and wreckers themselves at one time but later they became respectable and produced several vicars of Penhale; that meant they still smuggled, but they gave up wrecking. Probably, as my mother would have said, they felt they had to draw the line somewhere.

"I just don't understand," I said to Ginette. "How could you possibly have behaved in such an appalling fashion?"

She began to cry. I was aghast. I was not unaccustomed to seeing her in tears for she had always cherished the tiresome belief that weeping was a necessary adjunct of a heroine's passionate nature, but these tears were far removed from her usual histrionic displays of emotion. They filled her eyes and trickled down her cheeks in silence, and as I watched she bowed her head in despair.

"Ah Ginette, Ginette . . ." I did not know what to do. We never embraced. I was being educated in a culture that judged it very sloppy for a boy to make a spontaneous gesture of affection. In the end I merely sat down beside her on the window seat and suggested the only possible panacea. "Come home to Oxmoon."

"I can't. There was a dreadful quarrel. Didn't they tell you?"

"But they've forgiven you!"

"I haven't forgiven them. They were horrid about Conor, they said he wasn't what he seemed to be but that was the whole point: he was. He was real. But nothing else was. I'd been living in a fairy tale." She blew her nose on a grubby handkerchief before adding unsteadily, "I don't want to live in a fairy tale anymore."

"You're living in a fairy tale if you believe that villain will ever come back for you!"

"No. I'm going to marry him."

"But you can't! What about me? You can't just throw me over as if I no longer exist!"

She gazed at me helplessly. "I'm sorry, it's as if we don't even talk the same language anymore."

"But you swore I came first with you!"

"And so you did," she said. "You were there in the beginning, you were part of the magic of Oxmoon, and you'll be with me always in my memory, always to the very end of my life." She broke down again. I tried to grab her hand, as if I could lead her back to the strawberry beds, symbol of our paradise lost, but she jumped up and ran sobbing from the room.

I was alone.

VII

She did go back to Oxmoon but only for an occasional visit with Lady Appleby and the Applebys' son, Timothy, who had recently come down from Cambridge. The presence of Timothy annoyed me for I thought him a poor fish, and I became even more annoyed when Ginette, who had once described him as the lamppost the lamplighter forgot, never failed to giggle at his idiotic jokes.

"You don't care for Timothy, do you?" I said to her once on a rare occasion when we were alone together.

"Good heavens, no!" she said. "But he's very amusing, and it's nice to have an older friend who's been out and about in the world."

In the autumn she was sent to Germany to spend six months at a finishing school, but she had barely arrived home from Germany in the March of 1898 when she and Timothy announced their engagement. I was at Harrow but my father wrote, my mother wrote and this time even Ginette herself wrote to break the news. Her letter arrived first.

Darling Robert, she began. Advancing years had taught her how to be effusive, and I knew very well that the more nervous she was the more effusive she became. *Something simply too divine has happened and I'm engaged to be married!!! To Timothy!!! I'm so excited I can hardly put pen to paper but of course I had to tell you at once because after all you're so special to me and always will be,* quite *the best first-cousin-once-removed that anyone ever had, and I'm sure that when* you *marry I shall be madly jealous and gnash my teeth and long to be an absolute* CAT *to her!*

Now Robert, don't be too livid with me—a girl really does have to get married, you know, and Uncle William and Aunt Maud were having second thoughts about giving me a season because Timothy was so passionate about me and they thought it would be rather heavenly if I married him and I suppose they didn't like the idea of me meeting heaps of luscious gentlemen in London, and quite honestly I didn't care for the idea much either, I decided I'd already had more than enough of luscious gentlemen who promised to love me forever and then disappeared without trace.

Bobby and Margaret are thrilled, in fact they're both being simply wonderful, and darling Bobby says he's going to give a ball for me at Oxmoon on my eighteenth birthday next month, so hurry home from Harrow, my dear (what a collection of breathless aspirants!) because I simply can't wait to see you! Undying love, yours through all eternity, GINETTE.

I had barely recovered from this sickening effusion when my father's letter arrived. After breaking the news of the engagement, he wrote, *I myself am* convinced that this is the best possible solution for Ginevra and when you come home we'll have a talk and I'll explain why. Meanwhile behave like a gentleman and do nothing that would make me ashamed of you—but I have every confidence that your conduct, as always, will be exemplary. Ever your affectionate and devoted father, R.G.

This elliptical letter seemed curiously empty. I read it and reread it and felt more despairing than ever. I wanted immediate comfort; the promise of future explanations coupled with exhortations to behave like a gentleman merely increased my baffled misery. I wanted someone to say, "Yes, you must be appalled," and suggest if not a remedy, at least a road to resignation.

My mother's letter arrived two days later.

My dearest Robert, she wrote, Of course you will be appalled by the news of Ginevra's engagement. But try to be patient. It is a difficult situation but there are arguments in favor of the engagement which I must leave to your father to explain. It is not a mother's provenance to talk of the Ways of the World to her sons.

No doubt you will be feeling frustrated that your father hasn't written at length, but when considering the Ways of the World an oral discussion is more efficacious than an exchange of letters. Also your father is subject to uneasiness when he has to write long letters in English. Remember that he has not had the benefit of your first-class education, and try to understand how sensitive he feels on the subject. It was terrible for him to be sent home from school at the age of thirteen because his father would not or could not pay the bills, terrible for him later when no tutor would stay in a house so impregnated with immorality and corruption. Again, be patient. And have courage. Remember, everything passes, even the most unspeakable horrors. Believe me. I know. I send my best love, dearest Robert, and remain now and always your most affectionate and devoted MAMA.

VIII

I returned to Oxmoon two weeks later for the Easter holidays, and on the morning after my arrival my father asked me to accompany him to the library, a long tousled room dominated by the leather-bound collection of books ordered for Oxmoon by my eighteenth-century ancestor Robert Godwin the Renovator. My father, who used the library as an estate office, read only magazines when he was at leisure; he never opened a book. My mother read Mrs. Beeton's Book of Household Management and, occasionally, moral tracts which she felt might be suitable for the servants' hall. My parents, in other words, were a perfect example of how to succeed in life without benefit of a worthwhile education.

"Sit down, Robert," said my father, motioning me to the chair by his writing table, but he himself remained standing by the fireplace.

My father was a tall man, over six feet in height, and he looked like the hero he was. I cannot remember a time when I did not know he was a hero, saving his ruined inheritance, overcoming all manner of adversity, winning a reputation throughout the length and breadth of the Gower Peninsula as a just landlord, a hardworking farmer and a devoted family man. At that time, when I was two months short of my sixteenth birthday, he was still only thirty-six, three years older than my mother, but as he stood facing me in the library I thought neither of his youth nor of his hero's looks, which were so familiar that I took them for granted, but of his lack of education which my mother had recently underlined to me.

My father was a gentleman, a member of an Anglo-Welsh family which had survived in Gower for many hundreds of years, but at that moment I suddenly saw him through the English eyes I was busy acquiring at Harrow and I realized for the first time how hard it would be to place him within the conventional framework of the English class system. His casual country clothes were in impeccable English taste but there was something foreign about the way he wore them; Englishmen are prone to be shabbily, not elegantly, informal. Then his hands were wrong; they hinted at past manual labor, not gentlemanly pursuits. But his voice was the most marked anomaly of his gentleman's appearance, even more marked than the unfashionable beard which any English gentleman would have been tempted to shave off years before. He had a country accent. In the eighteenth century this would have been unremarkable in a provincial gentleman who seldom went to London, but here we were, almost in the twentieth century, and my father did not speak English as it should be spoken. His accent, the curious hybrid of Gower in which Devon meets and conquers Wales, was not marked, no more than a steady Welsh inflection mingled with Devonian vowels, but it was sufficient to label him an oddity in a society where every man is immediately placed as soon as he opens his mouth. My father was a Welshman living in a little corner of England which history and geography had combined to maroon behind the Welsh frontier, and in his English Welshness Oxmoon stood reflected, English yet not English, Welsh yet not Welsh, a cultural and racial conundrum endowed with an idiosyncratic charm and grace.

"Well, Robert," said my father, so charming, so graceful, so anxious to help me in any way he could, "let me explain why I approve of this engagement which you find so detestable. It's like this: a girl such as Ginevra, a beautiful girl, an heiress, lives in constant danger as soon as she's old enough to go out and about—and even before she's old enough; I don't have to remind you of what happened with Conor Kinsella. Now, an early marriage to a suitable young man is the best thing that could happen to a girl like

Ginevra, particularly a girl who's already got herself talked about in an unfavorable way."

"Yes, but—"

"Believe me, Ginevra could do worse—much worse. This is a good match. Socially the Applebys are beyond reproach, and I've no doubt Ginevra would enjoy the future Timothy has to offer—an amusing sociable sort of life divided between London and Gower. Also the two of them have plenty of friends and acquaintances in common and no one denies marriage is easier when the partners share a similar background. Besides, they find each other good company. I don't see why they shouldn't do tolerably well together, indeed I don't."

"I can see the truth of what you're saying, but—"

"I know what you're thinking. You're wondering how she could be happy with a plain boy who wears spectacles and likes collecting butterflies instead of playing cricket. Well, there's more than one kind of happiness, Robert. He'll make her happy because he'll give her a secure respectable status as a married woman. And if she wants a more exciting sort of happiness she'll be eligible to look elsewhere later."

I stared at him. "I don't understand."

"No. Well, that's the way of the world, Robert. A girl like Ginevra is certain to favor the kind of life that in our society only married women are allowed to lead."

I went on staring. "But surely when women are married they still have to play the game and stick to the rules!"

"I'm not talking about God's rules—we all know what they are. I'm talking about society's rules, and there are rules governing carnal behavior just as there are rules governing how to eat at table. The difference is that passion's more important than table manners, and if you break the rules of passion you can be smashed to pulp." He was still staring into the grate. Then abandoning the fire he moved to the window. As he slipped his hands into his pockets I saw that his fists were clenched.

"Passion . . . carnal desire . . ." He seemed to be working his way towards some vulgar colloquialism but in the end as usual he eschewed all Anglo-Saxon bluntness and when he next spoke I realized he had fallen back on the elliptical but time-honored phrase that had been sanctified by the Bible. He was entrapped not only by his Welshness but by the verbal restraint of his generation. "Acquiring carnal knowledge is like swimming in the sea," he said carefully at last. "The sea's so beautiful to look at, so wonderful to swim in, but you must never bathe unless it's safe. People so often drown in the sea and some coasts are so very dangerous . . . like the coast of Gower."

Drifting back to the writing table he paused to look down at the ink-stained blotter. "As you know," he said, "I saw a man drown once. I saw a man drown and a woman go mad. And one day, Robert," said my father, slowly raising his eyes to mine, "one day I'm going to have to talk to you about my mother and Owain Bryn-Davies."

I respected him far too much to ask what connection there could possibly be between this hoary old skeleton in the family cupboard and Ginette's disastrous engagement, and presently—as usual—he backed away from the subject without imparting further information.

"So you be careful of that shining sea," he said, and as he spoke I thought how Welsh he was, wrapping the truths of life in metaphors and serving them up to me on a salver of myth. "Be careful as I was—and as I am." He paused. His very blue eyes seemed unnaturally clear and when he looked straight at me again I found it was impossible to look away. "A good wife's the only answer," he said. "Anything else isn't worth the risk of drowning. You'll notice I don't just say marriage is the answer, because if you choose the wrong wife it's no answer at all. There's no hell on earth like a bad marriage. My parents . . . yes, I must tell you about them someday when you've seen a little more of the world. They didn't stick to the rules, you see—neither God's rules nor the rules of society—and in breaking the rules they were both destroyed."

There was a pause in which nothing moved in the room but the flames of the fire in the grate.

"So," said my father, suddenly altering the mood by giving me his most charming smile, "I'm sure you can understand now how dangerous life could be for Ginevra and how we must do everything in our power to ensure her safety by encouraging her to make a satisfactory marriage."

"Yes, of course she's got to have a husband to look after her, I quite understand that, but as far as I'm concerned there's only one possible solution: I must marry her myself. Now, I do realize I'm a little young at present, but—"

"I concede," said my father, "that I married at nineteen and it turned out to be quite the most fortunate thing that's ever happened to me, but I'm afraid I could never consent to you marrying while you're still in your teens."

"But this is an emergency!"

"I think not. I recognize that you feel a very deep affection for Ginevra, but you in your turn should now recognize that it's fraternal."

"Oh no, it isn't!"

"I'm sorry. I know you're jealous. I know you've been unhappy since she left Oxmoon. I know this is all a nightmare for you, but you must try to be grown up, try to be sensible, try to accept that this is something you can't change."

This maddened me beyond endurance. "I'd like to kill him!" I shouted in a paroxysm of rage. "That would change things soon enough!"

The next moment my father was slamming me face down across the writing table and the scene had dissolved with terrifying speed into violence.

IX

He never did it. He never beat me. I cried out in shock and the cry paralyzed him. For five seconds he held me in an iron grip but then with a short painful intake of breath he released my arm which he had doubled behind my back. As he walked away from me he said, "Never, never say such a thing again." He spoke in Welsh but as it was a simple sentence I understood it. However a moment later, realizing he had used the wrong language, he repeated the order in English. The English was broken, a foreigner's attempt at an unfamiliar tongue. He sounded like a stranger. I was terrified.

"We don't talk of murder at Oxmoon," said my father.

"Forgive me, I didn't mean what I said—"

"You ought to be ashamed of yourself, behaving like a spoiled child all over again—and to think you have the insolence to talk of marriage! It'll be a long time before *you're* fit for marriage, indeed it will—all you're fit for at the moment is the nursery!"

"I'm sorry but I'm just so damnably unhappy—"

"*Unhappy!* Don't talk to me of unhappiness, you don't even know what the word means! My God, when I was your age—"

"I'm sorry, I'm sorry, please don't be angry with me anymore, please—"

"Then sit down at that table and stop whining like a pampered puppy! That's better. Now take a sheet of notepaper and write as follows." My father hesitated before continuing with appropriate pauses: " 'My dear Ginette, I must apologize for not writing earlier to send my best wishes to you on your engagement, but I'm very much looking forward to celebrating the news with you at your birthday ball at Oxmoon. After all, I'd be a poor sort of friend if I couldn't share your happiness! I shall be writing separately to Timothy to congratulate him but meanwhile please do give him my warmest regards. I hope you will both be very happy. Yours affectionately'— or however you close your letters to her—'Robert.' "

I finished writing. My father read the letter over my shoulder and said, "Yes, that'll do," but on an impulse I scrawled beneath the signature: *P.S. Make sure you save a waltz for me at the ball!* I wanted a waltz not because it would give me the opportunity to hold her in my arms but because I knew she liked waltzes best and I wanted my dance with her to be a dance she would remember.

"Well, I don't care," I said as I watched my father seal the letter. "Let her marry whom she likes. My friendship with her will outlast any marriage."

My father said tersely, "Even if you'd been older your mother and I could never have approved of you marrying her. She's too alluring and you're too jealous. She'd make you very miserable."

But I was miserable enough already and my misery had hardly begun.

X

The ball to celebrate both Ginette's engagement and her eighteenth birthday was held on the twenty-third of April, 1898. That was when my life finally began. The previous fifteen years and ten months had been merely a rehearsal.

All Gower came to Oxmoon for by that time my parents were famous for their lavish hospitality. It was their weakness. Everyone, after all, must occasionally have a holiday from hard work, self-help, drawing the line and doing the done thing, and my parents were in many ways a very ordinary Victorian young couple. My mother specialized in what she called "little dinner parties for twenty-four," but her English talent for wielding power with implacable attention to detail was only truly satisfied by giving balls for a hundred. My father, displaying an inborn Welsh inclination to hospitality, seized the chance to abandon the austerity which he had been compelled to practice for so much of his life, and glide down the glittering road of extravagance. The result of their combined efforts to entertain their neighbors was unbridled sybaritic luxury served up with a shattering military precision.

At first I had no intention of making more than a brief appearance; I not only loathed the prospect of seeing Ginette with her fiancé but in my misery I knew another of those moments when I was overwhelmed with the drearier aspects of adolescence. Once again I was undergoing a bout of rapid growth; I looked ridiculous in my evening clothes, and as I stood before the looking glass I thought I had never seen a youth who looked more unappealing. There was even a spot on my chin. I never normally had spots. I did not believe in them. But now I found myself obliged to believe, and the next moment I was noticing what a distasteful color my hair was. In childhood it had been pale yellow and attractive. Now it was mud-brown and repellent. My eyes were blue but not bright blue like my father's; they were light blue, unendurably anemic. It suddenly occurred to me that my looks were second-rate. I would never be classically handsome. A sense of failure overpowered me. I was in despair.

Then my mother looked in to see how far I had progressed with my preparations and when she saw me she said briskly, "This won't do, will it?" and hustled me along to her room where my father, golden-haired, classically handsome and every inch a hero was somehow contriving to look elegant in his braces.

He lent me some evening clothes and life began to seem fractionally less hopeless. Finally I ventured downstairs. The house seemed to be throbbing with a powerful emotion and so strong was the aura of glamour that I did not at first realize that this powerful emotion lay within me and was not some mysterious miasma emanating from the walls. All the main rooms were adorned with flowers from the garden and the hothouses. In the ballroom the scent of lilies, very pure and clear, drifted faintly toward me from the bank of flowers around the dais where the gentlemen of the orchestra were busy tuning their instruments. No amateur trio scraped out the music whenever all Gower danced at Oxmoon; my parents imported a dozen first-class musicians from London. I glanced up at the chandeliers. Every crystal had been washed, every candle replaced. The room was mirrored. Perhaps Regency Robert Godwin had dreamed of Versailles, and as I stood in what I later realized was such a quaint provincial little ballroom I saw reflected in those mirrors the fairy-tale prince of my personal myth.

The guests began to arrive. The music began to play. The room began to hum with conversation and still I remained where I was, saying her name again and again in my mind as if I could will her back from the brink of her great catastrophe and deliver us both to the happy ending of a traditional nursery fairy tale.

I was in the hall when she arrived at last with the Applebys. Through the open front door I saw their carriage coming up the drive and although I wanted to retreat to the ballroom in order to pretend I was barely interested in her arrival, my feet carried me inexorably past the staircase, through the doorway and out into the porch.

I saw her and for the first time in my life I found myself old enough to recognize feminine perfection. I was reminded of the silver cups which I regularly collected at school in my compulsive quest for excellence. She was a prize. She was waiting to be awarded to the man who came first, and when I finally realized this I knew I had to have her; I knew I had to win.

True to the conventions of the fairy tale I was instantly changed. The long tedious journey through adolescence was terminated as abruptly as if my fairy godmother had waved a magic wand, and at that moment childhood lay forever behind me and only manhood was real.

"Robert! My dear, isn't this thrilling! *What* a birthday treat . . ." She swept on, radiantly oblivious of my transformation, and disappeared into the ballroom. Presently I found I had to sit down. Then I found I could not sit down but had to stand up. I was beside myself. All the famous love poetry which I had previously dismissed as "soppy" and "wet" now streamed through my brain until even the rhythm of the iambic pentameters seemed impregnated with a mystical significance. Like the author of the Book of

Revelation I was conscious of a new heaven and a new earth. I stumbled forward, broke into a run and hared after her into the ballroom.

"Ginette, Ginette—"

She heard me. I saw her turn her head idly and give me a languid wave with her fan. "Don't worry, I haven't forgotten!" she called. "I've saved the first waltz after supper for you!" And she began to dance away from me in Sir William Appleby's arms.

Some sort of interval passed which I can only presume I spent dancing with the girls I was supposed to dance with and behaving as I was supposed to behave. I must have shown some semblance of normality for no one inquired anxiously after my health. Did I eat any supper? Possibly. I have a dim memory of sipping a glass of champagne but giving up halfway through because I was afraid I might go mad with euphoria.

"Oh good, this is your waltz, isn't it, Robert? Thank goodness, now I can relax! I never before realized how exhausting it must have been for Cinderella having to be radiant to everyone in sight. . . . Lord, I'm in such a state, Robert, does it show? I feel so excited I don't see how I can possibly survive —in fact maybe I'm already dead and this is what it's like in heaven. . . . Oh, listen—Johann Strauss—yes, that proves it, I *am* in heaven! Come on, Robert, what's the matter with you? Let's dance!"

And that was the moment when we danced together beneath the chandeliers at Oxmoon as the orchestra played "The Blue Danube."

"Oh, this is such paradise!" exclaimed Ginette, echoing my thoughts word for word but glancing restlessly past me to the doors of the ballroom as if she could hardly wait to escape. "I'll remember this moment forever and ever!"

"I'll remember it till the day I die. Listen, Ginette, wait for me, you've got to wait—"

"What? I can't hear you!" The orchestra was blazing into a new coda and as we whirled by the dais I saw her again look past my shoulder at the open doors in the distance.

"I said you've got to wait for me because—"

She left me. The orchestra was still playing "The Blue Danube" but as she ran the full length of the ballroom all the couples stopped dancing to stare at her. She ran swiftly and gracefully, her feet seeming barely to touch the ground, and suddenly there was a flash of diamonds as she pulled off her ring, tossed it aside and carelessly consigned her engagement to oblivion.

He was waiting for her in the doorway. As I have already mentioned, I had no trouble recognizing Conor Kinsella. He was smiling that charming Irish smile of his and as she flung herself into his arms he kissed her with appalling intimacy on the mouth.

The music stopped. No one moved. A great silence fell upon the ballroom and then in my mind's eye I saw the mirrored walls darken, the chandeliers grow dim and my fairy tale turn to ashes to foul the perfumed festering air.

2

I

So MUCH for romance. Later I considered it fortunate that this early experience had granted me immunity, and I was never troubled by such irrational behavior again.

After the ball life went on. I admit I did wonder at the time how it could but it did, and presently the natural human instinct for self-preservation nudged its way to the forefront of my mind. I suddenly saw that no one must know how I felt. Sweat broke out on my forehead at the thought of people pitying me. Horrifying visions smote me of a future in which my unrequited love made me an object of derision throughout Gower, and in panic I realized that my only hope of avoiding such humiliation lay in exercising an iron will and concealing my feelings behind the facade of my quasi-fraternal friendship. If I followed this course I could permit myself a certain amount of fractious moping because it would be expected of me, but I had at all costs to beware of extremes; I had to keep eating, talk to people, go about my daily business. Eventually I would have to pretend to recover and this would be a formidable challenge, but sheer pride alone made it imperative that I should succeed.

I began to rehearse a series of appropriate remarks which I could use later to deceive my parents. "Ginette? Oh yes, I suppose I was a trifle possessive, wasn't I—rather amusing to look back on that now. . . ." Endless scenes in this endless charade of indifference slipped in and out of my mind. My inventive powers impressed me but unfortunately they were unable to relieve my misery whenever I thought of Ginette with Kinsella. My imagination, never normally intrusive, was now a torment to me. So was my sexuality. Together the two demons destroyed my sleep, gave me a consumptive look and did their best to destroy the grand illusion of resignation which I was trying so hard to propagate.

Meanwhile, as I floundered in the toils of my adolescent's nightmare, Kinsella had taken advantage of everyone's paralyzed stupefaction to sweep Ginette off on horseback to Swansea, our nearest large town, and bear her away by rail to Scotland where the lax matrimonial laws had long been God's gift to clandestine lovers. There he had married her despite the fact that she had been made a ward of court, and afterwards they had evaded legal retribution by slipping into Ireland on a ferry from Stranraer to Larne. They had sailed to America from Cork a week later.

There was much talk about what could be done to preserve Ginette's fortune but the debate soon lapsed as her well-wishers acknowledged their impotence to alter her fate. Before long general opinion favored treating the disaster as a *fait accompli* and making the best of it. No one knew how Kinsella was earning his daily bread, but later, when the lines of communication had been renewed, Ginette's letters indicated a life of affluence with no sign of an apocalyptic retribution hovering in the wings.

Timothy Appleby was dispatched on a world cruise to recover from the catastrophe and had all manner of adventures before meeting a rich widow in Cape Town and settling down in Rhodesia to make a study of the butterflies of Africa. Ginette's defection was undoubtedly the best fate that could have overtaken him, but the more I heard people remarking on his lucky escape the more I wondered how Ginette could have treated him so badly. The situation had no doubt been abnormal but her deliberate entanglement with a man who meant nothing to her continued to puzzle me and when we had drifted into a faultlessly platonic correspondence I asked her outright for an explanation. In reply I received a typical letter, full of romantic hyperbole and feminine flutter, which I knew meant she was still struggling with her guilt and remorse: . . . *yes, I know I behaved like a* serpent, *and believe me I'll have poor Tim on my conscience till my dying day, but the truth is quite simply that I was mad. Aunt Maud drove me mad, intercepting my letters from Conor and lecturing me about chastity and sending me to that ghastly place in Germany which was just like a prison—or worse still a convent—so in the end I saw clearly that my only hope of escaping her was to marry and the only man (or so I thought) who wanted to marry me was Timothy. I knew I'd still have to spend part of the year at All-Hallows but at least I would have been my own mistress instead of Aunt Maud's prisoner and at least I would have been able to spend most of the year in London where I would have met all sorts of exciting people and had a simply heavenly time.*

So that was why I decided to marry Tim. I had no way of communicating with Conor and (thanks to Aunt Maud) I'd given up all hope of hearing from him.

And then—just after my engagement had been announced—Conor finally managed to outwit my jailer! He sent over from Ireland the most extraordinary gentleman called Mr. O'Flaherty who posed as a jobbing gardener and managed to smuggle a letter to me by seducing the second housemaid—my dear, I can't tell you how romantic it was and the housemaid had a thrilling time too —and then I told Mr. O'Flaherty about the ball at Oxmoon and Conor sent word that I was to leave a packed bag beforehand with the second housemaid who would take it to Mr. O'Flaherty who would be waiting in the grounds of All-Hallows by the ruined oratory—my dear, I was simply ravished *by excite-*

ment, in fact when the orchestra was playing "The Blue Danube" and I saw Conor had finally arrived I'm only surprised I didn't swoon in your arms! At least when I die I'll be able to say: well, never mind, I've lived. Oh, but what a nightmare it was before Conor came, thank God I've escaped, thank God the ghastly old past can't touch me anymore. . . .

Years afterwards when she and Kinsella paid their first and last visit to England I said to her, "If All-Hallows was such hell, why didn't you come back to Oxmoon?"

"But my dear!" she exclaimed as if astonished that I could be so obtuse. "Margaret would have been just as bad as Aunt Maud! Can't you imagine all the homilies on drawing the line and doing the done thing?" And we laughed together, just two platonic friends, just first cousins once removed, just two strangers who had been childhood playmates long ago in a little Welsh country house in the back of beyond, but I wanted her then as strongly as I had ever wanted her and although I concealed my feelings I knew that they had remained unchanged. It was as if they had been frozen in time by the shock of her sudden desertion; it was as if, so far as my deepest emotions were concerned, I was still dancing beneath the chandeliers at Oxmoon while the orchestra played "The Blue Danube."

This should have been romantic. However in reality—the reality I had to master when I was sixteen—it was both inconvenient and bewildering. I had read enough novels by that time to know that a hero in my position had to yearn for his lost love in impeccable chastity and perhaps hunt big game in Africa to relieve his feelings, but I had no interest in game hunting and no interest, as I presently discovered to my horror, in being chaste.

It took me a few months to realize this, but when I returned home for the summer holidays I found I finally had to face the prospect of Ginette's permanent absence. In other words, for the first time in my life I had to live with the concept of losing.

I did not know where to begin. Then I gradually became aware that I wanted to conquer this new world of carnality and prove I was still capable of coming first. At that point I should have confided in my father but two factors inhibited me. The first was that I was so obsessed with acting my charade of indifference towards Ginette that I shied away from any conversation which would have betrayed my true feelings, and the second was that I could so clearly remember my father talking of the dangerous sea of carnality and telling me a good marriage was the only answer.

I struggled on in silence, utterly confused, utterly miserable, but then one morning I got up early and on wandering downstairs I found a very junior housemaid polishing the floor of the drawing room. Immediately I recalled my recent letter from Ginette on the subject of the erring housemaid at All-Hallows, and immediately I saw what possibilities had confronted the mysterious Mr. O'Flaherty. One thing led, as I fear it so often does, to another until at last, to put a turgid episode in the shortest, most salutary sentence, she stooped, I conquered and we both fell from grace. I was back at school by the time my father was obliged to make a financial provision for her and I was still at school when to the relief of all concerned she miscarried and emigrated to Australia, but when I returned home for the Christmas holidays I found a most unpleasant reception awaiting me.

It was my mother who had found out. Her chilling expression was bad enough but the worst part of the affair was that my father was entirely at a loss. He was stricken. His expression of bewilderment, his painful halting attempt to reprimand me, his air of misery all formed more of a punishment than any violent demonstration of rage, and in an agony of shame I begged his forgiveness.

"I'll turn over a new leaf, sir, I swear I will," I added desperately, and on this edifying note of repentance the conversation ended, but I knew, as soon as I had left him, that my problems remained unsolved. I was just wondering in despair if I could secretly ask the local doctor for a drug that would suppress my carnal inclinations and was just trying to imagine the celibate future studded with cold baths that lay ahead of me to the grave—for of course I could never marry if I could not marry Ginette—when Lion banged on the door and shouted that my mother wanted to see me.

She was making a blouse for Celia and her worktable was littered with various pieces of material, but my mother herself was, as I had anticipated, sitting at her dressing table in front of the triple looking glass. Her box of assorted buttons was open before her and she was sifting through the collection in search of a suitable set for the blouse.

"Sit down, dear," she said, not looking up. "I've just been talking to your father."

I sat down. The chair was cunningly angled so that I was reflected in all three mirrors, and as I noticed this unnerving multiplication of my guilty image I felt a queasiness form in the pit of my stomach.

"Your father," said my mother, poking away busily among the buttons, "is capable of considerable eloquence, but when a conversation is of a painful nature he often finds it difficult to be as explicit as he would wish. I have spoken of this to you before and attributed this characteristic to his Welsh temperament but we must also never forget that he was not brought up to speak English by his Welsh mother and his Welsh nursemaids and that in times of stress he thinks more easily in their language than in ours."

Poke-poke-poke among the buttons. A swift glance into the far mirror.

"So I thought," resumed my mother tranquilly, "that I should see you for a moment to . . . clarify your father's statements in the unlikely event that you might be feeling a trifle bewildered or confused." She paused, glanced into all three mirrors and then returned to the buttons before adding: "Now,

I want to talk to you briefly about your grandmother and Mr. Bryn-Davies—your father has not, I think, yet broached the subject with you in any detail."

I was so startled that it took me a moment to answer, "No, Mama."

"Well, that's as it should be. Your father is the best judge of when you should hear the whole story, but I think a word or two from me now wouldn't come amiss, especially as the case seems strangely . . . pertinent to what I have to say." She toyed with a large red button. Then putting it aside she continued with the same tranquil fluency: "Let me start with your grandmother. Now, you may be surprised to hear that I do not entirely condemn poor Grandmama for her liaison with Mr. Bryn-Davies. She loved him. Her husband had treated her vilely. She certainly deserved a little happiness. Of course her conduct was immoral and wrong, that goes without saying, but," said my mother, deciding to look at me directly, "everyone in this world is subject to temptation and since very few people are saints, most people cannot always succeed in living as they know they should live. So Grandmama's lapse was, in that sense, pardonable; she was guilty primarily of human frailty. However," said my mother, finding two more red buttons, "where Grandmama made her cardinal error was that she abandoned all attempt to keep up appearances. A secret liaison conducted with discretion would have been socially acceptable. A public performance as a harlot destroyed her. Remember that, Robert. Discretion is everything. And it has nothing to do with morality. It's a question of good taste, common sense and consideration for those you love and who love you. Have I made myself entirely clear?"

"I—"

"There are standards of immorality as well as standards of morality, Robert. Make sure yours are high. You may not end up a saint—I'm not at all sure I would want a son who was a saint—but at least you'll end up with an ordered civilized private life. Oh, and of course—though it's hardly necessary for me to add this—an ordered civilized private life doesn't include seducing family servants and causing extreme embarrassment to the parents who love you. There are to be no more seductions beneath this roof, Robert. I draw the line. What you do elsewhere is entirely your own affair and I neither expect nor desire to know anything about it—you should ask your father for further advice on the subject, and when you do you must *insist* that he's explicit with you. It is not a mother's provenance," said my mother, "to advise her son on subjects of a carnal nature."

After a pause I said, "No, of course not, Mama."

We looked at each other for one brief telling second in the triple glass. Finally I managed to add, "Thank you."

"Oh, there's no need to thank me," said my mother. "I'm merely clarifying what your father said—or what he would have said if he hadn't been subject to linguistic difficulties when distressed."

The interview was concluded. At first I was conscious merely of an overpowering gratitude towards her for reprieving me from a lifetime of cold baths, but later my attitude became more ambivalent. I was aware that in some nameless competition which I could not begin to define she had come a highly commendable first while my father had come a most ineffectual second, and this truth which instinct urged me to deny but which my intellect forced me to acknowledge ran contrary to my most deeply entrenched beliefs not only about my parents but about the male and female sexes. In the world in which I felt most comfortable men were always first and best, heroes were always more important than heroines and the father who idolized me could do no wrong. But my mother had unwittingly opened a window onto another world, the world which Ginette had shown me when she had eloped with Kinsella, the real world which I secretly knew I had yet to master and which I secretly feared I might never master to my satisfaction. In my dread of coming second there I resented that world and above all I resented the women who had shown it to me. I still loved Ginette—but there were moments when I hated her too. I loved my mother—but there were times when I resented her so much that I could barely keep a civil tongue in my head when I addressed her.

My mother's understanding should have brought me closer to her but in adult life I found we were estranged. We were each faultlessly polite whenever we met but nothing of importance was ever uttered between us, and later when my considerable success had deluded me into believing I had mastered the real world, my attitude mellowed from resentment into an affectionate contempt. Poor Mama, I would think, so plain, so dumpy, so unfashionable, so provincial—what did she know of life when she had barely ventured from her rural backwater since the age of sixteen? The only crisis she had had to surmount had been her mother-in-law's determination to live in sin with a sheep farmer, and even that droll little inconvenience had been smoothed aside by my father who had played the hero and visited his mother regularly in her Swansea asylum.

My father never did tell me the whole story about his mother and Owain Bryn-Davies, but the older and more sophisticated I became the less curious I was to hear about this amusing slice of Victorian melodrama which I felt sure by Edwardian standards would be judged tame. In my late twenties when I became involved with defending criminals of the worst type I quickly reached a state of mind in which no human behavior could shock me, least of all a little indiscreet adultery in South Wales in the Eighties, and when my father said after my grandmother's funeral that my mother had been urging him to talk to me of the past, it was all I could do to suppress a yawn and assume a look of courteous sympathy.

"It must be exactly as you wish, Papa," I said. "If you want to talk then

I'm willing to listen, but you shouldn't let Mama dragoon you into a course of action which at heart you've no wish to pursue."

"Your mother thinks you could be a comfort to me," said my father. "I feel so tormented sometimes by my memories."

We were strolling together across the heather to the summit of Rhossili Downs. It was a clouded winter day not conducive to walking, but after the ordeal of my grandmother's funeral we had both felt in need of fresh air. I was twenty-eight but considered myself worldly enough to look older; my father was forty-eight but considered himself lucky enough to look younger; we had reached the stage when we were occasionally mistaken for brothers.

"Yes, I must tell you," said my father. "I must."

We paced on across the heather in silence. I waited, but when nothing happened I automatically fell into my professional role of playing midwife to the truth.

"What were they like?" I said, throwing him a bland question to help him along.

"What were they like?" repeated my father as if I had astonished him. "Oh, they were charming, all of them—my mother, my father, Bryn-Davies . . . Yes, they were all the most charming and delightful people." He stopped to stare at the skyline and as I watched the color fade from his face he said in a low voice, "That was the horror, of course. It wasn't like a melodrama when you can recognize the villains as soon as they step on the stage. It wasn't like that at all."

"They were just three ordinary people?"

"Yes, they were just three ordinary people," said my father, "who failed to draw the line."

I suppressed a sigh at this fresh evidence of my mother's middle-class Victorian influence over him. It was only the middle classes—and in particular the *nouveaux-riches* middle classes—who made a professional occupation of doing the done thing and drawing moral lines. Anyone of any genuine breeding did the done thing without thinking twice about it and left drawing lines to clergymen who were trained as moral draftsmen.

"It was all a tragedy," my father was saying. "My poor mother, she was so beautiful. My father wasn't very kind to her."

"Because he was a drunkard?"

"He was the most splendid fellow," said my father exactly as if I had never spoken, "and so fond of children. I was the apple of his eye. Bryn-Davies was very civil to me too. Interesting chap, Bryn-Davies. Strong personality. Just calling him a sheep farmer gives no clear impression of him."

"But surely," I said, deciding to risk a little Anglo-Saxon bluntness, "you must have resented Bryn-Davies when he took over Oxmoon after your father died of drink. Surely it became an outrage when he lived openly with your mother and kept you from your inheritance."

"It was all a tragedy," repeated my father. "A tragedy."

I gave up. We walked on across the Downs.

"And afterwards," said my father, "after Bryn-Davies had had his little accident with the tide tables and drowned on the Shipway, it was all so difficult with my mother but Margaret was wonderful, such a tower of strength, and she found out all about the Home of the Assumption where the nuns were so kind to the insane. Sometimes I wondered if my mother should come home more often but Margaret said no, only at Christmas. Margaret drew the line and of course she was right—because terrible things happen," said my father, his face bleached, his lips bloodless, his eyes seeing scenes I could not begin to imagine, "when people fail to draw the line."

I said nothing. The silence that followed lasted some time, but at last he thanked me for listening so patiently and said he was so glad he had talked to me.

But as he and I both knew perfectly well, he had still told me nothing whatsoever.

II

When I related this incident to Ginette in my Christmas letter she wrote in reply: *Poor Bobby, but what defeats me is why he and Margaret make this big mystery out of the past when it's quite obvious to anyone of our sophistication, my dear, what was going on: the drunken husband developed a penchant for beating the wife, the wife dived into a grand passion in sheer self-defense and the lover, being both naughty and greedy, grabbed not only the wife but all the money he could lay his hands on when the husband obligingly died of liver failure. Heavens, such sordid goings-on happen all the time everywhere—and as always in such frightfulness, the people who suffer most are the poor innocent children. Really, it's a wonder some of them survive at all and if they do survive they're lucky if they're not scarred for life by their experiences!*

And it was then, as I read this passage in her letter, that it first occurred to me to suspect that my father was not a flawless hero but a deeply damaged man.

III

I was damaged myself although at that time I did not admit it. I had enjoyed so much worldly success that the prospect of private failure was inconceivable; it never even crossed my mind that anything could be amiss.

It would be immodest for me to record my achievements at Harrow so I need only say that it was taken for granted that I would achieve a first when I went up to Oxford to read Greats. This made life a little dull; success loses its power to charm if insufficient effort is involved in its acquisition and after I had demonstrated to my contemporaries, my tutors and the various females of my acquaintance that whatever I saw I conquered, I acknowledged my boredom by looking around for a new challenge that would make life more amusing. I had just finished my second year at Balliol when a friend invited me to stay with him in Scotland and for the first time in my life I saw the mountains.

There are plenty of mountains in Wales, but the spectacular ones are in the north, and since my parents never took holidays I knew little of Wales beyond the Gower Peninsula and little of England beyond Central London, Oxford and Harrow. There are no mountains in Gower, only the smooth rolling humps of the Downs, and although I had long been attracted to the spectacular cliffs by the sea, these were so dangerous that my father had always forbidden me to climb them.

However I was now presented with a challenge that no one had forbidden me to accept, and I knew I had to climb those mountains. I had to get to the top. I had to win. I was enslaved.

During the next few months I drove my parents to despair, nearly ruined my career at Oxford and almost killed myself. That was when I first realized something had gone wrong with my life; it occurred to me that when my desire to win had been channeled into academic excellence the compulsion had formed a benign growth on my personality, but when that desire had been channeled into mountaineering it had formed a cancer. I did recover but not before the cancer had been cut out of my life. I gave up mountaineering.

"I shall never come back here," I said to the doctor who attended me in the hospital at Fort William when I lay recuperating from the accident that had killed my three best friends. "I shall never go climbing again."

"They all say that," said the doctor, "and they all come back in the end."

But I was certain I could stay away; there was a void in my life but I thought I could see how to fill it. I had to fight the opponent I had discovered on the mountains, the one opponent who consistently mesmerized me. It was Death. Death had won my three friends; Death had almost won me. But now I was the one who was going to win—and I was going to win by outwitting Death over and over again.

I then had to decide on the arena best suited for my battles. I toyed with the idea of becoming a doctor but decided it would involve me in the study of too many subjects which I found tedious. I was interested in death, not disease. Then I considered the law, and the law, I saw at once, had considerable advantages. It not only blended with my classical education but it was a profession that could ease my way into public life, and since I knew my father dreamed that I might enter Parliament I thought I could see how both our ambitions might be satisfied.

As the eldest son I was heir to Oxmoon but my father's youth and the likelihood of him living until I myself was far advanced in middle age made it imperative that I had some occupation while I waited for my inheritance. I also had a very natural desire to be financially independent, and no one denied there was money at the bar for a young man who was determined to reach the summit of the profession.

I won my double first at Oxford in Greats and Law and was called to the bar of the Middle Temple in 1906. To my family I pretended it was sheer chance that I became involved with criminal law; I did not disclose how I had engineered a meeting with a famous K.C. and more or less hypnotized him into engaging me as his "devil"; I did not disclose that I had selected him as my master because a number of his clients ran the risk, in the formal words of the death sentence, of being hanged by the neck until they were dead. While I deviled for him I met the important solicitors and soon I was acquiring a few briefs of my own. Unlike many barristers I did not have to endure briefless years at the bar. I grabbed every opportunity I could and when there was no opportunity I created one. My career began to gather in momentum.

Of course I said it was pure coincidence that I ended up defending murderers who had no hope of acquittal, but the truth was I deliberately sought out the hopeless cases because there was more pleasure in winning a hard victory over Death than an easy one. I pretended to be nonchalant, claiming murder trials were somewhat tedious, but in my heart I loved every minute I spent fighting in court. I loved the excitement and the drama and the perpetual shadow of the gallows; I loved the jousts with Death; I loved the victory of saving people who would have died but for my skill. To compete with Death, as I had discovered on the mountains, was to know one was alive.

It made no difference that sometimes, inevitably, Death won. Some of my clients died on the gallows just as my three friends had died on the mountain, but that only made the next battle fiercer and enhanced my satisfaction when the lucky clients were saved.

My work became an obsession. Although I tried to deny it to myself I was suffering from cancer of the personality again, and gradually I became aware of the familiar symptoms appearing: the fanatical dedication, the withdrawal from other pursuits, the loss of interest in carnal pleasure, the isolation of the soul. I even found myself postponing my entry into politics. Westminster was not the Old Bailey. There was no shadow of the gallows there.

Then one day I saved a client whom I loathed and believed to be guilty, and suddenly I not only asked myself what I was doing but saw the answer all too clearly: I was wasting my life in order to satisfy obsessions I could not master. The cancer was upon me again and I knew I had to cut it out to survive.

That was when I discovered that some cancers spread so deep that no surgery can remove them. My cancer now had such a hold on me that I did not see how I could remove it and retain my sanity; I felt as if I were on the edge of some mental breakdown, but as I struggled to imagine a life in which winning no longer mattered I saw, far away and unattainable, across the abyss of the past and beyond the walls of the present which imprisoned me, the world where I knew I could be at peace. I saw the road to Oxmoon, the lost Oxmoon of my childhood, and Ginette was with me once more in her grubby pinafore as we ate strawberries together in the kitchen garden. I saw a world where winning and losing had no power to drive me because with Ginette's hand in mine I was always content, and when I saw that world I knew that she alone could cure my cancer because she alone could take me back to Oxmoon and resurrect that lost paradise of my dreams.

But Ginette still wrote regularly of married bliss with Conor Kinsella. Fifteen years after we had danced to "The Blue Danube" she was still living happily ever after in New York, and although time and again I asked myself how I could win her back I knew there was nothing I could do. I was powerless, and as I acknowledged my absolute failure to change my life I felt I must surely be condemned to live unhappily ever after in London, a man rich, famous and successful—yet losing, lost and alone.

IV

I awoke very suddenly in the middle of the night, and my first conscious thought was: She's coming home.

Using one of Cicero's favorite metaphors I told myself that the Wheel of Fortune of Conor Kinsella had finally spun him into extinction and now my own Wheel of Fortune was spinning me back into life.

I lit the gas and immediately my cold austere masculine bedroom was bathed in a warm sensuous glow. I drew aside the curtain. Below me the formal lawns below King's Bench Walk were bathed in a powerful white moonlight and far away beyond the Embankment the river glittered beneath the stars. I stood there, transfixed by this vision of an erotic enchanted London, and as I listened to the night I heard the bells of St. Clement Dane's chime a distant half-hour.

Letting the curtain fall I turned abruptly from the window and decided to take a long cool rational look at the immediate future. Tomorrow—which was in fact today—I would go down to Oxmoon for a protracted weekend. On the following day Ginette would arrive in Swansea on the Irish steamer for an indefinite stay in the Gower Peninsula. We would meet, possibly enjoy one or two quiet passionless talks on our own and then part; I had another important case pending and it was necessary for me to return to London to prepare for it. During the next twelve months further meetings would doubtless occur and, all being well, our platonic relationship would be comfortably reestablished. After that I would have to wait and see what my prospects were, but the one strikingly obvious aspect of the situation was that I could not now descend upon Oxmoon like some overheated knight of medieval legend, fling myself at the feet of the lady I loved and beg her to marry me immediately. I could think of nothing that would irritate Ginette more, particularly a bereaved Ginette who had lost her husband in unexplained but apparently tragic circumstances.

As promised in her wire she had written to my parents but still she had not clarified the mystery of Kinsella's death; indeed she had begged them not to inquire about it. Having wound up her New York life with extraordinary haste she had sailed to Ireland with her two sons within a week of Kinsella's death, and after the funeral she had resolved to leave her sons temporarily in the care of her husband's family while she visited Wales. She did not explain this decision in her letter to my parents. Perhaps she felt it would be better for the boys to remain with their father's family instead of being swept off into a milieu where their father had been disliked; perhaps she had simply wanted to be alone for a while; perhaps her decision represented a combination of these reasons, but whatever her motives the fact remained that she was due to arrive alone in Swansea on the morning of Friday, the twentieth of June, and that she had begged that no one, absolutely no one, was to meet her at the docks except my father's coachman with the family motorcar.

I want to fulfill a dream, she wrote to me in response to the brief formal letter of sympathy I had sent to her in Dublin. *I dreamt I was coming home to Oxmoon and all the family were lined up on the porch steps—it was like an old-fashioned photograph, I could even see the sepia tints! So don't be at the docks to meet me. Be at Oxmoon with the others and make my dream come true.*

I found her letter and turned up the gas to reread it.

So Ginette too had her dreams of returning to Oxmoon.

The bells of St. Clement's sang faintly again on the night air and beyond the window the sky was lightening but I could not sleep. Cicero's metaphor of the Wheel of Fortune had captivated my imagination, and moving to the bookshelves I found the volume written by that later philosopher who had restated the ancient metaphor for the men of the Middle Ages who had known little of Cicero. From King Alfred to Chaucer, from Dante to a host of other Continental writers, all medieval Europe had been mesmerized by Boethius, writing in *The Consolation of Philosophy* about the sinister Wheel of Fortune:

I know the many disguises of that monster, Fortune, and the extent to which she seduces with friendship the very people she is striving to cheat, until she overwhelms them with unbearable grief at the suddenness of her desertion. . . .

I thought of Ginette abandoning me for Kinsella in the ballroom at Oxmoon.

But now Fortune herself was speaking; the monster was making her classic statement about her notorious wheel:

I was inclined to favor you . . . now I have withdrawn my hand. . . . Inconstancy is my very essence; it is the game I never cease to play as I turn my wheel in its ever-changing circle, filled with joy as I bring the top to the bottom and the bottom to the top. Yes, rise up on my wheel if you like, but don't count it an injury when by the same token you begin to fall as the rules of the game will require. . . .

I saw myself facing a new opponent in the game of life. Death had been replaced by Fortune. I was riding upwards on her wheel at last but this time when I got to the top I was going to stay there. I was going to beat that Wheel of Fortune and bend Fortune herself to my will.

A variety of erotic images teemed in my mind. Then, thinking how appropriate it was that Fortune should be represented as a woman, I returned to bed and dreamed of conquest.

V

I left Bennett at my chambers in London, just as I always did when I went home. It would have been pretentious to take a valet to Oxmoon where under my mother's regime shirts seemed to wash, iron and starch themselves and where my father's man was always on hand to attend to any detail that defied the laundress or my mother's omnipresent needle. Bennett, who was a Cockney, never minded being left in London. No doubt he enjoyed the respite from ironing *The Times* and performing all the other minor rites which must have made life with me so tedious. As he handed me a perfectly packed bag to take to Oxmoon I made a mental note to give him an increase in wages.

My brother Lion had threatened to accompany me on the train journey to Swansea, but fortunately he had been dismissed that week from the bank where he had been pretending to earn a living and had already bounded back to Gower to resume his favorite occupation: the pursuit of idleness in pleasant surroundings. Justice compels me to add that Lion was not vicious, merely a young man of twenty-three with a limited intellect and an ingenuous disposition. In my opinion such people are much better suited to life in the country and should leave places like London well alone.

However despite Lion's absence I did not travel on my own to Swansea that day. My favorite brother John was at Paddington Station to meet me; he had recently taken his finals at Oxford and had been spending a few days with friends in London to recuperate. Term had ended, his rooms had been vacated, his possessions had been dispatched to Gower. He was, in short, in that pleasant limbo when one successful phase of life has ended and another is yet to begin, and he looked as if he had been finding the hiatus enjoyable. Having made some aristocratic friends up at Oxford he was fresh from sampling the pleasures of the London season from a base in Belgrave Square.

"How's the decadent aristocracy?" I said as we met on the platform.

"You sound like an anarchist!" He laughed to show he was redeemed from priggishness by a sense of humor but I suspected he was mildly shocked. John would not have approved of anarchists. Nor would he have approved of any decadence among the members of the aristocracy, for in our family John represented the final triumph of my mother's *nouveau-riche* middle-class values. With an apparently inexhaustible virtue he dedicated his life to drawing lines and doing the done thing.

He was twenty-one, ten years my junior, better-looking than I was but not so tall. Neither was he so gifted athletically and academically. This meant that jealousy would have been quite uncalled for on my part, and indeed I had never seen any reason why I should be other than benign towards this intelligent sibling who always behaved so respectfully in my presence, but occasionally—perhaps once every two or three years—I did wonder how he avoided being jealous of me. Lion did not compete. Neither did Edmund, my third brother, who was two years younger than John and a mere lackluster version of Lion. My fourth brother Thomas was at present too juvenile to take seriously but showed every sign of growing up stupid. But John had brains, and John, I knew, was ambitious, and John was just the kind of young man who might resent an older brother who always came first. However, he had apparently found some solution to this dilemma because I could tell he still hero-worshiped me. Perhaps he merely told himself that jealousy was not the done thing.

"It's so good to see you again, Robert! It seems ages since we last met—of course I know you've been uncommonly busy—"

"I should never be too busy to deny myself the opportunity for civilized conversation," I said at once. I felt guilty that although he had been in London for some days I had been too preoccupied with my obsessions to see him. "It's the fools, not the intelligent men, whom I find impossible to suffer gladly."

John relaxed. "Talking of fools, I suppose you know Lion's been sacked? I saw him at a ball last weekend and he told me how thrilled he was. He was rather squiffy and trying to teach some married woman the Paris tango."

"I trust you gave him a wide berth."

"The widest, yes. I spent an hour discussing the Marconi scandal with three elderly bores and praying that no one would ask me if Lionel Godwin was a relation of mine. . . ."

We found an empty first-class compartment, paid off the porters and settled ourselves opposite each other while John talked earnestly of the Marconi scandal and the absolute necessity for a strict morality in politics.

"Quite," I said, and to steer him away from the subject of morality which so entranced him I added, "So much for politics. Tell me about yourself. Met any interesting girls lately?"

John liked girls. For some years I had waited for him to ask my advice on the vital subject of premarital carnal satisfaction, but evidently my father had improved on his discourse on the shining sea of carnality because the appeal for useful information had never come.

"Well, I met this most fascinating suffragist at a tea dance—"

"Oh my God!"

"—and she knew the woman who threw herself under the King's horse at Epsom the other day—"

"If you ask me *The Times'* leader put the entire matter in a nutshell by saying the woman showed a thorough lack of consideration for the jockey."

"—and did you realize, Robert, that the woman had actually won a first at Oxford?"

"Then that woman's suicide is the best argument I've yet heard against higher education for women. All women should be educated at home by a governess—as Ginette was."

The name was out. I, who prided myself on my immaculate self-control, was apparently reduced to dragging in the name of my beloved at every conceivable opportunity as if I were some addlepated schoolboy who had fallen in love for the first time.

"I say!" said John, so young, so innocent, so utterly unaware of my chaotic thoughts. "Isn't it splendid to think that Ginevra's coming home! How long is it since we last saw her? Four years?"

"Five." The train lurched forward at last and my heart lurched with it as the station began to recede before my eyes.

"It was a shame she only managed to visit us once during her marriage but I don't think Kinsella liked us much, do you? Robert, now that he's dead, do tell me—what was your final opinion of Conor Kinsella?"

"I've been educated as an Englishman. The English don't have opinions about the Irish. They have prejudices," I said, determined to repel all memory of Conor Kinsella, but the next moment the view from the train window had faded and in my mind I was once more drinking port with him five years ago at Brooks's, once more longing to smash my glass against the nearest wall.

VI

"I'm clean overpowered by the honor you're doing me!" said the villain. "Dining in a famous London club with a true English gentleman! I never thought I'd ever rise so high—or sink so low, depending on which side of the Irish Sea you're standing!"

"I'm a Welshman."

"To be sure you are—a Welshman with one of the most famous Saxon names of all time! Wasn't it Earl Godwin's son who fought William at Hastings?"

How does one talk to such people? If they somehow avoid talking about religion then they talk of race, and all the time they drag in history by its hind legs as if the past were a recalcitrant hero who obstinately refused to die.

Of course I had been obliged to ask him to dine. I had wanted above all to perpetuate the myth that I no longer cared about Ginette's marriage so I knew I had to make some demonstration to convince her husband that I wished him well. But beyond my compulsion to shore up my pride with such a charade I was aware of a terrible curiosity to examine my successful rival at close quarters. I think I hoped I could write him off as a failure, someone who was patently inferior to me despite his achievement in winning Ginette.

During our dinner I tried to size him up but this was difficult. I found myself increasingly aware that he came from a part of the British Isles that I had never visited, and because it was such an alien part I found it impossible to place him against any background that was familiar to me. The Welsh may be Celts as the Irish are but they are a different kind of Celt. To know the Welsh well was no passport to understanding that mysterious race which lay on the other side of the St. George's Channel.

To make matters still more confusing I sensed that the life he now lived in New York had little connection with the life he had led in Ireland. Ginette had told me his father had been the manager of a small shipping firm in Dublin, a fact which implied that Kinsella had come from a respectable middle-class home, and she had also told me that Kinsella himself had received a Catholic education, whatever that meant, in a reputable Dublin school, but as I faced him across the table at Brooks's that night it seemed to me that he had discarded both his religion and his respectability a very long time ago. Despite the fact that he dressed well and knew how to behave I sensed that he was a criminal. He had the kind of soft dark eyes which I often found among my clients, eyes that could watch iniquity with indifference. He drank too much without any noticeable effect. And in his well-kept hands and in the occasional turn of phrase I saw the cardsharper and heard the gambler speaking.

"Cards on the table!" he exclaimed at last after the waiter had brought us our port. He had a variable accent which in one sentence could range from Dublin to New York and back again. "We've been watching each other like hawks throughout the meal—why don't we now strip off the mask of courtesy and exchange our true opinions of each other?"

I had no objection. Far from it. I seized the chance to annihilate him with my perspicacity. All I said was, "Who goes first?"

"We'll toss for it!" said the gambler and flicked a florin in the air.

I called heads and won. With a smile I said, "I'm to be entirely frank in giving my opinion of you?"

"Altogether and entirely—with no offense given or taken on either side!"

"Very well." I lit a cigar. "I think you're the black sheep of your respectable Dublin family. You say you own two restaurants in Manhattan but I think your money comes not from the dining rooms but from the gambling hells—and worse—upstairs. Perhaps you have other interests too which are equally dubious because I think you've got the nerve and the flair and the sheer amoral greed to sail dangerously close to the wind in your business ventures and emerge unscathed. Some men are born criminals. I believe you're one of them. Crime really does pay for men like you. You have the well-oiled veneer of a man who's constantly on the receiving end of glittering dividends."

He roared with laughter and drank a glass of port straight off. "Oh, for shame!" he said. "And me an innocent man who goes to Mass every Sunday!" Then he poured himself some more port and leaned forward with his forearms on the table. He was still smiling. "And now," he said, "we come to you."

I was unperturbed. What could he say? I was impregnable behind the massive walls of my success, and it was inconceivable that he could reduce them to ruins.

"I look at you," said this gambler, this criminal, this personification of all my misery, "and what do I see? I see a tough customer who's made a career of grabbing what he wants and profiting out of it. You have as much amoral greed as I have but you cover it up by masquerading as an English gentleman —ah yes, you may be Welsh by birth, Robert Godwin, but it's an Englishman you are through and through and like all Englishmen you think you should be top dog. And being top dog means getting what you believe is owing to you—money, power, fame, fortune . . . and women. But you don't think of women as women, do you? You see them as prizes—glittering dividends, if I may quote your own phrase against you—but the prize you've always wanted, Robert Godwin, is the prize you can never win, and that's why you're sitting there, God help you, hating my guts and wishing I was dead. Ah, to be sure it's a terrible tragedy you've suffered! To lose your best prize to another man would be enough to break your heart—but to lose your best prize to an *Irishman* must be enough to destroy your English soul entirely! How can you dine with me and feign friendship? I swear I'd find your pride contemptible if I didn't already find it so pathetic!"

I drank a little port and eyed the glowing tip of my cigar. When I was sure I had myself in control I said, "An inaccurate survey of my private thoughts —but an amusing one."

"Are you denying you still want her?"

"There are other women in the world."

"Women who can match that childhood sweetheart?"

"Playmate," I said, "would be a more appropriate word to use, I think."

"Little girls don't stay playmates. Little girls become big girls and big girls become sweethearts."

"I was only fourteen when she left home to live at All-Hallows Court."

"I started doing all manner of things when I was fourteen," said Conor Kinsella.

There was a pause. I said nothing.

"In fact if I'd had a sweetheart like Ginevra when I was fourteen I sure wouldn't have let the grass grow under my feet."

"I happen to be exceedingly partial to grass. What the devil are you trying to say to me, Kinsella?"

"You had her, didn't you?"

I got up and walked out.

He followed me to the cloakroom.

"So I was right," he said. "Well, cynic that I am, I've always found it hard to believe in platonic friendship!"

"You're wrong," I said, "and to hell with your bloody cynicism."

"Oh, don't misunderstand!" he said after only the most fractional pause. "Of course when I married her she was as virginal as three nuns knocking at the gates of heaven—lucky man that I was!—but one can travel far, can't one, without meddling with virginity, and you can't blame me for wondering in the circumstances if the two of you had been in the habit of taking long journeys together."

I returned to the dining room, signed for the meal, stubbed out my cigar and left the club. He was just putting on his top hat as I emerged into the street. It was raining. I remember the cabs splashing mud and a motorcar sidling along like a noisy crab while nearby a bunch of inebriated young sprigs were trying to sing "Hullo Dolly Gray."

"Not a word of this to Ginevra," said Kinsella, very much the sophisticated older man telling his junior how to behave. "The poor woman wants to think we're bosom friends—ah, such a romantic she is!—and loving her as we do we've no choice but to humor her, have we? But I'll not bring her back here in a hurry—I wouldn't trust you not to try and win her when my back was turned. Oh, I know you English gentlemen! You'd lay waste the world to get what you wanted and afterwards you'd claim it was the will of God!"

And off he sauntered along St. James's Street on his way back to Claridges and his wife.

VII

It was late in the afternoon when the train approached Swansea on that June day in 1913 and John offered a paraphrase of William Blake:

"Here come the dark satanic mills."

The familiar bizarre landscape once more met my eyes. As the full curve of Swansea Bay came into sight we could dimly perceive through the pall of smoke the blue expanse of the sea and the masts of the many ships which crowded those shining, polluted waters. John hastily pulled up the window to keep the smell out as we passed through the copper-smelting area, and we both averted our eyes automatically from the scars of coal mining that marked the industrial wasteland on the ruined east side of the city.

Yet beyond the east side in the central district lay the Swansea which had provided us with our first experience of urban life, a teeming, tousled town flung against the steep hills overlooking the bay like some Naples of the North. The main streets had English names but Swansea always seemed to me as Welsh as its male choirs. Welsh dynamism pulsed through the busy streets and throbbed daily in the vast market; the Welsh lust for culture was on exhibition at the great library which was one of the city's finest buildings; the Welsh addiction to music continually floated in some form or another upon the Welsh air where the tang of the sea persisted in mingling with the reek of the smoke. Swansea might have been raped by the industrial revolution but she had survived with her vitality, if not her beauty, intact.

"I feel such a foreigner in England sometimes," said my brother John, gazing out of the window at our native land. "I feel so torn between one culture and another."

"Well, stitch yourself together again because here comes the station." I always felt John exaggerated the conundrum of belonging to two countries. Wales was home but England was the center of the world and if one wanted to get on in life one moved freely between the two without making a fuss.

To our surprise and pleasure we found that my father had dispensed with the services of his coachman and had motored himself to Swansea to bid us welcome.

"It's not often you come home nowadays, Robert," he said as we shook hands, "so I felt this was a special occasion." Scrupulously fair to John he then added: "And you deserve a royal welcome too after three such successful years up at Oxford!" I might be my father's favorite, but my father was always most conscientious about not neglecting his other children.

We retired to my father's motorcar which, though new, looked elderly because it was covered with white dust from the Gower lanes. My father loved his motorcar with a passion which John shared. The two of them spent much time discussing the merits of this new soulless brute, which was called a Talbot, while I yawned and thought what a bore the subject of mechanics was. A passion for horses I can understand; a horse is an aesthetically pleasing animal with an honorable history of service to mankind, but a passion for a few scraps of metal slapped on four wheels seems to me not only irrational but also indicative of an unintellectual, possibly even of a working-class, cast of mind.

With my father at the wheel we were soon careering through central Swansea. We roared past the ruined Norman castle, blazed past Ben Evans, the largest store, and swept by the grandest hotel, the Metropole. Other motors hooted in friendly admiration, the carriages and carts jostled to escape and the pedestrians dived for cover. While my father and John laughed, I amused myself by planning how I would defend my father against a charge of manslaughter by motor but presently I was diverted as we ascended the hill out of the city and our pace became funereal. John offered to push but my father said that would be an admission of defeat. We toiled on.

With the summit of the hill behind us we soon found ourselves on the outskirts of the city, and then with that suddenness which always took my breath away we entered a different world. A wild moorland wilderness stretched before us. Mysterious hills shimmered in the distance. We had crossed the threshold into Gower.

"Swansea's secret—the Gower Peninsula!" said my father in Welsh with a smile, and John, exhibiting somewhat showily his parrotlike trick of bilingualism, made a swift response which I failed to comprehend.

We drove on into an England beyond Wales, into a hidden land, pastoral and idyllic, which basked innocently in the summer sun. Beyond the moorland stretch which bounded the outskirts of Swansea, fields drowsed between English hedgerows and little lanes twisted through the countryside to villages which looked as if they had been transplanted from far beyond the Welsh border. We might have been a thousand miles now from teeming Swansea and a thousand years from that industrial wasteland on the bay.

"How peaceful it looks!" said John to me, but as soon as he said that I thought of Gower's lawless past. This was a land where the King's writ had so often failed to run, a land soaked in the crimes of smuggling, wrecking and piracy, robbery, murder and rape. I have always thought it an irony that we have become so civilized that we can now regard places such as Gower as "romantic" and "colorful." Personally I can think of nothing more terrifying than to live in a land where law and order have no meaning and violence is the rule of the day.

On and on we traveled through South Gower, that ancient Norman stronghold, and now on our right Cefn Bryn, the backbone of Gower, rose to form a long treeless line of land beneath the blue sky. To our left the sea at Oxwich Bay flashed far away, sometimes hidden, sometimes revealed by the gates set in the hedges. And ahead of us at last, shimmering with promise and seemingly beckoning us on into a mythical kingdom, the hump of Rhossili Downs marked the end of the Peninsula and a view that I believed no land in Europe could surpass.

We turned off before the Downs. The motor picked up speed as we roared into the parish of Penhale. Moors dotted with wild ponies stretched before us again, but we could see the trees of Oxmoon now, and presently the high wall of the grounds bordered the land on our right.

"Hurrah!" cried John as we reached the gates.

Oxmoon lay ahead of us, droll little Oxmoon, an eighteenth-century parody of the classical architecture made famous by Robert Adam. We had arrived. My father halted the motor with a triumphant jerk and as the noise of the engine died I at once felt in a better humor. We had been traveling with the roof closed and all the windows shut in order to keep the dust out, so when we flung open the doors the fresh air came as the most exquisite luxury. I got out, stretched my long legs which had not been designed to suffer gladly fifteen-mile journeys in motorcars, and took a deep breath. The air was fragrant with the scent of new-mown grass mingled with lavender. I could hear the larks singing and suddenly, for one precious moment, I was back in my childhood with Ginette so that when I turned to face my home again I saw not the provincial little country house of reality but the fairy-tale palace of my dreams.

My mother opened the front door.

Instantly the past was wiped out and I was left with all my most ambivalent emotions in a highly uncertain present. Assuming an impregnable mask of filial respect I exclaimed with warmth, "My dear Mama, how splendid to see you again!" and moved swiftly up the steps to embrace her.

"Dearest Robert," said my mother, regarding me tranquilly with those pale eyes which saw far too far and much too much, "welcome home."

VIII

I was at Oxmoon waiting for Ginette. It was seven o'clock on the evening of my arrival and I was dressing for dinner. Fifteen hours to go.

When I had finished I paused to survey my oldest possessions which, arranged around me on shelves, created a powerful atmosphere of nostalgia. Here were the silver cups I had acquired during the course of my academic and athletic career as a schoolboy. Here were the favorite books of my boyhood, the dog-eared collection of Robert Louis Stevenson's work, the battered copy of *Eric*, the haggard edition of *The Prisoner of Zenda*. Here were my school photographs hanging at regular intervals on the wall above my bed to record my progress from stony-faced small boy to supercilious young man. Why had I kept this amazing collection of trivia? I could only suppose that despite my well-ordered mind I had fallen victim to one of Oxmoon's most exasperating traditions: everything was hoarded; nothing was thrown away.

Tucked discreetly behind a cushion on the window seat I even found the toy dog which I had been given in infancy, his white woolly coat worn threadbare and his ears sagging with age. To my astonishment I saw that his tail had recently been repaired. This seemed to indicate either the presence in the house of a demented housemaid or a tension so profound in my mother that she had been obliged to scour the bedrooms for something to sew. I was just picking up the dog tenderly by the front paws and remembering how I had screamed when Ginette had once tried to annex him, when the door of my room was flung open without warning to reveal a small intruder in a nightshirt.

"You're wanted," said my youngest brother Thomas, and seeing the toy in my arms he added, "I want that dog. I took him last week but Papa said I had to ask you if you minded. We had a tug-of-war over it actually and his tail came off. The dog's, I mean, not Papa's. Well, Papa doesn't have a tail. Anyway it didn't matter because Mama sewed it on again. Can I have him?"

"No. Who wants me?"

"Mama. She's in her room. Why can't I have Dodo?"

"Because you haven't said Please and you didn't knock before you came in. Run away and learn how to behave."

"Yah!" said the infant, sticking out his tongue at me, and stumped off angrily to the nurseries.

In a large family it is not uncommon to find a sting in the tail and the sting is usually referred to as an "afterthought." This afterthought, far from being ignored as befits the youngest and least significant member of a tribe, is often most foolishly pampered until he has ideas far above his station. Thomas was six and his ideas of his own importance were so elevated that they probably, like the occupants of the recent record-breaking balloon, needed oxygen to survive.

How he had come to enter the world was a mystery to me, and not a pleasant mystery, either. In fact I had been much disturbed when in my mid-twenties I was informed that my mother was expecting another child. My feelings arose not because I felt it was in poor taste for my mother to indulge in parturition at an advanced age; at that time she was still only forty-two, a curious but by no means preposterous age at which to embark on pregnancy. The truth was that I was disturbed by the news because it seemed my father had lied to me about his private life.

I was twenty when I found out he was unfaithful to my mother. There was no dramatic scene. The dénouement arose from my observation that he had formed the regular habit of going up to town once a month and staying three or four days at his club. My mother said this was a good idea because he tended to work too hard at home and now that he was older she felt it was important that he should go away to relax occasionally. I thought no more about this reasonable explanation for his absences, but one day during the long vacation when he and I were out riding together I said casually, "What do you do with yourself when you're up in town, Papa?" and he had answered with regret but without hesitation: "I knew you'd ask me that one day and I made up my mind that when you did I'd be honest with you."

He then told me he kept a woman in Maida Vale.

"Of course," he said, "your natural reaction will be to think me a hypocrite after all I've said to you on the subject of reserving that sort of pleasure for marriage but in fact my views haven't changed. I don't like what I'm doing and I don't ask you to condone it. All I ask is that you should try to understand and not judge me too harshly."

He said the intimate side of marriage had become repugnant to my mother and added that this was hardly surprising after so many pregnancies.

". . . certainly I don't blame her, how could I, she's the most wonderful wife in the world and I'm the luckiest man on earth and I love her with all my heart, as you know. But . . . well, on religious grounds your mother don't hold with anticonception, and as for chastity that's a gift I don't possess, not at the age of forty after twenty-one years of perfect married life."

He revealed that my mother herself had suggested that he kept a mistress.

"She said she wouldn't mind so long as it was a business arrangement conducted a long way from home—she said it would even be a relief to her because the last thing she wanted was to make me unhappy. So . . . well, we thought London would be best. I didn't want to go into Swansea. In fact I couldn't. You see, my father used to go into Swansea and . . ." He stopped. As usual he could never bring himself to talk about his father but this time I saw to my horror that he was about to break down altogether. There were tears in his eyes. Hastily I gave him my word that I quite understood his predicament and thought none the worse of him for his solution.

The conversation then closed and I never raised the subject again until he told me Thomas had been conceived.

"But my dear Papa, I thought you told me that side of your marriage had ceased!"

He laughed and said quickly, "It was the night of our silver wedding—just an isolated occasion."

"But you said my mother—"

"Oh, now that she's had a rest from childbearing she's anxious for one final pregnancy."

I was a trained lawyer by that time but an inexperienced one; it was not until later that my professional instincts told me my father had had something to hide. This fact by itself, however, was neither remarkable nor a cause for alarm for there was no reason why my father should have told me every salient detail of his private life, particularly as any marriage is a very private affair. But what troubled me was that I sensed my father had brought off a *tour de force* which I could only regard as sinister: I suspected he had blended fact and fiction with the skill of an uncommonly gifted liar.

As soon as I had formed this judgment I dismissed it as ridiculous, but Thomas always reminded me of it and I knew I was more abrupt with the child than I should have been. Making a mental note to bestow the toy dog on him with my blessing I remembered the message he had brought me. It was time for battle again at Oxmoon. Smoothing my hair I looked in the glass to ensure that my appearance was immaculate, and then I set off to wage war with my mother.

IX

"Hullo, dear," said my mother, barely glancing up as I entered the room. She was seated at the dressing table and sifting through one of her jewel boxes for a suitable adornment for her dowdy evening gown. As I closed the door she retrieved a dreary trinket studded with jet and began to pin it on her ample bosom. "Do sit down," she added as an afterthought, nodding at the customary victim's chair nearby.

I moved the chair back against the wall so that it stood facing her but out of reach of the triple looking glass. Then I manifested nonchalance by sitting down and crossing one leg over the other but immediately she readjusted the far mirror until against all the odds my reflection was recaptured. Embarking on a study of the ceiling I prayed for patience and heartily wished myself elsewhere.

I wondered not for the first time if she really had told my father to take a mistress or whether my father had invented this magnanimous gesture in order to gloss over the wifely failings that had driven him elsewhere. Anger pierced me suddenly. I sensed she had made my father unhappy, and if she had rejected him I felt I could only find her attitude repellent.

It also occurred to me, as I continued to observe her, that her rejection showed a lack not only of charity but of gratitude. A plain middle-aged woman should surely be so thankful to have a handsome successful devoted husband that she should make every effort to accommodate him. I remembered how my father never uttered one word of complaint about her *nouveau-riche* background and her appalling relations in Staffordshire. He had married beneath him when he had married her, and although her Midlands accent had long since disappeared and her more unfortunate social attributes had been ironed away by a formidable air of refinement, she could never be his equal in rank. The marriage had been arranged to save Oxmoon from bankruptcy. If my father had been older and if his mother and Owain Bryn-Davies had been less desperate for money, I had no doubt that my father would have looked elsewhere for a wife.

However the marriage had been successful enough in its own way and my mother did have many virtues. Reminding myself how fond I was of her I made renewed efforts to be charitable.

"What did you wish to speak to me about, Mama?" I said, knowing perfectly well that she had diagnosed the state of my heart with unerring accuracy and had resolved to advise me against marrying Ginette.

"Well, dear," said my mother, poking around in her jewel box, "I just thought we might have a little chat before Ginevra arrives tomorrow. Your father told me of the conversation he had recently with you in London."

"Ah yes," I said; "I did wonder if you'd think his report needed clarification."

We exchanged smiles.

"Oh no, dear," said my mother. "You told your father, I believe, that you had every intention of behaving like a mature intelligent man. What sentiment could be more clearly expressed? I simply wished to reassure you that like your father all I want is your happiness, Robert. I wanted to reassure you of that in case you were harboring some suspicion that I had every intention of making you miserable."

"Far be it from me, Mama, to suspect you of such an unworthy aim."

We laughed politely together. There was a pause. I waited.

"I do so disapprove," said my mother, extricating a pair of jet earrings from the jewel box, "of mothers who meddle in the lives of their grown-up children, so you need have no fear that I'm going to meddle. After all, why should I? You're a man of the world. You don't need your mother to remind you of the hazards of marrying a widow of thirty-three with two growing sons and a somewhat . . . unusual past. Nor do you need your mother to tell you how much better you could do for yourself. Nor need I point out to you the danger of relying on illusions which bear no relation to reality—naturally you're well aware of the dangers of carrying an adolescent infatuation forward into adult life. So all in all, Robert—bearing in mind that you're a supremely rational man and thoroughly experienced in the Ways of the World—I have decided to say nothing whatsoever on the subject and to hold my peace in order to display my utmost confidence in the ultimate triumph of your good sense."

There was another pause. When I was sure I had my temper in control, I said, "Mama, it's hard to believe you've never studied Cicero. One of his favorite oratorical tricks was to declare, 'I shall say nothing about this' and then to say everything in the most excruciating detail." Standing up abruptly, I moved beyond the range of the triple looking glass before saying, "You seem to be implying I'm a complete fool."

"It's a sad fact of life, dear, that not even men of a brilliant intellectual caliber are incapable of making a mistake where affairs of the heart are concerned. Indeed quite the contrary, I've always thought."

"I'm not interested in your opinion of some idiotic state of mind which as far as I'm concerned exists only in the pages of romantic fiction."

"Oh my dear Robert—"

"I'm sorry, Mama, but really this skirmishing is exhausting my patience!"

"Then let me be direct." Leaving her dressing table, she moved swiftly to my side, gripped my shoulders and spun me to face her. "Let me speak straight from the heart. Your father believes you when you imply you've recovered from Ginevra, but you haven't recovered, have you, Robert? I think you're bound to see Ginevra's bereavement as an opportunity for you to rewrite the past and wipe out the memory of that time when you were humiliated. You're such a very clever man, but very clever men can be capable of such disastrous emotional naivety!"

"Why are you so against Ginette?"

"When she visited Oxmoon five years ago, I had the chance to sum her up and I saw exactly what kind of a woman she had become."

"A beautiful woman necessarily finds it hard to win the approbation of her own sex—"

"Oh, don't misunderstand me! I don't disapprove of her because she's the sort of woman who wouldn't think twice about being unfaithful to her husband—such women often manage to sustain successful marriages. No, I disapprove of her as a wife for you because I think she's a complex woman with all kinds of problems you couldn't begin to solve."

"Mama—"

"You see, I know you, Robert. I know you better than you know yourself. You're like me. At heart your emotional tastes are really very simple."

"I'll be the best judge, thank you, Mama, about what my emotional tastes really are. And if you think I'm like you then all I can say is that I can't see the resemblance."

There was a silence. For a moment we stood there, inches apart, and stared at each other. Then she covered her face with her hands and turned away.

"Mama . . ." I was immediately appalled by my cruelty. "Forgive me, I—"

"It was my fault," she said levelly, letting her hands fall and moving back to the dressing table. "I shouldn't have meddled."

"I do have the greatest respect and regard for you, Mama—"

"Oh yes," she said flatly. "Respect and regard. How nice." She found a garnet ring, shoved it onto her finger and snapped shut the box.

"I have always entertained the very deepest affection—"

"Quite." She made no effort to respond as I stooped to touch her cheek with my lips. I had a fleeting impression of eau de cologne and anger. Her plump cheek was cold. When she said abruptly, "Hadn't we better go downstairs?" I made no effort to detain her, and after opening the door in a formal gesture of courtesy I followed her in silence from the room.

X

Unable to sleep that night I lay awake remembering the aspersions which my mother had cast on Ginette's capacity for marital fidelity.

In the old days Ginette had been conspicuous for her loyalty. I could remember her standing shoulder to shoulder with me in the nursery, writing to me at school every week without fail and even after her marriage keeping in touch with me when a less faithful friend would have permitted the relationship to become moribund.

Yet although I did not question her capacity for loyal friendship I knew well enough that sexual fidelity was a game played to different rules. Friendship might be forever but people fell in and out of love, and marriage was far from immune to this well-known ebbing and flowing of desire. Would I blame Ginette for being unfaithful to Kinsella? No, of course not. A man like Kinsella deserved an unfaithful wife. But I wasn't Conor Kinsella and my marriage would be played to different rules.

Not only would I give Ginette no cause for infidelity, but I would make it clear to her from the beginning that she was to behave as a wife should. Like servants, women need to be told what to do; they like firm guidance, and that is why I am so unalterably opposed to votes for women. In reality it would not mean independence for females. It would mean that all the masterful husbands, lovers, fathers and brothers would have two votes instead of one. A woman's talents are limited to managing a home and bringing up children. One can no more expect a woman to show independence of mind by casting an intelligent vote than one can expect a woman to debate an important issue in the House of Commons with implacable oratorical skill.

I thought of my mother reminding me of Cicero, the greatest orator of all time.

But that proved my point. All my mother had ever wanted to do was to manage a home and bring up children. My mother was a clever woman, possibly the cleverest woman I had ever met, and she had no interest whatsoever in women's suffrage.

When I finally fell asleep it was well after midnight but by six o'clock I was already awake and picturing Ginette asleep in her cabin on the steamer that had been carrying her overnight from Dublin to Swansea. Would she be nervous? She had been nervous when she had returned for her visit five years before, although she had tried to hide her feelings behind a mask of exuberance.

"Robet darling, how heavenly to see you again—give me a divine platonic kiss to celebrate our eternal friendship!"

I shuddered at the memory and wondered how I was going to survive the inevitable sexual frustration which lay in store for me. She herself would be safe, locked up in her role of the bereaved widow, but what on earth was going to happen to me as she dabbed her eyes with a black lace handkerchief and succeeded in looking seductively haggard?

I groaned, and then gritting my teeth I began to plan a debonair speech to welcome her home.

XI

Four hours later I was awaiting her imminent arrival. I had made some excuse to escape from the mob milling in the hall and was standing motionless at the landing window which faced the drive. As I nervously embarked on smoking a cigarette I wondered what to do with the ash, but in the end I was in such a state that I merely let it drop to the floor.

Various inane remarks floated up the stairs.

"Let's all pose for a photograph!" Celia was calling breathlessly.

"Celia, give me your camera!" That was the infant, being obstreperous as usual.

"No, Thomas—no, *Thomas*—oh, Mama, do stop him—"

"Edmund," said John, intelligent enough to remain urbane amidst all this hysteria, "what about a quick game of billiards? I bet the steamer's been delayed."

"But supposing it hasn't?" Edmund, even though he was now nineteen, suffered from a constitutional inability to make up his mind.

"I think she'll be arriving at any minute," said Lion, "and if you go off to the billiard room you'll be fools. Lord, isn't this a thrill? I keep visualizing this splendid creature swathed in black and looking unutterably sumptuous—"

"Shhh! Here comes Mama."

"Boys, have you seen Robert anywhere?"

"No, he's gone off to be wonderful somewhere else, thank God," said Lion, revealing that he was less than respectful when my back was turned.

"That will do, Lionel. No, Thomas, you *cannot* have Celia's camera. Edmund—"

"Here's the car!"

"She's coming!"

"Quick, quick, quick—"

"Papa—quickly, Papa, the motor's here!"

"Out to the porch, everyone—"

"Come on, Celia—"

"Come on, Edmund—"

"Come on, everyone!"

There was a stampede of feet below me. Meanwhile I had dropped my cigarette and was making the most intolerable mess. Having unforgivably ground the butt beneath my heel I drew back for cover behind the curtain as my father's Talbot bore the bereaved widow at an appropriately funereal pace up the drive to the steps of the porch.

"Hurray!"

"Welcome home!"

"Welcome back, Ginevra!"

"Shhh, boys, a little less noise and a little more decorum, if you please— remember she's in mourning."

My brothers fell obediently silent but as soon as the motor halted they rushed forward to catch a glimpse of the passenger. It was impossible for me and probably difficult for them to perceive her with any degree of clarity. The white dust from the Gower roads had once more laid a pale mask upon the windows.

"Ginevra!" cried Lion, beaming from ear to ear as he flung wide the door of the motor, and then the next moment his mouth dropped open in astonishment. Everyone gasped. My father was suddenly motionless. My mother appeared to be rooted to the ground.

Evidently our visitor was making some shattering impact but since I could see only the roof of the motor I still had no idea what was happening. In a fever of curiosity I flung up the window as far as it would go so that I could lean out over the sill, and it was at that exact moment that she began to descend from the motor. Then I understood. As soon as I saw her I too gasped, for she was not wearing mourning. The image of the widow swathed in black was at a stroke smashed to smithereens.

"Darlings!" cried Ginette, gorgeously clad in a brilliant turquoise traveling costume and sporting a corsage of orchids. "How simply and utterly divine to see you all again!" And as everyone continued to stare at her in stupefaction she glanced carelessly upwards and saw me framed in the window above.

A great stillness descended on her face but a second later she was blowing me a kiss with a smile. "Heavens, darling!" she called richly. "Just like Romeo and Juliet in reverse—all you need is a balcony! What are you doing up there?"

"I was on my way to the kitchen garden to pick you some strawberries!" I said laughing, and at once saw the past recaptured in her dark and brilliant eyes.

3

I

WE DRANK CHAMPAGNE in the drawing room, a spacious room which Robert Godwin the Renovator had called a saloon and filled with eighteenth-century furniture. Unfortunately this elegant collection now lay under dust sheets in the attics, for my parents, whose aesthetic tastes could most kindly be described as eclectic, had long since decided to cram the Oxmoon reception rooms with overstuffed chairs, obese sofas and a bewildering jungle of bric-à-brac.

Oxmoon was famous for its ready supply of champagne to complement important occasions. It was the only alcoholic beverage which my father permitted himself to enjoy; he would take two glasses and, very occasionally, a third. Now that I was older I admired his abstemiousness the more because his cronies among the Gower gentry were a hard-drinking bunch, and I knew from experience how difficult it was not to drink to excess when in the company of men determined to be inebriated.

On this current momentous family occasion my father permitted himself a third glass of champagne. My mother, according to a custom which she never varied, took two glasses with enjoyment and declined another drop. Lion seized the opportunity to join my father in a third glass, John followed my mother's example to show how good he was at drawing the line, and Edmund, as usual, could not make up his mind whether to continue drinking or to abstain. Celia, who had a weak head, was still conscientiously nursing her first glass while I, who could normally take my drink as well as the next man, was keeping pace with her. It is one of the idiosyncrasies of my constitution that under great stress my emotions are not soothed by the consumption of alcohol but exacerbated by it.

Meanwhile in the midst of this studied moderation Ginette was drinking the champagne as if it were lemonade. As the celebration progressed we all stole uneasy glances at my mother to see how she was tolerating this further manifestation of conduct unbecoming to a widow, and although my mother continued to smile serenely the tension steadily increased. I was just wondering how I could abort this sinister emotional momentum when Ginette tossed off the remains of her fourth glass of champagne and said rapidly to my mother, "Margaret, you must be quite horrified, do forgive me, but I'm simply overwhelmed by the desire to rebel against the way I was treated in Ireland—everyone behaved as if my life was finished, and suddenly I couldn't bear it any longer, as soon as I reached the steamer I wanted to throw all my mourning clothes into the sea . . ." She stopped. She was on the verge of breaking down.

"Even your hats?" I said promptly.

"Oh my dear, you know what I'm like about hats!" she said, laughing through her tears. "Even the black ones are much too gorgeous to throw overboard!"

"You'd make any hat look gorgeous!" said Lion roguishly.

"Darling Lion, how adorable you are!"

"Where did you get those incredibly vulgar orchids?" I said to put an end to this cloying exchange of compliments.

"I forced poor Williams to drive up and down the main streets of Swansea until we finally found that very grand florist near the Metropole. No wonder I was late getting here!" She had recovered her equilibrium. Her hand moved automatically back to her glass.

"Orchids and champagne!" said my father who became subtly more carefree under the influence of alcohol. "Good friends—amusing company—laughter—happiness! Yes, that's the remedy I'd prescribe to anyone recovering from terrible times—and we know all about recovering from terrible times, don't we, Margaret?"

"Yes, dear," said my mother.

"Ginevra," said my father, "I insist that you permit me to write a prescription for you: I propose a little dinner party for twenty-four as soon as possible!"

Celia protested amidst the ensuing cheers: "But Papa, I don't suppose Ginevra wants to see anyone outside the family just yet!" She glanced nervously at my mother.

"And what would all the neighbors think?" said John, so driven by his desire to do the done thing that he failed to shrink from exhibiting a lamentably bourgeois cast of mind.

"Oh, damn the neighbors!" exclaimed Ginette, and in the absolute silence that followed I was acutely aware of my mother straightening the garnet ring on her right hand.

Ginette blushed, and in the panic-stricken glance she sent me I read a desperate appeal for help but I was already speaking. Moving to her side I said casually, "I expect women say 'damn' all the time in New York, don't they? *Autre pays, autres moeurs.*"

"What a rotten French accent you've got, Robert," said John, valiantly collaborating with me in helping the conversation along, but Ginette proved quite unable to permit us to gloss over the disaster.

"Margaret, I'm so sorry—please do excuse me—awful vulgarity—frightful taste—" She was in agony.

Ignoring her my mother said serenely to my father, "I think a little dinner party would be acceptable, dearest, provided we have only our oldest friends. But it must be quiet. No champagne; I think champagne would look too eccentric in the circumstances."

"I agree," said my father obediently. "A good claret—perhaps a touch of hock somewhere—but no champagne."

"And of course," said my mother to Celia, "you and I must wear dark gowns, dear, to acknowledge the fact that there's been a tragedy in the family."

"Yes, Mama," said Celia.

"Dearest Ginevra," said my mother, smiling to conceal how implacably she was wielding her power, "you must think us so provincial and old-fashioned in our ways, but we're so far removed here from a modern city like New York! I do hope you understand."

"Yes, Margaret," said Ginette. "Of course." She was clutching her glass so hard that I thought the stem would snap.

"Naturally," pursued my mother, "I wouldn't dream of dictating to you on the subject of dress. I have every confidence, dearest, that you'll contrive to look dignified as well as fetching on any occasion when people outside the family are to be present."

"Yes, Margaret." Her hand shook as she put down her glass. She stood up clumsily. "I must go upstairs and unpack—all my black gowns will need ironing—I wonder if perhaps your maid—"

"I'll send her to you at once," said my mother, clinching her victory with a single succinct sentence.

"I'll come and help you, Ginevra," said Celia, and we all rose to our feet. Lion, John and Edmund all tried to open the door in an orgy of chivalry, and there was much laughter as they bumped into one another. The women departed. My father said, "Who's going to volunteer to deliver the dinner invitations? Time's short as Robert's going back to London on Monday, so we'll have to give this party tomorrow night."

An argument began about how quickly the invitations could be delivered but I did not stay to listen to it. Opening the garden door I slipped out onto the terrace and the next moment I was escaping across the lawn.

II

Cutting a straight line past the freshly painted croquet hoops I circled the lawn tennis court and paused on the edge of the woods by the summerhouse, a two-roomed frivolity built at the whim of my grandfather Robert Godwin the Drunkard in the days before his unfortunate habits had driven his wife to seek consolation with her sheep farmer, Owain Bryn-Davies. In the open doorway I turned to look back at the inheritance his son had resurrected from the grave.

Oxmoon's original name had been Oxton-de-Mohun, which in a loose translation of the three conquerors' languages involved meant "the settlement by water belonging to Humphrey de Mohun." Of the three aggressive races who had battered the Peninsula the Vikings, prowling the coasts in their longships, had probably had the least effect; the Saxons, trading continuously from North Devon, had steadily insinuated their influence among the indigenous Celts, and the Normans had blasted their way into the seat of power with their usual brutal efficiency.

Humphrey de Mohun had been a twelfth-century Norman warlord who had delegated the running of his Gower estate to a Saxon mercenary called Godwin of Hartland. Hartland is the Devonian peninsula that lies south of Gower across the Bristol Channel, and in English-speaking South Gower—called "The Englishry" to distinguish it from "The Welshery" of the Welsh-speaking northeast—Devon is reflected like a mirror image, a little distorted but plainly recognizable, the result of centuries of communication between Wales and England across the busy waters of the Channel.

Godwin set the seal on a successful career when he married de Mohun's younger daughter. When de Mohun died, the elder daughter received her father's vast estates in the Welsh Marches but the younger inherited the fiefdom in Gower which included the fortified tower in the woods below Penhale Down. Financially, socially and territorially Godwin had arrived, and giving his son the Norman name of Robert he settled down to become more Norman than the Normans.

The Norman tower remained the home of the Godwin family until Tudor times when fifteenth-century Robert Godwin tried to celebrate the Battle of Bosworth by building a moated manor, but after this architectural innovation had been razed by a faction from Llangennith he retired to the Norman castle of his ancestors. In the seventeenth century the master of Oxmoon attempted to build a Jacobean mansion on the site of the Tudor manor, but he abandoned the attempt when it became obvious that the result would be a disaster. However the founder of modern Oxmoon, Robert Godwin the Renovator, decided that this uncompleted monstrosity could be finished and given a new look. He had met Robert Adam in Italy during a typical eighteenth-century tour of Europe, and later he became acquainted with the architects of the Wyatt family. Inspiration inevitably followed, and in the library we have one of his letters declaring his intention of making Oxmoon the grandest house in Wales.

A highly idiosyncratic vision of classical architecture was thus initiated, a rustic rendering of a magnificent dream. The portico was rather too large, the windows a fraction too narrow, pediments and chimneys appeared in unexpected places. But if not the grandest house in Wales it must have been one of the most unusual; in South Wales particularly such places are few and far between.

That was the end of the rebuilding of Oxmoon although various additions to the house and grounds occurred later. Robert Godwin the Regency Rake added the ballroom after a visit to Bath, and experimented with an orangerie which collapsed. My grandfather Robert Godwin the Drunkard later restored it before turning his hand to designing the summerhouse.

The results of these centuries of idealistic efforts to bring civilization to this formerly remote and lawless land lay now before my eyes. Despite the small failures of design, which were less noticeable at a distance, the house was at least passably proportioned. It had no basement, two floors and an attic. Virginia creeper, clinging to walls that should have been left bare, gave it an unorthodox look of shaggy coziness, and this unorthodoxy was enhanced by the presence of the ballroom, a startling excrescence upon the Georgian symmetry which looked as if the architect had been reading too many of the Gothic novels of Mrs. Radclyffe during a fatal visit to Brighton Pavilion. However the balance in favor of the conventional was somewhat restored on the other side of the house where the kitchen wing meandered into courtyards which embraced the servants' quarters, the stable block, the farmyard, the timberyard, the kitchen garden and the blighted orangerie where nothing would grow except stunted grapes. Provincial and relaxed, sunlit and cherished, twentieth-century Oxmoon faced its future master across the manicured lawn of the eighteenth-century "pleasure garden" and shimmered beguilingly in the hot noon light.

I felt at peace.

Yet the very peace, which was so unfamiliar, served to remind me of my intractable problems. Rising to my feet to shut them from my mind I sought refuge in the soothing shadows of the woods but at the ruined Norman tower I turned back. Another path led me out of the trees on the far side of the tennis lawn, and strolling down the lavender walk I found myself heading into the walled rectangle of the kitchen garden.

Most of the fruit lay at the far end where an ancient orchard flourished, but nearby I was aware of the strawberry beds exuding their old seductive fragrance. I paused. My senses sharpened. I felt that nothing had changed—despite the fact that everything had changed. I felt time had stood still—and yet I knew it had moved inexorably on. Stooping impulsively I plucked a strawberry from beneath the leaves, and then as the past repeated itself by sliding ahead of the present I knew immediately, without looking up, that Ginette was once more moving down the path to my side.

III

"Robert."

She had changed into a plain black skirt and an elaborate black blouse which opened at the neck to reveal a string of pearls. She had looked striking in turquoise and orchids but in stark black with chaste jewelry she was alluring beyond description. I found myself smiling as I realized how effortlessly—and no doubt unconsciously—my mother's veiled demand for seemliness had been outwitted.

"You shouldn't have let my mother dictate to you in the matter of dress," I said abruptly, offering her the strawberry in my hand.

"My dear, whenever Margaret opens her mouth and says 'dearest Ginevra' I'm immediately reduced to a mindless mass quivering with terror! Heavens, how delicious this strawberry is. Do you remember—"

"Vividly."

"—how we overate and were sick and Margaret put us on bread and water as a punishment—"

"Are all children so mindlessly preoccupied with food, I wonder?"

"Of course! Eating's the first of the great sensual pleasures of life—although of course children don't believe heroes and heroines should be sensual at all. Do you remember how you said you wanted to be a hero?"

"I remember expressing considerable doubt that you'd ever be a heroine."

"I suppose it all depends how you define heroes and heroines, doesn't it? I've come to the conclusion they're unheroic people who flounder around, stagger in and out of awful messes and somehow manage to survive without going mad. Oh, I became a heroine, Robert! But the big question is . . . what became of you? Who are you now? Are you still there?"

I knew at once what she meant. "Yes," I said. "I'm still here."

"Thank God. You terrified me when I arrived. All I could see was this formidable stranger encased in glamour." She stooped to pick another strawberry. "Darling, for heaven's sake take me away from here before I make a complete pig of myself."

We smiled at each other. Our hands clasped. We said no more but walked away without hurrying, and around us past and present kept shifting and interlocking like a constantly shaken kaleidoscope. Bees hummed lazily along the lavender walk and as we drew nearer the tennis lawn the scent of lavender once more gave way to the scent of new-mown grass, drifting towards us on the limpid summer air.

"I can hear the larks singing," said Ginette suddenly.

"Oxmoon Redux."

"What does that mean?"

"The past recaptured."

We reached the summerhouse and turned in unison to look back across the lawn.

"Oxmoon!" said Ginette, and as the tears filled her eyes she said in a shaking voice, "I've done it. I've come home."

I gave her my handkerchief and helped her sit down on one of the wicker chairs. As I sat down beside her she whispered, "I did love him."

"Yes." I watched the curve of her neck below her auburn hair. "I saw that when you were eighteen and I saw it five years ago when you were twenty-eight. Why should I start disbelieving in your love now?"

"Because I'm behaving as if I'm mad with relief. But I'm mad with pain and grief too—it's hard to explain, I'm in such a muddle, oh Robert, Robert, why do I always end up in these ghastly messes?"

"You need someone who can train you to be orderly. Let me offer my services by attempting to dissipate this air of mystery which is clinging to you like a fog—no one can hope to be orderly while they're wallowing in mystery. How did he die?"

"He was shot."

"What! How?"

"With a gun."

"Oh, don't be so stupid, Ginette! I meant how did it happen?"

"Oh, that sort of thing happens quite often in New York. It's that sort of place. I hated it at the end but I loved it in the beginning. It was the city of my youth, the place where all my dreams came true—"

"Never mind that sentimental twaddle for the moment. Let's keep this a well-ordered narrative. Just tell me why he was shot."

"Oh God, I don't know, how should I know, I suppose he got on the wrong side of the Sicilians over his gambling debts, certainly his Irish friends said it would be safer if I left town as soon as possible—"

"But this is barbarous! Are you trying to tell me—"

"Oh yes, it was barbarous, it was hell, it was ghastly beyond belief, God knows why I'm not dead with shock and horror—"

"Tell me exactly what happened."

"He was shot dead on the sidewalk outside our apartment block. We'd been to the theater. He died in my arms." She was sitting on the edge of her chair, my handkerchief clenched in her hands. "That sounds romantic, doesn't it, but it wasn't. It wasn't romantic at all." Tears streamed down her face again. "He screamed in pain and choked on his blood," she said, her voice trembling, "and his last word was an obscenity. 'Shit,' he said. That was all. 'Shit.' Then more blood came out of his mouth and he died." She covered her face with her hands, and although by this time instinct was telling me that her married happiness had not been unflawed, she sobbed with a grief which I had no choice but to acknowledge was genuine.

I took her hand in mine again. No further words were necessary. She knew I sympathized, she knew I understood the horror she had endured, she knew I was there to stand beside her and give her all the help I could, and gradually her tears ceased. She was just turning towards me in gratitude at last when we were interrupted. Far away across the lawn the garden door was flung wide as Lion, John and Edmund bounded out onto the terrace.

"Oh God," I said. "Let me go and fend them off."

"No—no, it doesn't matter, I'm all right now. . . . Oh, look at them, how adorable they are, so fresh and new and unspoiled—"

"Spare me the sentimentality. They're noisy, tiresome and ignorant, and at present they're no use to you at all. Now look here, Ginette. This is what you must do—"

"Robert, I must see you on your own again before you go back to London, I simply must."

"Don't interrupt. Just pay attention to me for a moment before those three boys get within earshot. Are you listening? Very well, now summon all your energy to survive luncheon. Then retire to your room and *rest* for the remainder of the day—you're obviously worn out. But we'll meet tomorrow. In the morning I have to go out with Papa to see the estate but in the afternoon I'll borrow the motor and we'll escape."

"But Robert, what will Margaret think?"

"My dear Ginette, I don't care what she thinks and neither should you! Why this slavish preoccupation with my mother?"

"Because she's the only mother I can remember, and daughters who are so hopeless at doing the done thing and sticking to the rules are automatically paralyzed with guilt whenever they come within fifty yards of a mother like Margaret."

"But it's irrational to be so intimidated! After all, who is she? Just an ordinary little woman with a provincial mind and conservative tastes! For God's sake, take no notice of her if she implies you should behave like Queen Victoria after Prince Albert died!"

Our conversation was at that point terminated by my brothers who were halfway across the lawn.

"Coo-ee!" called Lion idiotically. "What are you two up to? Reciting all your old nursery rhymes?"

"Darling Lion!" murmured Ginette, incorrigibly sentimental. "Who would have thought that monster of a baby would turn out to be so amusing? I'm passionate about his *joie de vivre!*"

I could think of more rewarding objects for her passion but I kept my mouth shut and contented myself with repossessing her hand.

All things considered I felt my prospects were not unfavorable.

IV

"Murdered!" exclaimed my father. He reined in his horse and stared at me.

"She herself doesn't want to talk about it, but she asked me yesterday to tell the rest of the family so I thought you should be the first to know."

We were riding down one of the narrow country lanes that crisscrossed the Oxmoon estate in the center of Gower. Penhale Down towered on our right, Harding's Down shimmered ahead and the lie of the land beyond the Oxmoon woods prevented us from seeing the long high line of Rhossili Downs which protected the inland plain from the sea. We were on our way to Martinscombe, the only one of my father's four major farms that specialized in upland sheep. I could see the sheep now, dotted over Penhale Down, but we were still half a mile from the farmhouse.

I was feeling very hot. I rode often enough in London for exercise so I could not complain I was unaccustomed to the exertion, but the weather was unusually warm and my mind was in an uncharacteristically overheated state. As the conversation turned towards Ginette I felt the sweat break out afresh on my back.

"But how appalling for Ginevra," said my father, "to see her husband killed before her eyes!"

"Appalling, yes." Following his example I too reined in my horse and we faced each other in the lane.

"How did it happen?"

I told him and added, "Obviously New York is the most barbarous and uncivilized place."

"As Gower used to be." My father stared at the tranquil rural landscape that surrounded us. "Barbarity's everywhere, that's the truth of it. Absolutely anyone is capable of absolutely anything."

"My dear Papa, I had no idea you were such a cynic!"

"That's not cynicism, that's honesty—as you well know, dealing with criminals as you do, seeing the human race continually at its worst."

"My profession has only underlined to me the importance of civilized behavior—a civilizing influence can be a powerful deterrent to iniquity. . . . But you're thinking of Bryn-Davies, aren't you? Some people, I agree, are certainly capable of anything." As I spoke it suddenly occurred to me that I had been living with the mystery of his past for over quarter of a century and that now was the time to solve it, analyze it and file it away once and for all. "What exactly did Bryn-Davies get up to, Papa?" I said, adopting the tone of mild interest that I used with nervous witnesses. "I know he seduced your mother and plundered your estate, but was that the limit of his crimes?"

My father said nothing.

"Did my grandfather really die of drink?" I said, and started counting. A bad liar will let a silence of several seconds elapse while he tries to frame a reply. A good liar will play for time while he keeps the silence at bay.

"Your grandfather died of something-or-other of the liver," said my father without a second's hesitation. "The doctor wrote it down for me but the word looked so uncommonly odd that I could never work out how to pronounce it, but of course you'll know the word I mean; I believe the disease is very common among drunkards." He paused. He had now worked out what he considered to be the perfect reply. Smiling at me he said, "You mustn't start seeing murder in every death, Robert! I'm sure you'd never have thought of asking that question if you hadn't been working in a world where murder is commonplace."

That was a valid criticism, and smiling back I made a gesture to acknowledge it. We said no more on the subject. As we rode on my father began to talk of the Martinscombe sheep and soon he was recalling Bryn-Davies' famous dictum that Penhale Down might have been designed by God to produce strong ewes and twin lambs.

My father managed all four of the major farms on the estate himself and his four foremen answered directly to him instead of to a bailiff. He always said a bailiff would be guaranteed to annoy the laborers and make the wrong decisions, but no doubt he had been influenced by the memory of his father who had made a disastrous habit of hiring the wrong men for the post.

My father was also in a position, exceptional among his fellow squires, of having experienced the practical side of farming in his impoverished early years. The men in his employment knew he was no idle landowner who kept his hands clean and talked through his hat. They knew *he* knew what it was to shovel manure, rise before dawn to milk cows, bore himself into a stupor with hoeing and generally endure all that is most tedious in agricultural life.

". . . and then I had this chance to buy into a closed herd . . ."

We had left Martinscombe after drinking tea with the foreman and his wife, and as we wound our way across the valley to Daxworth my father began to talk of the cows that awaited us there. Of the three other major farms beyond Martinscombe, Daxworth and Cherryvale were concerned with cattle breeding, while the task of the Home Farm was to supply a wide variety of food to the main house.

". . . so taking it from a financial point of view, Robert, it works out like this. . . ."

I tried not to yawn and succeeded but the truth was that I had no fundamental interest in farming. I loved Oxmoon; I enjoyed every leisure hour spent roaming around the countryside; I savored the peace and permanence of a home where my family had lived for generations, but whenever my father embarked on a cattle-breeding panegyric I felt my brain begin to atrophy.

". . . and the cost of feeding a cow through the winter works out at . . ."

As my mind wandered I recalled Cicero's rhapsodies about the glory of farming. But of course his life had been centered on Rome. If he had lived all the year round in the country his views might have been less romantic.

My life was and would be centered on London but I saw no conflict in the future; there was nothing to stop me maintaining a successful parliamentary career while I kept Oxmoon as my country house. I would have to employ a bailiff but because I had mastered the necessary agricultural theories in order to please my father, I would be capable of the appropriate supervision, and I saw no reason why such an arrangement should not be a success. Certainly I judged myself more than adequately prepared to take the minimum interest required to pass on a prosperous estate to the next generation.

But the thought of my parliamentary career, which so far existed only in my mind, brought me once more back to my problems and I was acutely aware of not knowing what I really wanted from life. For a second I yearned for the mountains, but told myself I was only longing for the cancer that would kill me.

". . . and Emrys Llewellyn tried to sell me this bull; you never saw such an animal, looked as if it would run a mile at the sight of a cow . . ."

My ill-fated grandmother had been a Llewellyn. The Llewellyns were one of the few Welsh-speaking families in The Englishry of southern and central Gower and were unusual in owning their own land in the parish of Penhale. My father was estranged from his Welsh cousins. He had never forgiven them for refusing to receive his mother when she had tried to leave her drunken husband.

"Is Emrys still referring to Grandmama as 'Aunt Gwyneth the Harlot'?" I inquired idly. I was becoming unable to sustain an intelligent interest in cows and bulls.

"We don't mention her nowadays. I've no patience with Emrys. Whatever I do he don't like it. It's all jealousy, of course. He'd like to be a squire with two thousand acres and an entry in *Burke's Landed Gentry* instead of a yeoman with two hundred acres and a pedigree which goes back to Hywel Da

—and we all know that's a fable. I'm willing to treat him as an equal, I'm no snob, but it makes it worse when I'm friendly to him, he'd far rather I was breathing fire and making a nuisance of myself."

"I think it'll be a long time before the Llewellyns intermarry again with the Godwins!"

"Yes, thank God you've no desire to marry your cousin Dilys."

There was a silence as we remembered the other cousin who was now only too eligible to be my wife.

My father suddenly reined in his horse again. "How do you find Ginevra?" he said abruptly.

"In a state of shock and grief."

"No, I meant . . ." He hesitated, sifting through his English vocabulary but finding only an obsolete phrase which could express the nuance of the Welsh question in his head. "Will you pay court to her, do you think?"

"How quaint that sounds! Papa, I intend to be what she needs most at this time: a good friend."

"Is that possible? I saw the expression in your eyes when you were refilling her glass of champagne yesterday morning."

"What expression?"

"Oh, your mother and I both noticed it. Robert, I want you to promise me something. If you're going to pay your addresses to Ginevra, will you please not do so at Oxmoon? Your mother's never forgiven her for causing such a scandal, engaging herself to one man, eloping with another, and you can hardly now expect Margaret to welcome any signs that you still want Ginevra to be your wife."

"All I expect from my mother," I said, "is that she should mind her own business."

"And all I expect from you," said my father, "is that you should keep a civil tongue in your head and do as you're told in a house which don't yet belong to you."

There was a pause. Our horses fidgeted restlessly but we ourselves were very still. I was aware of a cow lowing far away by the river and a gull soaring overhead and a faint breeze swaying the poppies by the wayside but most of all I was aware of shock. It had been many years since my father had spoken to me so roughly. Too late I realized he was deeply distressed.

"I'm sorry," I said at last. "Yes, of course I'll behave as you wish—I regret if I've given you cause for concern."

We rode on but it was as if a cloud had passed over the sun and it was not until later as we were leaving Daxworth on our way to Cherryvale that I summoned the nerve to say to him, "Papa, I'm afraid your edict about Ginette puts me in an awkward position." And I told him how I had promised to take her out in the motor that afternoon. "I assure you my behavior towards her will be entirely fraternal—"

"Of course. Yes, by all means make the excursion—I'm sure it would do her good," said my father, obviously anxious to avoid a quarrel, and with mutual relief we exchanged smiles and rode on to Cherryvale.

V

"The sea! The sea!" exclaimed Ginette with a sigh of pleasure as I halted the car on top of the cliffs.

"That," I said, "is the most famous line in Xenophon's *Anabasis.*"

"Of course," she said, teasing me. "What else?" And we laughed.

We were at the extreme western end of the Gower Peninsula and before us lay the matchless curve of Rhossili Bay. On our right Rhossili Downs rose from the vast empty golden sands which were marred only by the blackened timber of shipwrecks. Beyond the little village that slumbered beside us on the cliff top there was no sign of human habitation except for one house, built above the beach at the foot of the Downs.

Ginette was still wearing black but she had exchanged her flimsy shoes for a pair of walking boots and had donned a large hat with a suitable motoring veil. Now that the motor was stationary she was setting aside the veil and adjusting her hat.

"Thank God this brute of a machine behaved itself," I said, carefully ascertaining that the brake was in the correct position. Only an imbecile could fail to master such a simple skill as driving a motor but I was never at my ease with machinery, particularly as I would have been helpless in the event of a breakdown.

"Let's go and look at the Worm," said Ginette.

The Worm's Head is Gower's most striking claim to fame. It is an extension of the south arm of the bay; the cliffs beyond the village of Rhossili slope steeply to sea level and there, across the tidal causeway of rocks known as the Shipway, a long narrow spur of land arches its way far out into the sea. It has all the allure of a semi-island and all the glamour of a myth. "Worm" is an old word for dragon, and with a little imagination one can look at this unusual land formation and see a monster thrashing its way into the Bristol Channel.

The Mansel Talbots of Penrice who owned the land kept sheep on the Worm's Head, and it had been on his way to inspect this flock that Owain Bryn-Davies had met his death in the tidal trap of the Shipway. Bryn-Davies, born and bred in The Welshery of northeast Gower, had misjudged the dangers awaiting those unfamiliar with the landscape in the southwest.

"You're thinking what I'm thinking, aren't you," said Ginette suddenly. "Robert, did Bobby ever tell you—"

"The whole story? No, of course not, but what intrigues me is why my mother should keep so resolutely silent. It's as if she feels the story must come from him because she herself doesn't have the right to tell it."

There was a pause. We stood there on the exposed headland and stared out across the silver-blue sea towards the coast of Devon which was hidden in a heat haze. The powerful light played tricks with the seascape and created optical illusions. The Shipway seemed a narrow strip of rocks instead of a curving swath of land many yards wide. The Inner Head, the first of the Worm's three humps, seemed close at hand and not half an hour's hard scramble away. On our right the shimmering sands seemed as remote as some beautiful mirage, and on our left the cliffs stretched away towards Porteynon into another haze. At that moment I was conscious of the shifting quality of reality, of the elusiveness of truth, and as my thoughts returned to the tragedies of my father's past I heard Ginette say, "Why would Margaret feel she hadn't the right to tell the story?"

"Because I believe," I said, "that my father connived at concealing a murder and she would think it to be her duty to protect him, not to confess to his children on his behalf."

"Good God! Are you trying to say—"

"Yes, I believe the lover poisoned the husband and that the wife knew of it but convinced the authorities he died of cirrhosis. I think Papa guessed but as he was only a child then, no more than fourteen, he was too frightened to do anything but keep quiet."

"Heavens!" She was staring at me wide-eyed. At least I had temporarily diverted her from her own tragedy. "But what makes you think this?"

"Well, first of all I don't believe the disintegration of a bad marriage is sufficient by itself to explain Papa's paralyzed reticence on the subject of his parents and Bryn-Davies. For a long time I've suspected there was more to the story than that, and this morning I finally subjected Papa to a cross-examination."

"Poor Bobby!"

"Not at all. He stood up to it well although he made the fatal mistake of assuming, without any open declaration from me, that murder was the subject under discussion. Of course he lied, but the really interesting question is Why did he bother? I gave him the perfect opening to make a clean breast of this story which I know he's wanted to tell me for a very long time. So why on earth didn't he take advantage of it?"

"Perhaps he simply felt it was the wrong time to launch himself upon a confession."

"But in that case when *will* be the right time? The whole thing's most odd."

We discussed my theory further during the journey down the cliff path to the Shipway, but presently the conversation drifted towards nostalgia again.

"Do you remember that picnic at Rhossili beach when you found a starfish and I helped you smuggle it home?"

"Ah, those picnics at Rhossili beach!"

"And at the Worm. Do you remember when we asked Bobby why Margaret would never go there? That was the first time we heard that Bryn-Davies had drowned on the Shipway."

I was conscious that we were back with Bryn-Davies again and Ginette was conscious of it too for the next moment she was saying, "How strange it is that the happy home Bobby and Margaret created for us was always permeated by that old tragedy. . . . Those ghastly Christmases when your grandmother was brought home from her asylum! How could we have laughed at the time and regarded poor old Aunt Gwyneth as a figure of fun? In retrospect it all seems unspeakably sinister and tragic."

"Tragedy and comedy often go hand in hand. Think of Shakespeare."

"Oh darling, must I? Let's go and look at the rock pools."

We had reached the foot of the cliffs and were standing on the grassy bank that lay on the brink of the Shipway. The ensuing scramble over the rocks was too arduous to permit conversation but when we had paused on the brink of a large pellucid pool Ginette murmured, "Oh Robert!" and heaved a sigh of pleasure.

"Yes?" I said neutrally, wondering how much longer I could repress the urge to embrace her.

"I was just thinking how wonderful it is to reminisce with someone who shares one's memories—and how even more wonderful it is to be with a man who simply treats one as a friend! To tell the truth, darling"—another sigh, another misty-eyed gaze into the rock pool—"I've absolutely exhausted the possibilities of grand passion."

"Ah," I said. "Yes. Well, I've always suspected grand passions were grossly overrated. Shall we go on?"

We began to flounder at a snail's pace across the rocks to the next pool but Ginette soon stopped to gaze out to sea. The entire seascape was, as I now realized, disastrously romantic. If we had been in a Swansea back street I was sure I would have had perfect control over my emotions but as it was I felt I was walking a tightrope suspended between two steadily sinking poles.

"I want to talk about the present," said Ginette. "I want to ask you all about your career and your London life. But I can't. All I can do is talk about the past. How do I escape from it? Sometimes I don't believe there's a present or a future; there's just the past going on and on."

I saw my chance. The poles supporting my emotional tightrope promptly collapsed as all reason and common sense slumped into abeyance, and putting my future at the stake I gambled, playing to win.

"No, Ginette," I said. "The past is over. The past is done. You may not be in a frame of mind to admit that at the moment, but later when you're more recovered from your husband's death, I'll help you see that a very different future is possible for you."

She looked at me. Then she turned away and stared again past the rocks to the alluring serenity of the sea.

I waited, outwardly calm yet inwardly furious with myself for disclosing my true feelings at such a premature stage of our reunion. Yet I failed to see what else I could have done for the truth was I was on the horns of a dilemma. So relieved had I been that Ginette and I should have slipped back with ease into our old friendship that I had not at first realized I could be setting out on the same road to failure by inviting the past to repeat itself, but now I could visualize a future in which I nursed Ginette back to emotional health only to see her turn to someone else when a platonic friendship no longer satisfied her.

The vision horrified me. I knew I must somehow re-form our relationship immediately in order to avoid such a disaster, but since she had just made it clear she wanted nothing from me but friendship, any change seemed doomed to repel her. I was thus in the unenviable position that whatever I did I lost. I was losing now as I sensed her emotional withdrawal. I would have lost ultimately if I had persisted in keeping my hopes for the future to myself. In despair I groped for the words to put matters right but the words —if they existed—continued to elude me. All I could say was "I'm sorry. I didn't mean to disclose my true feelings."

She turned in surprise to face me. "Disclose your true feelings? But my dear Robert, I've always known exactly how you felt!"

I was stunned. "But you couldn't. Not possibly."

"Oh, I agree you've acted superbly! But a woman always knows when a man's in love with her." She moved restlessly back to the first pool and it was not until she was standing by the water's edge that she added, "Has there been no one else?"

"Well . . ."

"Oh, of course you've had mistresses, I understand all that, but—"

"You're the only woman I've ever loved and you're the only woman I'll ever want and that's that. However I quite understand that this kind of sentimental twaddle is the last thing you want to hear at this particular moment, so—"

"I adore sentimental twaddle!" She was smiling at me. Then she said suddenly, "What a gloriously simple man you must be. Oh God, that sounds insulting, doesn't it, but what I meant was—"

"I know what you meant. Yes, I suppose single-mindedness is a form of simplicity."

"It's very attractive." As she moved forward again, I heard her say, "I'm so sick of complexity, so sick of mess and muddle and unhappiness."

"You were unhappy?"

"Yes, but saying I was unhappy is meaningless, it's too simple, it describes nothing here." She turned impulsively to face me. "I loved Conor," she said, "and he loved me, but it wasn't a restful sort of love. Quite the contrary."

I said nothing. I knew better than to interrupt anyone bent on confession but when she spoke again I sensed she was already retreating into generalities. "We were too alike, that was the trouble," she said idly. "When a marriage runs into difficulty it's always supposed to be because the couple grow apart. Nobody ever tells you how difficult it is when the couple grow too alike. To live with one's own faults is hard enough. To live with one's own faults mirrored in someone else is like looking into a glass and watching oneself grow ugly. . . . But sometimes even ugliness can exert its own irresistible fascination." She laughed briefly and I heard her murmur, "But we couldn't have parted. We were too attracted physically. That brought us together in the beginning and it kept us together at the end. . . . Odd, wasn't it?" she demanded unexpectedly, her voice crisp. "Most affairs of that kind fall apart after six months. Oh, what a white-hot muddle it all was! And then suddenly one bullet . . . a rush of blood . . . and after fifteen years of perpetual clamor—silence. I still can't get used to it. I wake in the middle of the night and the silence goes on and on."

"Naturally it'll take you a long time to recover."

"You keep making these wonderfully simple remarks which have nothing to do with reality. Recover, you say? How do I recover? Do I suddenly discover a talent for leading an orderly, peaceful life? I've never had a talent for that—I barely know what peace and order mean! Yet I long for them. . . . Yes, I long to be safe . . . and protected . . . with someone I can trust, someone loyal who won't let me down. . . . Oh God, what on earth's going to happen to me when I get to London? I'm so frightened, Robert, so frightened of all the predatory men, so frightened of getting into yet another appalling mess, sometimes I think I can't face London at all, but where else am I to go? I can't stay indefinitely at Oxmoon—oh, all thought of the future paralyzes me, I don't know how I shall ever survive—"

"I give you my word of honor that I shall come riding up on my white horse to slay every London dragon who breathes fire at you!"

"Oh Robert! Dear, *dear* Robert! How romantic!"

We were laughing together, just as I had intended. Meanwhile I had moved closer to her and the next moment I was aware of nothing save the muffled boom of the surf on the other side of the Shipway and the throb of the blood beneath my skin. The expression in her eyes changed. Unable to stop myself I held out my arms.

"Ginette—"

But she interrupted me. "Come to my room tonight," she said in a low voice. "After the dinner party. I'll be waiting for you."

The scene froze. It was as if the violins had once more stopped playing "The Blue Danube."

I was appalled.

4

I

My FEELINGS must have been clearly written on my face. I saw her turn so white that I was seized with the melodramatic notion that she might faint, but the moment of crisis passed and instead of fainting she managed to say carelessly, "Sorry! Wrong move. I stole your lines, didn't I? What a *faux pas!*"

I drew breath to speak but she forestalled me.

"If a man says to a woman, 'May I come to your room tonight?' they both think he's a very fine fellow," she said in a shaking voice, "but if a woman issues a similar invitation—even to a man she loves—the man automatically classes her as a whore."

"I could never think—"

"You thought it. I saw you. Well, maybe you're right. Maybe, according to your book of rules, I *am* a whore. But who wrote that book of rules, I'd like to know? Men! *Damned men!* They make the rules and have all the fun of breaking them while we women have to stay locked up in our straitjackets!"

"I absolutely deny—"

"Oh, don't bother!"

"But—"

"I've talked like a whore and now I'm behaving like some ghastly suffragette and I know perfectly well you're wondering how you could ever have loved me and oh God, I've done it again, I've made a mess of everything and I hate myself so much that I don't know how to bear it!"

She burst into tears. For one long moment I was transfixed by this harrowing display of feminine emotion but finally I recovered my wits and pursued the only intelligent course of action that remained to me.

She was still weeping. "Oh Robert, forgive me—please forgive me—"

"My dearest Ginette," I said, and took her in my arms.

II

There followed a somewhat predictable interval in which I lost the capacity for rational thought and made a number of declarations which sounded as if they had been invented by the worst kind of nineteenth-century poet. However most of the time I had the good sense to keep my mouth shut—or at least, to be accurate, to keep my nineteenth-century maunderings to myself; my mouth was busy proving the maxim that actions speak louder than words.

This extraordinary scene was interrupted all too soon by a party of jolly strangers on an excursion. The secluded beauties of the Gower Peninsula have never been entirely unspoiled since Baedeker wrote of them, but at that moment I felt I could resign myself to any intrusion, even the advent of four noisy fiends with Lancashire accents who sang "Rule, Britannia" as they strode down the cliff path.

"Maybe they'll drown on the Shipway!" murmured Ginette.

"Not a chance—the tide's barely past low water!"

We smiled into each other's eyes.

"Oh Robert . . ."

"Ah Ginette, Ginette . . ."

And so on and so on. I was not surprised when the strangers boggled in response to our polite "Good afternoon." They probably felt the landscape was quite romantic enough without two starry-eyed lovers cluttering up their path to the Worm.

"Darling, what time is it?"

"There is no time," I said, "only eternity." Of course I was still thoroughly demented.

"Darling, that's simply lovely and I'd adore to stay here in eternity with you forever, but unfortunately I promised Margaret that we'd be back for tea."

Eternity was terminated. "Why on earth did you do that?" I said annoyed.

"Because Margaret said to me before we left, 'Dearest Ginevra, have a lovely time and don't forget that there'll be a special tea waiting when you come back—you will be back for tea, won't you?' and I said, 'Dearest Margaret, yes, of course.' "

"I despair of you both."

"Oh Robert, she doesn't trust us an inch!"

"Yes, we'll have to reassure her by acting a charade of unblemished chastity among the teacups and the cucumber sandwiches."

We laughed. Then I said again, "My dearest Ginette!" and we paused for one last lingering luscious kiss before toiling back up the cliff path to Rhossili.

III

It took half an hour to reach the motor, and the interval proved salutary. By the time I was helping Ginette into the passenger seat I had recovered my capacity for rational thought, and although I was still in a fever of happiness I had at least emerged from my delirium. Thus when the engine stalled I made no attempt to restart it. I remained motionless, my hands gripping the wheel, my eyes watching the white lines of the breakers sweeping the beach far below.

"Ginette."

She turned to me. Her dark eyes were brilliant beneath their long black curling lashes. Her flawless skin was flushed from her walk. Her wide full-lipped mouth was irresistible and again I made no effort to resist. I kissed it.

"What's the matter?" she said when I released her.

"I can't come to your room tonight." I paused before adding levelly: "There are reasons—good reasons—why it's not possible."

All she said was "Go on."

I bent all my concentration towards translating confusion into clarity. "In my opinion you shouldn't go to bed with anyone at the moment," I said frankly. "The truth is your husband's been dead less than a month, you're in a thoroughly unstable state and if I took advantage of you now I think you might come to resent me later—I think I might become just another of those 'damned men' who you implied take what they want at the woman's expense. And I don't want you ever to think of me in that way, Ginette. I want you to think of me as a man who cares enough for you to postpone winning what he wants most."

Still she looked at me steadily. And again she said, "Go on."

"I also have to consider my parents. I promised my father this morning that my attitude towards you would stay fraternal while I remained at Oxmoon, and we both know why he extracted that promise from me; we both know my mother not only disapproves of the idea of any intimacy between us but is absolutely opposed to any irregular behavior beneath her roof. And annoying though I find my mother at present, I have to concede that I have a duty not to offend her in this respect."

"Yes, I understand. Go on."

"Well," I said, finally disconcerted by this continuing request to proceed, "that's it. All things considered I sincerely believe—"

"Are you sure there's no other reason? Can you promise me you're not acting out of anger?"

"Anger!" I was astonished. "But why should I be angry?"

"Because I was the one who took the initiative in suggesting that we meet tonight."

"What an extraordinary notion! No, of course I'm not angry with you because of that!"

"Then are you worried about Conor?"

"Worried about . . . my dear Ginette, what in God's name are you talking about?"

"Nothing. I'm sorry." She leaned forward to kiss me. "Shouldn't we be going?"

But after that kiss I was conscious only of my physical arousal. I said abruptly, "How soon can you come up to London?"

"I don't know. It depends what I do about the boys."

"Well, never mind, we can discuss that later." The thought of her two sons was not a stimulating one.

She was drawing on her gloves and as I watched Kinsella's rings disappearing from sight I was aware for the first time of complex emotions which I could not begin to analyze. I thrust them aside. Then with my confusion safely buried at the back of my mind, I got out of the car and made renewed efforts to start the engine.

Twenty minutes later we were motoring hell-for-leather up the drive to Oxmoon and praying we were not too late for tea.

IV

The special tea which my mother had promised Ginette consisted of a sumptuous repast on the lawn below the terrace. There were three different kinds of sandwiches, four cakes, a batch of scones, a heap of currant buns, assorted biscuits and, to add the final touch of luxury, strawberries and cream. When Ginette and I emerged from the house we found the meal had already started. Lion, John, Edmund and my father had all been playing lawn tennis; they were wearing whites, my father looking just as lean and strong as any of his sons. Celia had been sketching; her drawing board and pencils were tucked beneath her deck chair and she had a hot flustered look as if she had just beaten back Thomas's efforts to purloin them. Thomas himself, looking like a sulky cherub in his white sailor suit, was busy pouring his glass of milk over my father's dog. Meanwhile Bayliss and Ifor were circulating with the large plates of sandwiches, and beneath a striped umbrella which shaded the wrought-iron table my mother presided over the silver teapot. I was acutely aware of her watching us as we descended the stone steps to the lawn.

"No, no, Thomas," my father was saying mildly to the child. "Glendower doesn't like being christened with milk. Perhaps cold water, as it's such a hot day."

"Here come the childhood sweethearts!" caroled that idiot Lion.

"Where did you go?" called John cheerfully.

"Rhossili!" exclaimed Ginette. "My dear, that Worm's Head! Too divine! We toiled all the way down to the Shipway—imagine! I feel exhausted!"

"Have my chair, Ginevra—"

"No, have mine—"

"Mine's the best—"

"Darlings," said Ginette, reclining gracefully upon the nearest proffered deck chair, "how heavenly you all are!"

"I'm sorry we're late, Mama," I said, sitting down next to my father.

"That's quite all right, Robert. I hope you had a pleasant outing." She turned to the footman. "Ifor, we're going to need more hot water."

"So sorry we're late, Margaret!" said Ginette, accepting a cucumber sandwich from the butler. "I'm afraid it's my fault—Robert didn't realize that I'd promised we'd be home for tea."

"That's quite all right, Ginevra. Milk or lemon?"

"Oh, lemon would be delicious, as the weather's so hot! In America, you know, they have iced tea—it sounds horrid but actually when the weather's absolutely steaming . . ."

Settling down to join her in a bravura performance of our grand charade I began to discuss the merits of the motorcar with my father.

V

The next ordeal on the agenda was my parents' "little dinner party for twenty-four" which, since not all the invited guests were able to come at such short notice, had turned out to be a little dinner party for eighteen. The Mowbrays were up in town and the Byrn-Davieses had a previous engagement in Swansea, but the de Bracys, the Stourhams and the Applebys all professed themselves eager to welcome Ginette home.

I was sorry the Byrn-Davieses were to be absent. My father had long ago befriended Owain Bryn-Davies the Younger, and with admirable determination had persisted in demonstrating his belief that the sins of my grandmother's lover should not be blamed upon the next generation of the family. Owain the Younger had also suffered as the result of the debacle in the Eighties; his father had walked out on a wife and five children when he had gone to live at Oxmoon with his mistress. However later, well educated on the money his father had plundered from the Oxmoon estate, Owain the Younger had made an excellent marriage to the daughter of a Swansea coal-mine owner, and now he lived in immaculate middle-class respectability on the outskirts of Swansea. His only son Alun, a contemporary of mine at Harrow, was so grand that he barely knew one end of a sheep from the other.

"By the way," said Lion after tea when the conversation turned to the approaching dinner party, "there's something I want to ask." He glanced around to make sure Ginette and the servants had retired indoors. "Do we admit Kinsella was murdered?"

"Absolutely not!" said my mother, effortlessly drawing the line. "We say he had an accident with a gun and of course everyone will be much too well-bred to make further inquiries."

"Oh Mama, I don't really have to wear black, do I?" begged Celia queru-lously. "I'll look such a fright!"

"Well, I think navy blue *would* be permissible for you in the circum-stances, dear. After all, Mr. Kinsella was not a blood relation and indeed was barely known to us. I of course shall wear black, but I see no reason why you shouldn't allow yourself a little latitude so long as the color of your gown remains discreet."

"My dear Celia," I said later as we found ourselves going upstairs to change, "you're twenty-nine years old! Can't you make your own decisions about what to wear for a dinner party?"

"Oh, leave me alone, Robert—you're always so beastly to me! Do you think I like being reminded that I'm nearly thirty and still living at home?"

For some reason which I failed to understand, conversations with my sister always sank to this fractious level. Celia seemed to think I despised her but I thought her worthy enough despite her plain looks and lack of intelligence. She occupied herself a great deal with charity work and was famous for her volumes of pressed wild flowers.

In my room while I waited for hot water to be brought to me I thought what a very different life Ginette had lived far away in unknown barbaric New York, and the next moment before I could stop myself I was seeing Kinsella's rings on her finger and hearing her talk of her marital intimacy. "It brought us together in the beginning and it kept us together at the end. . . ." That disturbed me. I began to pace up and down. Finally I even shuddered, and when the hot water arrived it was all I could do not to cut myself as I shaved. I knew from my experience in criminal law that women, even good women, can become as addicted to carnal pleasure as many men, and it seemed to me that Ginette now sought not me at all but an opiate which would shut out her fear of the future.

I told myself firmly that I had reached the right decision on top of the cliffs at Rhossili that afternoon. I did not want to be treated as a soothing

medicine contained in a bottle marked TAKE REGULARLY AT BEDTIME. Nor
—and this was an even more horrific possibility—did I want to be treated as
a substitute for Kinsella. I wanted to be wanted because I was myself, because
I was the best man in the world for her, and bearing this in mind I had no
alternative but to wait until she could give me the response I deserved. Any
other solution was quite unacceptable.

I felt better, and congratulating myself that my thoughts on this most
complicated subject were now in order, I set off briskly downstairs to the
drawing room.

VI

She entered the room and my well-ordered mind fell apart into chaos. She
wore a rich black satin gown, very décolleté and trimmed with yards of erotic
black lace. A diamond pendant, sparkling against her creamy skin, pointed
downwards like an arrow as if to emphasize her breasts, and her thick glowing
auburn hair, piled high, was secured with a diamond clasp.

"How very fetching you look, Ginevra," said my mother in a studiedly
neutral voice.

"I'll have to keep you away from Oswald," said my father lightly, "or he'll
be so overcome he'll swallow his soup spoon!"

Oswald Stourham, a great crony of my father's, lived in an ugly modern
house at Llangennith with his wife, his unmarried sister and his daughter.
The daughter was too young to attend the dinner party, but his wife and
sister accompanied him to Oxmoon that evening and when they all arrived
Stourham, who looked like a *Punch* cartoon of an English gentleman and
talked like an old-fashioned masher, predictably dropped his monocle as soon
as he saw Ginette. He was a good-natured, brainless fellow who had thoroughly deserved to inherit the fortune of his father, a Birmingham manufac-
turer who had patented an interesting form of hip bath.

His unmarried sister Angela, a woman of about thirty-five who had once
shared a governess with Ginette, was just giving her old friend a warm welcome when Bayliss announced the arrival of the de Bracys with their daughter and two sons. The evening was gathering momentum. Taking care not to
look in Ginette's direction I did my best to resume my grand charade.

Sir Gervase de Bracy, a gouty old roué who had seen better days, was
already heading purposefully in my direction, jowls quivering with excitement.

"Robert, my boy—delightful to see you—heartiest congratulations on all
your recent successes—"

Little Mrs. Stourham swooped down on me. "Why, Robert, how well you look—isn't Robert looking distinguished, Sir Gervase! I declare those photographs in the newspapers don't do him justice! Have you seen the photographs of Robert in the newspapers, Lady de Bracy?"

"I only read *The Times*, Mrs. Stourham."

Meanwhile Oswald Stourham had cornered me. "I say, Robert, uncommon clever of you to win that latest acquittal, don't you know—I didn't like to think of a pretty little thing like that ending up on the gallows—"

"But what I want to know," interrupted the de Bracys' daughter Gwen, "is how she got hold of the arsenic! I never quite understood—"

"Gwen dear, murder's so vulgar. Must you?"

Ginette and I were facing each other across the room. Hastily glancing in the opposite direction I found myself looking straight at my mother, and my mother, I was unnerved to discover, was looking straight at me.

"—yes, yes, I *know* she was acquitted but that was entirely owing to Robert's brilliance—"

Meanwhile Oswald Stourham had turned aside to gossip with his crony. ". . . and how the deuce did poor Ginevra's husband die, Bobby?"

"Oh," I heard my father say easily, "it was just a little accident with a firearm."

"Margaret"—Mrs. Stourham darted between me and my mother—"I hardly expected to see Ginevra looking so *thriving!*"

"Dearest Ginevra," said my mother, "has great recuperative powers."

At that moment Bayliss announced the arrival of Sir William and Lady Appleby, and out of the corner of my eye I saw Ginette steel herself for new horrors.

"Dear Ginevra, you must have been quite prostrated . . ."

The Applebys, who had long since decided to thank God that Kinsella had saved their son from a disastrous fate, were now more than willing to inundate Ginette with benign platitudes to conceal how much they disliked her.

"Dear Aunt Maud," said Ginette, kissing Lady Appleby on both cheeks, "how kind you are! Yes, I'm sure it'll take me simply years to recover—"

"Are you all right, Robert?" said John at my elbow.

"No. I think I've got a touch of sunstroke."

"Lord, how awkward! Tell Mama."

"No, I'll struggle on."

I struggled. Gallantly I took Lady Appleby in to dinner. Valiantly I labored through watercress soup, vanquished my lobster and feinted an attack on my roast duck. Doggedly I toiled in the coils of some formidably forgettable conversation. And all the while across the table Ginette glittered in her satin and diamonds and made a mockery of my charade of indifference.

"Robert, you're shifting around on your chair as if it were a bed of nails!" protested Gwen de Bracy on my left.

"I'm so sorry, I thought I was showing matchless stoicism in the face of discomfort."

I was indeed in discomfort but the discomfort was of a nature inconceivable to an unmarried woman.

"Do tell us more about London, Robert!" urged Mrs. Stourham across the table. "I suppose you go absolutely everywhere—what's it like at Number Ten?"

I duly trotted out my Margot Asquith stories and before I could be asked how much her husband drank I deflected the conversation towards his eldest son Raymond whom I had known up at Oxford; like myself he was a Balliol man.

Somehow I survived the introduction of pudding, cheese and dessert and sustained the illusion that I was still eating. My glass of claret remained untouched, an impressive monument to my sobriety, but in contrast all the other guests had become very merry indeed and I had to spend a considerable amount of energy trying to pretend I was equally carefree.

Finally to my unutterable relief the ladies retired and the cloth was drawn. I hardly dared stand up as the ladies left the room, but managed to do so with a subtle flourish of my napkin. Sinking back into my chair as the door closed I then allowed myself to hope that my physical condition would be eased now that Ginette was no longer shimmering before my eyes, but I was to have no respite. Oswald Stourham embarked on some long story about a friend of his who knew someone who knew someone else who had slept with Lillie Langtry, and the very thought of a man fortunate enough to go to bed with any woman, even an aging Lillie Langtry, was enough to make me start shifting again in my chair.

My father had by this time noticed that something was amiss. "Robert, are you quite well?"

"I think if you'll excuse me, sir, I'll retire to the cloakroom for a moment."

More sleight of hand with my napkin followed, but everyone was much too busy talking of Mrs. Langtry to pay any attention.

I was just washing my hands some minutes later when my father knocked at the cloakroom door and called my name.

I drew back the bolt to let him in. "I'm afraid I've just been sick," I said, dredging up my remaining strength to lie convincingly. "I must have caught a touch of the sun this afternoon at the Worm. Would you and Mama think it very bad form if I excused myself and went upstairs?"

Five minutes later I was sitting on the edge of my bed and wondering, amidst the ruins of my well-ordered mind, what the devil I was going to do.

VII

Although I was by no means sexually inexperienced I had never before been rendered irrational by physical desire. Periodically I had felt the need to have sexual intercourse and periodically I had done so. I had always tried to behave well; I had not consorted with prostitutes; I had not made trouble with husbands; I had never had more than one mistress at a time; I had always terminated the affair as painlessly as possible when it bored me; I had done my best to be courteous, honest and kind. However it had never occurred to me before that this splendidly civilized behavior had only been possible because my deepest emotions had remained unengaged.

This uncomplicated private life had suited me well, perhaps better than I had realized at the time. I actually have very simple emotional tastes. (Someone else had commented on that recently but I could not quite remember who it was.) My prime concern when I embark on a liaison is that there should be no fuss and no mess. Naturally I expect to do what I want in bed but there again my tastes are straightforward and no woman has yet appeared to find them tiresome. Sexual athletics require skill, of course; I have no wish to imply that Burton's translation of the *Kama Sutra* escaped me at Oxford, but in my opinion the skill is easily mastered and although I enjoy the game there are other sports I enjoy as much and more. I would put it below mountaineering, on a par with rugger and slightly above cricket in any list of sports in which a gentleman should wish to excel.

Yet as I sat on the edge of the bed that evening I found that mountaineering was a distant memory, while rugger and cricket seemed as irrelevant as a couple of Stone Age tribal rites. I even felt that my entire previous life was not only remote but fantastic, a bloodless dance by a machine to a barrel organ that played only one tune. I supposed I was very much in love. This fact, I knew, was worthy of euphoria and I was indeed euphoric, but I was also alarmed. The unknown is often alarming and to be deeply in love was for me an unknown experience. Before that day my love for Ginette had been little more than a romantic myth but now it was a reality, and I felt confused, nervous, ecstatic, appalled, irrational and dangerous. I knew I should remain in my room but the next moment I was padding to the head of the stairs to see if the guests were on the brink of departure.

They were. In the hall all was noise and confusion, laced with fond farewells and fatuous remarks. I retreated to my room to think. It came as a relief to me to find I was still capable of thinking, but unfortunately I was thinking reckless thoughts of nocturnal expeditions; I was realizing the impossibility of running around Oxmoon in my nightclothes. I had to be able to say to anyone I met unexpectedly, "Oh, I'm feeling so much better that I thought I'd go out for a breath of air before I turn in." I felt like a murderer plotting his crime. Stripping off my evening clothes I pulled on a pair of white flannels, thoughtfully packed by Bennett in anticipation of lawn tennis, and found the accompanying shirt. White socks and white canvas shoes completed the picture of a gentleman in quest of sport, and after a quick glance at my transformed reflection in the glass I opened the door again to gauge the advisability of a further reconnaissance.

The guests had gone. Everyone was drifting upstairs to bed. I decided to remain where I was.

A seemingly vast span of time elapsed which was probably no more than half an hour. At last, taking no candle, I risked another reconnaissance but all the lights were out in the hall and everyone seemed to be safely stowed out of sight.

Returning to my room I waited for sleep to vanquish even the most active brains, and another eon passed. I finished the last cigarette in my case but fortunately perfect Bennett had included an additional packet in my bag. I mentally awarded him yet another increase in wages.

When the clock on my bedside table told me it was one o'clock I decided that to prolong the suspense would be more than my beleaguered flesh and blood could stand. I put out the candle. Darkness descended, rich and sensuous as the black satin of Ginette's evening gown. I felt intense sexual excitement, and beyond it the old hypnotic vision of winning was beating its familiar drum to lure me on to the end of my dreams.

Leaving my room I moved swiftly and soundlessly down the corridor, tiptoed across the landing past the door of my parents' room and glided down the passage into the other wing.

Time warped in the darkness around me and bent back in a great curve before running forward once more in a straight line. I was the child Robert again, tiptoeing through the night for a midnight feast with a bag of boiled sweets in his hand, and the child Ginette was waiting with licorice hidden beneath the eiderdown of her bed. Then I remembered that Ginette was no longer in her old room. My mother had put her in Foxglove, the best spare room, as if a line had to be drawn beneath the past.

When I reached the spare rooms I found the darkness unbroken. Foxglove, still named after its former wallpaper, was now only six feet away but there was no light visible beneath the door.

I knocked lightly on the panels and at once I heard a match flare in response. The bed creaked as she left it, and seconds later she was opening the door.

We looked at each other for one long exquisite moment in the candlelight, and after that there was no need for explanations. All I said in the end was, "I've changed my mind."

VIII

As I stepped past her she closed the door behind me and moved into my arms. We kissed. I drew her hard against me both to gratify myself and to prove to her how unmistakable my need was, and she laughed softly and yielded her pliant mouth to mine.

"Come to bed."

I smiled, recognizing her desire, and withdrew my hands from hers to strip off my clothes.

My fingers grazed her rings.

My fingers grazed the rings that Kinsella had given her.

My fingers—her hand—Kinsella's rings—and suddenly I was in a nightmare, the most horrific nightmare of my life, half-dressed, wholly paralyzed and absolutely and unquestionably impotent.

I was on the Shipway again and Ginette was saying, "It brought us together in the beginning and it kept us together at the end." I was in the dining room at Brooks's and Kinsella was saying, "The prize you've always wanted is the prize you can never win." Having come second to an Irishman in the past I was now coming second to an Irishman again, and the prospect of defeat was dancing before my eyes like a demon. I was failing, I was losing, I was lost, unable to do anything but stare at the floor as the sweat trickled down my naked spine, unable to be rational by telling myself I was a better man than Kinsella, unable to summon the willpower which would convince me that I could outshine him in the most important contest of my life. Panic beat around my brain like a demented hammer. I had a hellish glimpse into an unutterably complex world that was far beyond either my comprehension or my control.

"Robert." She slipped her arms around my neck and stroked my hair. "It's all right, I understand—I understood this afternoon—oh, I shouldn't have told you so much about my marriage, but I was so consumed with the desire to put Conor behind us forever—"

"Forever?" I said, hearing the one phrase I could understand and grabbing it.

"Oh darling, I long to set him aside—wasn't that obvious when I invited you here?"

"But you implied that physically, despite all your troubles—"

"Yes, but the marriage was so ghastly, such a nightmare, and now I just want someone utterly different—I want you, Robert, you, you, you—"

"Yes, but—"

"There's no competition. He's dead and you're different and you're going to win, Robert. You're going to win because there's no one now, *no one*, who can possibly stand in your way."

She took off her rings. She tugged them from her finger in a single impulsive gesture and the next moment she was flinging them into the farthest corner of the room. The past merged again with the present. In my memory I saw her throw away Timothy Appleby's ring as she moved into Kinsella's arms, and now as she threw aside Kinsella's rings I saw her moving into mine.

I held her tightly. "I'll always come first with you now, won't I," I said, "no matter what happens next."

"Always!" Her eyes were brilliant with love.

"And you really love me?"

"Yes. Best of all. Always."

"Promise?"

"Cross my heart and hope to die!" she said laughing, echoing our old nursery oath.

She lived.

We went to bed.

IX

I had not been in bed for more than a few seconds before I realized that the pleasure awaiting me there far exceeded even my most imaginative expectations, but I was in such a state by that time that the word pleasure seemed to bear little relation to what was going on. Despite all she had said I found myself consumed with worry. This was another new experience for me. In the past I had assumed that if one possessed physical fitness, the necessary desire and the required modicum of knowledge biology would do the rest, but now I found that although I was physically fit, beside myself with desire and well-nigh gasping to put my knowledge into practice, I was obsessed with the fear that biology would let me down. Fortunately impotence was now the least of my worries but other disastrous possibilities were jostling for pride of place in my fevered imagination. Caught between trying to remember the *Kama Sutra* on the one hand and my fear of an early ejaculation on the other, I was soon floundering around like a virgin schoolboy.

Then she put everything right. She whispered, "Darling, I'm sure you don't want me to speak but I can't help it, I've simply got to tell you what heaven this is," and suddenly I forgot my fears and started thinking about heaven instead. This was a much more profitable exercise, and presently I found that no further ordeal divided me from the pleasure which exceeded all my dreams.

Afterwards for some time I was much too happy to speak but when she too remained silent I found I needed to hear her voice. Tightening my arms around her I asked if everything was well.

"Darling!" She gave me a radiant smile. "What a question!"

I felt compelled to say, "I'll be better next time. The truth is I'm out of practice. I've been on my own too long."

"Robert, I despair of you! No sooner have I convinced you that you're not in competition with anyone than I find you're still in competition with yourself!"

We laughed and kissed. I felt so much better that I even thought how pleasant it would be to smoke.

"I wish I'd brought my cigarettes with me."

"Do you want one?" Opening the drawer of her bedside table she produced a packet. "So do I."

"I shall never again disapprove of women smoking!"

We smoked pleasurably and intimately for a time. I was just about to tell her that I had never been so happy in my entire life when she asked idly, "Why has it been so long since the last occasion?"

"Oh . . ." I could hardly bore her with an explanation which involved disclosing the more convoluted aspects of my personality. "I've been working too hard. There's been no time for pleasure."

"What a mistake!"

I smiled. "But everything will be different now I have you," I said, and it occurred to me that I would no longer even miss my mountaineering. We kissed. I extinguished our cigarettes and it was then, just as I was preparing to caress her again, that we both heard the soft footfall in the corridor.

X

We stared wide-eyed at each other. Then we both sat bolt upright and held our breath.

The footsteps halted. There was a long pause, followed by a tentative tap on the door.

Too late I remembered that in the drama of my arrival we had failed to turn the key in the lock.

"Who is it?" called Ginette unsteadily.

"Bobby. Ginevra, do forgive me but I'm so worried about Robert and when I was outside just now for a breath of air and saw a light was still burning in your room—" As we watched, both paralyzed with horror, the door began to open. "—I wondered if I could possibly talk to you—just for the briefest moment, of course; I'm sure you must be very tired after the dinner party . . ."

His voice stopped. There was a short terrible silence. Then he began to back away.

"So sorry . . . unpardonable intrusion . . . should have waited for permission to enter . . . very remiss . . . just so worried . . . forgive me—it never occurred to me . . . forgive me."

He left. The door closed behind him but before his footsteps had faded into the distance Ginette had jumped out of bed and was fighting her way into her dressing gown as she ran across the room.

"Bobby—" She opened the door and rushed out into the corridor. "Bobby, please—come back."

I was pulling on my white flannels. My shaking fingers slipped futilely among the buttonholes of my fly as my father with great reluctance returned to the room.

"Bobby," said Ginevra in a shaking voice, "you mustn't betray us to Margaret. *Please*, Bobby, promise me you won't."

"Of course he won't!" I said abruptly. I drew her aside so that I could face him. "I'm sorry, sir—you've every right to be very angry. I'm also sorry that you've been so worried about me, but I assure you I'm going to settle down now, I'm going to be happy at last and I'm going to live my life very differently in future."

My father said nothing. He looked at me, he looked at her, he looked at me again but he was quite unable to speak. The silence seemed to last a long time. Then he said simply, "Please excuse me," and once more he left the room.

XI

We sank down on the bed. Ginette was trembling so I put my arm around her and kept it there until she was calmer. Then I said, "Never mind my mother. Never mind my father. Never mind either of them. I've apologized for my bad manners in flouting their rules and as far as I'm concerned that's that." I waited again before adding firmly, "Of course you'll marry me."

"Darling Robert!" she said and burst into tears.

An emotional interval followed during which she clung to me and swore weeping that she wanted to marry me more than anything else in the world but she was so frightened, frightened, frightened in case the marriage never happened and she lost me and wound up in a mess for the rest of her life.

"My dearest Ginette! How can you lose me? Friendship's forever! Don't you remember how we used to tell each other that?"

The memory calmed her. She said tearfully. "Nothing can ever destroy that shared past, can it?" and I answered, "Nothing."

After we had embraced she whispered, "Don't go back to your room, sleep here, I don't want to be alone."

I locked the door, returned to bed and, thoroughly exhausted by this time, slept almost as soon as I had pulled her into my arms.

XII

My last conscious thought was that I had to wake no later than five; my mother always rose early to supervise the start of a new day in her household, and I had no wish to encounter her as I slipped discreetly back to my room.

When I opened my eyes again the hands of the clock on the chimneypiece told me five o'clock was still ten minutes away so I stayed where I was, savoring my good fortune and struggling with my guilt. Shuddering at the memory of my father's intrusion and blotting it from my mind before it could mar my happiness, I drew Ginette closer to me and wondered if there were any joy on earth that could compare with the joy of waking up for the first time beside a woman one has single-mindedly desired for more than fifteen years.

She awoke, clung to me, pulled my mouth down to hers. Yet I knew further intimacy was impossible at that time and in that place. My guilt that I had broken my word to my father seemed to lie physically on my body like a lead weight, and in my mind I could hear my mother saying as she had said so often in the past, "Here I have my standards, and here I draw the line."

After one last kiss I left the bed and pulled on my clothes.

"It's much too early to announce our plans," I said as I smoothed my hair into place. "If we did we'd simply shock everyone to the core and estrange ourselves from those we most respect. We'll have to go on with the charade for a while. No choice."

"None. Oh God, Robert, I'm so frightened—"

"Don't be. I can manage this—I've always been able to manage my father. I'll see him in private directly after breakfast and make a clean breast of the situation so that he can help me tame my mother—he won't turn his back on me once he realizes my happiness is at stake, I know he won't." I kissed her. "Courage!" I said smiling. "Be brave!" And I kissed her again before slipping out of the room.

I met no one. On the landing I could hear the housemaids beginning work downstairs, but the door of my parents' room was still shut and there was no sound behind the panels. I skimmed past, silent as a ghost, but by the time I reached the sanctuary of my room I was breathing hard not, I realized with contempt, because of the sudden exertion but because I was overcome with nervousness about my mother. After rumpling my bed to give an impression it had been occupied, I drew back the curtains to reveal another brilliant midsummer's day. Then just as I was turning aside I glanced across the garden and saw a figure moving on the far side of the lawn.

It was my father. He was still wearing the casual clothes he had donned for his nocturnal walk, and as I recognized the old tweed jacket it occurred to me that he might have spent all night wandering around the garden to ease his insomnia. I stared. There was an aimless quality in his strolling which hinted at some profound disorganization. He paced around the tennis court in a semicircle, doubled back, headed for the summerhouse, doubled back again. My bewilderment sharpened. Kneeling on the window seat I leaned out over the sill.

He had his dog with him, the latest in a line of golden Labradors all called Glendower, but just as I was wondering what the dog was thinking of his master's erratic movements, my father sat down on the bench by the tennis court and drew the animal close to him as if for comfort. This strange childlike gesture disturbed me still further. Leaving the room I headed abruptly downstairs to the garden.

As he saw me coming across the lawn he rose to his feet. The dog looked up, tail wagging, but my father ignored him. My father had eyes only for me.

"Robert."

"Papa?" I was unsure why I made a question of the word. Perhaps it was because he seemed so unlike himself; perhaps I used an interrogative to imply I wanted to know what was wrong; or perhaps I sensed I was finally in the presence of the stranger who had always kept himself hidden from me.

We paused. We were some six feet apart. Above us the sky was very pale, very clear, and the sun was already hot. The lawn was sparkling with dew.

"Papa?" I heard myself repeat at last.

"Oh Robert," he said, the words tumbling from his mouth, "the moment's finally come—I can't put it off any longer. I've got to tell you, Robert. I've got to tell you about my parents and Owain Bryn-Davies."

5

I

PAST EXPERIENCE with clients had taught me that people in trouble often make confessions which at first appear irrelevant but which in fact have a profound bearing on a truth not easy to approach. So when my father made his statement about his parents and Owain Bryn-Davies I did not say, "What on earth's that got to do with last night's disaster which has obviously upset you so much?" I said instead, "Let's go into the summerhouse and sit down."

"No," said my father. "Not the summerhouse. That's where my mother used to meet Bryn-Davies before my father died. I saw them once and Bryn-Davies caught me and said he'd kill me if I told anyone. I was so frightened I couldn't speak. I didn't think my mother would let him kill me but I wasn't sure. She let him do what he wanted. He was a powerful violent man.

"Yet after my father died—of course I knew they'd murdered him—Bryn-Davies was kind to me, took trouble, I knew he was just doing it to please my mother but I liked him for it, it made life easier. But I was always frightened of him, I was always frightened of her and I thought they might kill me one day because I knew of the murder and they knew that I knew—my mother had confessed to me. After my father died I said to her, 'It was the arsenic, wasn't it, the arsenic you got for the rats,' and she broke down, she said she'd be hanged if the authorities found out, she said if I made trouble Bryn-Davies would kill me and she wouldn't be able to stop him. She was weeping, she was terrified and *I* was terrified to see her in such a state—I was just a child, only fourteen and I was so frightened. I was so frightened that I couldn't sleep at night, I used to go and hide in the stable loft and cover myself with straw before I could sleep without fear of being killed.

"I didn't ask why she'd murdered my father, I knew how unhappy he'd made her, but Bryn-Davies was afraid I might take my father's side and hate my mother so he spared me nothing, he told me everything, oh God I can't tell you, I was so appalled, so frightened, I was just a child, only fourteen, God Almighty, I used to think I'd die of the terror.

"So I took my mother's side and said I forgave her for the murder, my poor mother, she'd suffered so much, my father had been so cruel to her. I used to wonder why they had ever married. It was an odd sort of match, he from the gentry, she the daughter of a Welsh farmer, but as you know the Llewellyns are such an old family, and when Henry Tudor granted them their land after Bosworth that set them apart from all the tenant farmers in Gower. . . . But even so to marry a Godwin was a social triumph for my mother, yes, I can see why she married him. And he would have married her because she was so beautiful and he prized beautiful things, I suppose he thought that if he married anyone he might as well marry someone beautiful, and he had to marry because of Oxmoon, he loved Oxmoon so he had to have a son. . . . But he shouldn't have married. He shouldn't have married anyone.

"In the beginning I think he drank to suppress his vice and in the end I think he drank because he'd given way to it. You wouldn't believe how he drank. I loved him but he frightened me. He frightened her. He'd start drinking brandy after breakfast and he'd be dead drunk by noon. Then he'd get violent and start shouting at her. He used to beat her . . . and worse. I'd run out of the house and hide in the woods because I couldn't bear to hear her screams. . . . She left him in the end, it was when he started bringing boys home from Swansea, she ran away back to her father and took me with her, but her father was a religious man and said he wouldn't have a deserting wife in the house. So she had to go back, and when she did Bryn-Davies escorted her. He was visiting the Llewellyns' farm at the time to sell her father a ewe, and it was then, when she was rejected by the family who should have helped her, that she came to know him well. They already knew each other slightly because although he was born in The Welshery his farm was nearer, he used to graze his sheep on Llanmadoc Hill. My poor mother, how absolutely she fell in love with him . . . but it was all my father's fault. It was his wickedness that drove her to adultery, it was his wickedness that drove her to murder and it was because his wickedness had driven her to such evil that I myself was driven to . . ."

He stopped.

His face was white, beaded with sweat, but his voice had remained level throughout this shattering monologue. He was looking across the lawn at Oxmoon, and as I watched he clenched his trembling hands and shoved them deep into his pockets in a pathetic attempt at self-control.

"Sit down, Papa. Sit down again on the bench here."

We both sat down on the bench by the tennis court, and the dog Glendower, resting his long nose on his master's knee, gazed up at him with devotion. My father stroked the golden coat, kneading the fur with strong repetitive movements of his fingers.

"But you do see, Robert, don't you," he said. "It was the vice that lay at the root of the disaster, it was the perversion. I couldn't forget that. I can't forget it. That knowledge came to dominate my whole life, and you have to understand that in order to understand me—oh God, I was so frightened, Robert, always so terrified that I'd inherited the vice and would grow up like my father.

"I didn't look much like my father but I had his build, I kept growing taller and taller, and I thought if I had his build that might mean . . . Oh God, how it horrified me, I thought I'd go mad with the horror, but meanwhile other horrifying things were happening—Bryn-Davies taking control of Oxmoon—my mother living with him openly—the estate going to ruin—the rats infesting the house . . . For a while I just went my own way and tried not to notice but in the end I wasn't allowed to be passive, in the end I had to act. Well, it couldn't go on, could it? He was stealing my inheritance, robbing me blind, shaming my mother, ruining us all . . . Oh yes, I knew it couldn't go on.

"But I was afraid of my mother ending up on the gallows. I was afraid that if I once embarked on revelations to the law there was no knowing where those revelations might end. And above all I was afraid of Bryn-Davies. But of course the situation couldn't go on, and after you were born, I looked around, I saw the world I'd brought you into, and I knew I couldn't tolerate it anymore. I had to change it for you. I had to cleanse it and put it right. I did it for you, Robert; I did it for you and for Margaret. You gave me the courage to act.

"I talked it over with Margaret and decided the best plan was to arrange a meeting with Bryn-Davies at the Worm's Head. This was a favorite spot of mine, I often took your mother there to escape from Oxmoon, even after you were born we used to take the pony trap to Rhossili and walk out to the Worm and you'd be strapped in a little pack on my back. I knew the Worm like the back of my hand. But Bryn-Davies didn't. He'd never been there but he talked of going because the sheep there were legendary, wonderful quality, and he was interested in buying into the flock.

"But on the day he died he didn't go out to the Worm to see the sheep. That was just what we told everyone later. He went out to see me. I wrote him a note saying I'd meet him there to discuss my father's murder and the future of Oxmoon, and then I left immediately for Rhossili—with you and your mother, of course. I didn't dare let either of you out of my sight.

"Well . . . We got to Rhossili and . . . and I realized I'd made a little mistake with the tide tables . . . silly of me. . . . I saw at once, as soon as I looked down at the Shipway, that it would be going under in half an hour.

"Well . . . I settled you and Margaret in a secluded spot farther along the cliffs and then I went back . . . but he'd already started out. The Shipway's so deceptive, it looks safe long after it's begun to be dangerous. He was caught in the middle. And he didn't have a chance.

"You know what happened next. My mother arrived. She'd found the note and realized . . . well, no doubt she was worried about what might happen. She came and I was there and there was nothing we could do but watch him drown.

"It drove her mad. It wasn't just that he died before her eyes, it was because she thought I'd killed him. I told her over and over again it was . . . well, just a little accident with the tide tables, but she refused to believe me. And she went mad. But I was glad of this because it gave me an excuse to lock her up. She had to be locked up, you see, because she was a murderess, she'd poisoned my father—and besides, I wanted Oxmoon purged, I couldn't have had her there, polluting the house with her memories of adultery and murder. . . . No, she had to be locked up. As Margaret always said, in the circumstances what else could I possibly have done?

"And so we come to Margaret. We come to your mother. You think she's so commonplace, I know you do, but my God, you've no idea, Robert. You've no idea at all.

"She got me through all this. I couldn't have survived without her. And I don't just mean she stood by me before and after Bryn-Davies died. She gave me the will to pull Oxmoon back from the grave. I stood in the ruined hall with her and said, 'I can't manage, I don't know where to begin.' I felt so helpless because I knew nothing about the estate, but she said, 'I *know* you can manage,' and suggested searching the library for papers that might help me. We found nothing but later she said, 'Let's take one last look,' so we went back and there in the library the most enormous rat was sitting on the table and chewing a candle. It was a vile moment. Beautiful Oxmoon, ruined, infested, decayed . . . Margaret screamed and I grabbed the nearest book and flung it at the rat and killed it. And then when I replaced the book I found there were papers stuffed behind it—the journals of my grandfather in which he'd described in detail exactly how he'd managed the estate. . . . Margaret just said, 'Where there's a will there's a way.'

"But it was her will. And her way. She made everything come right, you see, even when we were first married. I was so terrified that I might be like my father, but Margaret proved I wasn't. And you proved I wasn't. That was why I wanted a lot of children because every time a child was born it proved how different I was from my father, who, so Bryn-Davies told me, only consummated his marriage twice in the normal way. So every time I was in bed with my wife . . . being normal . . . do you see what I'm trying to say? It was like an erasure, like a victory over memory, until in the end bed became not just a way of forgetting my father but a way of forgetting everything I couldn't bear to remember. And gradually . . . as time went on . . . I found . . ."

He stopped again. I waited but when he clearly found it impossible to continue, I said in the neutral voice I used to clients when I was playing midwife at the birth of some terrible truth, "As time went on you found Margaret alone couldn't help you forget." I used my mother's Christian name deliberately to foster the illusion that I was a mere lawyer who bore no personal connection to my client or anyone he knew.

"Yes," said my father. He had stopped caressing the dog and now he closed his eyes as if the truth were a physical presence which he could not bear to see. "But I'm afraid I haven't been very honest with you about that, Robert. I'm afraid I lied to you about the past. You see—" He opened his eyes again but he could not look at me. "—I wanted you to go on thinking of me as a hero. I couldn't endure to think you might be disillusioned."

"I understand. But now—"

"Yes, now I must tell you—I *must*—that it wasn't your mother's fault that I was driven to adultery. I lied when I implied it was. I know your mother's a stickler for convention but as a matter of fact she's very down-to-earth about marital intimacy, I always thanked God I didn't marry some well-bred lady who hated it. Your mother and I always got on well in that respect and she wanted children just as much as I did so there was no conflict. Actually I liked her being pregnant and she liked it too so that never created any difficulties either—rather the reverse, if anything. But then . . . I couldn't help it . . . I just had to go elsewhere as well—"

"Did you really discuss the problem with Margaret? Or did you lie when you told me you did?"

"Oh God, of course I discussed it with her, how could I avoid it? I was beside myself with horror, I couldn't face what I'd done, she helped me get through it all, she saved our marriage—"

"You mean when it all began?"

"Yes," said my father, "when it all began." He paused before saying, "My infidelity had begun a long time before you found out about it." And after another pause he said, "You were fourteen and away at Harrow when it all began."

"I see," said the lawyer, a model of neutrality and detachment. "I was fourteen, you were thirty-four, Margaret was thirty-one—"

"—and Ginevra was sixteen," said my father, and covered his face with his hands.

II

"Of course," he said at once, letting his hands fall as he swiveled to face me, "I didn't seduce her, never, never think I could be capable of such wickedness, but . . . I was foolish. And the direct result of that foolishness was that I went to London and committed adultery for the first time with a woman I met there."

Several seconds passed. When I could finally trust myself to speak I said, "This . . . this incident with—"

"Incident, yes, that's all it was—utterly appalling, utterly wrong, but just a little incident in the music room—"

"How did it happen?"

My father seemed to relax. I had seen criminals relax like that when they thought they were past the most harrowing section of their story. He started to knead Glendower's golden coat again.

"I was out riding one day with Oswald Stourham," he said conversationally, "and we were just chatting about women as we so often did when Oswald said to me, 'By Jove, Bobby, that little cousin of yours is turning into quite a peach!' and I said, 'Oh yes? I can't say I've noticed'—which was true because I still thought of Ginevra as a child—and as a daughter. Well, Oswald laughed so hard he nearly fell out of his saddle. 'By Jove, Bobby!' he says again in that hearty voice of his. 'A man would have to be a second Oscar Wilde not to appreciate the charms of your little cousin Ginevra!'

"I said nothing but I couldn't forget that gibe about Wilde. Then a disastrous thing happened: Margaret had to visit her sister and once she was gone I found I was thinking continually about Ginevra . . . I suppose it became an obsession. Anyway, to cut a long story short, I kissed Ginevra one afternoon when she was practicing her piano in the music room. She was upset and, I saw at once, very frightened. I tried to reassure her, swore I wouldn't do it again, but I suppose she felt she couldn't trust me and that was why soon afterwards she rode to Porteynon and tried to elope with Kinsella—she wanted to run away from Oxmoon . . . and from me. . . . But her action took me wholly by surprise. I didn't know she'd been having clandestine meetings with him ever since Margaret had left.

"Well, I was in a terrible state but as soon as I'd confessed to Margaret she sorted everything out. She sent me to London to get me out of the way for a while, and then using Kinsella as her excuse she arranged for Ginevra to go to the Applebys'. . . . Oh God, Robert, if only you knew how wretched and ashamed I felt—"

"You went to London."

"Yes. For two weeks."

"And there you committed adultery for the first time, you said."

"Yes. I was in an appalling state and kept remembering all I didn't want to remember—my father—Bryn-Davies—the little accident with the tide tables —my mother raving—Oswald talking about Oscar Wilde, it was all jumbled up together, I couldn't sleep, I couldn't eat, I tried drinking but I was so frightened of getting drunk, I thought that too would mean I was ending up like my father—"

"So you found a woman and managed to forget. When did Margaret find out?"

"Oh, I told her as soon as I got back," said my father. "Of course."

I suddenly found I was on my feet.

He looked up. His very blue eyes were bright with fear. He had to struggle to stand.

"Oh God, Robert, forgive me—oh my God, my God, what a retribution this is—"

"You told my mother," I said, "and what did my mother say?"

"She said she could understand but no one else would so it had to be kept absolutely secret. She said I must do what I apparently had to do but it must always be done in London."

"So she sanctioned the adultery. And eventually, I suppose, she took you back."

"Oh, we were never estranged. We always shared a bed."

"You mean . . . I'm sorry, I think I must have misunderstood. You're surely not trying to tell me—"

"Yes. She never rejected me. She knew I'd have gone to pieces utterly if she'd done that."

After a moment I managed to say, "I see. So everyone, it seems, then lives happily ever after—until Ginette comes home and you and Mama realize that I'm still dead set on a marriage which you can only regard with horror. No wonder you were driven to approach Ginette last night when you saw the light was still burning in her room! You were under a compulsion to find out how far I'd gone with her!"

"No, you misunderstand. By that time your feelings were no mystery but what I *had* to find out was how Ginevra felt. If she just wants to be your mistress then I don't think Margaret will interfere, but if she wants to be your wife—" He covered his face with his hands again.

"Quite." I looked across the sparkling dew-drenched lawn to Oxmoon, shining in the morning light. The maids had now drawn back all the curtains on the ground floor.

"But at least now I've spoken to you," said my father. "At least now I can tell Margaret you know everything and that there's no need for her to tell you herself. And perhaps eventually . . . after you've thought over all I've said about my parents and Bryn-Davies . . . you might find it in your heart to understand . . . and make allowances . . . and possibly one day forgive me for . . . Oh Robert, if only you knew how much I regret that past foolishness with Ginevra—"

"Quite," I said again.

He was crying. My clients, both male and female, usually cried at the end. The birth of truth can be so painful. I was well accustomed to witnessing such ordeals, so accustomed that the sight of the emotional aftermath had long since lost its power to move me.

"I must thank you for confiding in me, sir," I said. "Please don't think I'm unaware of the considerable strain such confidences have imposed upon you. And now I have only one question left to ask: did you tell my mother that you found me in bed with Ginette last night?"

He simply looked at me. The tears were still streaming down his face. I shrugged, turned my back on him and walked away.

III

Sodomy, adultery and murder; robbery, madness and lust. The Greeks would no doubt have considered this catalogue standard fare at the table of life. I thought—I tried to think—of *The Oresteia*. I felt that if I could reduce my father's story to the remote status of Greek tragedy, I would somehow transform it into a saga I could contemplate with equanimity—or if not equanimity, at least with an ordered mind, the mind which I had applied at

Harrow to translating Aeschylus. But my nerve failed me as I remembered my father's appalling understatements.

Just a little accident with the tide tables. Just a little incident in the music room. The phrases rasped across my consciousness, and as I recalled that voice speaking of the unspeakable I knew I had no defenses against the horrors he had revealed.

I was in the woods by Humphrey de Mohun's ruined tower. I was in the woods thinking of sodomy, adultery, murder, robbery, madness and lust but I dared not think of guardians who abused a position of trust. There my couraged failed me. I thought only of the evil which existed in the realms of Greek literature—although such evil was more commonplace than civilized people dared believe; I knew that well enough. Had I not always seen the Gower Peninsula not as the pretty playground eulogized in the guidebooks but as the lawless land soaked in blood where the King's writ had so often failed to run? It was the peace and order of my parents' Oxmoon that were unusual; the nightmare of the Eighties had merely represented Gower running true to form.

I now fully understood my parents' obsession with setting standards and drawing moral lines. Having been to hell and back their central preoccupation lay in keeping hell at bay, and as far as they were concerned they believed that observing the conventions was the best way to stop hell encroaching. Within the fortress of their self-imposed morality they could feel they were safe, but after their experiences neither of them could doubt that beyond the fortress walls lay violence and madness, perpetually hovering to destroy all those who failed to draw the line.

I thought of my parents fighting from their moral fortress but not, as I had always supposed, winning the battle against the forces which besieged them. I saw now that they were slowly but inexorably losing as my father, my desperate damaged father, sank ever deeper into the mire of his guilt and his shame.

Trying at last to consider my father's disastrous weakness rationally, I told myself that he was a victim and that any civilized man could only regard him with compassion.

I waited for compassion to come but nothing happened. Then into the void which compassion should have filled I felt the darker emotions streaming, emotions which I knew I had to reject. But I could not reject them. I was too upset. In fact I was very upset, very very upset indeed, more upset than I had ever been in my life, and my thoughts were spiraling downwards into chaos.

"Just a little incident in the music room . . ."

I was trembling. I gripped the ivy that clung to the walls of the ruined tower, and above me the jackdaws beat their sinister wings and cawed as if in mockery of my collapse.

I was thinking of Ginette at last. I tried not to, but I could no longer stop myself. I knew she should have told me but I knew too that it would have been impossible for her to confess. I decided I could not blame her. There was only one person I could blame and that was my father.

I went on gripping the ivy as first rage and then hatred overpowered me. That kiss in the music room had set Ginette on the road to Conor Kinsella, the road which had led to the destruction of my adolescent dreams and the blighting of my adult life. How farcical to think that during all those years I had continued to regard my father as a hero! As I could see now with blinding clarity he was no hero; he was a lecher, a cheat and a fool.

I vomited. Afterwards I still felt ill but I was mentally calmer, as if my mind had rebelled against the violence of my emotions and forced my body to make a gesture of expulsion. As a rational man I knew I had to forgive my father, that victim of past tragedy, and I did indeed believe I would eventually forgive him—but not yet. And perhaps not for a long while.

Washing my face in the stream I tried to pull myself together by considering the immediate future, and at once I saw how imperative it was that no one should know I was so distressed. In other words, my father was now not my immediate difficulty; I could deal—or try to deal—with him later. My immediate difficulty lay in summoning the strength to return to the house, change into a suit, appear at breakfast and later go to church with the rest of the family as if nothing out of the ordinary had occurred.

I vomited again. Then, disgusted by such an exhibition of weakness and humiliated by my loss of control over my emotions, I forced myself to leave the woods, return to the house and face the full horror of my new grand charade.

IV

Breakfast was not until nine on Sundays so I had plenty of time to prepare for my ordeal. I wondered whether my father would ask my mother to read the customary prayers before the meal, but I came to the conclusion that this was unlikely. He too would be bent on hiding his distress by keeping up appearances; he too would have decided, just as I had, that no other course of action was available to him.

I thought of us both saying to ourselves: No one must ever know. No one must ever guess.

I found myself quite unable to think of Ginette now. I knew that at some time in the future I would have to talk to her about my father, but that future was apparently beyond my power to imagine at that moment. In my room as I washed and changed I told myself I could cope with only one ordeal at a time, and my first ordeal without doubt was surviving the family breakfast in the dining room.

I set off downstairs to the hall.

When I arrived at the foot of the stairs I found to my dismay that my watch was five minutes slower than the grandfather clock which traditionally marked the correct time at Oxmoon. That meant I was late. That also meant a bad start to my charade, and I was still staring at the clock in futile disbelief when far away in the distance I heard the dining-room door open.

A second later my mother was bustling into the hall.

"Ah, there you are!" she said with satisfaction. "Come along, we're all waiting—you mustn't miss prayers!"

But I was transfixed. I looked at her and could not speak for suddenly I was seeing her not as the woman who was so familiar to me but as the unknown girl of sixteen, brought up in a cheerful moneyed home and catapulted into the moral and financial bankruptcy of a terrifying alien world. I thought of her standing by my father in the beginning when a lesser woman might have run sobbing home to her parents; I thought of her sticking by him through thick and thin; I thought of her mastering crises that most women would have found not only insuperable but unimaginable. And I thought how I had misjudged her, dismissing her as narrow and limited when in truth the narrowness and limitation had been all on my side. I saw her helping me at that crucial moment in my adolescence when she realized my father had failed me; I saw her trying to talk to me although I had always been too proud to listen; I saw her understanding me far too well for my own conceited contemptible comfort, understanding me as my father never had and never could. In my memory I heard her say, "You're like me—you really have very simple emotional tastes," and for the first time I realized what she must have suffered from that complex man she had married and whom she had apparently loved, as single-mindedly as I had loved Ginette, from the age of sixteen.

"Come along!" she was repeating briskly. "You mustn't keep your father waiting!" But hardly had she finished speaking when I was stepping forward to take her in my arms.

For a brief interval she was silent. Then she patted my back and said kindly, "There, there. We'll sort it all out later. Now come along and let's do what we're supposed to do."

Still mute I followed her to the dining room.

V

I noticed at once that Ginette was absent. That disturbed me. By this time I was so obsessed with the desire to pretend that everything was as it should be that any small deviation from the normal was unnerving.

"Are you feeling better, Robert?" inquired John when the prayers were finished.

"Better?" I said blankly.

"Your sunstroke, dear," said my mother. "I nearly sent a tray up to your room this morning, but then your father told me you were quite recovered. I'm so glad."

"Mama decided to spoil Ginevra instead!" Lion informed me. "And incidentally, Mama, how tired do *I* have to be before I'm allowed to miss family prayers and have breakfast in bed?"

After the laughter had subsided I accepted coffee, fried eggs, bacon, sausages and toast and sat toying with my knife and fork. My father chose bacon alone and managed to slip it slice by slice to Glendower. At the other end of the table my mother had cunningly ordered a boiled egg, and since no one could see through the shell no one could tell how much of it she ate. She drank two cups of tea and looked tranquil.

Meanwhile an animated postmortem on the dinner party was being conducted. I had forgotten what a noise large families make but although I winced periodically I was glad of the opportunity to remain silent.

"Well," said my father, making a great business of pulling out his watch, "there are one or two things I have to do before church, so if you'll all excuse me—"

The door of the dining room opened and in walked Ginette.

VI

"Ginevra!" chorused my brothers in delight.

"Darlings!" said Ginette radiantly to them. "I simply couldn't stay in bed, it made me feel too guilty!" She looked down the table at my mother. "Margaret, it was so kind of you to send up a tray but I really did feel I wanted to join the family for breakfast. I'm sorry I missed prayers."

She was wearing a plain black day frock with no jewelry. She had not replaced Kinsella's rings and in my fevered state I thought this omission a disastrous error, but when I glanced around the table I soon realized that no one had noticed such a minor detail of her appearance. I willed myself to keep calm.

"Good morning, Robert!" she was saying as Ifor drew out the chair next to mine. "How's your sunstroke?"

"He's decided to live!" said Lion promptly. "We're all mortified!"

"Well, I really mustn't linger," murmured my father, and to my envy he finally managed to escape.

But I knew I had to stay at the table. I could hardly abandon Ginette now that she had flung caution to the winds by walking into the lion's den, and as I glanced at her tense smiling face I recognized a pattern of behavior with which I was not unfamiliar: the prisoner became so exhausted by the strain of waiting in his cell that he could barely be restrained from rushing into court to confront the judge and learn his fate.

"Papa looks awful, Mama," John was saying with concern. "Is anything wrong?"

"No, dear, just a little touch of insomnia as the result of last night's lobster."

"Mama," said Celia, preparing to leave the table, "how are we all traveling to church? Will there be room for me in the motor or are Robert and Ginevra accompanying you and Papa?"

"Oh, there'll be room for you, dear," said my mother. "Robert and Ginevra won't be going to church."

Everyone looked at her in astonishment.

"But it's the rule!" shrilled Thomas scandalized.

"No doubt they'll go to Evensong, dear, but this morning they have an important matter to discuss."

"What's that?" said Lion automatically.

"Lion dearest," said my mother, "it's a personal and private matter connected with Ginevra's recent sad loss, and I think it would be indelicate of you to inquire further. A widow," said my mother, sipping her tea, "naturally has many legal and financial problems which require the attention of someone experienced in such matters."

"Oh, I see." Lion subsided into a puzzled silence.

"Shall I eat this third rasher or not?" mused Edmund, who was still pondering over his breakfast. "I can't make up my mind."

"Leave it," said John, standing up so suddenly that I knew he had sensed the tension in the room. "Come on, fellows, time to play hunt-the-prayer-book."

"Can I get down, please?" said Thomas perfunctorily. He was already moving to the door with his mouth full.

"Very well, Thomas. Edmund, make sure you change your tie before church. You've got an egg stain on it."

"Oh, Lord, so I have! Thank you for telling me, Mama."

"That will do, Bayliss," said my mother to the butler. "I shall ring later when I want you to clear."

"Very good, ma'am." Bayliss left with Ifor at his heels. Thomas and John were already in the hall and as I watched both Lion and Edmund followed them.

"I wonder which hat to choose," mused Celia. "I think I'll wear the one with rosebuds."

She drifted away. The door finally closed. My mother remained at one end of the long table and Ginette and I remained side by side some distance away on her right. In the silence that followed I felt Ginette's hand groping unsteadily for mine.

"I'm sorry you saw fit to come down, Ginevra," said my mother pleasantly at last, replacing her teacup in its saucer. "I intended to say what has to be said in the privacy of your room. I didn't want to embarrass you in front of Robert." She paused before adding: "Perhaps you'd prefer Robert to leave now?" Her voice was solicitous. She made it sound as if she had only our welfare in mind.

I pulled Ginette's hand above the table so that my mother could see our fingers were interlocked. "I'm staying," I said.

"Oh, I don't think you want to stay, Robert," said my mother. "Not really. I think you'd be much happier if you let me have a little talk with Ginevra on her own."

I put my arm around Ginette's shoulders. She was trembling. Holding her tightly I repeated, "I'm staying."

"Very well." My mother paused to reorganize her thoughts. Finally she said, "Ginevra, I must tell you that Bobby had a long talk with Robert this morning, and Robert is now aware that you haven't been honest with him."

I both heard and felt Ginette's horrified gasp but I said with lightning speed as if she were a client in great danger, "Don't say a word."

Ginette was rigid with fear. I was painfully aware of the color suffusing her face but still I kept my arm around her and we remained silent.

"Now, Ginevra," said my mother, suddenly becoming very businesslike, "I think that if you intend to marry Robert you really should be honest. You may well be content to deceive him but in my opinion such a deception would be quite wrong and I could not possibly condone it. But perhaps I'm mistaken and you have no intention of marriage? If you merely intend to continue as his mistress then of course Robert must take you as he finds you and I'll say no more."

I said, "We're getting married."

"Ah," said my mother, "then I fear I have no alternative." She stood up, a small neat square figure in gray, and we stood up too, Ginette leaning against me, barely breathing, fingers frantically clutching my free hand.

"I am now going to church," said my mother. "While I'm gone, you,

Ginevra, are going to tell Robert exactly what happened at Oxmoon when you were sixteen, and when I come back I shall discuss the situation further with him. If I find you haven't told him the truth, then believe me I most certainly shall."

I intercepted her. "Ginette can tell me nothing," I said, "that I don't already know."

She looked at me steadily. Her pale eyes seemed darker than usual as they reflected the somber shade of her dress. She had a wide plain broad-nosed face with a mouth that could harden in a second to express implacable resolution. It hardened now. As I instinctively recoiled from her, I heard myself say—and to my horror my voice was unsteady—"I know what you're trying to tell me but I don't believe it. I don't, I won't and I can't. You're just acting out of spite and revenge."

She turned abruptly to Ginette. "We must put him out of his misery at once. Are you going to tell him or shall I?"

"Oh Margaret, no—*no*—"

"My dear, you can't fool him indefinitely. He's much too clever and he deals daily with criminals and liars—look at him, he already knows although he refuses to believe it—"

"*I can't tell him!*" screamed Ginette. "I can't, I can't, I can't!"

"Very well," said my mother. "Perhaps I was expecting too much. Perhaps I should have made greater allowances for you considering all you've been through." Then she turned to me and said kindly, with a complete lack of all the emotion to which she was entitled, "I'm sorry, Robert, but your father didn't tell you the whole story. It's not his fault, it's just that he's emotionally incapable of it. The truth is simply this: he seduced her. She slept with him. And it nearly destroyed us all."

PART TWO

GINEVRA

1913–1919

But you are wrong if you think Fortune has changed towards you. Change is her normal behavior, her true nature. In the very act of changing she has preserved her own particular kind of constancy towards you. She was exactly the same when she was flattering you and luring you on with enticements of a false kind of happiness. You have discovered the changing faces of the random goddess. To others she still veils herself, but to you she has revealed herself to the full. . . .

—Boethius
The Consolation of Philosophy

1

I

"AND IT NEARLY destroyed us all," said Margaret.

I fainted.

No, that's not right. That's fantasy and in this journal I must be concerned with reality. I'm like one of those wretched women who suffer from some disorder of the womb yet lie to their doctors because they fear having their private parts examined. If you don't tell the truth to your doctor how can you expect to get better? And if I don't tell the truth to my journal how can I hope to extricate myself from the messy lies of my ghastly private life?

So no more lies, not here. No more writing, "I fainted" as if I were the virginal heroine of a romantic novel. (Oh, how divine it would be to be a virginal heroine! I wouldn't even mind pressing all those frightful wild flowers.) What I have to do is to record in the past tense what, to the best of my recollection, seemed to be happening, and then to comment in the present tense on what was—and is—really going on. Then perhaps I'll master reality and avoid the horror of a future based on illusion.

So bearing all this in mind, I must be brave, resolute and blindingly honest (all the things that I'm not). Cross out "I fainted." And start again.

"The truth is simply this," said Margaret, rather as if she were discussing some troublesome dinner-party menu with Cook. "He seduced her, she slept with him and it nearly destroyed us all."

I thought: Well, that's that. All over. And I sank down on the nearest chair. I was conscious of nothing but relief that disaster, long anticipated, had finally struck. I thought of my childhood heroine, Mary Queen of Scots, finally being obliged to put her head on the block. What bliss! What relief! Nothing else to do but wait for the ax.

So I sat at the dining-room table in a passive stupor amidst the ruins of breakfast while nearby a very tall man was facing a very small woman who was saying in a passionless voice, "I shall now go to church. However, should either of you wish to resume this conversation with me later, I shall be only too willing to help in any way that I can."

Neat little footsteps tip-tapped past me, and after the dining-room door had closed neat little footsteps tip-tapped away to the hall. I went on waiting for the axe but when nothing happened I eventually nerved myself to look at my executioner. He was staring at the dirty plates on the table, the crumpled napkins, the sordidness, the disorder, the mess. Then he said in an abrupt voice, "Go and wait for me in the music room." He might have been marshaling a tiresome solicitor out of his chambers; I almost expected him to advise seeing his clerk for a further appointment.

He held the door open for me as I left the room but I did not dare look at him and I suspected he did not dare look at me. Stumbling down the corridor I prayed I wouldn't meet anyone and I didn't. (Why is it that God so often answers trivial prayers but not the prayers that really matter?) The little music room, where I had spent so many hours thumping out those boring scales, lay off the passage that led to the ballroom, and there by the window stood the same table where long ago I had teased my ineffectual governess Miss Sale by drawing grossly sensual treble clefs.

I went to the piano.

"How well you play!" said Bobby in my mind, the Bobby I could bear to remember, the man who was always so kind and good with children. Another Bobby had existed but he could be allowed no place in my memory. Sometimes he tried to slip in—he was trying to slip in now—but fear made me strong and I shut him out. The road to remembrance was guarded by a terrible coldness and as soon as I shivered I thought, I won't think of that. Yet I was always terrified I would. I was terrified now. I knew I was going to have to remember that other Bobby but I did not see how I could speak of him and remain conscious. I thought I would die of the shame.

To distract myself I began to play "The Blue Danube," but I was in such an agony of terror that all the notes came out wrong, and I had just broken off in despair when the inevitable happened; footsteps echoed in the corridor and Robert walked into the room.

I struggled to my feet. He was expressionless but exuding a businesslike efficiency. My terror deepened.

"Sit down, please," he said, gesturing to the table.

We sat down opposite each other by the window. There was a pile of sheet music between us, and as I stared at the treble clefs they became meaningless, mere recurring symbols between those recurring parallel lines.

"Now," said Robert briskly, "this is what we're going to do. You're going to tell me the truth, the whole truth and nothing but the truth. Then once the truth is established beyond all reasonable doubt I shall reduce it to order so that we can conduct a rational survey of our dilemma. However before I begin . . . Are you listening?"

I whispered that I was.

"Then look at me."

I somehow raised my eyes to the level of his watch chain.

"That's better. Now before we begin there are two points I wish you to understand. One: don't lie to me because I'm on my guard now and I'll be able to spot a lie almost before it's spoken. I'm trained to recognize lies, and in fact although I shut my mind against the knowledge I knew earlier that my father hadn't told me the whole truth; he was very plausible but I noticed how he relaxed in relief when he thought his big lie had been safely delivered. . . . So you see, you must always tell me the truth because if you don't I'll know and that'll mean the end."

"Yes." I heard the word "end" and realized dimly that he spoke of it not as if it were in the present but as if it were in the future, and not just in the future but in a future that was not necessarily inevitable. I was apparently being granted some fearful stay of execution. I thought of the rack and disembowelment and began to see the advantages of a simple beheading. Perhaps Mary Queen of Scots had been luckier than I had ever realized.

"Very well, that's the first point I want to make," said Robert, "and the second point is this: whatever the truth is don't be frightened of confessing it to me because I can't possibly be shocked—I'll have heard it all before. May I remind you that I don't just defend murderers at the Old Bailey. I go out on circuit, and at the assizes I defend people accused of robbery, assault, rape, sodomy, bestiality, incest and any other criminal offense you care to name. You do see what I'm trying to say, don't you? You do see what an enormous advantage my profession gives us here?"

I managed to nod but I still couldn't imagine how I was ever going to speak of the unspeakable. However Robert saw my difficulty and tried again.

"If you can help me by doing as I ask," he said, "then I can help you. Regard it as a new charade to play: I shall think of you as my client, someone in great trouble who requires all my professional skill, and you must think of me as your lawyer, the only person on earth who has a hope of getting you out of this mess."

I suddenly understood not only his proposal but the logic that lay behind it. He was trying to distance us from the horror by making it impersonal. We were no longer lovers. We were lawyer and client. I was in ghastly trouble but he could help, he had seen it all before; he was calm, he was professional, he could cope. All I had to do to survive was to trust him.

"This sort of case is in fact not uncommon," said Robert, shoring up my confidence. "You may be surprised to hear that there's even sometimes on the part of the child a degree of acquiescence which can amount to encouragement. I say that not to imply that this was true in your case but to reassure you that I'm wholly familiar with such incidents. Now . . . shall we begin?"

I nodded but was immediately plunged into panic again. As far as I could see no beginning was possible.

"Ginevra." That snapped me out of my panic as abruptly as a slap in the face for he never called me Ginevra as everyone else did. "You must trust me," he said, and when I looked into his eyes I found I could not look away. "You must."

"Yes . . . I will . . . I do . . . but I can't see where to begin."

He smiled. Like so many juries I had surrendered my mind to his and the first hurdle had been overcome. I was so relieved to see him smile that tears came to my eyes, and when he offered me a cigarette (a noble gesture from a man who hated women smoking) I nearly wept with gratitude.

When our cigarettes were alight he said, "The first matter I want to clarify is the chronology. This case is all mixed up with your first encounter with Kinsella, isn't it? What I'd like to establish is whether the two incidents were related or whether they were merely running concurrently. Let's start with Kinsella. You met him at the Mowbrays', didn't you, in the May of 1896, shortly after your sixteenth birthday?"

"Yes." This was easy. I thought of Conor and how divinely glamorous he had looked at twenty-four, a fascinating rough diamond in a pearls-and-primness setting. "It was a grown-up dinner party," I said. "I wasn't 'out,' of course, but it didn't matter because it was just a gathering of old friends. The Porteynon Kinsellas came with Conor, and the Bryn-Davieses were there as well. I remember saying to Conor, 'Mr. Bryn-Davies's father and my cousin Bobby's mother were involved in a simply scorching grand passion!' and Conor was very entertained, but Margaret overheard and was livid with me afterwards."

"What was Bobby's attitude to you at this time?"

"Normal." I was grateful to him for using Bobby's first name instead of any word that would have underlined their relationship.

"Very well. What happened after this dinner party when you created such a deep impression on Kinsella?"

"Nothing. There was no deep impression. You see, I was so young, I still wore my hair in plaits—I hadn't a hope of winning any serious attention from a sophisticated man of twenty-four. Besides, he was after his cousins' money—the money that went to that wretched dogs' home in the end—and so he had to be on his best behavior. He couldn't afford any unwise flirtations."

"But he did like you."

"Oh yes, I think he found me amusing but I soon realized nothing was going to come of it. Margaret hadn't cared for him at all so I knew he'd never be invited to Oxmoon."

"Very discouraging for you. What happened next?"

"I mooned around at home, shed a few tears of frustration and decided my life had finished at the age of sixteen."

"All very normal behavior, in fact, for a young girl in the throes of calf love."

"Oh yes, everything was absolutely normal. But then . . ."

"Just take it in strict chronological sequence. There you were, you say, shedding tears like a lovesick heroine—"

"—in the summerhouse, yes, I was just weeping over my volume of Browning when . . . when Bobby turned up with Glendower—or at least the Glendower of seventeen years ago. He asked me what the matter was and when I poured out my heart to him he was so kind and understanding." This was the Bobby I could allow myself to remember. I was able to speak the words without difficulty.

"Was there any manifestation of an abnormal interest at this stage?"

"No, but after that he became nicer and nicer to me, and I kept meeting him by accident at odd moments—only of course the meetings were no accident—"

"I'm sorry, I've lost track of the time here. Is this still May or are we in June?"

"It must have been still in May. I met Conor at the beginning of the month, and I don't think this unusual interest from Bobby went on for more than a fortnight or so—three weeks at the most."

"But there was still no hint of impropriety?"

"No, I knew his interest was unprecedented but I just thought he was making an extra effort to cheer me up."

"He didn't kiss you here in the music room, for instance, when no one was around?"

"No, never. But it's odd you should mention the music room because he did come here more than once when I was practicing the piano." I tried to recall the incidents. I had spent so many years trying to forget that my memory had become shadowy, but I now found as a matter of pride that I wanted to dispel the shadows in order to impress Robert with my courage. "Wait a moment," I said to him. "I must try and get this right."

"Take your time."

I went on thinking. I now felt no pain, no fear, just a consuming desire to confess as accurately as possible, and as I sat there in silence the past seemed no longer an emotional nightmare but an intellectual puzzle which I felt morally bound to solve.

At last I said slowly, "I think the truth is probably this: Bobby may well have wanted to kiss me—or hold my hand—or something—by that time, and I think if I'd been older I'd have realized that he was thinking of me sexually, but I didn't realize and he didn't actually do anything."

"Very well, I accept that."

"You see, when it did happen it was as if I'd had no warning . . ." My voice shook and I had to stop.

"Yes, I understand but don't jump ahead—keep to the sequence. Margaret went away at about this time, I think."

"Yes, to Staffordshire to see Aunt May whose baby had died. Poor Aunt May, she was so nice—trust awful old Aunt Ethel to be the sister who survived—"

"A tragedy, I agree, but don't let's be diverted by Aunt Ethel's indisputable awfulness; let's concentrate on the May of 1896. Now: Margaret was away in Staffordshire and Kinsella, presumably, was still at Porteynon. How did you manage to see him after Margaret left?"

"I didn't. I never saw him. That story of the clandestine meetings was invented by Margaret later to hush up what had happened."

"I see. Very well. So there you were at Oxmoon, but you certainly weren't alone with Bobby. You had your governess and Celia bobbing around you whenever you weren't being pestered by the babies in the nursery, so Bobby must have had to choose the moment for the seduction very carefully."

"Yes. He did."

"If I were Bobby I'd have gone to your room at night."

"Yes," I said again. "He did." As I crushed out my cigarette I heard myself say rapidly, "That was what was so awful, Robert, about last night when Bobby interrupted us. Of course I knew perfectly well he only wanted to find out how likely I was to marry you—I knew he had no sinister purpose in mind—but when he came in it was as if the past was repeating itself—oh God, I can't tell you what a nightmare last night was—"

"It was a nightmare for all three of us. But let's return to the nightmare of '96."

"That's why Margaret didn't put me in my old room this time. She knew —she understood—"

"Never mind 1913. We're in 1896 and Bobby's come to your room to show he can no longer think of you as a daughter."

"Yes, he . . . he kissed me and . . . I'm sorry, I *will* be able to go on in a moment—but you'll have to ask me another question; I can't see where to go next—"

"Did he seduce you then or did he merely set the scene for a later seduction?"

"Oh God, the answer's both yes and no. I'm sorry, I know that sounds ludicrous, but—"

"Not at all. He seems to be conforming to a well-known pattern. What you're saying is that he did seduce you but he didn't—he left you a virgin physically but not mentally and emotionally."

"Yes, it was all so . . . oh, so indescribably awful, *awful* because . . . because . . . well, you did say just now, didn't you, that in such cases the child sometimes acquiesces to the point of encouragement . . . and I did acquiesce, it was because he frightened me. I knew it was wrong, but what shattered me was that I could see *he* knew it was wrong yet he couldn't stop himself—and when I saw him like that, a changed man, a stranger—oh God, it was so terrifying, all I wanted was to put things right. . . . He said he was unhappy, you see, so I thought that if only I could make him happy he'd become the Bobby I knew again—"

"Did he explain why he was unhappy?"

"He said that with Margaret away he was afraid to sleep alone because he knew he'd have nightmares, and he asked if he could sleep with me for a little while to keep the nightmares at bay. And the awful thing was, Robert—"

"He was telling the truth. He was genuinely desperate and of course you longed to help him—oh yes, the really consummate liars of this world always use the truth as far as they possibly can! Very well, so the truth gave him the excuse he needed to get into bed with you, and you were much too terrified by this revelation of the unbalanced side of his personality to do anything but consent. I accept all that. Now—"

"He did say he wouldn't do anything I didn't want him to do, but the trouble was . . . well, I didn't really know what he meant, I'd never discussed passion with anyone—'sex' as Mr. H. G. Wells calls it—well, you just thought it was soppy, didn't you, and Margaret had only said she'd have a little talk with me later before I had my first dance—of course I had inklings of what went on because of all the animals, but I was still so ignorant—"

"I understand. Now, what was Bobby's reaction afterwards? Did he immediately ask if he could return the next night?"

"Oh no—no, quite the reverse! Robert, he was horrified, absolutely appalled—and of course that made me more terrified than ever because at that point he seemed irrevocably transformed into someone wicked who did terrible things. He sat on the edge of the bed and said, 'I've done a terrible thing and no one must ever know about it'—oh, God, how he frightened me! Then he got in a state about the sheet because . . . well, I said I'd sponge it off but he didn't trust me, he had to do it himself. He was in a panic. He said, 'You mustn't worry, you're still a virgin, I haven't harmed you,' but when he looked at my expression he saw how he had harmed me, and he said, 'Oh God forgive me,' and I thought he was going to break down but he didn't, he just repeated he'd never do such a thing again, and then he left."

"But he came back—"

"The next night, yes."

"—and completed the seduction."

"Yes. I couldn't bear to see him so distressed, and when he broke his word I was almost relieved. I thought: Now I'll be able to put matters right. But—"

"How many times did full sexual intercourse take place?"

"There were two more occasions but I didn't mind, I was just so relieved to make him happy because afterwards the stranger disappeared and he was himself again."

"And after the final occasion—"

"Margaret came home and the horrors began." I closed my eyes for a moment and when I reopened them I found myself again staring at the sheet music on the table. "He told her straightaway," I said. "I think that shocked me more than anything that had happened previously. I knew by that time that he couldn't be trusted to keep his word, but he'd sworn he'd never tell her and he'd made me swear too . . . all for nothing. It destroyed him for me when he did that. I hated him. I felt betrayed. It was vile. I felt so filthy, so unclean, so absolutely *defiled*—"

"What did Margaret do?"

"She was very fierce and very ruthless. 'I'm not going to let my home and family be destroyed by this,' she said to us. 'I've been through too much in the past and I'm damned if it's all going to be for nothing.' Then she said, 'Let me think about what has to be done and then we'll meet again in the morning.' It was late at night by that time. I went to bed but I was so wretched, so overcome with shame and guilt and grief, that I knew I couldn't bear to stay in the house. It was Margaret, you see . . . I knew I'd lost her love forever . . . the only mother I could remember . . . I didn't know how I was going to bear it."

"Yes." He paused before asking, "What happened next?"

"I ran away. I thought the least I could do to make amends to her was to run away so that she would never have to see me again. And of course I was frightened of Bobby still, frightened that he would come to my room in spite of everything. I knew I could never live at Oxmoon again—it was all destroyed, the Oxmoon I loved, the Oxmoon of our childhood—the fairy tale had come to this terrible end and I had to escape somehow into the real world outside."

"So you turned to Kinsella."

"It was the only solution I could think of. I was so desperate—naturally I'd never have dared to approach him under normal circumstances, but I thought he might help me start afresh in Dublin—I thought he was the sort of unconventional man who might possibly be bold enough to come to my rescue. Well . . . you know what happened next. I rode to Porteynon, roused the whole household by mistake and wound up making a complete mess of everything. More horrors. Scandal. Ghastliness. The only gleam of light in the ink-black landscape was that I finally succeeded in capturing

Conor's imagination—that was when he realized that I was just the sort of woman he wanted. . . . But I didn't tell him the truth. I just said I was unhappy at home. I never told him the truth, never, he tried to make me when he found out two years later that I wasn't a virgin, but I said I'd had an accident riding and I stuck to that story through thick and thin. You see, I couldn't talk about it, even to him. It belonged to the horrible evil fairy tale I'd left behind; I felt that if I once talked about it to anyone afterwards it would become part of the real world and I didn't see how I could possibly live with it. . . . Oh God, I was so frightened that he'd find out but luckily although he never quite believed in the riding accident, he always thought the lover was you—and he never suspected Bobby at all."

There was a pause. Presently when I was more composed I said, "There's not much more to tell you. Soon everyone believed I'd had a row with Bobby and Margaret about Conor and that I was being sent to live with my godparents because I'd behaved so disgracefully. I didn't mind by then what people thought. I was just so glad to escape to the Applebys."

"And Kinsella? How had you left matters with him?"

"In all the uproar we barely had thirty seconds alone together but he told me I was magnificent and that I was to wait for him while he went to America to make some money. He swore he'd never forget me and that when he came back we'd be married."

"And you believed that."

"Oh yes, I was much too young and romantic to do anything else. But in fact, as even a cynic would have to admit, his attitude was credible enough. I did have thirty thousand pounds. I was, as Margaret would say, 'fetching.' Conor was proud, too proud to marry when he was penniless, but once he had a little money behind him it wasn't so surprising that he thought it worthwhile to return to Europe to collect me."

"True. But you lost faith in him, didn't you? Otherwise you wouldn't have become engaged to Timothy."

"I never entirely lost faith in him, but Robert, as time went by I began to see another horrible prospect drifting towards me and I knew I simply had to marry to escape it. I didn't dare wait for Conor any longer."

"Oxmoon?"

"Exactly. I was terrified that in the end I'd have to go back. You see, once Margaret became confident that she had Bobby in control she was quite shrewd enough to realize how odd it would look if they didn't offer to have me back; they couldn't go on exiling me indefinitely because of my mad behavior with Conor."

"Margaret discussed this with you, I assume."

"Yes, she was very kind to me. She guaranteed Bobby's good behavior and said I was never to think she wouldn't welcome me back to Oxmoon whenever I chose to come. Oh Robert . . . I cried when she said that. I was old enough then to see how absolutely she'd saved us all . . . but of course I knew I couldn't go back. I couldn't trust Bobby, you see, no matter what she said. I knew I could never trust him again."

"No, of course you couldn't. So, in conclusion, you became engaged, disengaged and—finally—married."

"Yes—out of the frying pan into the fire as usual. But that's another story," I said, and when I managed to look at him I saw he was smiling at me.

"Oh Robert . . ." I began to cry. I sniffed and snorted and huge tears streamed down my cheeks and I'm sure I looked a perfect fright. I've never had any patience with those romantic heroines who weep beautifully into dainty pieces of lace while the strong silent hero tells himself she's A Woman Sorely Wronged.

"Why the devil is it," said Robert exasperated, "that you never have a handkerchief? Here you are, take mine and start mopping."

"Oh Robert, you do believe me, don't you? I've told you the whole truth, I swear I have—"

"Yes, I realize that. Have another cigarette."

I started weeping again because he was being so nice to me. I was in far too emotional a state to wonder how genuine his mood was and what it all meant. I was simply living minute by minute, second by second, and marveling that I should still be conscious after such an ordeal. I now thought of the ordeal as "over." Where it left us I had no idea but I was for the present too relieved to care. At that point, I told myself, matters could only improve. Now that Robert had all the information at his fingertips he could sort it out, file it away, erase all trace of the mess and tell me how to live happily ever after.

Looking back I can see I was positively unhinged by my relief. In fact I was almost on the point of hallucination; as Robert lit my second cigarette I had no trouble seeing him as the hero who would forgive me everything and swear never again to mention my past.

"Very well," he said, extinguishing not only the match but my sentimental delusions. "So much for 1896. Now let's turn to your marriage. How often were you unfaithful to Kinsella?"

That shocked me out of my tears fast enough. It also brought me face to face with reality. My ordeal wasn't over. On the contrary it had just begun, because although Robert had got what he wanted as usual—the truth—he couldn't cope with it. Unable to bear the thought of me with his father he was now ricocheting in self-defense toward the murky waters of my subsequent sexual experience.

I knew very well that he had loathed Conor. In fact I was almost tempted to confess that Conor had been unable to keep me to himself, but fortunately despite my panic I still had the sense to see that any pleasure Robert might derive from this information would be utterly outweighed by his horror that I had given myself to other men. Robert was deeeply jealous and very possessive. (This was now part of his attraction for me; in his jealousy and possessiveness I saw the shield that would protect me against predators.) However although I was willing to tolerate and even embrace this side of his personality, I did clearly see that a little jealousy could go a very long way.

Discretion was obviously called for.

"What makes you think I was unfaithful?" I said to play for time while I decided what to say.

"Ah come, Ginette, you may as well tell me about your marriage—why not? What could be worse than what you've already told me this morning?"

He had called me Ginette again. My spirits soared. Whatever happened I now had to avoid the disaster of falling at the final fence.

"But I was never unfaithful to Conor," I said, assuming my most candid expression. "I loved him too much to look at anyone else."

Robert gave me one long contemptuous look. Then he stood up and walked out.

"Oh my God." I'd fallen at the final fence. Rushing after him I caught him up in the hall. "Robert, wait—Robert, *please*—"

"I can't talk to you anymore." He began to hurry up the stairs. "I can't listen to lies."

"All right, I'll tell you the truth, I swear I will, I swear it, I'll do anything you want . . ."

He took no notice. He never even looked back.

I hitched up my skirts and tried to race after him but I nearly fell flat on my face. Sometimes I think women's fashions should be abolished by act of Parliament. I was wearing not only a hobble skirt but a vile corset, currently much in vogue, which reached almost to my knees in order to ensure that the skirt fell in the right lines.

I was still teetering absurdly up the stairs when I heard the door of his bedroom slam in the distance but I never faltered, and seconds later I was bursting across the threshold. "Robert," I panted, "Robert, *listen*—"

I had grabbed his arm but he wrenched it away. "No hysterics. I can't stand hysterics. I won't tolerate them."

"All right, I'll be calm, look how calm I am, I'm so calm I'm virtually dead. Robert, I admit I wasn't faithful to Conor, but I only lied to you because I couldn't bear the thought that I'd make you even more upset—"

"*Upset!* That word's so shattering in its banality that I hardly know how to respond!" It was now obvious that he had lost his grip on the situation. He could no longer pretend he was my lawyer; our new sexual intimacy precluded him from assuming his familiar role of platonic friend and my revelations had turned his role of lover into a nightmare. He was beside himself. He had nowhere to go. His only escape lay into rage.

"You've consistently lied to me." He could hardly speak. "You've tricked me, you've deceived me, you've—"

"Every word that I spoke about Bobby was the truth!"

"Oh yes! Just now! When you knew you had no choice! But last night—when I came to your room—"

Amidst all my terror I knew that my one hope of saving us both lay in forcing him to face reality.

"Oh, for God's sake, Robert!" I burst out. "How on earth could I have embarked on the truth last night? Don't be so absurd! A woman doesn't say to a man who's obviously got nothing but copulation on his mind: 'Oh darling, I'm so sorry but I slept with your father when I was sixteen and I was just the tiniest bit unfaithful to my husband later on!' God Almighty! Wake up! This is no dream, this is—"

"Reality. Quite. That's precisely why I want to know how many men you've slept with."

"Very well, I'll tell you," I said. "I'll tell you exactly how many men have slept with me just as soon as you've told me exactly how many women have slept with you."

He stared at me. In the baffled silence that followed I had a glimpse of that curious naivety which lay beyond his intellect at the hidden core of his personality.

"But I don't understand," he said, too astonished to sustain his anger. "What have my mistresses got to do with you?"

"Absolutely nothing, Robert. And my lovers and my husband have absolutely nothing to do with you either."

He was floored. And he hated it. He could never bear anyone to get the better of him, and as his injured pride streamed to his rescue I saw him once more go white with rage.

But I stood my ground. I was convinced now I had nothing left to lose and in my sheer soul-splitting misery I wasn't afraid of his rage and I no longer cared how much I shocked him as I used the truth in my defense. I heard him shout, "A man has a right to know the past of a woman he's promised to marry—" but I cut him off.

"Shut up!" I screamed. "Don't talk as if my past is a closed book to you when you've just put me through hell by forcing me to recall every damned minute of it! My lovers meant no more to me than your mistresses meant to you, so what the hell do they matter now? The past is over, it's finished, it's done!"

"But I was a bachelor—you were married! You had duties, obligations—"

"We're not talking about marriage; we're talking about copulation!"

"No, we're not, we're talking about marriage—*your* marriage—and what I want to know is—"

"All right, just you listen to me! You're a criminal lawyer, you say, you've heard it all before, you say, very well, just you listen to this and see if you can make head or tail of it, because I don't think you've heard it all before at all! It's no good trying to give you an orderly rational explanation of my marriage because there isn't one. Conor and I were the victims of what's popularly known as a grand passion except that grand passions aren't as they're described in story books, in real life they're quite different, you hurtle around between heaven and hell until you want to commit murder—or at the very least a dramatic suicide—my God, no wonder all the famous lovers in history killed themselves, I'm not surprised, that sort of passion's enough to drive anyone round the bend!"

"You mean—"

"I mean Conor and I fought and screamed and yelled and laughed and loved and were passionately happy and utterly miserable and he wasn't faithful to me and I wasn't faithful to him and he was a bastard and I was a bitch and we each got the partner we deserved and we were wild about each other and it was all awful and wonderful and chaotic and appalling—and thank God it's over because I couldn't have stood it much longer, and if you understand all that mess and muddle better than I do, then you really *are* brilliant and not just a man with a first-class brain which you've trained to go through legal hoops!"

"But—"

"The trouble with you, Robert, is that you know nothing about life. Oh, you know it all in theory—my dear, those criminal cases! Do tell me about the bestiality sometime!—but you're always on the sidelines looking at other people, you've no idea what it's like to be so damned involved that you can't see the sidelines for dust. So don't you pass judgment on me—you're not in court now and anyway you're not a judge. If you want to go back on your offer to marry me, then go back on it—God knows you're entitled to revoke it utterly after all you've heard this morning and I certainly shan't blame you if you do. But don't start losing your temper with me just because I'm not the fairy-tale princess of your dreams—lose your temper instead with yourself for being romantic and foolish enough to propose marriage after a few hours' reacquaintance and a passing victory between the sheets!"

I stopped speaking. He was ashen. Nothing happened, but I knew I now had the upper hand and must ram my advantage home. A magnificent exit was called for so I swept out of the room across the landing, I swept halfway down the stairs—I was traveling on a tidal wave of emotion, but tidal waves don't last forever and on the half-landing I found myself beached in the most intolerable shallows. I stopped. I knew I had to flounder out of the shallows but I knew too that I couldn't go on.

Drying my eyes I crept back and listened at the door.

There was no sound.

I went on listening and suddenly I could endure his silent grief no longer.

What was unendurable was not that I'd made my lover miserable; all's fair in love and war, and love can be as brutal in its own way as war can be. What was unendurable was that I'd made my friend unhappy. No one could have wished for a more loyal and devoted friend than Robert. I remembered how pleased he had always been to see me when he returned from school, I remembered his precocious letters sprinkled maddeningly first with Latin and then with Greek, I remembered him spending his pocket money on gifts for me when I was ill, I remembered the midnight feasts and the secret picnics and the illicit raids on the strawberry beds . . . And then I saw the road to Oxmoon, the lost Oxmoon of our childhood—and I knew that only Robert could lead me back there to the peace I so longed to find.

I thought: Well, I may have been a disastrous mistress and of course I'll never now be his wife, but at least I can still be a good friend and comfort him when he's so unhappy.

I tapped softly on the door and peeped in. He was sitting on the bed with his head in his hands.

"Darling Robert," I said as he kept his eyes shaded. "How unkind I was to you, I'm so sorry. Isn't this crisis a nightmare? I do so wish we could go off and plunder the strawberry beds and forget all about it."

He gave a short awkward laugh and let his hands fall. Of course his eyes were tearless. "If you can apologize to me," he said in his best rational voice, "then I can apologize to you. You weren't the only one who was unkind." Then, movingly, he covered his eyes with his hands again and whispered in despair, "I feel so confused."

"Oh darling . . ." I put my arms around him and when he made no attempt to push me away I saw he had reached the end of his resources and had no idea what to do next. I saw too more clearly than ever that salvation was turning out to be a double-sided ordeal. He had saved me by playing the role of the detached attorney and eliminating all falsehood between us, and now I had to save him not only by insisting that he faced reality but by unraveling the complex emotional aftermath which he was far too proud to admit he couldn't master.

"Listen," I said gently, taking his hand in mine, "I know the situation couldn't be more confusing, but think of all the things that haven't changed. I'm still your friend and whether we marry or not I'll still need someone loyal who'll stand by me in the future."

"Yes, but—"

"No, never mind marriage for the moment. Marriage is complicated. Let's keep this situation very, very simple. We'll be friends. We're very good at being friends; I think we've got a unique gift for it—perhaps it's because we're like brother and sister without all the bore of being confined in a close blood relationship."

"True, but—"

"No, don't worry about bed. That's not important at the moment either. If later on you find you do want to sleep with me now and then, well, that would be heaven because I thought we got on rather well in that direction, but meanwhile you probably feel that having me as a mistress would be too complicated for you, and don't worry, I quite understand, we'll just wait till the way ahead seems clearer."

"What makes you think the way ahead will get clearer?"

"Well, it usually does, you know. One crashes around in a fog but eventually one does see a gleam of light in the distance—"

"I never crash around in a fog."

"That's the point, darling—that's why you must trust me about this business: because I'm so much more used to crashing around in fogs than you are."

We smiled at each other. His hand tightened on mine. After a long silence he said unsteadily, "I love you," and started kissing me. When he paused for breath he added more to himself than to me, "I've got to have you, I swore I'd have you, I've got to win."

"Well, that's certainly what I want, darling, and don't think for one moment it isn't, but—"

"Marry me."

"Of course I'll marry you, but don't you think it would be better if . . . Oh heavens, how difficult it is to know how to say this! Listen, Robert, I don't want you turning on me later and accusing me of taking advantage of you while you were too confused to make the right decision. You've had some dreadful shocks this morning—and I don't think you should marry me until you've recovered from them."

"Very well, I'll wait six months. But not a day longer. We'll marry at Christmas."

"Well, that would be wonderful, darling—wonderful . . . but only if you're absolutely certain—"

"I know what I want and by God I'm going to get it." He got up, locked the door and began to unbutton his trousers.

"Heavens, do we have time?" I couldn't help saying nervously. "They'll all be coming home from church soon!"

"I don't give a damn."

"Well, now you come to mention it," I said, realizing that he needed a display of enthusiasm to shore up his confidence, "neither do I."

The next few minutes weren't pleasant, but I wasn't so naive as to expect rapture from a man who has been seriously hurt emotionally and who is far more angry than he can admit either to himself or to anyone else. As I forced myself to go limp I thought, Everything passes, even this, and sure enough it passed and afterwards his violent feelings were sufficiently purged to enable him to whisper a plea for forgiveness as he buried his face guiltily in my hair.

I automatically reassured him, but as I spoke my thoughts were elsewhere. I had just realized that emotionally he was color-blind. I saw human relationships as a great glorious splodgy painting where every color in the spectrum was represented in unending ever-changing patterns. Robert saw human relationships as a black-and-white geometrical design which, being fixed, was always orderly and subject to rational interpretation. This meant that whenever he encountered a piece that was neither black nor white he was lost. He had no way of placing it in his design; he had no way of creating a new pattern that made sense.

"You do love me, don't you, Ginette?"

"Darling, you know I do. Very, very much."

"Then nothing else matters," said Robert, resolutely sweeping aside all the messy garish colors from his design and masterfully calling his black-and-white world to order. "I'll go and see Mama just as soon as she arrives home from church."

Very well, that was reality as I remember it. But now for the gloss on reality; now let me write about what was—and is—really going on; now let me try and pin down the chaotic thoughts in my head.

What do I truthfully think of Robert? Oh yes, we all know he's six feet two and divinely glamorous, but what do I really *think?* How attractive do I actually find him? Robert said gloomily to me once that he would never be classically handsome and he was right, but nevertheless he *is* good-looking and far better-looking now than when he was a fierce lanky spotted adolescent. I like that tough mouth of his. How does it ever manage to relax into such a charming smile? A mystery. Yes, I'm wild about that, and as for his eyes . . . Who would have thought that eyes the color of dishwater could be so alluring? Remarkable. Oh yes, he's very attractive but not in an obvious way and I like that; I'm getting to an age when I can appreciate the more subtle forms of masculine appeal. Robert may not radiate sexual charm as Conor did, but do I really want a man who's carnal knowledge personified? No. Not now. A brilliant good-looking man like Robert will suit me very well, thank you, and I shall adore living in London and basking in all the reflected glory of his inevitably dazzling political career. (Can't wait to meet the Asquiths!)

However . . . beyond all the divine glamour . . . oh, let's be honest, I've no doubt he can be very tricky. There are bound to be times when I shall find him willful, selfish and thoroughly pigheaded, but so what? I shall only be faced with that extraordinary emotional simplicity—I'll just need a bit of guile when he's difficult, but that's not a problem because I'm an old hand at the art of being beguiling. There's something curiously endearing about that simplicity. It attracts me. Heavens, what a contrast to Conor he is! Conor's emotions were as volatile as my own, and my God, that's saying something.

How restful it'll be to live with someone so simple and straightforward! I feel quite entranced by the prospect.

Am I madly in love with Robert? No. But that must be good. I've had enough of being madly in love, and besides, my feelings for Robert are far more stable than that. There's our shared past, that old, old friendship which nothing can destroy, and that must surely be a good basis for marriage, far better than that lethal sexual affinity I shared with Conor.

Yes, that's the truth. That's reality. Oh yes, I must marry him, I must! It's the wisest decision I could possibly make. . . .

"All's well," said Robert half an hour later when he returned to the bedroom. He embraced me with a smile. "She's resigned herself to the inevitable and says she's prepared to give us her blessing."

Clever, *clever* Margaret. I tried to imagine the depth of her horror and rage but my imagination failed me. I felt weak. In my overpowering relief that Robert still wanted to marry me my mind had neatly glided around the problem of how we were going to face his parents. Whenever I have a severe problem in my private life (which is most of the time) I always say, "I'll cross that bridge later," and put the problem out of my mind. So when Robert and I had been conducting our long crucial harrowing conversation earlier I hadn't once thought, even at the end: My God, what are we going to do about Bobby and Margaret? I had remained acutely aware of the problem, just as one would be continually aware of a vast wardrobe in an underfurnished room, but I had classified it as a bridge to be crossed later. And now "later," to my absolute terror, had without doubt arrived.

"I'll give you a blow-by-blow description presently," said Robert, who was looking naively pleased with himself. Endearing emotionally simple Robert didn't quite see the problem as I did, of course. He probably thought he had mastered the entire situation after a ten-minute chat with his mother. "But meanwhile Mama would like to see you on your own for a moment. She's waiting in her room."

"Oh *God.*" I now felt so weak that I even swayed in his arms but Robert merely laughed, patting me kindly as if I were a lapdog, and told me to stop being so melodramatic. I would have slapped him but I was too weak with fright. Instead I looked in the glass, smoothed my skirt and made sure that every hair on my head was in place before I sallied forth at a funereal pace to meet my future mother-in-law.

The bedroom which by tradition belonged to the master and mistress of the house was a high wide sunny chamber which Bobby and Margaret, purging it after its occupancy by Gwyneth Godwin and Owain Bryn-Davies, had filled with their usual junk-shop furniture. At least, the furniture had been purchased new from a respectable Swansea store but it still looked as if it had been acquired in a junk shop because each piece was in such execrable mid-

Victorian taste. Possibly Margaret's *nouveau-riche* background among the Potteries of Staffordshire had given her a penchant for vulgar grandeur, but Bobby also had a weakness for oversprung comfort, and between the two of them they had accumulated a collection of objects, all of overwhelming ghastliness and all displayed against the background of a garish flock wallpaper. When I eventually became mistress of Oxmoon . . . but that was far in the future and meanwhile I had this dreadful bridge that had to be crossed. I knocked on the door, Margaret tranquilly bade me enter and somehow I found the strength to creep into her presence.

Margaret was only fifteen years my senior but she looked older, partly because her clothes were always ten years out of date and partly because her hairstyle (which she never altered) had gone out of fashion at least ten years before she was born; her dull straight brown hair was parted in the center and drawn back into a bun at the nape of her neck. In spite of her lack of interest in fashion she was a feminine woman in appearance. She was very round, very curvy—but in a maternal, not a seductive way. Of course plenty of men like that overweight, motherly, comfortable look; although Margaret wasn't in the least pretty I could see she did have her attractions. She had the most exquisite skin, flawless and velvet-smooth, and a mild benign expression, which she no doubt believed to be the essence of seemly femininity, but unfortunately this mildness was marred by that straight tough mouth which I found so attractive on Robert. It looked very odd indeed on a woman—and particularly odd on a woman like Margaret who in every other respect looked so cozy and conventional.

When I entered the room she was seated at her dressing table and engaged in a favorite occupation of hers, poking around in one of the several large jewel boxes which were all full of worthless trinkets. She disliked precious stones. I think she had read somewhere once that *nouveau-riche* women had a vulgar habit of wearing too much flashy jewelry. As I edged reluctantly towards her I saw she was lining up her mourning brooches (sordid little squares filled with dreadful swatches of faded hair) and piling her jet brooches into a pyramid.

"Oh, do sit down, Ginevra," she said casually, nodding towards the nearest chair. "How good of you to come so promptly. Thank you."

As I sat down speechlessly I was aware of a terrible desire to burst into tears.

"Well, we mustn't be emotional about this, must we," said Margaret, idly arranging four mourning brooches into a quadrangle. "There's no room in this situation for petty little displays of hysterics."

"No, Margaret." I realized at once that she was handling me in the cleverest possible way. I need to be handled firmly when I'm quite beside myself with guilt and terror.

"So," said Margaret, surveying her quadrangle of brooches before glancing at me in the glass to make sure I had myself in control, "Robert still wants to marry you. Very well. If you two now decide to marry in spite of what you've been through this morning, all I can say is that you've certainly earned the right to do so. However—"

I had never realized until that moment that "however" could be quite one of the most sinister words in the English language.

"However," repeated Margaret, suddenly abandoning the quadrangle and turning to look directly into my eyes, "I think this marriage, if it ever takes place, would be a very big mistake. Robert's marrying you for all the wrong reasons. He's marrying out of pride; he's marrying because he's invested so much emotional energy in you that he feels he can't change his mind without looking a fool and suffering a fatal loss of self-respect. And as for you—" She turned aside and taking another brooch she converted her quadrangle into a pentagon. "—well, I won't embarrass you by saying what I think is going on in your mind, but I'll say this: you shouldn't marry anyone until your husband's been dead a year—and I'm not just talking about the proprieties when I say that; I'm talking about the dangers of marrying on the rebound."

She paused. Then she took me by surprise. As I braced myself for her next verbal assault she stretched out her hands to mine which were clasped in agony in my lap, and when she next spoke her gentle voice reminded me of days long ago when she had looked after me with as much love and care as if I had been her own child. "Ginevra . . . my dear, don't think I don't understand. I of all people know why you're so afraid to be alone and unprotected—I of all people will never forget what happened to you once when I left you defenseless and alone. Do you think I can ever forgive myself for not realizing what was going on in Bobby's mind during that dreadful summer of '96? I shall always feel guilty about you, and I shall feel even guiltier if you now make the wrong decision as the result of that past tragedy."

I began to cry. I tried to find Robert's handkerchief but I'd lost it. I tried to blink back my tears and failed.

"You're a very beautiful woman," said Margaret in her most passionless voice as she efficiently passed me a lavender-scented handkerchief from the top drawer of her dressing table, "and as such, as you well know, you're the prey of unscrupulous men. Of course you feel you need a strong man like Robert to protect you and keep you safe—that's quite natural and I utterly understand it. But my dear, you don't have to *marry* Robert to ensure the love and security you need. He'll look after you whether you're married or not, so why not simply continue as his mistress? I'm sure that would suit you both far better and be much more in keeping with your old friendship."

After that there was an interval of some minutes because I broke down and could do nothing but weep. Margaret was very kind and very patient and even passed me a second lavender-scented handkerchief. I hardly knew how to bear it.

Eventually I controlled myself sufficiently to whisper, "But Margaret . . . why wouldn't marriage be in keeping with our old friendship too?"

"Oh, friends find it very difficult to live together," said Margaret. "Haven't you noticed? In fact it always seems to me that the quickest way to end a friendship is for the parties to try to live in harmony beneath the same roof. But if you're Robert's mistress you'll both have your own establishments, and then the dangers of too much proximity won't arise."

"But Margaret—"

"Just think it over," she said. "You do at least have six months to reflect on the situation before you journey to the altar—I only wish Robert would wait longer, but never mind, the gossip caused by a hasty marriage is the least of our problems. Ginevra—" She was now crisp and businesslike again; I watched her cram all the mourning brooches but one back into the jewel box and snap shut the lid "—this may come as a surprise to you, but I think the real difficulty in this situation lies not between you and me. I think we'll both try hard and manage tolerably well. No, the real problem for the future lies between Robert and Bobby—and that, I confess, is worrying me almost to death. Will you help me?"

"Oh, Margaret, you know I'd do *anything*—"

"Then don't cut Robert off from Oxmoon. It would break Bobby's heart if Robert withdrew utterly to London."

"Well, of course I give you my word I wouldn't persuade Robert to do such a thing, but surely Robert himself would never—"

"Robert will try to give you the life you want, and you like the glitter, don't you, Ginevra, you like the glamour and the fame. You want a smart London life with a thoroughly successful husband, and Robert's going to see that you get it."

"But surely that's what Robert himself wants!"

"I don't think Robert knows what he wants," said Margaret, "but he'll use you to clarify the confusion in his mind." She began to pin on her selected mourning brooch. "You don't know Robert very well, do you?" she added casually. "But then how could you? You've lived apart for so long. A great deal can happen in fifteen years—and that reminds me: have you discussed your boys with him?"

"Well, actually . . . no. No, there hasn't been time."

"Has he asked about them?"

"No, not exactly. I mean, no, he hasn't. But you see, what with one thing and another—"

"Quite. Well, never mind. I don't need to remind you, do I, how much Robert has always disliked children. I'm sure you can remember that all too clearly." She stood up to terminate the interview. "You'll have a great many problems to sort out between you," she said, "and all I can do is wish you well. But do remember what I've said. Marriage is very different from a love affair and very, very different from a romantic fraternal friendship, no matter how powerful that friendship may be."

"Yes, Margaret."

"Oh, and Ginevra—"

"Yes?"

"I should be greatly obliged if you and Robert would observe the proprieties while you're under this roof. What you do elsewhere is of course entirely your own concern, but here I have my standards—and here I draw the line."

"Yes, Margaret. Of course. I'm so sorry, please forgive us," I stammered, and somehow managed to escape from her in an agony of guilt and shame.

Now that I've calmed down, what do I think of Margaret's advice? Not much. I've got to be married. Otherwise I shan't feel safe. Besides, how could I manage on my own in London with the boys? (That was a very nasty gibe of Margaret's about Robert and my boys and at some time I'll have to consider it, but not just yet; I'll cross that bridge later.)

No, I've got to be married—and so has Robert. He's reached the age now when he really has to have a wife, particularly as he's about to enter politics. We simply can't settle for a smart little love affair; it wouldn't work. If I were unmarried I'd flirt with other men, I know I would, and then I'd be sure to end up in a ghastly mess, whereas if Robert were my husband, watching over me and frightening away all the predators, I know I'd never be lured into naughtiness. The trouble is that although I'm terrified of men in some ways I adore them in others; men are my great weakness but at least I'm terrified enough to want to fight it by vowing to be utterly faithful to darling Robert.

My God, what a muddle my emotions are. Can Robert cope? Yes. Robert will slip the wedding ring on my finger, iron out my problems and then take whatever steps prove necessary to ensure that we live happily ever.

I'm going to marry him.

I'm in London and it seems so gray and dispirited, so different from shining Manhattan with its glittering vistas and gaudy crowds and rowdy celebration of life. I loved New York once and now that I'm away from it I have this terrible suspicion I love it still. But I mustn't start thinking of New York. If I do I'll start thinking of Conor and then I'll feel so unhappy, and God knows there's quite enough muddle going on at the moment without me deciding to play the part of the grieving widow.

But I miss New York and all my friends there. They all promised faithfully to write, but they won't. Once or twice perhaps but no more. Do I mind? No, not really. I need to make a fresh start. I don't want to be reminded of that life I shared with Conor.

I find London intimidatingly grand. Life in the raw exists here, just as it does in New York, but the British have drawn the line as usual and the rawness has sunk obediently out of sight behind it. There's the East End and there's the West End and ne'er the twain do meet. Was any city so absolutely divided between the acceptable and the unspeakable? Of course the West End too has its unspeakable side but it's all veiled discreetly by the twin gods of Tradition and Propriety which have to be ceaselessly appeased in order to keep the real world, the chaotic world, under control. No race knows better than a conquering race how anarchic the real world can be, and no race knows better than the British how to master reality by subjugating it, by setting those chilling standards and drawing those brutal lines.

Yet after all isn't this exactly what I want? There's comfort in convention, security in being ruled by the rules. Don't think of gorgeous free-and-easy vital New York which made you feel so intoxicatingly liberated. Liberation has to be paid for, just like any other social amenity, and the price I paid was chaos, the chaos symbolized by Conor's violent terrible end. No. No more New York, no more violence, no more chaos. Welcome to London, welcome to Robert's well-ordered world.

Robert has taken a short lease on a furnished apartment in Kensington. The English call it a "mansion flat," which means it's spacious and comfortable, and downstairs in the reception hall a porter in Ruritanian uniform presides over acres of red carpet. My apartment is on the second floor—which the English call the first—and faces south over a pastoral square. I adore it and when I wake up in the morning I rush to the window and fling back the curtains and feel lyrical. Robert's chambers near Temple Bar are some way away, but fortunately the underground railway is very accommodating in London and it doesn't take him too long to reach me. Meanwhile I'm only two minutes (on foot) from Kensington Gardens and five minutes (in a cab) from divine Harrods, which is just as good as any store in New York and where I know I shall be perpetually lured to spend too much money.

I'm rather naughty about money, I know I am, but I'm going to reform. How lucky it was that although Conor spent all the money that became mine outright on my marriage (he was *very* naughty about money and he *never* reformed), ten thousand was locked up on trust to me for life with the remainder to my children, and this meant he could never get his hands on the capital. Heavens, what rows we used to have about the income—and about money in general—but I won't have to go through all that ghastliness with Robert. Robert's bound to have his financial affairs under iron control, and anyway he must surely earn thousands so I daresay he won't mind if I'm a little bit naughty with money now and then.

Robert is paying for this heavenly mansion flat, but we haven't actually talked about money yet. I've been too busy settling down in London and recovering from the ordeal of my visit to Oxmoon. It was dreadful that I couldn't stay on there for more than a week after Robert left. I wanted to. I know it must have looked so odd to come home after many years and then rush off to London ten days later, but I couldn't bear to stay. I'm still trying to work out why. Bobby and Margaret were faultless and the boys were adorable, but . . . it was ghastly. I suppose my guilt must have been responsible for the fiasco. Or Bobby's guilt. Or—oh God—maybe even Margaret's guilt. How *dreadful* I feel when I think of Margaret feeling guilty; but I must blot that out of my mind and think instead of how exciting it was to move from Oxmoon into this gorgeous apartment in London.

It has a drawing room, a dining room, a bathroom, a very elegant water closet, a kitchen with a scullery, four bedrooms and a sort of cupboard beyond the kitchen where a half-witted maid sleeps; a cook-housekeeper arrives daily to provide rudimentary intelligence and food. One of the large bedrooms has been set aside for housing the luggage, the other large bedroom I sleep in and the two remaining bedrooms, which are smaller but still comfortable, will be allotted to darling Declan and darling Rory when they arrive from Ireland. I think they'll be able to manage there without too many fights. That reminds me: I must write to Dervla and Seamus to say I'm now ready for the boys to join me. But before I do that I simply must raise the subject of the boys with Robert and make sure he understands that I can't bear to be parted from them any longer.

Perhaps if I were to show him the letters that arrived this morning . . .

Dear Ma, wrote Declan. *Thank you for your letter. We were glad to hear you are not in a decline but remembering how prostrate you were all the way across the Atlantic, not to mention how you nearly fainted into the grave at the funeral, I don't think you should be on your own any longer. It's not safe. You might kill yourself in a fit of passion and then regret it afterwards. You know what you're like. So all in all I think it would be best if we came over and collected you and brought you back here where I can keep an eye on you. I know you have the apartment in London, but I'm afraid I can't live in England, it would be quite contrary to Pa's wishes, so I'm making inquiries through uncle Seamus about the possibility of renting a place in Dublin. The sooner you get here the better, in my opinion, because I'm becoming worn out with worrying about what might be happening to you. With fondest love from your respectful and anxious son,* DECLAN KINSELLA.

That letter touched me but made me feel very nervous. Rory's letter simply touched me. The little love wrote: *Dear Ma, I miss you, I can't sleep at night for crying for Pa and wishing you were here, please come and get us, to be sure if you don't we'll die of grief altogether completely, and you'll be left with nothing to do but sob on our grave. Love,* RORY.

My darling boys! I spent the whole morning feeling so sentimental that I forgot to dwell upon all the problems they represented, but long before Robert arrived that evening with his customary bottle of champagne I was asking myself in absolute panic how I could tell my darlings that I was already planning to remarry.

"Darling," I said to Robert after we had made love, "I'm rather anxious about Declan and Rory. Please could we talk about them for a moment?"

We were lying languidly in bed, and far away at the other end of the flat the half-witted maid who always retired early was safe in her cupboard. It was half-past ten. We had dined out as usual and as usual we had not lingered at the restaurant because we had been so anxious to spend as much time as possible alone together. Robert never stayed the whole night, not merely because he had no wish to enthrall the morning porter downstairs but because he worked hard at hours when less successful men were asleep. Sometimes I wondered if he worked a little too hard, but I put this down to his bachelor life. Bachelors do tend to keep irregular hours, but I was sure his habits would be quite different once he was married.

"You see, darling, it's like this . . ." I took a deep breath, delivered what I had planned as a calm unemotional statement of the problem and finally, when I had sunk into incoherence, thrust the boys' letters mutely into his hands.

"Hmm," said Robert, pale cool eyes seeming to become paler and cooler as he skimmed through the pages. "Very un-English." He handed the letters back to me.

"Well, darling," I said nervously, "they're *not* English, you know. They're two American boys who have been brought up to think of themselves as Irish to the core."

"I agree that's unfortunate but never mind, it needn't necessarily be fatal." He smiled at me. "I assume you're telling me you want to pay a visit to Ireland."

"I—"

"I'm glad the subject's come up," said Robert, and at once I knew I was being manipulated around an uncomfortable truth as if I were some peculiarly awkward witness, "because although I guessed the situation had become as obvious to you as it's become to me I was naturally reluctant to broach the matter myself. I thought it better if the suggestion came from you."

"What suggestion?"

"The suggestion you've just made—that you should visit them in Ireland."

"I didn't make that suggestion, Robert."

"Yes, you did—you said you wanted to see them again as soon as possible, and it must be as obvious to you as it is to me that it would be better if they didn't come to London until after we're married."

"But Robert—"

"To be honest I never thought much of the idea in the first place. You've got quite enough to do, settling down here, looking for a house and preparing for the wedding, and if those boys come you'll soon be utterly worn out. Besides, how are we ever going to have any premarital privacy when you're perpetually chaperoned by two boys on the threshold of adolescence?"

This indeed was the question which I had always been unable to answer.

"But what shall I do?" I said in despair. "I must see them soon, I simply must—look at Rory's letter! The poor little love's crying every night because he's missing me so much!"

"Yes, it's disgraceful that a boy of his age shouldn't be able to control his emotions better. A boy crying for his mother at the age of twelve! I've never heard such nonsense, and anyway I don't believe a word of it. He's just saying that to tug at your heartstrings."

This also had occurred to me. Darling Rory did so enjoy exaggeration.

"Go to Ireland for a fortnight," said Robert, "and see them. I absolutely understand that a visit is necessary and of course I shan't stand in your way."

"But Robert, I can't leave them in Ireland for the next five months!"

"Why not? If you explain to them carefully that this is a temporary situation which has arisen because you're in the process of setting up a new home for them, I'm sure they'll accept it. Of course they'll miss you, but I'd be prepared to wager a large sum of money that their father's relatives are at this moment lavishing affection on them and making sure they're having a splendid time."

I was in despair not because he was wrong but because he was right. What he said was logical, sensible and true. The only trouble was that this superbly rational approach to the problem took no account of my emotional muddle.

"Darling . . ." I took another deep breath, made a new great effort. "There are two difficulties. One is that I hate the thought of going to Ireland for regular visits because I feel I can't face Conor's family. They'll . . . well, they'll remind me of Conor and I can't cope with Conor's memory at the moment—"

Robert began to shift restlessly against the pillows.

"—and the second difficulty," I said frantically, "is that I love my boys so much and I want to make sure they know it. They've just lost their father, and if I tell them I don't want them in England at present they're going to be terribly hurt and upset."

"It sounds to me as if you spoil those children abominably. Good God, boys of their age shouldn't expect to have their mother in constant attendance and drooling over them daily! Very well, have them here for the summer if you must, but I think it's a very big mistake and I'm quite sure you'll soon be regretting it. If you want my opinion—"

"No, I don't!" I cried. "You don't understand anything—*anything!*" And I burst into tears.

Robert sighed. I could almost feel him praying for patience. "There, there!" he said kindly, taking me in his arms. "It's not the end of the world."

"It feels like it." I felt horribly upset, not only because he seemed to be incapable of understanding my point of view but because I was apparently incapable of explaining it to him. And suddenly I thought: Conor would have understood. But I pushed that truth from my mind.

"This is simply a problem which requires a solution," Robert was saying with that superb confidence which was so very hard to resist, "and of course we're going to find the solution and overcome the difficulty."

"Are we?"

"What an extraordinary question! Why the doubt? Solving awkward problems simply requires the right attitude of mind. Now listen to me, Ginette. Please don't think I'm hostile to those boys. They're your children and I'm more than prepared to treat them as if they were my own. But you must realize that I can see this situation more clearly than you can at present because as usual you're wandering around in one of your emotional fogs. Now, do you or do you not want order in your life?"

"I do."

"And do you or do you not want someone to look after you and stop you getting into a mess?"

"I do."

"Then kindly oblige me by taking my advice and desisting from feminine tantrums."

"I'm sorry but I'm in such a state that I've forgotten what your advice was."

"Leave the boys in Ireland until we're married and content yourself with regular visits to see them. You'll just have to grit your teeth about facing your husband's family. Be honest—in the long run it'll be easier to grit your teeth than to enter into a situation which is likely to reduce you to a state of exhaustion."

"True." I was still in despair but by that time I was so hypnotized by the power of his personality that I no longer had the energy to resist. "I'm sorry, darling; I know I'm being hopelessly emotional as usual."

"Never mind, after thirty-one years I'm used to your vagaries. Now for God's sake let's put all that emotional energy to better use," said Robert sensibly, and seconds later all was well but for a moment I couldn't help comparing this down-to-earth invitation of his with Conor's imaginative and outrageous seductions in similar circumstances.

"Ginette . . . what are you thinking about?"

Of course I couldn't tell him. I just said, "I was wondering how on earth I'm going to break the news to Declan and Rory that I'm planning to remarry."

"My God, don't let's start arguing about those boys again! Give the subject a rest, there's a good girl—the whole problem's bound to seem less harrowing in the morning . . ."

Robert was wrong. It's more harrowing than ever. I'm in a terrible state because although I know that rationally Robert's right, I know too that I can't leave my darling boys in Ireland. If they're so far away from me they'll be unhappy, and if they're unhappy I'll be a failure as a mother, and if I'm a failure as a mother I'll be unable to live with my guilt. I know this is emotional stupidity, I know it is, but I can't help it. It's what being a parent is all about, but Robert's never been a parent and so he doesn't understand.

I'm in such a state that I can't look at houses today. I go to Harrods instead and buy three enormous picture hats, all costing twenty and a half guineas, all lavishly decorated with flowers and feathers and all looking exactly what they are—the last word in foolish extravagance. But I always feel better when I buy things.

This sinful shopping expedition has helped me get through the morning, but now it's afternoon and I still can't relax so I think I'll go out again and buy some cream cakes for tea—terribly naughty, and I can almost hear my corset groan in anticipation, but I simply can't rest until I've sunk my teeth into a divine mille-feuilles . . . or perhaps an éclair . . . or—oh God—an utterly sumptuous meringue . . .

"There's a gentleman waiting to see you, ma'am," said Edna the half-witted maid when I returned later with the wickedest assortment of cream cakes I could find. It was my cook-housekeeper's afternoon off and Edna, in sole charge, had scurried out to meet me as soon as I had opened the door.

At first I wasn't sure that I had understood her. Her cleft palate made even the simplest words enigmatic.

"Is it Mr. Godwin?" I was surprised because I hardly expected to see Robert before half-past six.

"Yes, ma'am, but—" Incomprehensible syllables followed.

"Very well, make tea, would you, Edna, and put these cakes on a plate."

I walked into the drawing room and there I found not Robert but Bobby, looking very formal and very embarrassed, and as soon as I saw him I knew that familiar coldness which always assailed me on the rare occasions when he and I found ourselves alone together.

"Bobby, what a lovely surprise!" I said.

"Good afternoon, Ginevra," he said, remaining rooted to his spot on the far side of the room. "I spoke to Robert on the telephone this morning and he suggested that I met him here, but I'm afraid I'm a little early. Perhaps I'll go for a walk. I don't want to distract you when you must have so many things to do."

Of course I wanted to get him out of the flat and of course I knew I couldn't. He was going to be my father-in-law and we were both morally bound to pretend the past had never happened.

"Don't be so silly, Bobby," I said. "Sit down and have some tea. Excuse me, I'll just make sure the maid brings two cups—she's rather a half-wit."

I escaped. When I was sufficiently composed I reminded Edna about the cup, steeled myself against the inevitable repulsion and returned to the drawing room.

"I'm only up here for a couple of days," he said as I came in. "I wasn't even going to bother Robert, but Margaret said it would be wrong not to telephone so I had a word with him and he was uncommonly civil, said his case had been postponed and that he'd meet me here at teatime—of course, I won't stay long—"

I couldn't bear his horrible humility. "How's everyone at Oxmoon?" I interrupted, sitting down some distance away from him and praying Robert wouldn't be delayed.

"Oh, everyone's very well, thank you, in capital form. . . . But how are you, Ginevra? You look a little tired. I hope nothing's wrong."

And suddenly I saw not the sad and pathetic stranger who angered me but my cousin Bobby, so kind, so gentle, so understanding.

"Oh Bobby!" I exclaimed in despair, and the next moment I was pouring out my troubles to him. I talked and talked and Edna brought the tea and Bobby said, "By Jove, look at those meringues!" and I answered laughing through my tears, "Aren't they wonderful?" and at last I began to feel better.

"But my dear," said Bobby when I gave him the chance to respond to my dilemma, "the answer's very simple: I'll have the boys at Oxmoon and then you can visit them as often as you like. It's such an easy journey to Swansea nowadays, far easier than that long exhausting journey to Dublin."

I was so grateful I could hardly speak. "Oh, but it never occurred to me to think of Oxmoon—all the awkwardness—"

"Never mind about that. Ginevra, at last I have the opportunity to help you and Robert. Don't deprive me of it—and don't worry about those boys either. I'll make sure they're as happy as larks."

I knew he would. Bobby had brought up four sons and was still bringing up a fifth. He understood boys and had a gift for managing children.

"Bobby, I can't tell you how grateful I am—"

"Would you like me to go to Ireland to fetch them for you? I'd enjoy that."

I stopped weeping with relief by embarking on an éclair. "No," I said. "I wish you could but I really must go myself. I have to tell them I'm going to remarry."

"Do that at Oxmoon. The last place you want to disclose your future plans is in the bosom of your husband's family."

Here was advice far removed indeed from Robert's rational but useless conclusions. Here was sound, sane, utterly realistic common sense.

"My God, that's true!" I said. "But . . . oh Bobby, how on earth do I break the news to those boys?"

"Well, tell them the truth, my dear, why not? After all Declan's fourteen. Tell them that no matter how much you loved their father you can't be alone in the world without a strong man to look after you, and Robert's the strongest man you could ever hope to find. I think you'll find Declan at least is at an age when he can understand your difficulty. You needn't stress the romance, of course. Just say you've no choice but to be practical about the future—for their good as well as yours."

I felt a new woman. I was even able to abandon my éclair.

"In fact," added Bobby, "if you have difficulty explaining I'll help you out. So even if Robert don't accompany you when you visit the boys, you won't have to face the difficulty on your own."

"Robert . . . yes. Bobby, I'm a little worried . . ." But I stopped. In the vastness of my relief I had gone too far. The one thing I could never do was discuss Robert with his father.

"A capital fellow, Robert," said Bobby as he saw my difficulty. "There's no challenge he can't master if he has a strong motive for succeeding so you can wager he'll manage those boys well enough when the time comes. Look how good he was with John."

"So he was!" I said, much cheered. I had a memory of dear little Johnny, chattering away in Welsh and English, bright as a button and delectably naughty. It was sad to think he had turned into such a boring priggish young man. "But what strong motive did Robert have for succeeding with Johnny?"

"He wanted to kill two birds with one stone—please Margaret and make Lion jealous."

We laughed—but then the next moment the smiles were wiped off our faces as we heard Robert enter the hall.

I feel much better about Bobby now, and not just because we managed to share something that resembled a normal conversation. I feel better because I can see how desperately anxious he is to put our relationship on a tolerable footing so that we don't inevitably go through hell whenever we see each other. He's realized—and so have I—that my boys can provide us with a common ground upon which we can meet as two normal people instead of two people perpetually crucified by guilt. I know I shall never be fully at ease with him and I'm sure he'll never be fully at ease with me, but at least our compulsory charade can now become more of an automatic reflex and less of a harrowing effort, and that must surely rank as an improvement.

I'm beginning to think Margaret was right when she said that the problem in future will be the relationship between Bobby and Robert. Look what happened today. Robert sailed in, shook hands with his father and was impeccably courteous throughout the remainder of Bobby's visit, yet although no one could have faulted his behavior, the atmosphere was nonetheless subtly cold, indefinably wrong. Sometime in the future—after we're married and can relax sufficiently to iron out all our problems—I'm going to have to talk to Robert about Bobby because I've come to realize that it's much better if horrid subjects can be aired instead of being buried to fester at leisure. The one subject which I could never discuss, Bobby's seduction, has been a terrible burden to me in the past, and the reason why I can now see this so clearly is because I feel the burden's been eased by my confession. I shall never, never be able to recall the incident with indifference but at least now I don't have to say to myself, "I can't talk of that or I'll go mad." I can say instead, "I talked about it to Robert and stayed sane."

Robert needs to talk to someone about that morning last month when he heard in shattering detail exactly what kind of man his father was, but the trouble is that if I suggest as much to him he'll simply say, "Why?" Robert, I suspect, is in the deepest possible muddle over this, but that's not the main problem. The main problem is that he doesn't know it, and even if he does he won't acknowledge it. Emotionally color-blind Robert has made up his mind that so long as he can adopt certain attitudes (courtesy to his father, passion to me), the past can be tied up in pink ribbon, like a legal brief, and locked safely away forever in the vault of his mind. But I'm not color-blind like Robert and I don't think the answer to his difficulty is that simple. In fact I don't think it's any answer at all.

"Ginette, what the devil are these three new hats doing on your bed?"

"Oh darling, yes—well, you see—"

"I gave you fifty pounds last week to spend on essentials, not to descend on Harrods like Attila the Hun!"

"Oh, I know, darling, but it's all right—I've hardly spent any of your fifty pounds yet! I saw the most charming man in the Harrods credit department—"

"Are you trying to tell me you bought these hats on credit?"

"Yes, isn't it wonderful! I took along the letter from my bank manager to say that my trust money had been safely transferred from New York, and—"

"But you told me you'd already spent your income for the rest of this quarter!"

"True, but I didn't think that mattered, as you were being so divinely generous—"

"Sit down, Ginette," said Robert, "and listen to me. I think it's time you and I had a serious talk together."

We've had the most horrible row about money, quite different from any row I ever had with Conor. At least Conor never made me feel a fool and we always ended up going to bed together. Robert merely made me feel a half-wit and then he walked out and didn't come back.

Well, maybe I deserved his anger. Maybe I *was* a fool to lose my temper and call him a cold-blooded bastard, but what else can you call a man who has just told you he now believes more firmly than ever that the law is right when it classifies married women with lunatics and children? How dare he behave as if I'm incapable of adult behavior, how dare he!

Very well, I *am* naughty about money. But I'm not stupid. In fact when I have to be clever with money I can be brilliant (think of that time when I had to pay for the boys' clothes out of my housekeeping money because Conor had had a disaster at poker). So I don't like being treated as an imbecile who's not responsible for her actions. It's not my fault I had no education. I regret it but Margaret always said the last thing any future wife and mother needed was instruction in academic subjects, so my brain was allowed to atrophy at Oxmoon with a stupid governess.

The trouble with Margaret is that she married at sixteen and coping with the resurrection of Oxmoon, the raising of a large family and the rigors of an unreliable husband has absorbed every ounce of her energy throughout her adult life. That's why she's never been able to imagine that an intelligent woman might like the idea of acquiring an education before she acquires a husband and children; Margaret sees education as irrelevant—as in her case indeed it was. Well, I've certainly never had any wish to be a bluestocking, but when Robert slings a Greek quotation at me and translates it by Tennyson's line "Woman is the lesser man," I'd love to be able to sling back a quotation in Latin to the effect that practice makes perfect and although God did create Adam he was more accomplished when the time came for him to create Eve.

Is Robert one of those male monsters who pride themselves on being thoroughly patronizing on the subject of masculine superiority? That's a chilling thought, but no, brilliant, rational Robert could surely never be guilty of such stupid irrational opinions. He just wanted to show me how vexed he was by my behavior.

Yes, Robert takes what he's pleased to called my "feminine foolishness" very, very seriously but never mind, now that I know how he feels about money I'll be scrupulously careful, and I've no doubt that when we're married we'll never have another cross word on the subject.

We've just had the most divine reconciliation. On the morning after our quarrel telegrams of repentance arrived, and the florist's boy staggered upstairs to my front door with a lavish bouquet of flowers. Fortnum's delivered the champagne after lunch. Finally at eight Robert swept me off to dinner and a most successful evening later culminated in a most memorable night in the bedroom. It really is remarkable how much can be achieved with the aid of orchids, champagne and a heavenly dinner at the Ritz.

And now . . . is this the moment when I can finally compare Robert with Conor and dispose of the problem of comparisons once and for all? Yes, I think it is, because at last I feel I've got that particular difficulty solved. What bliss! At least there's one bridge I've managed to cross before the wedding.

In that brief but nerve-racking crisis which blew up immediately before Robert and I went to bed together for the first time, I told him glibly that there could be no competition between him and Conor in the bedroom, but I said this (a) because it was obvious his confidence needed boosting and (b) because I knew that if he had crowned his romantic dreams by being impotent our affair would have been finished before it had begun.

However the awful truth remained that Robert *was* a competitor in a nightmarish trial of sexual prowess, and although Robert's mind might have been in an uncharacteristic fog at the time my mind was (for once) as clear as crystal because I knew without a shadow of doubt that I was going to compare him with Conor. How could I have avoided it? The situation, in short, could easily have dissolved into disaster, but to my relief the gods decided to smile on us because Robert *was* very different from Conor in bed, and although I did make a comparison or two, I soon realized that comparisons were more meaningless in the circumstances than I'd dared to hope they might be. To compare Conor and Robert was like trying to compare "The Blue Danube" with the latest Paris tango; both compositions rank as musical entertainment but they appeal to the audience in completely different ways.

Despite Robert's Welsh background he's an Englishman by education and temperament, and he's very much the Englishman in bed (contrary to what scornful foreigners think, this needn't necessarily be a disaster). For Robert passion is a sport, like cricket or rugby football, and being Robert he's bent his will to ensure he knows how to produce a first-class performance. If Oxford University awarded blues for passion, as it does for cricket and rugger, then Robert would undoubtedly have won his blue at passion. And because passion is a sport for him and because he's an Englishman he obeys the rules and would never dream of breaking them. Breaking the rules wouldn't be playing the game; only damned foreigners and cads break the rules, every Englishman knows that.

Conor was a damned foreigner and a cad. He made up all the rules as he went along and then had the most glorious time breaking every one of them in the most amusing way his limitless imagination could conceive. Robert would be appalled by such wildly disordered antics, but interestingly this doesn't damn Robert for me. I think I enjoy him as he is first because he really is very competent and second because this rational well-ordered sportsmanship is such a novelty that I find it erotic.

This leads me inevitably to myself. What do I truly think about physical love? I've been truthful about my two men and now I must put myself alongside them to complete an honest picture of my private life.

I think I would like to record once and for all that I enjoy passion not because I was seduced at sixteen, but in spite of it. Men have such odd ideas about early seductions and seem to assume such an episode automatically converts a woman into a furnace of sexuality, but the truth is that I wasn't in the least keen about passion at first. It raised too many appalling memories for me, and the chief among those memories was fear. I'll never forget how much Bobby frightened me by turning into someone else. I've always thought the tale of Dr. Jekyll and Mr. Hyde is quite the most beastly story ever invented.

I don't believe I exaggerate my situation if I write that Conor saved me. I was very frightened when I first went to bed with him because I thought he too might turn into an evil stranger but he didn't; he merely became more gorgeous than ever. That was the major hurdle overcome, and eventually my cure was completed (and it was by no means an overnight miracle) because Conor cared enough about me to be patient and I cared enough about him to respond to his patience. I was so lucky not just because (as I now realize) I was born with a considerable capacity to enjoy myself in bed but because at that crucial moment of my life fate presented me with a man who was able to free that capacity from its burden of fear.

I've been naughty about passion in the past. I can't deny that, but all I can say in my own defense is that I'm not by nature promiscuous. When I was unfaithful to Conor it was for a variety of reasons but never because I merely fancied an exciting roll in the hay. I was unfaithful because he was unfaithful to me and I wanted to get even with him, or because it seemed an escape from problems I couldn't face, or because I was so depressed that it seemed easier to say yes than to say no. The fact is I don't think I *would* have been unfaithful to Conor if life with him had been less racked by ghastly crises. Conor satisfied me sexually. So does Robert. I want, I long, I yearn to be faithful to Robert. The rock-bottom truth is that I can't stand infidelity. Such a mess, such a muddle, such hell.

Hell makes me think of Bobby again. Do I now write down what Bobby was like in bed? Or is that aspect of the subject still absolutely *verboten* despite my confession to Robert? I always thought it would remain *verboten* for the rest of my life or at the very least until I was eighty and past passion altogether (or will I ever be past it? Horrid thought!) but maybe writing down my opinion will help, just as talking to Robert of the seduction helped. But perhaps all I need say is that after I'd first been to bed with Robert I thought, Thank God he'll never remind me of his father. Yes, that was certainly a moment for heaving a sigh of relief. Disciplined, competent Robert . . . Perhaps that was when I first consciously formed the judgment that Bobby was no good in bed, although of course I had always felt that the experience with him was one which I never wished to repeat. However perhaps with other women Bobby's different; perhaps he was too disturbed when he was with me to give an adequate performance, but one thing I know for certain: sex wasn't a sport for him. What it was exactly God only knows, but it wasn't a game at all.

Enough. No more Bobby. No more Conor. I've just had the most wonderful night with the man I'm going to marry, and all that's left for me to say is thank God we're never likely to have a row about sex . . .

We've just had the most ghastly row about sex. At least, that's what Robert thinks the row was about. Actually although he refused to admit it we were having a row about my previous sexual experience. The stupid thing is that Robert would hate it if I were still the miserable timid woman whom Conor acquired when he married me; Robert can't stand the incompetent or the second-rate, and he enjoys me exactly as I am. What he doesn't enjoy—and what he can't face at all—is the thought of how I acquired my competence.

When I realized what the problem was I tried to allay his fears that my past adultery meant I was hopelessly promiscuous, but he cut me off. He couldn't bear to hear me talk of other men, he couldn't bear to hear me talk of Conor, he couldn't bear to be reminded that I had ever loved someone else.

He couldn't admit that, of course. That was why the whole row took place on another subject: my bedroom manners. He had the nerve to say that "a woman who plays an assertive role in bed isn't very womanly." Honestly, if I hadn't been so upset I would have laughed. Anyone would think from that statement that I was some fierce suffragette who bellowed orders at the top of her voice! The truth is that I'm sensitive and considerate in bed, and although I never lose sight of my own pleasure, I do my imaginative best to give a man what he wants. And the last thing Robert wants is some female who does no more than lie on her back with her legs apart—he'd be bored to death.

This time I didn't lose my temper and indulge in what he would have described as "a feminine tantrum." I said politely but firmly that he might not think much of my bedroom manners but I thought still less of his if he treated an intelligent, devoted partner as if she ought to be a mere mindless receptacle for male seed—at which point *he* threw a tantrum by yelling, "Bloody women, bloody sex, bloody hell!" and retiring in a rage to the lavatory. I know men and women are utterly different but sometimes the little similarities of behavior make one wonder if the differences are as great as everyone says they are.

We were soon reconciled but afterwards it hardly seemed the right moment to insist that he faced the reality of my marriage to Conor, and what now worries me is whether the right moment will ever come. It's obvious that Conor represents a serious problem for us, but it's equally obvious that Robert's decided to solve the problem by locking it up at the back of his mind and refusing to speak of it. Is this a solution? No. It's merely another example of Robert's curious emotional naivety; he simply can't see that before we can hope to resolve the difficulty we have to discuss it frankly together.

The trouble with this particular difficulty is that I'm not very good at facing Conor's memory myself at the moment. I'm too afraid that if I start thinking of him my bereavement will overwhelm me, just as it did at the funeral in Ireland, and then I shall have a nervous collapse which Robert would find an awful bore. The only way I can cope with my life at present is to keep going steadily towards my goal—marriage with Robert—and not look back. If I lose my nerve, disaster will be sure to follow, and then chaos will descend again.

Perhaps I should be optimistic. After all, it's a fact of life that all second marriages somehow have to adjust to the idea that previous partners existed, and in the majority at least an adjustment is made. The truth is that time will distance us both from Conor and so eventually he's bound to seem less important.

Yes, I'm sure that after our marriage we'll find that darling Conor will simply fade away. . . .

"Marriage!" shouted my darling Declan, looking at me as if I were the original serpent in the Garden of Eden.

"And Pa not yet cold in his grave!" shrilled my darling Rory, who adores being dramatic and emotional.

"Oh darlings, *please* don't be upset—"

We were at Oxmoon a week later. After a joyous reunion I had lured them up to my bedroom to give them two new watches (bought on credit from divine Harrods), and as soon as I was sure both boys were delighted I embarked on my confession. I had spent hours rehearsing my speech, and by that time I was so nervous that I could delay no longer. I was afraid sheer terror would drive me into forgetting my lines.

"I'm sorry, Ma," interrupted Declan, "but I can't allow this."

Declan was taller than I was and already an expert in the art of intimidation; he had walked up to me and was glaring into my eyes. Amidst all my fright I was aware of thinking what an attractive young man he would be when he grew up. He had a great look of Conor, particularly around the eyes and mouth.

"Darling, just listen!" I pleaded weakly, backing away until I could subside onto the edge of the bed. "I'm doing this for all of us!"

"Then you'd best go on strike and do no more!"

"She must be mad, Declan—look at her, destroyed with grief, just like Aunt Dervla said—"

"That's enough!" I screamed. "Be quiet, both of you!"

"Now Ma, there's no need to be hysterical—"

"None at all," said Rory, sitting down close to me on the bed and grabbing my hand for comfort.

I put my arm around him and planted a kiss on his red hair. I felt racked by guilt, driven by the need to lavish affection on them to compensate for my behavior and beside myself with terror for the future. In short I was in my usual mess.

"Look, Ma," said Declan briskly, "I know you need looking after, Pa always said you did, but *you don't have to get married to be looked after*. I'll do it. I'll make it my permanent occupation."

"Oh darling, that's heavenly of you, but—"

"Now that I'm fourteen, I don't need to go to school anymore, I know all there is to know and anyway as I can use a gun and play poker I'm sure I'll have no difficulty taking Pa's place."

"But Declan—"

"No, don't worry about anything, Ma; I'll organize your life now. We'll have a swell apartment in Dublin, and you can turn over your income check to me every month and I'll give you the money for housekeeping just as Pa did, and I'll be so soft-hearted I'll even let you smoke in the parlor. And when I eventually get married, you can come and live with us, I'll take special care to find a girl you can get along with—"

"Oh Declan—darling—"

"But Ma, you can't get married, not again, not ever, it would be so disrespectful to Pa, so disloyal—in fact how could you even think of such infidelity to the man you always swore was the Love of Your Life? No, no, you've got to dedicate yourself to chastity and wear black forever—and maybe now at last you can turn to the Church, just as every decent widow should, you know it was the tragedy of Pa's life that you stayed a Protestant—"

"Darling, please," I said, "not religion. Not now. My nerves can't stand it."

"But Ma—"

"No, my love, you've been simply adorable and I'm deeply moved but now I'm afraid you must listen to me. Listen, pet, I did love Pa. You know I did. And he was without doubt the Grand Passion of My Life, just as I've always told you he was. But there are different kinds of love, and the man I love now I love in quite a different way. Robert's my friend. He's like a brother to me. I'm terribly lucky that he wants to look after me because he's a fine man, brilliantly clever and successful, and he wants to do his very best for all of us, not just for me but for you too."

"I'm not living in England," said Declan, "and I'm not living with an Englishman. It would be contrary to my principles as an Irish patriot and an insult to Pa's memory."

"Robert's a Welshman, Declan—and before you make any more of those dreadful anti-British remarks please remember that before I went to live at Oxmoon I was born in Warwickshire and that makes me English. I know darling Pa always preferred to gloss over that, but—"

"All right, if you insist on living here I guess I'll have to live here too to look after you, but I'm not receiving an English education. Rory, you wouldn't go to an English school, would you?"

"I wouldn't mind so long as I saw Ma every day," said Rory, "although of course I couldn't approve."

"Darling Rory!" I hugged him lavishly again. "Declan, there are some very, very good Catholic schools in England, places where even Pa would have been proud to be educated. Robert's been making inquiries at Downside which is a very famous Catholic public school—a private school, as we would say in America—"

"I'm not letting Robert organize my life," said Declan, "and hell, Ma, I'm not letting him organize yours either. Maybe Robert hasn't realized I could keep you in the lap of luxury by playing poker and working for Irish republicanism—in fact maybe he's just offered to marry you out of kindness because he thinks there's no better fate awaiting you, but don't worry, I'll talk to Robert, I'll set him straight, you just leave it all to me."

Are there any two people on earth doomed to clash as disastrously as Robert and Declan? I can see the clash coming—I've seen it coming from the beginning, although I was too frightened to dwell upon it—and now I'm well-nigh gibbering with terror.

I have four days to devise some master plot that will solve the insoluble, four days before Robert arrives here for the weekend and Declan tries to sabotage our future. Can I confide in Bobby who's being a tower of strength, winning the boys' liking and respect and giving them exactly the kind of cheerful, friendly, sympathetic attention that they need? No, I really can't start hatching schemes with Bobby. Robert might think we were conspiring against him and that would lead to some new frightfulness. And the awful thing is I don't need to confide in either Bobby or Margaret because it must be as plain to them as it is to me that Robert's not going to be able to cope with Declan.

No, that's not true. Robert will cope with Declan. Robert can cope with anyone. But *I* won't be able to cope with the way he copes with Declan, and Declan won't be able to cope with it either.

Horrors.

There's only one thing to do: warn Robert that this is a situation which will require all his professional skill. That will appeal to his vanity in addition to putting him on his guard. And while I'm about it I may as well stop talking of "Darling Declan" and start talking about "Difficult Declan" instead.

Oh God, how on earth are we all going to survive . . .

. . . *and so, darling, I* wrote, scribbling away feverishly as I sat at the desk in the morning room, *although the last thing I want to do is mention Conor I really think that you'll understand Declan better if I tell you just a little more than you already know about the background of my marriage. The truth is Conor wasn't exactly a restaurant owner. He was a professional gambler who had a financial stake in what he used to call a "cabaret," meaning a drinking place where they have low entertainment downstairs and even lower entertainment upstairs—a sort of brothel-pub. Of course he kept his family well apart from all this, in fact I never even saw the cabaret (well, actually there were several of them) and neither did the boys, but they've grown up thinking it's the height of manhood to play poker, so you see they're not exactly very English in that respect . . .*

I paused. I was wondering if I could avoid the subject of Irish patriotism, but I knew that if I didn't mention the Brotherhood, Declan most certainly would.

I gulped some air and bent over my pen again.

. . . *and I'm afraid they're not very English either, darling, when it comes to discussing Ireland, but that doesn't matter, does it, because I know you've always held the most advanced Liberal views on the subject of Home Rule. All the same, I think you ought to know that Conor was involved with some rather rabid patriots, and I'm afraid boys of Declan's age do think that sort of thing is very glamorous. I was never happy with the situation, but what could I do? I felt it wasn't my place to criticize Conor when he entertained these people— although I did feel so nervous when they started talking about the beastly English, but Conor just told them I was Welsh and they used to say, "Ah yes, another race crushed beneath the Saxon heel!" and quite honestly, darling, it somehow seemed so very much safer just to say, "Oh yes, those beastly Saxons, such a bore." However, never mind, I'm sure the boys will soon realize that being rabidly anti-British simply isn't the done thing at all . . .*

I paused for another deep breath. Now I had to turn to the subject of the boys' education but I had trouble phrasing my next sentence. Those boys had to go to boarding school. I accepted that not only because British upper-class boys always went to boarding school but because I knew Robert wouldn't settle for anything less. However I wasn't being entirely feeble here, meekly letting Robert dispose of my children for two-thirds of the year. Although I adored my boys, I was still sensible enough to see that they needed both the discipline and, after the great upheaval, the stability of a good school that could provide them with a familiar Catholic atmosphere. I also honestly believed that the massed company of British boys of their own age would help them make the difficult adjustment to another culture and another way of life. But although Robert was in favor of packing them off to Downside as soon as the term began in September, I was now convinced that they needed more time before they were sent away to school. Conor's death had been a dreadful shock to them.

. . . and talking of doing the done thing, darling, that reminds me of our decision to send the boys to Downside in September. Bearing in mind how very un-English they are, don't you think it might be better if we postponed boarding school till the new year? I'm not saying they should be with me in London—I do accept that this solution of Oxmoon is ideal, but if Bobby and Margaret consent perhaps we could engage a tutor to spend the autumn here with the boys . . .

I wondered what Robert would think of this suggestion. It seemed reasonable enough, but when I read through what I'd written I thought, He's not going to like me making regular visits to Oxmoon for the next five months. He's not going to like it at all.

"I don't like the idea of you making repeated sorties to Oxmoon during the next few months," said Robert four days later. "That may be pleasant for the boys, but I think you're going to wind up exhausted. Why, look at you now—you're worn out! No, I'm afraid it won't do. You're in a muddle as usual, and you must let me sort you out."

My heart felt as if it had plummeted straight to my boots, but I was aware to my interest that I wasn't angry with him. What Robert said was true. I was indeed worn out, and repeated visits to Oxmoon would indeed put me under severe emotional strain.

"Those boys now have six weeks to recuperate from their bereavement in eminently suitable surroundings," pursued Robert, "but by September they'll be ready for school and to school they must go. If they loaf around any longer they'll get into mischief; in my opinion they'd mince a tutor in no time and eat him with bacon for breakfast."

I knew he was right. That, I was beginning to discover, was the great difficulty in dealing with Robert. Rationally he was always right. But not all situations can be mastered by reason alone.

I said fearfully, "Declan will argue with you."

"Good," said Robert. "Let him try."

I suddenly found I had to sit down.

It was after dinner at Oxmoon on the evening of Robert's arrival, and at Bobby's suggestion Lion and Johnny had taken the boys off to the billiard room so that Robert and I could snatch a little time alone together. We had wandered across the lawn to the summerhouse, and now as the twilight deepened over the woods I sank down on one of the wicker chairs and found myself once more struggling against my tears.

"Don't be too severe with Declan, Robert. He's not nearly so grown up as he pretends to be."

"I've no intention of being severe with Declan. Nor, I must tell you, do I intend to be sentimental. I intend to be a stepfather whom he can respect."

"Oh God, I'm in such a muddle over this—"

"Obviously, but do try and be calm. The situation is in fact very simple: we're discussing what kind of stepfather you want for those boys—or in other words, whether you want me to be active or passive. Now, if I'm active I treat those boys as if they were mine, and that means that they've got to recognize that I, as the Boers say, am the boss. If I'm passive I simply stand by and let them run wild while you undermine all discipline by your misplaced maternal indulgence—no, don't interpret that as a criticism! You can't help being overemotional, and anyway, the truth is that no woman's fit to cope single-handed with two boys verging on adolescence."

"Yes, darling. But—"

"Ginette, if I adopt a passive role here I think those boys will wreck our engagement in no time. After all, that's what Declan wants, isn't it? So now you have to decide what *you* want. Do you want our engagement wrecked or don't you?"

"I don't. I couldn't bear it—"

"Very well. That means you authorize me to be an active stepfather. Thank you. I shall now take whatever steps I deem necessary to preserve our future—in other words I'm going to have order, discipline and respect, and I'm going to have them now, right from the beginning. In my opinion children are like wives and servants: you've got to start as you mean to go on."

Children are *nothing* like wives and servants. And anyway wives aren't like servants—or they shouldn't be. I can't say that to Robert, though, because I'm too afraid of another ghastly quarrel. It was bad enough quarreling about money and sex, but if we quarrel over the boys I shall have a nervous collapse and then Robert will decide he'd do better not to marry me after all and oh God, what would I do, how would I manage, no, *I must stave off* a nervous collapse and I can start by making up my mind that whatever happens we must avoid quarreling over the boys.

I can also help myself by acknowledging that once again Robert's right—in theory. He's got to be an active stepfather in order to win the boys' respect, but the trouble is that Robert's idea of being an active stepfather is certain to embrace behavior I shall hardly know how to endure.

And yet . . . Let's be honest; the truth is there's a dreadful secret relief in letting Robert try to annihilate this problem. I can't control those boys, never could. Conor was good with them but he was out at work most of the time, and I was the one who had to try to keep them in order while the nursemaids gave notice and the cook had hysterics and the apartment began to look like a lunatic asylum.

Yet now Robert's going to reduce chaos to order with his usual skill, and of course he's going to succeed; he's going to win. But what about me? I think I'm going to lose. I'm going to end up being forced to side with Robert against the boys and Declan will never forgive me. He'll think I'm betraying them just as I've betrayed his father. Rory's sufficiently young and frightened and lost to forgive me anything, but Declan has a hard fanatical streak, like Conor, and he'll violently oppose anyone he believes has wronged him.

I can see horror approaching, no, not just horror but HORROR in capital letters. But what can I do to avoid it? Nothing. If I don't let Robert win here I'll lose him and if I lose Robert I'll collapse, I'll be driven mad by predatory men, I'll be wrecked and ruined in no time at all. No, I can't stand alone, how can I, I'm too vulnerable, *too frightened*—and that means I've got to marry Robert, got to protect myself, got to, got to, got to, and besides . . .

If only we can get these frightful problems sorted out before the wedding I'm sure our marriage will be blissfully happy.

"If you think I'm going to be locked up for two-thirds of the year in an English prison, you'd better think again!"

"Declan, Downside isn't a prison—it's a very fine school run by monks—"

"Holy shit! I don't want to live in a monastery!"

"Declan, how dare you use such language to me!"

"Why not? Pa did! But you wouldn't remember that, would you—all you can think about is that English bastard Robert!"

"Declan, *I will not have you behaving like this*—"

"*Who's going to stop me?*"

"I was wondering when you were going to ask that question," said Robert blandly from the doorway.

At his request I left them alone together in my room. I managed to walk away steadily down the corridor but on the landing the tears overwhelmed me and I rushed up the stairs to the attics. The Oxmoon attics were not set aside for the servants, who were housed in the kitchen wing which overlooked the stable yard, and the long chain of rooms was filled with junk and rejected heirlooms. Nothing was ever thrown away at Oxmoon, and as I blundered around among the memorabilia I came across the well-remembered portrait of my aunt Gwyneth, Robert's grandmother, who had gone mad as the result of her love affair with the sheep farmer Owain Bryn-Davies.

Feeling on the brink of madness myself I sat down by her picture and wondered if she too had ever felt divided beyond endurance between her lover and her son. Poor Aunt Gwyneth, I could remember those bright blue eyes of hers so clearly, the eyes Bobby had inherited. Johnny too had inherited those eyes, and as I looked at the portrait of Aunt Gwyneth in her prime I was struck by the fact that Johnny was far more like her than Bobby was. Johnny was the only one in the family who had her dark hair.

I tried to go on thinking of Johnny in order to avoid thinking of Declan. Why had Johnny, once an adorable little boy, bright as a button and delectably naughty, turned into this prim dreary young man of twenty-one? This was a mystery that could occupy me for some time but no, I was unable to concentrate on it, and the next moment I could think only of Declan.

Burying my face in my hands, I once more abandoned myself to despair.

Margaret and Bobby are being immaculate as usual at keeping up appearances; they're behaving as if nothing's happened, but Robert's brothers are less expert at concealing their feelings. Johnny manages well but Lion keeps glancing at us in fascination while Edmund is too embarrassed to look at us at all. Celia is being kind (she thinks) and has offered to show me her pressed wild flowers, but I've muttered some excuse and escaped to my room for an early night. I want Robert but I know he won't come to me. We must observe the proprieties at Oxmoon, no choice, so I'm alone and weeping, I shouldn't weep, I know I shouldn't, but I can't help myself.

I haven't seen Declan since the ghastliness began. Robert's locked him in his room and forbidden me to go near him, and of course I daren't disobey. It's not that I'm frightened of Robert (although I am—petrified); I just feel that if I'm to support Robert I must support him utterly and then perhaps the horrors will finish sooner. If Declan once believes I could be won over to his side he'll go on and on and on in the hope that I'll give way.

But I won't. Everything's at stake, Robert, my marriage, my future, my entire life, and I've now reached the stage where I can't go back. I've come so far, salvation is in sight and whatever happens I've got to go on.

"If you don't want me anymore I'll go and live in Ireland with Uncle Seamus and Aunt Dervla."

"Oh Declan darling, you *know* I want you, you know it . . ."

It was the next morning, a Sunday, and Robert had given me permission to see Declan so that I could take him to Mass with Rory at the Catholic church in Swansea. Declan was white and there were dark shadows under his eyes and he was trying so hard to be brave but when I put my arms around him he began to cry. As I had told Robert, Declan was still so young even though he wanted so much to be grown up, and Conor's death had been very terrible to him.

"I want Pa. . . . Why did he have to get killed like that . . . I don't believe in God anymore. I don't want to go to Mass. . . . I want Pa, I don't want that bastard Robert. . . ."

"Declan, I can't hear a word against Robert, I'm sorry."

"But he hurt me, *he hurt me—*"

"He won't hurt you if you behave well, Declan."

"But Pa never hurt me, he never laid a finger on me!"

"Pa's dead. It's terrible, it's tragic but it's true and you must try to accept that I've no choice but to give Robert permission to treat you and Rory as if you were his sons."

"But in New York—"

"We're not in New York, Declan, not anymore. Here Robert sets the standards, and here he draws the line."

"Don't worry about the boys—I'll cheer them up, I promise," murmured Bobby to me when the time came for me to return to London with Robert, but Margaret merely remarked with chilling truth, "They'll be well enough once no one's here to upset them."

I had wanted to stay on at Oxmoon with the boys but this was impossible, not only because Robert would have been angry but because we had social engagements to fulfill and cancellation would have caused considerable awkwardness. Rory shed a tear to see me go but Declan was dry-eyed and withdrew into the house without bothering to watch the motor drive away.

When we arrived in London some hours later Robert escorted me to the flat, sent the housekeeper home early, dispatched the maid on an errand to Kensington High Street and then to my extreme distaste drew me into the bedroom to make amends for the nights at Oxmoon when we had been obliged to conform to Margaret's standards. By that time I was feeling so ill with distress that all I wanted was to be alone, but of course I couldn't have told him that. Instead I tried to display enthusiasm, but when were in bed together I found that competent sportsmanship of his no longer seemed so erotic, and at once the effort of acting a charade was almost more than I could bear.

Robert withdrew from me. At first I thought with relief that his desire had died but I was mistaken. He was merely pausing to clear up the muddle.

"Are you angry with me?"

"No. You're right to want to be an active stepfather, and I'd be a fool if I stopped you. But"—I prayed for courage—"I'm afraid I *am* upset. Please try not to mind. It's just that I'm a mother and I can't bear to think of my children being unhappy."

He considered this carefully. He applied the full force of his formidable intellect to the problem. At last he said with touching simplicity, "I thought this would make you feel better."

It was a logical assumption to make. The only trouble was that it was quite wrong.

We went on lying there, unjoined, Robert propped up on his elbow, I lying inert on my back, but when I saw his anxiety increasing I couldn't bear it. He was so concerned and loved me so much. A powerful affection for him overwhelmed me. I heard myself say, "Time to raid the strawberry beds again!" and then I pulled him back once more into my arms.

I can't stop thinking of those boys. They're going to hate boarding school. Downside may be the finest school on earth but they'll loathe it. I'm a mother who can't bear to think of her children being unhappy, and I know they're going to be unhappier. But what can I do? Nothing. Robert must have me to himself for two-thirds of the year, and if he can find some way of decimating that final third he'll do it.

Robert doesn't like sharing me. He never did. I remember how furious he became when I spent time playing with Lion—darling Lion, what a huge gorgeous captivating baby he was! But in the end I had to call Lion a monster and say I hated him; I had to pretend to hate all babies otherwise Robert would be upset.

What on earth is he going to be like when we have a child of our own?

No, I must stop. It's pointless worrying about the distant future at the moment, and anyway I'm sure that as soon as we're married and living happily ever after, that sort of problem will turn out to belong to the very distant past . . .

"We've been invited to the Wharf!"

"Robert, how exciting!"

The law courts were about to close for the long vacation and the invitation to the Asquiths' country house on the Thames was only one of a number of important invitations that Robert had received from various well-wishers in Society. Because of my bereavement we had not announced our engagement formally, but word of our proposed marriage had soon circulated with the result that the invitations had been extended to include me.

This was very gratifying, and now I had my first delicious glimpse of the affluent political world that would be waiting for me on the far side of the altar. As I immediately blossomed in bliss I found that the shady glamour of my New York life seemed—thank God—more than a million miles away, and in fact I was so captivated by the change in my fortunes that I bought rather too many smart clothes in celebration. But I told myself how important it was for Robert's sake that I should make a suitably fashionable impression.

We did not mingle much with the aristocracy for the Liberal Party had alienated this section of Society during the constitutional crisis of 1911, but nonetheless there were a number of lords and ladies who had succeeded in advancing from the nineteenth to the twentieth century by embracing the Liberal creed, while the Asquiths themselves, commoners and self-made, generated a frenetic and somewhat eccentric social life of their own. Oddly enough I was more intimidated at first by the Asquiths than by the aristocrats, but fortunately Margot Asquith chose to regard me kindly and showed her benign interest by bestowing on me one of her outrageous remarks. ("At last Mr. Godwin's found someone who hasn't had to poison her husband to win his attention, Mrs. Kinsella—or did you perhaps poison your husband after all?")

Wherever we went that summer I found that my bedroom was always next to Robert's, and this escape from the standards set at Oxmoon also added to my enjoyment. In fact I was in ecstasy—or so I told myself. Probably it would be closer to the truth to say I was feverishly trying to divert myself from the ghastliness to come. At some stage during all this hedonism I had ordered two sets of school uniform, and at the beginning of September I returned to the flat to start sewing on name tapes. Bobby brought the boys up to town a day later, but although Rory was willing to see the sights of London Declan shut himself in his room and refused to go out. I was terrified he would also refuse to go to school when the time came, but Bobby had persuaded him to give Downside a try, and after a tense miserable week I think Declan was willing to go anywhere to escape from Robert.

Robert visited us every day and took trouble to be pleasant to both boys, but Declan could hardly bear to be in the same room with him. However Robert's behavior continued to be immaculate. He escorted the boys himself to Downside; he made sure that a watchful eye would be kept on them; he did everything possible to lessen the ordeal of beginning a new life. That was why he was so angry and I was in such despair when three weeks later Declan ran away. Robert was quite justified in feeling he himself had done all he could to avoid such a disaster.

To make matters worse Declan didn't run away to Oxmoon, where he would have been assured of a nonviolent, if disapproving reception. Anxious for money which would take him to Ireland he came to London to see me, and arriving late at night he found me with Robert.

A hideous scene followed.

After Declan had been locked in his room Robert stayed the rest of the night at the flat to ensure that I exhibited no criminal weakness, and then he took Declan straight back to school the next morning. I didn't think Declan would go but he did. He knew Robert would beat him again if he refused. I tried to kiss him goodbye but he spat at me, and although I at once cried out, "No, Robert—" Robert only exclaimed, "You don't think I'm going to let him get away with that, do you?" and more horrors ensued.

Returning from Somerset soon after six, Robert reported that the school authorities had been most understanding and had told him he had done entirely the right thing. This failed to surprise me. Robert always did the right thing. However at least this time he was expecting me to be upset so I didn't have to pretend that everything in the garden was lovely once the two of us were alone together again. He made no attempt to lead me to bed but sat on the sofa and put his arm around me as he held my hand.

"You're being a great comfort, Robert," I finally managed to tell him when my tears were under control.

"I'd be a poor sort of friend if I wasn't!" he said surprised, and when I thought of all those times he had stood by me in the past I dimly saw, far away in the distance, a gleam of happiness.

"Oh Robert!" I exclaimed passionately, aching for reassurance. "We'll be all right, won't we?"

"How can we possibly fail?"

That settled that. Robert had decided our marriage was going to be a huge success. In exhausted relief I surrendered all my fears, all my anxieties and all my battered emotions to his irresistible self-confidence, and told myself that everything was bound to come right in the end.

Let me see, it must be three months since I wrote anything in this journal. Why did I stop? Because having finally made up my mind that everything was under control, I no longer had an urgent need to set down my conflicting emotions in an effort to understand what was really going on. I was also diverted by the fact that after the crisis with Declan I had to spend much time house hunting and preparing for married life (and spending too much money but I won't think about that just yet). However now is the time to pick up my pen again because here I am in Gower on the nineteenth of December, 1913, and tomorrow at five o'clock in the afternoon I shall be marrying my formidable second husband in Penhale parish church.

I'm in such a muddle about this bloody wedding that it almost beggars description. (Oh, what a relief to write that down in black-and-white!) What I really wanted was to marry Robert quietly in London in the briefest of ceremonies and then leave immediately for some destination like Timbuktu where the past would seem a thousand years away. But what I wanted was impossible. Margaret made that clear to us well before we had embarked on our wedding arrangements, and I knew I could not possibly oppose her.

Robert's attitude to his mother has changed from a patronizing filial courtesy to a profound filial respect. We've never discussed this but I know it's connected with his discoveries about his father (that's why we don't discuss it). Very well, I don't mind him respecting Margaret. God knows she's earned his respect, and God knows I respect her myself. But when iron-willed Robert, who normally stands no interference from anyone, least of all from a woman, prepares to listen in meek obedience as his mother tells him how he should get married, I want to scream with exasperation.

Margaret declared—in a long sinister highly Victorian letter liberally sprinkled with the words "Ginevra dearest" and "dearest Robert"—that we had to be married at Penhale and endure a reception at Oxmoon afterwards because from the point of view of keeping up appearances this was the right thing—indeed, said Margaret, the only thing—to do. All Gower would expect the wedding of the heir to Oxmoon to be a big occasion, and all Gower could not be disappointed. Otherwise there might be unfortunate comment that the marriage was unpopular and this, Margaret explained serenely, would be "tiresome." The church ceremony must necessarily be austere, since I was marrying within months of being widowed, but this "little awkwardness" could be glossed over with the help of a magnificent reception at Oxmoon. A ball and supper would "suit admirably" and she looked forward to conferring with us further as soon as possible.

Robert said he really didn't care what happened so long as he danced with me to "The Blue Danube," and I then discovered to my absolute horror that he had every intention of making this waltz our special tune.

"For me it symbolizes the moment when my life really began," said Robert, "the moment at your ball in 1898 when I held you in my arms beneath the chandeliers at Oxmoon and knew I'd never be content until I'd married you—and that's why when we do marry I'm going to dance with you there again to 'The Blue Danube' and then the past will be rewritten, all my unhappiness will be cancelled and that tune will become a symbol of the greatest triumph of my life."

"Oh darling, how romantic!" I said, heart sinking, because of course for me "The Blue Danube" belonged to Conor. It symbolized that moment when he had appeared in the ballroom to save me; it symbolized the end of the horrors at Oxmoon and the beginning of a new life. How was I ever going to cope with a second marriage haunted by the strains of "The Blue Danube"? I had no idea then and I have no idea now.

What a prospect! Can Robert honestly fail to realize how awful this wedding at Oxmoon is going to be for me? No. Emotionally color-blind Robert has simply shut out all the aspects of the situation that might interfere with the celebration of his mighty victory but meanwhile, half-blinded by the gory colors of my own emotional spectrum, I can't help but visualize ghastliness at every turn.

Anyway here I am, staying at Penhale Manor with the de Bracys in order to fulfill the traditional requirement that the bride and groom shouldn't meet on the night before their wedding. It's very kind of Sir Gervase and Lady de Bracy to offer hospitality because they probably think it's dreadful of me to rush to the altar before my first husband's been dead a year, but Gwen's such an old friend of mine and no doubt she's been campaigning vigorously on my behalf. This evening the whole family has nearly driven me mad by telling me how romantic it is that I'm marrying my childhood sweetheart. When Gwen said cheerily, "Now all you have to do is live happily ever after!" I had a hard time suppressing the retort "Never mind living happily ever after— the main question is whether I can survive the next twenty-four hours."

I wonder if my boys are all right. Dearest Bobby said he would take special care of them. He *is* kind. How bizarre it is to think that someone as decent as Bobby should ever be capable of doing what he did to me. How sinister life is, how frightening. I remember Robert saying once that some of the murderers he had met had been quite charming. Ugh! A vile thought. Well, at least poor Bobby's not a murderer.

I wonder if Declan really will come to the wedding. He's promised Bobby he will, although how Bobby extracted that promise I can't imagine. But Bobby's such a magician with children. He doesn't have to beat them to get his way. I think Declan will be there but only to please Bobby. He won't want Bobby to be disappointed in him.

Let me cheer myself up by thinking how simply stunning I'll look in my pale green velvet wedding gown with those luscious dark green trimmings and that sumptuous matching shallow hat with the gossamer-thin veil (twenty-five guineas from divine Harrods). I hope to God naughty little Thomas doesn't throw a tantrum at the wrong moment. I didn't want a page but Margaret said Thomas would enjoy it so that was that. However at least I've had the brains to recruit little Eleanor Stourham as a bridesmaid so that Thomas has an eleven-year-old partner to keep him in check. Maybe they'll fight. Oh God, I wish the whole nightmare were over. . . .

But I must stop groaning and be for one moment, as Robert would say, rational. How do Robert and I stand as we prepare to sally forth upon our greatest adventure of all? I think our position is favorable but I can look back now and see how far I was deceiving myself when I hoped we'd have our problems solved before the wedding. We've got them under control but nothing's been solved. We don't talk about Bobby, we don't talk about Conor, we don't talk about what's going to happen to those boys—and these three areas of silence represent three huge bridges to be crossed. But we don't have any other problems, do we? And I'm sure everything will come right in the end.

So am I ready to promise to love, cherish and obey Robert till death us do part? Yes. Absolutely. But how stern that marriage service is, how forbidding. Till death us do part . . .

I hate death. I hate all thought of death. I want to live and love and have a wonderful time . . . and that's exactly what I'm going to do.

Darling Robert, what a dear little boy he was, offering me his boiled sweets and saying he wanted to be a hero when he grew up. . . . Yes, Gwen's right after all. It *is* romantic that Robert and I are finally getting married, it's a fairy-tale happy ending, it's a dream come true and I'm *passionate* about it. Forget Conor. Forget the rows and the lies and the cheating and the adultery and the tears and the rages and the misery and the sheer soul-destroying awfulness of disillusioned love. Down with reality, long live romance! I'm marrying the man I *really* love at last and nothing on earth can now stand in my way.

"I Ginevra take thee Robert . . ."

We were married.

It was gorgeously romantic, the ceremony taking place on that dark winter afternoon in Penhale's old candlelit church which had already been decked for Christmas with holly and evergreens. But all through the service I could not forget that I was due to be the belle of the ball again at Oxmoon and that Bobby would be waiting to kiss me under the mistletoe.

Oh, the horror, the horror . . .

"Dearest Ginevra—welcome home again!" I was there. I was at Oxmoon. And Margaret was holding out her arms to embrace me.

Ghastly. God help me. Please don't let me break down.

"This is the happiest day of my life!" exclaimed Robert to the guests.

Don't think of the past. Don't think, don't think, *don't think*—

"Are you happy, Ginette?"

"Darling, how can you ask? This is the happiest day of my life too!"

"Truthfully?"

"Truthfully—cross my heart and hope to die!"

And may the Lord have mercy on my soul.

But I had to lie. I had to survive. Was I going to survive? Could I? Yes, of course I was but—

"Ginette, Ginette!"

—but I was in the ballroom at Oxmoon and the past was about to repeat itself.

The ballroom was dazzling, a glittering dream glowing with winter flowers, and all the mirrors reflected a glamorous celebration of life as the gentlemen of the orchestra raised their bows to their violins.

"The waltz, Ginette! The first waltz this time!"

I looked back over my shoulder to the ballroom doors and all I saw was the emptiness where Conor had stood fifteen years before. He wasn't there. He would never be there again, and as I realized that I realized I was alone among the radiant crowds at Oxmoon, alone and bereaved and longing for the dead man I still loved.

The music began.

"Isn't this romantic, Ginette?"

"Darling," I said, "it's sheer unadulterated heaven!"

And then we danced again beneath the chandeliers at Oxmoon as the orchestra played "The Blue Danube."

It was hell.

I'm rather horrified that I experienced quite such an overwhelming sense of my bereavement at a time when I should have been thinking only of Robert, but I suspect the explanation lies in the fact that for the past few months I've been resolutely refusing to contemplate Conor as I struggled towards the blessed security of my new marriage; I've been suppressing my grief and that was probably unwise, but the truth is that my feelings for him are so deep and complex that I was afraid to dwell upon them in case they diverted me from my goal. However all will be well now that I'm safe with Robert. I'll have the courage to grieve secretly every now and then, and soon the awful pang of bereavement will be dulled until finally I shall have Conor securely locked up in the past where he now belongs.

Meanwhile perhaps I should start savoring the fact that I've survived the wedding, God knows how, and here I am, strolling with Robert down the Champs-Élysées just as a quarter of a century ago we used to pitter-patter hand in hand along the lane to the village shop at Penhale. We're enjoying ourselves hugely, rushing off on exciting expeditions as if we were children again, only this time, as Robert points out amused, nobody's going to be cross with us if we turn up late for tea. Yes, I think I'm recovering from that ghastly wedding—and certainly a heavenly honeymoon is a useful start to the rigors of married bliss. . . .

What a wonderful honeymoon! Darling Robert's spent money like water and this proves he's quite capable of being generous when it suits him. He did make one edgy remark about my weakness for lavish spending but I pretended not to hear, and anyway I'm absolutely determined to reform. (Yes, I really am. I *must*.)

We're now back in London again at our heavenly little house in Ebury Street and everything in the garden couldn't be lovelier—except that Declan and Rory are due to arrive from Oxmoon tomorrow, and new horrors are without doubt about to begin.

The boys have gone back to school after four frightful days and Robert has told me frankly how pleased he is to have me to himself again. To do Robert justice I have to admit he has good reason to be pleased; when the boys are with us I'm in such a state of excruciating tension that I'm very poor company and a most inadequate wife. I'll have to pull myself together but it's hard to be serene when Declan calls me a whore and encourages Rory to be as disobedient as possible. I daren't tell Robert who's fortunately out of the house most of the time. If Robert knew what I was going through there would be more beatings and I couldn't stand the strain.

However now they've gone so I have a breathing space for eleven weeks— although I shall visit them next month at the school. But I don't have to think about that yet. All I have to think about now is my delicious new social life as Mrs. Robert Godwin. For a day or two I had this frightful worry that I might be pregnant, but thank goodness it was a false alarm. As I told Robert at the beginning of our affair when he finally roused himself from his passion to consider the potential consequences, I've never had an unwanted pregnancy, although I've certainly had some bad scares in my time.

I do want another baby, of course—I'd like two more, a boy and a girl—but not just yet. Robert would be livid if he couldn't have me entirely to himself once the boys were out of the way, so I must be careful—and in being careful I'm being realistic. Some marriages can take the strain of an early pregnancy, some can't. Ours couldn't, and it's much better to face this truth and acknowledge it. In a year or two it'll be different—after all, Robert's told me he wants a son and I believe him—but at this particular moment little unborn Robert Godwin would most definitely not be welcome.

I hate to admit it but I'm uneasy. Having acknowledged that our marriage isn't yet stable enough to welcome a child, I now have to acknowledge that our unsolved problems are assuming a sinister clarity of outline. I can't keep saying to myself, Oh, everything will come right after we're married. This statement may well be true—my God, it's got to be true!—but here we are, married, and we now have to grit our teeth and solve these problems. Or, to be accurate, *I've* got to solve them, since Robert won't admit there are problems to be solved.

Heavens, how worrying it all is! In fact I'm so worried I can't even begin to think of divine Harrods and their slightly overwhelming blizzard of bills. . . .

"Ginette, I'd like a word with you, if you please."

"Yes, darling, of course. What about?"

"Money."

I inwardly quailed but somehow managed to give him a brilliant smile.

We were browsing through the Sunday papers on a snowy day at the end of January. Outside in our little walled garden which stretched to the mews, the morning light was bleak but in our drawing room the fire was burning in the grate and all was warmth and coziness.

I was very pleased with our house in Ebury Street. I would have preferred something bigger and more positively Belgravia, but I recognized that there was no sense in thinking in those terms without a substantial private income, so I had done my best to find an attractive house and make it as charming as possible. I had succeeded, but sad to say, such a success could hardly have been achieved without generous expenditure.

Robert had approved the cost of the renovations to the main reception rooms but had urged economy on redecorating the rest of the house, so I had made up my mind to skimp wherever possible. But of course the hall and stairs had to look well, to match the standard of the drawing room and dining room, and of course some alterations were essential in the kitchens, which were positively medieval, and of course I couldn't skimp on the boys' rooms because I did so long for Declan and Rory to be happy in their new home. I was sure Robert would understand the need for this additional expenditure so I didn't ask his permission beforehand, and anyway I planned to pay for the boys' rooms out of my own income—but something seemed to have happened to my quarterly payment (could I really have spent it all in advance?), and then I had some bills from Harrods which I thought I would be wise not to open, so I hid the unopened envelopes at the back of my desk and said to myself, "I'll think of all that later."

However I kept thinking of those unopened bills, so to divert my mind from this little awkwardness I took a stroll along the Brompton Road, and I was just drifting past Harrods—of course I never intended to buy a thing—when I saw in the window this dressing table which was quite exquisite and I couldn't help thinking how ravishing it would look in our bedroom where I'd skimped and saved until it looked no better than a monk's cell. Frankly, I'm not too keen on monk's cells. Anyway I bought the dressing table but then I found I couldn't rest until I'd bought one or two other items to go with it. Well, three or four. Or five or six. What does it matter, the point was that our bedroom suddenly became divinely exciting and I adored it. I knew I'd been naughty but in my opinion the result made my liberality (what a much nicer word that is than extravagance!) worthwhile.

"Don't worry, darling," I said glibly to Robert in the hope of forestalling his complaints. "I'm going to reform."

Robert tossed aside his newspaper, stood up and moved to the window to watch the falling snow. He looked very tall, very authoritative and very menacing. Then turning to face me he said, "I had a letter from Harrods yesterday and I've decided it would be better for our marriage if I have complete control over our financial affairs. Otherwise quarrels over money will be a recurring feature of our married life."

"You mean—"

"I want your credit account terminated and the income from your trust fund assigned directly to me."

Silence.

"Let me reassure you," said Robert, pleasant but implacable, "that I intend to be generous in the amount I shall give you to cover the cost of housekeeping and your general expenses."

Another silence.

"So you'll have no cause for complaint," said Robert, still speaking in a pleasant voice, "and in fact I'm sure you'll find such an arrangement will make life much easier for you. The truth is it's no good expecting a woman to balance a checkbook. The feminine mind is quite unsuited to even the lower forms of financial management."

I at once thought of Conor telling me how clever I was as I eked out the housekeeping money to cover his disaster at poker.

"You were always hopeless with money," said Robert, slicing through my memories. "Right from the beginning you were always borrowing the odd penny from me to buy extra humbugs and then forgetting to pay me back."

"Licorice. I never liked humbugs. And I always paid you back!"

"No, you didn't! Oh, I admit you gave me the occasional boiled sweet, but—"

"I borrowed money from Celia to pay you back!"

"Exactly. You borrowed from Peter to pay Paul, as the saying goes, and you're doing exactly the same thing now with appalling results. I'm sorry, Ginette, but my mind's made up. I'm your husband and I can't allow this situation to continue."

"But Robert—"

"You want order in your life, don't you?"

"Yes, but—"

"Well, this is it. This is order; this is freedom from chaos. Now run along like a good girl and fetch your bills so that I can see the exact dimensions of your latest mess."

"How dare you talk to me like that!"

"What do you mean? I'm your husband, aren't I?"

"That doesn't give you the right to talk to me as if I were a mentally deficient schoolgirl!"

"And being my wife doesn't give you the right to behave like one! Now pull yourself together and face reality. We're married now, the rules of the game have changed and it's my absolute moral duty—"

"Oh my God."

"—to look after you in as kind, as considerate and as generous a way as possible, and it's your absolute moral duty to be loyal and obedient and to do as I say in all matters regarding the welfare of our marriage. I know perfectly well you have an inclination to be strong-willed and independent, but I'm going to be the boss of this marriage, and I think the time has come—"

"If you talk of drawing lines I shall scream."

"—to make it clear exactly what I will and won't tolerate. Now, I know this is difficult for you. Our old friendship gets in the way here because you can still look at me and see the small boy two years your junior whom you used to order around, but—"

"What! I never ordered you around! You were ordering me around as soon as you could talk! 'Ginette, do this, Ginette, do that'—all the time, every day, God knows how I ever stood it—"

"I'm sorry, I realize women can seldom resist the urge to digress but I must recall you to the subject under discussion. As your husband, I—"

"Oh, be quiet! You're not behaving like a husband, you're behaving like a jailer! Oh, how dare you treat me like this, how dare you—"

"I'll tell you exactly why I dare. Because you're no good with money. Because I'm ultimately responsible for your debts. Because you asked me to stop you getting into messes. Because I care about our marriage and rows such as this are something we have to avoid in the future at all costs."

"If you care about our marriage you'll treat me as an adult woman ought to be treated!"

"I am," said Robert.

I stormed out and slammed the door.

I've married a male monster. Is this a fatal mistake? Not necessarily. Male monsters can often be absolute pets. I've flirted with a number of delicious ones in the past and I've adored feeling that I'm the only chink in their antifemale armor, but I've always thought what a bore they would be as husbands and my God, now I know I was right.

However I'm not a feminist. I'm enjoying myself much too much being a first-rate woman to want to be a second-rate man, and I've no quarrel with the way the world's arranged. I don't care whether I have the vote or not. Certainly I would never bother to chain myself to the railings of Number Ten Downing Street; I'm much too busy wondering when I'm going to be invited to dine there. But despite my indifference to feminism there's one belief I hold very strongly and no one can talk me out of it: women are not born inferior to men. They're born different, but not inferior. And I resent, *deeply* resent being treated as if I were something less than a normal human being.

Why did I never realize Robert could be like this? Because he was playing the game according to the rules and making no attempt to be a male monster until he became my husband and acquired (he thinks) the right to be one. He did give me inklings, though; I can remember him saying the law was right to class married women with lunatics and children, but I just wrote that off as male arrogance, something to be taken with a pinch of salt. However I can't take the loss of my income with a pinch of salt. I'll need a huge indigestion pill to enable me to absorb an outrage like that, but for lack of alternative I'd better start swallowing one.

Is there really no choice but to acquiesce? I must try to be dispassionate; I must ask myself what the truth of this situation is, and the truth is that Robert *is* my husband. He can cancel my credit account and if I refuse to assign the income of my trust fund, my life soon won't be worth living.

Let me now try digesting that very unpalatable verdict. Well, the first fact which stands out like a sore thumb is that rationally Robert's right—as usual. I've been very naughty and very extravagant. No more using that delightful word "liberality" now; I must confront my problem. I'm not incapable of handling money but I can't blame Robert for deducing that I am. I should also admit that Robert's not taking an unusual line here; plenty of husbands refuse to let their wives buy goods on credit, and plenty of husbands refuse to let their wives have checkbooks, and this may even be good for their marriages, particularly if their wives have the brains of a cotton reel.

Yet the fact remains that although Robert's logically right he's emotionally wrong. That trust money is mine. It was left to me—*me*—by my father. I may be only Mrs. Robert Godwin in the eyes of the world, but to my bank manager I'm still an individual, not merely an extension of my husband—I'm the recipient of those funds, a human being who deserves to be treated with respect, not an idiot wife who can expect no better fate than to be the target of remarks like "the feminine mind is quite unsuited to even the lower forms of financial management." I have this horrid feeling that if I assign the income from my trust fund there won't be any *me* anymore, and I'll be diminished in some way quite impossible to describe to someone like Robert.

I feel wretched about this, and not merely because I'm furious with myself for not anticipating the severity of Robert's reaction. I feel wretched because I know our marriage now has another problem. I can manage; I can cope with a male monster if I have to, but the fact that Robert and I have different notions of what marriage should be like is hardly going to make life easier. I believe marriage should be a partnership aided by a reasonable amount of give-and-take and based on mutual respect and trust. Robert apparently regards it as a variation of a master-servant or parent-child relationship. Why on earth didn't I realize this before? How can one sleep with a man for six months without discovering this fundamental difference of opinion?

I blame the old friendship. I assumed we'd jog along on more or less the same lines after we were married. How spine-chilling it was just now when Robert said the rules of the game had changed! He would put it that way, of course. Typical.

Yes, I'm horrified but never mind, the first year of marriage is notorious for unwelcome revelations, and most partners manage to adjust to the unpleasant home truths in the end. Meanwhile it's certainly no good prolonging the quarrel. Robert won't behave as Conor did, seducing me whenever he wanted to get his hands on my money. If Robert doesn't get what he wants he'll withdraw from me emotionally, and I couldn't stand it; I want a loving Robert at my side, not a monster labeled HUSBAND; I want *my friend,* my companion at the strawberry beds and the loyal confederate who lent me the extra pennies to buy that mouth-watering licorice long ago in Penhale. . . .

I really should have given him more boiled sweets in compensation. I might have known that little mistake would catch up with me in the end.

"I'm sorry I lost my temper, Robert."

"I'm sorry if I upset you."

"Well, I do realize I've been very stupid and I do concede you have the right to cancel my credit account. But the trust fund . . . Robert, that fund is special to me, it comes from my father, and I'm sorry but I really do think a wife shouldn't be utterly dependent on her husband for money—"

"And I think she should be."

Another fundamental difference of opinion. I tried not to panic. "I can't think why," I said evenly, "we didn't discuss all this before we were married."

"We did. I made it very clear what I thought of your extravagance."

"You never said you thought I should be utterly dependent on you financially!"

"Naturally I had to give you the chance to manage your affairs. I did want to be fair."

"If you could give me just one more chance—"

"No. It would only lead to another scene like this, and I won't have it. We're not going to quarrel all over again, are we, Ginette?"

I shook my head, went to my desk and extracted the hidden bills from Harrods. Then at his dictation I wrote a letter to my bank manager to say that I wished the quarterly income from my trust fund to be paid directly into my husband's account.

"Thank you," said Robert. "Now we need never again have a row about money."

I stared in silence at the blotter. I could not bring myself to ask how much he intended to give me each week. I only prayed it would be sufficient and that I wouldn't have to beg for more.

Robert was glancing at his watch. "It'll take me a day or two to survey our expenditure and decide how much you need," he said, "so we'll conclude this discussion later. And now if you'll excuse me I must go to my study and work. I've got a lot to do." And with my checkbook in his pocket he left me on my own in my beautiful but extravagant drawing room.

Robert's working much too hard. I had no idea he could be so obsessed with his work. How could I possibly sleep with a man for six months and not realize . . . But I mustn't start saying that again. The brutal truth is that a love affair puts the partners on their best behavior. It takes marriage to ensure that all the unpalatable truths come sidling out of the woodwork of the happy home.

Robert is now rushing off to his chambers in the Temple at six in the morning so that he can work in peace before all the other barristers and clerks arrive to distract him. At first he used to leave without having breakfast but I put a stop to that by conspiring with Bennett.

Bennett used to be Robert's man before our marriage, and he's now our butler, wielding authority with great skill over Cook, the kitchenmaid and the parlormaid. I don't have a personal maid; they're usually an awful bore and anyway I learned how to live without one in New York. The trick is not to economize on a laundress and to track down a retired lady's maid who is willing to come in now and then to attend to the more difficult aspects of hairdressing. I'm good at sewing, thanks to Margaret, so mending presents no problems. When Robert becomes very grand I dare say I shall acquire a maid but meanwhile I manage well enough without one.

Bennett and I get on well, which is fortunate because valets often lapse into paroxysms of jealousy when their masters acquire wives, and when I told him how worried I was by Robert's increasingly eccentric working hours, he was sympathetic. Eventually we agreed that he would provide an early breakfast and I would coax Robert to eat it, but the trouble is that since this conversation of mine with Bennett, Robert has lost all interest in food and is eating the early breakfast only in order to keep me quiet.

Food isn't the only subject that no longer interests him. After our social engagements have been fulfilled he retires to his study to work into the early hours of the morning, and when he finally comes to bed he sinks instantly into unconsciousness while I'm left lying awake in the dark and wondering what happened to that lover who won his blue at passion.

Last night I said, "Darling, how long is this peculiar behavior of yours likely to go on?"

This embarrassed Robert but I'm sure I was right to signal to him that in my opinion he's carrying professional dedication too far. The entire trouble is this wretched murder case which he jokingly told me he took on in order to pay for the honeymoon. His client is accused of murdering his wife, chopping up the body and distributing it in bags deposited at various left-luggage offices all over London. Robert won't discuss the case with me so I have no idea whether he thinks his client is innocent or not, but I find the whole affair repulsive and can't imagine why Robert should find it so all-absorbing —not that he spends all his working hours on this case; he doesn't. He works so hard in order to keep up with his other cases, but I'm beginning to think that the murder alone is responsible for this sinister aura of fanaticism. It's the first murder case he's accepted since I came back into his life from America, and he seems to be turning into someone else altogether.

Nothing could frighten me more.

"No, no—stay away from me, *stay away!*" shouted Robert, and I awoke to find him in the middle of a nightmare.

"Darling, it's only a dream—"

"He was there again, he was coming towards me across the snow—"

"Who?"

"Death." He slumped back exhausted on the pillows.

I thought: What a vile nightmare. But I judged it tactful to remain silent so after switching on the light I merely slipped my hand into his to comfort him.

He clasped my fingers tightly and seemed grateful for both the light and the silence, but at last he said, "I seem to be in a mess again but I don't understand why. I thought I'd be cured once I had you."

I was astonished. "Cured of what, Robert?"

"I've got this bloody awful obsession; it's like a cancer of the personality."

"Cancer!"

"Don't be idiotic; I'm speaking metaphorically—oh God, I forgot you were terrified of illness—"

"But what on earth is this obsession of yours?"

"I'm obsessed with death."

There was a pause. We lay there, our hands clasped, and listened to the silence. I tried to speak but nothing happened. I was too revolted.

"It's all mixed up with this other obsession—"

"Other obsession?"

"Winning. I have to compete, I have to win, I can't stop myself. Now I thought this was all the result of my third obsession—"

"Third obsession?"

"Yes. You. It was a terrible thing when I lost you, Ginette; it was as if my whole life was dislocated—I kept trying to push it back into position by winning everything in sight. So I won and won and won until the easy victories no longer satisfied me, and then finally I found the challenge I needed, I found a competitor who would give me the most enthralling game of all—"

"And who was that?"

"Death."

My hand went limp in his but he didn't notice. He was too absorbed in his explanations.

"I thought," he said, "that once I had you back, I wouldn't feel the need to compete anymore. I thought I'd be able to go home again to Oxmoon—"

"What?"

"Oh, not literally! I was thinking of the lost Oxmoon of our childhood—I was seeing Oxmoon as a state of mind, a symbol of happiness."

"Oh, I see. For one moment I thought you meant—well, never mind, go on."

"But I'm still looking for the road back to Oxmoon, I'm still locked up in a way of life which is fundamentally meaningless to me—"

"Oh come, Robert, don't exaggerate! You love the glamour and the fame of your life at the bar!"

"No, I've come to hate all that. Glamour and fame have become symbols of my imprisonment. I'd give up the bar but—"

"*Give it up?*"

"—but I can't now that I have a wife and family to support, and besides if I'm to go into politics I must have a lucrative career. But do I really want to go into politics? Won't Westminster ultimately be just another cage like the Old Bailey? Oh God, how muddled I feel sometimes, how confused—"

"But my dear Robert, surely you don't doubt that you're cut out for great political success?"

"But what does that mean?" said Robert. "What's the point of pursuing a career which has nothing to do with what one's life should really signify?"

"But what do you think your life should signify?"

"That's the conundrum. I don't know. All I know is that I'm not at peace. I ought to be; I've won you, I've cancelled out my loss and now I can be happy—except that I can't. It's almost as if I hadn't won you after all—oh God, what a mystery it is; how bewildered I feel, how despairing, how utterly tormented by the irrationality of it all—"

"Darling." I finally managed to pull myself together. "The first thing you must do is to stop talking of 'winning' me as if I were one of those ghastly silver cups which clutter up your bedroom at Oxmoon. One doesn't win people—they're not inanimate objects. The fact is that you've married me, which has more to do with existing and surviving than with winning or losing, but never mind, that's not a disaster, that's good, because of course I'm going to do my best to help you, just as a good friend should, and I'm sure that together we'll be able to sort out these horrid problems of yours. But to be quite honest, darling, I think you're suffering from nervous exhaustion brought on by overwork."

"You've understood nothing." He got out of bed and groped for his dressing gown.

"I understand that you need a thorough rest!"

"But I can't rest. That's the point."

"Yes, but once this murder case is finished—"

He walked out. I stared after him. Then I jumped out of bed and pulled on my kimono. By the time I reached the dining room he was drinking brandy by the sideboard.

"Robert, I do want to help—you're not being very fair to me—"

"I'm sorry. That's true. I haven't told you the whole story, that's the trouble. But perhaps I should." He looked down at the brandy in his glass. Then he said slowly, "This reminds me of the morning when my father talked to me about you. He didn't start by saying he wanted to talk about you, of course. He said. 'I want to tell you about my parents and Owain Bryn-Davies.' It was because he knew that only by talking of his adolescence could he explain why he did what he did to you, and I now feel that only by talking of the mountaineering can I attempt to show you why I feel my present life has very little connection with the kind of man I really am. . . . Or should I keep my mouth shut? You're looking appalled. I'm sorry, I didn't mean to upset you by mentioning my father."

I gave him the only possible response. "Pour me some brandy too, please, and let's sit down at the table."

Robert poured me some brandy. We sat down. And then the horrors really began.

"All my life," said Robert, "I've been made to understand that I'm unusually gifted. This has been my father's attitude to me ever since I can remember. This was the attitude of my teachers at school. And finally at Oxford the tutors at Balliol confirmed that I could have an outstanding career in law and politics, the road to the highest offices in the land—and of course I had no quarrel with this vision. It all seemed so attractive that I accepted it unquestioningly. But I didn't think, Ginette. Until I saw the mountains I never applied my so-called exceptional intellect to asking the simplest and most important of questions: what did I really want to do with my life? And then I saw the mountains and I knew. I just wanted to climb. Nothing else mattered.

"Afterwards—after it was all over—I told myself I'd undergone a form of insanity which had resembled a cancer on my personality. So I cut out the cancer: I abandoned mountaineering. But now I feel dead. And lately I've come to ask myself, Which was the real cancer? The academic life followed by fame and fortune at the bar? Or the climber's life which I rejected? And I have this terrible suspicion that it's the life I now lead which is killing me, strangling my personality and blighting my soul.

"Why did I actually give up mountaineering? I'd had a shock, of course. I was stunned not only with grief but with a rage against death—the rage which ultimately led me to the Old Bailey; I found I had to fight death in order to come to terms with the loss of my friends, but I found too that I couldn't fight death anymore on the mountains, I had to find another theater of war.

"But I know now that I didn't give up mountaineering just because I'd had a shock. I gave it up because I was a coward—yes, I gave it up because I was afraid, that was the truth of it, afraid of death. And I'm still afraid. Dying is losing. To die is to fail—and to fail utterly because once one's dead there can be no second chances; one can never go winning again.

"So I turned back to the academic life where there was no risk of dying. I'd been on the brink of wrecking my university career but at that point I realized I could still save it, I could still emerge a winner ready to master this brilliant future which had been forecast for me. So I did it—coward that I was, I did it: I took the easy way out. Back I went up to Oxford to conform, to crucify myself and to win.

"But I can see those mountains so clearly in my mind's eye. Oh Christ, how I loved those mountains. . . . When one's climbing one exists in a very simple world from which all the trivialities and irrelevancies have been cauterized. It's all so beautiful, so exciting—and best of all there's the unique comradeship with one's fellow climbers and the satisfaction of being a man among men—"

I could keep silent no longer. "And what consolation was that to you," I said, "when your three friends were killed?"

"You don't understand. Well, you're a woman, I suppose you can't. It doesn't matter."

"Of course it matters and it's possible—just possible—that I'm capable of understanding this peculiarity better than you yourself do. You seem to be describing some sort of compulsion to escape from the realities of life. I believe it's very common among young people growing up—they can't face adult life so they retreat into a fairy-tale world of their own creation—"

"What nonsense! Mountaineering *was* my reality!"

"Then tell me more about it so that I can understand. Tell me exactly what happened on this last climb of yours."

"You'll never understand."

"Why not? Think of me as an asinine juror who has to be conquered!"

This challenge proved too tempting for him to resist. Pouring himself some more brandy he said, "Very well, try and imagine a January day in Scotland—we'd reached the stage, you see, when we found winter climbing more exciting. It had snowed but the snow was crisp and conditions were good. We set off from Fort William, my friends and I, and I was so happy, I remember how happy I was—I suppose when all's said and done I prefer the company of men, and if it wasn't for sex I wouldn't bother with women at all —apart from you. My dearest Ginette! Putting the bedroom aside for a moment, I can honestly say that you're the only woman I've ever met who can be good company just like a man.

"Well, there we were heading for Ben Nevis, and both women and bedrooms were far away, thank God, so we were able to concentrate on our . . . is 'calling' too strong a word? The term 'obsession' describes nothing here. It omits the spirituality. That morning I felt at one with God—in whom I didn't believe—and at one with the universe; I felt as if I were playing an allotted part in the scheme of things; I felt intensely happy and completely fulfilled—and *this* for me was real life. Everything else was makeshift and make-believe."

"Yes, but . . . No, I'm sorry. Go on."

"We decided on an easy climb up the Tower Ridge. The main difficulties lie in the first three hundred feet, but we overcame those easily enough and we then decided for fun to take the last stretch as a diagonal climb to make the expedition more of a challenge." He paused as if he expected me to make some disparaging remark, but when I said nothing he continued: "There was a very high wind, and this had two results which were crucial. The first was that it meant a large amount of new snow had accumulated, and the second was that we didn't notice when the temperature suddenly began to rise. We were all roped together. I was the last man. We were skirting an overhanging rock as we moved around the corner of the mountainside. The other three had completed the stretch successfully and were out of sight when my rope snagged and I had to stop. The only thing to do was to untie the rope from my waist so that I could unhook myself, and I was just flicking the rope free when the end came.

"There was a tremendous roar. It was like the end of the world. I flung myself under the overhang and saw the loose rope whipped from my fingers. Then at last the silence fell. I can't begin to describe my emotions. Eventually when I managed to get around the corner for a look, I saw that the whole face of the mountain had moved—a huge block of snow had broken free and slid a thousand feet or more towards the valley. There was no sign of my friends.

"I tried to go back but it was impossible without a rope and *then* I was frightened because I knew that if I had to spend a night on that mountain I could die of exposure. So I willed myself to keep warm. All through that night I fought to live but I knew Death wanted me, I could feel him there, and when the dawn came I saw him coming to claim me as he walked across the snow.

"He wore red—yes, red, not black—and he had a white face with no features.

"Of course I was hallucinating. The dawn light was playing tricks with the snow. But to me at that moment he was intensely real. 'Stay away from me!' I shouted, and I was so terrified because I thought he was going to win. But he didn't. He receded and vanished as the sun came up. The rescue party reached me soon afterwards. The doctor at Fort William was surprised not only that I was alive but that I wasn't suffering from frostbite. 'You'll survive unmarked!' he said, but he was wrong. There are some marks no doctors can see.

"I was marked by the guilt that I was alive while my three friends were dead. I was marked by my need to atone for my guilt by fighting death in revenge. And worst of all I was marked by my fear of death, because I had now seen so clearly that to die is to fail once and for all.

"As I've already said, I couldn't face that knowledge. I found I couldn't go back to the mountains because I was too afraid that next time I confronted death I'd lose—and yet . . . I was wrong, wasn't I? Death's everywhere, that's the truth of it. You can't hide from him, he'll come and get you when he wants you no matter where you are. So in that case the way to outwit him, in the limited time available, isn't to retreat into a way of life which is alien to you; the way to outwit him is to live the life you were put on this earth to lead. It's wrong to waste yourself in work that means nothing to you. It's not only a waste of talent. It's a prostitution of the soul.

"I've begun to think I'm wasting my life but I can't bear to think of that so I don't, and when I'm working like a demon I don't have to think of anything but the case in hand. But I want to go back to the mountains, and if I inherited a suitable fortune I'd abandon my London life without a backward glance and . . . I'm sorry, you obviously think I'm talking like a maniac so I must stop. Perhaps I was a fool to have said so much."

"Don't be absurd! It's vital that you should be absolutely frank with me—how else am I to understand your dilemma? But darling, I still think this huge pessimism of yours is largely due to the fact that you're worn out. Come back to bed and let's discuss it further later."

"I've horrified you, haven't I?"

"No, of course not, darling; don't be silly. I'm just deeply concerned about your health."

"My God, if you start wishing you'd never married me—"

"Now you really are talking like a maniac!" I said, laughing, and at last I succeeded in coaxing him back to bed.

He's right. I'm horrified. Who would ever have thought Robert could be so convoluted and disordered? I mean, *I'm* the one who's supposed to be perpetually in a mess. One of the most important reasons why I married him was because I thought he could sort out my problems but now I find I have to sort out his. Well, I wouldn't mind doing that, but they're so bizarre and I'm not sure I can. Can Robert be on the brink of losing his mind altogether as the result of this case? But it seems he's been secretly like this for years. *Why did I never guess? Why did I never know?* I feel so shattered by the entire episode that I can hardly nerve myself to dwell on it, but I suppose I must try.

Robert is in love with mountaineering. Well, we all have our little peculiarities, but why can't he see this "calling" of his (honestly, what romantic exaggeration!) as just an undergraduate hobby which went disastrously wrong? And why does he have to talk like a demented disciple of muscular Christianity—all that rubbish about being a man among men (and to think men say women have the monopoly on sentimentality!) and all that rot about how women and sex pale in comparison with platonic masculine comradeship. Laying aside all sexual prejudice the rock-bottom truth of life is that women and sex mean the perpetuation of the human race and that platonic masculine comradeship is, as the Americans say, a dead-end street. Well, I mean, sex *is* life, isn't it? So how can Robert possibly argue that his obsession with mountaineering is in some way superior? And let's be honest: Robert likes sex as much as anyone, and he's absolutely normal there, thank God, and he'd be the first to object if he were condemned to perpetual chastity on a mountain with a bunch of male chums. I admit he's temporarily lost interest in sex but that's just the strain of this appalling case.

As for him saying he'd give up the law and London tomorrow if he had the means, that's just laughable. Robert would be *miserable* without his glamour and his fame, and he'd die of boredom if he were deprived of his life here for more than a month! He's a brilliant man and he enjoys worldly success. That's natural. To turn his back on it would be most unnatural and he'd soon be racked with regret.

Yes, I understand him better than he himself does. Poor Robert, what a state he was in; I did feel so sorry for him . . . But how simple Conor seems in retrospect! He knew what he wanted from life well enough, no muddled agonizing for him. "I want to have one hell of a good time!" I can hear him say it now—I can even hear him laughing. No obsession with death ever clouded his mind. All he cared about was life and that was all I cared about too.

Oh, I keep thinking the grief will fade, but it doesn't; it's still there and I miss him, I miss him dreadfully, I miss him and want him to come back. . . .

I nearly scratched out the above maudlin paragraph because I'm so ashamed of it, but I'll let it stand as a monument to the shock I felt at the time. I don't miss Conor as much as that; I only think I do when I'm feeling depressed. I'm so happy with Robert, and anyway he's better now because the case is over.

He lost. I was most apprehensive when I heard the news but Robert took his defeat better than I'd dared hope, although he was very quiet as he went off to see his client for the last time. However that's understandable. What on earth does one say to someone whose next appointment is with the gallows? Presumably Robert has a formula but nevertheless it must be a harrowing experience. However afterwards he went for a ride in the park and came back saying 'Mens sana in corpore sano,' so presumably he now believes himself to be on the road to recovery. Even *I* know what that Latin tag means. It means Robert's no longer sound asleep while I'm lying awake frustrated in the dark. It means I'm no longer seized by the urge to ransack Harrods to take my mind off my troubles. It means Robert is dining tonight with his friend Raymond Asquith, the Prime Minister's son, in an attempt to explore the future with someone who can give him sound advice.

Robert has a special respect for Raymond because Raymond's about the only person in London who's cleverer than he is; Raymond, with his numerous Oxford prizes and multiple academic honors, leaves even Robert, with his double first, outclassed. A gap of four years separates them in age but because of their Balliol background they have all manner of interests and acquaintances in common so I can well imagine them chatting away happily to each other, both thrilled to dine with someone of their own intellectual caliber for a change. Robert told me once that one of the worst things about being brilliant is that one finds most people dreadfully dull. Well, at least that'll never be one of my problems. I find people endlessly fascinating, and I like Raymond who, not content with being an intellectual phenomenon, is good-looking and charming, just like Robert, and normal enough to have a wife and two children as well as a successful career at the bar. If Raymond can apparently manage his life so happily and adroitly, then surely Robert can too.

But someone mentioned to me the other day that Raymond's problem was that he was without ambition. Perhaps Raymond too is convoluted and disordered beneath the shining surface of his life. How little we know even of those who are closest to us. How can we hope to know those with whom we're barely acquainted?

I'm becoming pessimistic again, so I must stop. But I can't help it, I'm still very worried indeed . . .

All's well. Thank God. Robert's decided to give up criminal law, since it undoubtedly feeds his obsession with death, and move to chancery chambers specializing in trusts. However that will take time to achieve, and while this rearrangement is taking place he'll start pursuing a political career in earnest. He's dining again this week with Raymond, and with them will be two successful Liberals of their own age, "Bluey" Baker and Edwin Montagu. At least Robert has first-class political connections, and I'm sure it won't be long before he's adopted as the prospective Liberal candidate for some promising constituency.

I couldn't be more pleased by this evidence that Robert's recovered his equilibrium. Really, I can't think why I let myself get so upset! I might have known that brilliant rational Robert would be able to sort out his problems efficiently in the end. . .

Robert's just told me he wants to give everything up—the law, London, any hope of a political career—and live cheaply in the country so that he can afford to return to mountaineering.

I realize at once that this is some form of delayed nervous breakdown so I don't have hysterics. I keep very calm and ask him what we're going to do about money, because even the smallest gentleman's residence in the country can hardly be run on a shoestring.

He tells me there's only one solution. We must live at Oxmoon—not in the main house, he hastens to add (no doubt I looked as if I were about to faint), but on the estate. He can ask his father for a portion in advance of his inheritance, and if Bobby cedes him one of the major farms, then the farm-house itself can be improved and extended into a residence suitable for a gentleman; Bobby would probably even offer to pay the cost of the alterations because he would be so pleased to have Robert back in Gower. Then we could rent the house in Ebury Street to boost our income, and it would certainly need boosting even though Robert thinks he might be able to earn the odd sum here and there by writing, first about his famous trials and later about his mountaineering. However he has a little capital, I have the income from my trust fund and we would both have the small income from our future farm, so, as Robert himself points out, we wouldn't starve; he would be able to return to the mountains, and whenever he came home I would be waiting for him at Oxmoon, just as I'd been waiting in the old days, and then the Oxmoon of our childhood would finally be recaptured and we would live happily ever after encased in a glowing aura of romantic nostalgia.

I've asked for time to consider this ridiculous fantasy—I really can't dignify it by calling it a plan—and Robert has said yes, of course I must have time, and of course he realizes what a shock he must have given me, and he's very, very sorry but he can no longer go on living a meaningless life.

Quite.

Oddly enough now that I've stopped burying my head in the sand and telling myself that everything in the garden's lovely, I do feel much better. This is because I'm no longer worrying about what might happen; I'm worrying about what *has* happened and can concentrate on solving a specific problem. For of course I can't let him make this catastrophic mistake. I've got to stop him, and as far as I can see my only hope of doing so lies in presenting him with the brutal truths he's apparently unable to face.

"We've been married eight weeks today. What a mess. Never mind, once we're over this crisis, matters must surely improve. God knows they could hardly get any worse.

"Robert, before I start I want to apologize for what I'm going to say. I'd never be so brutal unless I honestly felt I had no alternative."

"Go on."

"I can't live on your parents' doorstep. But that's not my major objection to your plan. My main objection is that I don't believe you could live on their doorstep either."

There was a silence. We had cancelled our evening engagement and were alone after dinner in the drawing room. Robert was standing by the fireplace, his eyes watching the flames flickering in the grate, but as the silence lengthened he turned to face me, one hand remaining on the mantelshelf as if he felt the need to steady himself. I was sitting on the edge of the sofa. We were some eight feet apart.

"It's no good you pretending that we can ever have a normal relationship with your parents," I said, "because we can't. It's impossible."

He said evenly, "I've forgiven my father. He's a deeply damaged man. I must forgive him."

"I was damaged too. And he damaged me."

"That's all in the past now."

"That's exactly where you're wrong, Robert. We may all pretend everything's forgiven and forgotten, but that's just to keep ourselves sane. The reality is much more appalling than you've ever allowed yourself to acknowledge but if we were to move to Gower you'd have to face that reality every day, and quite frankly I don't think you could do it."

"I—"

"The truth is that every time I see Bobby and Margaret I remember—we all remember—all that past horror lives again in our minds. I admit you're a latecomer to this horror, but no matter what you say you can't persuade me you're unaffected by it. I think you're very affected by it, but you've managed to gloss over the problem in your mind because we're two hundred miles from Oxmoon and living a life in which your parents have no part to play. You forgive your father, you say. That's admirable. But is it true? You're a jealous possessive man and I don't believe you could ever tolerate for long the company of a man who you knew had gone to bed with me. I suppose you think that with sufficient willpower anything's possible, but I think this is the kind of situation, Robert, that could break your will in two, put us all through hell and wreck our marriage."

He made no effort to dispute this. After a protracted pause he said with distressing awkwardness, "You don't think that if we were both back at Oxmoon we could recapture the magic of the lost Oxmoon where we were so happy?"

"No," I said. "That's a romantic and sentimental notion which has nothing to do with reality. I can't take you back to that magic Oxmoon, Robert, because the magic was destroyed and can never now be recaptured. I'm sorry but I can't work that particular miracle for you."

"Yet sometimes," he said, "in your company, I see those days live again."

"Well, you certainly wouldn't if we removed now to Oxmoon. All you'd see in your mind would be your father crawling into bed with me and pulling up his nightshirt."

He flinched and turned away. Jumping up I ran to him. "Darling, forgive me, I'm being so cruel, I know I am, but I've got to make you see—"

"Won't you ever want to go back?"

"Yes," I said. "When Bobby's dead and Margaret's pensioned off somewhere and you're Prime Minister, I shall be delighted to spend part of the year there. We can make it into a weekend retreat for all the most famous people of the day!"

He gave a small painful smile and said nothing.

"Darling . . ." I put my arms around him. "Don't think I'm unsympathetic about the mountaineering—I do understand how much it means to you; but treat it as a hobby. To devote your life to it would be to give way to an obsession—it would be most unhealthy. Why don't you at least give politics a try? I can't understand why you've recoiled from it like this."

"Raymond was talking the other day of the futility of it all."

"But he's been adopted as the prospective candidate for Derby!" I was now definitely having second thoughts about Raymond Asquith. I wondered what *his* wife had to go through whenever he suffered a bout of nihilism.

"Raymond's feelings are very complex," said Robert. "But it can't be easy to be the son of the Prime Minister."

"Well, at least you're spared that problem! Maybe you should see less of Raymond and more of someone like Edwin Montagu, who's so brilliant and so ambitious and thinks politics is the only life for a man."

Robert said nothing.

"Darling . . ." I kissed him. "Please—for my sake—do nothing rash. Do nothing you might regret later."

He nodded, still mute. I kissed him again and suggested we went to bed, but he said he wanted to think a little more so I went upstairs alone. Naturally I was too nervous to sleep. I lay awake and at last, well after midnight, he joined me.

"Do you love me?" he said as we lay beside each other in the dark.

"Darling, you know I do."

"Then all's well," said Robert. "I'd give up everything for you, even mountaineering."

"But I'm not asking you to give up mountaineering!"

"I couldn't treat it as a hobby. Either I devote my life to it or I don't, but so long as you love me I don't much care about anything else. Anyway, if we can't go back to Oxmoon I can't afford a removal to the country, and if we can't live cheaply in the country I can't go back to mountaineering. Problem solved."

He began to make love to me with his usual efficiency but the performance went wrong, and afterwards I had to hug him tightly to show I didn't mind. Conor would have said, "Holy shit!" and hugged me back before falling asleep, but Robert was silent and tense in my arms, and I knew he was racked by a sense of failure.

"Darling, *don't* worry, please don't—I know ten seconds isn't such fun as ten minutes—or longer—but no one can be perfect in bed all the time!"

"What about Kinsella?"

I knew a moment of horrified panic but I somehow managed to answer briskly, "Good heavens, Robert, surely you know hard drinkers aren't always perfect in the bedroom!"

That satisfied him. He went to sleep but I continued to lie awake, and despite the renewal of his decision to enter politics, I knew our marriage was still in very great trouble indeed.

I'm praying that was rock-bottom. Surely after this matters can only improve. If only Robert doesn't have to wait too long for the opportunity to enter Parliament! I'm sure that once he reaches Westminster he'll be thoroughly happy and then our worst problems will be at an end—or at the very least considerably eased.

Meanwhile his career at the bar is still worrying him. He's decided he would be a fool to leave his common-law chambers, since it would inevitably entail a drop in income while he built up a new reputation for himself as a chancery lawyer, and anyway he thinks he'd be bored to tears with trusts or tax. In his opinion he would be better off staying with the criminal cases and trying to specialize in nonviolent crimes such as fraud, but I do wish he could get right away from crime. However in a few years' time it won't matter because he'll be in the Cabinet with a substantial salary and then he can retire from the law altogether.

But first of all he must get into Parliament. Since the Prime Minister's taking such a benign interest in him I doubt if he'll have to wait long, but any wait is tiresome, particularly in these nerve-racking circumstances, so I've made up my mind to do all I can to make life smooth for Robert at home.

I'm counting not only the pennies but the ha'pennies and farthings in the generous allowance he gives me, and I'm drawing up elaborate accounts so that he can see how clever I can be with money when I put my mind to it. I'm also refusing to go anywhere near Harrods. In fact I'm at the point where all I need is polish for my halo, but it's such hard work being parsimonious that I've barely had the strength to tackle the problem of the boys.

Nevertheless I managed to dredge up sufficient nerve to tell Declan that if he could survive till the end of term without being expelled I'd let him spend the Easter holidays in Ireland. So now he's in Dublin. It was the only answer, as my marriage couldn't have stood another onslaught from Declan at the moment. However Rory I summoned to London, and now here he is, good as gold without Declan and enjoying his outings with me to galleries, museums and picture theaters. I must say, I feel rather dashing going to picture theaters—so amusingly *déclassée!* Robert doesn't approve of me going to a darkened room frequented by the lower classes, but he quite understands that darling Rory would punch any man who tried to be uppish with me when the film broke down.

I'm much happier about Rory, and I really think he'll survive this chaotic year intact. He does moan that he hates school, but I'm not going to be upset by that (a) because I can't afford to be and (b) because Rory's gregarious and I honestly think that once he's thoroughly settled he'll enjoy school very much. He's not as clever as Declan but he's good at games, and in an English public school this is a guarantee of happiness; the poor little love said they stopped calling him Yankee scum when they realized he was good at rugger.

I did say I was willing to spend Easter at Oxmoon but Robert just said, "No, that's not necessary," so I think my speech about the ever-present nature of the past horrors must have sunk in. We'll have to go down for Christmas, of course—there's no way out of that obligation, but I've told Robert I accept this and that he's not to worry about me when December comes. What a relief to have that situation clearly defined! I can face Oxmoon once a year. Just.

Bobby visits London regularly, but although Robert conscientiously sees him, I don't. I must say, I do admire Robert for maintaining the trappings of a normal relationship with his father. I'd love to know what he says in his weekly letters to his mother but Margaret in her elaborate replies gives little clue. After transforming the task of saying nothing into a high art, she always sends her love to me and she never, never reproaches either of us for avoiding Oxmoon. This makes me feel so guilty that I try not to think of her, but even this coward's course isn't available to me at the moment because she's just written to ask if we can have Lion to stay. He's got a new post in a City bank, and he needs a roof over his head while he finds himself some bachelor chambers.

Lion is traditionally accepted as being Margaret's favorite, and this, of course, is why she writes to me with her request and not to Robert. She knows Robert would make some excuse not to have Lion, just as she knows I can't possibly refuse her, but nonetheless Lion's arrival will create an awkward situation because Robert is very possessive at the moment; it's as if he has to be constantly reassured that I love him, and this means I have to give him my undivided attention whenever he comes home. He won't want me to be distracted by any visitor, least of all Lion. Personally I adore Lion and I can quite see why Margaret turns to him in relief after struggling with the more tortuous-minded members of her family, for Lion's nature is so simple and open. He's always cheerful, always bursting with high spirits, always exactly what he appears to be—ingenuous, naughty and, beneath the bombastic manners, as gentle and kind as Edmund. Yes, darling Lion is blissfully straightforward and darling Lion must definitely come to stay, but to keep the peace I'll need every ounce of diplomatic skill I possess.

Was there ever a first year of marriage like this one? Honestly, I think if I survive to celebrate the first anniversary I ought to be given a gold medal—or perhaps one of those ghastly silver cups awarded to Robert during the course of his morbid and sinister career as a winner . . .

Darling Lion has confided in me. He *is* a pet. He says he doesn't think he was designed by nature to earn his living, so he's had a brilliant idea: he's going to marry an heiress. He tells me this as if no penniless young man had ever thought of it before, and adds quickly that his only requirement is that he must be passionately in love.

"However," says sunny-natured Lion, beaming at me from ear to ear, "that's no difficulty because I fall in love all the time, nothing to it, easiest thing in the world. I'm sure I can very easily fall in love with a girl who's rich if I put my mind to it."

Robert tells me Lion's being ridiculous because no rich girl in her right mind would dream of marrying him.

But I'm not so sure. Lion may be plain and he may be brainless, but he's six feet five in his stockinged feet and he has a splendid physique to complement his engaging personality, and I think there might well be an heiress who'll find him irresistible.

Anyway I've promised to do all I can to help. It'll take my mind off my marital problems, and besides . . . poor darling brainless penniless Lion really does need all the help he can get.

Life has been transformed—salvation is at hand! A Labour M.P. has dropped dead in South Wales, and Robert has been adopted by the Liberal Party as their candidate in the inevitable bye-election! The only trouble is that although Wales is a Liberal stronghold, this constituency of Pwlldu beyond the Rhondda Valley is so impoverished that the dreaded Labour Party has gained a grip on its voting population. The area is so scarred with coal mining that it looks like a fouled desert, the long bleak streets are lined with terrace-house slums, the children are barefoot, the women are old at thirty and the men are wizened and choking with coal-dust disease.

What can Harrow-and-Balliol Robert, one of Britain's charmed elite, say to such people? The new Labour candidate is a man of the working classes, a Welsh-speaking demagogue who wants people like Robert exterminated and the nation's wealth redistributed. I shudder but Robert is greatly stimulated. What a challenge! He can't resist it. Soon he's forgotten all his problems. He's too busy perfecting his rusty Welsh by hiring a tutor to converse with him, too busy planning strategy, too busy going respectfully to Mr. Lloyd George for tactical advice.

Mr. Lloyd George has always been friendly towards Robert, though in a detached way because Robert is an Asquith protégé, but now Mr. Lloyd George is beginning, like a baby, to "sit up and take notice." Mr. Lloyd George, naughty man, is certainly taking notice of *me* but luckily I find him absolutely resistible: too old, too crooked, too full of empty charm.

For the coming election I've ordered some new clothes, absolutely plain, all black and navy, no trimmings, and I'm cultivating a serious austere air so that no one will want to murder me for being a Society woman with a penchant for raiding divine Harrods. I've also been practicing "You *will* vote for my husband, won't you?" in Welsh in front of the looking glass. I can't remember much of the Welsh that we all picked up in a haphazard fashion from the Welsh-speaking nursemaids whom Margaret employed, but at least I can brush up a few choice phrases, and Mr. Lloyd George tells me my accent is superb.

Robert laughs admiringly as I trot out my Welsh phrases, and when he laughs I laugh too so that suddenly, miraculously, we're happy once more, no longer an ill-assorted husband and wife but *friends*, rushing off hand in hand into a thrilling new adventure.

"My dearest Ginette!" says Robert shining-eyed, and as he kisses me I know he doesn't mind anymore about his absurd plan to withdraw from London, just as I know that he's grateful to me for standing by him in his hour of need, just as a friend should, to stop him making such a terrible mistake.

"I love you," I say, and I do. I'm deeply connected to him by some unique emotion which has nothing to do with any conventional idea of passion—and suddenly as I realize this I know that in our minds we're back at Oxmoon, the lost Oxmoon of our childhood, and I can see the strawberries ripening beneath the powerful summer sun.

Life is still absolutely stunning—oh, I *am* enjoying myself! Robert has just made his last speech before the election, every word in Welsh, and his audience has cheered him to the echo. How did he do it? He's told his listeners that he's a Welshman but because he's had an English education he has a unique insight into those English minds at Westminster, and therefore he, unlike his opponent, is qualified to play the English at their own game with lasting benefit for Pwlldu. This is all nonsense, of course, but by playing on their nationalism he avoids the issue of class on which his opponent had hoped to impale him. And then, thrill of thrills, triumph of triumphs, Mr. Lloyd George, the greatest Welsh statesman since Owen Glendower, appears on the platform to endorse Robert's views and the audience go wild.

Victory is still touch-and-go, but if Robert does win tomorrow it will be a tremendous triumph not only for him but for the Liberal Party, which has lost too many seats to the Unionists in various bye-elections since the second general election of 1910. In fact the Unionists now have more seats in the House than the Liberals, and although at present the Labour Party backs Mr. Asquith, such support might prove unreliable in shifting circumstances, and obviously the Liberals would prefer to have their own man representing Pwlldu rather than a Labour ally who might or might not be loyal in the days to come.

I've been modest and retiring, loyal and admiring, bold and courageous, meek and mild, depending on which performance each occasion has required. I've been asked regularly for my views on the suffragettes, but I just say, "I love my husband and I think a woman's place is in the home."

However I'm beginning to think I'd rather like to be a Member of Parliament. All that glamour, that excitement, that intrigue, that power—delicious! I can see myself wearing trousers and smoking a cigar, like George Sand, and briskly calling the Cabinet to order.

Enough! No more idle fantasy. I'll never have the vote and I'll never have a seat in the House and I'll certainly never be Prime Minister. But I really do think darling Robert's going to be a huge political success, and that, when all's said and done, will be quite enough for me.

He did it. He won. He had a majority of over a thousand votes, and when the result was announced the waiting crowd began to sing "Land of Our Fathers." I cried. The party organizers cried. Robert wanted to cry but his English stiff upper lip was too much for him and he couldn't bring himself to do it. But he was very moved and very thrilled and afterwards, long afterwards when we were finally alone together, he thanked me for pushing him into politics and said he realized now that I had been absolutely right and he had been absolutely wrong on the subject of our withdrawal from London.

There's nothing mean about Robert. He's warm and honest and generous to his friends. We'll live in amity now, I'm sure of it, and all those horrid marital quarrels will belong entirely to the past as I continue to share his new career. Am I really being too optimistic if I write that I feel our long-delayed marital happiness is finally about to begin?

I wasn't being too optimistic. Our long-delayed marital happiness has begun, and please God may it go on forever. We've swept back to London in triumph and now everyone, but *everyone*, is panting to know us and we've been scooped into a frenetic social whirl.

I'm now passionate about London. All the trees are lush and green, all the flowers are glowing in the parks, a brilliant sun is blazing from cloudless skies. High noon in the capital of the world, high summer in ravishing glorious 1914 and there's no limit to the glamour and the gorgeousness—it's like the finale of some stupendous symphony except that unlike any other symphonic finale this one is set to stream on indefinitely with no end in sight. How lucky I am to be moderately young, moderately rich, vastly fortunate and vastly happy in such a place and at such a time! I feel now that nothing can stop all my dreams coming true.

Robert says we're riding the Wheel of Fortune; we've been at the bottom and now we're being carried right to the breathtaking top. What an alluring picture that conjures up! Robert says it's not an original metaphor of his as it was made famous by some old pet called Boethius who lived in the year dot. Darling Robert, always so intellectual! However I must confess that at the moment my thoughts tend to center on more prosaic matters, such as how I can acquire the evening gowns I need without propelling Robert into bankruptcy.

However Robert is perfect when I confess to him that I'm worried about my wardrobe, and he quite understands how important it is for me to be well dressed. In and out of all the famous houses we go—from Taplow to Panshanger, from Alderley to Avon Tyrrell, from Mells to the Wharf—we eat, we drink, we dance, we patronize the theater, the opera, Ascot and Henley—life's one long sumptuous party but like all parties it's hard work. One needs plenty of stamina. But I feel so full of *joie de vivre* that I barely notice any weariness, and Robert, still working hard at the bar, somehow manages to look radiant on four or five hours' sleep a night. He wants to accumulate as much money as possible this summer so that he can give his full attention to politics after the coming recess.

I simply doted on Number Ten when we were invited to dine there. I know they say Mr. Asquith drinks too much (When? Where? I've never seen any sign of it), but he's *such* a pet and I think he's just as keen on women as Mr. Lloyd George is although no doubt he's kept in check by the terrifying Margot. Or is he? I heard someone say . . . But no, I will *not* let this entry degenerate into vulgar tittle-tattle, no matter how much I adore finding out what *really* goes on behind the scenes! I always feel sorry for men having to pretend to be above gossip. So dreary for them, poor dears.

Anyway I'm in such a whirl I can hardly fit my appointments with my dressmaker into my crowded calendar, but I haven't forgotten Lion, who's busily bounding around looking for an heiress, and he has an open invitation to call at our house whenever he likes. I thought he might share chambers with Johnny, who's also working in town now, but they preferred to go their separate ways. In order to be fair, though, I've also given Johnny an open invitation to our house so now here I am with these two eligible young men on my hands, and I'm beginning to feel like Mrs. Bennet in *Pride and Prejudice*, a woman unable to think of anything except matrimony for her loved ones. Actually Johnny's too young for marriage; he's only twenty-two, whereas Lion's twenty-four, but Johnny is looking for a wife, I can sense that just as I can sense that he too is after money. But he doesn't confide in me. I used to think he confided in Robert, whom he hero-worships, but I now realize they talk only of intellectual matters.

Enigmatic Johnny, Bobby and Margaret's male replica of Bobby's beautiful, doomed, passionate mother—but unfortunately this romantic resemblance is only skin-deep. Johnny may be beautiful in his masculine way but he'll never wind up doomed; he's much too clever and ambitious, and he hasn't a scrap of passion in his prim puritanical little mind.

However I feel mean criticizing this paragon because he's pleasant and courteous and he really is doing very well. Having won a first in modern languages at Oxford he passed third out of four hundred entrants in the

Foreign Office examinations and is now settling down to be a success as a diplomat. Obviously he's toiling away trying to follow in Robert's brilliant footsteps, but this must be an unrewarding occupation, because Robert is so exceptional that Johnny, despite his considerable achievements, is always going to end up coming second. A first but no double first for Johnny at Oxford, no blues at cricket or rugger although he's good at games, no glamour and fame at his worthy but possibly dull position at the F.O. In fact if I were Johnny I'd loathe Robert but he doesn't. Johnny doesn't loathe anyone because that wouldn't be the Done Thing, and Doing the Done Thing is Johnny's prime delight in life. He's such a single-minded prig that I even wonder if he's a virgin but no, he can't be, he's much too good-looking, although his personality is so aseptic that I don't find him sexually attractive. That's just as well because no doubt Johnny would think that being sexually attractive isn't the Done Thing at all.

"Ginevra," he said to me the other day, "would you mind not calling me Johnny? I'm not in the nursery now and I find the name somewhat undignified."

I find it the only available antidote to his dreariness. Poor Johnny! So dull.

However Johnny can look after himself without my help. Lion can't. We toil away together hatching elaborate schemes as we plot the downfall of every heiress in sight, and whenever he wants to give up in despair I harangue him until he's feeling more cheerful. We usually end up giggling together. Robert hates this so we have to be careful not to giggle in his presence. Lion's terrified of Robert, and although he resents Robert's coldness he would secretly love to be friends so that he wouldn't have to be terrified anymore. He has a deep admiration of Robert's achievements and speaks reverently of Robert's intellect. I find this touching and tell Robert so.

"I'm getting very tired of Lion perpetually occupying my drawing room" is all Robert can say in reply. "Can you make it clear that I'd prefer him to call less often?"

Back we are in the nursery again. Robert isn't sexually jealous of Lion, of course, but he just can't bear not being the center of my attention. It reminds me of those dreadful scenes he made after Lion was born when he realized there was another little boy who had a claim on Margaret's time.

I somehow conceal my impatience and resentment but I'm determined not to abandon Lion. Without my constant encouragement he'd drift away brokenhearted to Oxmoon, but in my opinion he deserves a rich wife. After all, these rich girls have to marry, and think what ghastly men they constantly choose! Lion's not ghastly. He's affectionate and lovable, and he'll be so pleased to be saved from the dreariness of earning a living that he's bound to adore his savior. I think she'll be a very lucky girl . . . if we can find her.

Luckily Robert's been diverted from Lion by politics because he's now absorbed with the ordeal of making his maiden speech in the House. As a woman I was brought up to be uninterested in political issues. Margaret said all I needed to know was that the Liberals were for change and freedom while the Tories (as they were called when I was young) were wicked enough to want everything to stay exactly the same, even the poverty and suffering. The Godwins were a Whig family in the eighteenth century, and in the nineteenth they drifted along with the Liberal tide. Bobby is actually quite radical, despite his place in that established order which the Unionists seek to preserve unchanged. Bobby said to me once that anyone who had known impoverishment could never vote for the Unionists.

When Robert entered politics I wondered whether to study the big political issues such as Free Trade and Home Rule, but Robert said the last thing he wanted was a wife who held forth on politics, so I didn't bother. However I'm beginning to be interested in the major issues of the day and I do wish Robert would speak on Ireland. Declan would be impressed by his advanced views, but Robert is shying away from that graveyard of political reputations and says he intends to speak on foreign affairs. Such a pity, because what could be more dreary than foreign affairs at this time? Something's going on in the Balkans as usual but honestly, who cares? Something's always going on in the Balkans; it's a standing joke, just like that hoary old warning regularly issued by the Job's Comforters that we're on the brink of war. I've been hearing that for years and I'll believe it when it happens. Meanwhile the Balkans are a big bore as usual. Let the Balkanese get on with it, I say, and good luck to them. I've got more important things to worry about.

What am I going to wear when Robert makes his maiden speech?

What a stunning success we both were yesterday! I wore royal blue, the skirt of the costume so narrow at the ankle that I could barely glide, and the material draped and swathed in gorgeous curvy lines over my hips and legs. A new corset and three days' rigorous banting had ensured a slim waist, and all the surplus flesh above was pushed upwards so that my bosom, discreetly swathed beneath pale blue trimmings, was guaranteed to rivet the male eye. I also wore a sumptuous new hat decorated with osprey feathers (thirty guineas at divine Harrods), and when I entered the gallery even the male monsters on the benches below dropped their eyeglasses and gaped. Sometimes I do think the suffragettes are very stupid. They shouldn't go around wrecking everything in sight. All they need to do to get the vote is wear splendid hats and look lavish.

Darling Robert made a wonderful speech about the boring old Balkans and was warmly congratulated. Later so was I—in fact we were both positively weighed down with "dewdrops" and the evening finished in a haze of champagne. What heaven! I adored every minute of it, and in the midst of so much euphoria I quite forgot Lion but lo and behold, today he's appeared again, madly in love, and says this is *it* and please could I help him and he's utterly desperate because he knows his whole future happiness is at stake.

She's perfect for him. Her name is Daphne Wynter-Hamilton, and her father, Sir Cuthbert, has a house in Belgravia and thousands of acres in Scotland complete with castle and grouse moor. Daphne is an only child. Her father dotes on her—and her wretched mother, of course, wants her to marry someone with a title and ten thousand a year.

But this is a nice, sensible girl, not pretty but very jolly, and she doesn't mind Lion having no money. She's passionate about him and he's passionate about her and whenever they're not giggling together they're sighing into each other's eyes. Yes, they must certainly marry but how are we going to overcome the cold-eyed mother who thinks a penniless younger son of an untitled Welsh squire is about as low as one can go without sinking into the middle classes?

I'm going to ask Robert if he can cultivate Sir Cuthbert.

"Good God, certainly not!" said Robert. "Let Lion fight his own battles! Ginette, you'll oblige me, if you please, by doing as I say and terminating this consuming interest you have in Lion's affairs. I'm not prepared to tolerate it any longer, and for the good of our marriage I'm now drawing the line."

I'm back with my husband again. My friend has vanished. I'm back with this ghastly male monster who says that for the good of our marriage I should obey him unquestioningly—even when he's being unreasonable and wrong.

Of course we've just had the most appalling row. I felt so angry with Robert after our clash this afternoon that this evening I flirted with a charming American at a reception in Grosvenor Square. I knew at the time that it was a stupid thing to do, but I wanted Robert to know how livid I was with him.

I'll never do it again, though, because just now, when we were shouting at each other in the bedroom, I felt genuinely frightened. Violence always frightens me and Robert is potentially a violent man. Curiously enough Conor, who was certainly a violent man in some ways, was never violent with me; when he wanted to hurt me he just slept with someone else or perhaps extorted my money to lose at poker. But that's not Robert's style. Robert's style is first to slap me so hard across the mouth that I fall backwards across the bed and second to assert himself in the most obvious way available. It's not rape exactly because I'm sensible enough to give in without a fight, but whatever it is, it's vile. All I could think in the bathroom afterwards was: Conor would never have done that, never, never, never. And to my horror I found myself grieving for Conor all over again.

Robert apologized afterwards but spoiled the apology by adding: "Nevertheless I'm your husband and I'm entitled to make a strong demonstration of my marital rights if you appear to need reminding of your marital duties." Anyone would think I'd been guilty of the grossest infidelity, yet all I had done was flutter my eyelashes at this inoffensive diplomat over a glass of champagne.

However with great self-restraint I made no comment on Robert's monstrous statement and presently in bed in the dark, he slipped his hand into mine to show he wanted to be friends. What's my final verdict? Oh, I daresay we shall be friends again in a day or two. I don't mind Robert when he's trying to be a friend. It's when he's trying to be a husband that he's so absolutely bloody impossible.

I now feel quite exhausted with getting Lion off my hands, almost too exhausted to consider the problem of the school holidays. Declan is determined to go to Ireland again and Rory is determined to go too, but although I'm not keen on this I feel I can't cope with them here while Robert's being even more possessive than usual. With reluctance I shall tell them that they can spend the first month of the holidays with Dervla and Seamus but the second month must be spent with me—and yet I'm sure now, if I drum up the courage to be honest with myself, that this time when Declan goes to Ireland he'll have no intention of ever coming back.

How did the war creep on me like this? One moment I was thinking of Lion battling for Daphne and worrying what in God's name I was going to do about Declan, and the next moment the ultimatum was expiring and the Germans were on the rampage. I know a great many people felt they had been taken by surprise but I thought I should have been more aware of what was going on.

"Why didn't you tell me how crucial matters had become, Robert?"

"I thought all you cared about was getting Lion married."

Robert's still being thoroughly impossible. I know I should put matters right by being especially warm and loving to him, but frankly I can't be bothered. I want someone to be warm and loving to *me*. I'm desperately upset about Declan, and I'll never forget that dreadful scene two weeks ago on the eve of his departure for Ireland. . . .

"Declan, you're not coming back, are you?"

"No, I'm sorry, Ma, but it's impossible. I promised Cousin Bobby I'd stick it for a year to see if things got better, but they haven't. I loathe that school. I loathe England. I loathe Robert."

"Do you loathe me?"

"Yes, sometimes. But generally I just feel you're no use to me and I'd be better off on my own. Are you going to raise hell if I don't come back?"

"There's no point, is there?"

We were silent for a time. We were in his room, which only so recently I had planned for him with such care. It still looked new and unused, a symbol of his hatred of the house and everyone in it. Declan looked older than fifteen because he was tall. His dark hair grew exactly like Conor's and even waved in the same places. His dark eyes, also exactly like Conor's, regarded me with gravity. A lump formed in my throat. I turned away.

"Will you remember," I said to him, "that this separation's not of my choosing? Will you remember that whatever happens I love you and will always want you to come back?"

"I couldn't come back so long as you're married to Robert, Ma. So it's no use wanting the impossible."

"But you'll write to me?"

"No. I don't want any correspondence. I want to start again without having to read your letters telling me how miserable I've made you."

"I wouldn't reproach you, I swear it—"

"The very letters would be a reproach. I'll send news regularly to Aunt Dervla, and if you want to know what's happening you can write to her."

"Oh Declan—"

"No, it's no use crying, Ma. You've brought all this on yourself, behaving like a whore, betraying Pa's memory, smashing all my faith in you by marrying a bastard like Robert—"

I left him, and the next day he left me. I managed to control myself at the station but when I arrived home I shut myself in my darkened room and cried as I had not cried since Conor's death fourteen months before.

"I'm sorry," said Robert. "Very sorry. I know how you must feel. But it may all be for the best."

My nerve snapped. I flew at him, hit him, screamed that I wished we'd never married. Then I burst into tears again and flung myself down upon the bed.

I felt him sit beside me but he said nothing, and when at last I felt compelled to look at him I saw his face was stricken with grief. His pain was obviously so genuine that I couldn't bear it. One can be driven to be cruel to a husband, but no matter how adverse the circumstances one should never be cruel to a friend.

Struggling upright I pushed my tangled hair away from my face and put my arms around him. After I had apologized I said, "You did your best, you tried so hard, this failure isn't your fault. Some problems really are insoluble and Declan's one of them. There's nothing we can do but let him go."

He seemed not to hear. He whispered, "Do you really wish you'd never married me?"

"Darling, I wish no such thing, and I don't hate you either, but do try to understand. I've just lost my son. I'm demented with grief—"

"Of course. Yes. Forgive me—oh God, what a fool I am sometimes," said my poor friend, pathetically acknowledging how baffling such a complex situation was to his simple emotional nature. He put his arms around me and we hugged each other. Finally he said in a low voice, "I'm beginning to think I've been a most obtuse and unhelpful husband. I must try and put matters right. You mean everything to me, Ginette, everything in the world, so . . . what can I do? Tell me how I can help you get over this tragedy."

I kissed him to show how precious he was to me. Then when I was calm enough to speak, I said, "I want to have a baby."

Robert's response is perfect. He says it's the best possible idea and he's only sorry he didn't think of it himself because he wants a child just as much as I do.

No more douches of vinegar. No more sordid little chunks of sponge tied with flesh-colored thread. The dreary side of physical love will be eliminated for nine blissful months, and at the end of it all will be another adorable bundle in a shawl, a new little Robert Godwin for Oxmoon—or perhaps a little Ginevra for myself. I've always longed for a daughter. What a pity it was that my first marriage was so arduous that I never had the strength to embark on a third pregnancy, but at least now I can make up for lost time. Conor wanted a daughter. I'll never forget the rows we had after Rory was born and I, encouraged by a sophisticated friend, started to conspire against pregnancy with the aid of vinegar and sponges. I can so clearly remember Conor shouting that it was contrary to his religious principles and he wanted me to have a baby every year.

"And who's going to look after them?" I screamed, demented with motherhood as I struggled to survive two small boys with the aid of incompetent nursemaids. "And who's going to pay for them?"

Sulks. Then a smile. Then a laugh. And finally acquiescence, laced with the charm that made me forgive him everything. "Suit yourself, sweetheart, but say nothing more. Then I'll lie more easily in the confessional."

What a villain he was, but how we laughed! And we did so enjoy my pregnancies, our times in bed became better than ever—and of course that was why he wanted me to be constantly pregnant, the rogue; it had nothing to do with his religion at all.

I understood him and he understood me but now Robert finally understands me too so all's well. Oh, I simply can't wait to conceive. . . .

This war is really rather alarming. At first, reassured by Harrods' notice that business would be as usual, I thought the squabble would be a nine-day wonder, but ghastly things have been happening in Belgium and someone's now invited me to a charity bridge afternoon to raise money for the refugees. I don't play bridge but I'm going to learn. The Asquiths are mad about it. However I can't learn just yet because there's no time. Darling Lion, triumphantly engaged to be married at last, is busy telling me I'm the best sister-in-law a man ever had and I'm just wholeheartedly agreeing with him when we hear that our joint victory has been eclipsed by his younger brother. Johnny has announced his engagement to the beauty of the season, Blanche Lankester. How typical! Lion huffs and puffs, I moan and groan, we both end up in a stupor of exhaustion securing a nice plain little girl who apart from her money is nothing out of the ordinary, and then Johnny, without any apparent effort, walks off with the catch that richer and more blue-blooded men than he have been fighting for since the season began.

"How did you do it?" gasps poor Lion, overcome with admiration. "You're just as penniless as I am!"

"True," says Johnny, who I'm beginning to think is a very cool customer indeed, "but my prospects at the F.O. are excellent, and Mr. Lankester is convinced that I have a first-class diplomatic career ahead of me."

The benign Mr. lankester has a large estate in Herefordshire, a house in Connaught Square and a private fortune which Margaret might describe as "useful." Like Daphne, Blanche is an only child. I would love to write that she's a spoiled bitch of an heiress certain to make her smooth-tongued Lothario unhappy, but honesty compels me to admit the child is perfect. She's eighteen, charming, lovely, modest and accomplished. In fact she's the kind of girl who makes a married woman like me feel like a garish old war-horse. I'm probably jealous of her youth. Let me combat my jealousy by saying how lucky Johnny is. I feel her musical talent, which is considerable, is quite wasted on him, since he's one of those people who only recognize "God Save the King" because people stand up.

I still say he's too young to get married, but if Mr. Lankester's happy with his daughter's fate, who am I to criticize? I think Bobby and Margaret are perturbed, though, for Bobby's been dispatched to London to size up the situation, but Bobby is charmed by Blanche and confesses himself unable to object to the match.

Silly Lion's talking of enlisting. I tell him it's pointless as the war will be over by Christmas, but he thinks being a soldier would be a terrific lark. Apparently down at Oxmoon Edmund thinks so too. Men *are* odd. I can't see the point of enduring all sorts of tedious discomforts like poor food and primitive lavatories unless there really is a chance that the war will last, but Sir John French will soon mop up the Germans and everyone will be on their way home again before Lion can emerge from some dreary training camp. Thank God I'm a woman and can sit at home and knit Balaclava helmets. Who in their right mind would want to do anything else?

Silly Lion.

I can't conceive. At least I'm sure I can, but I haven't yet. I tell myself it's because I'm still so upset about Declan, and that's true; I am. But Rory was so nice to me when he came back from Ireland, and I'm sure he'll be less difficult now that Declan's gone. I wonder what he'll think when I have the baby. Declan would have hated it but I suspect Rory will be generous. He's more forgiving and has such an easygoing nature.

Oh, I do hope I conceive soon! Perhaps this time next year I'll be preparing for the christening. . . .

Excitement about the war is rising to fever pitch and all we need now, as Robert says sardonically, is a panegyric from Kipling. However Robert takes a bleak view which is quite out of step with all this raging Jingoism. He says he knows death too well to be deceived; he says death often appears brilliantly attired in the theater of life, but once that mesmerizing figure starts to move downstage the gorgeous garments dissolve to reveal the horrors beneath. What a revolting image. I thought Robert had finally set aside that morbid obsession with death, but it would take a morbid mind to imagine that death could ever seem glamorous. It's war that's glamorous, not death. It's death that makes war vile. I know war is vile, of course I do, but nevertheless unlike Robert I do see the glamour of this great European convulsion. It's jolted everyone out of their ruts, sent a thrill of excitement crackling through all the ranks of society and united our unstable problem-racked country in an electrifying comradeship against the common foe.

However as usual I have Lion to divert me because it now looks as if he'll be sent to France in the new year and he wants to marry before he goes. (I thought the war would be over by Christmas but it seems everyone's got bogged down in France. Such a bore.) I told Lion to press for an early wedding day, and to my surprise the Wynter-Hamiltons have now given way. But no doubt they feel that our fighting men have to be humored wherever possible, and certainly everyone's rushing to the altar at the moment. Even Johnny's taking advantage of the current rage for the quick marriage, although there's no obligation on him to rush into uniform; his position at the Foreign Office would exempt him from military service even if military service were compulsory—which it isn't. However I can see Johnny's becoming muddled about his position because although he wants to do the Done Thing as usual, he can't work out what the Done Thing is. Should he resign and enlist? Or should he stay where he is? Robert tells him in no uncertain terms that anyone can enlist but not everyone can do Johnny's work at the F.O., and that as the Home Front will ultimately be as important as the Front Line, Johnny has an absolute moral duty to stay where he is. That settles it. He stays.

Robert sets Johnny an example, thank God, by deciding from the start to stay at Westminster, and he says he's determined to stick to that decision no matter how long we're bogged down in France. Of course being a Member of Parliament is more important than being a Foreign Office clerk, but Robert says the principle is the same: he can be of more service to the nation at home than overseas. And now this truth has just been confirmed by Mr. Asquith himself who has dropped a hint that Robert will be given an Under-Secretaryship at the earliest opportunity. Robert can hardly flout the Prime Minister's plans for him so there's nothing he can do now but remain in London—unlike his friend Raymond, who isn't yet a Member of Parliament and will probably enlist. But perhaps Raymond, like Lion and Edmund, is keen to be a soldier. At least it'll give him a respite from the legal and political worlds for which he apparently has so little enthusiasm.

"You're not secretly longing to escape into uniform, are you, Robert?" I say nervously, just to make sure.

"Good God, no," says Robert. "I wouldn't want to compete with death when the odds are stacked against me."

That chills me. It chills him too—but we're chilled for different reasons. Robert's chilled because he's afraid I'll think him a coward, but I don't, I just think he's appallingly rational; I could never doubt Robert's courage after hearing the details of that fearful climbing accident. No, I'm chilled because he's implied how badly the war's going and because he probably has secret information about the current situation in France.

"Asquith's got us into the war," says Robert, "and now he thinks all he has to do is let the generals get on with it. But I don't share Asquith's touching faith in generals. God knows where it'll all end."

I say, "Don't let's talk about it anymore." Honestly, I'd rather not face such pessimism, and Robert, seeing he's distressed me, falls silent.

I'm not worried about Lion. Lion will bounce in and out of danger with his usual insouciance and regale us all later with amusing stories about how he won the war. But it's Edmund's fate that terrifies me—twenty-year-old mild gentle Edmund who loves gardening and whose biggest problem has always been how many rashers of bacon to have for breakfast. Could anyone be less suited to a military life? Yet he says he wants to do his bit to ensure that the Huns are kept out of Oxmoon. Edmund loves Oxmoon. Since he left school he's been pottering around there, officially helping Bobby on the estate, but I think he spends most of his time growing roses. Bobby and Margaret, who are both so insistent that Lion should be employed in London, are far more lax with Edmund because they accept how unworldly Edmund is, how un-suited to earning a living in a city. How can he ever survive this nightmare waiting for him in France?

I can't bear to dwell on that so I won't.

I'll think of Celia instead. Poor Celia has been staying with us for a few days, and I've been drumming up eligible men for her to meet, but alas! I know she hasn't a hope of suiting them. She's thirty now and yearns to be married but has never had anyone in love with her. What can it be like to be a virgin of thirty, six feet tall with mousy hair, protuberant eyes and a flat bosom? I think I'd cut my throat and pray for reincarnation in a more tolerable form. How unfair it is that women's entire lives depend on their physical appearance! I honestly do feel very sorry for Celia, and so although she drives me to distraction with her boring conversation, I make every effort to be nice to her.

Robert just treats her as an imbecile, of course, but then Robert would. It's men like Robert who make life hell for women like Celia.

Anyway poor Celia's rather a strain, and then on top of that I now have a fearful servant problem because perfect Bennett, butler and valet *par excellence*, has regretfully decided that it's his patriotic duty to enlist. Really, it's small wonder I'm not pregnant. I've got much too much on my mind.

Lion looks gorgeous in his uniform. He says he adored his training camp and can't wait to get to France. Poor Daphne looks up at him with shining eyes. Can it really be two weeks since they were married? It seems like yesterday. Johnny marries Blanche tomorrow at St. James's Piccadilly, and Robert, who's to be the best man, has taken him out tonight to celebrate his last evening as a bachelor. Not that Johnny's interested in getting drunk and having a good time; he'll go home early and be tucked up in bed by midnight.

But Robert will come home and I'll seduce him. Oh, how I wish I could get this baby started. . . .

Christmas at Oxmoon. Bobby and Margaret utter not one word of reproach that we haven't visited them since our wedding a year ago, but I talk too much out of guilt about how frantically busy we've been. Margaret asks me in private if all's well, and I say yes, simply divine and I'm trying to have a baby. I shouldn't have mentioned the baby before it's been conceived—not the Done Thing—but I had to find some way of convincing her that Robert and I are in the seventh heaven of marital bliss.

Margaret says, "That's nice, dear; I'm so glad" and rearranges her mourning brooches into an octagon.

Robert seems closer to his mother than ever, and now I notice that his feelings go beyond mere filial respect. Neither of them shows emotion to the other; they're much too English for that, but in a crowded room he seeks her out as if she's the only person worth talking to, and in his company she seems to relax her grip on that relentless air of refinement and become blunter, pithier and wittier. She doesn't quite slip back into her Staffordshire accent, which I can dimly remember, but I can now look at her and see that tough energetic forthright little girl in her teens who looked after me so conscientiously during my earliest years long ago.

To my horror I find that I'm jealous of her close alliance with Robert. He treats her as an equal. He treats her as if she's capable of balancing a checkbook. He treats her as a friend.

I don't get treated as a friend anymore. That thrilling campaign at Pwlldu was just a romantic interlude. I've now been permanently converted into an object labeled WIFE, and I hate it, I hate being treated as if I'm an inferior being incapable of understanding a subject like politics. I know much more about politics now and I would certainly vote sensibly if I were given the chance. . . . Heavens, I'm beginning to sound like a suffragette! I must stop before I succumb to the urge to chain myself to the nearest railing.

The truth is it's no good grumbling about Robert. He has his tiresome side, just as we all do, and I've no choice but to resign myself to it until we can embark on our joint venture, parenthood. Once I'm pregnant matters are bound to improve because of course the baby will draw us together.

Or will it?

Yes, of course the baby will draw us together. I was feeling drenched in pessimism when I wrote that last sentence because the most ghastly things have been happening in France. But I won't think of them. Robert's become convinced that the country can't continue in wartime with a one-party government, and he talks privately of coalition and reorganization. I now actively enjoy Robert's reports from Westminster not only because I'm becoming increasingly interested in politics but because it stops me thinking about what might be happening in France.

Lion's left now and Edmund's also due to leave soon. They're in different regiments, which I think is a good thing because one hears frightful stories of multiple fraternal casualties sustained during a single offensive.

London seems full of men in uniform now and the whole atmosphere of the city has changed. People say the tough new liquor laws are at the bottom of the new sobriety, but it's not as simple as that. Everyone I know is still drinking like a fish—more so than ever, in fact, and the social life goes on at a hysterical pace as if to compensate for the abnormal times we live in, but London is darker, mentally darker; mentally London is now gunmetal-gray, and the symbol of this bleakness is DORA, the Defence of the Realm Acts, which give the government dictatorial powers to keep us all in order. Nobody talks about "Business As Usual" now. The talk is all of DORA and the servant crisis and whether so-and-so really is a Swiss and not a German who ought to be locked up.

But perhaps London seems so bleak to me because today I had the most depressing consultation with a gynecologist who told me I may have damaged myself by indulging in what Mrs. Sanger has described so neatly as "birth control." It's the only explanation he can offer for my failure to conceive. I hated him, although I'm not sure why. I hated him for being the bearer of gloomy tidings but perhaps there was another reason too for my deep antipathy. He made me feel like an imbecile. He was Robert in a different guise.

Damn it, why shouldn't a woman practice birth control if she wants? It's her body and no man has the right to dictate to her what she should do with it.

Oh, I feel so angry sometimes, so *angry* . . .

"Ginevra!"

"Julie? Is it—can it be Julie?"

It was indeed Julie Harrington, who had been at boarding school with my old friend Gwen de Bracy. Gwen and I had for some years shared a governess with Angela Stourham, but at the age of fourteen Gwen had been sent to finish her education at Eastbourne and later Julie, her new friend, had spent more than one holiday with her at Penhale Manor.

"Ginevra, it's been years! How are you?"

"My dear, quite overcome that we should bump into each other like this in the middle of Piccadilly—do you have time to pop into the divine Ritz for a cup of coffee?"

Julie is thirty-four, a few months younger than I am, but unlike me she's not married and she has a job. Why, I ask her (I know she doesn't have to work for a living). She says she does it because she likes it. She has a good job. She's not just an office clerk working for a pittance. She's an editor on that dreary magazine *A Woman's Place* which instructs its readers how to embroider tablecloths, but Julie's trying to broaden the magazine's outlook by including articles on modern life. It sounds interesting. *She's* interesting. I'm so puzzled about why she's never married (obviously she must have had her chances) that in the end I ask her directly. She says she's never fancied it. How peculiar. Can she be a Lesbian, I wonder? How exciting! I've never met a Lesbian before and have always longed to find out what they actually *do*.

Julie lives *all alone* in a little flat in Bloomsbury and *she has a checkbook*. I saw it when she opened her smart leather handbag. (How did we all manage without handbags a few years ago?) Naturally I suspect her of being a suffragette but somehow I can't quite see her attempting to strip Mr. Asquith naked on a golf course. She's far too busy enjoying her independent life.

I wouldn't like a life like that, of course, but I admire her for having the courage to live it, and we get on very well—so well that finally I tell her what a beastly visit I've had to the gynecologist and how horrid doctors can be to women sometimes.

"Why not go to a doctor who's a woman?" says Julie carelessly. "I do."

A woman doctor! Heavens, how daring. But I like the idea, and when I tell Julie so, we arrange to meet again. I won't tell Robert, though. He'd just say women are temperamentally unsuited for the upper reaches of the medical profession, and besides . . . I don't think he'd care at all for Julie Harrington.

"How do you do, Mrs. Godwin. I'm Dr. Drysdale—do sit down."

The lady doctor was tweedy and foursquare but so kind and she quite understood why I'd spent so much time cutting up sponges into little chunks and drenching myself in oceans of vinegar. She also assured me that it was most unlikely that I'd done myself any harm because she could see no evidence of scarring or infection.

"However," she added honestly, "I do think this: if you've managed to avoid pregnancy for thirteen years with only douches and sponges to help you, you might well be less fertile than the average woman." But she added to encourage me: "Even so, that's no reason why you shouldn't have a baby eventually."

She then asked me about Robert. "He's anxious for this baby, is he?"

"Oh yes! He's been so understanding about it!"

"Excellent," said Dr. Drysdale satisfied. "I only ask because sometimes when all isn't well between husband and wife, the wife becomes too tense to conceive."

"Oh, that couldn't apply to me at all," I said glibly, but as soon as the words were spoken I began to wonder.

"Robert, you remember Julie, of course."

"Indeed I do—how are you, Miss Harrington—but I don't think we ever had much to do with each other in the old days, did we? You two girls went off with Gwen while I went off with Gwen's brothers and the two sets seldom met. . . ."

Julie had telephoned me earlier to ask if she could interview me for an article she was writing on the servant problem, so I had invited her to tea and soon after her arrival she had asked me if I had ever thought of writing professionally. Would I be interested, for instance, in writing a thousand words about life in New York?

"How long's a thousand words?"

"A lengthy letter to your best friend."

I had been excited by this idea because I knew it would take my mind off the subject of pregnancy. I had told Julie I would try, and then just as our delightful tea party was concluding Robert arrived home from his chambers in the Temple, and having no alternative I had reintroduced him to her.

For a time all went well. They chatted about the old days at Penhale Manor and discussed the de Bracys. In fact I was just thinking with relief that I had been wrong in assuming they would detest each other when the conversation started heading for disaster.

"But you would agree, surely," said Robert to Julie in response to a remark of hers about working women, "that most women find fulfillment in the home."

"Yes," said Julie, "I think I would agree with that. A canary shut up in a cage will find fulfillment by singing. Otherwise it would die of melancholy."

"Darling," I said quickly to Robert, "shall I ring for more tea or are you in a rush to get to the House?"

"No—no tea, thanks. Am I to take it then, Miss Harrington," said Robert, settling down to annihilate her with his usual forensic skill, "that you don't believe women find their greatest happiness in being wives and mothers?"

"Not being a wife or mother, I wouldn't know."

"Exactly. In other words—"

"All I know is," said Julie, "that I'm very happy exactly as I am."

"But you don't pretend to speak for the majority."

"No, I speak for myself. I don't pretend to speak for all women—how could I? All women are different."

"But nevertheless, despite the minor differences, you must surely concede that all women want at heart to be wives and mothers."

"No. They don't. I don't. I disprove that entire thesis simply by my happy existence."

"Robert darling," I said in a rush, "we really mustn't delay you if you're on your way to the House."

"But Miss Harrington, don't you find your solitary life very lonely?"

"Why should you assume my life is solitary?"

"No doubt you have a wide circle of friends, but when you're at home don't you miss the companionship of a husband?"

"Good God, no!" said Julie amused. "I see my lover two or three times a week and that's quite enough for me, thank you!"

I was stunned. I realized I had just seen Robert outtalked, outwitted and outmaneuvered in a debate—I had just seen Robert *defeated—and by a woman!* Amidst my horror that the meeting should have ended in disaster, a small voice at the back of my mind whispered: "Good—and about time too."

"My dears!" I said, somehow finding my tongue, "what an enthralling dialogue! But now I must ask you to excuse Robert, Julie, because he really does have to rush off to Westminster—"

"—and besides," said Robert, recouping his losses with professional smoothness, "no matter how enthralling the dialogue I feel too handicapped by my upbringing as a gentleman to bring the argument to any rational conclusion. Chivalry insists, Miss Harrington, that I allow you to have the last word."

"How charming of you," said Julie smiling at him, "but isn't this supposed to be the twentieth century? We're not in the Middle Ages now, you know!"

Robert somehow restrained himself from slamming the door as he walked out.

"Darling, how lovely—you're back early!"

He arrived home soon after eight but not before I had prepared my defenses. I was going to say "Heavens, these feminists—such a bore!" but when Robert immediately announced, "I trust you won't ask that woman here again—I don't want you associating with anyone who talks like Rebecca West in *The Clarion,*" I suddenly found my patience was exhausted.

"It's heavenly of you to be so concerned for me, darling," I said, "but I think I might be allowed to choose my own friends."

"Any woman who leads a Bohemian way of life and who is almost certainly a suffragist, if not a demented suffragette, is certainly not fit company for any wife of mine!"

"Oh, what absolute—" I paused to choose between the New York obscenity and the raw English slang but (no doubt fortunately) he did not allow me to finish.

"I'm sorry, Ginette, but I refuse to allow you to associate with a woman who despises marriage—she'll introduce you to the wrong people, she'll encourage you to take a lover—"

"You don't seriously think I'd take a lover, do you?"

"Well, why not?" he said. "You've done it before."

I felt as if I had been assaulted, not merely slapped in the face but slammed in the stomach. Turning my back on him I groped my way to the *secrétaire* and sat down abruptly on the chair beside it. I wanted to remind him that I was trying to have his child and that other men had never seemed less important, but all speech was impossible.

"I'm sorry," said Robert at last. I thought he was going to embark on some conciliatory speech but when he could only repeat in misery "I'm sorry," I saw he had shocked himself as much as he had shocked me. Eventually he added: "I suppose I'm uneasy because I know you're restless and dissatisfied."

"Only because I haven't been able to conceive! And you don't make life any easier when you refuse to let me choose my friends and refuse to allow me any control over my money—"

"Oh God, not that old quarrel again!"

"It may seem nothing to you!" I shouted. "But it means a very great deal to me! I hate having nothing of my own—God, no wonder I want a baby, what else do I have that's even partly mine? Everything is yours—yours, yours, yours! It's *your* house, *your* money, *your* career and *your* friends whose wives I have to cultivate—boring silly women though most of them are! And then on top of that I find I have no individuality anymore, I'm just *your* wife, someone who can be treated with contempt!"

"Christ Almighty, how dare you say that!" He was white with rage. "I've made all manner of sacrifices to give you what you want! I love you more than anyone else in the world and yet you spend your whole time being discontented, nagging me because I've finally reduced *your* life to the order *you* wanted and offered you a world which is compatible with *your* idea of happiness! Very well, just what the devil is it you want from me—and from life? I'm beginning to think you're just a spoiled pampered Society woman who can think only of herself!"

I did not reply immediately. I could only stare down at the sloping surface of the desk but at last I said in despair, "Perhaps that's true. I don't know. I just know I'm upset at the moment because I'm still not pregnant. I'd no idea before how awful it is to want a baby and not be able to start one."

"Well, I want a child as much as you do," said Robert, "but if this is what happens when you attempt maternity I'd rather we remained a childless couple."

"Oh yes," I said drearily, too exhausted to do more than retreat into passive acquiescence, "I daresay I've been difficult lately. But you see," I added, somehow dredging up the strength to make one final effort to clarify my feelings, "that's why I've so enjoyed meeting Julie again. She's helped to take my mind off the awful problem of pregnancy—she's suggested that I write an article for her magazine—"

"Oh, I couldn't permit that," said Robert.

"But I want to!"

"I'm sorry, I hate having to repeat myself, but I can't have you associating with that woman."

"Robert." I rose to my feet, dashed away the tears that had collected in my eyes and walked straight up to him. "Robert, you mustn't go on treating me like this. It's disastrous. You're acting as if you're so uncertain of my love that you have to resort to tyranny to feel secure!"

"What nonsense! I'm just trying to be a good husband!"

"In that case could you possibly try not to be such a good husband? You used to behave so differently when we were merely friends—"

"Of course I did—before we were married we were two independent people! But marriage isn't about independence, Ginette, it's about dependence. It's a mutually beneficial arrangement, guarded by a web of rights and duties, to encompass the biological fact of life that women are weak and need to be looked after while men are strong and seek to protect them."

"Yes, of course, but—"

"You wish to be unmarried and independent, perhaps?"

"No—oh, God, no, I'd hate to live Julie's kind of life—well, how could I, all those awful men battering away at my defenses, I'd be half-dead with terror in no time, no, I must have someone to look after me, I absolutely must—"

"Then I fail to see how you can criticize me as a husband."

I gave up. I was miserable, baffled and in utter despair. As usual I knew that rationally he was right—and as usual I sensed that in some way beyond my powers of definition he was absolutely wrong.

Robert is as thoroughly upset by this conversation as I am, but he won't give in and eventually, to make life more bearable, I let him think that he's achieved a reconciliation. How chilling that competence in bed seems now. I lie awake in the dark and think so longingly of Conor that when I fall asleep I dream of him and know all the pleasure that Robert's failed to give me. I wake up full of joy but then I remember. Conor's dead. The man next to me in the dark is Robert. This is 1915 and Conor's been dead nearly two years.

I don't suppose I'll have the baby now. I'll always be too upset to conceive. Maybe it doesn't matter but yes, it does, it matters terribly. Both Daphne and Blanche have confided to me that their husbands didn't spend their honeymoons in idleness, but although I'm trying so hard to be happy for the girls I can't help feeling twinges of jealousy. I must beat them back before I start to share Robert's belief that I'm just a spoiled selfish Society woman. *Am* I so spoiled and selfish? I don't mean to be, I honestly don't, I do try not to want the baby but it's no good, I have such an urgent need to fill the gap that Declan's left in my life and I find I'm longing for the baby more than ever.

I shall divert myself by thinking of that article on New York. For of course I'm going to write it. And of course I'm going to see Julie again.

Oh, I've had such fun! I wrote a very racy article and Julie says it's mesmerizing. The only piece she's cut is the anecdote about the preacher and his three wives—she's kept my description of cabarets and she's even kept my explanation of why streetwalkers are called streetwalkers! (But she says her senior editor may strike this out.) I feel very proud and very happy and for hours and hours I haven't thought of the baby at all.

I'm to be paid ten guineas. I daren't ask for the sum in cash; that would give rise to the suspicion that I was working behind my husband's back. But what do I do with the check? Would the bank hand over the money to me without telling Robert? Whatever happens Robert mustn't hear about this. I think the only answer is to endorse the check to the Red Cross and look upon my writing as war work. That'll help alleviate my guilt, and nowadays I'm not just guilty that I'm deceiving Robert; I'm guilty because I haven't been knitting socks or visiting maimed young men or canteening or organizing a bridge afternoon to raise money for war orphans. One longs to do *something*, but I loathe hospitals, and I tend to shy away from the bossy worthy souls who flourish in charitable organizations.

I've stopped trying not to think of the war. It's impossible not to think of it. One can hardly believe that a year ago there was cricket at Lords and racing at Ascot and everyone was chattering away about what they were going to wear at Cowes. Now there's no formal sport at all and everyone's talking of the Zeppelins whenever they're not whispering about the report of the Royal Commission on Venereal Diseases. They've even revived that awful old play *Damaged Goods* which Robert says he doesn't have the time to see, but I wouldn't mind seeing even a play about venereal disease—I'd welcome anything that would take my mind off the ghastly events in the Gallipoli Peninsula which have followed the disaster in the Dardanelles. I thank God daily that both Lion and Edmund are embroiled in the stalemate in France, although God knows there's little to choose between one hell and the other.

It's such a relief to turn from the news of the overseas horrors to my personal reports from Robert on the Home Front. Robert says a coalition is now certain but he's sure Asquith has the power to come out on top. Churchill will have to be dropped, though, after the Dardanelles debacle, and how many other Liberals will have to be butchered to make room for the leading Unionists? To my astonishment I find I'm becoming quite obsessed with politics, but better to be obsessed with what might or might not be happening at Westminster than to be obsessed with what might or might not be happening in France.

Darling Lion writes that he's at last found the life that suits him: eating, sleeping and gossiping in an amusing little billet behind the lines. He's somewhere near Neuve Chapelle where the British recently pierced the German lines, but Edmund is nearer the front than Lion. Edmund is at Ypres. How frightened I feel when I remember Edmund but he sent me a placid little letter recently saying what a bore it was to have to cart around a gas mask.

Men have been gassed during this second battle of Ypres. They say the results of gassing are—no, I mustn't think of such things, I *mustn't.*

I'll think instead of Mrs. Pankhurst proclaiming the suffragists' desire to help in the war effort. Even Robert is impressed by this desire of the suffragists to put patriotism before their cause, and yesterday he asked me idly if Julie had voiced an opinion on the subject. I said I had no idea as I hadn't seen her.

I meet Julie regularly at The Gondolier, a cozy little restaurant which serves light luncheons and heavy teas to ladies who shop in Kensington High Street. It's so middle-class that I know I'm safe; no one Robert knows will ever see me there. Since Julie wouldn't normally patronize such a conservative backwater either I've had to confide in her to explain why it's such an ideal meeting place, but she was sympathetic, offering no criticism of Robert but merely accepting that he was a man who would drive his wife to hide behind steak-and-kidney pie with two vegetables in a middle-class coffin like The Gondolier.

Julie wants me to write another article, this time on transatlantic travel. Apparently the readers of *A Woman's Place* are now in retreat from articles on war work and yearn to be reminded of the more glamorous aspects of peacetime. I say I'll do my best but do I or do I not disclose what goes on in the lifeboats when everyone's awash with champagne?

"Oh, toss it in!" says Julie. "Sex is all the rage now that everyone's either racing to the altar or wailing about the illegitimate issue of our gallant soldiers or rushing around pretending V.D.'s just been invented."

We laugh. Full of ideas for my new article I rush home and there I find a lovely surprise: a letter from Daphne to say that Lion's coming home on leave.

"I'm immensely flattered!" said Lion impudently. "I'd no idea the Huns thought I was so important—I leave the Front for a little peace and quiet and what happens? I'm pursued by Zeppelins in London!"

Only Lion could have had the nerve to joke about the Zeppelins. As I laughed I felt nearly overcome with emotion; I could hardly believe he was back in my drawing room, a thinner, paler Lion but still just as full of bounce and charm. On the sofa Daphne was looking radiant, her plain little face transformed with happiness. They were staying at the Wynter-Hamiltons' London house for the duration of his brief leave, and both Bobby and Margaret had come up to London to visit them there.

"Darling Lion, how wonderful to see you again—and looking so well! One hears such ghastly rumors—"

"Oh, I never believe rumors," said Lion breezily. "The truth's always so much more entertaining. I'm enjoying this war hugely—never had such a good time in my life! Of course it's a bit muddy in the trenches but one meets such fascinating people . . ." And he embarked on a series of amusing reminiscences before his new daughter woke up and began to cry. Daphne, who had been holding the baby, immediately panicked and begged Lion to call for the nanny, but in an effort to beat back my jealousy by being helpful I exclaimed, "No, let me hold her for a moment!" and I took little Elizabeth in my arms. She was plain and bald, just as most new babies are, but when she luckily stopped crying, I said warmly how angelic she was and Daphne blushed with pleasure.

"I'm glad it's a girl," said Lion later. "I don't want a baby who might one day wind up in even the most entertaining of trenches. I wonder what John and Blanche will produce. I suppose a cherub with a halo is the least they can hope for."

We all giggled. Johnny and Blanche, who had established themselves as the perfect couple, were without doubt destined to be the perfect parents of an intolerably perfect child.

I could feel the jealousy creeping over me again so I said firmly, "Lion, you're being *very* naughty!" But Lion just exclaimed outrageously, "That's what makes life such fun!" and burst into peals of laughter.

The casualty lists are so appalling that I feel numb now whenever I hear someone I know has been killed. I say, "How dreadful!" and I know it *is* dreadful, but the full dreadfulness has somehow become impossible to absorb. I felt overwhelming terror when Lion left, but I've recovered from that now and I still believe he'll go on bouncing his way to safety. Meanwhile my worry about Edmund has eased. He's had dysentery and is being sent to a convalescent home in Surrey to recuperate.

I shall conquer my horror of medical institutions and go to see him just as soon as I can.

"Ginevra!"

Edmund was looking so ill, so waxen and gaunt, that I found it hard to believe he was going to live, but the sister in charge of the ward said he was much better and well on the road to recovery.

"Poor Edmund!" I said, forcing myself to kiss him despite my irrational desire to shy away from someone who had been so sick. "What an awful time you've been through."

He looked vague. His mild blue eyes were untroubled. All he said was "It doesn't matter."

"But of course it matters!"

"No, nothing matters. Chap I knew wrote a poem about that. I rather liked it. Wish I could write poetry."

"Does he write much?"

"Oh, not now, no; he's dead."

"I'm so sorry, I—"

"It doesn't matter, one gets used to everyone being blown to bits. In the end it's the little things one minds most, like the rats and the lice."

"Oh my God—"

"Sorry, bad form, should be saying it's all tremendous fun. . . . Poor Ginevra, don't be upset—I've been so lucky! I'm not dead, I'm not blind or mutilated, I'm soon going to be fit as a fiddle again! Now . . . tell me all about your life in London."

What could I say? The chasm between the Home Front and the Front Line suddenly seemed not only bottomless but obscene. Gripping my handbag tightly I willed myself to be calm, and in an effort to convince us both that London had not been entirely untouched by the horrors he had survived, I began to talk in a steady voice about the Zeppelins.

Christmas at Oxmoon, and everyone's thrilled because Edmund's been judged fit enough to complete his convalescence at home. This is probably the first time in his life that Edmund's been the center of his family's attention but he seems not to notice; he's eerily placid and I find his monosyllabic responses soon become unnerving.

Lion is in France and Daphne and little Elizabeth are with the Wynter-Hamiltons in Scotland, but Johnny and Blanche are at Oxmoon for three days before joining Blanche's father in Herefordshire. With them is their new daughter Marian and everyone is busy saying with truth what a perfect baby she is. However Blanche really is a dear child and I hate myself for being catty enough to think she's much too good to be true. Meanwhile Johnny's as priggish as ever and looks at me as if I'm a Soho trollop just because I have a divine new evening gown that's a trifle décolleté. Well, at least I'm not married to Johnny. Thank God for small mercies.

Robert and I are rubbing along somehow and I'm determined not to complain—things could be worse so a complaint would be hard to justify. We're pleasant and affectionate to each other, and as I never mention my longing for a baby there's never a cross word spoken on either side. Margaret eyes my figure but says nothing. I immediately find I have to tell her how blissfully happy Robert and I are. Margaret says she's so pleased. Robert gives her special attention as usual and I keep coming across them chatting privately in corners. I hate it, I hate being here, I hate Oxmoon, *hate* it. Oh, I can't wait to escape to London again. . . .

I feel so depressed, so absolutely cut off from Robert by our mutual pretense that we have an untroubled marriage, that I'd like to take a lover. But I won't—and not just because I'm terrified of what would happen when Robert found out. (Of course there'd inevitably be someone only too willing to tell him.) I won't have an affair because I proved conclusively to myself during my first marriage that adultery solves nothing when it stems from despair. It may temporarily alleviate one's misery but one's problems remain not only unsolved but exacerbated by guilt.

I do think a case can be made for adultery but only when the misery of the partners reaches huge proportions: if the husband is impotent, for example, or the wife hopelessly revolted by the sexual act—or if venereal disease, habitual drunkenness, perversion and cruelty persist in raising their vile heads to blight the matrimonial landscape. But my marriage is far removed from such a marital hell and I've no right to behave as if it isn't.

The truth is I have a husband who loves me. The way he expresses that love may not be particularly acceptable to me, but I must at least try to love him loyally in return. I daresay our marriage will jog along well enough in the end. Certainly I feel better able to tolerate it since I started writing magazine articles and meeting Julie for luncheon at The Gondolier.

Julie has suggested that I might like to answer the readers' problem letters in the new year. What an irony if I end up advising women on their marital difficulties! But at least no one can complain that I'm inexperienced. . . .

Edmund's gone back to France. I really must stop crying and telling myself I shall never see him again.

I keep thinking the war can't get any worse but it does. Robert says there'll shortly be a handbook issued which advises on the correct behavior in the event of an occupation. Everyone assumes an occupation can never happen, but can it? *Can it?* The inconceivable has a nasty habit of coming true these days. Everyone said gold sovereigns would go on circulating but they've stopped. Everyone said there'd never be compulsory blackout but it's coming. Even the public clocks are shortly going to cease to chime. We're no longer mentally gunmetal-gray; we're slate-gray edging towards black but nobody can stand that thought so everyone's rushing to the overflowing theaters and dancing themselves into a frenzy in the Soho nightclubs and drinking and drugging themselves into a stupor.

Yes, I've heard some very unsavory stories recently about girls with a yearning for morphia, but here, handed to me by Julie, are some very different though in their own way equally hair-raising stories. I know just what goes on among the rich, but now I'm about to find out how the other ninety-five percent of the country live.

"Dear Nurse—" The magazine pretends its problem-letter page is in the charge of a nurse because this is supposed to stimulate the readers' desire to confess their most intimate troubles. "—I am twenty-five years old and am not sure what is meant when gentlemen 'take liberties' but I met a soldier on leave last week who said it was my patriotic duty to . . ."

"Dear Nurse, I have three children under four with twins expected next month and my husband is in France and I don't know how I can go on . . ."

"Dear Nurse, I have allowed a sailor to kiss me on the lips. When will I have the baby?"

"Dear Nurse, My husband has just run off with a land girl and I have no money and nowhere to turn . . ."

"Dear Nurse, My husband has been wounded . . ."

"Dear Nurse, My husband has been blinded . . ."

"Dear Nurse, My husband has been castrated . . ."

"Dear Nurse, I'm a war widow and feel I have nothing left to live for . . ."

I stop. The well of undiluted misery and ignorance is so appalling that I feel as if God has reached out, seized me by the scruff of the neck and given me a violent shake. Here are hundreds of women, all far, far worse off than I am. Yes, pull yourself together, Ginevra Godwin. Robert was right—as usual —and it's time you stopped behaving like a rich spoiled bitch. This is your chance to do some worthwhile war work at last and alleviate the suffering on the Home Front. Roll up your sleeves, stop thinking of yourself and make a big effort to help those who are so much less fortunate than you are.

I like the effect of the new summer-time act. It means the evenings are so light that I can sit at my *secrétaire* after dinner and draft my answers to the problem letters while the sun's still shining in the summer sky. Robert's at the House so much at the moment and I always seize the chance to work when I'm on my own.

I was glad to be alone this evening because I have a horrible letter to answer—not a letter from a reader of *A Woman's Place*, but a letter from France. It's from Lion. I shrink from reading it again but I can't delay my answer so I must somehow drum up all my courage and confront that terrible message for the second time. . . .

My dearest Ginevra, Lion had written, *things are busy here for a change, although I haven't mentioned this to Daphne as I didn't want her to worry about me. Ginevra, if anything happens please will you always keep in touch with her? She's frightened of Mama and she thinks Celia's a bore and she finds Blanche maddeningly pi, but you she genuinely likes. You were so nice to us when I had my leave after Elizabeth was born. What a wonderful sister you've always been to me, it seems strange to think you're really just a cousin. God bless you, and my love always,* LION.

I read the letter a third time but found myself unable to write a word in reply. I merely sat with my pen poised over the blank paper as the sun finally set and the darkness began to fall.

Later I tried to think of Edmund, who so clearly had the mark of death on him, but I found I couldn't worry about Edmund anymore. Edmund, I knew, was safe behind the lines, whereas Lion . . . well, obviously Lion was right at the front.

Robert came in at ten, and after kissing me he asked in concern if I felt well. I assured him I did. Then I heard myself say in a calm voice, "Robert, there's a big show brewing, isn't there?" and he answered after only the briefest hesitation: "Yes. The British Army's lining up along the Somme."

Nobody knows what's happening. It's July the first, 1916, and nobody knows what's going on. Robert says this will be the greatest action of the war so far, an action by a British army of continental size. Robert is optimistic. Lloyd George believes Haig is about to win the war, and Robert is Lloyd George's man at heart now even though they both still claim allegiance to Asquith. But the war's proving too much for Asquith. The war's proving too much for us all.

I'm thinking of Lion all the time, I'm praying and praying to my nice kind Church of England God, the God whom I first met long ago during my magic childhood with Robert and whom, like Robert, I've always been unable to abandon. During my marriage to Conor I nearly turned Catholic three times but I always balked at the last minute; I felt the Roman Catholic God would be too demanding and we'd be forever having rows which would leave me a nervous wreck. My Church of England God doesn't mind if I go to church only at Christmas and Easter; he sits up in heaven quiet as a mouse but if I ever want him he's always there to listen even though he can seldom be bothered to reply. But perhaps out of sheer horror he'll now intervene and look after Lion for me. It's only as I pray that I wonder if God really is benign. Perhaps he's evil. Or indifferent. Or simply not there at all.

"Any news?" I keep saying, but there never is. The Somme. What a vile name. It reminds me in shape of the word "tomb." But that's an unspeakable thought which I must erase at once. I must think of the name as a clean-cut shining syllable, sharp as the edge of some invincible sword; I must picture the word as it will appear in future history books. "The Great War, which began in 1914, was triumphantly concluded in July, 1916, by the mighty victory of the British Army on the Somme. . . ." Yes, I can see it all: the battle that will go down in history as the battle that won us the war, the greatest British battle since Waterloo, the last huge battle of the twentieth century—

THE BATTLE OF THE SOMME.

They say there are nineteen thousand dead. They say there are nearly sixty thousand casualties and nineteen thousand dead—in a single day. And nobody's winning. The battle's just going on and on and on.

How does a nation survive such a hemorrhage? I feel like a damaged nerve in a body that is fatally ill.

Nineteen thousand dead. And that's just the beginning.

I can't eat. I can't sleep. I can't work. I can't do anything. I just sit and wait for the telegram from Oxmoon to arrive. The official telegram will go to Scotland, where Daphne's retreated with her parents, but the Wynter-Hamiltons will wire Bobby and then Margaret will wire us.

Nineteen thousand dead, and all over the country the telegrams are starting to arrive; all over the country there are people like me, sitting, waiting, listening for the ring of the doorbell—but no, there's no ring of the doorbell for me, only Robert returning home at eleven o'clock in the morning. I look out of the window and see him paying off the cab, and the instant I see his face I know all there is to know.

"I'm afraid . . ."

"Yes." I turned away and went upstairs to our bedroom. I was trying to remember how many clean shirts Robert had. With Bennett gone it was so easy to lose sight of what was happening in Robert's wardrobe. When I reached the bedroom I moved to the tallboy and started counting shirts. I wondered how long we would be at Oxmoon and decided a minimum of three days would be required. Putting down the shirts on the table I stood looking at them. I remember the sun shining. I can see the sun shining on those shirts. They were achingly white.

"Robert—"

But he was there, and as he took me in his arms I knew I had my loyal friend back again. It seemed like a miracle. I had feared my grief might irritate him but now that I had my loyal friend restored to me I knew there was no need to suppress my feelings. For he was grieving too, grieving for the life that had been lost, and beyond the grief lay his old rage against death which now set fire to our emotions with the violence of a torch thrust into a tinderbox.

We were embracing but without passion. We were merely two friends locked for comfort in each other's arms, but as I sensed that rage exploding in Robert's mind we felt the sexuality vibrate between us and the next moment we were overpowered by a force which neither of us attempted to resist. Robert locked the door. I pulled the curtains. We shed our clothes, fell on the bed and copulated. It had no connection with any conventional notion of passion. What I chiefly remember is that it seemed the obvious natural thing to do, and the act was strangely functional, as if all sensuality had been cauterized by grief. It was our violent protest against the war, our savage litany for the men who had died on the Somme, our unyielding determination to defy death by celebrating life. Lion was dead. His joyous life had been brutally laid waste but we were still alive to rebel against his end.

Later, much later, when I had resumed sorting our clothes for the visit to Wales, I began to cry, but Robert was there still, my beloved Robert, the best friend anyone could wish for. Robert took me in his arms and when he said, "My dearest Ginette," it was as if by some miracle we were back at Oxmoon, the lost Oxmoon of our childhood, and in our shared memories we saw it live again.

Oxmoon's in a shambles because Margaret's withdrawn to her room and Celia is distractedly trying to manage a household in which the servants seem as mindless as lost sheep. I'm shattered by this new evidence that without Margaret Oxmoon falls apart; against my will I'm reminded of that time when she visited her sister in Staffordshire and my childhood came to such a horrific end.

However I try not to think of that. I do my best to be strong and capable, but that's not so easy because the most unnerving aspect of this unnerving situation is that Bobby's useless. With a glass of champagne in his hand he drifts around talking of wartime farming and how splendid all the land girls are, and at regular intervals he pauses to pronounce that all will be well once Margaret's recovered—as if Margaret will miraculously iron out the tragedy by bringing Lion back to life.

Robert soon loses patience with his father and yells at him to be quiet but Johnny's with us, thank God, and—yes, I have to conquer my antipathy and admit it—Johnny's a tower of strength, not only soothing poor Bobby but coping with little Thomas, who's obviously so disturbed by Margaret's withdrawal that he's seizing every opportunity to create havoc.

I'm not sure at first how I should approach Margaret but in the end I send in a little note of sympathy to indicate that she needn't see me if she doesn't want to. However she decides I have to be seen, so we have a short interview during which she thanks me for coming to Oxmoon to help. She's not in bed. She's sitting by the window in a shabby old dressing gown and looking much older than her age, which must now, I suppose, be fifty-one. Her eyes are tearless but she frowns when she says how special Lion was to her, a baby so miraculously full of life after the three babies who had died.

"Yes, he was lovely, Margaret. I can remember him so clearly in the nursery."

And I can. I want to cry but Margaret stops me when she starts to speak again in that low passionless voice.

"I don't know whom Lion resembled but I loved him the better for not reminding me of anyone. It's so difficult when a child, poor innocent little thing, reminds one of someone one loathed, but I never had that difficulty with Lion. I can see why people thought he was my favorite. If one could choose one's favorites I would indeed have chosen him, but one isn't allowed to choose, is one? There's always one child for whom one cares so much that his existence becomes almost an ordeal, but that sort of relationship has nothing to do with choice; it exists whether one likes it or not. I tried to explain that to Robert yesterday and I think he understood. Now that Lion's dead it's finally possible to have a rational conversation with Robert about him."

I nod to show her I understand, but all the time I'm thinking neither of Lion nor of Robert but of the child who reminds her of someone she loathed. She's thinking of Johnny reminding her of her mother-in-law, I know she is, but she and Johnny get on so well together and Johnny's the most devoted son. If only Robert could have got on equally well with Declan, who must have continually reminded him of Conor, but Declan was hardly his own flesh and blood, just a little Irish-American second cousin who came from a world Robert was unable to comprehend.

Thank God Declan's survived the Easter Rising in Dublin. I hope he can escape to America—but oh God, supposing his ship's sunk by U-boats! I worry about Declan all the time still so I know what Margaret means when she says one can care so much for a child that his existence becomes an ordeal. I love Rory because he's so cheerful and uncomplicated—like Lion— but Declan is to me as Robert is to Margaret, and I know he'll always be the son who's closest to my heart.

I seem to have missed this month, but I'm sure I can't be pregnant so I suppose this is a physical reaction to the shock of Lion's death. I'm trying to arrange a visit to Scotland to see Daphne, but Robert refuses to go, despite the fact that it's August and many of our friends will be in Scotland too. But the Wynter-Hamiltons' castle is a stone's throw from Fort William and you can see Ben Nevis from nearly every window, and this must surely be why Robert shuns a visit; he can't bear to be reminded of his climbing days and the dreadful accident which scarred his mind.

However I must see Daphne so I've nerved myself to go without him, and at least I have Rory to look after me on the long train journey. As soon as I leave Robert will go down to Pwlldu to deal with various constituency problems, and then he'll journey south into Gower to make sure Bobby's pulled himself together.

Thank God that for once I have a genuine excuse not to accompany him to Oxmoon.

I seem to have missed again, but of course I can't be pregnant; this is the product of nervous strain resulting from my visit to Daphne. I found it a great ordeal. I could have borne it better if she'd been distraught but she was so brave that I felt *I* was the one in constant danger of breaking down. However I know she was glad to see me, so I did the right thing by forcing myself to undertake the visit. Little Elizabeth is nearly a year old now. She's fat and happy and has Lion's impudent blue eyes, and as I cuddle her I can't help longing again for the baby I know I'm never going to have.

"Raymond's dead."

"Oh Robert, no—not Raymond—"

"He's dead. The army's dying. It's the biggest graveyard the world's ever seen."

It was my turn now to comfort him, but what could I say? I thought I had become immune to the full horror of the casualty lists but now that someone like Raymond had died I felt the horror batter me afresh. Someone like Raymond . . . But there was no one quite like Raymond Asquith. So much brilliance, so much charm, so much wit—and all obliterated one September day by a German bullet in a French hell. Although to me Raymond had been no more than a delightful acquaintance I knew he had meant far more than that to Robert who could so readily associate Raymond's image of brilliance with his own, and as I sensed Robert thinking, There but for the grace of God go I, I suddenly had an intuition of what was to come.

"Christ, what a bloody coward I am," whispered Robert, and covered his face with his hands.

"Rubbish," I said at once. "It takes great courage to stay on the Home Front when both the new law and public opinion push men to enlist."

"I deserve to be thought a coward. I *am* a coward. I'm just so bloody afraid of dying—of losing—"

"Anyone in their right mind should be afraid of dying. That doesn't mean you're a coward."

"I ought to enlist, I know I ought to enlist—"

"How can you? You've been ordered by the people who are running this war to stay where you are!"

"Raymond was told to stick to his staff job. But he had the courage to go back to his men—"

"You're not Raymond, Robert. Not only is your position quite different as an Under-Secretary in the Commons, but I suspect your personalities are more different than you've ever realized. The truth is we don't know much about Raymond, but I'll say this: if he was so keen to go back and dice with death in very adverse circumstances then I suspect he was a far more complicated man than you are. You're a simple man with complex problems. Raymond seems to have been a complex man with complex problems. There's a difference."

"But—"

"To put it bluntly, Robert, if you rushed off to enlist now you wouldn't prove you were courageous, you'd simply prove you were suicidal. Don't be ruled by guilt! Be ruled by reason—and *that*, in the circumstances, will require just as much courage as the courage displayed by most men in uniform."

He made no attempt to argue. Some time passed while I held him close but finally he said in a low voice, "This'll knock the heart out of Asquith. Lloyd George will disembowel him now." And then he began to talk of Raymond's intellectual glamour, of his own golden days up at Oxford and of a vanished world that had been blasted beyond recall.

Today I've been shopping, partly to distract myself, partly to recuperate from the ordeal of writing to Raymond's wife and partly because I thought I might buy some charming but inexpensive cuff links for Rory in the Burlington Arcade. I always like to take him a little present when I visit the school at half-term. However I couldn't find what I wanted at the right price so I abandoned the Arcade, and I was just wandering idly through Fortnum's, as one so often does when one's marooned in Piccadilly a long way from divine Harrods, when I saw the most sumptuous blackberries. Good fruit is hopelessly expensive nowadays but I was seized with the urge to pamper myself so I went wild. I bought six oranges, six peaches and two pounds of blackberries, and the price I paid was almost enough to buy off the German blockades.

I can't help but think now how curious that impulse was, just as I can't help but remember my passion for fruit, particularly oranges, when I was pregnant with both Declan and Rory. The craving would strike in the early months and last several weeks. Conor used to say it was like living in a Florida orange grove, and we had such fun peeling the skins off and chasing the pips around the sheets.

I don't dare hope too much for fear I might be disappointed but a visit to my kind Dr. Drysdale would surely settle the question in no time. . . .

"Are you sure?" said Robert.

"Darling, *yes!* Isn't it wonderful!"

"Wonderful, yes, but how extraordinary! I wonder when—"

"Lion's death. It's the only date that makes sense."

"That's more extraordinary than ever! The occasion was so bizarre that the question of reproduction never even crossed my mind!"

"Yes, that was absolutely the last thing I was thinking about too, but oh Robert, isn't it thrilling! I'm in ecstasy—let's have some champagne!"

We drank some champagne.

"What a relief it is to see you happy again!" said Robert, smiling at me.

"Oh darling, I'm sorry I've been so difficult over the last eighteen months, but our married life will be utterly changed now, I promise you!"

"Splendid!"

I waited for him to say, as Conor would have said, "Let's go to bed and celebrate!" although why I should have thought Robert would choose that moment to display a belated resemblance to Conor I have no idea.

"Well, I must be off," said Robert presently, glancing at his watch. "Don't wait up for me because tonight's debate may be a long one."

Then he kissed me. He turned his back on me. And he left me on my own.

I suppose I know what's going to happen but I can't face it, so I'm turning the problem into a bridge we can cross later. The only trouble is that Robert and I aren't good at crossing bridges. Crossing bridges has become for me a synonym for marital hell.

To divert myself from the crisis that I know is now approaching, I start to read the political news again in *The Times* and soon I realize that Robert has a genuine excuse to avoid me by immersing himself in affairs at Westminster.

They've got rid of Asquith at last. Lloyd George has made his bid for power and this puts Robert in a cruel dilemma. He wants to be loyal to Asquith, his original patron, and with Raymond's memory still in the forefront of his mind his natural inclination is to stand by Raymond's father, but there's no room for such sentiment in politics and now Lloyd George is beckoning; the Welsh wizard is weaving his divisive spells. Lloyd George has had his eye on Robert for a long time, and now he's offering him the prospect of a major role in a glittering future. Robert's seduced. He's going to leave the Asquith camp and back the new leader who has emerged from the dramatic *coup d'état.*

Nothing can stop Robert's career now, nothing—except possibly a failed marriage and a session in the divorce court.

But that's a future I refuse to accept. How could I even think of such a disaster! Pregnancy must be making me unbalanced so I must recover my equilibrium without delay. Perhaps I'll just fly off to Fortnum's and buy some more fruit. . . .

"Robert, are you awake?"

"Barely. What is it?"

"Robert, I know this'll make you angry because you always like to take the lead in such matters, but *please* don't be cross—"

"At the moment I'm merely exasperated. Would you mind coming to the point?"

"Yes, well . . . Robert, are you leaving me alone at night because you think you might harm the baby? If so you needn't worry—now that the beginning of the pregnancy is over it's safe until the seventh month."

"Yes, I did know that."

"Oh. Well, in that case why—"

"Oh for God's sake, Ginette! Go to sleep and stop nagging me! Why is it you're never satisfied? I've made you pregnant—isn't that enough for the time being?"

A long, long time passed while I lay on my side and pretended I was asleep. I made no noise but my pillow was soon sodden. Even though the rejection was not entirely unexpected I still found it very hard to bear.

Then he made a fatal mistake. He too was pretending to be asleep but when I failed to stifle a sob he shouted in a paroxysm of guilt, "I suppose Kinsella wanted it all through your pregnancies!" and I screamed back, "Yes, he did—he wasn't an overgrown spoiled child who hated babies!"

Our peaceful interlude of friendship was brutally terminated and once more the marital horrors began.

I blundered out of bed, I blundered across the landing, I blundered into Declan's room. It was a desperate flight through the dark, and when I sank onto the bed I burrowed under the eiderdown as if all thought of light terrified me.

"Ginette." I heard the click of the switch by the door and felt him sit down on the bed, but when he tried to pull aside the eiderdown I clung to it so fiercely that he abandoned the struggle. As the silence lengthened I knew he was frantically groping for the emotional subtlety that would have reduced the scene to order.

But Robert was capable only of emotional simplicity. He said touchingly but uselessly, "This is our child, yours and mine, and I want it and it has nothing to do, so far as I'm concerned, with those babies I found so tedious at Oxmoon long ago."

I thought: Yes. That's the situation as it should be. That's the situation that you, emotionally color-blind Robert, believe it to be. But that's not the situation as it really is.

I felt so cold then that I burrowed more deeply beneath the eiderdown than ever to ward off the chill of that terrible truth.

"But the trouble is," persisted Robert, struggling on, never for one moment allowing himself to believe that any problem could be incapable of a rational solution, "that I don't find pregnant women desirable. Some men do, some men don't. I don't. I don't know why."

I said nothing. Pregnancy to Robert meant not being the center of attention. Not being the center of attention meant not winning. And not winning to Robert meant a failure he couldn't endure.

I knew him so well that I could see so clearly each contorted fold in that powerful mind which his reason was powerless to iron smooth. I was powerless too. I was seeing truths he was too emotionally simple to recognize. I was seeing a gory pattern which had no place in his rational black-and-white world.

"So the truth is this," said Robert, moving from one statement to another with matchless but impotent logic, "I love you, I want the child but for the moment I can't express these feelings in bed. Of course," he added carefully, "all will be well again after the child's born."

I no longer had the strength to cling to the eiderdown and he was able to ease it away.

"I'm sorry," he said rapidly when he saw my face, "but I had no idea beforehand that this would happen."

I merely waited for him to go but he lingered, fidgeting with the cord of his dressing gown and twisting it continuously between his fingers. At last he said humbly, "Won't you come back to bed? Despite everything I don't want to sleep on my own."

"Don't you?" I said. "I'm afraid I do. Indeed I'm afraid I must. I can't go on sleeping chastely with you night after night like this; it's driving me mad."

He was too shattered to speak.

"I accept that I can't change you," I said, "and I accept that all will be well after the baby's born, but meanwhile you must let me choose my own way to survive this horrible crisis as best I can."

He managed to stammer, "But you've no right to reject me like that!"

"Why not? You've rejected me!"

He crept away without another word.

Robert comes back at dawn in a terrible state and says he's been quite unable to sleep because he now realizes he's being a bad husband, failing in his marital duty to make me happy. He says he's sorry, desperately sorry, he knows he's deserved every ounce of my anger but please, please could I forgive him because he so much wants to make amends.

But I see only that he's locked into the most disastrous competition with a dead man and that he can't rest while he feels he's coming second.

I beg him to leave it for a night or two. I say I do want him, but we're both tired and upset and it would be far better to postpone our reunion.

But he can't listen to me. He daren't. He's got to prove himself, he's got to win, so he gets into the single bed with me and then, inevitably, the worst happens, probably one of the worst things that could ever happen to a man like Robert, and we wind up in a far worse mess than before.

"I don't understand, I simply don't understand—"

"Darling, listen for a moment, *listen*. There's only one thing to do with a nightmare like this and that's to come to terms with it. We've got to accept that our marriage has been dislocated and that the dislocation will last until next spring. That's ghastly, I agree, but it's not permanent and fatal, it's transitory and curable, so we must both make up our minds to endure the present in the knowledge that we can look forward to the future."

"But why am I failing like this? I just can't understand it—"

"Well, it's no vast mystery, Robert! You said frankly earlier that you didn't find me desirable."

"Yes, but I want to! I'm willing myself to! So why can't I succeed?"

"Robert," I said, "there are certain situations in life which aren't subject to the power of your will, and very unfortunately this seems to be one of them. Let it be, I beg of you. Let it rest."

"Was Conor ever like this?"

With horror I noticed the change of name. My first husband was no longer "Kinsella" to Robert, no longer a cipher who belonged to a past which could be conveniently forgotten. He was a rival. He was present. And he was winning.

"Oh Robert, *please*—"

"I can't help it, I've got to know. Did Conor ever fail you as completely as this?"

"Oh God, yes, lots of times!"

"You're lying, I don't believe you."

"Robert, he drank! He drank too much too often! He was often far from perfect in bed—why, I told you that before; I distinctly remember telling you—"

"But was he ever actually—"

"Oh, of course he was impotent occasionally! He wasn't a machine, he was a man!"

"But what did he do when he suffered from impotence?"

"He usually said 'Holy shit' and went to sleep."

"And at other times? What did he do then?"

"I think you'd call it breaking the rules."

"You mean—"

"No, Robert, I absolutely refuse to say any more—"

"I don't mind breaking the rules. I'd never normally suggest such a course to my wife, but if you don't mind then I don't care."

"I do mind—I don't want to do with you what I did with Conor!"

"Why not?"

"Well, because . . . because Conor had this knack of making forbidden things come right, but they weren't the sort of things I'd normally—"

"You mean he was better in bed than I am."

"No! Oh God, no, no, no—"

"You loved him so much that you didn't care what he did, but you don't love me so much so you do care!"

"*No! No, no, no!*"

"You love him—you still him—you'll always love him—and you love him better than you'll ever love me!"

I screamed and screamed in denial but he had already stumbled from the room like someone maimed.

Horrors. Robert's wrecked, I'm wrecked, the marriage is wrecked, and all the time the little baby is growing millimeter by millimeter, fluttering every now and then to remind me how joyous I should feel.

Of course we're keeping up appearances, but I'm now in such a state that I'm quite incapable of answering my problem letters, so I telephone Julie with the excuse that my doctor's advised me to take life at a more leisurely pace until the spring. Julie says never mind, I can always come back to the work later, and how lovely it is to think of someone having a *wanted* pregnancy for a change.

I immediately start weeping into the telephone. Julie says, "Meet me at The Gondolier at one," and as soon as I've controlled my tears I rush off to Kensington High Street.

"What shall I do, Julie? What on earth shall I do?"

"Take a deep breath and calm down. I agree the situation's awful but you're going to get out of it."

I had been weeping all over my steak-and-kidney-pie-with-two-vegetables but when Julie gave me this hope for the future I managed to control my tears again. I knew then that she was the best woman friend I would ever have. Every woman needs a special friend of her own sex with whom she can "have a haircombing" about everything from menstruation to male monsters, and Julie had become that kind of special friend. It made no difference that she had never been married. She was a woman of the world and she had an intuitive sympathy that was almost telepathic in its grasp of a situation. I hadn't had to regale her with every detail of my horrors; I'd merely sketched the outline and she'd penciled in the rest.

"For a start," she was saying, "forget about the truth, whatever the truth is. It doesn't matter which of those two men you love best. All that matters is that Robert should believe it's him."

"But what can I say to convince him?"

"Anything. You've got to mount a propaganda campaign in his favor. Forget about bed—obviously you can do nothing there at the moment—but treat him as if he's God and be passionate about him."

"But won't he be suspicious and skeptical?"

"Don't be silly—he'll be weak with relief and only too willing to believe every word you say!"

"But supposing he drags up the subject of Conor again?"

"I agree Conor's ghost will have to be exorcised. But Robert's not going to try—he'll be much too scared. You're the one who'll have to perform the exorcism."

"Oh God, Julie—"

"No, don't panic. All you have to do is to convince him that it's a compliment, not an insult, that you don't want to do with him what you did with Conor. Tell him you never liked what Conor did when he was drunk, although you wanted to believe out of sheer wifely loyalty that anything he did was right. Then say you simply couldn't bear the thought of Robert the Greek god feeling driven to descend to Conor's pagan Irish level. What explanation could be more rational and comforting?"

Hope now succeeded despair and overwhelmed me. Once more I began to weep into my steak-and-kidney pie, but afterwards I felt so encouraged by this conversation that I even had the energy to walk to Harrods to buy a present for Johnny and Blanche's second baby. It was due to arrive at any moment, and I told myself it would never do if I were so preoccupied by my troubles that I failed to have a gift waiting to welcome the baby into the world.

More ghastliness. Blanche had a little boy but he only lived a few hours. The clergyman came as soon as it was realized that death was inevitable and the baby was christened John before dying in Blanche's arms. I feel very, very upset and condemn myself utterly for my past cattiness about Johnny and Blanche when I mocked them for being a couple who were much too good to be true. I was just jealous because the marriage is so blissfully happy—and there's no charade going on there either; they're both far too young and innocent to fool a cynical old hag like me.

The tragedy has made me nervous about my own baby although Dr. Drysdale assures me that all is well. Certainly the baby feels healthy enough. I'm always so excited when the baby becomes active, and despite my troubles I'm excited this time too. I can picture the baby gritting his toothless little gums and flailing away with his little legs and wondering where on earth he is. Why do we think of the womb as cozy? I think it must be terrifying, a dark padded cell. Poor little baby. But never mind, he'll be free soon, and once he's free Robert and I can begin to emerge from this nightmare which has overtaken us.

It's quite a challenge trying to treat Robert as if he were God, display endless loving solicitude and still keep the charade reassuringly sexless, but I'm battling on. Julie was right when she said that Robert would be relieved. He is. No doubt he imagined he would be burdened with a frustrated sulky lump for the remainder of the pregnancy, so in his gratitude he's sending me flowers every day and giving me extra money to spend at Harrods to ensure that I keep smiling.

Of course he feels guilty because he's made me miserable, and of course I feel guilty because . . . Well, I made him miserable too, didn't I, but I didn't mean to, it was an accident, I got in a panic and said the wrong thing, that's all. Darling Robert, what a dear little boy he was; I can see us picking those strawberries in the kitchen garden, I can hear him saying, "I'll always come first with you, won't I?"—oh yes, I love Robert so much, he *does* come first, and Conor's just a skeleton in the closet who periodically rattles his bones too loudly.

That's the truth. That's reality . . . or is it? Yes, of course it is, and I shall now prove it by conducting the conversation that will triumphantly exorcise Conor's ghost once and for all. . . .

". . . and I can't believe any decent woman would approve of such behavior, but because he was my husband . . . well, it was my duty as his wife to obey him, wasn't it, and he did have the right to do what he liked in bed . . ."

Would Conor have recognized this description of our marriage? No. He would have burst into incredulous laughter, but I couldn't stop to think of that. I didn't dare.

I struggled on.

". . . and that's why I was so horrified when you suggested . . . well, you do understand, darling, don't you? I didn't want our marriage dragged down to that level, and I didn't want *you* dragged down to that level because I think of you as a much finer person than Conor, far more civilized, far more . . . well, to be frank, far more the sort of man I want to be married to."

I paused. I decided it was time I gave him an honest look so I dredged up my courage and gave him one. We were sitting side by side on the sofa in the drawing room before dinner. I had had to conduct the interview before dinner because otherwise I would have been unable to eat.

Robert's eyes were steady. "I see," he said. "Yes. Thank you."

I almost collapsed with relief. The hard part of the story was over. All I now had to do was to add the finishing touches.

"I love you better than I ever loved Conor," I said, and added in a rush: "Oh darling, you do believe that, don't you?"

"Oh yes," said Robert. "Of course." And as soon as he spoke I knew how deeply I'd lied—and what was far, far worse, I knew *he* knew how deeply I'd lied. For one terrible second we were back in the music room at Oxmoon in 1913. I could hear him saying brutally, "Always tell me the truth because if you don't I'll know and that'll mean the end."

To my horror I started to cry. "I've told you the truth," I whispered. "You've got to believe it's the truth, you've got to—"

But he stopped me from betraying myself further. His mouth closed protectively on mine for three seconds, and when he withdrew I found myself beyond speech. I could only listen as he said with perfect calmness, "We'll both accept that what you've said is true, shall we? And I think we should also accept that although we've been distressed we've discussed the matter satisfactorily, with the result that we can now put it behind us once and for all."

I nodded dumbly, still weeping. He passed me his handkerchief.

"Oh Robert . . ." I felt my tears flow faster than ever.

"My dearest, think of the baby, calm down and be sensible. I love you just as much as I ever did, and I'm sure everything will come right in the end."

It's a lie. The entire conversation was a lie. He knows it, I know it, but because we love each other we've invented this charade which will enable us to go on. I can't ask myself how long we can go on or where the charade is going to end. I can't ask because I can't face the answers. I can't even confide in Julie. I'll just tell her all's well—and so it is, in a way. Robert's affectionate and considerate; I'm loving and cheerful, but it's all an act, it's false through and through, and beneath the falsehood I can feel our marriage disintegrating.

I must be very near my time because I've joined in my housemaid's spring cleaning. I can't sit still, I'm turning out my wardrobe, I have to be constantly busy. Conor said I was like a bird who had suddenly realized at the last moment that it had forgotten to feather its nest. Now I'm rushing around feathering it.

I do wish the baby could be a girl, but Robert would never love a daughter, not a hope, he'd simply regard a daughter as a failure to have a son, so it's got to be a boy and I must reconcile myself to the fact that I'm destined to be the mother of sons.

Stop. I feel the first twinge. Oh God, how thrilling this is, and how sad, how very very sad that Robert can't share my joy.

"Is it a boy?" I gasped, and when I heard it was I fainted not from the ordeal of giving birth but from relief. However panic returned the instant I recovered consciousness. "Is he normal?" I said wildly. "Is he deformed? A cretin? An imbecile?"

My kind Dr. Drysdale hastened to end these agonized inquiries, and while she was speaking the midwife placed the baby in my arms.

He was washed, shining, serene.

"Oh!" I was speechless.

"Isn't he lovely?" said the midwife pleased. "I don't see them like that every day, I can tell you!"

I felt confused still after the gas and I had the dreadful desire to hide the baby from Robert as he entered the room a few minutes later, but I soon stopped feeling terrified. After he had kissed me he gazed down at our immaculate pink-and-white infant, so different from the messy red-faced babies who had cluttered up the nurseries at Oxmoon, and to my joy I realized he was stupefied with delight.

"What a *tour de force!*" he exclaimed with complete sincerity, and as I wept with joy I thought, If we can survive this we can survive anything. Yet despite all my euphoria I knew the fate of our marriage was still very far from being resolved.

I'm taking infinite trouble. I've decided (with reluctance) not to breast-feed because I sense Robert would find this repellent. I've bought a new brassière—how on earth did we manage before with those awful camisoles?—and I'm lacing myself daily into a fiendish corset so that I can regain my figure as quickly as possible. I've bought a gorgeous nightgown, wickedly décolleté, for the coming seduction. I'm reading the parliamentary reports from end to end so that I can be an interesting companion. I display unflagging absorption in the news of all Robert's activities, I hang on his every word, I pet him, cosset him and utterly exhaust myself with the effort of being the perfect wife.

It's such a relief to be with the baby because then I don't have to be perfect, I can just be myself. Dear little baby, he's quite adorable, and we've decided to call him Robin. He'll be christened Robert Charles after his father and grandfather, but to address him as Robert would be too confusing and of course there's no question of calling him Bobby. Robert did say that "Robin Godwin" sounded odd and the baby might well object to it in later life, but I said we'd cross that bridge later.

Why worry about the future? There's quite enough to worry about in the present because although Edmund's safe in hospital again, this time with an attack of typhoid, Declan's still on the run in Ireland, and meanwhile the war gets worse and worse. The food shortages have now begun in earnest. I'm bribing both the butcher and the grocer so I've had to ask Robert to increase the housekeeping money, but this was inevitable anyway because food prices have soared out of sight. There's some demented Food Controller at the Food Ministry at Grosvenor House who's covered up the Rubens murals to protect the virgin typists from corruption and is issuing a stream of orders forbidding the consumption of crumpets. It gives a new mad dimension to a life of rushing into the Underground stations to escape from the latest air raids, skimming through the casualty lists and writing the mechanical sympathy letters. To conform to the new regulations, The Gondolier can now only serve a two-course meal in the middle of the day, but I don't mind because I'm banting.

America will come into the war soon after her three sunlit years of sitting on the fence. Her soldiers will saunter across the Atlantic to save us, and how surprised they'll be when we regard them with anger and resentment! They won't realize that they've waited too long and that we're now beyond their naive notion of saving; we've bled too much, and the wounds are too deep. We may survive to live again, but it'll be a very different kind of living from the life we knew before.

Meanwhile we still haven't won and the war's going as badly as ever, and I know I'm going to start worrying about Edmund again as soon as he returns to France. . . .

Wonderful news! Dervla writes to say that the authorities have dropped the charges against Declan: they accept that he didn't shoot the British soldiers after all. Thank God. Dervla tells me Declan's come out of hiding and plans to join Michael Collins, the famous Irish leader, so this is only a brief respite for me. But at least I know Declan's not in immediate danger of execution.

I've written a note to tell him about Robin but I know I'll have no reply. Yet I think one day there might be a letter. I shall never give up hope of a reconciliation, never, but meanwhile I can only console myself by looking at my old photographs of Conor and remembering those happy days we all shared in New York.

I've just survived the christening at Oxmoon. Everyone adored the baby and said how wonderful it was to see that Robert and I were so happy. Margaret was so relieved that she even confessed to me how worried she had been in case Robert had disliked the baby on sight, but fortunately I only needed to smile in reply because Robert is in fact behaving very well. It helps that the baby is greatly admired; Robert can consider his venture into father-hood a huge success and regard himself once more as a winner.

That was the right moment to stage the seduction so I staged it. We were pathetically out of practice but I'm not worried; we achieved what we wanted to achieve and so logically, rationally, it should only be a matter of time before our private life returns to normal.

And yet . . .

There's something going on here, but I'm not sure what it is. Robert seems as interested in sex as ever, but . . . No, I really don't know what I'm trying to say.

I won't think about it.

Another wonderful piece of news—Edmund's been wounded at Passchen-daele! And he wasn't permanently maimed—he just suffered a severe leg wound which has rendered him unfit for further service! It's so wonderful that I want to cry when I think of it. Edmund's coming home. He's won, he's safe, he's going to live. . . .

Thank God Edmund was invalided home because if he'd remained he'd be dead by now. The past seems to be bizarrely repeating itself as if the war were completing some macabre circle. The old names are recurring again; we're on the Somme, we're at Ypres, we're on the Aisne and now at last, in the June of 1918, we're back once more along the Marne. The same few miles of mud, the same terrible suffering, and only the names of the dead have changed.

I suddenly long to turn my back on it all by accepting Daphne's invitation to spend August with her in Scotland. It would suit Robert too because he's been working much too hard and his doctor has recommended a holiday, but I know very well I'd have to go on my own. . . .

"I'll come with you," said Robert.

I was both amazed and delighted. "Darling!" I exclaimed, kissing him warmly. "Nothing could please me more, and I'm sure it would do you good, but . . . well, don't think I wouldn't understand if you refused to come. I know why you always shy away from the thought of returning to the country around Ben Nevis."

"I shall be all right." He made no other comment and I made no attempt to pursue the matter, but of course, as I realized later, I had no understand-ing whatsoever of his aversion to the sight of Ben Nevis. I merely thought he was reluctant to be reminded of a past tragedy but the truth was I was like a wife who had offered her drunkard of a husband a bottle of brandy—and, what was worse, just poured it into the largest glass she could find.

"But you swore you'd never go climbing again!"

"I'll only go once. Just once."

He went back to mountaineering. At first he had merely contented himself with long walks in the company of one of the ghillies from the Wynter-Hamiltons' estate, but soon he had gone riding into Fort William to buy climbing equipment and renew his acquaintance with the mountain guides.

"Just once," he said. "Just once." But he could no more satisfy himself with one expedition than a drunkard could satisfy himself with a single glass of brandy. He went climbing once but he didn't stop. He couldn't. He went out every day. He cut all the social engagements the Wynter-Hamiltons had arranged and he even ignored the start of the grouse season. I was deeply embarrassed by this rudeness to our hosts, but my embarrassment, as I was finally coming to realize, was the least of my problems. After so much physical activity during the day he would sleep as soon as his head touched the pillow at night—and that, I realized as the truth slowly dawned on me, was exactly what he wanted.

"Today I climbed that same stretch where my friends were killed," he said later. "It looks so different in summer."

I could think of nothing to say except "Did you reach the top?"

"Oh yes," said Robert, and I knew he was thinking: I won.

I understood then the exact nature of his obsession. In the black-and-white world of mountaineering, a climber either won or he lost; he either reached the summit or for some reason he turned back and waited till he could try again. There were no grays there, no shadows where one appeared to succeed yet ended in failing, no hellish competition with a dead man who somehow still managed to be alive. Mountaineering was the sport in which Robert knew he could always come first but he had come to believe that sex was the sport where he would always come second.

I saw now the depth of his humiliation when he had failed to consummate our marriage during my pregnancy, and I knew that even though he was no longer impotent he was unable to forget the memory of that failure to live up to Conor Kinsella. No doubt he had wanted to forget. No doubt he had struggled to come to terms with the memory, but when all was said and done this had proved impossible for him, so impossible that in his confused despair, mountaineering had represented the only escape from emotional problems he knew he could never solve.

As the end of the holiday drew near he told me he intended to go to the Inner Hebrides and would join me later in London.

"I want to go to Mallaig," he said, much as a devout Moslem might have expressed the yearning to go to Mecca. "I want to get the boat to the islands. I want to experience again that magic moment beyond the Isle of Eigg when one can look across the glittering sea to those mystical Coolins of Rhum."

I looked at him. He was in a dream. I saw then what a hopeless romantic he was, talking of glittering seas and mystical mountains, conjuring up a fantasy world like Valhalla where happiness was always endless, winning was always guaranteed and everyone lived forever in a haze of glory and masculine comradeship. I was a realist who adored romance. Robert was a romantic who adored realism. We might have been two people inhabiting different planets.

"What about your work?" I said, not exactly trying to drag him down to earth but at least trying to ease him back as painlessly as possible. "What about Mr. Lloyd George?"

"He can wait."

That was when I formally acknowledged to myself that we stood on the brink of disaster.

We were in our room at the castle, and one of the Wynter-Hamiltons' maids was helping me pack. Beyond the long window the rain was gusting across the loch and the mountains were half-hidden in mist. Turning my back on the view I dismissed the maid, waited till the door was closed and then said in the firmest voice I could manage, "Robert, the cancer's growing again on your personality and you must cut it out to survive."

"No," he said. "This is my personality as it should be. This is the man I really am."

I was too appalled to speak. The silence lengthened. Then he said, "I'm such a bloody coward that it's taken me years to face up to this, but now I'm determined to have the courage to live my life as it should be lived."

"But Robert—"

"Life's short. Life's precious. I can't go on wasting my time like this in London; it's not only wrong, it's obscene. During the war I've lived while others—men like Raymond, better men than I—have died. That's a terrible truth to have to live with, and I can only live with it by leading the kind of life I was put on this earth to lead. Then I shall feel that my survival, unmerited though it is, has some point."

So he was using his guilt about the war, not the failure of our marriage, to explain his behavior, and I knew then that he would never realize he was running away from problems he couldn't solve. His nature was too simple, his emotional understanding too limited.

We stared at each other and the void of our estrangement yawned between us.

At last he said, "So long as the war lasts I must stay at Westminster. That's my duty. But as soon as the war's over I'm giving up London and I'm giving up politics."

No longer able to look at him I turned away towards the half-packed trunks. The clock told me it was four o'clock. I dimly remembered my promise to Nanny to look in at the nursery for tea.

"I'm sorry," said Robert, not unkindly, "but perhaps I can save us both from emotional scenes if I tell you that my decision is unalterable. I gave in to you once on this subject and regretted it. I'm not giving in to you again."

That settled that. Over. Finished. Done.

"We'll go back to Gower," said Robert, "just as I originally planned."

I whispered, "What about Bobby and Margaret?"

"Oh, I don't care about that difficulty anymore—and anyway that's your problem to solve, not mine, because I'll be away climbing most of the year. Time's short. I'm thirty-six and that's old for mountaineering. I must go to train in the Alps if I'm ever to tackle the Himalayas, and I must go as soon as possible before I'm forty."

I sat down on the bed. "If you still loved me, you wouldn't condemn me to Gower."

"I do still love you but I can't go on pandering to this abnormal sensitivity about something that happened over twenty years ago."

"But surely we could stay in London—I wouldn't mind if we had to move to a small flat—"

"I can't afford London."

"Then perhaps I could earn a little—find employment—"

"*Find employment?* Good God, no, I don't want my wife earning a living! I want her looking after my home and child wherever I choose to live, and I don't choose to live in London, I choose to live in the parish of Penhale—and not merely for financial reasons, either. I want Robin to grow up in Gower as we did."

"But—"

"I'm sorry, but I'll stand no argument. I've given you what you want for damn nearly five years, and now it's my turn to have what I want—and that, I'm afraid, Ginette, is really all I have to say."

I have but one thought, and that is I mustn't quarrel with him. If Robert and I part I'm bound to take a lover eventually, and then unforgiving, implacable Robert will take me straight to the divorce court and wind up with custody of Robin. But that's never going to happen. *Never.*

I've got to struggle on somehow. At present I can face only one day at a time. Better not to think of Bobby and Margaret just yet. I'll cross that bridge later.

One day at a time. A little sex would help. I don't want Robert but without sex I eat and drink too much, and I feel quite miserable enough already without feeling miserable because I'm fat.

But supposing he can't be bothered to make love to me again?

Oh God, what shall I do, what shall I do, what shall I do . . .

He's made love to me again, though I found I was too bitter to enjoy it. I might have known he'd stick to the rules and do his marital duty in the bedroom, just as he's now doing his patriotic duty by attending sessions in the House.

But the war's coming to an end. I do believe it's almost finished, and now I can see the bridge called New Life looming ahead of me, the bridge which represents the final crisis in a marriage wrecked quite beyond repair.

The war's ended today. I know I should feel joy, so after I've stopped grieving for Lion I try to drink champagne with a smile. But the joy's a charade. I feel the word "joy" can never be the same again, and suddenly I see that golden summer of 1913, the summer I returned to Oxmoon; I see us all laughing and lounging on the lawn while little Thomas pours milk over Glendower and Margaret presides over the silver teapot and Robert and I are in an ecstasy of romantic excitement. All gone now. A lost world utterly vanished. I'm alive in a grim drab postwar London and enduring a grim drab marital reality for which I can see neither amelioration nor cure.

They say Parliament is to be dissolved and the election held at once, so my days of respite are coming to an end. Robert won't change his mind about his career so I shall soon have to tell our friends that we're about to sink without trace into Wales. I've decided I shall be quite brazen about it and pretend to be thrilled—it's the only way of concealing my horror, but what our friends will think God only knows. Most of them will drop us immediately. It's at times like this that one discovers who one's friends really are.

Julie will stay my friend. I think I would have gone mad by now without my lunches with Julie at The Gondolier. I even go to her flat sometimes when Robert's at the House, and she's introduced me to the most delicious drink based on gin. Of course it would be dreadfully common before the war for a woman to drink gin but this is after the war and everyone's much too busy trying to keep sane to worry about being common. "Bugger being common!" says Julie, who as a socialist believes not only that we'll all be common one day but that we'll all absolutely love it.

I absolutely love gin so I suppose my next problem will be chronic drunkenness. What a bore, but oh God, what *am* I going to do, how can I stop Robert living in Gower, never mind the mountaineering, let him climb every mountain in sight, but I've got to stop us winding up on the doorstep of Oxmoon.

I haven't told Julie about Bobby. That's *verboten*, but she sees clearly that I can't bear the thought of living near my parents-in-law and that this has now become my major nightmare.

"Ginevra, why not try to enlist his mother's help? I can't believe any mother in her right mind would welcome her brilliant son wrecking his career in order to pursue an undergraduate hobby, and if he sticks to his career he'll have to stay in London, won't he?"

This strikes me as shrewd advice. I don't honestly believe that anyone can now stop Robert climbing, but if anyone can it's Margaret.

I decide to act on the principle Nothing venture, nothing gain.

We're going down to Oxmoon for Christmas as usual, and Robert's talking of advancing the date of our departure because he's so anxious to discuss the future with his father. This means that I'll soon see Margaret, but nevertheless I think it would pay me to write a little letter warning her that everything in the marital garden is rather less lovely than it appears to be . . .

"Here you are, Robin my angel, have some of Mummy's heavenly licorice."

Nanny said strongly, "It'll all end in tears, Mrs. Godwin, if you don't mind me saying so. Little children weren't designed by the Almighty to digest licorice on trains."

"I want it!" said dear little Robin, reminding me of Robert, and grabbed the licorice from my hand.

"Say Thank you, my pet," I said dotingly, but Robin was too busy cramming the licorice down what Nanny called "the little red lane."

It was early in December and Rory was still at school when we all left London. We had a first-class compartment on the train to ourselves, but Robin, who was twenty months old and very active, kept Nanny busy by rushing up and down the corridor at high speed. Nanny was right about the licorice. My fatal indulgence did end in tears but darling Robin was so adorable that I couldn't resist spoiling him. Fair-haired, blue-eyed, rosy-cheeked, sunny-natured and divinely intelligent, he was the one ray of sunshine in my dark private life, and although I detested mothers who doted excessively on their offspring, I was quite unable to stop myself being detestable. As Robert sat in his corner of the carriage with *The Times* and tried to pretend he had no connection with two distracted women and a child who was screaming of nausea, I ignored him and lavished all my attention on poor sickly little Robin instead.

Poor sickly little Robin was eventually borne off by Nanny to the lavatory to vomit. I was just heaving a sigh of guilty relief when Robert suddenly put down *The Times* and covered his eyes with his hand.

"That's uncommonly odd." He let his hand fall, squeezed his eyes shut, shook his head violently and opened them again. "I'm seeing double. Reminds me of the time when I was hit on the head by a cricket ball."

I was most alarmed. "Oh God, Robert, do you think it's a recurrence of the injury? One hears such extraordinary stories about head wounds."

"I'll probably be all right in a minute."

But at Swansea his condition was unchanged. As we left the train he said to me, "Don't mention this at Oxmoon. I'll see a doctor tomorrow if I'm not better."

I was concerned but he seemed only mildly troubled, so I did my best not to think of damaged retinas and concentrated instead on the task of greeting Bobby who had come to Swansea to meet the train.

The great ordeal of the 1918 Christmas was finally about to begin.

We're not the only ones in a mess apparently—what a relief it is to hear that other people too have their troubles! Poor Celia, who's more spinsterly than ever now that she's in her mid-thirties, has fallen madly in love with a German P.O.W. whom she met while she was doing V.A.D. work at the Cottage Hospital. The P.O.W. was removed from his camp in order to have an appendix operation and Celia nursed him back to health. She says he's a chemist from Heidelberg and she shows me a photograph of a cherubic youth who must be at least ten years her junior.

"My dear—a younger man—how do you do it!" I say to cheer her up, because of course Bobby and Margaret are livid and Bobby swears that even now the war's over he won't have "that damned Hun" in the house. Well, I'm not mad on the idea of her marrying a German either, but the boy looks rather a pet, and anyway if I were nearly thirty-five and had never been to bed with a man I'm sure I'd be capable of marrying anyone, even a damned Hun.

Ironically it's Edmund, the one who's suffered most from the Germans, who says, "The Huns are no different from us. They bleed and die just as we do."

Edmund's looking a little better but not much. Apparently he had a bad bout of shell shock, complete with rigor, while he was recuperating from the leg wound, and he's still odd at times, odd enough to spend several days without talking, but he seems reasonably normal at the moment although he still limps as the result of his wound. He looks at least ten years older than twenty-four.

However I've no time to meditate on Edmund's suffering because Celia's demanding all my attention. She asks what on earth should she do because Dieter is bound to be repatriated soon and this is her One Chance and if she ignores it she'll have nothing to do but press wild flowers for the rest of her life, and she can't bear it, she simply can't, and she's tried to explain to dearest Mama and dearest Papa, but they refuse to listen.

There's only one answer to give, and as one woman to another I give it.

"Celia: your dearest Mama and Papa married when they were in their teens. Obviously they haven't the remotest idea what it's like to be a spinster approaching thirty-five. I agree with you; this is your one chance; grab it and to hell with them."

This sort of advice is hardly likely to endear me to my mother-in-law, the one person whose help I so desperately need, but I'm safe for the moment because Celia can't elope with her cherubic Hun while he's still in his prison camp.

I must plan my interview with Margaret. If I were still religious, now would be the moment to pray.

"Yes, come in, Ginevra," said Margaret. "I thought it might be suitable if we had our little talk before dinner. Do sit down."

As usual we were in her room, and as usual she was sitting at her dressing table, and as usual the jewel boxes were open before her, but as I slowly crossed the room she piled the stray jewelry back into the boxes and shut the lids with ruthless movements of her fingers. I felt exactly as if I were watching a boxer hang up his gloves and prepare to fight with his bare hands.

"You mentioned a little trouble in your letter," said my mother-in-law politely. "I'm so glad you've seen fit to confide in me. Do please go on." And she set her straight mouth in it hardest, most implacable line.

I stammered away, repeating myself, contradicting myself, making the worst possible mess of my prepared speech. When I finally ground to a halt in misery all she said was "You don't seriously think I'm going to side with you against my son, do you?"

I was annihilated in a single contemptuous sentence. Amidst all my chaotic emotions I was shattered by the revelation of how much I was disliked. I wanted to cry but I was too appalled, and I was still groping futilely for words when she said, "You broke your promise to me. You said you wouldn't keep Robert from Oxmoon but you did. And you've made him very miserable, haven't you? Well, that's no surprise, not to me, I never thought you'd make him anything else, but thank God all that London nonsense is going to stop now, and if you've a grain of sense in that frivolous selfish head of yours you'll pull yourself together as fast as you damned well can and be a good wife to him for Robin's sake."

The word "damned," coming from Margaret, was more shocking than any common obscenity. I found I could barely speak. "I—I just thought the mountaineering . . . not what you would want—"

"I want Robert to be happy. If climbing mountains and setting up a home in Gower will make him happy, then I want him to climb mountains and set up a home in Gower—and what's more that's what you should want too if you've got any conception at all of what a decent marriage should mean. Of course it would be hard to imagine a woman less suited to a country life than you are, but now that Robert's made his decision you have an absolute moral duty to make the best of it. Life can't always be one long dance to 'The Blue Danube,' Ginevra. There comes a time when the music stops and life—real life—has to begin."

There was a long, long silence. I felt there was so much I could say to her but I knew that whatever I said she would never understand. She saw the world in black-and-white. Like Robert she was emotionally color-blind, and for the first time in my life I caught a glimpse of her marriage from Bobby's point of view.

When she next spoke I realized she was retreating again behind her mask of refinement. Her mouth softened; she assumed a milder expression, and as I watched she became once more the Margaret who was so familiar to me, the placid, provincial little woman who emanated that subtle sinister air of authority, the self-made Victorian lady who pursed her lips in disapproval if a word like "damned" was uttered in her presence.

"Dearest Ginevra," I heard her say as she idly opened her favorite jewel box again, "don't think I'm entirely unsympathetic. Marriage can be very difficult, can't it? But then it's only the fools who think it should be a bed of roses." She stretched out her plump little hand to examine the rings on her wedding finger. "However," she said presently, "I believe even a difficult marriage has its rewards, and I'm sure that when you remember your sons you'll agree with me—in fact there's no reason, as far as I can see, why even the most arduous marriages shouldn't in the end prove happy and successful. Happy and successful marriages," said Margaret, looking me straight in the eyes, "can be sustained simply by the right attitude of mind. One needs willpower, courage and an invincible determination to keep up appearances."

I said nothing. Having drawn the line against marital failure Margaret seemed to think my problems had been resolved—or at least reduced to manageable proportions. But as far as I was concerned she had offered me no solutions; she had simply restated my dilemma, and this dilemma had become even more intractable since she had refused to help me.

I could see why she had refused. I realized she had hated Robert being swallowed up by London just as I had hated Declan being swallowed up by Ireland. I realized that although she had been proud of his achievements, she had also resented them because they had served to cut Robert off from his family. Margaret wasn't about to shed a tear because Robert was abandoning his chances in the world of politics. All she cared about was having him back in the world of Oxmoon where he would see more of his family and make Bobby happy.

So much for Margaret. So much for my hope of an ally.

Somehow finding the words to excuse myself I crept away and began to cry.

Robert's double vision has disappeared overnight but I've sent him off to see Dr. Warburton anyway. I like Gavin Warburton. He's in his mid-thirties, just as we are, and I met him during our visit to Oxmoon two years ago when I was pregnant and the Boxing Day goose had disagreed with me. When he paid his call I could see he didn't think, Here's a silly woman who's made a hog of herself and deserves to be sick. He was cheerful and sympathetic and prescribed me some delicious medicine which made me feel better.

Yes, he's a good man, someone who reminds me that not all male doctors are horrid. I wonder what he'll say to Robert.

I know I ought to consider the future again, but I can't face it at present. Margaret upset me too much and if I start remembering that interview I'll only cry, and that would be disastrous as someone might notice my eyes were suspiciously red.

Must keep up appearances.

Mustn't let anyone know.

Warburton says the double vision could be the result of the old injury but he doesn't believe it is. He thinks it's more likely to be a form of eyestrain, and he recommends that Robert has his eyes tested as soon as he returns to London. What a relief! At least, amidst all the current horrors, I don't have to worry about Robert's health.

Bobby's thrilled that Robert wants to settle on the Oxmoon estate, and the two of them have gone off this morning to inspect Martinscombe Farm which is situated below Penhale Down a mile away. I expect he minds, just as Margaret obviously does, that I'm being brought back into their lives but they're both so glad to have Robert home again that I've assumed the status of a tiresome inconvenience. They'll adapt to my presence in the end. Margaret will say, "Tolerating dearest Ginevra is simply an attitude of mind," and that'll be that. After all, anyone who can deal with the kind of problems posed by Aunt Gwyneth and Owain Bryn-Davies would find me child's play in comparison.

How brutal they were to Aunt Gwyneth, keeping her locked up year after year and only letting her visit her home at Christmas! Poor Aunt Gwyneth, now that I'm older I don't think she was mad at all, just vilely unhappy—as I shall be, shipwrecked at Martinscombe, sipping gin from dawn till dusk and trying not to seduce every shepherd in sight.

Enough. No more suicidal pessimism. I must face the problem squarely and try to work out what I can do.

As far as I can see—after prolonged and painful thought—there's one most unpalatable truth here which I have to acknowledge. If I want to save my marriage (and in order to keep Robin I've no choice but to try), then I must throw all my energy into creating an attractive home which will periodically lure Robert away from his mountains and console him when he's too old to climb seriously anymore. The prospect of embracing with enthusiasm a permanent country life on my inlaws' doorstep is repellent indeed, but at present it seems I've no choice but to admit this is the only course I can take. The one question that remains is Am I capable of taking it?

It's tempting just to answer "no," but I must try to be constructive. I think the answer could be "yes"—but only in the context of a marriage that is very, very different from this current nightmare. If I knew I could visit London regularly, if I had an interest like my journalism which I could develop without fear of Robert's disapproval, if I could keep in touch with my loyal friends like Julie, if I could even discreetly take a lover now and then to make up for the fact that Robert no longer genuinely wants me in bed—*then* I could say, Yes, very well, I love the Gower Peninsula, it's a wonderful place for Robin to be while he's growing up and I'm content with my lot. It wouldn't be the ideal life, it would certainly require some sacrifices on my part, but as Margaret said, life can't always be one long dance to "The Blue Danube." However the major difficulty about launching myself on an unconventional marriage is that Robert's never, never going to consent to the suggestion that I become an unconventional wife.

However he's bound to feel guilty if he goes away climbing for months at a time. He might make concessions later, and besides there's always the possibility that he'll wind up bored stiff, decide he's made a mistake and move back to London.

No, I mustn't despair. I must live in hope, dredge up all my strength—and somehow summon the nerve to go on.

Christmas is only a day away now, and Johnny and Blanche, that perfect couple, have joined us with their perfect child little Marian, who's now three and very pretty and wonderfully well behaved. Blanche is expecting another baby soon and is radiant. Johnny's bright-eyed with happiness. There was a point in 1917 when we all thought he would have to go to France; the authorities had a "combing-out" at the Foreign Office to sweep the less useful members of that gilded fraternity into the army, but perfect Johnny was deemed essential so he was ordered to stay where he was. He was also promoted. However, as I know from my experience with Robert, those who served on the Home Front have wound up half-dead with guilt, so I've no doubt there are some complex thoughts churning away behind Johnny's immaculate facade.

But we don't talk of the war now and we certainly don't talk of politics and the "coupon" election. It's a relentlessly merry Christmas and Robert's as merry as anyone, laughing and joking and acting as if he hasn't a problem left to solve. Without bothering to consult me first he's declared that we'll stay at Oxmoon while the Martinscombe farmhouse is prepared for us. The house is structurally sound and by no means a hovel, but it will need to be substantially extended and refurbished before it can be classed as a gentleman's residence. Bobby says he knows an architect in Swansea, a charming fellow, who would be delighted to help us, and I say, What fun, I can't wait to consult him.

I drink more champagne than usual and Robert makes Margaret livid by breaking another glass from her best set. That's the second champagne glass he's dropped recently and the shattered fragments seem horribly symbolic of our marriage.

However at least his double vision hasn't recurred.

What a Christmas.

We've seen the architect and I've displayed boundless enthusiasm for his schemes. Much good that did. Robert says he intends to spend the rest of January in Scotland, and would I mind putting the Ebury Street house on the market while he's away. We only have a short leasehold interest in the property, but Robert's decided on reflection that it would be more prudent and less wearying to dispose of it and invest the proceeds than to let the house to tenants who might prove unreliable.

He almost forgot to make love to me before he rushed off to make love to his mountains, but luckily his training as a gentleman reasserted itself and he resigned himself to playing the marital game for ten minutes. After all, if one had a wife one had to copulate with her now and then. That was the Done Thing, a ritual which had to be performed to keep up appearances.

What a farce.

Robert's returned to London from Scotland after only three days. I was most surprised but apparently he's worried about the hand that dropped the glasses; his fingers seem to be liable to occasional muscular spasms, and since this makes him a danger on the mountains, both to himself and to his companions, he's going off this morning to consult our family doctor.

Tiresome for him.

Good news for a change. Celia's eloped to Heidelberg with her pet of a damned Hun, and meanwhile here in London Blanche has had her baby, another boy, but in contrast to the poor baby who died, this infant is strong and noisy and is clearly going to thrive.

A worrying thing happened when we went to drink champagne at Johnny's house to celebrate Harry's arrival. Robert dropped his glass yet again as he suffered another muscular spasm in his hand. We'd both thought he had recovered. On the doctor's advice he had been wearing his arm in a sling, and after a few days Robert had been convinced the rest had cured the trouble.

He's so upset that I can't help feeling sorry for him.

"Let's go and dine at the Ritz."

"Robert! What a heavenly idea—but can we afford it?"

"No, but let's go anyway."

I could not make up my mind whether he was issuing the invitation to divert himself from his worry about his physical fitness or to alleviate his guilt that he had been neglecting me, but whatever his motives I was delighted. I decided to treat the offer as a gesture of friendship, and indeed once we reached the Ritz we slipped easily into our role of old friends, chatting away about amusing trivialities until I sensed we were more relaxed in each other's company than we had been for months.

"Darling Robert!" I said afterwards as we held hands in the cab that drove us home. "I know you think I'm loathing everything you do at present, and up to a point I am, but I'm truly glad if you're so much happier."

"And I'm truly sorry if I'm making you so miserable," he said, and I knew, in one of those moments of comradeship which had become so rare between us, that he was just as sincere as I was.

Our concern for each other still survived, and as I saw our old friendship, bruised, battered but apparently unbeaten, still shining amidst the ruins of our marriage, I heard myself say strongly, "Friends must stick together. I shall be all right."

"Friendship's forever?" said Robert, smiling at me.

"Apparently!"

We laughed, kissed and were happy, but after we had arrived home he said with a yawn, "I'm afraid I'm hopelessly sleepy—too much claret, I suppose," and I knew I had been rejected again. It was as if a curtain had descended abruptly on our friendship and I was alone once more in our unhappy marriage.

He sensed my feelings and immediately the marital tension began to grind between us.

"Well, never mind the claret," he said. "Perhaps I can wake up after all."

As soon as he said that, I wanted to snap back: "Oh, please don't bother—I really couldn't care less." It was so obvious that he was only doing his duty as a husband, and I felt both humiliated and repulsed. However I knew it would be fatal to refuse him. If I did that he might not offer again, and besides I spent so much time resenting his lack of desire for me that I could hardly fly into a sulk on one of the rare occasions when he felt obliged to make amends.

We undressed in our room. Drearily I trailed to the bathroom, drearily I performed my dreary rites with the vinegar and sponge and drearily I returned to bed. He performed some more dreary rites to ensure that his body did what he wanted it to do, and since there was no serious impediment, like my pregnancy, which prevented his body from obeying instructions, copulation drearily ensued for precisely sixteen seconds. I was counting for lack of anything better to do while I waited for it to be over.

"Sorry about that," said Robert, acting the perfect gentleman. "I'm afraid the claret told after all."

"Never mind," I said, and in fact neither of us minded in the least. Trailing to the bathroom I prepared for more tedium, but was awoken from my stupor of distaste by finding that the little flesh-colored thread had become detached from the sponge while the sponge itself had been shoved beyond the reach of my longest finger.

I sighed, prayed for contortionist skills and returned to the fray but in the end I gave up. I spent some time debating whether I should use the douche again, just as I always did, but in the end I was too nervous. Supposing I washed the sponge so far up that I had to have an operation to remove it? I shuddered. I was unsure what went on in the nether reaches of the feminine anatomy, but I pictured some unspeakable nastiness taking place among the ovaries. Wholly repelled I abandoned all thought of douching and toiled exhausted back to bed.

Men have no idea what women have to go through sometimes, no idea at all.

The lost sponge has finally turned up. Thank God. Really, that sort of incident is enough to put anyone off sex for life.

Robert's having his hand X-rayed, although what good that will do I don't know. Robert now tells me he's been unable to move the middle finger of his right hand for three days, and with a shock I suddenly realize how sinister this is. Could he be suffering from a series of minor strokes? It seems unlikely but this recurring weakness—we don't call it paralysis—must surely mean there's something wrong with the part of the brain that controls the muscles. Or does it? I don't know. Robert doesn't know. The doctor doesn't know.

It's all very worrying.

We've found someone who wants the house but I can't think of that at the moment. I'm too worried about Robert. He's recovered the full use of his hand but the specialist says he must have a thorough examination, and as I'm terrified of illness I'm now in a great state.

No wonder I've missed this month. Supposing Robert has a brain tumor? Supposing he only has three months to live? Supposing he drops dead tomorrow? I could do without my husband but how could I manage without my friend? Even if we eventually separate once Robin's grown up, I must have Robert in my life. Who else would stand by me through thick and thin? Who else would always be there when I needed him?

I panic. I'm demented with anxiety. In fact I'm in such a state of hysteria that I even go to Brompton Oratory, where I used to take the boys to Mass, and make a feverish attempt to pray.

Robert's all right. Oh God, the relief! The exhaustive examination found nothing—no brain tumor, no stroke, no diabolical illness. Very strange about his hand, but I suppose it was just one of those inexplicable physical vagaries like the double vision.

Odd how these little ailments come and go. . . .

"Oh my God!"

"Robert—what is it?"

"I've got that double vision again. Damn it, *damn* it—I thought I'd finished with those bloody doctors . . ."

He's seeing another specialist. Oddly enough I'm not so worried this time. After all, the double vision can hardly be connected with the trouble in his hand.

Or can it?

I'm suddenly so frightened that I can't even get to Brompton Oratory to pray.

I did go to the Oratory later but I couldn't feel God listening so I walked down the road to Harrods instead. There was a fruit stall on the corner of the Brompton Road and I automatically bought two pounds of oranges. Then I came home.

Five minutes ago I finished eating my third orange and now I want to eat a fourth.

I know what that means. It means I made the wrong decision when I failed to reapply the douche after that dinner at the Ritz. It means that sixteen seconds of unwanted copulation has had a very unwanted result. It means . . . but no, I simply can't face what it means.

I'll think about it later.

"Ginette, I'm afraid I wasn't entirely honest with you when I came home from Harley Street just now."

We were in the drawing room having tea and I was eating a slice of gingerbread. My hand paused halfway to my mouth. "What do you mean?"

"The specialist wasn't encouraging."

I put the gingerbread down on my plate. On my right the fire was burning, warding off the chill of a dank April day, but all the warmth seemed to have vanished from the flames.

"What did he say?"

"He thinks I have some obscure illness, but there's no method of proving the diagnosis. We can only follow an Asquith policy of 'Wait and See.' "

"Oh."

Robert continued to drink his tea. His vision had returned to normal before he had seen this second specialist, and his hand was once more unimpaired. He looked fit and strong, glowing with good health.

"But why didn't this specialist believe as the other one did that the trouble was caused by mental strain?" I said baffled at last.

"He didn't rule out that possibility. He merely said this odd combination of disorders in the eyes and hand suggested that a specific illness was responsible."

I finished my tea. "What is this illness?" I said as I put down my cup.

"He didn't go into detail. He said it involved paralysis but apparently remissions are common and people can suffer the disease yet have few symptoms."

"That doesn't sound too bad, does it," I said relieved. "How long does one take to recover?"

"Oh," said Robert, "one doesn't recover. But one needn't die prematurely either. He said the moderate cases could experience a normal life-span."

I looked at my empty teacup. I looked at the spring flowers on the sill. I looked at the pale afternoon light beyond the window. And I felt Death lay his finger on us gently, very lightly, from a long, long way away.

"There are three possibilities here," said Robert, summing up the situation with unperturbed logic. "One: this diagnosis is wrong and my physical troubles are resulting from a stress which will ease once we remove to Gower. Two: the diagnosis is right but I experience a continuation of the remission I'm enjoying at the moment. And three: the diagnosis is right but my remission isn't sustained. This uncertainty is without a doubt most tedious but one fact at least is crystal-clear: if I do have this illness I can never go climbing again. Even if I were temporarily capable of doing so it would be too dangerous because I could be stricken with paralysis at any time."

My mind was in such chaos that I hardly knew how to reply but I managed to stammer: "I'm sorry. I know how much climbing means to you—"

"Yes, well, don't let's wallow in sympathy just yet. I may not have this illness. I may recover completely, and meanwhile it seems to me all we can do is continue with our plan to remove to Gower."

I struggled to match his calmness. "You still won't consider staying in London?"

"That would be no more possible financially if I were ill than it would be if I spent my time mountaineering."

"No, I suppose not. I'm sorry, I wasn't trying to nag you again about London—"

"Besides, I want to go home. If I can't climb at least I can still go back to Oxmoon and give my son the kind of life I had when I was young."

"I understand." I thought of him still yearning for that lost Oxmoon and my throat began to ache. I knew no mere physical removal to Gower could recapture it, nothing could recapture it, it was lost and gone forever.

Robert finished his tea. "There are two matters of immediate importance," he said briskly as if he suspected I could barely contain my emotions.

"The first is that I don't want anyone to know about this or else I'll have everyone staring at me as if I'm an animal at the zoo. And the second is that we must stop the builders at Martinscombe. We must have new plans drawn up in order to provide for every eventuality."

I was struggling so hard for self-control that I could only say, "What kind of plans?"

"I think it would be better to abandon the farmhouse and build a bungalow nearby. A single-story dwelling would be easier for a wheelchair."

In the grate the fire now seemed to be raging. I was so overwhelmed by the heat that I thought I would faint.

"I'll open a window," said Robert as I put my hand to my forehead.

He flung wide the casement and as he paused beside it I was able to say, "You think you do have this illness, don't you. What's it called?"

"Oh, it has some hopelessly long-winded medical name which for the life of me I can't remember."

I knew what that meant. It meant he didn't want me to look it up in the medical dictionary. It meant he himself had looked it up and been appalled.

Panic overwhelmed me.

"Darling . . ." I hardly knew what I was saying. "Forgive me, obviously we must talk more about this, but I'm afraid I simply must go and lie down for a while; I'm feeling thoroughly worn out."

He said he was so sorry and of course I must rest and he did hope I would soon feel better.

I escaped.

I'm much too frightened to think about the future, my mind shies away from it, so I ponder instead about whether God intends me to find some deep meaning in the fact that I'm pregnant while my husband is incurably ill.

For of course I know Robert's ill, just as I know I'm pregnant. I know it, feel it, I don't have to wait for a diagnosis.

After prolonged meditation I've come to the conclusion that there's no deep meaning in this situation and almost certainly no God. I haven't truly believed in God anyway since the Battle of the Somme, but if God does exist and has some purpose in mind for this baby, I'd very much like to know what that purpose is. As far as I can see, this pregnancy is quite the most pointless thing that's ever happened to me; I've got to endure the removal to Gower and Robert's illness and I just can't face any additional ordeal; I can't bear it. But I've got to bear it, haven't I? Can't face an abortion, too squeamish; couldn't. Other women can do as they like, I don't mind, let them get on with it, they should be able to do just what they like with their own bodies, but I know what I can do with mine without going mad with guilt.

I could arrange to erase this embryo physically but I could never erase it mentally. I'd remember it every year on the anniversary of the day it was never born—or perhaps on the anniversary of that dinner at the Ritz—and I'd picture it, as adorable as Robin, holding out its arms to me and asking to be loved. Yes, that thought's hideously emotional and hideously sentimental but it also happens to be hideously true. It's what would happen. I know myself, I know the kind of woman I am and I know I can't get rid of this child, I've got to endure it.

Can I endure Robert taking years and years to die of this unnamable paralytic disease? That question reminds me of the time I asked myself if I could endure a country life on his parents' doorstep. The obvious answer is "no" but one has to try to be constructive.

Perhaps I could survive with someone who was hopelessly ill, but my state of mind would have to be so radically different from its present state that I can't begin to imagine it. How does a woman who loathes illness stick with a sick estranged husband who insists that she remain a conventional wife? A brave woman would stick it. A religious woman would stick it. A strong woman like Margaret would stick it. But I'm neither brave nor religious nor strong. I'm cowardly, agnostic and feeble. I'm not cut out to be a heroine. All I'm cut out to be is a broken reed and a mess.

"I'm going to be a heroine when I grow up!"

"I want to be a hero!"

Dear little Robert, what fun we had . . .

"Friendship's forever!"

How sad to think of us saying that. For of course friendship's not forever. Friendship can be destroyed by adverse circumstances just as Robert's body can be destroyed by this illness. Nothing's forever, nothing—except the memory of Oxmoon, that lost Oxmoon of our childhood, the memory that no adverse circumstances have ever been able to destroy.

I think I'm on the brink of imagining the unimaginable, but wait; I must beware of sentimentality; I must deal only with what is real and true.

Robert asked me once if we could recapture the magic of Oxmoon and I just said brutally, "I can't work that particular miracle for you."

But that in fact is what I now have to do. I somehow have to lead us back into the world we knew as children because that's the one world which no tragedy will ever be able to annihilate.

How do I do it? We'll go back to Gower, but as I've already realized, that removal by itself means nothing. I have to re-create something intangible, a world that exists only in our heads but a world that is as real to us as Mount Everest is to a mountaineer.

It's all a question of friendship in the end, isn't it? The marriage can't help us. That's dead, and our present friendship is such a maimed pathetic affair that it's small wonder I've been tempted to discount it. But we gave friendship a unique meaning at Oxmoon, that lost Oxmoon of our childhood, and if that old bond's recaptured we'll go home again at last.

"Are you asleep?"

"No, come in, darling, I'm about to get up. I must have a word with Cook about dinner." As he entered the room I rose from the bed and drew back the curtains. It had turned into a beautiful evening and below us in the courtyard the daffodils were blooming in the jardinière.

"Are you better?"

"Yes. Sorry I collapsed like some feeble Victorian heroine."

"Unlike a feeble Victorian heroine you had good reason to swoon. Ginette, can we have just one honest conversation before we go on?"

"Why not? Life's so awful at the moment that the prospect of an honest conversation doesn't even send a shiver down my spine." I straightened the bed and we sat down on it. "Where do we begin?"

"Where we left off. With the illness. Ginette, I do think I've got it. What's more, I suspect this is going to be a far worse experience than anything we can begin to imagine, so what we should do now is try to work out how we're going to face it."

All I said was "Go on."

"You loathe illness; it repulses you. You enjoy physical love; the prospect of you being tied to a cripple is ludicrous. You love London; the thought of a country life appalls you. To sum up, I can't believe you want to continue with this marriage and therefore I think it's only right that I should offer to release you from it."

"Robert—"

"Wait. I haven't finished. You must hear me to the end. Our marriage has been a failure. You know that—I know that. We've both been very unhappy, but at least I still love you enough to do all I can to put matters right. I can't drag you through this ordeal that lies ahead of me—well, to be frank, I don't think you could stand it, so if we're going to part it's far better that we should do so now. We'll forget about Martinscombe. I'll live at Oxmoon with my parents and that'll mean I'll have sufficient funds to maintain you in London —in a flat, though, I'm afraid, I couldn't afford a house. As for Robin, he must be with you while he's young although I do hope you can bring him to visit me. I wouldn't dream of asking you to come often, as I know how you hate seeing my parents, but the occasional visit would mean so much to me, and—"

"Darling—"

"No, you must let me finish, I'm sorry but you must let me have my say. The occasional visit would mean so much to me, and I would find it easier to bear the divorce if I knew I wasn't going to be entirely cut off from you both. Now, it'll be awkward about the divorce, because neither of us have any grounds, and even if I manufacture some infidelity you can't divorce me on the ground of adultery alone, but once we've lived apart for two years you could claim both adultery and desertion and then you'd be entitled—"

"No," I said.

He stared at me. "No what?"

"No divorce."

"But surely—"

"No divorce, Robert."

"Well, I admit it would be far less messy if we merely entered into a legal separation, but—"

"No. No legal separation."

He was dumbfounded. "No legal separation either? Oh, but I think you should consider it for your own sake. It's best to tie these things up formally —you should see a solicitor, have the legal situation explained to you."

"That's unnecessary. I want to remain married to you."

"For Robin's sake, you mean? But . . . how could we sustain a normal marriage?"

I said nothing. We went on sitting on the bed, he looking at me, I staring at the rings on my wedding finger.

"It would be impossible for me to be a conventional husband to you," said Robert. He paused to consider the logical deductions which could be drawn from this fact. Then he said with his characteristic simplicity, "Therefore I couldn't expect you to be a conventional wife. That wouldn't be fair at all. That wouldn't be playing the game." And as he paused again, frowning as he tried to imagine the complex relationship which lay far beyond the bounds of the marital game as he perceived it, I covered his hand reassuringly with mine.

"There are all kinds of marriages, Robert. Ours will simply be a little different from most marriages, that's all."

"Yes, but . . . well, it wouldn't be a marriage at all, would it, because it would be absolutely essential to me that you lived entirely as you wished—"

"It would still be a marriage, Robert."

"—because, you see, I couldn't bear it if you came to hate me for blighting your life—"

"I understand."

"—and that's why I shan't mind if you can't bring yourself to visit me much—I couldn't bear you to look at me with loathing—or repulsion—or worst of all pity—I'd rather set you free altogether, no matter how much I came to miss you—"

"Very well. Set me free. But set me free within the bounds of our marriage."

He still did not understand. He looked at me trustfully, waiting for an explanation, and when I saw that trust I knew time was completing its circle at last and we were moving back to where it had all begun.

I thought: Nearly there now, nearly home. And as I clasped his hand in mine I could see in the distance the strawberry beds and the mellow walls and the sunlight streaming down upon the kitchen garden long ago.

"But are you sure," said Robert when I remained silent, "that you'll wish to stay married once you're living apart from me in London?"

"I'm not staying in London," I said. "I'm coming with you to Gower."

I saw the trust in his eyes eclipsed by the blackest despair. He said in a shaking voice, "That's just sentimentality! You're being stupid, emotional and unrealistic! You're embarking on a charade you'll never be able to sustain!"

But I could see the strawberries, large and juicy among their thick leaves. I could feel the sun blazing down upon us, and at that moment the circle was completed, time was displaced and *we were there*, side by side in the kitchen garden at Oxmoon with the magic past recaptured and the strawberries in our hands.

"No, Robert," I said. "This is no charade, no illusion and no lie. There's one absolute truth in this situation, and it's the truth I intend to prove to you till the day you die."

"But for God's sake, what truth can that possibly be?"

Speaking in a voice that never faltered I completed the reformation of our marriage which he himself had had the courage to begin. "Robert," I said simply, "I could always walk out on a husband. But I could never turn my back on a friend."

PART THREE

JOHN

1921–1928

Why then do you mortal men seek after happiness outside yourselves, when it lies within you? You are led astray by error and ignorance. I will briefly show you what complete happiness hinges upon. If I ask you whether there is anything more precious to you than your own self, you will say no. So if you are in possession of yourself you will possess something you would never wish to lose and something Fortune could never take away. . . .

—Boethius
The Consolation of Philosophy

1

I

"SHE SAID, 'I could always walk out on a husband, but I could never turn my back on a friend.' "

"What an extraordinary remark."

"She's an extraordinary woman."

"Quite."

I moved restlessly to the window. The spring sun, shining on Ginevra's chaotic garden, emphasized herbaceous borders crammed with a variety of unsuitable shrubs, most of which had failed to survive the winter. A group of vulgar stone cherubs, part of a dismantled fountain acquired at an auction, were grouped beyond the swing where Robin was playing, and his nanny was staring at them as if she were wishing she had a supply of fig leaves. A wail from a nearby rug indicated that the baby was as usual oppressed with his peculiarly vocal variety of unhappiness.

"Shut the window, would you, John? I can't stand the way that child cries all the time. It gets on my nerves."

It was not one of Robert's better days. He was sitting in his favorite armchair by the hideous modern fireplace and fidgeting with his crutches as if he longed to break them in two. Ginevra had gone to London for a week, but when I had ventured to suggest that a wife's recurring absences from home could hardly be in the best interests of her husband, he had become angry. In vain I had tried to explain that I merely wished to sympathize with him in his depression; that had made him angrier than ever. He had said he loathed sympathy. Again I had tried to apologize and again I had been shouted down. Grudgingly conceding that my intentions had been good, he had said he had no alternative but to show me that my sympathy was misplaced, and the next moment, to my embarrassment, he had launched himself upon an explanation of his relationship with his wife.

I had always accepted that despite their recent adversity Robert and Ginevra had the happiest and most perfect of marriages, so it came as a considerable shock to me to hear that the marriage had been highly unorthodox for over two years.

I did not care for unorthodoxy. When Robert told me he had not pursued his marital rights since the onset of his illness, I was uncomfortable enough to rise to my feet; when he added that Ginevra was the kind of woman who would find intimacy with a diseased man repulsive, I hardly knew where to look and when he told me neither of them cared anyway that this aspect of their marriage had ceased, I found myself moving aimlessly around the room to cover my extreme distaste for the conversation. Robert completed this Bohemian marital portrait by declaring that he had no idea what Ginevra did in London, but he hoped she drank plenty of champagne, visited Harrods every day and had at least three lovers.

". . . because if that's the price I have to pay for having a good friend at my side, then by God I'm more than willing to pay it," he concluded truculently.

My diplomatic training ensured that I answered: "Quite so. I entirely understand," but I was appalled. I did not blame Robert. Obviously for the children's sake he had no choice but to be a complaisant husband, but I felt that Ginevra, never noted for either her decorum or her good taste, had sunk even lower than I had always feared was possible.

"I must make a move," said Robert. "Ring the bell, would you?"

I did not offer to assist him to the cloakroom. His man Bennett had been a hospital orderly during the war and was more adroit than I was at giving the help necessary when Robert was finding his crutches a trial. As Bennett entered the room I said, "I'll just say hullo to the children," and then I escaped through the French windows into the bungalow's untidy garden.

Robin came running to meet me as I crossed the lawn. He had recently celebrated his fourth birthday and was tall for his age. Since neither Robert nor Ginevra had any talent for parenthood he had been abominably spoiled, but he was a good-looking intelligent little fellow who with luck would survive his upbringing. Meanwhile he was merely precocious and tyrannical.

"Hullo, Uncle John! Mummy sent me a postcard from London!" And pulling a crumpled picture of Buckingham Palace from his pocket, he read the message in order to show off his formidable reading ability.

I knew people thought Blanche and I were old-fashioned, but we still preferred the dignity of "Mama" and "Papa" to the mediocrity of "Mummy" and "Daddy." However as usual Ginevra had no taste in such matters. Her Kinsella sons actually called her "Ma" although allowances had to be made for their New York background.

I inspected the picture, commented admiringly on the gushing message and paused to bid the nanny good afternoon before turning my attention to the baby, who was sitting moodily on his rug. He was eighteen months old but backward, disinclined to walk or talk. His pale blue eyes looked up at me fearfully; his large nose quivered; he was very plain.

"Silly Kester!" said Robin, trying to tug me away.

The baby had been named Christopher after the patron saint of travelers because Robert and Ginevra had felt they had such a difficult journey ahead of them, but although I liked the name it was never used. Ginevra had adopted this coy rustic abbreviation because she claimed to find it "romantic," and Robert was too indifferent to the child to object.

To divert Robin, I gave him my watch and asked him if he could tell the time. Then I knelt on the rug and tried to encourage the baby to take a few steps. He managed three and fell down. Howls ensued. "Pernicious infant," said Robin, showing off the vocabulary that Robert taught him as a jest, and handed me back my watch. "It's quarter past four. Are you staying to tea?"

But I had planned to be home for tea. Extricating myself from a situation that threatened to become increasingly noisy, I patted both children on the head and retreated to the drawing room. I was very much aware that I had not yet disclosed to Robert the main purpose of my call at the bungalow that afternoon.

Bennett was helping Robert into his chair again as I closed the French windows.

"Will you be staying to tea, Mr. John?" said Bennett as he prepared to leave the room.

I glanced at Robert but he said nothing. I knew he was too proud to ask for fear I might think he was begging for company.

"Yes, I will," I said abruptly, "but could you telephone my wife, please, Bennett, and say I'm staying on?"

As soon as Bennett had left the room Robert said, "John, I hope you didn't abandon a promising career at the Foreign Office because you thought you had some repellent moral duty to be my unpaid companion."

"Don't be absurd! I hated the F.O. and was only too pleased to begin a new life in Gower for reasons which had nothing to do with my moral duty!"

"I still find your decision surprising—and to some extent hard to explain. Why did you really come back here? You're a dark horse, John! I sometimes wonder if even you yourself have any idea of what's really going on in your head!"

"Good heavens, how very sinister you make me sound! I assure you I'm just an ordinary, simple sort of chap—"

"A touching description—but I suspect hardly a truthful one. Never mind, let it pass. Personally I'm only too glad that when Papa's senile and I'm a vegetable there'll be someone in Gower who's capable of ruling the Godwin roost—and now you're going to fling up your hands in diplomatic horror! My God, is it really so impossible to have an honest conversation with you?"

"Damn you, I *am* being honest! As you well know, I came back here because I was unhappy in London. Naturally I was influenced in my decision by the fact that Papa isn't getting any younger and your health isn't what it should be, but—"

"A truly magnificent euphemism. Go on. I can hardly wait to hear what you're going to come out with next."

"—but above and beyond my moral duty to give my father and brother any assistance which may become necessary in the future, I was concerned primarily with my family's happiness and welfare—which I feel will be better served if I live the life of a country gentleman in Gower than if I pursue a life of ambition in a career which means nothing to me."

"It all sounds most implausible," said Robert mildly, lighting a cigarette, "but since I benefit so profoundly, why should I start worrying that you've gone off your head? Very well, I accept what you say. You're a saint who yearns for the simple life. Very nice. I congratulate you."

I was silent. This was evidently one of Robert's more difficult days not only physically but emotionally as well, and I had no wish to continue a conversation which could so easily become acrimonious. I too lit a cigarette in order to provide an excuse for my continuing silence, but I was still wondering how I could turn the conversation towards the subject I wished to discuss when Robert said, "Forgive me. I know you genuinely believe in what you say and that means I've no right to treat you as a *poseur*. I suppose I'm cynical about your decision because I know you enjoyed the glitter and glamour of London far more than I ever did, but I must say you've given no indication that you miss your old life—and that in turn, as I said to Papa the other day, makes me wonder how well I ever knew you in the first place."

I saw my chance. "Talking of Papa, Robert," I said swiftly, "I've reached the stage where I can no longer condone his disgraceful situation—in fact I feel so embarrassed by him nowadays that I hardly like to take my family to Oxmoon every Sunday. Something's got to be done. His conduct is absolutely beyond the pale."

"I agree it's regrettable. However—"

"Regrettable! What an odious understatement! For Papa to keep a mistress in London is one thing; for him to keep a mistress in Gower is quite another—and for him to keep a former Oxmoon parlormaid in a tied cottage in Penhale is simply beyond the bounds of all permissible behavior."

"I do see it must be awkward for you and Blanche. But if Mama can tolerate the situation then I think you should too."

"I'm afraid I'm finding that old argument of yours increasingly unsatisfactory. Obviously Mama can no longer cope. She needs active assistance, not tactful silence."

"When Mama wants assistance she'll ask for it."

"Obviously she's to proud to do so. Robert, in my opinion it's your moral duty as the eldest son to tell Papa—"

"Any reprimand from me would be futile because unfortunately a man as troubled as Papa can rarely be cured by censure."

"But how dare he break all the rules like this!"

"I agree it's tragic. But try to remember the mitigating circumstances."

"What mitigating circumstances?"

"His sufferings in adolescence."

"How can they be mitigating circumstances? They should have taught him that the wages of sin are death!"

Robert sighed as if praying for patience.

"Well, look what happened to Owain Bryn-Davies!" I shouted, maddened by his obtuseness.

"Ah yes," said Robert blandly. "Mr. Owain Bryn-Davies and his little accident with the tide tables."

I looked away but not quickly enough and Robert saw the expression in my eyes. I heard his quick intake of breath. Then he said, "So you know. How the devil did you find out?"

"I haven't the slightest idea what you're talking about."

"My dear John—"

"I know nothing, absolutely nothing."

"Then why don't you demand that I explain myself? For someone who's asserting ignorance of the past you show the most remarkable lack of curiosity!"

There was a silence. I tried to speak but nothing happened, and at last Robert said mildly, coaxingly, as if I were some peculiarly difficult witness, "You've known for some time, have you? Who told you? And why did you never confide in me? It's the devil of a shock for a man, as I well know, to discover that his father's committed—"

I found my tongue just in time. Before he could utter the unutterable I said with all the force I could muster, "I'm sorry, Robert, but this is a matter which I refuse to discuss either now or on any later occasion. I also refuse to be diverted from the subject of Papa's present behavior, so let me now ask the vital question again: Do you or do you not intend to tell him he must pull himself together and mend his ways?"

"I most certainly do not. It would only exacerbate a situation which is already quite painful enough."

"Very well." I rose to my feet. "Then if you won't tell him, I shall."

"Oh for God's sake, John, don't be such a bloody fool!"

"I hate to contradict you, Robert, but I absolutely deny being a fool, bloody or otherwise. I'm a man intelligent enough to have high standards— and here I draw the line."

II

"What an odd boy you are," said my father. "Impertinent too."

"I'm not a boy, sir. I'm a man of twenty-nine."

"Then behave like one."

We were in the billiard room at Oxmoon shortly after six o'clock that evening. I had found my father and Edmund between games, and when I had asked for a word in private, Edmund had drifted away before my father could suggest we withdrew to the library, the room where he usually chose to conduct private conversations.

There was a superficial physical resemblance between us but this was muted by a difference in manner. My father, unmarked by the stamp of an English education, concealed his Welsh shrewdness behind an informal, almost indolent charm. So appealing was this charm that one tended to underestimate his strength, which was considerable. He was not a weak man. He had strong feelings, strong opinions and a strong inclination to be stubborn in the face of opposition. Although gentle and affectionate with his children he was capable of violence if his temper was roused, and the moment I finished speaking I knew I had roused it.

I was already nervous but now I became more nervous than ever. I did love my father but the love was confined in a straitjacket of fear because whenever I looked at him I could never forget that I was seeing a man who had committed murder and got away with it. I knew that the murder had been justified. I knew he was a good man. But always I was aware that he was capable of anything, and that was why I felt it was so important that he stuck to the rules of a civilized society when conducting his private life.

"Sir, please believe me when I say I speak only out of respect and concern—"

"I don't know what the devil you're speaking out of, but I doubt if respect and concern have much to do with it." He turned away from me, flung open the door and shouted, "Margaret!"

I was horrified. "Papa, for God's sake—you can't drag Mama into this conversation!"

My father lost his temper. As I backed away, automatically keeping the table between us, he shouted, "How dare you try to tell me what I can or can't do! How dare you have the insolence to preach to me in this hypocritical fashion!"

"I'm no hypocrite. I'm just doing what I honestly believe to be right."

"Your trouble is that you'd like a mistress in Penhale yourself but you know your wife would be a lot less understanding than mine!"

I was so angry that I forgot my fear of his violence and walked right up to him. "That's a bloody lie!" I shouted. *"You* may have no more morals than your bloody mother, but at least *I* have the bloody decency not to follow in your footsteps!"

A plump little hand closed on my arm. My mother said in a voice cold with fury, "That's a disgraceful thing to say to your father. Apologize this instant," and her manner shocked me into composure.

I said, "I'm sorry. I'm very sorry, I—" but even before I could finish speaking my father was addressing my mother.

"Margaret, I can't manage this boy, I can't talk to him, he makes me too angry."

"Yes, don't worry, dear," said my mother, "I'll straighten out this little difficulty for you."

He kissed her and left the room. My mother's hand was still gripping my arm, but as his footsteps receded she released me, stepped back a pace so that she could more easily look me in the eyes and then said with a coarseness which shocked me to the core, "You damned fool—why in God's name couldn't you come to me if you wanted to complain about Mrs. Straker? For an intelligent man you seem to have behaved with the most unforgivable stupidity."

III

I had anticipated neither my mother's anger nor her attitude to my father's behavior, and for a moment I was too distressed to marshal my defenses. I was very fond of my mother. Lion was supposed to have been her favorite, but it seemed to me I had been favored too because I sensed she made special efforts to be loving towards me. In early childhood I had taken this warmth for granted but later when I was all too aware that my resemblance to my grandmother might make me repulsive in my parents' eyes, I had gratefully interpreted my mother's marked affection as a sign that I was not to be condemned to a low place in her esteem.

But this resolute determination of hers to be just was characteristic behavior. What I admired most about my mother was her infinite capacity for rejecting wrongdoing, and whenever she said, "I draw the line," I felt an overwhelming relief and gratitude. My mother was the bastion against madness, chaos and catastrophe. In a world where I had known from childhood that absolutely anyone was capable of absolutely anything, my mother offered an infallible recipe for normality: one set oneself high moral standards, one drew the line against what was wrong—and one survived with one's sanity intact. My fear of my father had long been ameliorated by the knowledge that my mother would always stop him if ever he began to breach his own rules too flagrantly.

I thought she would stop him now.

"Mama, please do forgive me but I came here this evening with the very best intentions—"

"Your father is not to be upset like this! He needs compassion and understanding, not pigheaded intolerance!"

"Well, all I can say is I think it's time *he* showed some compassion and understanding! What about us? What about his family? I can't stand Blanche being exposed to scandal like this—"

"Have you told her?"

"What about?"

"The past."

"What past?"

"Oh, for God's sake, John! Sometimes I think this Welsh evasiveness will drive me mad!"

"I'm not Welsh, not at all, I'm English by education, inclination and temperament."

"Good. Then perhaps you'll now practice the Anglo-Saxon virtue of calling a spade a spade. Have you or have you not told Blanche that your father was driven to kill his mother's lover and shut his mother up in an asylum for the rest of her life?"

"Good God, no! Of course I've never told Blanche that!"

"Then may I suggest that you should? Quite apart from the fact that she's your devoted wife and deserves your confidence, she's also a compassionate intelligent girl, and I think if she knew the full tragedy of your father's past she would be willing to forgive him now for putting you both in such a difficult position."

"I'm sorry," I said, making a great effort to remain calm, "we're ostensibly conversing with each other but I'm beginning to think no communication's taking place. Are you trying to tell me that you're refusing to draw the line against Papa's immorality despite the fact that this is an occasion when the firmest possible line should be drawn?"

"I do draw the line," said my mother. "I draw the line against your unChristian, uncharitable and unforgivably priggish behavior. I find it repellent."

"But it's his behavior that's repellent! How can you tolerate him keeping Mrs. Straker in Penhale—Straker the parlormaid whom you had to dismiss from Oxmoon because he couldn't keep his hands off her! I think the entire episode's disgraceful, and how you can stand there and criticize me when all I'm trying to do is prevent innocent people from suffering as the result of his despicable conduct—"

My mother slapped me across the mouth. As I gasped, I saw not only the rage but the dislike blaze in her eyes.

The world went dark. The past began to suppurate. Chaos had come again.

"I don't pretend to understand you," said my mother. "I never have. I've always made a special effort not to be prejudiced, but really it's very hard not to be prejudiced when I see Bobby upset like this. I know just what's going on in his mind—he used to lecture his mother about her immorality and now he must feel as if her ghost has crawled out of the grave to lecture him in return!"

"But I had no idea I'd remind him of—"

"Oh, be quiet! Can't you see how you're tormenting Bobby by treating him as if he's in danger of ending up like his mother?"

"I just want him to live up to his own high standards—"

"He would if he could but he can't. That's the truth of it. Your father's haunted by the past. He thinks it'll drive him mad unless he uses every means he can to control it, and I think he's right; it'll drive him mad if he can't live with the memory of what happened. Women help him live with it. I don't know why. He doesn't know why. It doesn't matter why. What matters is that women keep him sane. I don't care about the mistresses. I did once, but not anymore; I don't give a damn. I'm the one he loves and that's all that counts—and as for Milly Straker, I tell you frankly that she's the best thing that's happened to Bobby for a very long time. I concede it's unfortunate that he has to keep her in Penhale, but now that he's getting older it's no use expecting him to travel up to London or even as far as Swansea in order to get what he must have. I accept that she has to live in Penhale, but that's all right; that's a concession I'm prepared to make because Mrs. Straker, provided she's paid well, won't cause trouble; quite the reverse. She's clever and discreet, and if he has to have a whore at least I have the satisfaction of knowing he has a whore who has high standards and sticks to them. I can respect someone like that, no matter how common and vulgar she is, and besides I'm sufficiently practical to understand that there are worse fates for an elderly lecher than Mrs. Straker. Gervase de Bracy died of syphilis. Oswald Stourham's taken to drink. In contrast Bobby's healthy and reasonably happy—whenever you're not making him miserable by reminding him of his mother. Now go home, talk the whole matter over sensibly with your wife and never, never let me find you making such a scene here again."

She left the room. For a long time I stayed by the billiard table, my forefinger tracing meaningless patterns on the green baize, but at last I slipped furtively out of the house and drove home in misery to my family.

IV

"Hullo, darling! There you are, Marian, didn't I tell you Papa would be back in time to say good night? Let me see if Harry's finished his bath. . . . John, is anything the matter?"

"No, everything's fine," I said. "Couldn't be better."

"Papa, I've chosen my bedtime story," said Marian, who was going to be six in the autumn.

I read a fairy tale about a handsome prince who fell in love with a ravishing peasant girl. After interminable vicissitudes they succeeded in getting married and living happily ever after.

"That's like you and Mama, isn't it, Papa?"

"Well, Mama was hardly a peasant girl, Marian, but yes, we did get married and live happily ever after."

Blanche returned to the night nursery with Harry in her arms.

He was two years old. He looked very clean after his bath and very fresh in a newly laundered little nightshirt. A faint scent of talcum powder drifted towards me. His dark hair, much darker than mine, had been neatly parted and brushed.

"Kiss Harry, darling," said Blanche to Marian as Nanny hovered in the background with the customary approving expression on her face, "and then Papa will hear you say your prayers."

Harry yawned again. His small head drooped against my chest to betray how tired he was after yet another stimulating day. Then, conscious that I was smiling at him, he looked up and smiled brilliantly back at me.

I thought of spoiled little Robin and tedious little Kester and knew a moment of intense pity for Robert, but a second later I had recognized this pity as an ambivalent emotion and was suppressing it rigorously. It would never do to enjoy Robert's misfortune, and it would certainly never do to savor the notion that my life was turning out to be more satisfactory than his. These were contemptible thoughts indeed, suggesting hidden jealousies which could not be permitted to exist.

Chaos as always was waiting. And as always I drew the line.

"Darling," said Blanche uneasily several hours later when we were in bed. "I know something's wrong, and I do wish you'd tell me what it is. I must be a poor sort of wife if you feel you can't confide in me."

"Don't be absurd; you're a perfect wife, you know you are!"

"In that case—"

"I'm worried about my father, but I don't want to talk about him."

"Ah." I heard her sigh in the dark. "I wish there was something I could do when you're troubled," she said, laying her cheek gently against my shoulder. "I hate feeling I'm incapable of helping you."

I knew at once how she could help me but I spent a great deal of my married life trying not to exploit her love by giving vent to selfish inconsiderate behavior, and I now shrank from taking advantage of her. She had been exceptionally generous to me only the night before.

"I wouldn't dream of—"

"It doesn't matter."

There was a silence while I tried to work out what was the right thing to do. No decent husband imposed himself on his wife on two consecutive nights. On the other hand if the wife expressed willingness this could be held to exonerate him, although if she was merely expressing willingness in order to be a good wife, then the consent failed to be genuine and restraint was called for.

"Darling . . ." She pressed closer to me. To my humiliation I was conquered, and despising myself I embarked on the most pleasurable way I had yet discovered of forgetting what I had no wish to remember. The exquisiteness of that pleasure never failed to appall me, and that night after Blanche had fallen asleep I found myself struggling afresh with memories that not even the most exquisite pleasure could annul. I knew all too well what could happen to those who became addicted to carnal pleasure—and the next moment I was back in the past again while my grandmother screamed for mercy, my mother struck her to control the hysterics and my father shouted at me in Welsh at the top of his voice that insanity and ruin lay waiting for all those who failed to draw the line.

V

I had no respite when I fell asleep because that night she invaded my dreams, just as she always did when I was seriously upset. My grandmother had died in 1910 but for me in 1921 she was still alive. The straight line of time bent so that 1903 kept recurring interminably in my mind, the Christmas of 1903 when I had been eleven years old.

My grandmother had been sixty-two. She had not aged well. She was thin and haggard. She had bony hands which she twisted together continually. Her glance darted furtively hither and thither among her grandchildren, as if she were trying to pin us all in her mind so that she could savor us during her lonely months in the asylum where we never visited her. We all thought her both pathetic and a bore, a perpetual blight on our otherwise exuberant family Christmas, a cross which we had to undertake in the name of Christian charity. Grandmama was mad and not normally a fit subject for discussion, but once a year her portrait had to be brought down from the attics and hung in the dining room, and once a year for a few hours we had to endure her presence. We sighed and groaned and yawned but every Christmas submitted ourselves to the tedium of the inevitable.

The Christmas of 1903 began in unremarkable fashion. On Christmas Eve my father fetched my grandmother from the Home of the Assumption. On Christmas morning we all racketed around in our noisy fashion, pulling all the gifts out of our stockings, eating a huge breakfast and setting off for church. The presents under the tree were never unwrapped until after dinner which at Christmas, in order to spare the servants, was taken in the middle of the day. When we all returned from church my mother went to the kitchens to see how the dinner preparations were progressing and my father remained in the drawing room to keep an eye on my grandmother. It had only recently occurred to me that my parents never left my grandmother alone with their children.

Robert, always aloof, had wandered off somewhere in search of solitude. Ginevra was absent in America. Celia and Lion were playing an acrimonious game of cribbage while Edmund looked on. I was reading a book, *Kidnapped* by Stevenson it was, I remember it well, just as I remember glancing up from the page and seeing my grandmother watching me from her position by the hearth.

My father was talking to her casually in Welsh about his plans to redesign the kitchen garden. He was just saying, "And I've a good mind to double the asparagus beds" when Ifor the footman rushed pell-mell into the room and gasped that the head parlormaid was having what he described as a "pepperleptic" fit in the dining room.

"Good God!" said my father, and hurried out.

"Heavens!" said Celia, and rushed after him.

"This sounds too good to miss!" said Lion outrageously, and bounded away with Edmund, the constant shadow, pounding at his heels.

I was just setting aside my book after making the obvious decision to follow them when my grandmother said suddenly, "Johnny."

I was called Johnny in those days. I had always thought the name John very dull, redolent of John Bull and English stuffiness, and I had long been envious of Lion's racy evocative first name.

"Yes, Grandmama?" I said politely in Welsh.

She beckoned me. Trying to disguise my impatience, I drew closer and thought, Poor mad old crone.

"I want to give you a little present," she said, "a special present, every year I've brought it to Oxmoon to give to you and every year I've never had the chance to see you on your own." She looked nervously at the half-open door. Her eyes were bright with fear. "Take me somewhere private, Johnny, where they won't find us."

I thought this was possibly some new manifestation of madness, but I was intrigued by the thought of a special present and she seemed harmless enough.

"Very well," I said politely, helping her to her feet. "We'll go to the music room. We'll be quite private there."

We set off, she clutching my arm in an agony of nervousness, I feeling gratified that I had been singled out for special attention. Bayliss the butler was passing through the hall when we left the drawing room, but he was too busy to do more than cast us a passing glance, and a minute later we had reached our sanctuary. I was just saying kindly, "There! You're quite private now!" when to my horror my grandmother embraced me amidst floods of tears.

"Forgive me." She saw how alarmed I was and at once she withdrew, but the tears continued to stream down her cheeks. "I couldn't help myself," she whispered, "I've loved you so much for so long, such a fine boy you are, the finest in the family and so special to me, but of course I never dared say so in front of Margaret because that would make her angry and then she might not let me come home anymore, and if that happened I'd never see you and that would break my heart because I love you so much, so much love I have and no one to give it to, not anymore, but just for a little while at Christmas I can look at you and love you without Margaret knowing about it—oh, how frightened I am of Margaret, turning my son against me, keeping me from my grandchildren, so hard your mother is, Johnny, so cruel and unforgiving, but never mind that now, all that matters is that I have you on my own at last and I mustn't waste any time."

She produced a carefully folded handkerchief and held it out to me.

"Here, take this, take it, it's something to remember me by, something that will always remind you I love you better than anyone else does, better than your parents do, such a large family they have, so many claims on their affection, but never mind, you come first with me always although you mustn't tell Margaret or she won't let me see you anymore. Yes, unfold the handkerchief, I used my best handkerchief specially for you, yes, it's a ring, a man's signet ring, it'll be too big for you now but you can wear it later in memory of me. It belonged to the man I loved. They took it from his corpse after he was drowned. I asked Bobby for the ring and he saw that I got it but I don't know if he ever told Margaret. Margaret wouldn't have wanted me to have it, oh I'm so frightened of Margaret, and that's why you must hide the ring from her, Johnny, hide it until you're grown up, because if Margaret ever finds out that I've given you the ring which belonged to—"

She stopped. Her eyes dilated in terror. Spinning round I found that my mother had soundlessly opened the door.

"So there you are," said my mother, very composed. "Bayliss said he saw you disappearing together down the corridor to the music room." Stepping back into the passage she called, "All's well, Bobby. I've found her."

My grandmother began to tremble. She had backed away against the wall. As I watched, paralyzed by the guilt and fear that emanated from her, I saw the tears flow down her cheeks again.

My mother stepped back into the room. "Dearest Grandmama," she said kindly, "how generous of you to give Johnny one of your little mementos. Mr. Bryn-Davies's ring, isn't it? Yes, I thought I recognized it. However I'm afraid Johnny couldn't possibly accept such a gift. It wouldn't be fitting."

She spoke as always in English. I had never heard my mother speak a word of Welsh and yet I suspected she understood more than she would admit. I had no idea how much of my grandmother's speech she had overheard but I could see that my grandmother feared the worst and was petrified.

"Johnny dear, give Grandmama back the ring, please."

"Mama, please don't be cross with poor Grandmama—"

"Give her back the ring."

"What ring?" said my father from the doorway.

My grandmother covered her face with her hands and began to sob.

"Dearest Grandmama, Bobby," said her daughter-in-law, "has decided to single out Johnny for special attention by giving him the ring which belonged to Mr. Bryn-Davies."

"My God," said my father to his mother, "you bloody whore."

"Bobby, no—Margaret, please—Margaret, stop him—"

He slammed the door and seized me by the scruff of the neck. I was terrified. As my relaxed cheerful familiar father dissolved into a taut violent stranger, I felt as if I were witnessing a shining surface cracking apart to reveal unspeakable horrors beneath. Certainty, security, safety, peace—all the cherished attributes of a happy childhood—all were blasted from my life in seconds. I had been catapulted into a chaotic darkness. I knew instinctively that we were each one of us in hell.

He snatched the ring, shoved me aside and shook his mother by the shoulders. "You filthy, disgusting old woman, how dare you ask any son of mine to wear a ring which belonged to that thief, that blackguard, *that bloody villain Bryn-Davies* who ruined you and robbed me blind and soaked us all in evil—"

"I'll take the child out, Bobby," said my mother crisply. "This isn't good for him."

"Oh no!" shouted my father. "He stays where he is! He's going to find out all about this vile old woman who's singled him out for special attention!" And he began to talk in Welsh in graphic detail about how she had poisoned her husband in order to live a life of debauchery with her lover.

My grandmother went down on her knees and begged him to stop. He hit her and went on. Then she went down on her knees to my mother.

"Send Johnny away, Margaret—spare him—please—"

"No, it must be as my husband wishes," said my mother without expression, and stood by unmoved as my father hit my grandmother again until she cowered sobbing at his feet.

". . . and it was her wickedness which drove me to evil . . ." He never stopped talking, even when he was hitting her. He was talking all the time. ". . . and I killed Bryn-Davies, yes, I killed him—I trapped him and drowned him on the Shipway so that Oxmoon could be purged and we could all be saved—"

My grandmother saw my expression and could bear the torture no longer. She began to scream for mercy.

My mother stepped forward. "She's hysterical, Bobby. You'll have to hit her again."

"I daren't. I might kill her."

The door opened. Celia was revealed on the threshold.

"Mama, what on earth—"

"Celia, leave us at once and keep the little ones out of the way. Very well, Bobby, I'll deal with this."

My mother walked up to my grandmother and slapped her firmly twice, once on each cheek. That ended the hysterics, but not the scene. My father, sweat streaming down his face, then took advantage of the silence to shake me as if I were a bunch of rags and shout, "Look at her! Go on, look at her! She picked you out because she thinks you're like her, but if ever you're tempted to depravity just you remember this vile filthy old woman, utterly ruined, hated by those she loves, damned through all eternity—yes, just you remember her and never forget—*never forget for one moment*—that insanity and ruin lie waiting for those who fail to draw the line!"

He released me. My mother said to him, "Lock her up in one of the attics. She's not fit to dine. She'll have to go back to the asylum this afternoon."

My grandmother whimpered but was too terrified to speak.

"If you behave now," said my mother to her, "we might let you come back next year. I'll have to think about it. But if you do come back, you are never, never, *never* to address another word to any of my children. You're to keep silent and speak only when you're spoken to. Very well, Bobby, take her away."

My father removed the object. I could not think of her as a human being anymore. She had become evil personified, a threatening force which had to be perpetually kept at bay. Overpowered by fear I hid my face from her and hurtled blindly into my mother's arms.

"There, there," said my mother soothingly as I tried without success to cry. "You're quite safe, Mama's here and I'm going to tell you what you're going to do in order to feel better. First of all, you're never going to mention this scene to anyone—we'll draw a line neatly underneath it and then it'll belong to the past where it can no longer trouble us. Then afterwards you're going to be a specially good boy so that your poor papa is never reminded of his mother's wickedness."

I finally managed to cry.

"There, there," said my mother again. "Papa's a good, brave, thoroughly decent man and you must never think otherwise. He was just driven to wickedness by that evil woman, but that's all over now and I'm in control and there's no more wickedness at Oxmoon, not anymore—because *here I have my standards,*" said my mother, uttering the magic incantation that warded off all evil, "*and here I draw the line.*"

My grandmother paid six more visits to Oxmoon before her death, but she never spoke to any of her grandchildren again. She was too frightened, and whenever I saw her I was frightened too, terrified by the sinister possibilities of heredity. I had changed myself as far as possible, rejecting my Welshness, calling myself John and devoting myself to an austere life, but there remained the physical likeness which was beyond alteration, and so often when I saw my face in the looking glass I would fear there might be other inherited traits, now dormant, that might one day burgeon beyond control.

I was frightened of the uncontrollable. I was frightened of myself. As I passed from adolescence into adult life I realized that for my own peace of mind I had to keep my life in perfect order. Nothing, I told myself, must flaw the perfection and any drift towards chaos must be immediately checked. I knew I was jealous of Robert, but I saw how I could master that by pursuing a brilliant career in the one field in which I knew I could outshine him: modern languages. I knew I resented the fact that as a younger son I was unlikely to inherit my family home, but I resolved to do so well in life that I would wind up with a far finer home than Oxmoon—which, after all, was merely a pleasant Welsh country house of no great architectural merit. I knew I had to make some arrangement to neutralize the potential dangers of my sexuality, so I married young. I knew that in order to realize my ambition I had to surmount the handicap of being penniless, so I married money. I had overcome problem after problem, defused danger after danger, and now here I was, twenty-nine years old, with a perfect wife, a perfect home, two perfect children and a perfect life as a gentleman farmer.

It had been difficult to leave the Foreign Office, even though I had hated working there. How could I continue to equal Robert, I had asked myself in despair, if I abandoned all thought of the diplomatic service? But then Robert, fortunately, had abandoned his own career and soon afterwards his illness had ended our competition forever. I no longer had to be jealous of Robert. I have been set free to love him as I should, and in the relief of this liberation I had found I was also set free to do as I wished with my life.

I knew then what my real ambition was. I wanted—in the most tactful sympathetic way imaginable—and of course for the best possible motives—to take Robert's place. I knew my father had been greatly upset by Robert's illness. He had been looking forward to the prospect of Robert following in his own footsteps in Gower, but now Robert was following in no one's footsteps. Neither was Lion. Edmund was shell-shocked and ineffectual. Thomas was troublesome and appeared unintelligent. That left me, and I . . .

I was going to be the son my father had always wanted. No more coming second for me, not now. I was going to come first with my father at last; I was going to redeem myself wholly for my unfortunate resemblance to his mother, and we were all going to live happily ever after. I would be the prop of my father's old age and a pillar of strength to Robert, and by being indispensable I would wipe out the guilty memory of how much I had resented my father for idolizing Robert and how jealous I had been of Robert for being idolized. No more resentment! No more jealousy! My life would be in perfect order at last, and I could relax in the knowledge that I was permanently safe from a moral catastrophe. It was the most attractive and alluring prospect.

I might even inherit Oxmoon in the end. If my father outlived Robert he would certainly turn to Robin, but supposing Robin were to turn out badly, as spoiled children so often do? Nobody took any notice of Kester, so I could discount him. As the next son in line I thought my prospects were promising, but I kept my imagination in tight control because it was safer to believe I would never have Oxmoon than to evisage some possibly chaotic future in which the title deeds fell into my lap.

Oxmoon was the joker in the Godwin family pack, and the joker was circulating as we all played our cards. So far it had not appeared in my hand but I sensed it was coming nearer, and meanwhile I was bunching my cards closer together to leave a gap where the joker could slip in.

Naturally I could not acknowledge my hopes in regard to Oxmoon. That would have been a breach of taste while Robert lived and quite definitely not the done thing at all. Nor could I actively pursue my ambition to be master of the estate. That would hardly have been the done thing either. But I saw no reason why I shouldn't be a good son and a good brother and secretly hope a little. That appeared to be well within the bounds of civilized behavior, and it was of course unthinkable that I might ever step beyond those bounds. That way chaos lay.

I drew the line.

2

I

IT TOOK ME some time to recover my equilibrium after the disastrous scene with my parents in the billiard room at Oxmoon, but I concealed my distress from Blanche. I felt better after I had written my parents letters of apology. To my father I regretted behavior which he had justifiably regarded as lacking in filial respect, and to my mother I wrote that although I could not condone my father's conduct, I was willing to keep up an appearance of amity by continuing to bring my family to Oxmoon on Sundays for tea.

My father wrote back by return of post: *My dear John, Least said soonest mended. I remain always your affectionate father,* R.G.

My mother did not reply.

That upset me. It made me remember that dislike in her eyes; it made me remember my grandmother saying how hard my mother was and how unforgiving. I had suffered many nightmares about my grandmother but the one that never failed to horrify me was the nightmare in which the traditional roles were reversed. Supposing my grandmother were the tragic heroine of the story and my parents were the villains of the piece? This was a horrific thought indeed. I could not endure to think that my grandmother had loved me but that I had repudiated her as a vile and loathsome object in order to please my parents. Neither could I bear to think that my parents were villains, unjustified in their cruelty to a pathetic old woman, because if this were the truth then their high standards were a mockery and chaos had remained unconquered. These ambiguities tormented me, and after my quarrel with my mother I found the torment deepening. I felt my mother had to approve of me in order to put the situation in order and be the mother I needed her to be. If she continued to dislike me I might feel driven to turn for consolation to the memory of my grandmother, who had loved me so much, and once I started to embrace this symbol of evil, God only knew what might happen.

When I next saw my mother after church the following Sunday I said, "I trust your failure to reply to my letter doesn't mean we're estranged," but she merely replied, "If any estrangement exists, John, it's entirely of your own creation," and then my father joined us so that further opportunities for private conversation were curtailed.

I spent some time analyzing my mother's reply but I could not make up my mind what to think of it, and finally I was in such confusion that I appealed to Robert for help. I found him unsympathetic about my continuing moral stand against Mrs. Straker but he was willing enough to help with my mother, and presently I received a note which ran: *Dearest John, Robert tells me you're quite tormented by our little difference of opinion. I'm sorry. I would not wish any of my children to be tormented. Our best course would seem to be to consider the matter entirely closed, but I am sad to find you still so lacking in humanity in regard to your father's predicament. Never doubt that I remain always your most devoted mother,* MARGARET GODWIN.

I disliked this note so intensely that I burned it on the spot. Then I began to feel angry, an unacceptable emotion for a devoted son to feel towards a devoted mother. I finally controlled myself to the point where I was able to behave in her presence as if nothing were wrong, but I felt I had suffered some profound injury. I longed to confide in someone, but Robert, echoing my mother's sentiments with monotonous regularity, was clearly unsuitable, and naturally I would never have burdened Blanche with my complex resentment. In my misery it became more important to me than ever that no hint of trouble marred the perfection of my home, for at least when I was with my family I could pick up the script of my life, which I had worked out so painstakingly in my teens, and resume my familiar, comfortingly unflawed role of the perfect husband and father.

Fortunately several matters at this time conspired to divert my attention from my mother. The most obvious was the state of the nation, which was dire. We had survived the miners' strike and the threat of a general strike, but as far as I could see revolution was only a stone's throw away and the class war was about to begin. I had always leaned towards the conservative in politics. While wishing to alleviate the sufferings of the working classes I believed that the only way to keep Britain well ordered was for it to remain exactly as it was. God only knew what would happen if the Labour Party came to power but I had no doubt chaos would immediately ensue.

This air of political crisis was diverting enough but I was diverted still further by the problems of my new estate which I had acquired a year ago, soon after Robert and Ginevra had established their own home in Gower.

It was now the May of 1921, two years since Robert's illness had been diagnosed and seventeen months since the Christmas of 1919, when he had awoken at Oxmoon to find his right leg was paralyzed. Before that the illness had been a secret between him and his wife; after that no concealment had been possible.

They had been making their plans for some time. My father had already given Robert Martinscombe, the sheep farm below Penhale Down, but the farmhouse was now let once more to a foreman, and a bungalow, specially designed for the future wheelchair, had been built a quarter of a mile away.

As the result of Ginevra's dubious taste, this most eccentric new home consisted of a single-story block sandwiched between two towers, and had been nicknamed "Little Oxmoon" by the baffled villagers of Penhale. Pursuing a course of unflagging diplomatic tact whenever my opinion was sought on the structure's aesthetic qualities, I made every effort to ensure that Robert never guessed how sorry I was for him having to live there.

I was much more fortunate. My father-in-law died in the influenza epidemic of 1919, and although he could not leave me his country home, an ugly Jacobean mansion entailed on an heir in Canada, he did leave me his three thousands acres of Herefordshire farmland and his house in Connaught Square. To be accurate, I should record that he left them to Blanche, but naturally Blanche wanted to share her inheritance with me, and after I had made my decision to leave the F.O. I think she hoped we might settle in Herefordshire. However when I explained that it was my moral duty to return to Gower to help my father and Robert she was most understanding, and after engaging a manager to run the Herefordshire farms for me, I sold the town house in Connaught Square and began to cast around for a suitable property in Gower.

Fate stepped in with admirable neatness. Early in 1920 Sir Gervase de Bracy died, his widow and unmarried daughter removed for reasons of health to Bournemouth and the Penhale Manor estate found its way to the auction block. Both the de Bracy boys had been killed in the war.

I was the highest bidder. I had never ceased to thank God I had had a respite from financial worry since my wedding day, and I felt sorry for Robert, who must often have been obliged to wrestle with money troubles. He had written two books, one a memoir on Lloyd George and the other a dissertation on his famous trials, and both books had been well received, but, as everyone knows, there's no money in writing. He had some money saved, but Ginevra was an expensive wife and I suspected her extravagance was hard to control. I was appalled when I saw how much she must have spent on furnishing the bungalow to reflect her vulgar taste. Penhale Manor also needed refurbishment, but Blanche had exquisite taste and never made any purchase without my permission, so we managed to achieve beauty without profligate expenditure and elegance without vulgarity.

My one item of extravagance was a new grand piano which I bought for Blanche to thank her for her loyal support when I had left both the Foreign Office and our smart life in London. Blanche's great passion was music, and she was wonderfully accomplished. I myself am not musical; my talent for languages means that I have the most acute ear for sound, but the only instrument my ear can master is the human voice engaged in phonetic patterns. However because of my musical shortcomings I doubly admired Blanche's talent, and indeed I often felt sorry for Robert having a wife whose only talent lay in dressing in a manner which recalled the Edwardian *demi-*

monde. I would not have permitted my wife to dress as Ginevra dressed. I constantly marveled that Robert allowed her such latitude, but it was not my place to criticize, so I took care never to make any inappropriate remarks.

Blanche always looked matchlessly beautiful. She was dark and slender and had a pale creamy skin. Naturally she dressed to perfection. I never had to worry about Blanche looking raffish and hinting at an unfortunate past. I was very, very lucky to have such a flawless wife, and when we removed to Penhale Manor I knew I was very, very lucky to have such a potentially flawless home. As soon as I was settled, I applied myself conscientiously to the estate to iron out the remaining flaws.

Judicious expenditure might have been sufficient to make the house charming, but the estate required both brains and hard work to master and I spent long hours pondering on the problems it represented. It was not a large estate. There were less than three hundred acres attached to the Home Farm, which lay a mile from the house, but the land had been indifferently farmed by a succession of inadequate bailiffs, with the result that when I took over the farm it was little better than derelict. Much capital investment was required, but that raised no difficulty; I had only to sell off some land in Herefordshire to finance my schemes. Meanwhile I had resolved to manage the land myself with the help of a foreman whom I would install at the Home Farmhouse, and my father, much pleased by this decision, offered to inspect the land with me in order to determine what should be done.

Having grown up on a thriving estate I had a good general idea of what farming involved, but I had no practical experience of farm management so I knew it was crucial that I found the right foreman. Delighted as I was that my father should be interested in my plans, I thought his enthusiasm would pall if I kept running to him for help when things went wrong, and I was just wondering how I could find the agricultural sage that I needed when my father, who must have feared my inexperience as much as I did, offered me the services of his foreman at Daxworth; apparently the man was ambitious enough to fancy the idea of transferring to a semiderelict farm which would test his skills to the utmost, and certainly I was willing enough to consider him. He was a Welshman from Carmarthen called Meredith, and he was two years my senior. We met, liked each other, shook hands—and in that brief commonplace gesture I sealed his fate, and although neither of us guessed it, he sealed mine.

However when we first met we did not think in melodramatic terms such as fate because we were much too busy considering my decision to gamble on the new opportunities offered by motor transport. The remoteness of Gower before the war meant that cattle breeding was the type of farming favored and that crops were grown primarily for winter feeding, but with improved communications other avenues of farming could now be explored.

I decided to continue with the cattle breeding but expand the growth of crops so that the farm would produce a surplus which could be transported by motor lorry to Swansea for sale. Endless cogitation then ensued about which crops would be best to grow, not only for sale but to feed the cattle during the winter. Did I or did I not grow mangolds? How profitable were swedes? What were the pros and cons of potatoes? How much clover should be grown? I became so absorbed with these vital questions that I could hardly tear myself away to inspect my new lorry, but soon my father and I were indulging our passion for mechanics as we examined the lorry's huge engine together. My father enjoyed himself immensely. He told me more than once how happy he was that I had returned to Gower, and I assured him how delighted I was to be back. After each meeting we parted in a haze of gratification.

Meanwhile Blanche was settling down well and involving herself in village life. She kept saying how kind my mother was to her and how lucky she was to have such a helpful affectionate mother-in-law. I was deeply pleased. I knew my mother had always approved of Blanche but it was very satisfactory to learn that she also found her so congenial. My mother had never cared for Ginevra and I knew my parents had been disappointed by Robert's marriage.

"I think we're doing well, sir," said my foreman, Huw Meredith, in the spring of 1921, and I answered, thinking not only of the farm but of my place in my parents' affections, "Yes, we certainly are."

That was before the quarrel and immediately afterwards I was besieged with problems, as if fate had decided to dent my pardonable complacency. First of all we had a problem with a stockman who drank too much and had to be dismissed. Then I had a row with my cousin Emrys Llewellyn, whose sheep had trampled across one of my fields with disastrous results for the crop; he claimed that de Bracy had granted him a right-of-way over the field in the Nineties, but when I asked for the legal evidence of the easement I was informed that none existed. My cousin told me he had merely taken the word of a gentleman although, he added sourly as he looked me up and down, in his opinion all gentlemen farmers, particularly English gentlemen farmers, ought to be abolished and their land redistributed.

Until that moment the conversation had been conducted in English, for nowadays, apart from the occasional remark in Welsh to my father, this was the only language I permitted myself to speak, but Llewellyn's gibe made me forget that any betrayal of my Welshness was like a declaration of kinship with my grandmother. I told him in his own language that I was just as Welsh as he was and that he spoke out of jealousy because he secretly wished he himself had been brought up at Oxmoon instead of in his commonplace rural hovel. His jaw sagged at my command of Welsh but he recovered, and for some time we shouted at each other in a thoroughly un-English fashion until he called my grandfather a drunken bastard and I called his grandfather a bloody peasant and we almost came to blows. Fortunately he then started talking about "Aunt Gwyneth the Harlot," and this reminder of my grand-mother pulled me to my senses. I told him in English to keep his sheep off my land and said that if he failed to do so I would sue him. Then I retired, still in a towering rage, to the Home Farm to consult Huw Meredith.

The hour had come. It was eleven o'clock on the morning of July the eighteenth, 1921, and my perfect life with my perfect family in my perfect world was finally about to unravel.

II

The farmhouse was about two hundred years old, a square little building of faded brick with a slate roof. There was no garden in the English manner, merely a vegetable patch on one side of the house and some grass shaded by an oak tree in the front. The farmyard lay at the back, and as I halted my Sunbeam abruptly, I saw two children peeping out of the hayloft above the stables. This surprised me. Meredith was married but childless. I remem-bered that the new stockman had progeny but could think of no reason why they should be playing at the farm.

As usual I entered the house by the back door. In the kitchen Mrs. Mere-dith was scolding the local servant girl, but when I came in she broke off with a smile and told me her husband had just departed for Standing-Stone Field, where Llewellyn's sheep had been running riot. I said I would go and catch him up. As I turned back to the door I added, "Who are your visitors?"

"My sister's here from Cardiff with her children. Ah, here she is! Bronwen, this is Mr. Godwin, whom we talk so much about! Mr. Godwin, this is my sister, Mrs. Morgan."

I glanced over my shoulder at the woman who had entered the room, and instantly I knew I had to make a crucial decision: either she was ugly or she was beautiful. I decided that she was ugly. She was pale and thin, with garish red hair which was scraped back from her face into a bun.

"How do you do, Mrs. Morgan."

She murmured something which ended in "sir" and bobbed a brief awk-ward curtsy, which indicated she had been in service. Her voice was heavily accented like her sister's but gruffer, somewhat harsh. I thought it most unattractive and found it hard to believe that dark, plump, loquacious Mrs. Meredith, whose vivacity made her pretty, could have such a pallid unprepos-sessing sister.

Excusing myself I retreated to the farmyard. The children were no longer visible in the hayloft but I could hear their laughter in the distance, and as I paused for no reason except that I could not remember why I had wanted to see Meredith so urgently, Mrs. Meredith's voice drifted towards me through the open kitchen window nearby.

She came from a Welsh-speaking area of South Wales, and now she had reverted to her native tongue.

"Yes, he's such a handsome gentleman, isn't he, and he has this beautiful wife, such a lovely lady, so sweet and kind and unaffected . . ."

I walked away.

Three minutes later I had caught up with Meredith in Willow Lane and was giving myself the pleasure of railing against Emrys Llewellyn to a thoroughly sympathetic audience.

Meredith was the best kind of Welshman, quick, industrious and with cultural tastes that would have put an Englishman of a similar class to shame. In truth they even put me to shame, for although I myself was by no means uninterested in intellectual subjects I was still suffering from a reaction to my exhausting labors at Oxford, and nowadays I seldom opened a book more demanding than an Edgar Wallace thriller. Naturally I did not disclose these Philistine's tastes to Meredith. He believed an Oxford education represented a passport to a perpetual intellectual Elysium, and I had no intention of disillusioning him.

"Emrys Llewellyn's reminding me of Pip's sister in *Great Expectations*," he commented brightly. "Always on the rampage."

I racked my brains to cap this reference and managed to say, "Well, he's made a mistake if he thinks I'm going to be as passive as Joe Gargery." I hastened to divert him from literature. "And talking of sisters, is Mrs. Morgan staying long with you?"

"Till her husband gets back from the sea. He didn't leave her enough money and the poor girl's been turned out of her rooms."

"How very unpleasant for her."

I dismissed Mrs. Morgan from my mind but three days later I saw her in Penhale. I was driving back from Llangennith where Oswald Stourham, an old crony of my father's, had been trying unsuccessfully to sell me a horse, and as I passed through Penhale I saw Mrs. Morgan and her children leaving the village stores. She was carrying two full baskets and looked paler than ever.

I was a gentleman. Though disinclined to burden myself with the company of an inarticulate working-class woman, I drew up the car and offered her a lift.

She reddened in embarrassment. Indeed she was so overcome with confusion that she was unable to open the door, so suppressing a sigh of impatience I got out to help her. Her little boy shot into the back seat with great excitement but the little girl lingered shyly by her mother.

"What's your name?" I said to the child when they were all settled in the back seat.

"Rhiannon."

"Rhiannon!" I remembered the fairy tales spun by a succession of Welsh nursemaids long ago. "After the heroine in the *Mabinogion?*"

"No, after my grandmother in Cardiff."

I laughed. Mrs. Morgan smiled. I noticed that although she had the true Celtic skin, so white that it was almost translucent, the bridge of her nose was peppered with freckles. Reminding myself that I had always found freckles unattractive, I returned to the driving seat.

"And what's your name?" I said to the little boy as I drove off, but he failed to reply.

"Dafydd doesn't speak much English yet," said Mrs. Morgan. "He's only four and hasn't started school."

"Ah, I see. Do you like motors, Dafydd?" I said in Welsh, and glancing in the driver's mirror I saw the woman stir in surprise as she realized I spoke her language.

The little boy said yes, he loved motors but he had never ridden in one before, he had only ridden on a motorbus in Cardiff and on a train to Swansea and in a wagonette to Penhale. I asked him if he had enjoyed the train journey, but before he could reply the little girl said to me, "You speak English like an Englishman and yet you speak Welsh just like we do."

"I'm somewhat like a parrot. When I hear strange sounds I find it easy to copy them."

"You don't look like a parrot," said Dafydd.

We all laughed. I noticed that Mrs. Morgan had very white, very even teeth. I wondered if they were false. The dental condition of the working classes was notorious.

Passing the gateway of the Manor we traveled another hundred yards down the lane before swinging off onto the cart track that led to the farm.

"And how old are you, Rhiannon?"

"Six."

"Say, 'sir,' " whispered her mother. "He's a gentleman."

"My daughter's nearly six," I said. "Perhaps you can come to tea in the nursery someday and meet her."

Mrs. Morgan said in a rush, "That's very kind of you, Mr. Godwin, indeed it is, but of course we couldn't presume—"

"Nonsense, Marian's always complaining that she has no little girls to play with." I felt irritated by her humility but at the same time I realized that I would have been even more irritated if she had failed to be humble.

We reach the farmyard. As soon as I opened the door of the back seat the children scampered away, the little girl thanking me in a very well-mannered way for the ride, and I was able to lean into the car to draw out the heavy shopping baskets. Mrs. Morgan then emerged awkwardly onto the running board; setting down the baskets, I turned to offer her assistance.

"Thank you, sir." Her hand grated against mine. The palm was clammy. It was a hot day, and I was conscious of the heat as we stood there in the sun. Mrs. Morgan was wearing a straw hat which concealed her ugly red hair and shadowed her pallid face as she glanced down at the baskets. "Thank you," she murmured again, and when she looked up at me the sun shone in her eyes.

They were bright green in the brilliant light. I was reminded of the color of the sea by the Rhossili cliffs on a midsummer day. It was an extraordinary color, most unnatural.

I found I was still holding her hand.

I dropped it.

"Good day, Mrs. Morgan."

"Good day, Mr. Godwin." As she turned aside, her face immediately fell into shadow and I could see again how nondescript she was. I returned once more to the driver's seat. She was already walking away with the baskets, but as I drove off I saw in the mirror that she had paused to stare after me. For a second her slim solitary figure remained silhouetted not against the farm buildings but, mysteriously, against some uncharted landscape in my mind, but the second passed and the next moment I told myself it had been forgotten. Treading hard on the accelerator I drove at a breakneck speed down the cart track and hurtled up the lane to the comforting familiarity of my home.

III

"We had such a nice nursery tea today," said Blanche a week later as she put on her diamond earrings. She was wearing a white satin gown and her dark hair was coiled into an elaborate knot on the top of her head. That night we were due to dine at Oxmoon to celebrate Edmund's twenty-seventh birthday.

"Nursery tea?" I said vaguely as I wandered in from my dressing room.

"Mrs. Morgan came with her children—what a good idea of yours that was! Marian enjoyed herself so much, and Nanny said afterwards how very well behaved Rhiannon was for a little girl of her class—and you know how discriminating Nanny is! But I wasn't surprised the children were well behaved because Mrs. Morgan is a most superior girl, as my dear Mama used to say, so quiet and dignified and polite."

"I'm glad the visit was a success. I must say, I did have second thoughts after I'd issued the invitation."

"Oh, I don't think these social differences matter much when children are young, darling. . . . There! I'm ready and we must go. Do you have Edmund's present?"

I retrieved the book on rose growing, which had been beautifully wrapped by Blanche in lemon-colored paper, and five minutes later we set off for Oxmoon. It was a dull summer evening, murky and cool, and Oxmoon had a moody look as I turned the car into the drive. Though built to conform to the classical conventions of architecture popular in the eighteenth century, it somehow contrived to hint that a wild unorthodox streak lurked behind its severe well-disciplined facade, and as I stared at it I thought again, as I had thought so often before: Oxmoon the enigma, the joker in the pack. Then suddenly in a bizarre moment of self-knowledge I realized I was seeing not the house but my own reflection in stone and glass. *I* was the enigma, the joker in the Godwin pack, and beneath my conventional English manners lay the Welsh stranger I was too afraid to know.

Edmund came out of the house to greet us. He was looking a trifle more animated than usual but still less than half alive, and once more I was acutely aware that the war had divided me from him, just as it had severed me forever from Lion. I had been becalmed on the Home Front while Edmund had been brutalized in the Front Line, and now an abyss of chaotic emotion lay scrupulously concealed between us; our conversations represented the nadir of social banality.

"Hullo, old chap. Happy Birthday and all that rot."

"Thanks. I say, what a beautiful parcel! Almost too good to open!"

Edmund had a square face with pale blue slightly protuberant eyes and pale brown thinning hair. He had put on weight since he had been invalided home in 1918 but although his limp was now barely perceptible and his general health had improved, he made no effort to leave home. Mild, vague and chronically indecisive, he drifted from one bout of melancholy to the next, so I was particularly relieved to find that evening that he seemed to be in good spirits. Whenever I saw how damaged Edmund was, I hardly knew how to endure my guilt as a noncombatant. Egged on by Robert, who had never known a day's uncertainty over his decision to remain on the Home Front, I had allowed myself to be persuaded that it was my duty to stay in my exempt position at the Foreign Office, but I had spent the war in such a miserable muddle that several times I had found myself wishing I could have died on the Somme with Lion. My guilt was one of the reasons why the Foreign Office had become intolerable to me; I had felt so debilitated by my self-disgust that I had wanted only to make a fresh start in a world where no one would look at me askance.

"Daphne wrote to wish me many happy returns," Edmund was saying, uncannily mentioning our sister-in-law as if he knew I was remembering Lion dying on the Somme. "She's coming to stay here next month with Elizabeth."

"How lovely!" exclaimed Blanche. "Marian will be thrilled! Isn't that good news, John?"

I agreed, although in fact I did not care for Daphne, who was one of those bouncy gushing Society girls dedicated to a vacuous life. I had heard from friends in London that she had become rather fast, but I had taken care not to mention this to Blanche.

"I'm surprised old Daffers hasn't remarried," said Edmund as he led the way up the steps into the house. "I know she's plain but she's tremendous fun. I like girls like that. Dash it, if I had a bean I'd marry her myself! Or is one forbidden to marry one's brother's widow? I bet one is. All the really amusing things in life are forbidden, aren't they . . . But oh Lord, I didn't come out here to talk of amusing things, quite the contrary, I came to tell you something awful: Robert's worse. He's in a wheelchair. Mama sent me out to warn you so that you'd be prepared."

My youngest brother Thomas chose that moment to come slouching down the stairs. Fourteen is a difficult age, and Thomas, who enjoyed being difficult, was making the most of his new capacity for obstreperousness. Spoiled by doting parents who should have known better, he seemed perpetually outraged that his much older siblings and beyond them the world in general paid him such scant attention. However he behaved well to my parents, and I had come to suspect that his pose of *enfant terrible* had been adopted to counter his fear of being overlooked as the last and least important member of a large family.

He had a square face not unlike Edmund's and a wide full-lipped mouth which he kept tucked down neatly at the corners. His golden hair and blue eyes gave a misleading impression of a cherubic nature.

"Hullo," I said to him, and added in an attempt to demonstrate a friendly interest, "When did you get back from school?"

"Why do you want to know?"

I sighed, gave up and followed the others into the drawing room, where my parents, having yielded to postwar social change, had authorized that cocktails as well as wine might be served before dinner. This was characteristic of them. My mother disapproved of spirits and my father drank little else except champagne, but when they entertained guests they were lavish in their hospitality and no one could have accused them of being either mean or old-fashioned.

I saw the wheelchair as soon as I entered the room, and at once I was grateful to my mother for having had the presence of mind to send Edmund to warn us. The wheels with their long spokes seemed symbolic of a medieval ordeal. I felt cold with pity for Robert, then sick with relief that I myself was healthy and finally rigid with guilt that my life should be so perfect while his should be so infused with suffering.

"Johnny darling!" cried Ginevra, who was clearly far beyond her first glass of champagne. "Come and admire the chariot! Robert now rattles around at a terrific pace!"

I said the first thing that came into my head. "Ginevra, I do wish you'd stop calling me Johnny as if I were some Edwardian rake who spent his time throwing roses to chorus girls."

"But darling"—Ginevra had acquired in America the vulgar habit of calling everyone darling much too often—"think how perfectly thrilling it would be if you were an Edwardian rake tossing roses to chorus girls!"

"Oh shut up!" said Robert, who often behaved towards his wife as if they were both back in the nursery. "Well, John? What do you think of this latest innovation?"

I thanked God for my diplomatic training. "My dear Robert, I'm sure it's a king among wheelchairs—forgive my lack of alacrity in making an immediate obeisance, but I wasn't prepared to encounter royalty when I arrived here tonight! Is it easy to maneuver?"

He was satisfied. All pity and sentimentality had been avoided and he could relax.

Robert's illness was erratic, striking severely and at random but then receding either wholly or in part. The temporary improvements tended to divert attention from the steady progress of the paralysis. His right leg was immobile, his left was now weak; I noticed he had slight difficulty turning his head, although his facial muscles were untouched and he had had no visual problems for two years. He looked closer to fifty than to forty. His muscles had run to fat, but the power of his intellect, sharpened rather than dimmed by his physical weakness, was kept ruthlessly honed by his incessant reading, and he was even talking of engaging a companion, one of his old Oxford friends, who could converse with him on the classics; he knew well enough that I had closed my mind against intellectual matters after my drudgery at Oxford.

My father offered me a glass of champagne, and I accepted it with relief. I was feeling in a nervous unreliable frame of mind for reasons which were ostensibly connected with the appearance of the wheelchair but which I sensed also derived from other sources beyond analysis. I was aware of sinister changes, of a fixed world trying to slide stealthily out of control.

"I say, I'm reading *The Mysterious Affair at Styles,*" said Edmund, providing me with a welcome diversion. "You read it recently, didn't you, John? Do tell me—who's the murderer? I simply can't work it out at all!"

"Edmund, you don't ask who did the murder! You read to the end and find out!"

"I think it might be that attractive girl with the red hair . . ."

But I did not want to think about attractive girls with red hair. Evading him I moved over to my father, but my mother intercepted me.

"Robert looks a little better, don't you think?" she said. "I think the unexpected mobility of the wheelchair has put him in better spirits."

We both glanced across at Robert, and out of the corner of my eye I saw my father drain his glass of champagne and reach automatically for a refill.

He too was watching Robert, and suddenly I knew all three of us were united by a grief beyond description. I had an absurd longing to say to them, "I'm here—I'll make it up to you," but of course the words could not be spoken, and my parents, as usual when Robert was dominating their thoughts, were oblivious of me. My old jealousy which I had thought dead now rose from the grave to sour my compassion for the brother I admired so much, and I was horrified. Chaos was approaching. At once I drew the line—and as always I felt safe and secure behind it. Consigning my vile jealousy once more to the grave, I too drained my glass and turned to the bottle of champagne for further sustenance.

The bottle was empty. My father had clearly been helping himself for some time.

"Open another bottle, John," he said idly as he saw my plight but my mother said in a voice of steel, "I think not," and turned her back on him.

My father, who had been lounging in his usual debonair fashion against the chimneypiece, stood up ramrod-straight and went white. At once I said, "It's all right, I don't think I want another glass after all."

"Have mine," said my father, thrusting his glass at me, and stumbled after my mother. "Margaret—"

My mother was ringing the bell to signal to the servants that we were ready for dinner.

"—only wanted to be hospitable—special occasion—Edmund's birthday—"

"Quite."

". . . and my dear!" Ginevra was exclaiming to Edmund. "I hear from London that all women are now to look like boys and pretend to have no bosom and no hips! What on earth am I to do?"

As Edmund guffawed with laughter I was aware of the wheelchair spinning across the room towards us.

Robert said, "Mama, are you all right?"

"Yes, dearest, just a little worried about the soufflé after last week's disaster with the Stourhams."

Robert looked skeptical. My father looked painfully anxious. Deciding it was high time I exerted my diplomatic talents to save the situation, I speculated whether Oswald Stourham had yet recovered from his disastrous second marriage to an errant platinum blonde.

IV

Despite the underlying tension, dinner passed off better than I had dared hope, first because a failed dinner party was unknown at Oxmoon, second because my parents were superb at keeping up appearances and third because we all drank steadily from my father's hoard of prewar wine—all, that is, except Thomas, who was too young, and my father, who having consumed far more champagne than normal before the meal now behaved like a man who had taken the pledge. I drank, I knew, far too much and this was most uncharacteristic of me. Indeed my father, whose drinking habits were normally so moderate, had always made it clear to his sons that drinking was not an essential adjunct of masculinity, and certainly I had always shied away from the more dangerous consequences of too much wine, the fatal sense of well-being, the risky loosening of the tongue and the sinister relaxation of the will to behave as one should. I had also shied away from the aftermath of alcoholic excess, the depression, the restlessness and above all the inexplicable frustration which made me feel as if I were a dog endlessly chained up in a backyard and endlessly obsessed with the longing to be free.

However that night, disturbed by my impression of a clear-cut world slipping inexorably out of focus, I drank to maintain the illusion that nothing had changed, and soon I found I could look at Ginevra's décolletage without being embarrassed and at my father without remembering Mrs. Straker and at my mother without resenting the fact that she found it hard to love me as she should. I could even look at Robert and not feel ashamed because I found it so much easier to be devoted to him now that he was sick and helpless; I could even look at Robert and pity him because he would probably die before he could inherit Oxmoon.

". . . and of course there's no denying we farmers have done well out of the war," my father was saying after the women had retired and the cloth had been drawn, "but times are changing so rapidly now, and sometimes I worry about the future of this place."

"Oh, Oxmoon's all right," I said, finishing my glass of port. "A large estate can always survive, given good management, Oxmoon's all right. I could run Oxmoon and run it bloody well, changing times or no changing times, although of course I don't want Oxmoon, wouldn't touch it with a barge pole, it all goes to Robert, everyone knows that. However if I ever did wind up with Oxmoon—"

"You never will," said my father, "so that's that. You're still going to outlive me, aren't you, Robert?"

Robert, who was smoking a cigar, said sardonically, "John evidently has his doubts."

"Oh, for Christ's sake!" I exclaimed, half knocking over my glass. "Just because you're in a bloody wheelchair you needn't act as if you're in a bloody coffin!"

"Steady on, old chap," said Edmund.

"You're not going to die just yet, are you, Robert?" said Thomas, who had somehow reached the age of fourteen without mastering the art of being tactful. He had just sneaked and wolfed a glass of port from the decanter while my father had been busy lighting a cigar.

"Unfortunately not," said Robert drily. "Sorry to disappoint you."

I spun round on Thomas. "What the hell are you doing swigging port on the sly and asking bloody stupid questions?"

"My God, you *are* bad-tempered!" exclaimed Thomas, livid that I had called attention to his stolen drink. "And don't think we can't all guess why! You're fed up because you have to make do with measly old Penhale Manor when you think you're so bloody perfect and so bloody wonderful that you ought to be ruling the roost at Oxmoon!"

I leaped to my feet with such violence that my chair was flung over behind me, but my father shouted, "Enough!" and my fury was checked. Then as I remained motionless, he said in a level voice to Thomas, "Did I give you permission to drink port?"

"No. But I didn't think you'd mind—as it's a special occasion—"

"Nobody drinks port in this house before they're eighteen, special occasion or no special occasion. Very well, that's the end of your evening. Excuse yourself to the ladies in the drawing room and go to bed." He waited until Thomas had slouched off in a fury before adding, "Robert, will you please oblige me by going with Edmund to join the ladies. I want a word with John on his own."

"I'm afraid I provoked John, sir," said Robert. "I must ask you not to hold him responsible for this debacle."

My father said nothing. Robert then apologized to me but I shook my head to indicate that no apology was necessary. Retrieving my fallen chair I stood stiffly by it as Edmund and Robert left the room.

"You've drunk too much," said my father to me as soon as the door closed.

"I know. Unpardonable. I'm very sorry."

"Why did you do it? What's the matter with you?"

"Nothing. Everything's fine. Couldn't be better."

"So it would seem, certainly. You've got well over two thousand acres in Herefordshire, haven't you?"

"Yes, sir."

"And you have nearly three hundred acres here together with one of the finest old manor houses in Gower?"

"Yes, sir."

"And you have money on top of all that, haven't you, and good health and good looks and a devoted wife and two fine children?"

"Yes, sir."

"You've everything a man could wish for, in fact?"

"Yes, sir."

"Then let's have no more nonsense about Oxmoon. It goes to Robert and if Robert dies before I do it goes to Robin and that's my last word on the subject."

"I absolutely accept that, sir, and what's more, I always have accepted it. I can't think why you should be taking Thomas's idiotic remark so seriously."

"A man's private feelings aren't so private when he starts to drink, and God knows I can recognize avarice when I see it. I remember how Owain Bryn-Davies used to covet Oxmoon while my father was still alive."

"I'm not Owain Bryn-Davies! And how dare you compare me to such a bastard, why are you always so bloody unfair to me, it's unjust and I resent it, *I resent it*, it's not my fault I look like—"

"Be quiet! That's enough! Take yourself home at once and don't show yourself here again until you're sober!"

"I'm not drunk!"

The door opened, interrupting me, and swinging around I saw my mother had returned. "Please," she said, not to me but to my father, "could you go to the drawing room and deal with Thomas. He's making a fuss and I can't cope. I'm afraid everything's quite beyond me this evening."

"Of course," said my father, greatly agitated by this unprecedented confession of defeat, and left the room.

My mother sank down on the nearest chair.

"Mama . . ." Shock sobered me. When I stooped over her in anxiety I found she was crying. "Mama!" I was appalled. I had never seen my mother cry, not even after Lion died. I drew up another chair and sat down beside her. "Mama, what is it?"

But she was already controlling herself. "Nothing. But I live under such strain and sometimes I hardly know how to bear it."

I was deeply distressed. "What can I do? I'm so sorry, I had no idea, tell me how I can help."

"Oh, you can't help," she said flatly. "You have too many problems of your own."

"What problems?"

"My God," she said, "how's that poor child Blanche ever going to cope?"

"Mama, I think you're a little overwrought—"

"Overwrought? Oh yes, I daresay. Lion dead, Robert dying, Edmund shell-shocked, Thomas impossible, Celia cut off in Heidelberg, you cut off in some dangerous world of make-believe—"

"My dear Mama—"

"—and Bobby," wept my mother, "Bobby no longer strong enough to live as he longs to live . . . a decent life . . . free of scandal . . . It's so terrible to see a good man, someone one loves, slip deeper and deeper into degradation—"

"There must be something we can do to stop it, there must be!"

"No. There's nothing." She wiped her eyes clumsily with the back of her hand before adding: "This is retribution. People pay for the wrong they do, and then hell exists not in the hereafter but *now*, right here on earth—and here we are, 1921, thirty-nine years after that terrible summer, and I'm in hell, Bobby's in hell and that man's still drowning on the Shipway and that woman's still being destroyed in her asylum." She wiped her eyes again and managed to say in a calmer voice, "Sometimes I ask God to remember how young we were. Young people are capable of such brutality but it's because they know nothing of life. All they understand is the instinct driving them to survive, but sometimes the price they have to pay for survival is so very terrible."

There was a silence. I did not know what to say. I was consumed with the longing to terminate this morbid stream of quasi-religious reflection which I found both tasteless and embarrassing, yet at the same time I was moved by my mother's grief and I desperately wanted to help her. I racked my brains for a consoling diplomatic response, but when it continued to elude me I realized that this was because it did not exist; no words were appropriate and she was inconsolable. In bewilderment, not knowing what else to do, I put my arms around her and kissed her gently on the cheek.

This was evidently the right approach. Her fingers clutched mine. She looked up at me with gratitude. "Dear John," she said, "how very good and kind you really are." Then she said with more than a hint of her old self, "You must have too much to drink more often!" and she smiled as she kissed me in return.

"Forgive me—I'm afraid I've just had an appalling row with Papa—"

"It doesn't matter. I'll put it right. So much has gone wrong tonight that I'm almost past caring. It's just so sad about Robert," said my mother, weeping again. "I couldn't bear to see him in his wheelchair."

If I had been sober I would have murmured a platitude. As it was I said painfully, "I couldn't bear it either, but you shouldn't retreat into religion, Mama, in order to make sense of the suffering—you shouldn't start flagellating yourself with concepts like retribution. You're the heroine of this story, not the villainess." And when she covered her face with her hands, I put my arm around her again and said, "I don't care what you did in the past. You're a wonderful woman—a magnificent woman—and we all love and respect you so much. If you're suffering now it's unmerited, I know it is—it can have nothing whatsoever to do with that vile summer back in the Eighties."

My mother let her hands fall. She stared at me. Her eyes shone with tears. "Oh God forgive me," she whispered. "To think that *you* should be the one who loves me enough to say that."

The door opened as my father reentered the room. "Margaret—"

"I'm all right now," said my mother. "I'm better. And so's John. I'm sure he's willing to drink a lot of black coffee, and so there's no need for him to leave yet." She rose to her feet, she squared her shoulders, she set her mouth in its familiar determined line. "We must all go to the drawing room," she said, "and we must all keep up appearances. Whatever happens that's always the right thing—indeed the only thing—to do."

V

"Are you all right, darling?" said Blanche, in our bedroom later. "When Thomas returned to the drawing room he mentioned something about a quarrel."

"Oh, that was nothing, just a little difference of opinion."

I was so anxious to put an end to these questions and so overwhelmed by my desire to forget, for a few precious minutes, the hellish evening I had just endured that I started to claim my marital rights while the light was still burning. Blanche never complained about anything I did but this time she did whisper, "Darling—the candle," and I had the grace to mutter, "Oh, God, I'm sorry" before I clumsily extinguished the flame.

I had once heard up at Oxford that a surfeit of alcohol damages a man's performance in bed, but all I can say is that exactly the opposite now happened to me. Under cover of darkness I stripped off my pajamas and almost asked Blanche to remove her nightdress, but fortunately I had not drunk four cups of black coffee in vain, and I somehow managed to restrain myself. Then I found I was obsessed by the desire to prolong the episode beyond five minutes. Usually I tried to restrict myself to three or four. I also had other desires which are without doubt better left unrecorded. I was appalled by myself but at the same time hopelessly engulfed in pleasure. Blanche tolerated it all like a saint, God knows how. I loved her so much for her tolerance that I finally, after an interval which I fear was at least ten minutes, managed to conclude the episode and spare her further embarrassment. Pleasure ended. Self-hatred and guilt began. I begged her to forgive me, but she said she loved me so nothing mattered. At that point my alcoholic excesses caught up with me and I sank mercifully into unconsciousness.

I dreamed I was a dog chained up in a backyard but someone was calling to me from a long way away and suddenly I longed to be free. Slipping my collar I sprang over the wall of the yard, and there ahead of me was a vast space where Edmund's voice echoed, "I think it's that attractive girl with the red hair."

Then a rope encircled me and began hauling me back to my kennel. An anxious little voice kept saying, "John! John!" but I took no notice because John was no longer my name. I was Johnny again, Welsh-speaking Johnny who got into scrapes with Lion and lived adventurously at Oxmoon. I could see Oxmoon clearly now and it was Welsh, all of it, every brick beneath the creeper, every slate upon the roof.

"John, wake up! Darling, it's three o'clock in the morning and the telephone's going on and on and on—"

I scrambled back over the wall, pounded to my kennel, dragged the collar of my Englishness over my head and woke up. Pain immediately shot through my head and made me gasp. My mouth was desert-dry. Far away in the hall the telephone was shrilling like a demon.

"Good God, who the hell can that be?" I woke up further, apologized for my language and crawled out of bed. To my horror I realized that I was stark naked. I groped frantically for my pajamas as Blanche lit the candle.

"I'll go," Blanche said, seeing that I was hopelessly befuddled, and slipped out of bed.

"Lord, I'm sorry." I struggled into my discarded pajama trousers and plunged next door for my dressing gown. I was then delayed because I thought I was going to vomit. A stream of embarrassing memories threatened to overwhelm me but I shut them out, and when vomiting proved impossible I raced to the head of the stairs just as the demonic bell ceased to ring in the hall.

"Penhale three," said Blanche anxiously. "Who is it, please?"

I hurried down the stairs. During the pause that followed I saw her become rigid with shock. "Oh, Edmund," I heard her whisper. "Edmund . . ."

I was beside her. The phone was cold as I seized it from her hands.

". . . and there's no doubt about it," said Edmund's frantic voice at the other end of the wire. "She's dead, Blanche, Mama's dead—oh Christ Almighty, what in God's name will happen to us all now?"

3

I

Oxmoon was in darkness. My headlamps raked the opaqueness of the night and shone on the black windows. When I emerged from the car the darkness seemed suffocating. There was no moon and the distant woods formed a sinister mass beneath the sky.

The front door opened. Edmund stumbled down the steps.

"Johnny—" The old nursery name trembled on his lips, and I did not need to see his face to know that the semblance of normality which he had assumed for the dinner party had been destroyed.

"Where's Papa?"

"Upstairs—with her." He began to sob.

"Tell me exactly what happened." I grabbed the lamp from his hand and led the way into the house.

"Papa woke me. He'd just come back from Mrs. Straker. He asked me to telephone Warburton because he thought Mama was ill. He was so odd that I went with him to their room, and of course as soon as I saw her I realized—"

"Yes. Very well, telephone Warburton. Telephone Robert. Wake Bayliss. Get dressed." I headed for the stairs.

"I can't," whispered Edmund. "I can't." He was crying again. "Oh Johnny, I did so want to make it up to her, and now I never shall—"

"Make what up to her?"

"The fact that I survived instead of Lion."

I recoiled from him. Then I said savagely, "Don't talk such rubbish. I'm sure she was only too glad you weren't both killed," and I rushed up the stairs to escape. On the landing I looked back and saw that he had sunk down on the bottom step and was weeping helplessly, a pathetic figure in his faded dressing gown. Guilt gnawed me. I wanted to console him but I knew my father must come first.

I reached my parents' room and tried the handle but the door was locked, and although I banged on the panels there was no response. Visions of suicide gripped me. Lighting one of the candles arrayed on the landing table, I stumbled down the corridor to the door of my father's dressing room. It opened. With lightning speed I moved to the door that led into the main chamber.

"Papa!" The childish name which even in adult life none of us had had any inclination to change suddenly sounded ridiculous. I thought of my contemporaries who referred to their fathers with antipathy as "the governor," but my father had never been a mere figurehead at the top of the family dining table. I saw him as he had appeared to me in the early years of my childhood, tall and tranquil, gentle yet authoritative, a golden double image of father and hero.

"Papa!" I shouted. "It's John! Let me in!"

The key clicked in the lock. The door swung wide. The old memory disintegrated as I faced the complex stranger I feared.

He was fully dressed and unmarked by grief. His eyes were a brilliant empty blue.

"Not so much noise," he whispered disapprovingly. "Your mother's asleep."

I groped for my diplomatic skills. "I heard Mama was unwell," I said, obediently keeping my voice low. "Perhaps I could see her for a moment."

"Did Edmund telephone Warburton?"

A reassuring affirmative seemed necessary. "Yes," I said, and edged my way into the room. All the candles had been lit, and I could clearly see my mother in bed, her head tilted to one side, her hair gray against the pillows.

"I found her like that," said my father, "when I came home. After all the guests had gone, I walked to Penhale and visited Milly. Have you met Mrs. Straker, John? I can't remember."

"No. I was in London during that brief time she was employed at Oxmoon." My mother's face was pulled down on one side. I knew she was dead but to make sure I carefully reached for her wrist. There was no pulse.

"Milly's husband was killed at Jutland," said my father. "He came from these parts and he met Milly in London—a wartime romance—they didn't have long together. After he was killed she had no money so she came down to Swansea to stay with his sister and she worked in a munitions factory, awful it must have been, I don't know how these modern women do it. But after the war she went back into service. A wonderfully efficient parlormaid she was—Margaret said she was the best we'd ever had. 'Straker's got the brains to be a housekeeper,' she said; I can clearly remember her saying that. Margaret was sorry she had to dismiss her after only three months, but there we are. Got to stick to the rules. Terrible things happen to people who fail to stick to the rules."

On the dressing table lay the jet brooch which my mother had worn that evening. Opening the jewel box, I put the brooch away.

"I closed her eyes," whispered my father. "I didn't think it was right that she should sleep with her eyes open, like a sleepwalker."

I took a deep breath. "Papa . . ." I began but it was no use. Speech was too difficult. I waited, then tried again. "Papa, I'm afraid there's nothing Warburton can do."

"Nonsense, he's a very clever doctor and so good with Robert. Make sure you tell him how cold she is. I held her in my arms to warm her up but it was no use so she'll have to have an injection."

I waited again before saying, "Come downstairs with me and I'll fetch you some brandy."

"Oh, I never drink brandy," said my father firmly, but allowing himself to be led from the room. "Never. My father used to start drinking brandy after breakfast and he'd be dead drunk by noon. But when he was sober he was the most charming fellow, I wish Margaret could have met him, but of course he died before I knew her. She met Bryn-Davies. He was nice to her, much nicer than my mother was. My mother wasn't kind to Margaret, such a mistake, Margaret never forgot. I was very fond of my mother, though, devoted to her, and Bryn-Davies was the most remarkable fellow in his way. A pity about Bryn-Davies, but I made amends by befriending his son and helping him marry that heiress, although luckily Owain the Younger's not in the least like his father, and anyway he was a victim just as I was so it was easy to be friends with him. Of course he never knew the truth. I just told him it was a little accident with the tide tables."

We were on the landing. Down in the hall, Edmund dragged himself to his feet and looked up at us. His face was blotched with weeping.

"Yes," said my father meditatively, "Margaret was the one who thought of the tide tables, but as soon as she mentioned them I saw it was the right thing—the only thing—to do. Margaret always knows what the right thing to do is. That's why I couldn't possibly live without her. You do see that, don't you, John? I couldn't live without Margaret. Impossible. You must explain that to Warburton, but doctors are so clever nowadays and Warburton's such a delightful chap and I'm sure he'll know just what to do."

"Edmund," I said, "take Papa to the library and sit with him while I make the telephone calls. I'll wake Bayliss and ask him to make tea."

"Oh, I don't want tea," said my father. "I want champagne. Ask Bayliss to bring a bottle from the cellar."

I could see that Edmund was about to lapse into hysteria, so I said crisply, "Very well" and led them to the library. My father at once began to tell Edmund the well-worn family legend of how he had found the means of saving Oxmoon as the result of encountering a rat chewing a candle on the library table.

". . . and I flung book after book at the bloody rat before I succeeded in killing him, and then when I went to the space on the shelves where the books had been I found my grandfather's records showing exactly how he had managed the estate . . ."

Returning to the hall I unhooked the telephone and began the lengthy task of recalling the postmistress to the village switchboard.

II

Ginevra answered the telephone at Little Oxmoon. I wanted to tell her that my father was demented, but since I knew the postmistress was eavesdropping with an excitement that just failed to be breathless, I confined myself to the fact of my mother's death. I had expected Ginevra to become hysterical, but to my surprise although she was shocked she remained calm. She said she and Robert would be at Oxmoon within half an hour.

With relief I then summoned Warburton, but afterwards I found I was too exhausted to wake Bayliss. Taking the cellar key from the board in the butler's pantry I retrieved a bottle of champagne and headed for the dining room where the glasses were kept in the sideboard. While there I helped myself to a double brandy from the decanter. I remembered hearing at Oxford that the best cure for a hangover was another drink, but this was the first time I had been obliged to put this repellent piece of folklore to the test.

In the library I found my father telling Edmund all about his courtship of my mother.

". . . and her father was a wonderful old tyrant, no manners or breeding but a great personality, called a spade a spade and stood no nonsense. He'd built that pottery business up from nothing, and he was in Swansea because he wanted to explore the possibility of shipping china clay across the Bristol Channel from Cornwall. All the copper ore used to come that way in the old days to be smelted. Anyway he was out drinking somewhere and feeling fed up with the Welsh when he ran across Bryn-Davies, who had just sold some sheep at the market for a great price and was celebrating in his usual way. Well, they got on like a house on fire and Bryn-Davies invited him to Oxmoon—Bryn-Davies was master by that time—and as soon as Mr. Stubbs saw Oxmoon he realized he had an opportunity to marry one of his daughters into the gentry—"

"Do you want some champagne, Edmund?"

Edmund said, "No. Whisky," and disappeared in search of it.

"—and of course he thought Ethel would do, she was the eldest, but I didn't fancy her, she was stuck-up, pretentious, I knew she'd be a bore. The younger girl May was only fourteen so she didn't count. That left your mother but that was all right because she was down-to-earth and sensible and I liked the way she laughed. Afterwards, after Bryn-Davies had drowned and my mother was in the asylum, Margaret and I stood in the ruined hall at Oxmoon and I said, 'I want to hear you laugh.' She said, 'My God, what a thing to say at a time like this!' and sure enough we both laughed. And later I said, 'In the future we're going to laugh all the time, I'm going to make you happy even if it's the last thing I ever do,' and years later when we held our first ball at Oxmoon I gave her a red rose and we drank champagne, just as we'd promised ourselves we would, and then we opened the first dance beneath all those glittering chandeliers while the orchestra played 'The Blue Danube.'"

"Here's your champagne, Papa."

"Thank you, John. Delightful! Yes . . . I can remember Ginevra dancing to that tune years later, how terrible it was about Ginevra, but Margaret says we mustn't talk of that anymore. Dear me, John, you don't look at all well! Here—take this glass you brought for Edmund and have a little champagne —yes, I insist! Do you good. There you are. Now, where was I? Oh yes, Ginevra. Yes, it was terrible when Robert married her, terrible how he cut himself off from us, but I accepted it, it was retribution. Margaret didn't accept it, though, Margaret hated it, blamed Ginevra, but poor Ginevra, I didn't blame her, Margaret's so hard sometimes, but never mind, Robert's always uncommon civil to me, he makes such an effort that I think perhaps he might still be a little fond of me after all . . . Sorry, did you say something?"

"I said, 'You're not making sense.' "

"Am I upsetting you? Well, we won't talk about it. We must never talk of things that upset us—I said that to Oswald Stourham after that tart of a second wife of his had run off with the American sailor. All he could do was sob 'Belinda' into his brandy, but I told him to stop thinking about her, wipe her clean out of his mind and then he'd be all right. He shouldn't have remarried so soon after his first wife's death—and of course he shouldn't have married a girl young enough to be his daughter, silly old chap, a platinum blonde, I knew it would never do. Margaret didn't even want to receive her but I said Oswald was one of my oldest friends and I had to stand by him . . . Where are you going?"

"I must just see what's happened to Edmund," I said, and escaped.

In the dining room Edmund had emptied the whisky decanter and was seated sobbing at the table.

"Edmund, you've got to pull yourself together—"

"Fuck you, why the bleeding hell can't you leave me bleeding fucking alone?" bawled Edmund in the language of the trenches, and tried to hit me.

I retreated, paced up and down the hall, looked in on my father, listened to some more disconnected monologue and then escaped again to the front doorstep, where I spent some time peering into the dark. At last I heard the sound of a motor. Robert or Warburton? I waited, straining my eyes to pierce the gloom, and finally recognized the old Talbot which my father had ceded to Ginevra after buying his new Bentley. Leaving the front door open, I returned to the library.

"Papa, Robert's here."

"Robert! But what a wonderful surprise!" He sprang to his feet. "Get another glass from the dining room!"

"Papa, you mustn't—you can't go on pretending like this—"

"Don't argue—if Robert's come all the way from London he must certainly be offered champagne!"

My nerve snapped. I pushed past him into the hall just as Ginevra, white and tired in a black coat, hurried through the open front door.

"Johnny—can you give Bennett a hand with the chair . . . Bobby—darling—I'm so very sorry—"

I ran outside. Bennett had helped Robert into the chair and was standing beside him at the foot of the steps.

"Robert, thank God you've come—Papa's demented—the situation's quite beyond me—"

"So I see," said Robert. "Very well, help Bennett lift this bloody thing up the steps. Where's Warburton?"

"He's not here yet. I told him I thought she'd had a stroke. Oh God, Robert, I can't begin to tell you—"

"Then don't."

We reached the top of the steps. I was just moving aside to allow Bennett room to maneuver the chair over the threshold when Ginevra rushed out to join us. She looked gray enough to faint.

"Robert, he mustn't see you in that chair, he's forgotten the illness, he'll have such a shock—oh Johnny, help me, don't let Bobby see—"

But she was too late.

"Where's Robert?" demanded my father, opening the front door wide, and the next moment he was confronted by the invalid in the wheelchair.

He stopped. Then he said confused, "I want Robert" and added, "I want Margaret." He looked around in panic. For a second we were all transfixed, but when Ginevra and I darted forward instinctively to protect him, he shouted, "Margaret! Margaret!" in a terrified voice before keeling forward into unconsciousness.

III

"He'll be all right," said Warburton, closing his black medical bag. "He'll sleep through the rest of the night and wake around noon."

We were in the bedroom which had belonged to Lion and which after his death my mother had ruthlessly refurbished for the use of guests. My father lay asleep in Lion's old bed, his hand finally limp in mine.

"When he does wake," Warburton was saying, "don't force the reality of the death upon him but on the other hand don't join in any fantasy. I think with any luck he'll be normal—that's to say, he'll be deeply upset. I'll come back after lunch and see how he is, but if there's any trouble telephone me and I'll come at once."

Warburton was forty, a dark neat slender man who kept a boat at Porteynon and liked to sail and fish in his spare time. He was a distant cousin of Lady Appleby's and had become enamored of the Gower Peninsula during summer holidays spent at All-Hallows Court. He came originally from Surrey where he had attended Epsom College. Before the war my sister Celia had fancied herself in love with him, but he had married a London girl and although she was now dead he had shown no inclination to remarry.

"Warburton, now that you've dealt with my father I wonder if you could take a look at Edmund. I'm afraid he's in a bad way."

We found Edmund still in the dining room, his head pillowed in his arms as he lay sprawled across the table. Both the whisky and the brandy decanters stood empty beside him, and with horror I noticed he had even started on the sherry.

"Not much I can do there," said Warburton, "except give you a hand to carry him out."

We lugged Edmund into the morning room and arranged him on the sofa with a cushion beneath his head. He showed no sign of waking.

"And now," said Warburton, "we come to you."

"Oh, I'm all right, absolutely fine, no need to worry about me at all."

"Nonsense, you've had a bad shock!"

"I'm all right now Robert's here."

"He won't be here for much longer. It's essential that he should go home to rest."

But Robert had other ideas. Warburton and I both tried to argue with him, but he flatly refused to listen. "I've got to be there when my father wakes," he said to Warburton, "and that's that. Ginette, tell Bayliss to make up a bed for me on the morning-room sofa."

I explained that the sofa was already occupied.

"Ridiculous!" said Robert. "Turn Edmund out and tell him that he's bloody well got to pull himself together. No one else goes to pieces in this house, not while I'm here; I won't have it!"

Warburton and I were just glancing at each other in despair when there was an interruption. The door opened and in walked Thomas in his pajamas, his eyes puffy with sleep.

"What's going on?" he demanded. "Why's everyone rushing around in a frenzy at four in the morning?"

"John," said Robert, "you're good with children—take the boy away and deal with him. Ginette, organize Edmund's removal. Warburton, you can go. Thank you for your help. We'll telephone if we need further assistance. Well, don't just stand there gaping, all of you! *For Christ's sake do as I say!*"

We all gave in, collapsing in exhaustion beneath the power of his personality. Piloting Thomas away to the far corner of the room, I broke the news to him as gently as possible.

He looked livid as if his mother had offered him an unforgivable insult. Then his mouth became softer and his eyes brighter. He glanced away.

"I want Papa."

"He's sedated," said Robert, who had begun to draft a cable to Celia. "He won't wake till noon. John, how does this sound? 'Prepare shock regret Mama dead you essential Dieter prohibited Erika optional'—do you think that makes it sufficiently clear to a woman of Celia's limited intellect that although she can bring the baby with her she's on no account to bring the damned Hun?"

Watching Thomas I saw a tear drop pathetically into the cup of tea I had just given him, and a lump at once hardened in my throat. Grief is very contagious.

"I'm sorry, Robert, I can't—quite—"

"Conjugate Latin verbs—that's always an infallible recipe for keeping a grip on oneself. Now pay attention, please, while I read the message again. 'Prepare shock—' "

"He doesn't care," said Thomas to me in a shaking voice. "I hate him."

"For Christ's sake!" yelled Robert in a fury, and with his stronger arm hurled both pencil and paper at the wall.

When I had retrieved them and promised to send the wire, all he said was "I've got to rest," and I knew he was worn out. "Bloody hell," he said, raging against the illness that impaired him, but he was so weak he could hardly speak above a whisper. I wheeled him into the morning room. Edmund had been carried out. A bed was being prepared on the sofa. Bennett and Ginevra were both there. "John, give me your word you'll wake me in time to deal with Papa."

I gave him my word and hurried back to look after Thomas.

IV

"What a pretty blue paint Margaret chose for the walls," said my father, waking to find he was in Lion's refurbished room, and his eyes filled with tears.

We waited, I by the window, Robert in his chair by the bed, and eventually my father, wiping his eyes on the sheet, whispered, "I want to see her."

"Now or later?" said Robert with a bluntness which I could never have emulated.

"Now. I always think one ought to see the body. Otherwise one wonders whether the person's really dead. Better to make sure."

"Quite right," said Robert as I inwardly shuddered. "Very sensible."

"Such a relief it was," murmured my father as I helped him into his dressing gown, "when Bryn-Davies was washed up. I had nightmares that he'd somehow survived and swum ashore." He said no more at that moment, but when we all reached my parents' room he went without hesitation to the bed and looked down at the lifeless figure. "Yes," he said, "there's nothing there now. Just the shell." He covered the face again with the sheet, withdrew to the window and paused. Then at last he said, "I shall think of after-the-funeral later. Now all I shall think about is the funeral itself, and of course it must be a perfect funeral, everything done properly, nothing omitted, not a rule broken. I shall be all right, you see, absolutely all right so long as I stick to the rules."

We promised to help him organize a perfect funeral.

"And no atheism," said my father sternly. "I don't hold with it. Atheism's not the done thing at all."

We assured him we would behave as correctly as the devoutest members of the Church. He was satisfied. Methodically his thoughts turned elsewhere. "And now I must take care of the children," he said. "Let me see. You two are here, Lion's dead, Thomas . . . where's Thomas? Who's looking after him? Find him, John, I want to see him at once. And where's Edmund? He's got to be looked after too. And what's happening about Celia?"

"John's sent the wire. I'm sure she'll come at once."

"I won't have that damned Hun in the house!"

"Don't worry, I made that very clear."

We returned to Lion's room, but to my relief we did not have to coax my father back to bed; he was still affected by the drug Warburton had administered, and for another hour he was too groggy to consider getting dressed. Later Warburton said to me, "He's better than I thought he would be, but I'm worried about how well he'll be able to stand the coming stress. I suppose there's no chance of the funeral being a quiet one?"

"None whatsoever," I said levelly, and we found ourselves once more regarding each other in despair.

V

My father then proceeded to astonish us all by giving a bravura performance as an indomitable *paterfamilias*. He relieved me of the responsibility of looking after Thomas, he attended to Edmund with such success that Edmund became capable of conducting a rational conversation, he addressed the weeping servants with such skill that they pulled themselves together, he gave calm audiences to the vicar and the undertaker, he chose hymns and flowers with meticulous care, he even redrafted Robert's notices for *The Times* and the *Morning Post*. Afterwards Robert was finally sent home to rest, Ginevra's emotional but clearly reluctant offer to stay on to manage the household was refused and I myself to my great relief was dispatched to Penhale Manor. Now, I thought, I would at last be free to grieve in peace.

Yet when I arrived home I felt as if the mechanism for grief had jammed in my consciousness. I told myself how devoted I had been to my mother and how much I was going to miss her, but the words echoed emptily in my mind until I realized with horror that I was unable to connect them with a genuine emotion. Genuine emotion lay elsewhere, and suddenly I was aware of an anger which represented forbidden thoughts such as She should have loved me better, She didn't understand me, I doubt if I'll miss her much once the shock's worn off.

This reaction, which was so far outside any conventional idea of grief, shocked me so much that I hardly knew what to do with myself. Blanche was kind, as gentle a wife as any bereaved man could wish for, but her attitude only made it more impossible that I should confide in her. Amidst all my deplorable emotions the sheer perfection of her response seemed almost more than I could endure.

Blanche told the children their grandmother was dead. We were both present but she was the one who spoke. Marian shed a tear but was consoled by the thought of Granny happily ensconced among the angels in heaven. Harry was uninterested and obviously did not understand, but Blanche thought it better not to stress the death by further explanations, and I had no doubt she was right.

The funeral was perfect. It was everything my father wished. People came from all over Gower and South Wales to attend. Every villager in Penhale was crammed into the churchyard. My father had some antique notion that motorcars were unsuitable for transporting coffins, so the traditional black hearse drawn by black horses was used. Edmund, Thomas and I joined the undertaker's men in shouldering the coffin. Aunt Ethel, my mother's surviving sister, tried to tell Thomas he was too young but since he was as tall as Edmund and considerably more robust, we had all supported his wish to participate. Aunt Ethel, a massive figure in black veils, was proving a great trial to us all, but my father was so charming to her that her natural inclination to be frightful was temporarily muted. In fact my father was quite faultless, faultlessly dressed, faultlessly tearless, faultlessly demonstrating how a genuine grief could be displayed with dignity and good taste. I had never admired him more.

However unfortunately not everyone could follow his example. My sister Celia, a foolish but kindhearted woman of whom I was moderately fond, sat beside Edmund, her favorite brother, and snuffled and sniffled until I thought I would lose my patience entirely. Edmund himself wept without ceasing but then, as I reminded myself, allowances had to be made for Edmund. Ginevra sobbed in a most vulgar manner, but what else could one expect? Ginevra had never been renowned for either lack of emotion or good taste. Robert, who ignored her, looked bored as if the whole occasion were beneath his notice, and once even glanced at his watch. That horrified me. I too could hardly wait for the agonizing ceremony to be concluded, but I knew I could never have manifested open impatience.

Afterwards in the churchyard the only people with dry eyes were my father, Robert and I myself. I wondered vaguely what was on the menu for luncheon.

Luncheon, served that day at two tables joined in a T, turned out to be a five-course banquet for thirty-three, the food plain but perfectly cooked and accompanied by no more than a light hock, just as my mother would have deemed appropriate. Those present consisted of my father, my sister, my brothers, Ginevra, Blanche and me; Aunt Ethel with her three unmarried daughters, Dora, Rosa and Clara; her son Montague, who ran the family pottery business, and his wife; dead Aunt May's daughter Evadne and her husband Frank; Lion's widow Daphne with her parents, Sir Cuthbert and Lady Wynter-Hamilton; Ginevra's son Rory Kinsella; Oswald Stourham with his sister Angela and his daughter Eleanor; Owain Bryn-Davies the Younger with his wife and his son Alun; Sir William and Lady Appleby; Lady de Bracy and her daughter Gwen; the vicar, his wife and Gavin Warburton. The conversation was universally appalling. Sandwiched between my cousins Dora and Clara, both keen feminists, I came to the conclusion that postfuneral lunches should be banned by law.

"My dears!" exclaimed Ginevra, who was seated opposite us. "What fun you girls are! Johnny, why did we always write off the Staffordshire crowd as a dead loss in the old days?" It was obvious she had had too much hock.

"Dead loss?" said Aunt Ethel, who had the kind of hearing that would have permitted her to eavesdrop at fifty paces. She turned to my father. "Bobby, did you hear that?"

"Well, as a matter of fact," said my father with great courtesy, "I didn't." He suddenly looked very tired. Pushing away his glass of hock, he turned to the butler. "Bayliss, bring me a glass of champagne."

"*Champagne?*" said Aunt Ethel. Unlike my mother, she had never fully conquered her Staffordshire accent. "Bobby, I don't know how you can think of drinking champagne when my poor dear sister has been laid to rest only an hour ago, but all I can say is—"

"John," said Robert at once, but I was already on my feet. We had long since worked out a plan of action in case Aunt Ethel's frightfulness assumed intolerable proportions.

"Papa," I said, moving swiftly towards him, "let me take you into the library for a quiet cigarette."

"But I can't abandon my guests," said my father. "That wouldn't be the done thing at all."

"Oh, don't mind me!" said Aunt Ethel. "I know I'm only here on sufferance to keep up appearances! I realized long ago I wasn't considered good enough for Oxmoon!"

I looked at Cousin Montague for help. He had been educated at some minor public school and I thought he might have the decency to keep his mother's vulgarity in check, but evidently he shared her grudge against my family, for he merely toyed with his fruit knife and said nothing. Meanwhile silence had fallen with lightning speed over the table, and into that silence Robert suddenly unleashed his fury.

"You stupid woman!" he shouted at Aunt Ethel. "How can you have the insolence to talk of your 'poor dear sister' when we all know you were so jealous of her that you could hardly ever bear to visit this house! I've had enough of you simulating grief in the most vulgar way imaginable—just you leave my father to grieve in peace!"

"Well!" said Aunt Ethel, puce with rage. "*Well!* Never in all my life have I been so—"

"Papa," I said, stooping over him, "you can leave your guests now—the meal's over. Edmund—Celia . . ."

Edmund, Celia and Thomas all rushed to the rescue.

"Poor dearest Papa," said Celia, "you've been so brave—don't take any notice of that horrible woman—"

"Montague," said Aunt Ethel, "are you going to let your mother be insulted like this?"

Cousin Montague said, "I must say I find this behavior most uncalled for and quite definitely not the done thing at all."

"You are, of course," said Robert, "referring to your mother's conduct. In which case I utterly agree with you."

"How dare you!" shouted Aunt Ethel.

"And how dare you," shouted Robert, "degrade my father's hospitality like this!" He turned to Ginevra. "Take me out of here; get me out."

"—never been so insulted in all my—"

"Please!" My father was on his feet. Silence fell. His children stepped back a pace as if allowing him room to speak. He was ashen. "I must apologize," he said to his guests, "for this unforgivable scene. Ethel, I apologize in particular to you because I know my children's insults are the last thing Margaret would have wanted you to suffer. And now, if you please, I must beg you all to excuse me." Exquisitely polite, shaming us by the very perfection of his manners, he walked out of the room.

Edmund, Thomas, Celia and I all looked at one another and then turned as one to follow him.

He was waiting for us in the hall. "Margaret will be very angry when she hears about this," he said severely. "Very angry indeed."

As we stared at him in appalled silence, Ginevra wheeled Robert into the hall, and in panic I swung to face them. "Robert, Papa's unwell again—"

"I'm not surprised!" Robert was still shaking with rage. "I'm only surprised that we're not all raving lunatics after this bloody unspeakable charade!"

We all gasped. My father was suddenly very white, very still, and the next moment Robert was turning on him with a horrifying brutality.

"Why couldn't you bury her quietly?" he shouted. "She was English and she deserved an English funeral—why did you have to give her this Welsh circus? You talk so much of doing the done thing and sticking to the rules, but all you're capable of is vile pageantry and bloody hypocrisy!" And covering his face with his hands, he began to shudder with inaudible sobs.

We were all staring appalled at him but no one was more appalled than my father. At last he whispered humbly, "I'm so sorry if I've offended you, Robert. Please forgive me," and blundered away towards the library. Thomas ran after him, but my father said, "I'm sorry, I must be alone. John will look after you till I'm better."

The library door closed. Robert let his hands fall. His bold strong striking face was battered with grief. I saw him reach for his wife's hand and saw too that it was waiting for him.

"Robert's right," said Ginevra. "I don't know why we're not all raving." She turned the chair and began to wheel him away from us. Over her shoulder she added: "We're off to the kitchen garden to raid the strawberry beds."

"The season's over!" called Edmund the gardener automatically, but Ginevra did not stop, and the next moment he was seizing the chance to escape by dashing after them to help her maneuver the chair into the garden.

Celia and I looked at each other.

"I'll deal with the other guests," she said, "if you can cope with Aunt Ethel."

I glanced at Thomas. "Will you be all right?" I said. "Celia and I have to go back, no choice, but you can stay here if you want to."

"I'm staying."

I could hardly blame him. Celia said with admirable resignation, "I'm afraid it's a case of 'Onward Christian Soldiers,' John," and seconds later we were reentering the dining room.

VI

I had already received the hint that some deep fissure existed between Robert and my father. In his dementia following my mother's death my father had referred to it obliquely, but in my distress I had discounted his words as the rambling nonsense of a sick man. Yet now, having witnessed Robert's unprecedented hostility to him, I began to wonder anew and to try to recall what had been said. My father had talked of Robert's marriage. That much I could clearly remember. But had he in fact disclosed anything which I did not already know?

We were all aware that my parents had opposed Robert's marriage to Ginevra, even though they had ultimately given in with good grace. As Celia had said in one of her more acid moments, "Who in their right mind would want their son to marry a woman who acts like a courtesan and was married to an Irish-American brigand?" However Ginevra was certainly a lady, despite her raffish manners; a broken engagement and an elopement may rank as deplorable incidents, but they hardly turn a woman into a courtesan. Yet what kind of a lady was she? She had a foreign air, no doubt acquired in America where all women, so I had heard, were bossy and independent, unmarked by the virtues of English tradition, and even though I had no evidence that she had been unfaithful to either of her husbands, I thought her untrustworthy; there was a shadiness about her which hinted at all manner of private eccentricities, and although Robert was devoted to her, I had been far from surprised when my parents looked askance at the match.

What now surprised me was that their disapproval had apparently deepened. I thought they had accepted the marriage. I had been well aware that Robert and Ginevra visited Oxmoon only at Christmas—how could I have been unaware of it when I was so meticulous in visiting my parents far more often?—but I had not imagined that this could have led to bitterness. I had done well at the Foreign Office, but I had been no more than a clerk promoted later to a personal assistant; Robert, on the other hand, had been maintaining a brilliantly successful career, and I had fully understood that unlike me he had found it almost impossible to find the time to visit Oxmoon. However my parents had evidently found understanding not so easy. Why had my mother blamed Ginevra, who had always seemed to bend over backwards to please her? And what had my father meant when he had called the separation from Robert retribution?

I was too busy salvaging the shreds of the luncheon party to indulge in speculation beyond this point, but to my relief the guests now showed signs of departing. Presently the de Bracys, who were staying at All-Hallows Court, left with the Applebys; the Bryn-Davieses left in the company of Warburton; the Stourhams gave the vicar and his wife a lift to Penhale on their way to Llangennith; Daphne and her parents swept away in their chauffeur-driven Rolls-Royce to the Metropole Hotel in Swansea while Rory Kinsella, now a volatile undergraduate of twenty, slipped off through the grounds to his mother's bungalow at Martinscombe.

That left the crowd from Staffordshire. They were all staying at Oxmoon but not, Aunt Ethel assured me, for a day longer than was necessary; she said it was against her principles to remain in a house where she had been so grievously insulted, and were it not for the fact that she was about to be prostrated by a migraine brought on by mourning for her poor dear sister, she would have left immediately. Her daughters somehow coaxed her to bed and then departed with Montague and his wife for a very long walk. Aunt May's daughter Evadne said she was exhausted and she hoped we wouldn't mind if she and her husband retired to rest. Somehow we restrained ourselves from saying we were delighted. After they had disappeared upstairs, Celia and I, who had by this time perfected our act as host and hostess, thanked Bayliss and the servants for making the luncheon such a success, and then we withdrew to the hall to decide what to do next.

My father had not emerged from the library, but Blanche, who had been playing the piano quietly in the music room, appeared to ask what she could do to help. She volunteered to stay on at Oxmoon, but I did not want to worry about her any longer; I considered she had been exposed to quite enough distress, so I asked my father's chauffeur to drive her home to the Manor, and as soon as the motor had departed I said to Celia, "I think we should have a family conference to plan how we're going to survive the rest of the day."

Celia agreed, and collecting Thomas from the hall, we retired to the drawing room where a glance from the windows revealed that Ginevra and Robert were sitting by the summerhouse on the far side of the lawn. After separating Edmund from his whisky in one of the greenhouses, I hid the decanter under a large flowerpot and shepherded my flock out of the kitchen garden.

Robert and Ginevra saw us coming as we moved down the lavender walk, and suddenly I experienced a longing for Lion. I could almost hear him saying, "Let's draw lots for who murders Aunt Ethel!" and I thought how he would have bounced out of his deep grief for my mother to raise our spirits with his vitality. The sight of Robert and Ginevra too heightened my longing for a past that had been lost. In my earliest memories I could remember the two of them in the summerhouse, Robert wearing his first pair of long trousers and looking immeasurably grand, Ginevra a remote goddess with thick plaits, a white frock and holes in both her stockings. "Here come the babies," I had so often heard her say as Lion, Edmund and I advanced to invade their privacy, and now in an eerie echo of the past I heard those same words repeated.

"Here come the babies," she said idly to Robert as we crossed the tennis lawn to the wheelchair.

"You've come at the right time," said Robert to us. "I'm feeling too hot out here—lift the chair into the summerhouse, would you?"

He seemed composed again. In the summerhouse, I did say, "Robert, if you want to go home now, I shan't blame you in the least," but he answered at once, "Don't be ridiculous—how can I leave without apologizing to Papa for that monstrous scene I created with Aunt Ethel?" and various sympathetic comments were made about Aunt Ethel's frightfulness before I called the meeting to order. I then declared that we should plan the rest of the day like a military operation in order to avoid further ghastliness.

"An idea which is none the less brilliant for being obvious," said Robert. "Continue."

Thus encouraged, I launched myself on a forecast of the next stage of the nightmare. "With any luck," I began, "Aunt Ethel won't emerge from her room again today, but if she does, leave her to me. I think I can just manage to survive her."

"John should never have abandoned a diplomatic career," said Celia to the others. "He's been quite wonderful."

"Well, you were wonderful too, Celia—"

"Enough of this mutual admiration," said Robert, "or I shall start to remember how I allowed Aunt Ethel to reduce me to her own appalling level of vulgarity. Go on, John."

"I suggest we divide the entire tribe between us and swamp each section with charm and good manners."

"What a revolting prospect," said Edmund.

"I think it's all rather heavenly," said Ginevra. "Shall I take on Dora, Rosa and Clara? I simply adore it when they talk about Emmeline and Christabel!"

Robert groaned. More comment on our frightful relations followed, but eventually I divided them as equitably as possible between Edmund, Thomas, Celia and Ginevra.

"And what do you and I do, John," said Robert, "while our siblings struggle with these repulsive duties you've assigned them?"

"We cope with Papa."

We all looked at each other.

Edmund said unexpectedly, "I think he'll crack now. I saw it happen in the trenches. When the brave ones cracked they cracked utterly. One just can't keep up that kind of performance forever."

Robert said to me, "He's right. This is where our troubles really begin," and I thought again of that moment in the hall earlier when my father had started talking of my mother in the present tense.

"I don't understand," said Thomas truculently, trying to keep the panic from his voice. "What do you mean when you say he'll crack?"

"Break down and cry," said Celia soothingly before anyone could mention the words "go mad."

"He's postponed his grief by organizing that appalling luncheon," said Robert acidly. "What a mistake! We should have forced him from the start to face reality."

"I'm sorry, Robert," I said, "but with all due respect, I couldn't disagree with you more. This *is* Papa's way of facing reality. It may not be your way but that doesn't mean it isn't equally justifiable. He had to go through this charade. It was essential to him to make a ritual of her death so that he could believe in it."

"Do you understand any of this, Edmund?" said Celia.

"Not a word, old girl, no."

"I do," said Ginevra unexpectedly, "but I'm not at all sure who's right."

"I am," I said. "I think he's done the right thing so far, although I do concede that another breakdown is now a real danger. He's finished being the perfect mourner at the perfect funeral, and what we now have to do is to help him over the interim that must inevitably exist before he can start playing the perfect widower at perfect Oxmoon."

They all stared at me as if I were talking some esoteric Welsh dialect.

"Well, isn't that what life's all about?" I said, exasperated. "You write the script, pick your role and then play that role for all it's worth! Papa's between roles at the moment, that's all."

"What's he talking about?" said Thomas to the others.

"He seems to be saying," said Robert, "that one must never on any account face reality—either the reality of one's true self or the reality of one's true circumstances. I've never heard such a recipe for unhappiness in all my life."

"But what is reality?" demanded Edmund moodily before I could launch myself on a heated protest. "Who knows?"

"Well, I agree," said Robert, getting into his stride, "that Kant says it's virtually impossible to know reality. However—"

"Oh darling, surely everyone knows what reality is!" protested Ginevra. "Why do intellectuals always tie themselves into such absurd knots? Reality is—"

"Reality is—" began Celia and I in unison.

"Reality," said Thomas, "is that Papa's walking across the lawn towards us at this very minute—what on earth do we do now?"

VII

My father had changed into a black lounge suit and was strolling idly across the lawn in the company of his golden Labrador Glendower. A light breeze ruffled his hair and emphasized his casual grace of movement. Behind him Oxmoon, shimmering in the July sun, heightened the impression of mirage and illusion. I was unnerved, and a quick glance at the others told me that my tension was shared. This, we had agreed, was going to be the moment when my father broke down again, yet never had he seemed more composed.

"Still living in his fantasy," muttered Robert.

"No," I said suddenly, "it's all right, Robert—he's playing his old self. This is the interim role."

Robert looked scandalized, but when he refrained from arguing, I realized he was reluctantly coming to accept my point of view. Meanwhile my father had raised his arm in greeting and we were all waving back much too heartily.

"Shouldn't we be talking?" whispered Ginevra, and added in a normal voice: "It's a new Glendower, Celia—did you guess? Old Glendower died last Christmas—hardpad, poor darling. We were all devastated."

"How simply too frightful," said Celia with nauseous brightness. "Hullo, Papa, how lovely to see you again!"

Ignoring this drivel Robert said crisply, "I do apologize, sir, for my behavior earlier—I'm afraid I chose quite the wrong moment to give way to my grief. And of course I do apologize too for my remarks about the funeral. I'm sure everything was exactly as Mama would have wished."

My father was by this time on the threshold of the summerhouse. "That's all right, Robert," he said with an easy smile. "Least said soonest mended." His smile broadened as he glanced at the rest of us. Then he said with his most winning charm, "I'll wager you've all been on your knees thanking God I didn't marry Ethel forty years ago!"

We laughed vigorously. In the deadly pause that followed, my father stooped over the dog. "Sit, Glendower, sit . . . that's it. Good boy." He gave the dog a pat and added without looking at us, "I've been thinking things over. Just thought I'd like to say a few words." Still fondling the dog, he glanced up at Robert as if waiting for encouragement.

"Yes, of course," said Robert in the mild neutral voice I had heard him use in court to soothe frightened witnesses, and at once looked immensely sympathetic.

"Well," said my father, duly encouraged and straightening his back as he faced us all, "I just thought I'd like to say thank you to everyone for being so good to me during these past few days. I've got a wonderful family. Don't know what I'd have done without you. Luckiest man in the world. Especially glad to see you again, Celia," he added suddenly. "Bury the hatchet and all that. I've missed you since you've been away."

"Darling Papa!" cried Celia, much moved.

I wondered what all this was leading up to. Sweat began to prickle beneath my collar.

"And I just wanted to reassure you all," resumed my father, his mild casual manner masking his unknown but clearly implacable purpose, "that I shall be all right now—I've had a little think in the library and I've worked everything out." He moved forward to slip his arm around Thomas's shoulder. "Sorry I closed the door on you like that, old fellow," he said, "but I knew it was very important that I should have my little think."

"And what did you decide, Papa," said Robert with extreme delicacy, "as the result of your little think?"

My father moved on from Thomas and drifted to the far side of the room before turning to face us once more. "Well, I can tell you this for a certainty," he said: "I shall never marry again. I shall be loyal to Margaret till the day I die. No one could ever take her place as my wife." He stood up straight and looked both proud and dignified. "You won't find *me* following in Oswald Stourham's footsteps and marrying a platinum blonde young enough to be my daughter!" he said. "I wouldn't dream of embarrassing my children and shaming myself before my friends in that fashion. I shall keep up appearances and live exactly as a widower ought to live. Although of course," said my father, stooping to pat Glendower, "I shall have to have a housekeeper. But that's not the same thing at all."

"Of course not, Papa!" cried Celia, blinded by sentimentality.

I was transfixed. I saw Robert dart me a warning glance, but I ignored him. My voice demanded roughly: "What exactly are you trying to say?"

"Shut up, John," said Robert. "Leave this to me."

"Celia my dear," said my father with his most exquisite courtesy. "Ginevra —please would you be so good as to excuse us? I'd prefer to be alone with my boys for a moment."

"Of course, Bobby," said Ginevra. "Come on, Celia, let's go and organize tea. Thomas, why don't you come with us?"

"Why should I?" said Thomas rudely, and moved closer to my father.

Ginevra looked at Robert, who said pleasantly, "Are you sure you want Thomas to be present at this conversation, Papa?"

"Certainly," said my father. "You can't treat a fourteen-year-old boy as if he were fit only for the nursery. That would be quite wrong."

Thomas, who was still very much a child despite his strapping physique, looked smug.

"Nevertheless—" I began.

"No," said my father, suddenly showing the tough side of his personality. "No 'nevertheless.' That's my decision and you'll oblige me by accepting it."

Robert shot me another warning glance. I kept my mouth shut. The two women began to walk away across the lawn.

When they were out of earshot my father said in a low but level voice, "Now I must speak frankly. I don't think that you boys have faced the—" He fumbled for the right English word. "—the *reality* of your mother's death. Your mother's death is, of course, a tragedy—a tragedy," he repeated, as if greatly relieved he had been able to file the episode away under some comprehensive heading which needed no further explanation. "I know all about tragedies. I'm good at them—sorry, that sounds absurd, wrong phrase. I mean I'm good at surviving them. Done it before. Do it again. Quite simple —just obey a few elementary rules. Rule one: don't dwell on the tragedy, don't think about it. Rule two: take stock of what's left and work out what you need to go on. Rule three: get what you need. Rule four: go on. Well, I've spent the afternoon taking stock and I know what I need—I need the best possible woman to manage the house, and it just so happens I know the best possible woman for the job." He hesitated to drum up the nerve to complete his speech but the pause was minimal. "This evening," he said, "I shall go to

Penhale and offer Mrs. Straker the post of housekeeper. Then—once I have my house in order—I know I shall have the strength to go on."

He finally stopped speaking. Edmund, Thomas and I all turned automatically to face the wheelchair.

"Thank you so much, Papa," said Robert with a courtesy that not even my father could have bettered. "I'm sure we're all most grateful to you for explaining the position and advising us of your plans before you consult Mrs. Straker. I needn't remind you, of course, how devoted we all are to you and how deeply concerned we are for your welfare at this most crucial and difficult time. May I venture to hope that bearing our concern in mind, you'll permit me to make one or two observations which I cannot help but feel are pertinent to the situation?"

After a moment my father said, "Very well."

"I think we're all a little troubled," said Robert, "by the effect of any immediate visit of yours to Mrs. Straker. While we perfectly understand that you should wish to see her, we can't help but wonder what people will think when they find out, as they inevitably will, that you visited your mistress on the day of your wife's funeral. Would it not be possible for you to postpone the visit for a day or two?"

My father considered this carefully and said, "No."

"My God!"

"John, *you must leave this to me.* Now, Papa: is it possible for you to explain to us why you have to see Mrs. Straker tonight?"

My father brooded on this but finally said, "I'm afraid I'll go mad if I have to spend another night utterly alone. If I see Milly tonight then perhaps she can move to Oxmoon tomorrow."

"Jesus bleeding Christ!" said Edmund, and sank down on the nearest chair.

"He's out of his mind," I said rapidly to Robert. "This is it—he's lost his mind."

"Just a minute." Robert was still calm. "Papa, don't listen to them, just listen to me. I understand every word you've said but now you must try and understand me because I'm going to tell you a very simple but very vital truth: you cannot bring your mistress into this house, in no matter what capacity, within a week of your wife's death. That wouldn't be sticking to the rules, you see, and terrible things happen, as you well know, to people who fail to stick to the rules."

"I've drawn up some new rules," said my father. "I've spent all afternoon drawing them up. I won't marry her. Nor will she be just a nominal housekeeper. She'll occupy a genuine position in the household, with her own room in the servants' wing, and she'll call me Mr. Godwin and I'll call her Mrs. Straker whenever we're not alone together."

"But my dear Papa—"

My father suddenly shouted with great violence, "Margaret would have understood!"

That silenced even Robert.

I had to speak. It was beyond all my powers of endurance to keep quiet a second longer. "How dare you say such a thing!" I cried in fury. "How can you conceivably think she would forgive such an insult to her memory! What you propose to do is absolutely unforgivable!"

"I agree," said Edmund, scarlet with emotion as he struggled to his feet. Until that moment I would have judged him incapable of opposing my father, and his blast of rage stunned us all. "I don't give a damn whom you sleep with, Papa, I don't believe in God or religion anymore and I can't stand people who preach about morality, but John's right for once, this is vile, this is the worst possible insult to my mother—on the very day of her funeral . . ." His voice broke. He turned away.

"You bloody fools, both of you!" said Robert angrily. "It's no good being emotional here—that's the worst course you can possibly take!"

"Robert," said my father, "just explain to them that I can't be alone. If I'm alone I'll have to drink to stop myself remembering the past, and if I drink I'll end up like my father—yes, tell them how frightened I am, Robert, always so frightened that I'll turn into a drunkard and start seducing boys as my father did—"

"Oh, my God—"

"Christ Almighty—"

"Get that child out of here—"

"Thomas, leave us at once—"

"*Quiet!*" shouted Robert. "Good God, there's no need for two grown men to throw a fit of hysterics just because they've found out their grandfather's hobby was seducing boys! Pull yourselves together! Now Papa, let's just try to be rational for a moment. Your father may well have been a drunken pederast who made a mess of his life, but he's been dead for well over forty years and in the meantime you've proved *beyond dispute* that you're a very successful man who's sustained a very successful marriage and shown himself to be a very successful father to six children. You never touch alcohol except on social occasions, when you spend the entire evening imbibing half a bottle of champagne, and bearing all that in mind, I can only say that if you see any similarity whatsoever between yourself and your father I'd very much like to hear about it."

"I don't want to talk about him," whispered my father. "I can't think of the past, I daren't, and that's why I've got to have Milly here as soon as possible."

"But that's irrational, can't you see?" cried Robert in despair. "It's quite irrational!"

"Of course it's irrational," I said violently. "He's mad." I swung round on my father. "Sir, if you bring that woman into this house either now or at any other time, neither I nor my family will ever cross your threshold again. And if you're depraved enough to sleep with your mistress on the night following your wife's funeral, all I can say is that I'll never forgive you. I feel thoroughly revolted by your behavior and I condemn it from the very bottom of my heart."

"So do I," said Edmund.

I turned to him. "You'll come and stay with me at the Manor, of course."

"Thank you. Yes, I couldn't possibly condone such an insult to Mama's memory by staying here."

"Thomas," I said, "you must live with me too. Papa's not fit to look after you anymore."

Thomas stared at me. His face had a white pinched expression. He looked very young and very frightened.

"There, there, Thomas," said my father, putting his arm around him again. "It's all right. They can't take you away from me. Don't let them upset you."

"I find it hard to believe, sir," said Robert, "that you—a man who's always taken such care in the upbringing of his sons—can be blind to the effect of your conduct on Thomas."

"Don't talk such bloody rubbish," said my father. "What do you know about bringing up children? A fine mess you made of those stepsons of yours!"

"And a fine mess you'll make of Thomas!" I shouted.

"Be quiet!" my father shouted back. "Thomas has just lost his mother, but he's not going to lose his father too! Children need love, not damned preaching! Now get out, the whole bloody lot of you, and leave me and Thomas alone!"

"That's the first sensible suggestion you've made for some time," said Robert, "and I'm sure we'll all be delighted to oblige you, but before we go I'd just like to say this: I shan't cut myself off from you because frankly I don't think you're fit to struggle on with only the support of Thomas and Mrs. Straker, but you should understand that I find your conduct very hard to condone and I certainly deplore the way you've deepened our bereavement by making a painful situation well-nigh intolerable. John—Edmund—"

We lifted the wheelchair from the floor of the summerhouse and carried it down the steps to the lawn. Edmund began to push the chair away, but I found I had to make one last attempt to talk to Thomas.

"If you change your mind," I said to him, "don't forget you can always have a bed at the Manor."

"Go away!" yelled Thomas, his face streaked with tears. "I'm staying with my father!"

Glendower barked as if to underline the statement, and as my father exclaimed, "Damn you, leave the boy alone!" something snapped inside me.

"Your father's a filthy disgusting old man!" I shouted to Thomas. "And the sooner you realize that the better!"

My rage carried me all the way across the lawn in my brothers' wake, but by the time I reached the house I was gripped by my next all-consuming problem: I was wondering how on earth I was going to break the news to Blanche.

4

I

I TOLD BLANCHE as soon as I returned to Penhale Manor. We were in the long drawing room which with the dining room next door had once formed the old medieval hall; it faced south over what had once been a moat and was now a rose garden. All the mullioned windows were open, and as I stood with Blanche beside her grand piano I could feel the warmth of the late-afternoon sun and hear the buzzing of the bees in the shrubs that clustered against the ancient stone walls of the house. Blanche had been arranging some white roses in one of the French crystal vases that had been given to us as a wedding present. No matter what time of year it was the drawing room never seemed to be without flowers.

"I hardly know how to tell you this," I said. "If there was any way of keeping it from you I would, but unfortunately the scandal will soon be notorious."

"Scandal?" said Blanche, pausing with a white rose in her hands. Her dark eyes, which slanted above her high cheekbones, were disturbed but trustful as she waited for me to continue. Naturally she knew that any incipient scandal could not possibly relate to me.

Rigid with embarrassment I told her that my father was planning to keep Mrs. Straker at Oxmoon. I could not tell her he proposed to sleep with his mistress on the night of his wife's funeral. I was too ashamed, too angry. As it was I had a hard time keeping my voice unemotional.

". . . and so we shan't be calling at Oxmoon once that woman's there. I refuse to condone such immorality."

"Of course," said Blanche. She fell silent, her face grave as she considered the situation. She was still holding the white rose. "How very sad it is," she said at last, and added more to herself than to me: "Your poor father."

I was shocked. "I really think sympathy's uncalled for, Blanche!"

"But obviously he's unhinged by your mother's death."

"That's no excuse! He has an absolute moral duty to his family not to degrade himself in this fashion!"

"Oh, I agree the immorality's dreadful," said Blanche rapidly as if she feared she had given me offense. "You mustn't think I'm arguing with you, darling. But my dear Mama used to say that it was easy to condemn sin but hard to be compassionate—to be Christian. I'd like to think I'd always try to be compassionate, even if the fault were very hard to understand."

"Well, no understanding's possible in this case," I said, "and I've used up all my compassion." But I kissed her to show how much I admired her goodness, and dropping her white rose on the top of the piano, she put her arms around me comfortingly.

"You look so tired, John—I do wish you'd rest."

"No, I'm too upset. I'm going for a walk."

"If there's anything I can do—"

"No, there's nothing," I said. "Nothing." And before I could break down and distress her with every detail of the sordid scene in the summerhouse I left her, a slender oddly forlorn figure beside her bowl of perfect roses.

II

I walked down the drive to the gates. The Manor stood on the edge of Penhale village, less than a quarter of a mile from the church but more than a mile from Oxmoon, which lay farther south along the road to Rhossili.

I headed into the village. It was a typical settlement of the Gower Englishry, complete with cottages grouped in traditional English fashion around a green, but it had a tousled casual air which an English visitor would have found alien. There was the usual village shop, which also served as the post office, and beyond the green lay the forge which still refused to cater for the motorcar. The church had been built on the orders of the two medieval warlords, Gilbert de Bracy and Humphrey de Mohun, and was resolutely Norman in design; the square tower was not a common feature among the churches of Gower. In contrast the interior was a monument to the excruciating taste of the Victorian de Bracys who had conducted renovations while my grandfather Robert Godwin the Drunkard had been too preoccupied with his troubles to care what was going on. The church had caused endless rows between the two families in previous centuries, for although the de Bracys had treated it as an extension of Penhale Manor, the living of the parish had been in Godwin hands. The poor vicars must have had a hard time surviving in the cross fire.

I hesitated in the shadow of the lych-gate. Then I walked around the tower, sat down on an iron bench and stared at the dying flowers on my mother's grave.

I wanted to forget my father by grieving for my mother, but again conventional grief eluded me, and rising to my feet in an agony of restlessness I began to walk in a clockwise direction around the Godwin tombstones. Then I turned and completed a circle anticlockwise. After that I realized I was beside myself not with grief but with a chaotic mess of emotion which I could not begin to subjugate, so I sat down again, put my head in my hands and gave way to uncontrolled despair; my father had failed to draw the line and beyond that line, as I knew so well, lay misery, madness and death.

I saw him following inexorably in my grandmother's footsteps, and at once I found myself wondering if some hereditary weakness could exist which might condemn a man to moral degradation against his will and his better judgment. That was a terrifying thought. I recalled my own sexuality and shuddered. At least I had it in tight control. But perhaps my father too had had his sexuality in control at the age of twenty-nine.

I rubbed my hand across my eyes as if I could wipe out my vision of intolerable possibilities, and suddenly I missed my mother. I wanted to hear her say, "Here I have my standards—and here I draw the line." But my mother's voice had been silenced, and although I was repeating her words the magic had gone from the incantation which warded off all evil, and now no one was listening to them.

I moved to the grave, stooped over the wreath of white roses which Blanche had made and pulled out the card which I myself had written. *In loving and devoted memory,* I read, *John, Blanche, Marian and Harry.* I spoke the words "loving and devoted" aloud, and at last I recognized an emotion that resembled conventional grief. Slipping the card into my breast pocket, I immediately felt better. I was now thinking not of whether my mother had loved me but of how much I had loved her for continually keeping hell at bay. I had been loving and devoted, just as the card had said. That was real, that was true. Then I remembered at last how my mother had embraced me on the night of her death and said, "Dear John, how good and kind you really are," and I knew those words had been spoken from the heart. "To think that *you* should be the one who loves me enough to say that," she had said, overcome with remorse for her past omissions when I had praised her, and suddenly I felt that whatever had been wrong had been put right. I too had spoken from the heart, and after years of dutiful formality we had at the end achieved an honest conversation during which love had undoubtedly been present.

I sank down on the bench again, shed a tear, stole a furtive glance around the churchyard to make sure I was unobserved and then cried for thirty shameful seconds. That cured me. I felt I had arranged my memory of my mother into an acceptable pattern which could be fitted into the script of my life; I felt I could now be, without difficulty, the devoted son of a loving mother.

That night I was so exhausted that I thought I would sleep as soon as my head touched the pillow, but I was wrong. Obsessed by the thought of my father sleeping with his mistress on the night of his wife's funeral, I tossed and turned in misery until dawn.

III

"I saw Mrs. Morgan today," said Blanche a week later.

"Oh, yes?" I said. I had just had a row with Edmund and was feeling distracted. "Which Mrs. Morgan?" Morgan is a very commonly encountered name in Wales.

"Mrs. Meredith's sister. I asked her if Rhiannon would like to play here again, but unfortunately they're all returning to Cardiff. It seems Mr. Morgan has returned from the sea and secured new accommodation for them."

"Oh yes?" I said again. "Well, I daresay that's for the best—we don't really want Marian becoming too friendly with a working-class child, do we. Darling, listen, I've just had the most appalling row with Edmund . . ."

In the week that had elapsed since my mother's funeral Mrs. Straker had been installed as housekeeper directly after the departure from Oxmoon of Aunt Ethel and her tribe. The entire parish of Penhale was now throbbing with a prurient delight, lightly masked as scandalized horror, and I was aware of the villagers observing me compassionately as if I were suffering from some monstrous affliction. From Llangennith and Llanmadoc in the north to Porteynon and Penrice in the south, from Rhossili in the west to Swansea in the east, the gossip was reverberating through Gower, and I was just telling myself that matters could hardly be worse when Edmund, who had been staying at Penhale Manor, announced his intention to return to Oxmoon to condone my father's conduct.

Edmund's argument—which was Robert's; Edmund was incapable of developing such a closely reasoned approach—was that if we were all to behave as if everything were aboveboard the gossiping tongues would at least be handicapped, if not silenced.

"That may be true," I said, "but I refuse to compromise my moral principles by condoning Papa's conduct."

"Oh, don't be so bloody pigheaded, John! Why don't you be sensible and give in for the sake of all concerned?"

"I might have known you'd take the line of least resistance!"

"I beg your pardon," said Edmund, "but it wasn't I who stayed safely in London throughout the war."

We did not speak again before he returned to Oxmoon, but when I next called on Robert he was very severe and said I had made Edmund utterly miserable.

"Well, what the devil does he think he's made me?"

Further protracted argument followed about the situation at Oxmoon.

"Intellectually what you say is right, Robert. But morally you're dead wrong, and I'm sticking to my principles. I draw the line."

"Well, I'm all for drawing lines," said Robert. "God knows nothing would be more boring than a world of unbridled excess where nobody bothered to draw any lines at all—sin would quite lose its power to charm. But has it never occurred to you that you might be drawing your lines in the wrong places?"

"Don't be ridiculous!"

"You're the one who's being ridiculous, drawing this brutal line between yourself and Edmund, who's actually showing great courage in a very difficult situation."

I was too guilty when I remembered the war to hold out for long against a reconciliation with Edmund, and on the following Sunday after church I offered him the olive branch of peace. My father had not returned to the church since my mother's funeral but had asked Edmund to take Thomas to Sunday Matins.

Edmund was pathetically pleased by my suggestion that we should end the estrangement. "If you knew how much I've regretted that bloody awful remark about—"

"Quite," I said, "but let's forget it. Least said soonest mended and all that rot."

The next night he came to dine at Penhale Manor, and after Blanche had left us alone with our port I asked him how he was getting on at Oxmoon.

"Well," said Edmund, welcoming the opportunity to confide and lowering his voice cozily, "it's not as bad as I thought it would be. The best part was that Papa was so pleased when I came back—honestly, I don't know how we each managed to maintain a stiff upper lip—"

"Spare me the sentimental drivel about how you and he almost sobbed in each other's arms. What about Straker?"

"My God, John, she's amazing! All the servants gave notice and sat back waiting for her to beg them to stay, but not a bit of it. 'All right, out you go!' she says, and brings in a gaggle of girls from Swansea, all terrified of her. She rules 'em with a rod of iron and the house runs like clockwork. Incredible."

"But surely not all the servants were dismissed?"

"No, Papa exercised clemency in a few cases. Bayliss is still there, white as a sheet and absolutely cowed—"

"All right, never mind the servants. How's Thomas?"

"Oh, fine! Actually he and Milly get on rather well."

"My God, Edmund, you don't call her Milly, do you?"

"Not before the servants—no, of course not," said Edmund blushing.

I was appalled.

After he had departed I said to Blanche, "If I were Edmund I'd leave Oxmoon and seek a position in London but of course he won't. It's a pity. I think his lack of ambition condemns him to great unhappiness."

"Perhaps," said Blanche, "but my dear Mama used to say that unambitious people often have a greater capacity for happiness than those people who yearn for worldly success."

I was becoming a little tired of hearing Blanche's Dear Mama quoted against me, but I said nothing because with our holiday fast approaching I wanted no cross word to mar our happiness.

I took my family each year to the Isle of Wight in August, not only because it was a delightful spot for the children but because the yachting at Cowes gave us the chance to keep up with our London acquaintances. I intended eventually to lease a flat in town but at present we seldom went to London. Blanche's aunt had a house near Knightsbridge and we occasionally stayed there, but I did not care for Aunt Charlotte, who thought her niece could have done better for herself than to marry the younger son of a Welsh squire. However Blanche was devoted to her aunt, the only sister of her Dear Mama, so I had to employ much diplomatic tact to avoid awkwardness in that direction.

Marriage is full of such trying little pitfalls. In fact I was not surprised that some couples were driven into regular quarrels. Blanche and I never quarreled, but now and then I did feel that we came dangerously close to a tiff. However I always labored diligently to suppress any cross word, and my reward for our unsullied marital happiness was our annual holiday when I could play with my children in the day, enjoy smart dinners in the evening and at night make love to my wife with a greater frequency than unselfishness usually permitted.

We had not been at Cowes more than a week when I realized that Blanche was hoping to conceive again. Nothing was said between us but then there was nothing to say. Certainly I was not about to object because my wife became subtly more gentle and loving than usual, but sometimes as we walked across the sands together I found our silence oppressive, as if we were divided by some gulf I did not understand, and then I thought I did not want another baby to divide us further. Yet that made no sense. How could it make sense when I wanted a large family and considered my marriage idyllic? Classifying such thoughts as morbid, I dismissed them firmly from my mind.

We were away a month, just as we always were, and returned home at the end of August. Still nothing had been said between us on the subject of pregnancy, but the fact that Blanche had been spared her monthly affliction had not passed unnoticed by me. Normally, when I pursued my marital rights once or at the most twice a week, it was possible for her to suffer her affliction without me knowing about it, but I had indulged myself at Cowes and I knew her health had been unimpaired.

I wondered when the symptoms would begin. Blanche spent a large part of her pregnancies lying either in bed or on a sofa to counter her general feeling of malaise, and to my distress I found this ill health annoying. I was not repelled by pregnancy itself but by the joylessness and lassitude that accompanied her infirmity. I did not want to be repelled. I was most upset that Blanche should be unwell, particularly when she never complained, but nevertheless I found her pregnancies dreary and knew they were made even drearier by my conscientious removal to a separate bedroom. Naturally I could not have forced myself on her at such a time. Only a savage would have been so inconsiderate.

"How nice it is to be home!" said Blanche as we reached the Manor. "Oh look, darling, the roses are lovelier than ever! Aren't they beautiful?"

"Beautiful," I agreed mechanically, and indeed my home did seem ravishing to the eyes, the garden glowing with flowers, the old house encircling us with its mellow charm, and beyond the Manor walls Gower too was ravishing, the Downs shimmering in the summer light, the earth of my lands a terra-cotta red, the cattle grazing peacefully in the water meadows.

Yet no sooner had I returned than I found that everything was going wrong. It had been one of the driest summers in living memory, too dry for the comfort of the cattle, and a freakish cold spell in June had laid a deathly hand not only on my new acres of crops but on the vegetables in our kitchen garden. Then just as I was wondering how in God's name I was going to water my cattle if the river ran dry, I heard that damned Llewellyn had been marching his sheep over my land again. I was so furious that I immediately drove into Swansea to see my solicitor, but he merely regaled me with legal obscurities till I lost patience. After telling him that he was to get me an injunction even if he were struck off the rolls in the attempt, I retired exhausted to Penhale.

The first person I saw when I entered the hall of the Manor was little Rhiannon Morgan. She was doubled up with laughter at the foot of the stairs as Marian slid down the banisters.

I stopped dead.

"Marian!" exclaimed Blanche, emerging from the drawing room in response to the squeals of laughter. There was no sign of Nanny. "Off those banisters at once!" She turned to greet me. "Hullo, darling—how did you get on in Swansea?"

I said blankly, "That's Rhiannon Morgan."

"Yes, isn't that nice! I saw Mrs. Morgan in the village this morning so I asked her to bring Rhiannon to play."

"But she returned to Cardiff."

"Oh, she arrived back at the farm last night for another little holiday! However I think she must have taken the Merediths by surprise, because when I saw them yesterday they didn't mention—ah, here she is! You'll stay to nursery tea, won't you, Mrs. Morgan?" she called. "Nanny assumed you would."

Mrs. Morgan had emerged from the kitchens. She wore a pale limp green cotton dress that needed ironing, and cheap white sandals. Her garish hair was scraped back from her face as usual and lay in a lump on her long neck. She looked tired.

"Thank you, Mrs. Godwin," she said awkwardly, and added to me with an even greater embarrassment, "Good afternoon, sir."

"Good afternoon, Mrs. Morgan," I said, and walked away into the drawing room.

"Papa!" cried Marian, rushing after me. "Come and have tea with us!"

"I'd love to, Marian, but I'm afraid today I've too much to do." I looked around the drawing room in search of some all-consuming occupation, but fortunately Marian took no for an answer and dashed away again into the hall.

"Dafydd's playing with a friend in the village," said Blanche, following me into the drawing room. "He's too young for the girls and too old for Harry—oh and darling, talking of Harry, I must tell you what he did today! He ran in here and played 'God Save the King' on the piano—with both hands and not a note wrong . . ."

There was a fresh bowl of white roses on the piano. While she was talking I stooped to smell them, but found they had no scent. They were perfectly formed, perfectly arranged, but they had no scent. I stared at them, and the more I stared the less real they seemed to me until finally it was as if they were made of wax, bleached of color, devoid of life.

"Darling, I don't think you've been listening to a single word I've been saying!"

"Sorry, I was thinking of wretched Llewellyn and his sheep."

After tea I retired to my study and tried to write some business letters, but I was unable to concentrate. I kept thinking of those white roses. Then I started thinking of color—the brilliant sea-green of the water by the Worm's Head and the flaming sunsets over Rhossili Bay. I remembered the white roses on my mother's grave, a symbol of death, but for one split second beyond them I glimpsed the fire of life, red-hot, all-consuming, terrifying.

I decided my Welsh blood was making me fanciful. Mixing myself a whisky-and-soda, I abandoned my correspondence, settled down in my favorite armchair and escaped into the very English world of John Buchan as I reread his famous shocker *The Thirty-nine Steps.*

IV

I remember every detail of that evening clearly. Blanche wore an evening gown of a most ethereal shade of yellow, paler than primrose, barely darker than cream, and with the gown she wore the amethyst pendant I had given her for her eighteenth birthday after our engagement had been announced. At dinner we discussed the possibility of inviting Daphne and little Elizabeth to stay in the autumn, as it was now out of the question that they should stay at Oxmoon, and soon afterwards I began to reminisce about Lion. I tried to explain how awful he had been and how wonderful he had been and how although I had expected to miss him less and less I found myself missing him more and more.

"He had more spunk than Edmund," I said, "and so much more warmth than Robert, and he was never sullen like Thomas—he was always so jolly and such fun. God, how we used to laugh when we were young! Yes, we had good times . . . but later we drifted apart, and at the end of our teens he called me a prig and I called him a rake and that was that. But I always remained fond of him. He was—" I hesitated before finding the right word. "—he was a very *real* person. There was no illusion there—he never played any roles, and he had such vitality—he was *so alive.*" I stopped to reflect on what I had said before adding in wonder: "How strange it is that I should say all that now, five years after his death! I thought I'd finished grieving for him long ago." And when I saw that Blanche was moved, either by my reminiscence or by the fact that Lion was dead, I said abruptly, "Well, we won't talk of him anymore. I'm sorry—I was being morbid. Will you play me some music instead?"

We retired to the drawing room and she sat down at the piano, her pale yellow gown shimmering in the light from the candle sconces; the fresh white roses, perfect as ever, in the same crystal vase nearby.

She began to play. The music meant nothing to me, but I enjoyed watching her and thinking how beautiful and talented she was. Then I started worrying about Harry, playing "God Save the King" perfectly before he was three years old. A musical inclination was no use to a boy at all.

I was just wondering if I could find a miniature cricket bat to give him for Christmas when Blanche suddenly stopped playing.

"Are you all right?" I said, springing to my feet as she put her hand to her forehead.

"No—I'm sorry, darling, but I've got the most beastly headache. It's come on very suddenly. Will you excuse me if I go up to bed?"

"Of course," I said sympathetically, and thought with a sinking heart: Pregnancy. To conceal this inexcusable antipathy I said quickly, "Shall I telephone the doctor?"

"No, don't worry, darling—it's only a migraine."

"I'll sleep in the dressing room so that I don't disturb you."

"No." She looked wretched. "I know you hate that."

"Don't be absurd! When you're not well I don't mind in the least!"

"You do," she said, and to my horror she began to cry.

"Well, we won't talk about that now," I said hastily, but she only wept harder and whispered, "We never talk, never, and there's so much I want to say."

"But my dear Blanche . . . what do you mean? We're always talking! We get on so well!"

"I feel so lonely."

"*Lonely?*"

"I'm frightened in case you don't love me."

"But I adore you! How can you possibly say—"

"I'm frightened in case I can't be the sort of wife you want me to be, I'm frightened that I won't be able to cope with our marriage much longer, I'm frightened that you don't confide in me, I'm frightened because I don't know what your silence means—"

"My darling, you must stop this nonsense—yes, I insist that you stop! You're simply tired and overwrought. I love you and you're the best wife in the world and—"

"Then why do you never talk to me?"

"I do and I will—but not now when you've got a bad headache. Come on, I'll take you upstairs."

"No," she said desolately. "I'll say good night here." She dried her eyes, gave me a chaste little kiss which I dutifully returned and vanished upstairs into the dark.

I felt very, very disturbed. I closed the piano and saw the roses shiver on their long stems. Then I shut all the windows. I felt as if I were battening down the hatches—but against what? I had no idea. Retreating to the study I mixed myself another whisky-and-soda and prepared to escape again into the world of John Buchan, but now Richard Hannay too was fleeing from forces that terrified him and in his flight I saw my own flight reflected.

Moving outside into the moonlit garden, I wandered down the path to the potting shed. An owl hooted above me, and as I remembered similar nocturnal expeditions with Lion long ago at Oxmoon I suddenly knew I wanted to be Johnny again, safe in an uncomplicated past.

But I was in a complicated present, and my wife was unhappy—except, as

I well knew, this was impossible because she had no reason to be other than contented. What had happened? What had gone wrong? I had no idea.

I thought of Blanche weeping, "I'm frightened that I won't be able to cope with our marriage much longer," and at once I heard my mother saying in despair, "How's that poor child Blanche ever going to cope?" That was the moment when I knew it was all my fault. I had no idea what "it" was, but I was going to find out. Glancing up at the dark window of our bedroom, I wondered if Blanche was still awake, and I hesitated, torn between my reluctance to disturb her and my compulsion to solve the problem. Naturally, I never doubted that the problem—"it"—could be solved.

"It" won. I hurried indoors, lit a candle and padded up the staircase. At the bedroom door I paused to listen, but all was quiet. I tapped lightly on the door.

"Blanche?"

There was no answer. Opening the door, I looked in.

"Darling, I hate to disturb you—"

But she was awake. Although she was lying in bed, her eyes were open.

"—oh, you're awake. Thank goodness. Blanche, I really must talk to you further about all this—"

I stopped.

She had not moved. Her eyes did not see me. She was looking at some point beyond my left shoulder. "Blanche?" I said sharply, but there was no reply. It was almost as if she were dead, but that I knew was impossible. Healthy young women of twenty-five did not die without warning in their beds. Setting down the candle, I touched her cheek with my hand.

It was cold.

I found it extraordinarily difficult to know what to do next, but since it seemed that some mysterious drop in her temperature had caused her to lose consciousness, I pulled off my shoes and got into bed beside her to warm her up. While I waited I tried to imagine what "it" could be. What had I done? I loved her, she loved me and we were happy. Except that we weren't. At least, I was. Or was I?

"Blanche?"

She was wearing a white nightgown, white as the white roses. Vile white roses. Odorless. Listless. Dead.

I got out of bed, pulled on my shoes again, picked up the candle and went downstairs to the telephone.

"Dr. Warburton, please," I said to the postmistress when she responded to my call.

I was now no longer baffled but incredulous. In fact I was outraged. How *could* she have been unhappy? I had done everything possible to ensure a successful marriage. I had told her lie after lie in order to protect her from my troubles. I had restrained my baser physical inclinations endlessly in order not to give her offense. I had toiled year after year at the task of behaving perfectly towards her—and as I thought of this, I could hear my mother's voice again. She was holding me in her arms in the remote past and telling me how I could feel safe and happy. "You're going to be an extra-specially good boy so that your poor papa is never reminded of his mother's wickedness . . ."

My mind suddenly plunged into chaos as past and present collided, instinctively I squeezed my eyes shut in a futile attempt to blot out the Christmas of 1903.

"Hullo? Warburton speaking."

"Warburton, it's John Godwin." I was so acutely aware of time being dislocated that I could not pin myself to the present. I said, "It's all to do with my grandmother, my grandmother and Owain Bryn-Davies," and then I hung up so that I could concentrate on the task of staying sane. Something seemed to be happening to my mind. I felt as if my capacity for producing rational interlinked thoughts were being savagely dismembered.

The telephone rang. I answered it. One always answered telephones when they rang. That was normal.

"Godwin, you need help, don't you?"

It was Gavin Warburton calling back, nailing me firmly to the September of 1921. The past receded. I was back, shattered but sane, in a horrifying present.

"My wife's dead," I said, "except that she can't be dead because she's only twenty-five and there was nothing wrong with her."

Warburton said he was on his way.

V

"I'm sorry," said Warburton, "but I'm afraid there'll have to be an autopsy. Of course there's no question of death from unnatural causes, but when a young person dies suddenly the cause of death must be conclusively established."

"You're saying she's dead."

"I'm saying she's dead. I'm very, very sorry. It could have been a heart attack," said Warburton, persistently talking in order to underline the truth which I was still trying to reject, "but it might have been a cerebral hemorrhage. Did she complain of a headache?"

I stared at him.

Warburton started talking again, but this time I could not hear everything he said. His voice seemed close to me at one moment, far away the next. "Possibly born with a weakness in one of the blood vessels of the brain . . .

could have happened at any time . . . or perhaps a blood clot . . . sometimes when a young woman is pregnant . . . very tragic . . . so much admired . . . deepest sympathy . . . My dear Godwin, I think you'd better tell me where you keep your brandy."

The next thing I knew I was drinking brandy in my study while Warburton telephoned for an ambulance. When he rejoined me I said, "I don't understand. This shouldn't be happening. It's as if my script's been torn up, it's as if someone's rung down the curtain in the wrong place and now I've got no lines, no part, nothing, I don't know what to do next, I don't even know who I am anymore."

Warburton waited a moment. Then he said, "Shall I telephone your father and ask him to come over? I think he'd understand what you're going through."

"Good God, no!" I said, shocked at last out of my wretched loss of nerve. I pulled myself together. "But I'll talk to Robert. He'll know what to do. I'll telephone him straightaway."

Warburton began to speak but checked himself. I looked at him coldly. "You needn't worry," I said. "I haven't forgotten he's an invalid. I'm not going to behave like my father, throwing a hysterical fit and mixing up past and present." I was going to say more but those last five words paralyzed me; I was too frightened to go on. I ran to the telephone but found I did not know what to do with it. I said, "This is September, 1921. Robert's in a wheelchair. My mother's been dead for two months. I'm twenty-nine years old. My grandmother's been dead since 1910, eleven years she's been dead, and this is now 1921."

"I'll talk to your brother," said Warburton. "Come and sit down again while I make the call."

He poured me some more brandy. I drank it. And gradually I began to be calmer.

VI

"I must establish straightaway," I said to Robert and Ginevra, "that I'm now on an even keel following my initial shock. No more dementia; we've had quite enough demented behavior in this family, thank you very much, so if you think I'm going to go to pieces like Papa, you'd better bloody well think again. Sorry, Ginevra, please excuse my language, I'm afraid I'm still a trifle upset."

"That's all right, darling," said Ginevra.

"Of course it's tempting to go to pieces because that would prove how much I loved Blanche, and I did love her, no doubt about that, although it wasn't a grand passion because I don't believe in grand passions, they're much too dangerous, think of Grandmama and Bryn-Davies—chaos, anarchy, madness and death. Awful. Stick to the script is the answer and don't deviate from it. Hold fast, stand firm and soldier on, as John Buchan might have said, although actually I don't think he ever did."

"Yes, darling," said Ginevra.

"Have a sedative, John," said Robert, "and go to bed."

"No, I'm going to sit by Blanche and grieve for her."

"They've taken her away to the mortuary, John, you know they have. You saw the body being taken out."

"Steady, Robert," said Warburton.

"I know I saw it," I said, "but I forgot for a moment, that's all, it was just a little slip of the memory, there's no need to treat me as if I'm a bloody lunatic. Sorry, Ginevra, please do excuse my language, I'm not quite myself yet."

"It doesn't matter, darling," said Ginevra.

I suddenly realized she was humoring me. "I'm not mad!" I shouted. "I'm not! I absolutely refuse to be mad! I draw the line!"

"It's all right," said Warburton, gripping me. "Don't panic; it's the shock, it's normal, you don't have to worry about madness. Now, if you can sit down and take off your jacket . . . Ginevra, can you roll up his sleeve?"

"My poor grandmother," I said, "it was retribution. But then the wheel turned a full circle and Papa and Mama knew retribution themselves. The wheel . . . Robert, you used to talk about that wheel—"

"All right, Godwin—just clench your fist and count to five."

"And to think it was *she* who thought of the tide tables—he did it but she thought of it—oh, the horror, I can't bear it, can't face it, blot it out, blot it out, blot it out—"

The needle found the vein. I started counting in Welsh and within seconds was fathoms deep in oblivion.

VII

I woke at six. Evidently Warburton had reduced the dose he had given to my father—or perhaps because I was younger and stronger the drug had had less effect—for I had no inclination to sleep till noon. I felt dull-witted but not ill. I did have one moment of bewilderment when I found myself lying semidressed beneath a blanket on the drawing-room sofa, but my brain was functioning normally again, and although I shied away from the memory that Blanche was dead, I could recall the fact without confusion. My main preoccupation was with Robert and Ginevra. I was just shuddering at the memory of the scene I had created in their presence when I was mercifully diverted by the sight of a note propped on the nearby table.

Darling, I read, *ring me as soon as you wake up and I'll come over to hold the fort. I've spoken to Nanny and she'll tell the children. All the servants know. Gavin will be returning to see you at nine. Much love,* GINEVRA.

My mind fastened on the word "children." I knew I had to tell them myself. That was the right thing to do. A glimmer of a new script presented itself. I had to be the perfect widower, and the first act consisted of surviving the funeral with decency and good taste. I had no idea what the second act would be about, but I could think of after-the-funeral later. Meanwhile I had to look after my children and behave properly.

Leaving the wings I began to move to the center of my new stage.

VIII

"Mama's gone to heaven?" repeated Marian dazed and burst into tears.

"When will she be back?" said Harry mystified. I saw that this second death in the family, coming so soon after his grandmother's, had made him feel death was a subject he wanted to understand.

"She's dead, you stupid baby, she's dead!" wept Marian before I could choose the right words for him. "And dead people never come back, never!"

"Shhh . . . Marian . . ." As I held her tightly, I saw Harry's dark eyes fill with tears.

"But that's not fair," he said.

There was no answer to that. Leaning forward, one arm still around Marian, I drew him to me as he started to cry.

IX

"My wife's aunt will of course be coming down for the funeral, Nanny, but she's suggested that you take the children now to her house in London for a few days." Ginevra had offered to have the children to stay, but Robin was always aggressive towards anyone who tried to share his nursery, and I thought Harry and Marian would be better off under Aunt Charlotte's roof.

"Oh, that would suit very well, sir—much better for the poor little lambs to be far away from here while the funeral's going on. . . . Oh sir, I can hardly believe it . . . such a *lady* she was, always so thoughtful to others, always so sympathetic and understanding . . ."

But I could not stop to think about Blanche. There was no time. My new script called for an audience with the vicar, and soon I was hurrying into Penhale on cue.

X

"I want the shortest possible service," I said to Anstey, who was a Swansea man about five years my senior. He did not have Gavin Warburton's County connections but my father, always conscious of his own lack of education, liked him the better for not having attended a public school. Anstey preached a brisk twenty-minute sermon, kept his services free of Romish tendencies and could be relied upon to discuss the weather intelligently. In my opinion no parish could ask more of its parson than that.

"But you'll have music, of course," he said to me. "Everyone will remember your wife's gift for music—although she was always so modest and unassuming—really, she was such an exceptional person, wasn't she, so sensitive to the welfare of others, such a very Christian lady—"

"But she's dead," I said, "and funerals are for the living to endure. I want no music, no hymns, nothing. This is to be a short plain private English funeral, and I'll have no Welsh circuses here."

XI

My butler was making an emotional speech telling me that all my servants offered their deepest sympathy.

". . . the best lady we ever worked for . . . always so ready to help . . . nothing was ever too much trouble or beneath her notice . . ."

I thanked all the servants for their sympathy and loyal support. Then I retired to my study to draft the notices for the newspapers.

XII

My father wrote me a note.

My dear John, I'm so very sorry. How seldom one meets someone who is beautiful and good and nice. It makes the tragedy worse. Tragedies hurt. I don't like to think of you in pain. Please come and stay for a while at Oxmoon. I want so much to help. Always your loving and devoted father, R. G.

I tore up the note. I burned the shredded paper. And I scattered the ashes from the nearest window.

Then, because I had a break between scenes, I started to think. That was a mistake because my thoughts were not in accordance with my script. I was aware that a portrait was inexorably emerging of someone I did not recognize, someone who listened to people's problems, someone who was deeply involved in caring for others, someone to whom people talked and who talked to them in return. My fragile exquisite wife whom I had preserved so conscientiously beneath the glass case of my love now seemed to be disintegrating in my memory while into her place moved a stranger I had never cared to know.

The world was grinding out of focus but I ground it back. I told myself I would think of all that, whatever "all that" was, after the funeral. Then I drove to Little Oxmoon to embark on the next scene in my script.

XIII

"Ginette and I feel we must talk to you," said Robert at Little Oxmoon on the night before the funeral.

I had gone there to dine with Aunt Charlotte, who had arrived that afternoon. Since I had temporarily dismissed all my servants from the Manor by giving them a week's holiday with pay, this meant—to my relief—that I was unable to invite Aunt Charlotte to stay, but although I had expected her to go to the Metropole Hotel in Swansea, Ginevra had compassionately offered her hospitality instead.

Dinner had now finished; Aunt Charlotte had retired, pleading exhaustion, and as soon as the drawing-room door had closed Robert was launching himself into the attack.

"We want to talk to you about your decision to spend a week entirely alone without servants after the funeral tomorrow."

"Darling," said Ginevra, taking the lead in a rush, "you *can't* be all alone in that house for a week! I know it's madly romantic to want to entomb yourself with your memories, and of course I'm simply passionate about romance, but—"

"Who's going to iron your shirts and wash your underwear?" said Robert with his usual brutal common sense. "Who's going to provide heated water for your shave?"

Ignoring him I said simply to Ginevra, "I know it must seem odd but I've got to be there."

"But darling, why?"

I thought carefully. It was hard to know how to express my complex emotional instincts in words, but at last I said, "I have to arrange my memories." I thought how much better I had felt after I had sorted out my muddled feelings towards my mother. "I have to arrange my memories into the right order before I can draw a line below the past and make plans for the future," I said. "And to do that I have to be alone in the house where Blanche lived."

They were silent but it was not a comfortable silence. I felt I could guess what they were thinking.

"Don't worry," I said, "I'm not about to go mad. I've rejected the grand folly of an elaborate funeral followed by a smart luncheon party. I'm quite in touch with reality, I assure you."

"I can think of nothing less in touch with reality," said Robert, "than shutting yourself up for a week in a manor house with no servants."

"Well, if I don't like it," I said, "I can always leave. What are you two getting so flustered about?"

They looked at me. They looked at each other. But they both decided there was nothing more they could say.

XIV

The air reeked of flowers, and all the flowers seemed to be white in remembrance of her French name. The servants' children had even offered wild white daisies from the hedgerows in little bunches tied with white ribbon. The September morning was warm but overcast; the sky seemed to reflect a burning white light which accentuated the aching glare of the white flowers. I had ordered a wreath of white roses and had instructed that the card should read: *In loving and devoted memory, John, Marian and Harry.* Later I planned to return to the churchyard, just as I had after my mother died, and put that card in my breast pocket. I was very mindful of how that small gesture had meant so much to me.

I had asked for the funeral to be private so the mourners in the church were restricted to the family, but outside all the village had gathered. Ginevra cried at the graveside. I knew she was prone to tears at emotional moments but nevertheless I was touched. I thought how kind she had been to me during the past few days, and I even wondered if I had judged her too harshly in the past. I resolved to be less censorious in future.

My father was there. He had tried to speak to me before the service but I had cut him dead. Edmund had been shocked. I thought, Silly old Edmund, and I started missing Lion again.

At last the service ended. I shook hands with Anstey and thanked him for conducting the service. I thanked Robert and Ginevra for being so kind. I thanked Aunt Charlotte for what I described as her understanding and patience in a time of great trial. Vaguely appalled by my diplomatic glibness, I excused myself from Blanche's Herefordshire cousins and promised to visit them later when I had recovered from what I described as "this sad and difficult occasion." I cut my father again, nodded to Edmund, said, "Thank you for coming, Thomas—that was good of you" and headed for the lych-gate. The silent crowds parted before me. My car was waiting. I drove off and two minutes later was halting the car outside the door of my home.

Now, finally, I could be alone to grieve. Taking a deep breath I expelled it with the most profound relief and then ran willingly, without a second's hesitation, into the nightmare that lay waiting for me beyond.

XV

The grandfather clock in the hall was striking noon. All through that day I remember the clocks chiming the passing hours and reminding me that time was moving on for those who were left alive. Only the dead were beyond time, and Blanche was most certainly dead—"gone to heaven," as I had told the children when I repeated the phrase that Blanche herself had used to break the news of my mother's death. I shuddered. "Heaven" in that context conjured up an image of a celestial concert hall, complete with harps and massed choirs, and since I had no ear for music I found this vision more hellish than heavenly.

Occupied with these comfortingly vacuous thoughts I drifted into the dining room, mixed myself a whisky-and-soda and sat down at the table to reflect further on life after death and other fables. Time filtered idly but not unpleasantly by until I found myself meditating on the meaning of life which I knew was a desperate subject for a man who had insufficient courage to believe in either atheism or God. I decided I had to pull myself together. Mixing myself a second whisky-and-soda, I set aside all metaphysical specula-tion and said aloud, "Now I shall grieve." I waited. Nothing happened, but that, as I realized, was because I was in the wrong room. I went into the drawing room and opened the lid of the piano so that I could more easily picture Blanche playing her music. Still nothing happened, but that, as I told myself, was because I needed time to unwind after the ordeal of the funeral.

The clock on the chimneypiece struck one, the fine French china clock that Blanche's ancestor had smuggled out of Paris during the French Revolu-tion. I had always thought this episode in the clock's history was most im-probable, but I had to concede that improbable things did happen. It was improbable that Blanche should have died yet she was undeniably dead and here was I, undeniably alone as I waited to grieve, just as every good widower should, for the wife I had so greatly loved and admired.

I debated whether to have another whisky but decided against it. Instead I began to wander around the house as I waited for the grief to come. I decided my trouble was that I had so many precious memories that I could not immediately decide how they should all be arranged, and suspecting I would think more clearly if I had something to eat, I entered the kitchens just as the clock in the servants' hall chimed two. Nosing around in the larder, I found a piece of cheese and ate it. " 'Appley Dapply, a little brown mouse, goes to the cupboard in somebody's house'!" Lion had chanted long ago. I could not accurately recall the rest of Beatrix Potter's rhyme, but I knew that Appley Dapply had been charmed by cheese. However I was less than charmed by the piece I ate, and closing the larder door I began wandering again.

Upstairs in our bedroom the little hand of the clock on the bedside table pointed to three, and when I opened the window I heard the church clock in the village boom the hour. Penhale church was as unusual in its possession of a clock as it was in its possession of a square tower. The previous Lady de Bracy, an Englishwoman who had found Wales distressingly unregulated, had installed the clock to encourage the villagers to lead more ordered lives, but nobody had paid it the slightest attention. Enraged by the continuing unpunctuality, Lady de Bracy had ordered that the chimes be made louder, and from that day onwards the clock of Penhale church had been famous for the manner in which it thundered the hour.

I stood by the window listening to it. I liked the thought of the clocks all chiming away, all doing what they were supposed to do, but that only reminded me that my own behavior was leaving much to be desired, so I embarked on my most serious effort so far to arrange my memories. My first task obviously was to picture Blanche with the maximum of clarity in order to conjure up the appropriate emotions, so turning aside from the window I examined the silver-framed wedding photograph that stood on top of the chest of drawers nearby.

I continued to stare at the handsome young couple in the picture but after a while they began to seem like an illustration from some old-fashioned book of homilies. I could imagine the text: "This is how you should look on your wedding day. This is how you must appear as you prepare to live happily ever after." Then it occurred to me that the photograph was just a pattern of black-and-white shapes. It had no reality, it was just a prop in my script, and when I looked at Blanche I could not see the Blanche I wanted to remember.

I shoved the frame face down on the chest of drawers and opened the wardrobe so that I could touch her clothes. Here was reality. Now I could visualize her clearly in the clothes she had worn. I saw her smooth, shining hair, so dark that it was almost black, the pale, creamy skin, the slender waist, the delicate breasts, the lovely line of her neck, her—but no, I could not see her face. In my memory, my glance traveled upwards from her neck and found a void beneath the cloud of dark hair.

I was unnerved. I had to see her face. I looked at the wedding photograph again but that was useless; her face was like a death mask. I had to see her being normal, laughing with the children, being the wife I remembered.

The grandfather clock in the hall struck four as I raced downstairs to the drawing room, but in panic I discovered that the photograph albums had vanished from the cupboard below the bookcase. This was bizarre indeed; it was almost as if Blanche had never existed, as if she had been a mere figment of my imagination, yet another prop in my script, but I knew I could not cope with a mad thought like that so I thrust it aside and dashed into the study. There was a photograph of Blanche on my desk, a studio portrait taken after she had recovered from the loss of our first son, who had died within hours of his birth. I stared at the new arrangement of black-and-white shapes. She looked like some actress who had been miscast in Shakespearian tragedy; I saw her as Ophelia, or perhaps as the poor queen in *Richard II,* someone struggling with adversity on a cold bleak stage, someone wearing a mask not of her own making, someone toiling in the wrong part assigned to her by some blockheaded producer who had entirely failed to understand her talents.

Reality began to grind into focus again, and this time I could not grind it back. I told myself I had to find those photograph albums. They were my last chance. Without the photograph albums I would be unable to visualize the Blanche I had loved, and if I could not remember her properly how could I arrange my memories? I started to ransack the house from top to bottom.

I ended up in the nursery just as the cuckoo clock on the wall was hiccuping five. It had occurred to me that Nanny had removed the albums from the drawing room and forgotten to replace them; no doubt the children too had wanted to see the photographs as part of the ritual of grief. I hunted among the toys, but at last ran the albums to earth on the bedside table in Marian's room. Sinking down on the bed I began to turn the pages.

I looked for a long time and in the end I even took the collection downstairs to the study where I could examine the pictures with the aid of a magnifying glass.

More time elapsed and on the chimneypiece the carriage clock struck six.

I glanced up at those two hands pointing in opposite directions. I was in my study at Penhale Manor, the room the de Bracys had called the library. That, I knew, was true. That was real. But nothing else was. All the albums showed me was my script. In a variety of charming scenes the perfect mother played and laughed with her perfect children; the perfect wife smiled adoringly at her perfect husband. But there was no sign of the other Blanche, the real Blanche who had wept and said we never talked to each other, the Blanche who had been so frightened and alone. I had never known the real Blanche. It had not suited me to know her. I had been too busy acting out my script in which I outshone Robert and secured my parents' approbation by making the perfect marriage. I had not cared for Blanche. The only person I had cared for had been myself. I had had this wonderful wife, who everyone now told me had been so exceptional, and yet I had never loved her enough to bother to become more than formally acquainted with her. And what was worse, I had made her desperately unhappy.

This was a different situation indeed from my mother's death. There I had been able to console myself that matters had been put right between us before she died, but Blanche had died when I was estranged from her; she had died alone and unloved.

The truth stood revealed in its full horror. I had been a bad husband. My marriage had been a failure. My life had been false. "I want to arrange my memories," I had said grandly. What memories? I had no memories of anything except lies, and now, I realized to my horror, I was going to have to live with them. But how did one live with such guilt and such shame? I had no idea. I felt I couldn't cope, couldn't manage, couldn't think how I was going to go on. I had never before experienced such a horrifying consciousness. The pain was excruciating. How did one live with such pain and stay sane?

The Victorian clock in the dining room thudded seven as I uncorked the bottle of champagne. I drank the first glass straight off and poured myself another, but seconds later the glass was empty again. I went on drinking, and gradually as the familiar lassitude stole over me I managed to control my panic. I knew I had been fond of Blanche. That was real, that was true, and I thought that if I could now grieve for her, not as a husband should grieve for his wife but as a man mourning the loss of someone precious, I would find my disastrous failure easier to accept. But my guilt defeated me; although I waited and waited and waited, the grief still refused to come.

I stopped drinking. I knew I should eat to avoid becoming ill but I had drunk too much, and in the kitchens all I could do was vomit into the sink. I returned to the hall, and as I entered the drawing room the silence came to meet me, the silence of those white piano keys, the silence of the white roses, the silence of reproach and estrangement. The room was utterly silent, utterly still, unbearably silent, unbearably still, and suddenly I was overpowered by the silence, choked and racked by it, and I knew I had no choice but to escape.

I burst into the garden. The evening air was clear but the rose garden was an intolerable blur of white light, and the next moment I had started to run.

I ran to the front of the house, I ran down the drive, I ran past the gates into the lane. I ran towards the village but even before I saw the church I knew what I wanted to do. I wanted to take the card from the wreath. I wanted to see those words *loving and devoted* and tell myself they did bear some relation, no matter how distorted, to reality. I thought that once that card was in my breast pocket next to my heart, I would finally be able to grieve as I had grieved for my mother.

I reached the lych-gate. I passed the porch. I turned the corner of the tower to confront the grave on the far side of the churchyard.

Some yards away in front of an ancient yew tree the white flowers, symbol of death, were heaped on the dark earth. But beyond them was color, a flash of shimmering red, the fire of life coruscating in the pale evening light.

I stopped.

A woman was seated casually on the ground by the grave. She was plucking the short grass nearby and throwing it aside in hypnotic rhythmic movements of her hand. Her brilliant red hair was very long, stretching all the way to her waist, and it waved over her shoulders like burning liquid gliding over molten rocks.

She went on tearing the grass, her head bent in deep, concentrated thought, but at last she became aware that she was being watched and her fingers were still.

She looked up. She saw me. She leaped to her feet. For a long moment we stood there, both of us transfixed with shock, and then above us, far above us in the belfry, the church clock began to thunder the hour.

5

I

SHE BEGAN to walk towards me. The evening sun, slanting across her face, lit those light eyes to a deep glowing sea-green. With a quick movement of her hand she pushed back her long fiery hair but again it slid forward to frame her face, and as the church tower cast its shadow across her translucent skin I knew, as indeed I had always known at heart, that she was ravishing. The clock, hammering her extraordinary beauty deep into my consciousness, struck again and again and again.

The last stroke died away. It was eight o'clock on the day of my wife's funeral and I was alone with Bronwen Morgan in the churchyard at Penhale.

"Mr. Godwin," she said rapidly in her low heavily accented voice, "forgive me for intruding. You want to be alone with your grief and I'll leave you at once."

I stopped her by raising my hand. "Why are you here?" I said. My voice was puzzled, confused.

"I couldn't be in the churchyard this morning with the rest of the village because Dafydd was sick, but I did so want to pay my respects . . . Mrs. Godwin was such a very lovely lady and so kind to me."

I had a brief poignant glimpse of Blanche being kind, and in that glimpse I saw both the familiar Blanche and the Blanche I had never known. The horror of my estrangement from my wife overwhelmed me afresh, and I leaned dumbly against the wall of the tower.

"Mr. Godwin, you're not well. Come and sit down, sir, you really should sit down, indeed you should."

I was too overcome by misery to protest. "I've done a very foolish thing," I said as we reached the iron bench by the yew tree. "I've dismissed my servants because I wanted to be alone to grieve, but solitude's proved too . . . difficult, and I don't know what to do next. I can't think clearly at all."

"Have you had anything to eat?"

I discounted the cheese and shuddered at the memory of the champagne. "No."

"Then if you like, sir," she said, "I'll make you some tea and a sandwich. You mustn't have too much but you should have something, and tea's so clear, so cool, you'll be able to think more clearly once you've had some tea."

I could at once picture the tea, fragrant and steaming, in one of the white Coalport cups. "That's very good of you, Mrs. Morgan," I said. "Thank you."

Leaving the churchyard, we crossed the green and walked down the lane to the Manor. No one was about. I supposed everyone was either at home or in the pub or at a meeting that was in progress in the church hall. In the lane the hedgerow glowed with wild flowers and the summer air was fragrant. Neither of us spoke. When we reached the house I led the way into the hall.

"I know where the kitchens are, sir," she said. "You go to the parlor—the room with the piano—and rest. I shan't be long."

"I'm afraid the fire in the range is out—"

"Then I'll light it," she said tranquilly, and disappeared beyond the green baize door.

Returning to the drawing room, I sat and waited. The room grew darker, and I was just rising to my feet to light a lamp when I heard her footsteps recrossing the hall.

She was carrying a tray. On it stood a teapot with a milk jug and sugar bowl, a plate bearing a cheese sandwich, and an apple. There was only one cup and saucer.

"I hope the bread's not too stale, sir."

"It doesn't matter. Mrs. Morgan, you've only brought one cup. Don't you want any tea?"

"I have a cup waiting in the kitchen."

"Then please bring it in here. I've been alone too much in this room today."

She retrieved her tea, and when she returned she brought not only more hot water but a second sandwich. The tea tasted exquisite. I ate and drank with single-minded concentration until finally I felt strong enough to look back over my shoulder at the piano, but although the image of Blanche returned to me I was still unable to see her face.

I said suddenly, "I can't grieve. I want to but I can't. I've set this time aside to grieve but now the grief won't come and I don't know how to summon it."

"There is no timetable for grief," said Bronwen Morgan. "Grief isn't a train which you catch at the station. Grief has its own time, and grief's time is beyond time, and time itself . . . isn't very important. It's the English who think time is a straight line which can be divided up and labeled and parceled out in an orderly fashion, but time isn't like that, time is a circle, time goes round and round like a wheel, and that's why one hears echoes of the past continually—it's because the past is present; you don't have to look back down the straight line, you just look across the circle, and there are the echoes of the past and the vision of the future, and they're all present, all now, all forever."

I looked at her and saw far beyond her into the remote comforting mysticism of Celtic legend. She leaned forward, putting her elbows on her knees and cradling her chin in her hands, and as her hair streamed over her shoulders to frame her face again, I felt the magic of that other culture beckoning me away from the down-to-earth brutality of the Anglo-Saxon tradition in which I had been educated. And then it seemed to me that the culture which had been hammered into me at school was not only inferior to hers but less in touch with the real truths of life, and I felt my familiar world shift on its axis as if pulled by some gravitational force far beyond my control.

"Tell me about the echoes of the past," I said. "Tell me how I can look across the circle and hear my wife's echo in time."

She said, "It may be tomorrow, it may not be for years, but you'll hear it. Perhaps the children will sound the first note, the first chord in time; perhaps one day Master Harry will go to the piano and when he plays you'll see her there and you'll think, Yes, it's sad I shall never hear her play again, and you'll grieve. Or perhaps you'll think, Yes, it's sad, but there was happiness before the sadness, and then although you'll still grieve you'll be grateful for the memory, and the memory will echo on in time. And later perhaps you'll hear one of her favorite tunes played by someone else and you'll remember again, perhaps less painfully, perhaps even with pleasure that the memory should bring her close to you again, and the echo may be fainter but still very clear, so clear that you'll tell your children about it, and then it'll be part of their memory too, and so it'll go on echoing again and again in time, and that time is beyond time, time out of mind."

She paused. She was still looking at the unlit fireplace, and behind her the soft light from the lamp made her hair blaze against her uncanny skin.

"When I was two," she said, "my father died in the Boer War. I have no memory of him. I thought later, How sad I can't remember him, can't grieve as I should—for of course to me he wasn't a hero, he was just someone who'd gone away and left us, and I resented him for being killed and then I felt guilty that I resented him, and what with all the resentment and the guilt I never thought the grief would come, I thought I'd never hear his echo in time, and indeed I forgot all about grieving, but gradually, as I grew up, other people would talk to me about him, and I thought, Why do they do this, what makes them speak now after so many years, and then suddenly I realized it was because of me, because *I was the echo* for those people, and for them the past wasn't lost far away down the straight line after all but coming back towards them in a curve. It was as if he was still alive, for when they looked at me they saw him, and when I understood this, when I understood he was present in me, then I knew him, then he became real to me, then the resentment died and the guilt fell away and at last, years after his death, I was able to grieve." She stood up and stacked her own cup and saucer with mine on the tray. "I'll take these to the kitchen and wash them up. Please excuse me, sir, for talking so much."

After a moment I followed her. She looked up startled as I entered the scullery.

"Thank you," I said. "I feel much better now." I was trying to decide how I could best express my gratitude to her. Obviously I could not offer her money but I felt some tangible gesture of thanks should undoubtedly be made, and after careful thought I said, "I must go through my wife's possessions soon. Perhaps you would accept something in memory of her."

"Oh, but I wouldn't presume—"

"Nonsense. She liked you, spoke well of you."

She was speechless. She set down the newly dried teapot as if she feared it might shatter to pieces in her hands.

"Perhaps you'd like some of her clothes," I said suddenly. "They're no good to her maid, she's the wrong shape."

"Oh, but I couldn't possibly accept—"

"I don't see why not. Why don't you at least have a look at them and see what you think?"

"Well, I . . . it's very, very kind of you. . . . When?"

"Now?"

"Oh! Oh yes—yes, indeed—if you wish." She hastily dried the last plate and hung up the cloth.

The twilight was heavy by this time but although the hall was in gloom it was not in darkness. Carrying a candle more out of courtesy than necessity, I led the way upstairs. We were both silent. I had fixed my mind on the subject of Blanche's clothes and was debating whether to donate them to the Red Cross or to the Salvation Army after Mrs. Morgan had made her selection.

In the bedroom I walked to the wardrobe and opened the doors.

"These are the clothes she usually wore," I said over my shoulder as I held up the candle to illuminate them. "But there's another wardrobe in the bedroom across the passage where she kept the clothes she wore less frequently."

Mrs. Morgan cast one glance at the contents of the wardrobe and said, "I'm afraid I couldn't possibly take any of them, sir. They're much too good for me."

In the pause that followed I was acutely aware of my hand setting down the candle. Then before I could stop myself I said, "You're too modest, Mrs. Morgan. You're far, far too modest."

Everything changed. I had never before realized that a mere inflection of the voice could destroy a world forever, but as I spoke I saw that Anglo-Saxon world in which I had always secretly been such a misfit keel over and begin to fall soundlessly, endlessly into the void.

The other world moved closer. I saw the open spaces, the timeless light, the freedom beyond imagination, and suddenly in a moment of absolute certainty I knew that this was the way, the truth, the life I longed to lead.

The chained dog finally slipped his collar. I rushed forward, she stumbled towards me and a second later we were in each other's arms.

II

I kissed her exactly as I wanted to kiss her. There was no question of worrying in case I offended delicate sensibilities, because I knew that she too was exercising no restraint. Her arms were so strong that they seemed almost as strong as mine, and her mouth was strong too, very free and supple, and her fingers were strong but sensitive as she caressed the back of my neck. Our tongues were silent together. I knew a moment of intense intimacy followed by such a violence of desire that I would have swayed on my feet if she had not been holding me so strongly, and in her strength I saw a reflection of my own.

I was aware of Blanche's bed behind her, and beyond the awareness lay the knowledge that whatever happened next could never happen there. I hesitated, and into the mental space created by my hesitation streamed the training and self-discipline of decades, no longer tormenting me with the image of imprisonment but offering me the only possible escape from the terror of my new freedom.

In panic I released her. I backed away, covering my face with my hands as my voice, the voice of an English gentleman, said with absolute correctness, "I'm so sorry; I do apologize. Obviously I'm unhinged by my grief."

There was a flurry of movement. Slim, strong fingers gripped my wrists and pulled my hands from my face. Great green eyes, fierce with the most desperate emotion, blazed into mine.

"Don't you lie to me!" she shouted in Welsh. "Never lie to me! *I don't deal in lies!*" And bursting into tears she rushed from the room.

I tore after her, and suddenly I was overwhelmed by the sheer reality of my emotion. I was blistered and bludgeoned by it, my old ways shattered, my past blown to bits and all my defenses incinerated by a white-hot heat. It was as though every mask I had ever worn, every lie I had ever told were being blasted from the face of my personality until at last, at the very bottom of my consciousness, my true self began to stir again in its long-forgotten, long-abandoned grave.

I caught her on the landing and grabbed her back from the head of the stairs. We were a long way now from the bedroom I had shared with Blanche, and nearby us a door led into one of the spare rooms which had never been used.

I remember how I noticed that door.

I opened it. The room contained only a narrow single bed with a shabby mattress but that didn't matter. Nothing mattered now except the door. It was the door I always remembered so clearly afterwards, the door leading from one world into another, the door which connected past and present and opened onto the future. I remember flinging the door wide, I remember shoving the door shut, I remember the door slamming with utter finality behind us—yes, it's the door I'll always remember, the door, the door, the door . . .

III

The miracle was the absolute cessation of pain. At one moment I was in such pain that I was incapable of imagining life without it and the next moment there was no pain, only a deep all-powerful forgetting, not a peace, for peace implies stillness, and not oblivion, for oblivion implies unconsciousness, but a freedom to sever myself temporarily from the unbearable sources of my distress.

We were together for a long time. Then the episode was concluded but within minutes, mysteriously, our strength was renewed. I use the word "our" deliberately because she was as exhausted as I was. I had never before witnessed feminine exhaustion of that nature, although I had known it could exist; I had heard stories about such phenomena, but I had thought only prostitutes could be so untroubled by reticence. However, I passed no judgment, registered neither astonishment nor disbelief; I was beyond such banal emotions. I was deep in my forgetting, only thankful that she wanted me again without constraint, so we went on and the new strength brought with it a gathering ease, but again I neither registered astonishment nor marveled in disbelief. I was wholly absorbed in the miracle of my painlessness and wishing only that it could last forever.

But passing time and the inevitably finite nature of all that one might wish to be infinite eventually conquered us. Exhaustion came again, and although we later achieved yet another renewal, it was short-lived. Unaccustomed to such excess my body had become sore, and I sensed she was sore too for the same reason. Her fingers hardened on my back; I felt our release uniting us for a few more precious seconds, but although I tried to sustain myself afterwards I failed. The force was spent and a moment later we had fallen asleep in each other's arms.

IV

When I awoke it was sometime in the dead of night but the moon had risen and the room was brighter. I was at first aware only of the body pressed to mine but presently I observed that the window was curtainless, the mattress was lumpy and the air was cool upon our nakedness. I shivered and she woke up.

"Bronwen." I sighed and kissed her and sighed again. I had never been face to face with a naked woman before. My knowledge of the feminine anatomy had been derived first from classical statues and later from tactful explorations of Blanche's body under cover of darkness.

After some time I said, "May I ask you something outrageous?" I was still existing entirely in the present. There was no past and no future. I was by a miracle suspended in time.

"Outrageous!" She laughed at the prospect. "You'd better ask in Welsh or I mightn't understand!"

I laughed too. Then I touched her below her narrow waist and beneath the curve of her hip. "Is your hair there," I said, "the same color as your hair here?" And I kissed the shining strands which, dark in the moonlight, streamed past her cheek to fall across her breast.

"Of course!" She started laughing again, and so did I. "Why should my hair be red in one place but not in another?"

"My brothers, who are all much fairer than I am, have hair that's darker on their bodies than on their heads," I said, and thought, What an extraordinary conversation! I began to laugh again. It amazed me that I should want to laugh with a woman in such very intimate circumstances.

"I know nothing about fair-haired men," she said simply. "My husband's dark and there's been no one else."

"I've had no one else but my wife. But that wasn't because I'm virtuous, as you undoubtedly are. It was because I felt I had to pretend to be perfect."

"But no one's perfect except in a fairy tale!"

After a pause I said, "Blanche was."

"No, she wasn't! That was why she was such a lovely lady—she wasn't cold and faultless like a stone angel in a churchyard; she was warm and human and real."

"But when I think how she slaved and slaved to be the perfect wife I so selfishly wanted her to be—"

"Ah, that reminds me of myself. I slaved and slaved to be a perfect wife to Gareth, but that wasn't because I was a saint. It was because I was afraid he'd fall out of love with me and leave me for someone else. I was weak and timid and dishonest. I wasn't a heroine at all."

"And did he leave you?"

"Yes—for the sea and the bottle. We still share a bed when he's home, but I don't bother to pretend to be a saint anymore, and now I'm much happier. Better to live in the truth, however terrible, than to murder your true self by living a lie."

I stared at her. Then I tried to imagine Blanche as weak and timid, perhaps even a little dishonest, not a saint but a flesh-and-blood woman who had loved me not perfectly but well enough to accept the burden of trying to be the wife I wanted. At last I said, "I never knew her. And she never knew me either. She only knew the English side of me; she only knew me as John. But in the old days I was Johnny and I was Welsh."

"What happened to Johnny?"

"I murdered him. I murdered my true self in order to live a lie." Pulling her closer I buried my face in her streaming hair.

"But he's come back, hasn't he?" she said. "Can't you see the curve of time? You didn't murder him after all. He's still alive."

V

Soon after four she said in English, "I must go. Myfanwy will be up before sunrise to bake the bread."

In alarm I asked if her sister would have waited up for her but she shook her head. "No, I always go to bed later than either Myfanwy or Huw. I don't have to be awake so early." She slipped out of bed. "I must wash," she said abruptly. "I'll go down to the scullery."

"What's wrong with the bathroom?"

"I'm not sure what to do there."

"What on earth do you mean?"

"Could you come with me?"

We removed to the bathroom which she had apparently visited during the night after using the lavatory next door.

"There are two taps," she said, "and I didn't know which one to use. The second sink in the scullery just has one tap so I knew I wouldn't have to worry there."

"Ah, I see." I stared at the bath and basin, two humdrum objects which I had taken for granted for as long as I could remember, and tried to imagine the background of someone to whom they represented a worrying challenge. "Yes," I said, pulling myself together. "Well, you can use either tap at the moment—it won't make any difference because the boiler's out and there's no hot water."

"Oh, I see. Yes, I wondered if the H on the tap stood for Hot but I wasn't sure. It's better to ask, isn't it, if one's not sure."

"Much better."

"I was afraid it might be some special drinking water which mustn't be used for washing. When I was in service there was no bathroom—river water came out of the pump in the yard and drinking water came from the well, and when the gentry wanted hot water it was heated in copper vats and carried upstairs to their bedrooms in jugs."

"Oxmoon used to be like that when my parents were first married. I daresay many country houses in remote areas took time to acquire modern plumbing and bathrooms."

"I've never seen a bathroom before," said Bronwen simply. Then she smiled and said with a trace of her old awkwardness, "I'll be all right now."

I kissed her and departed to my dressing room to put on some informal clothes. On my return to the spare room I said, "When's your husband coming home?"

"I don't know. It depends whether it's the Lisbon or the Naples run."

"Didn't you ask him which it would be?"

"No, I was too angry because he was leaving me with hardly any money and I knew we'd have to go back and live on Huw's charity again."

"Why couldn't he leave you more?"

"He'd drunk it."

We went downstairs in silence. I tried to imagine her life in cheap rented rooms in Cardiff but it was beyond me, so I thought instead of Disraeli, thundering three-quarters of a century ago about the two nations of Britain, the rich and the poor. Instinctively I recoiled from this vision; I reached out my hand as if I could bridge the unbridgeable, but as I looked across the void that separated her nation from mine I saw the glittering bayonets of the class system waiting to impale all those who fell into the abyss below.

"What are you thinking about?" she said suddenly as I opened the front door.

"Nothing."

She stopped. I saw her face and said, "Class. I shall never take it for granted again."

"What else can one do but take it for granted? It's the way of the world." She paused on the doorstep. "I want to say goodbye here."

"Can't I walk up the lane with you?"

"I'd rather say goodbye to you here, where you belong."

"But of course we'll meet again!"

"Where?" she said. "How?"

"But—"

"It doesn't matter," she said rapidly. "You needn't pretend that there could be more between us, you needn't try not to hurt my feelings. I accept that there's no future but I don't mind because I've had my one perfect night, the night I thought I could never have, and now on the dark days when life seems very hard I'll be able to look across the circle and hear your echo in time."

I could only say "I must see you again."

"How?" she repeated, and added: "Black is black and white is white and gray isn't allowed."

"Except in the bedroom."

"Oh yes! If the woman's a whore." She began to walk away.

"For God's sake, I didn't mean—"

"No, I know you didn't. But that's the truth, isn't it? And that's why I can't see you again."

We stood motionless facing each other. The sky was lightening in the east, and across the dew-soaked lawn in the opaque woods the birds had started to sing. I took her in my arms. After a long time, I said stubbornly, "I know we'll meet again, I know it," but she shook her head, said, "Goodbye, Johnny" and walked off down the drive to the gates.

VI

I sank down exhausted on the drawing-room sofa. My last conscious thought before sleep intervened was: Johnny. And in my dreams Lion was laughing once more at my side.

When I awoke I saw that the French clock had stopped. Outside in the broad daylight it was raining, but I barely noticed because memory was slamming through my mind with the force of a tidal wave and I was rushing out into the hall.

The grandfather clock, still ticking somnolently in its corner, told me that the time was twenty minutes past seven. I toyed with this fact, wondered what to do with it, but it meant nothing. All I knew was that there was still no past and no future and that I was still suspended in time.

I wandered around the hall, rubbed my face absentmindedly and remembered that I had to shave. The quest for hot water occupied me satisfactorily for quarter of an hour, but at last I was heading upstairs with a steaming kettle. I was enjoying the timelessness, savoring my detachment from the world, luxuriating in a mild but most delectable euphoria. Johnny! Not even Lazarus, raised from the dead, could have been so blissfully unconscious of everything save the fact that he was once more alive.

In the dressing room I poured the water into the basin, picked up the razor and glanced at my reflection in the glass.

I hesitated. I was wearing a blue shirt, and this performed the usual sartorial trick of making my eyes, never pale, seem bluer than ever. I looked into those eyes and saw my father looking back at me. And beyond my father, I saw my grandmother Gwyneth Llewellyn.

I dropped the razor. I got my back to the glass. Some time passed during which I stood leaning against the basin and gripping the edge to steady myself. I could think of nothing but madness. It filled my entire mind. Even if I had fought in the war I believe I could hardly have known such all-consuming terror. I had broken the rules and gone mad. Or had I? In my panic a thought so terrible occurred to me that I began to tremble from head to toe. I was wondering if my night with Bronwen had been the fantasy of a sick bereaved mind. I was wondering if my madness was even more profound than I had imagined.

I stumbled down the corridor, burst into the little spare room and rushed to the bed but I was safe because the mattress was stained. I touched the stains to make sure they were new and found them stiff. Colossal relief streamed through me. I was sane. It had all happened. It was all real, all true. The words formed a litany in my brain. All real, all true; all real, all true—

I was trembling again. I had just realized that I could not allow what had happened to be all real, all true.

I ran to the bathroom, found a cloth, soaked it, ran back and began to scrub the mattress. I scrubbed till my arm ached. Then I fetched the pumice stone and scrubbed all over again. The stains had long since vanished, but this made no difference because I could not believe the mattress was clean. I wondered how I could fumigate it. Finally I took it downstairs to air in the backyard but I had forgotten the rain and was obliged to leave my burden in the laundry room. In the hall I wrote *Replace mattress* on the note pad by the telephone, and as I wrote I became aware that the hall seemed unnaturally quiet. Then I realized that the grandfather clock had stopped.

I blundered into the study, but found that the carriage clock had stopped before six. The clocks were stopping, all of them; the wheel of time was standing still so that I could crawl aboard again and suddenly I knew that was what I wanted; I wanted to scramble back into Anglo-Saxon time so that I could shelter behind my Anglo-Saxon mask and feel safe.

But when I went into the drawing room I found the white roses were wilting on the piano, and the next moment Blanche was moving to meet me in my memory. I saw her clearly, very very clearly. I saw her standing by the white roses on the evening of my mother's funeral. I heard her talking about my father.

"I'd like to think I'd always try to be compassionate, even if the fault were very hard to understand . . ."

The memory became unendurable. I heard John Godwin, hard and selfish, smug and insufferable, commenting rudely: "No understanding's possible in this case and I've used up all my compassion."

I thought, I cannot be that man anymore.

The truth caught up with me then, but I found there was nothing I could do but face it because this particular truth could not be erased like a semen stain with soap and water and a pumice stone. I had betrayed my wife on the very day of her funeral, and now, as my mind turned back towards her, my one memory was of her talking of forgiveness.

Sinking down on the piano stool I bowed my head over the silent keys, and at last I was able to grieve.

VII

The car responded to my first attempt to start it. The rain had stopped. It was a cool morning, and I felt not only cool too as I drove down the lane but curiously older, as if I had grown up overnight instead of aging from adolescence to maturity over the conventional period of years.

As I headed south I drove into open country where stone walls intermingled with the hedgerows to enclose the fields of the valley. The road curved, the moorland drew closer and above the long line of the ridge that marked the summit of Rhossili Downs I could see huge white clouds billowing in from the sea.

The high wall of the grounds had already begun on my left. A moment later I was turning in at the gates, and there before me Oxmoon lay in an enigmatic challenge, goading me on to the end of my now inevitable mission.

It was seven weeks since my mother's funeral but I felt as if I had been away seven years or longer. As I parked the car I wondered if my nerve would fail me but I was conscious only of a fanatical determination to do what had to be done.

I rang the bell.

A new parlormaid, young and crisp in a spotless uniform, opened the door and said, "Good morning, sir" with a little bob of respect, but when she showed no sign of recognition I realized she was a stranger to the district, one of the untrained girls who had been recruited from Swansea.

"Good morning," I said. "I'm John Godwin and I've come to see my father."

The parlormaid displayed her inexperience by looking flustered. To spare her I stepped across the threshold without waiting for the invitation to enter, and as I paused in the hall a woman emerged from the passage at the far end. I took off my hat, she moved forward with a smile and the next moment I found myself face to face at last with my father's mistress Milly Straker.

6

I

I HAD SEEN her once or twice in Penhale but never at close quarters, so although I could recognize her, the details of her appearance had remained unknown to me. I controlled my immediate antipathy by telling myself that I of all people had no right to rush to judgment.

"It's Mr. John, isn't it?" she said courteously in a limpid voice. It was the voice of a Londoner, but not of a Cockney born within the sound of Bow Bells. I heard the inflections of the London suburbs—Wandsworth, perhaps, or Clapham—where drab little villas lined "respectable" streets, their windows festooned with lace, their parlors filled with obese furniture, and suddenly I felt I had stepped back fifty years into some erotic Victorian world where forbidden rites were enacted in secret rooms in which heavy blinds were perpetually drawn. Mrs. Straker was wearing a plain black dress with a cameo brooch pinned to her flat bosom. Below the severely parted black hair I saw a sallow face, sharp eyes and a foxy look. She gave the impression that she had seen a lot, done more, and what she had neither seen nor done she could intimately describe with the help of a bottomless imagination.

"This *is* a surprise, sir!" she said, still speaking in a well-modulated voice. "May I take the liberty of introducing myself? I'm Mrs. Straker." Dismissing the fascinated parlormaid, she added tranquilly: "Mr. Godwin's breakfasting in his room, but I'm sure he'll be ever so pleased to see you. If you'd care to follow me, sir, I'll take you up to him myself."

I wanted to tell her I could find my own way upstairs, but I knew I could hardly burst in on my father unannounced. In fact I would hardly have been surprised if Mrs. Straker had asked me to wait in the morning room while she found out whether or not my father wished to receive me. I decided I had no right to quibble about an escort.

"Thank you, Mrs. Straker," I said.

She led the way upstairs. She was thin, with narrow unfeminine hips, but her ankles were good. She moved well too, neither elegantly nor seductively but with a smooth unhurried self-confidence. It was impossible to guess her age but I doubted if she was younger than thirty.

"An unexpected visitor for you, Mr. Godwin!" she called mellifluously as she knocked on the door of my parents' bedroom.

"Come in!" was my father's cheerful response.

She opened the door. I heard her say "It's Mr. John," and the next moment I was moving past her into the room. Then she left us, and as the door closed behind her I found myself alone once more with my father.

He was sitting at the table by the window with the remains of his breakfast in front of him, and in his hands was a copy of *Country Life*. He was wearing the spectacles he used for reading, but when he saw me he pulled them off as if he feared they were deceiving him.

"John?" He struggled to his feet. His cup rattled in its saucer as he knocked it accidentally. The magazine fell to the floor.

"Good morning, sir," I said formally, but found myself so paralyzed with emotion that I was unable to embark on my prepared speech.

"But what a wonderful surprise!" said my father in a rush. "Please—sit down." He gestured towards the chair opposite him and nearly knocked over his cup again.

I managed to do as I was told but before I could make another attempt to speak my father said anxiously, "How are you? I've been so worried, I hardly slept a wink last night. Have you had breakfast? No, I don't suppose you have, you wouldn't feel like eating, but you must eat, that's important." He raised the lid of the silver dish in front of him and peered inside. "Yes, there's plenty here and it's still hot. I'll ring for an extra plate and some cutlery and a fresh pot of tea."

I somehow declined food and drink. I still could not remember my prepared speech, but now I no longer cared. "Papa," I said, "I've come to apologize. I was very cruel to you after Mama died. I don't expect you to forgive me straightaway, but perhaps in time . . ." I could say no more but it did not matter, for as soon as I stopped he began to talk to me in Welsh.

"My dear John," he said, "if only I had had just one-half of that courage which has brought you here this morning." He stooped, picked up the magazine from the floor and began to smooth the cover with his fingers. "I was just as cruel to my mother," he said, "but I never had the courage—or the humanity—to say later I was sorry. And after she was dead I regretted it."

I said, "You're giving me praise I don't deserve. I'm not showing nobility of character, just a shamefully belated understanding of what you must have suffered."

"Understanding's one thing. Having the courage to display it is quite another."

"But you don't realize—you don't know what I did last night—"

"Oh, I think I do," said my father, and when I looked at him I knew there was nothing else I needed to say.

After a while he said, "Your wife was a dear little girl but perhaps not entirely right for you. I daresay you feel guilty now that you weren't able to love her as she deserved. Guilt is a very terrible thing," said my father, staring at the rain which was falling again on the tranquil garden. "Believe me, I know all about guilt and how it can torture you when you're alone."

My fingers were interlocked on the table in front of me. Reaching out he covered them with his hand.

"It's strange," said my father presently, removing his hand and pouring himself some more tea, "how Margaret's absence has enabled me to see my children more clearly. I suppose it's because I keep looking for her in you all. Robert's the one who's most like her, of course, but do you know, I don't believe I ever really conceded that until Margaret was dead. I had a great need to idealize Robert always—to see him as myself, the self I would like to have been. It was all mixed with the fact that his birth gave me the courage to deal with Bryn-Davies and build a better world at Oxmoon. Robert was my justification, you see, and the more brilliant and splendid he was the more I felt justified in what I'd done—in fact I do believe that even if he hadn't been brilliant and splendid I'd have made myself believe he was. It was necessary to me. Very wrong, though," he added severely as he sipped his tea. "It did Robert no good to spoil him, and it was hard on you other fellows—and particularly hard on you. But you see, I didn't want to look at you and be reminded of myself. I only wanted to look at Robert and be reminded of the man I fancied myself to be. Very silly," said my father, watching the rain again. "But there we are. No parent's perfect. We all make mistakes. The great trick is to recognize them and put them right. Not always possible, of course. But one can try."

There was a silence as he continued to sip his tea.

"Yes," he said as if he had at last completed a satisfactory meditation on some particularly convoluted subject, "I was afraid, that was the trouble—afraid that you might be like me—and my mother—but now I can see how foolish my fears were. I don't care what brought you here this morning—all I know is that long ago I couldn't bring myself to do what you've done today. So the truth is, isn't it, that the likeness isn't all-important. What's all-important is that even if two men are dealt similar hands of cards they'll always play those cards in different ways." He smiled at me. "You'll play your cards far better than I ever have," he said. "I know you will. I know it."

I could not speak but we were at peace with each other. Indeed I thought perhaps I was at peace for the first time in my adult life. And then, before I could begin to absorb the full meaning of this new freedom, the door opened and in walked Mrs. Straker.

"Well, dears," she said as soon as the door was closed, "had a nice little chat? I've brought some extra dishes in case John was faint with exhaustion and longing for food—God knows, staging a reconciliation at breakfast is enough to beat anyone to their knees, but look at you both, dry-eyed and poker-faced, I don't know how you gentlemen do it, I really don't! Here, move your hands, John, and I'll set your place."

I kept my hands exactly where they were on the table and said, "Thank you, Mrs. Straker, but I don't require breakfast."

"Call me Milly, dear, all your brothers do except Robert but of course I don't see much of him, poor man. What ghastly things happen to people in this world, which reminds me, dear, let me offer you my condolences—you won't want them, but I'll offer them anyway for what they're worth. Well, there's no subject that kills a conversation like death, is there, so let's talk of something else. Bobby, is that all you've eaten? What's left in this silver dish? Oh, look at that, you've hardly touched it, you *are* naughty! Eat up at once before I get cross!"

"Well, as a matter of fact," said my father, smiling at her, "I do feel hungrier now."

I stood up abruptly. "I must be on my way."

"Oh, but you can't go back to that empty house!" exclaimed my father in distress. "Stay here!"

"That's very kind of you, Papa, but I've realized I must join the children in London."

This was a decision he could accept. "Very well, but when you come back—"

"I'll call on you," I said, "naturally. No, Mrs. Straker, you needn't see me out. Good day."

"And good day to you, John!" she said pertly, giving me a tough shrewd look with her amoral black eyes.

Somehow keeping my face devoid of expression I left the room and retired, profoundly shaken, to my car.

II

I was too disturbed to return home immediately. Instead I drove to Rhossili, parked the motor on top of the cliffs and stared through the rain at the windswept sands far below. Long lines of surf ceaselessly battered the black stumps of the shipwrecks. A mist hid both the Worm's Head on the left and the top of the Downs on the right, and above the three-mile beach in the fields of the rectory the sheep seemed pinned to the grass by the gale.

I realized, as I smoked several cigarettes, that I was trying to recover—and not merely from my rage, which was considerable. I was trying to recover from my shock that the scene at Oxmoon, in one respect more satisfying than I had dared hope, had evolved into a nightmare which I had no idea how to assimilate. How did one deal with someone like Milly Straker? As far as I knew, no book of rules had yet been written on the subject of how a gentleman could coexist in amity with his father's mistress, but I doubted if any book of rules could have solved the dilemma in which I now found myself. It looked to me as if I were going to be cut off from my father at the exact moment when we had finally come to understand each other.

I knew very well that my shock sprang from my naivety; I had had some sentimental notion that in forgiving my father I would automatically discover that Mrs. Straker was the most charming and delightful woman who would be only too willing to help us all live happily ever after. Because of this I had gone to Oxmoon prepared to bend over backwards to be civil to her; indeed I had felt almost under a moral obligation to like her, and so when she had revealed herself in her true colors I had been even more appalled than I would have been if I had arrived at Oxmoon expecting to meet a monster.

Once more I reviewed those true colors. Of course she was common, but I had been prepared for that. Of course she was vulgar, but even her intolerable familiarity, nauseous as it was, I could somehow have overlooked for my father's sake. But what I could not overlook was the unmistakable sign that Mrs. Straker was addicted to power. My years at the Foreign Office had taught me a good deal about power and the manipulation that inevitably accompanies it, and I recognized in Mrs. Straker a clever, ambitious, thoroughly unscrupulous woman. Her vulgarity had not been the artless chatter of a woman who knew no better; it had been carefully staged, and every word she had spoken in that bedroom had been designed to underline to me her influence over my father. Desiring above all else to avoid a new quarrel with him I had kept quiet, but nevertheless I had been horrified.

I could see exactly how the situation would appear to her. My father was fatally dependent on her company, Robert was a cripple, Celia was in Heidelberg, Lion was dead, Edmund was ineffectual and Thomas was a child. She was safe from all opposition there. That left me, and I was the one potential enemy. She must have long since realized that if anyone threatened her rule at Oxmoon it would be "Mr. John," and that was why she had staked out her territory so forcefully the moment I had recrossed my father's threshold.

Oxmoon was no stranger to predators. It had survived Owain Bryn-Davies, and I supposed it would survive Milly Straker, but nonetheless the prospect of an avaricious woman exercising her power there without restraint was chilling indeed. The only conclusion I could reach was that whatever happened I had to avoid quarreling again with my father.

It seemed a daunting challenge, and after grinding out my cigarette in despair I drove to Little Oxmoon to consult Robert.

III

"This is one of those nerve-racking situations," said Robert, "when one yearns for the gift of clairvoyance. Our main problem here is that we have insufficient information."

"I don't understand."

"Well, you're taking a dim view of the future on the grounds that Straker's a clever scheming woman, but on the other hand it's quite possible that he may have tired of her by Christmas. How long do Papa's mistresses last, I wonder? If he's like most men his affairs probably run a predictable course over a predictable period of time."

"She has an appalling air of permanence."

We were in the dining room where I had just finished an excellent breakfast. Ginevra had gone to Swansea with Robin and his nanny to see Aunt Charlotte off on the train to London. Kester was howling somewhere as usual in the company of his nursemaid. Outside it was still raining.

"I simply can't understand what he sees in her, Robert. She's neither good-looking nor particularly young. It's a complete mystery."

"My dear John, it's the commonest of all fallacies that sex can only flourish in an atmosphere of youth and beauty. I had the most extraordinary case once involving a man of forty, a woman of sixty-five and a youth of eighteen with a harelip . . ."

Robert talked on but I barely heard him. I had begun to remember another most extraordinary case of sexual attraction, the case of a gentleman of twenty-nine who had become obsessed overnight with a working-class girl six years his junior. I was thinking of their two separate worlds, coexisting in time yet unlinked by any bridge but the bedroom.

"Robert," I said, interrupting his saga of the homicidal youth with the harelip, "have you ever slept with a working-class woman?"

He naturally assumed I was still trying to make sense of my father's affair with Mrs. Straker. "Of course. Why?"

"Did you find the experience exceptional? I mean . . . did you find you could talk to such a woman more easily?"

"Talk! What about? How can one even attempt a serious conversation with such a person? There's no common ground. Anyway one hardly goes to bed with a working-class woman with a view to conducting a *conversazione* between the sheets!"

"No," I said, "I suppose one doesn't. . . . Robert, have you ever known a fellow who actually married a working-class woman?"

"One does, of course, hear of the occasional blockhead like Oswald Stourham who becomes besotted with a platinum-blond chorus girl, but fortunately such disasters are fairly rare. Don't worry, John, I believe Papa when he swears he'll never marry this woman. He's not a complete lunatic."

I was silent.

"The last thing he'd want is to commit social suicide," said Robert soothingly. "Even if he could face being ostracized by his friends, how could he ever face being humiliated before his children? No, he'll stay away from the altar, don't you worry—he'll draw the line there."

"Draw the line," I said. "Yes." I stood up to go.

"Well, John," said Robert, preparing to say goodbye, "I'm sorry you spent all last night being racked by loneliness, but if that's resulted in a better understanding of Papa then maybe you haven't suffered in vain. Now promise me you'll come back here tonight instead of incarcerating yourself all over again in that bloody Manor. There's nothing heroic, I assure you, about preferring suffering to comfort."

But I needed more time to consider my plans, and after promising to telephone him later I returned once more to Penhale.

IV

Back at the Manor I gradually began to realize that my situation had become intolerable for at least three reasons, and that once more my life required a radical change.

The first reason involved my father. If I remained in Gower, I doubted if I would be able to avoid clashing with him eventually over the subject of Mrs. Straker—and a clash would be just what my enemy wanted; in fact she would probably do all she could to promote it in order to drive a wedge between me and my father and keep me out of Oxmoon. My best hope of outwitting her undoubtedly lay in being a dutiful, affectionate but distant son until he came to his senses.

The second hard truth that I had to accept was that despite Bronwen's understanding words, Blanche's memory was intolerably painful to me and likely to remain so for some time. I did realize intellectually that my feelings about Blanche would become more quiescent as time passed, and I did think it likely that one day in different circumstances, I might well wish to live again in the house that was so conveniently close to Oxmoon, but at present I could see nothing but the piano and the white roses and know only that I had not loved my wife as I should.

The third reason which made a departure imperative concerned the woman I did love. If I stayed on in Penhale I would inevitably meet Bronwen again, and then I knew we would be drawn into an affair which she had made it very clear she did not want. It was useless for me to be foolish and romantic, dreaming of establishing her in a neat little terrace house in Swansea. Even if she were willing, such a scheme would be out of the question because the deserted husband would be sure to make trouble, and in the resulting scandal all the children, both hers and mine, would be certain to suffer.

I had a vision of chaos and shied away from it. I thought of my mother and of how horrified she would have been by the scandal. I thought of my father deciding I had played my cards disastrously after all. And finally, when there was no one else left to think about, I thought of my grandmother and Owain Bryn-Davies.

At once I made up my mind that I could never see Bronwen again.

Insanity threatened.

Destruction was imminent.

I drew the line.

V

I met Harley Armstrong three weeks later at a reception given by my former chief at the Foreign Office, and nineteen months afterwards Armstrong was introducing me to his daughter Constance. I had known for some time that he wanted me to marry her.

I have often examined this part of my life with scrupulous care, but I have come to the conclusion that in the worst possible way I was destined for Constance. I told Robert later that it was as if a *deus ex machina* were operating, and Robert promptly embarked upon a dissertation on the Greek concept of fate which incorporated the so-called "madness of doom," the hell where men rushed to destruction because they were driven by forces beyond their control. However at the time I thought I was being supremely sane and

Robert thought I was being commendably rational. Never were two intelligent men more deceived.

To have avoided Constance, I would have been obliged to avoid London for even if I had somehow managed to elude Armstrong in 1921, I would certainly have met Constance and her sister in 1923 when they were moving in Society. But I did not avoid London. I embraced it as a solution to my problems in Gower. I could have retreated to my lands in Herefordshire, but I recognized that I was going through an interim period of my life, and it seemed to me that such an interim could be most profitably passed in the capital. There I could slip back more easily into a social life which would help me recover from my bereavement, my children were bound to benefit from a stimulating environment and I would, if I were lucky, find some occupation far more congenial to me than my former dull routine at the Foreign Office.

I was unsure how long my self-imposed exile from Gower would last, but I suspected five years would see the conclusion of my problems. At the end of that time my father would surely have tired of Mrs. Straker, Blanche would be no more than a poignant memory and Bronwen would have faded into a Welsh myth. Then I would be safe.

Having arrived this far in the new script of my life, I looked around for someone who would lead me to the center of the stage, and immediately I was collared by Harley Armstrong.

Armstrong was an American of uncertain origins who had made and lost two fortunes on the New York Stock Exchange before the war, recouped his losses afterwards by profiteering in first canned food and then army surplus stock and was now in what he was pleased to call "Europe" to continue his profiteering in the new industries that had been developing fast since the war. He had acquired interests in petroleum, plastics and gramophone records, but his steady income came from his canning corporation, which was based in New York State. However Armstrong was bored with tinned food, and although he had opened a European subsidiary with a factory in Birmingham and occasionally toyed with the idea of launching a chain of grocery stores, his heart was now in plastics. I did wonder why he had abandoned America, but later he told me he regarded New York as an unlucky city for him, the scene of his two earlier lost fortunes, and he was one of those Americans who believe that if one cannot live in New York one might as well conquer Europe for lack of anything better to do.

During the period of his first fortune, he had contrived to marry a lady who independent sources assured me was far more respectable than he was, but she had not accompanied him to London, and later I learned that they had parted by mutual consent. Mrs. Armstrong lived with her two daughters in her native Boston. When I asked Armstrong what Boston was like, he said, "Even worse than Philadelphia" and shuddered. However he was very fond of his two daughters and dictated long, sentimental letters to them every week. Mrs. Armstrong was apparently interested in the idea that they should enjoy a season in London, and as soon as this possibility had dawned on the horizon, Armstrong was drawing up plans to crash his way into London Society.

"I've got to be in a position to launch my little girls in style," he explained to me, and at once I knew that at the back of his mind lurked the delicious notion that his "little girls" might marry Englishmen and settle down forever within a mile of his doorstep.

I thought at first he was equating himself with Vanderbilt, whose daughter Consuelo had married the Duke of Marlborough, but in fact Armstrong had the kind of vitality which ensured that he would find the upper reaches of the English aristocracy repellently effete. As a self-made man he also possessed what Constance told me later was called an inferiority complex. Shrewd enough to know he was vulgar and ambitious enough for his daughters' sake to want to do something about it, Armstrong decided towards the end of 1921 that what he needed was a well-bred, well-educated British private secretary—no one too grand, and certainly no one who had a title, but someone diplomatic and resourceful who could teach him how to behave in public.

He offered me the job on the morning after we had met.

My automatic inclination was to turn him down but then I thought, Why not accept? I had spent years loathing the stultifying English formality of life at the Foreign Office, and now here was an extraordinary opportunity to work for an unconventional bombastic foreigner. Whatever happened in his employment I was unlikely to be bored and I might even be greatly entertained. It would certainly divert me from the recent past. I therefore decided to accept his offer; the die was cast, and immediately I was whirled into the maelstrom of Armstrong's private life.

Within six months I had extricated him from his lavish but unsuitable nine-bedroom flat at the wrong end of Westminster and had installed him in a house with a first-class ballroom at Eaton Walk off Eaton Square. I gave Harrods *carte blanche* with the interior decoration and the acquisition of the necessary antiques. It seemed safer to trust the leading department store in London than to rely on some fashionable decorator, particularly as very peculiar things were happening at that time in the world of interior decoration.

Once the house had been decorated I engaged the staff and ensured that the housekeeper and butler reported directly to me. I paid the wages. I organized regular and successful "little dinner parties for twenty-four" to show that I was a true son of my hospitable parents. I reconstituted Armstrong's wardrobe and told him very firmly what ties he could never wear. I somehow got him accepted as a member of Brooks's and Boodles. I bought him a suitable country estate in Kent for weekend entertaining and an equally suitable villa in St. John's Wood for his mistress, a young French tart who had advertised herself as a governess. She had greedy tendencies but I enjoyed haggling with her in French over her allowance.

In fact I enjoyed every aspect of my new life, and the triumphant finale of my first months in Armstrong's employment came when I bought him a Rolls-Royce. I could not remember when I had last enjoyed myself so much. John Godwin would have hated the life, but my old self, my true self, was amused by these wrestling bouts with unbridled vulgarity. I kept thinking how Lion would have exclaimed, "What a lark!" and burst out laughing. I laughed too, frequently and spontaneously, and thought how many entertaining memories I would have when I finally retired to Gower.

Those were the innocent days. They came before that evening in 1922 when he invited me to dine with him to celebrate the first year of our association. We dined in great style. Then over brandy and cigars he told me I was the son he had always longed for and that he wanted me to become involved with his business empire.

I was staggered. I had never taken the slightest interest in his business empire; my heart was in neither plastics, nor petroleum, nor tinned food. I was also appalled, in the way that only a man educated at an English public school can be appalled, by this naked display of emotion. But above all else I was touched. Armstrong might be fifty, foreign, florid and frightful; he might periodically infuriate me with his tantrums and his pigheadedness; but there was an element both pathetic and endearing in his gratitude for rescuing him from loneliness in the country of his adoption.

However I knew I needed to be very careful, and after telling him in all sincerity that I was moved and flattered, I asked for time to consider his offer and retired to my little house in Kensington to analyze my new script.

To put it bluntly, in the smallest possible nutshell, I was being offered the chance to become a millionaire. I was also being offered the chance to exceed Robert's success, because with that kind of money behind me there was nothing I could not achieve. Oxmoon would finally cease to matter. I would be able to acquire a bigger and better home for myself than a quaint little Georgian conundrum set squarely on the road to nowhere, and all my old jealousies would be extinguished once and for all.

Yet if I accepted Armstrong's offer I would inevitably be cut off from my family, for I would be too busy to journey regularly to Gower. What had happened to those moral obligations about which John Godwin had once talked so loudly, particularly the obligation to be a pillar of strength to his father and brother in their declining years? I shuddered as the depth of my hypocrisy now stood revealed to me. I could see that although I had genuinely wanted to help my father and Robert, I had been concerned first and foremost with myself. I had wanted to take advantage of Robert's illness by ingratiating myself with my father and becoming the favorite son—a triumph which would have represented a final victory over Robert and which in turn would have been symbolized by my acquisition of Oxmoon.

For one long clear-eyed moment I thought of Oxmoon, that seductive focus of all my past discontent. I knew I still wanted it. Probably I would always want it. But at least now I was not obliged to regard it as the only panacea for my private unhappiness. Besides, the truth—the truth which I had always been too muddled and unhappy to accept—was that I was never going to inherit that place. If Robert outlived my father, nothing would stop Robin inheriting. If Robert failed to outlive my father, Robin would still inherit—as the favorite grandson. My father had made that perfectly clear, and no matter how strong his new affection for me I could not see him disinheriting the elder son of his eldest son when Robin was a child of such exceptional promise. I was already well provided for. My father could not be blamed for thinking his moral obligations lay elsewhere.

The only sane conclusion I could draw from all these clear-eyed deliberations was that I was not destined for a life in Gower; in fact, as I could now see so well, I would be a fool not to realize that my fortune lay elsewhere and an even worse fool to turn my back on the dazzling new script I was being offered by Armstrong.

Yet I was wary of dazzling scripts.

In the end I told Armstrong that I liked the idea but felt I needed another year to prove to us both that I had the necessary talents to master the world he was offering me, and Armstrong, impressed by the fact that I was making no immediate attempt to grab every penny in sight, suggested that I took charge of his two new charities to find out if I enjoyed wielding power from an office desk.

I enjoyed it. I also excelled at it. The Armstrong Home for Wayward Boys was in Battersea and the Armstrong Home for Distressed Gentlefolk was in Putney, and within six months I had organized them into formidable charitable machines. Throughout my labors I took care to ensure that Armstrong's name as a philanthropist was much quoted in the press, for by now it was 1923 and it was time for me to put the finishing touches to the American gentleman I had created out of the New York gangster I had met eighteen months before. Far away in Boston Mrs. Armstrong was preparing to launch her daughters across the Atlantic for their London season, and their social success was heavily dependent on my skill in promoting their father as a respectable generous benefactor who could be welcomed at even the highest levels of society.

"You'll like my daughter Constance," said Armstrong as the day of the girls' arrival drew nearer. "She's intelligent and well educated, just like you."

I knew an order when I heard one. My role in the script was being amended so that I could play Prince Charming as well as Heir Apparent, but although I expressed diplomatic enthusiasm, I knew I was still in no hurry to remarry. By that time I was well aware that my decision to marry at the absurdly young age of twenty-two had been prompted in part by the belief that sexual satisfaction could be safely obtained only within the framework of marriage, but now I knew that other frameworks were available. Naturally the idea of consorting with prostitutes was repugnant to me, and naturally I shied away from the loose-living Society women whom I met in increasing numbers, but eventually I encountered a gentle, unaffected young widow who was a seamstress. She visited my house regularly to attend to Marian's clothes, and one afternoon when I was on my way to the Boys' Home in Battersea I gave her a lift in my car to her room in Pimlico. Later I paid the rent on a flat for her near the Fulham Road, and when I realized how lucky I was to have found someone so pleasant, so grateful even for the smallest kindness and so anxious never to be demanding I started paying her a small income. Needless to say I spent much time worrying in case this arrangement marked the beginning of an inexorable decline into profligacy, but as the months passed I finally dared to admit to myself that I was doing the right thing. At least it guaranteed I did not rush into marriage a second time out of sheer sexual frustration.

Another reason why I had no wish to rush into marriage was because I was so aware how important it was that I should find the right woman to be my wife. I knew my father had been correct in saying that Blanche had not been entirely suited to me. I still wanted someone who could be gentle but paradoxically I now felt that what I needed most in a partner was strength. I had spent so much of my life in an emotional muddle that I longed for someone who could be guaranteed to see life clearly whenever I became bogged down in confusion, and for the first time it occurred to me how attractive my mother's personality must have been to my father. I had no desire to marry someone exactly like my mother, but her unflinching ability to discern the truth of a given situation and deal with it efficiently, no matter how horrific the truth might be, now struck me as a priceless asset.

The picture of my future wife began to form more clearly in my mind. I wanted someone strong, though the strength had to be entirely feminine; I wanted someone intelligent, like Blanche, but less musical and with more eclectic interests; I wanted someone not necessarily beautiful but certainly someone whom I found sexually attractive. I decided that although I could not contemplate a divorced woman, I might consider a widow. Virginity struck me as being overrated. I felt I had had enough bashfulness in my sexual history to last me for the rest of my life, and I decided it was high time I conquered those emotional constraints which I later discovered from Constance were called inhibitions.

By the time Constance arrived from America in the April of 1923, the portrait of my second wife had crystallized in my mind. I was now looking for a woman who was smart, sophisticated, good-looking, intelligent, efficient, sensible, sexually satisfying, popular with her contemporaries, admired by the world in general, affectionate towards Harry and Marian, devoted to me and altogether a paragon of womanhood. However as this extraordinary combination of feminine virtues not surprisingly proved elusive, it had slowly dawned on me that I might have to lower my impossibly high standards. I decided that I might after all marry a virgin if she showed unmistakable signs of sensuality. I also decided that I might marry a foreigner provided she could adapt herself without difficulty to my world. Armstrong's enthusiastic descriptions had made me suspicious, but when I met Constance I could see that he had by no means fabricated her attractions.

We were introduced at his house on Eaton Walk on the day of her arrival in London. Mrs. Armstrong never traveled anywhere on account of what were described as her "nerves," so her daughters had been chaperoned across the Atlantic by family friends who were heading for a grand tour of Europe.

Constance was nineteen. Dressed with severe smartness in a beaded black gown accompanied by a diamond necklace and earrings, she appeared more self-assured than her English contemporaries. Not a wisp of her fashionably bobbed hair was out of place. Her unobtrusive American accent gave her speech a formal tone, but beyond her apparent poise I sensed she was nervous in case she failed to appear suitably *soignée*. With the aid of my most polished manners I did my best to put her at ease.

"John!" Armstrong was surging towards me with his younger daughter bobbing saucily at his side. "Meet Theodora! Teddy my dear—Mr. John Godwin." And he gave her a doting look, a perfect example of a normally sensible man in the grip of a paternal sloppiness. Yet I knew Teddy was not to my taste. As soon as I saw her round blue eyes, bee-sting mouth and conscientiously "naughty" expression, I realized she would be a chaperone's nightmare, thoroughly unsuitable for me. However I took another look at Constance and decided she had possibilities.

Exerting the full force of my diplomatic charm I slipped casually and disastrously into the role of Prince Charming.

VI

At this point I needed someone to shout at me, "Don't you deal in lies!" and shake me till my teeth rattled but unfortunately no one performed these useful offices and I continued to think that I was behaving in a rational manner. Having made up my mind that it would be wonderfully fortunate if Constance turned out to be the kind of woman I wanted to marry, I now saw with striking clarity how wonderfully fortunate it would be if I decided to marry her. It would save me from disappointing Armstrong, who was offering me this wonderfully fortunate future which so neatly solved all my problems, and whenever I remembered those problems I became increasingly convinced that I did not care for the idea of disappointing Armstrong. I felt that Armstrong's disappointment was a prospect on which it was safer not to dwell.

However I did not forget my past experience with Blanche. Prince Charming, in other words, was a role I had played before with results that had been dubious in the extreme, and armed with this knowledge, I now decided the time had come to analyze my feelings for Constance with scrupulous honesty.

She apparently had everything to commend her. I found her sexually attractive; with her slim neat figure and her dark hair and eyes, she belonged to a physical type that I had always strongly admired, although despite this surface resemblance she was very different from Blanche. The most striking difference was that she was well educated enough to discuss French literature with me, an accomplishment which I regarded at first with antipathy but later with a reluctant fascination. It was by this time ten years since I had come down from Oxford, and I was ripe to recover from the anti-intellectual reaction I had suffered after so much exhausting academic toil. Deciding I would start to read novels in French again, I took Constance with me to Hatchard's where she bought all the novels that I bought so that we could embark on our literary journeys together. This joint venture resulted in some enthralling discussions, and I had to admit to myself that the prospect of a well-educated wife opened up vistas of hitherto unexplored intellectual pleasures.

Better still, Constance was no mere bluestocking but a well-informed articulate young woman who even read the reports of the political debates in *The Times*. The political state of the nation had been in turmoil for some time, with the Conservatives marching and countermarching, the Liberals continuing to hack themselves to pieces and the Labour Party waiting breathlessly in the wings as the Coalition fell apart. I found it all of absorbing interest, particularly since I had begun to doubt that the country would disintegrate if a Labour government came to power. Constance and I spent long hours debating the possibility of class war, revolution fermented by Bolsheviks and the elimination of all that was most inequitable in British society. In the election I voted Conservative out of loyalty to my class, but through the newspapers Constance and I followed Ramsay MacDonald with rapt attention as he inched his way closer to power. Constance said she found it so moving that he was illegitimate, and although I smiled, I knew what she meant. He proved that the socially unacceptable could still win their way to the top; he represented those who were discriminated against because of circumstances which they could not avoid; he stood for the victims of social prejudice, for all those in that unknown world where people did not know what H meant on a basin tap and were turned out of their rooms because their husbands had drunk the rent money.

"Nevertheless," said Constance, "I'm glad the Conservatives were elected. What would happen to the stock exchange if Labour came to power? *The Times* says today . . ."

To my amazement she started to quote from the City pages. As usual, she had read all the newspapers and knew everything. I began to wonder how she ever found the time.

She did play the piano, but it was a mere technical accomplishment and she preferred to listen to her gramophone or her crystal set. So did I. I bought her many records—classics, popular songs, dance tunes—and found she could comment intelligently on them all. Then we transferred our attention to painting, a subject about which I knew nothing, and Constance explained modern art to me. I still considered it was rubbish, but I thought it was wonderful how well she talked about it.

In addition to this exhausting intellectual activity, we somehow found the time to expend some energy on more mindless pursuits. I danced with her at numerous balls, dined with her at uncounted parties, escorted her to Ascot, to Henley and to Wimbledon, wrote my name against the most important dance in her program when Armstrong gave the coming-out ball for his daughters at Eaton Walk. Armstrong was now confidently expecting me to propose at the end of the season. So were Constance and Teddy. So was London Society. So was I. The only trouble was that I found it hard to imagine myself ever doing it.

Something was wrong, and because I admired Constance so much and longed so intensely for the happy ending to which I felt entitled after so much sadness and muddle, I made a new attempt to analyze my situation so that I could define the problem and put it right.

I knew she was a little too serious, but I liked that. The modern girl who constantly erupted with gaiety like an overshaken cocktail I found noisy, tiresome and unsympathetic. I did wonder if Constance's seriousness would affect her behavior in bed, but I came to the conclusion that this was unlikely, first because she struck me as an intense girl who would be capable of the most passionate emotion, and second because she was so competent in everything she undertook that I could not imagine her failing to master the basic pleasures of sex.

I had no doubt either that she would make an exemplary stepmother. "The subject of raising children is just so fascinating," she confided in me one day. "I've been reading the latest book on the subject of child psychology."

I had never even heard of the subject of child psychology. Gazing at her in unstinted admiration I thought yet again what a remarkable girl she was, and I was just telling myself I was a complete fool not to rush immediately to

Bond Street to buy a ring when my brother Edmund arrived to stay with me and announced that he was looking for a wife.

VII

"Between you and me and the bedpost, old chap," said Edmund as we smoked our cigars after dinner on the evening of his arrival, "I'm getting too old to turn out on a winter's night and drive all the way to Llangennith whenever I want a good you-know-what, and now that I'm almost twenty-nine I can see that marriage does have a lot to offer."

"I understand exactly," I said, remembering uncomfortable winter journeys down the Fulham Road.

I had become closer to Edmund since my reconciliation with my father two years ago. Whenever I returned to Gower we had plenty of opportunity for long talks together, because I had installed him at Penhale Manor to look after my house and estate for me. At first it had seemed merely a neat solution to an awkward problem, but to my surprise and gratification, it had turned out to be the best offer to Edmund that I could possibly have made. The opportunity to lead an independent life and the salaried responsibility of the position not only had diverted him from the chronic melancholy he had suffered since the war but had given him the confidence he had always lacked. All my father's children had known what it was to be overshadowed by Robert, but only Edmund had known the horror of being overshadowed by everyone.

I realized belatedly that he had grown up convinced he was useless, an opinion my parents had unwittingly reinforced when they had allowed him to live at home without earning a living, and it was only when I had offered him work that he had begun to believe he was not compelled to go through life as a failure who lived on his parents' charity.

His position was not arduous, since Huw Meredith was a first-class manager, but Edmund took his responsibilities seriously and applied himself with enthusiasm to the estate. However his chief interest remained horticulture, and at my request he had embarked on the task of removing all the scentless white roses from Blanche's garden.

"My one insuperable problem," said Edmund after he had revealed his decision to comtemplate matrimony, "is money. I know you and Lion each brought off the fantastic feat of marrying an heiress, but you yourself are so obviously cut out to be a huge success in life, and even old Lion was cut out to be a huge success as a bounder, while I'm not cut out to be a huge success at anything."

I recognized the plea for reassurance. "Stop talking drivel—you're earning your living, you've been to the right school, you're thoroughly respectable and you're a jolly nice chap. What more can any girl want?"

"Money for diamond hatpins."

"Edmund, girls don't go to bed with diamond hatpins. They go to bed with men."

This put us on safer ground. Edmund had overcome his conviction that no woman could possibly look twice at him; at least his experiences in wartime France had not all been hellish, and when he returned home he had embarked on a long affair with a land girl called Joan who worked at Stourham Hall. Unfortunately Joan, having decided that no wedding ring was ever going to be forthcoming from Edmund, had now announced her plans to marry a Swansea bank clerk, and it was this catastrophe, rather than his advancing years, which had led Edmund to consider that matrimony might have more to offer than a love affair.

"I was so upset," he confided in me, "that I damned nearly proposed to Joan myself, but Papa talked me out of it and I know he was right. It's simply no good marrying out of one's class, is it? Of course he and Mama did, but he was *déclassé* and she was exceptional and the circumstances were so peculiar that it didn't matter. But normally . . . well, you know what happens. The marriage winds up in a social mess, and it's always such hell for the children."

"True. I tried to explain to Armstrong once that to marry out of one's class here is like marrying someone of a different-colored skin. That's the only parallel that an American can understand."

"You don't think I'm being a bloody snob?"

"No, just bloody sensible."

Edmund visibly blossomed as I praised his good sense, but was still anxious enough to say, "All the same my position isn't easy. Do you by any chance know of a gorgeous young heiress who's simply panting to marry a man whose only talent lies in being a jolly nice chap?"

"Possibly—but what kind of a girl are you looking for? I suppose you'd like a sweet shy English-rose type of person who's fond of gardening."

"Good God, no!" said Edmund horrified. "What use would that be? Isn't it bad enough that *I'm* a sweet shy English-rose type of person who's fond of gardening? No thank you, I want someone utterly different! I want one of those marvelous modern girls who says outrageous things and laughs all the time, someone who smokes like a chimney and drinks like a fish and thinks sex is jolly good fun!"

"Say no more, Edmund. Let me introduce you to Teddy Armstrong."

VIII

I had spoken with the rashness that so often follows a pleasant dinner and half a bottle of claret, and when I awoke the next morning I was at once uneasy about my role of matchmaker. However I told myself it was most unlikely that Edmund and Teddy would discover a mutual passion which would drive them pell-mell to the altar.

Never was I more mistaken. Edmund was quickly reduced to a shining-eyed wraith who could neither eat nor sleep, and Teddy was quickly driven to confide that he was "every right-minded girl's dream come true." I noted the word "right-minded" as I acknowledged her determination to be besotted with him, and realized that Teddy had frightened herself by her fast behavior that season. After ricocheting in and out of love with a fine display of emotional pyrotechnics, she had lost her heart to a former army captain who had turned out to be not only a professional gambler but a married man. Her hired chaperone had washed her hands of her. Even the doting Armstrong had been shocked enough to talk of sending her back to America, but I had convinced him that his best chance of avoiding scandal lay in keeping her at his side.

"Of course nothing actually *happened*," confided Edmund to me. "She's told me all about it."

I thought it kindest to maintain a diplomatic silence. It was certainly possible that Teddy's virginity was intact but on the other hand hired chaperones seldom return their fees unless racked by the most profound sense of failure.

"Poor little Teddy's been awfully misunderstood," said Edmund. "She says all she really wants is to get married and live happily ever after near her father. She doesn't get on too well with that mother of hers in Boston."

That sealed Edmund's fate, and his fate made it well-nigh impossible for me to break with Armstrong even if I had wished to do so. If I now refused to marry Constance, I knew he would intervene in revenge to prevent his other daughter marrying my brother. I did wonder if he would object to the match, but I soon realized the bizarre truth that Edmund was even more of an ideal son-in-law for Armstrong than I was. Armstrong wanted to control his favorite daughter's life; this meant he needed a docile son-in-law whom he could manipulate, and in this respect Edmund posed no threat to him. He must have hoped that Teddy would do better for herself but after the scandal he was willing to concede that she could do very much worse, and as always he was keenly aware that if she failed to marry she would have to return to her mother in the autumn.

Deciding to approve of Edmund, Armstrong then asked me when I was going to propose to Constance.

"On her birthday," I said without a second's hesitation. The date was two weeks away.

"No, let's sew this up right now," said Armstrong, unable to resist pushing to conclude the deal that would scoop both his daughters away from his wife. "Constance isn't eating or sleeping properly, and I want her put out of her agony. Take the day off tomorrow, buy the ring and fix the date."

I said I would. Despite my anger that I had been the victim of an exercise in power, I was also conscious of relief that the decision had been taken out of my hands. Constance had not been the only one enduring an agony of uncertainty, and I went home convinced that proposing to her was the right thing—indeed, the only thing—to do.

I had just entered the house when my father telephoned. My nephew Robin, six years old and his parents' pride and joy, had fallen to his death from one of the tower windows at Little Oxmoon, and Robert wanted me to return to Gower at once to organize the funeral.

IX

"Have you ever noticed," said Edmund the next morning as our train thundered towards Wales, "how tragedy so often strikes at people who already have a surfeit of tragedy in their lives? I saw it happen again and again in the war. Men would have their balls blown off and then the next day they'd get a letter saying their wives had run away or their mothers had dropped dead or their children had died of diphtheria."

I said nothing. I was too busy thinking how I would feel if Harry's life had been cut short, and alongside my grief for Robert lay the memory of Robin, spoiled and precocious but still a child of exceptional promise and charm.

We were alone in our first-class compartment. I had thought Rory Kinsella would be accompanying us, but he was on holiday with his Dublin relations and would be approaching Wales from Ireland. Two years ago he had been sent down from Cambridge for incorrigible idleness, but Robert had somehow obtained a position for him in a well-known firm of stockbrokers and Rory had promised to turn over a new leaf. I was skeptical. Both those Kinsella boys had turned out badly, although since the formation of the Irish Republic, Declan was no longer in danger of being shot by the British.

"Of course it would be the best of the bunch that gets killed," Edmund was saying. "That always seemed to happen in the war too. Poor Ginevra! She hardly deserves yet another catastrophe."

I suddenly could not endure to hear him talking so calmly of such brutal chaos. "There's got to be some meaning in it all," I said in despair. "I just can't accept that life can be so disordered."

"Accept it, old chap," said Edmund placidly, "or you'll go mad. I found that out in the trenches."

"Oh, shut up about the bloody war!" Any talk of madness always had an adverse effect on me.

The rest of the journey passed in silence but as the train entered the industrial wasteland on the eastern side of Swansea I did apologize to him. Edmund promptly apologized in his turn for upsetting me, and with an uneasy peace established between us we steeled ourselves for the ordeal of our father's welcome.

He was waiting by the ticket barrier, and for once he looked his age. He was sixty-one, thirty years my senior. I noticed that he was stooping slightly and that his hair, which had once been a dark gold, was now a pale silvery yellow.

After I had embraced him I said, "This must have been a terrible shock for you."

"It was a tragedy," said my father so firmly that I knew he was incapable of discussing the subject. "Why, Edmund, how well you look! Tell me all about this nice little American girl you've met in London."

Edmund promptly began to chatter about Teddy, but when we reached the motor my father asked him to sit in front with the chauffeur and the paean was curtailed.

Somewhere beyond the Penrice Home Farm my father said to me, "He was such a game little fellow."

"Yes. I expect he reminded you of Robert, didn't he?"

"Just like him. It was a miracle. It made up for Robert being ill. Well, at least Margaret was spared this. No more little replacement, no more little miracle . . . and do you know, I can't face Robert, not yet, I'm too upset . . . that awful bungalow—the wheelchair—Ginevra—"

"Don't worry, Papa, I'll explain everything to Robert. I'll make sure he understands, just as I do."

My father wiped his eyes and said, "Oh, I'm so glad to see you, John! If only you knew how often I wish you weren't so far away in London . . ."

And that was when I first allowed myself to acknowledge how much I now wanted to come home.

X

"Oh, there you are," said Robert. "I heard you were rushing down from London, but to be frank I don't want to see you. I'd much rather be left alone."

"I'm sorry. Well, in that case—"

"However since you're here you may as well sit down, have a drink and drum up the strength to face the whole bloody mess. Ginette's gone to pieces, of course, constant hysterics and no use to anyone, I'm fed up with her. Oh, for Christ's sake don't look like that! If I had any bloody strength I'd bloody hit you. Get me some whisky. I'm not supposed to have any at the moment but God knows I could hardly be worse than I am now. No, that's not true: I could be infinitely worse. I could be blind, incontinent and only able to breathe in gasps. That's all to come, of course. What a bloody bore. Why don't I kill myself? Too much of a coward. I still want to shit whenever I think of death. God, how I despise myself. I think up wonderful excuses why I should live, though—my best one was that I wanted to see what Robin would be like when he grew up but that's no good now, so I'll have to dream up something new, but what excuse can I conceivably produce for putting Ginette through hell like this? Sheer bloody-mindedness liberally seasoned with sadism is now the only explanation I can offer—unless I confess my cowardice, but we can't admit to cowardice, can we, it's not the fucking done thing."

"You'll be better in a week or two, Robert. Warburton said this would just be a temporary setback."

"Oh yes—better! Back in the bloody chair! Fuck being better! Still, I agree it's an improvement on being bedridden like this. Christ, I always thought only overemotional women talked about being 'prostrated with grief,' but look at me, I'm literally prostrated. Ah, the whisky. Thanks. You'll have to get me a straw and prop me up . . . that's it. Now ease me back a bit. That's right. . . . God, that's a strong drink you've given me! Take it back and add some more water. No, on second thoughts don't bother. What does it bloody matter, nothing matters. We'd better talk about the funeral. The first thing you've got to understand is that neither Ginette nor I will be there. And for God's sake tell Papa not to go either—the last thing we want is him going round the bend again, that really would be the final straw. I want no fuss. Put the child in a box and bury him with the minimum of drama. He's dead and that's that. God, this whisky tastes good! Give me some more."

As I refilled his glass I said, "Is Ginevra seeing visitors at the moment?"

"God knows. I don't. We had a row and shouted at each other and I

haven't seen her since. She's probably drunk. Look, John, if you really want
to help here, get hold of Warburton, point a gun at his head and say that
woman's got to be carted off somewhere for a few days. She's got some idiotic
notion that she can't leave me, but I can't stand the thought of her turning
herself into a martyr, it's enough to make me stop shitting with fright at the
thought of death and fucking well cut my throat. I told her straight out that
she was being a selfish bitch and driving me to suicide, but that did no good
—she just had hysterics all over again and rushed off to get drunk—and she's
been drinking much too much for some time, I know she has, my spy Bennett keeps an eye on the gin bottle and anyway I can see the results for
myself. She's got too fat and she looks blowsy as a tart and damn it, she's in a
mess, that's all there is to say, a bloody mess, and *she's got to be helped out of
it.* Robin's dead. No one can do anything for him now, but Ginette's alive
and *someone's got to do something about her.* I'm frantic, I can't think of
anything else, I'm beside myself, she's now the only thing that makes my life
bearable, and I've *got to save her*—"

"Don't worry, Robert. I understand. I'll go and talk to her straightaway."

XI

"I'll quite understand if you don't want to see me, Ginevra, but Robert's
rather worried about you, and—"

"Don't mention bloody Robert to me! Just because he can't show grief he
thinks it's bad taste whenever anyone else does! God, how I hate him sometimes, I hate him, I wish he'd bloody well hurry up and die—"

"Ginevra—"

"Oh, *shut up!* What do you understand about all this? You just have no
idea, no idea at all! There you stand so bloody perfect and so bloody lucky—
you've never been in a situation where all you can do is scream with pain—"

"I do at least know what it's like to hold one's dead child in one's arms.
Ginevra, I'm going to phone Warburton. Will you promise me you'll do as he
says?"

"Do what you like, I don't care what happens to me now, I don't care, I
don't care, I don't care—"

"Well, *I* care," I said with a finality that I hoped would conclude the
conversation, and the next moment she had collapsed sobbing in my arms.

XII

"It's all right, Robert, she's agreed to go. Warburton's sent for an ambulance, and he's arranged for a bed at the Home of the Assumption. Apparently it's more of a rest home than a lunatic asylum nowadays."

"Thank God. Now I shall feel better. Are you off to see the vicar about the funeral?"

"No, I think my next task is to attend to Kester. Where is he?"

"No idea. Ginette sacked both the nanny and the nursemaid on the spot after the disaster and they packed their bags and left immediately."

"But who's looking after the child?"

"Don't ask me. Cook, probably. He knows his way to the kitchens. God, imagine us being left with that little freak! But maybe he'll turn out to be passable in the end. I don't *think* he's mentally defective. What's so bloody awful is that he looks just like a girl."

"I agree his looks are . . . unusual—but maybe he'll be striking later."

"Rubbish. The only way he could be striking would be as a transvestite. Christ, I sometimes feel like making sure he really does have a penis. It's all Ginette's fault for wanting a daughter. My God, if you only knew the fights I've had with her to keep his hair cut and his wardrobe free of Little Lord Fauntleroy blouses—"

"I can't believe Ginevra would deliberately—"

"Poor little devil, what a wretched life he's had, and I've contributed to that wretchedness by my indifference, I know I have, but never mind, I'll make it up to him now and that'll give Robin's death meaning, the death will make sense if I think of it as a punishment and show I've learned my lesson—"

"My dear Robert, I hardly think—"

"Shut up. I don't care what you think. I know you don't believe in God. I don't either. But this is a punishment whichever way you look at it, and if I have my way some good's going to emerge from this disaster to benefit that wretched child."

"In that case there's all the more reason why I should now—"

"Yes, find out where the hell the little bugger is and then tell me what the devil you think I should do with him."

XIII

"Hullo, Kester," I said, "I was wondering where you were! Are you all right?"

"Don't be frightened!" said Cook to him kindly. "It's your Uncle John!" She turned to me and whispered, "Poor little boy, he doesn't know what's happening, but don't you worry, Mr. John—Betty and I have been looking after him."

Betty was Watson, the parlormaid. Both servants were local women who had always been employed on the Oxmoon estate, and I knew they were reliable. Feeling matters could have been worse, I advanced on Kester. He was sitting at the kitchen table in front of a plate of sausages and mashed potatoes, but as he looked up at me the spoon trembled in his hand and he abandoned the attempt to eat. His pale eyes filled with tears. As I put out my hand to reassure him, I noticed with distaste that his thick reddish-brown hair waved to his shoulders.

"I expect you miss your nanny and nursemaid, don't you, Kester," I said. "Do you know why they had to go away?"

He shook his head. Two huge tears trickled down his cheeks. So no one had bothered to offer him an explanation.

"We told him Master Robin had gone on a visit to the angels," said Cook, who was a well-meaning soul, "but we didn't know whether Madam wanted us to say any more. Poor little mite, he's not four yet, is he? He wouldn't understand about D-E-A-T-H."

I picked Kester up, sat down with him on my knee and embarked on the necessary explanations.

XIV

"He's all right, Robert, but I don't think he should stay here with only the cook and the parlormaid to keep an eye on him. I've just telephoned Angela Stourham and she's very kindly said he can stay with her until Ginevra's better. Eleanor's driving over straightaway to collect him."

As far as I could remember, Stourham Hall, where the unmarried Angela Stourham kept house for her brother Oswald, was the nearest place where a nanny was still on active duty in the nursery. Eleanor, daughter of Stourham's first marriage, was now a young woman of twenty-one, but the fruit of his disastrous second marriage to the platinum blonde was only a child of three.

"That's very good of Angela," said Robert. "Can you convey my thanks to Eleanor when she arrives? I don't want to see anyone."

"I think you should see Kester before he goes."

"What for?"

"Because you're his father, Robert, and it's the sort of thing a father ought to do."

"Very well, what do I say?"

"Tell him you're sorry that everything's been such a muddle but you do hope he enjoys his little holiday with Belinda. I've told him what's happening so there's no need for you to embark on explanations."

Kester was summoned. As he was obviously nervous, I kept his hand clasped in mine after drawing him to the bedside.

"Well, Kester," said Robert abruptly, "I—good God, John, look at the length of his hair! Quick, get some scissors and chop it off before Eleanor arrives!"

Kester immediately began to cry. Startled I bent over him. "What is it, Kester? What's the matter?"

"Oh, don't take any notice," said Robert impatiently. "He's just terrified of scissors."

"But in that case how idiotic of you to suggest a haircut!"

"I'm not letting that child leave this house looking like a bloody girl!"

Kester howled. Robert cursed. I wished myself a thousand miles away.

XV

Order was eventually restored. Ginevra, heavily sedated by Warburton, was borne away in an ambulance to the Home of the Assumption, the Gothic mansion on the outskirts of Swansea where my grandmother had spent her final years. Robert's man Bennett managed to trim Kester's hair while I held the child in my arms and constantly assured him that he was safe. Later, after he had been collected by Eleanor Stourham, I interviewed the servants to make sure they knew what they were doing and then, leaving Robert to rest, I retreated to the night nursery, where Robin's pathetic little broken body lay beneath a sheet.

I wanted to say a prayer, but it was no use. The words refused to come and the faith I longed for remained absent. Chaos had broken into an ordered world but this time no drawn line could have stopped it, and although I tried again to make sense of the tragedy the pattern was too savage to comprehend. All I could think was that blind chance was on the rampage again, the same blind chance which had killed Lion and left Edmund alive, but then I wondered if the blindness lay not in chance but in the human beings who looked upon it. I could remember Robert saying in 1921 during our discussion of Milly Straker, "One yearns for the gift of clairvoyance . . . we have insufficient information." Perhaps chance was merely another name for a preordained future which had been conceived on such a vast scale that it was beyond the human understanding—but no, I found that a repugnant thought. I recoiled from the idea of a preordained future. I had to believe human beings could choose the way they played their cards; I had to believe they could be saved from suffering by drawing those lines to keep evil at bay. The alternative—a hopeless, helpless submission to uncontrollable, incomprehensible forces—seemed to me to be a vision of hell, a road that led straight to despair.

I stopped. I normally had no time for metaphysical speculation which had always seemed to me to be the enemy of a well-ordered mind, and I found my chaotic thoughts unnerving. A need to escape from the bungalow overwhelmed me. Leaving the nurseries in the west tower, I ran downstairs and seconds later was setting off at a brisk pace down the drive.

I decided a walk would help me relax after the harrowing scenes I had endured, but I did not take the path up to Penhale Down, where Robert's sheep now grazed among the megalithic stones. I headed straight on down the bridle path past Martinscombe towards Penhale village, and when the church spire came into sight among the trees, I turned away up the ancient track to Harding's Down.

The two hills, Penhale Down and Harding's Down, lay inland from the sea but parallel to the long ridge of Rhossili Downs which rose sharply from Rhossili beach. In the valley between this long ridge and those twin hills lay the parish of Penhale, and from the summits of all the Downs it was possible to see not merely Penhale but most of the Gower Peninsula, from Llanmadoc and Llangennith in the north to Oxwich Bay in the south, from the sea in the west to Cefn Bryn, the backbone of Gower, which stretched east towards Swansea. Harding's Down was a favorite retreat of mine; I could remember making secret camps long ago with Lion beneath the ramparts which crowned the summit. This hill fort, built by tribesmen hundreds of years before, was now no more than a vast ring enclosing a sloping wilderness of bracken, but it was still a powerful sight, and as I reached the grassy ditch and scrambled up onto the ramparts I knew again the exhilaration I had known as a child.

It was by this time early evening. The haziness of the warm July day had receded in the changing light, and the view stretched with eerie clarity before my eyes as I stood on the southern edge of the circle. I looked beyond Llangennith to the north arm of Rhossili Bay; I looked past Llanmadoc Hill to the bright water of the Loughor Estuary; I looked beyond the rolling farmland to the village of Reynoldston on the spine of Cefn Bryn. So deceptive was the extraordinary light that Penhale seemed barely a stone's throw away in the valley below, and as the sea wind hummed in my ears I heard the chime of the church clock and remembered how I had once listened to it thundering the hour.

I spun round. I was standing on the highest point of the wall so that the entire summit of the Down lay before me, and as I turned I saw that on the other side of the fort far below a slim figure in a pale green dress had scrambled up onto the ramparts. The wind hummed again across the ancient lonely landscape, and the evening sun shone fiercely on that unmistakable fiery hair.

She did not see me immediately but I made no effort to escape. I merely stood motionless, overwhelmed by all the memories I had tried so sensibly to forget, and then at last as she looked up across the circle I knew we both heard the same echo in time.

7

I

SHE WORE her hair up but the wind had whipped it into untidiness; shining strands blew about her face and her long lovely neck. Freckles still peppered the bridge of her nose before fading into that very pale, very clear skin. She wore with her old faded green dress white sandals and no stockings. Her eyes shone with joy.

Taking her in my arms I kissed her first on the cheek, as a valued friend who had helped me survive a past crisis, and then, before I could stop myself, on the mouth as a lover.

"How strange it is," I said at last, "that death keeps bringing us together."

"Ah no," she said, smiling at me. "It's life that keeps bringing us together. Death's only a part of life, isn't it?"

"God knows what it is. I don't understand any of it. All I do understand is that life's so precious and one wastes so much time doing things one doesn't want to do."

We looked at each other and both knew exactly what we wanted to do. The clasp of our hands tightened. Descending from the ramparts into the shelter of the embankment, we moved once more into each other's arms.

II

"Did your husband leave you penniless again?"

"Yes—for the last time. He died last month in a waterfront brawl in Marseilles."

We were lying in a little grassy hollow framed by gorse bushes which protected us from the sea wind. Around us the bracken grew waist-high, and we could see the fronds rippling in the breeze like a wheat field. It was quiet. When a lark burst into song above us we both jumped, but by the time we looked up he had gone and only two sea gulls were drifting across the sky.

"Myfanwy and Huw say I can stay on at the farm," said Bronwen, "but I can't live on their charity so I shall go back to Cardiff, rent a room from my in-laws and get work."

"What work?"

"Housework. I did it last year so that we wouldn't be turned out of our rooms again."

"It must be very dreary."

"No, it's all right if you find a nice lady. I like polishing all the beautiful furniture while I daydream."

"What do you dream about?"

"I dream I have a house with six bedrooms, like my last lady, with a lovely bathroom all tiled in blue and a big kitchen with a refrigerator in it and a garden with flowers, and I dream I have several teapots, I do so love teapots, they're such a pretty shape, and I dream I have a book once a week—a magazine, ladies call it—with a nice love story in it where the beautiful heroine marries the handsome hero and lives happily ever after." She laughed, showing her perfect teeth. "Life's not much like that, is it?" she said. "But that's why it's so important to dream a little."

"I like to dream too," I said, "but I dream all the wrong dreams." And I told her about Constance.

When I had finished she said, "What will you do?"

"I can't imagine. All I know is that I'm in a frightful mess—as usual—and I'd rather not think about it. Will you come away with me for a while?"

She considered this carefully. "Would it make things better if I did?" she said at last. "Or would it make things worse?"

"I don't know and I don't care. To be frank I wouldn't care if all life on earth ceased so long as I'd had a couple of weeks alone with you first."

She smiled. Then she said, "Where shall we go?"

When I had finished making love to her again, I lay on my back and pondered on this question. Finally I said, "Have you ever been to Cornwall?"

"I've never been out of Wales."

"I've never been to Cornwall either but they say it's like Wales' first cousin. I think we'd feel at home there."

As we dressed we made our plans. I told her I could leave directly after Robin's funeral. She said she could leave at any time; she knew her sister would be willing to look after the children.

"But I'll have to be honest with her," she added. "I'll have to tell her the truth."

I paused in the act of buttoning my waistcoat. "Must you?"

"You needn't worry, she'll hold her tongue."

"But won't she be very shocked?"

"Yes, but I think she'll be forgiving. She knows what a terrible time I had with Gareth."

"She'll certainly be angry with me."

"Why? Everyone knows gentlemen do this sort of thing. She'll probably think you do it all the time." She looked at me with a smile and said, "Maybe you do!"

"No." But I told her about my mistress in Fulham.

"Does she love you?"

"I think she's fond of me. I'm fond of her. But the fondness merely stems from a mutual convenience." I slipped my arms around her waist again. "You're the one I love."

She said nothing.

"Don't you believe me?"

"I don't know." She looked up at me steadily. "And I don't think you know either," she said. "Not really."

"Bronwen—"

"But I love you," she interrupted, "and all I want is to spend a few precious days alone with you. Isn't that all that matters for the moment?"

Two days later we were on our way to Cornwall.

III

I told Robert and my father that I had to return to London, but I wired Armstrong that I had to remain in Wales for a further two weeks. As for Edmund, rushing back to London directly after the funeral, he was far too preoccupied with thoughts of Teddy to query my statement that Robert needed me until Ginevra returned from the nursing home.

On the morning after the funeral my father's chauffeur drove me into Swansea, supposedly to catch the train up to town, and my disappearance began. First of all I entrusted my leather bags to the station's left-luggage office. Then I bought a cardboard suitcase, filled it with cheap off-the-peg clothes and finally, much stimulated by my escape from my upper-class identity, I retired to the men's lavatory at the station to change. In my new blue suit I certainly looked *déclassé*, but I was aware too that I looked foreign, un-British, a man outside the confines of the English class system. I knew my accent, that inexorable bondage, would give me away as soon as I opened my mouth but even that would cease to matter in Bronwen's company since we always spoke to each other in Welsh.

I felt liberated. I walked out of the station as if I had been reborn.

Bronwen was due to arrive at ten o'clock on the motorbus from Penhale, and as I walked to meet her I methodically reviewed my list of new possessions to confirm that I had forgotten nothing. Outside a chemist's shop I stopped. I knew what I ought to buy there, but I hesitated, thinking how ridiculous it was that I had reached the age of thirty-one without attaining more than the dimmest grasp of a subject which was of vital practical importance. An eighteen-year-old soldier issued with regulation French letters in the trenches would have known more than I did. After several miscarriages with her husband, my mistress in Fulham had had an operation to ensure that pregnancy never recurred, so the question of prevention had not arisen in her company. I had never bought contraceptives in my life. What did one ask for? Armstrong had at least stopped short of asking me to buy his French letters for him, and besides he had never bothered unless he went to a brothel and needed protection against disease. I shuddered. "The women I like can look after themselves," he had said, referring to his more respectable exploits. I wondered if Bronwen could look after herself. Dafydd was now six. I remembered her admission that she had shared a bed with her husband whenever he came home from the sea, but even though he had presumably been anxious to make up for lost time, she had not conceived again. I decided that indicated a knowledge of contraception. Or did it? I paced up and down outside the chemist's shop.

Finally, despising myself for my cowardice, I went in but there were women present so I left. The answer, as I knew, was to ask for the trade name but trade names had never cropped up in any discussion on the subject with Armstrong, and I had always shied away from mentioning the matter to anyone else. How *could* I have permitted myself to remain in such a state of ignorance? I mentally cursed John Godwin for keeping me a priggish adolescent until the age of twenty-nine.

In the end I decided to postpone the problem. Bronwen was a practical woman whenever she wasn't dreaming of blue-tiled bathrooms, and if she was worried I judged her sensible enough to say so. If she did, I would at once take action, but meanwhile it was undoubtedly pleasanter to go on loving her without any sordid impediment. Again I thought of Armstrong protecting himself against disease, and again I shuddered in revulsion.

Abandoning the chemist, I hurried on down the street to the bus station.

IV

In the train I took off the wedding ring Morgan had given her and slipped on her finger the plain gold band that I had bought before I had embarked on my quest for cheap clothes. Hours later in Penzance when I wrote *Mr. and Mrs. John Godwin* in the hotel register I felt as if I had been married to her for years but had somehow mislaid all memory of the wedding. The hotel was small and quiet, and from our attic room when we awoke next morning we could see over the rooftops to the sparkling sea beyond the promenade.

After breakfast we went out. We found our way down the hill past the harbor, and when we reached the esplanade we paused to gaze across the bay to the fairytale castle of St. Michael's Mount.

"It hardly seems real," I said, but it was. We bought a guidebook, and the next day we went across to the Mount and it was all real, all true. The fairy tale had become reality, and reality exceeded all our dreams.

Later our guidebook led us to Mousehole and Lamorna and Logan's Rock, to St. Mawes and the Lizard and Kynance Cove. The weather deteriorated but we hardly noticed. We were too busy sitting in country buses and missing much romantic scenery by kissing at the wrong moment.

At first we were muddled about meals, since Bronwen was unaccustomed to dining at eight, but I had no wish for such formality so apart from our breakfast at the hotel we ate in cafés or at small, casual harbor inns where we could order fresh seafood. Bronwen had never eaten lobster before. I had never eaten baked beans on toast. We laughed and laughed as we saw each other's expressions after the first taste. In the café where I tried tomato sauce on my fried potatoes, we both laughed so much that the good-natured proprietor, thinking us mad foreigners, gave us a free pot of tea and asked where we came from.

"We're from Wales," I said in English, and when I saw his astonished face as he heard my accent I began to laugh all over again.

We talked endlessly. She told me about the little village above the Rhondda Valley where she had been born and where her parents had worked as cook and gardener for the local vicar. After her father's death her mother had stayed on at the vicarage, but when she too had died Bronwen had traveled south to join Myfanwy, who was in service at a rectory near Cardiff.

". . . and then very luckily there was a vacancy for a kitchen maid at the Big House and I went to work there, but it was horrible, I hated it, the housekeeper was cruel and the other girls laughed at me because my English wasn't good and the footman tried to manhandle me and then finally, thank God, Gareth became one of the undergardeners and he began to take notice of me and I thought if I married him I'd be safe and live happily ever after. I was only sixteen and Myfanwy wasn't in the neighborhood anymore because she'd married Huw so there was no one for me to talk to—oh, I was so weak and silly, but sometimes I think one has to suffer a little in order to grow up strong."

I told her about Oxmoon. I talked about how awful it had been to have this great god Robert whom we had all had to live up to and how wonderful it had been when the great god had singled me out for special attention. I talked about Lion. I talked about school and what fun it had been once I conquered my homesickness.

"Poor little boy!" said Bronwen. "How cruel the upper classes are, getting rid of their children by shutting them up for two-thirds of the year in institutions!"

"But I loved it! At school no one compared me with Robert—the masters remembered him, of course, but even so, it was easier to escape from him there."

"Poor little boy!" said Bronwen again.

"No, no, I had this wonderful childhood—I was so happy! And then . . . when I was eleven . . ."

"Yes?"

"Something happened but I'll tell you about it later."

Later she said, "In Penhale they still talk of your grandmother and Mr. Owain Bryn-Davies. What was your grandmother like? Do you remember her well?"

And then I told her everything.

V

After some days we moved on to North Cornwall. The Cornish moors reminded us of the Gower Downs; even the mining territory around St. Just seemed to echo the industrial wilderness east of Swansea, and as we gazed at the ruined engine houses silhouetted against the sea, Bronwen said the coast must be almost as fine as the coast between Rhossili and Porteynon. But we agreed Gower was unsurpassable. Our bus crawled on along the coast road, through the hamlets of Morvah and Zennor until finally we reached the crest of a ridge, and there before us in a brilliant panorama of sea and sky lay the curve of a vast bay and the famous fishing town of St. Ives.

The town sparkled in a hot, bright foreign light, and beyond the beaches the sea was a rich glowing Mediterranean blue. We found a guesthouse in a cobbled alley in the heart of the town, and having shed our luggage we wandered through the narrow twisting streets to the harbor.

"I think the weather will stay fine now," I said rashly, and despite this tempting of fate, the sun continued to shine. We became idle, heading every morning for the beach and returning every afternoon to the seclusion of our room. From our window we could watch the gulls swooping among the crooked chimney pots as the fishing boats returned to the harbor, and in the evenings when the town became bathed in its golden southern light, we would wander to the summit of the hill behind the town and watch the sun sink into the sea.

"We're like pilgrims in a legend," I said to her once, and we talked of Welsh legends and read about Cornish legends in our dog-eared guidebook. I told her about French legends too, and described my visits to France before the war when I had been studying modern languages up at Oxford. She asked about Oxford but could not quite imagine it. I told her about Paris. She could not conceive of such a place, but was enthralled. We never mentioned London.

"I'd like to travel one day," she said. "I'd always accepted that I'd never leave Wales, but now that I have . . . oh, I must read books about travel, real books with hard covers; I shall talk to the lady of the traveling library and ask her advice, and then I shall read and read and read so that when I talk to you in the future—"

We looked at each other. She blushed painfully, but I pulled her to me. I did not want her hating herself for mentioning a future neither of us dared imagine.

When I had kissed her I said, "Of course I could never marry Constance now."

She made no effort to disguise her relief, and in her honesty I saw how vulnerable she was. But still she had the courage to say: "You must do as you must. I don't want you blaming me later and saying I ruined your life by spoiling all your fine prospects in London."

"I don't care about London anymore. I'm going back to Gower." We were watching the sun set again. The sun was a brilliant red, the blue sky was streaked with gold and the sea was a glowing mass of fiery light. It was the most alluring prospect, the kind of prospect that would tempt even an unimaginative man to see visions of paradise, and I was by no means an unimaginative man.

"Now that poor child's dead Oxmoon will come to me eventually," I said at last. "My father may promise Robert out of kindness that Kester will be the heir, but that promise will die with Robert. My father prefers Harry to Kester, and besides . . . I know very well that my father feels closer to me now than he does to his other sons."

After a pause Bronwen said, "But do you think you're suited to a country life at Oxmoon?"

I was startled. "Why should you think I'm not?"

"I remember Huw saying after your wife died that he wasn't surprised by your decision to go to London. He said he thought you'd become bored with being a gentleman farmer at Penhale Manor."

"Being a gentleman farmer at Penhale Manor is one thing; being master of Oxmoon is quite another and would certainly provide me with the challenges I need to stave off boredom." I tried not to sound annoyed. "That's a jaundiced judgment from your brother-in-law!"

"Oh, you mustn't think that," she said quickly. "He admires you so much. But he finds you a puzzle—and so do most people, if you really want to know. 'Mr. John's a dark horse,' they say. 'Doesn't seem to know what he wants. Up to London, back to Gower, up to London again—rushing around like an inklemaker in a drangway,' as they say in their funny Gower English—"

"I admit I've been confused in the past. But if I knew I had Oxmoon coming to me, all confusion would be at an end."

"Why? It's only a house. How can stone and slate solve muddle and unhappiness?"

I made a great effort to express my complex feelings simply so that she could understand. "I feel I need a reward," I said. "I want compensation for all those years I came second to Robert. I want compensation for all those years when I murdered my true self in a futile effort to please my parents as much as Robert did. I feel it's only fair that I should get Oxmoon; I feel it's owing to me."

"What's owing to you," said Bronwen, "is love, but you won't get that from Oxmoon. Nor can Oxmoon change the past. Forgiving your parents, not inheriting Oxmoon, is the only way you can stop the past from haunting you."

I stared at her and as she stared back I was aware, not for the first time, of the extreme clarity of her mind. It was as if she saw a spectrum of reality that was entirely beyond my field of vision.

"But of course I forgive my parents," I heard myself say. "I'm a good son, I always have been, so how can I not forgive them? To bear a grudge would imply I disliked and resented them—and how could I dislike and resent them, why, I'd despise myself, such feelings would be quite incompatible with being a good son."

Bronwen said nothing.

"My parents were innocent victims," I said strongly. "My grandmother's the one to blame. *She's* the one I loathe and resent as the source of all my unhappiness."

Bronwen kissed me and said, "Forgive her."

"How can I? If I don't blame her for what went wrong I must blame my parents and I can't—yet I've got to blame someone, I must, I've suffered, I went through hell, it distorted my whole life—"

"Yes," said Bronwen, "it was dreadful. But you must break free, you mustn't let it go on distorting your life, and the road to freedom isn't the road to Oxmoon. You won't be happy in a world where you think you need compensation, because the compensation will only chain you to the past."

There was a silence. The sun continued to sink into the sea and we continued to watch it, but finally I turned aside and said, "My father may well live another twenty years, so Oxmoon's not important now. What's important is that I should return to Gower so that we can have a life together there."

I saw her fear as clearly as I saw her joy.

"Of course," I said, "we'd be married."

She looked more fearful than ever. "But how would I manage?"

I kissed her. "We'll both manage very well." I kissed her again and began to sort through my pockets for coins. "Let's find a telephone so that I can discover what's been going on. I think I've got the courage now to return to the world we left behind."

As we set off through the cobbled streets I heard a clock chiming far away by the harbor, and when Bronwen's hand tightened in mine I knew she was aware of my thoughts. Anglo-Saxon time was waiting for us, and in that world of weeks, days and hours lay a crisis of catastrophic dimensions. I had realized, as I sent my last batch of postcards to my children, that I had been away for far longer than I had intended.

VI

"What the hell have you been doing?" shouted Robert. "Where are you? What's going on? That bloody American of yours has been persecuting us for information and saying you're supposed to be in London proposing to his daughter!"

"I've no intention of proposing to his daughter. I'm in Cornwall with the woman I love."

"You're *what?*" His voice receded; he had evidently turned aside to confide in his wife. "John's gone completely off the rails." He readdressed the telephone. "For God's sake, what woman?"

"Her name's Bronwen Morgan, and she's Huw Meredith's sister-in-law. Robert, are you better? And how's Ginevra? Do please forgive me for not telephoning you earlier—"

"Oh, don't worry about us," said Robert. "We're now the least of your problems. Tell me, is there any chance of seeing you in the immediate future, or do you intend to ramble around Cornwall in a romantic haze indefinitely?"

"I'm returning to Gower tomorrow. I have to take Bronwen back to Penhale before I go up to London."

"Good. I'll have the straitjacket waiting," said Robert, and hung up.

VII

"Of course you must realize," said Robert kindly, "that you're quite insane, but fortunately it's nothing to worry about; this form of insanity is very common, and there's no doubt you'll recover—probably sooner rather than later. Now, the most important thing is that you should start to come gently down to earth. Take your children to the zoo or something. Give those appalling off-the-peg clothes to the nearest branch of the Salvation Army. Read a newspaper. Have a haircut. Do all those boring little everyday things which remind one constantly of how drab life really is. And above all, my dear John, abandon this romantic pose of the Celtic Twilight Visionary—set aside this nauseous Celtic mysticism and try to see the situation not with Anglo-Saxon clarity—I don't ask the impossible—but at least with true Welsh hardheadedness and good sense. It's only the English who think the Welsh spend all their time wandering around singing at a perpetual Eisteddfod, so if you must see yourself as a Welshman, for God's sake see yourself as an intelligent one and don't wreck your life while you're not responsible for your actions."

It was early evening, and we were alone in the drawing room at Little Oxmoon. Ginevra had tactfully left after giving me a brief embrace; I was relieved to see she was looking better. So was Robert. He was no longer bedridden and had returned to his wheelchair.

"Robert, you don't understand. This is the way, the truth, the life I long to lead—"

"What way? What truth? And for God's sake, what life? John, have you really no idea how absurd you sound? Look, I'm going to get to the bottom of this. Contrary to the romantic poets, I don't believe falling in love is a random phenomenon—in my opinion it's always the symptom of some underlying disorder of the personality."

"If you think that," I said, "then obviously you've never been in love."

"It's precisely because I've been in love that I know what I'm talking about. Sex should be a sport, not a destructive obsession."

"You don't seriously regard sex as a mere sport, do you?"

Robert stared at me. "Well, how do you regard it?"

"Sex is life—real life. Sport is just a way of keeping real life at bay—it's just a poor substitute for what life's really all about."

"What an extraordinary remark! It's hard to believe you ever went to

Harrow. Have you by any chance come under the influence of that turgid little writer D. H. Lawrence?"

"My knowledge of modern English literature stops with John Buchan. Anyway why are we talking about sex? I'm talking about love!"

"Oh yes, yes, yes, of course you are—people who can think of nothing but sex always ennoble their emotion by calling it love, but don't worry, I refuse to let myself be defeated by this problem. You're my favorite brother and I'm very fond of you and I'm going to save you from yourself even if it's the last thing I ever do."

Robert was at his most formidable. He was carefully dressed in a black suit with his Old Harrovian tie, and although his right side was too weak to permit him to sit entirely straight in his chair, he still gave the impression of being bolt upright. His thinning hair, neatly cut and severely parted, was the color of iron. His deep-set, somewhat hypnotic eyes were steel-blue. Even his useless right hand, curled inwards like a claw, seemed to express aggression, and I had to make a considerable effort not to be mentally pulverized by the full force of his personality in top gear.

"There's obviously some lack in your life," he was saying, "which has driven you to compensate yourself by escaping into this addle-brained Celtic sloppiness. Now, let me see. What is it that's lacking? You're rich, healthy and good-looking. You enjoy your work. You have two attractive children to whom you're devoted. You have loyal servants and a wide circle of admiring friends—you even have a saintly mistress tucked away in Fulham who apparently never gives you a moment's anxiety—and on top of all this quite extraordinary good fortune, you have an American millionaire who thinks you're God's gift to a middle-aged buccaneer with a paternity obsession, and you have a good-looking, cultivated girl who can't wait to make you a matchlessly competent wife. Yet are you satisfied with this Elysium you've created for yourself? No, you're not. You rush off to Cornwall with a cleaning woman from Cardiff, gaze into golden sunsets and talk twaddle about ways and truths and lives you long to lead. Very well, I give up, you tell me: what's wrong with your London life? What's missing?"

"Bronwen."

"That's no answer. That just restates the conundrum. Christ, give me some more whisky! It's hard work providing a rational explanation for such thoroughly irrational behavior."

There was a pause while I removed our glasses to the decanter and refilled them. It was not until I was adding the water that Robert said slowly, "But perhaps I'm entirely wrong. Perhaps there's no lack in your life—quite the reverse. Perhaps there's a superfluity. Perhaps you've simply decided you don't need London anymore, and perhaps this raging love affair with a Welsh peasant is your peculiar way of celebrating your liberation. . . . But why would you feel you no longer need London?"

"All I care about is living with Bronwen in Gower."

"You couldn't conceivably be quite such a fool."

"Robert—"

"You wouldn't give up all for love—you're much too ambitious. You'd only give up your present Elysium if you thought you saw another more attractive one on the horizon—and so the big question is, isn't it, what's more attractive to you than a million pounds and all the worldly success you've ever wanted?"

"Oh, for God's sake! Listen, Robert—"

"No, I'm sorry, John, but you're going to have to listen to me, because I'm now quite beside myself with horror. I can see that your whole behavior has been the result of a most disastrous miscalculation."

"What the devil do you mean?"

"You're not going to get Oxmoon, John. Not now. Not ever. Drink up that scotch. Pour yourself some brandy. And I'll explain."

VIII

He said he was going to make sure Kester was the heir.

"Well, of course you are," I said without a second's hesitation. "I'd do the same for my own son if I were in your shoes." I took what I thought would be a sip of whisky and found myself draining the glass.

"You know what I told you after Robin died: Kester's going to benefit. It'll make sense of Robin's death."

"Yes, don't worry, Robert, I absolutely understand." I revolved the empty glass in my hands to give the impression it was still half full.

"No, I'm afraid you don't understand, not yet, but I'm equally afraid that I'm going to have to make sure you do. It may result in us being permanently estranged, but I can't help that. I've got to save you from messing up your life as the result of a misapprehension about the future of Oxmoon."

"Whatever you say we couldn't wind up permanently estranged."

"I wonder. Very well, listen to this. You think everything will still come right for you because I don't have a mild case of this illness and with any luck I'll be dead in ten years."

"My dear Robert—"

"Shut up. You think Papa's bound to outlive me and that once I'm out of the way he won't hesitate to make you his heir—but you see, John, that's where you make your big mistake. I'm going to tell Papa that he has to make Kester his heir and Papa's going to do what I say. There's no question about it. I've got him by the balls."

I stood up, took a clean glass from the salver and poured myself some brandy. "How?"

"He did something once that was so bloody frightful that it had a profoundly adverse effect on my life. He's been racked by guilt ever since, and he'll see my blackmail as a chance to cancel his guilt and finally be at peace with himself."

"I see." I drank some of the brandy. "I knew something had gone wrong between you," I said, "but I didn't realize it was so catastrophic. What happened?"

"It's not necessary that you should know that. All that's necessary is that you should believe that Oxmoon will never be yours."

I was silent.

"I'm sorry," said Robert, "but all I can say in my own defense is that I don't believe the loss of Oxmoon will ultimately matter to you. In my opinion you're not suited to the life of a country gentleman. You're like Ginette. You're drawn to the city lights and the glamour of worldly success; you enjoy money and power and smart women and smart cars. Your recent past with Armstrong proves that to the hilt. Have you ever enjoyed life more than during these last eighteen months in his employment?"

I drank some more brandy and said, "My recent past shows the worst side of me. But I do have a better side."

"There's nothing bad about thriving on a smart London life, John. You're in the company of numerous charming and talented people. It's nothing to be ashamed of."

"You make me sound contemptible."

"Not at all. You're only saying that because you want to deny your true self; but let me reintroduce you to your true self, John, the true self I've been watching so intently from this wheelchair since 1921. Why did you really go to London after Blanche died? 'To build a new life away from my tragic memories,' you say, but I say you went because you knew you'd made a mistake trying to play the country squire and after the novelty had worn off you were bored, restless and frustrated. In fact I think you ran to London gasping with relief, and what happened when you got there? 'I'll find some quiet civilized sort of work,' you say with charming modesty, but within a month you're hobnobbing with Harley Armstrong. 'I can't bear Americans!' you used to say at the F.O., but in fact Americans excel at being successful on a vast glittering seductive scale, and of course you now allow yourself to be seduced. Are you horrified by your new employment? No, you're thrilled and stimulated. You look well, sound cheerful and everyone remarks how splendidly you've recovered from your bereavement. 'I couldn't consider remarrying for at least five years!' you say earnestly at regular intervals, but when Armstrong plays the matchmaker do you laugh and tell him to go to hell? No, you most certainly do not. You—I'm sorry, do you want to comment?"

"No. Go on." I set down my empty glass.

"You start seeing a good deal of this girl and you even decide to marry her —and why? Because she's the symbol, isn't she, John, the flesh-and-blood symbol of your way, your truth and the life which you not only long to lead but which quite frankly I don't think you can do without. Forget Oxmoon, John. You'd only find it was an unnecessary and tedious drain on your increasingly valuable time. And forget Mrs. Morgan too—or if you can't forget her at the moment, then make some sensible provision for her until you've exhausted her possibilities. But what you mustn't under any circumstances forget is the life you deserve, the life that's owing to you and the life which can satisfy you as no other life can. Now go up to London, make your peace with Armstrong and slam that ring on his daughter's finger, because believe me, any other solution to your present crisis can only end in misery."

There was a long silence. I walked to the window and looked out at the garden. Then I began to roam around the room until I stopped by the brandy decanter. Removing the stopper, I poured myself another measure.

"Everything you say is absolutely right," I said at last, "and yet everything you say is absolutely wrong."

"But you must surely concede that I'm presenting a rational argument!"

"There's more to life than being rational."

"Not much more."

"I disagree. All the most profound mysteries of life are inexplicable in rational terms."

"My dear John, I hope you're not going to dive from Celtic mysticism into full-blooded Neo-Platonism!"

"God knows what I'm going to do." I drank my brandy and headed for the door. "I'll telephone you from London."

"We're parting friends?"

I had opened the door, but I abandoned it and moved back to his chair. "Yes. Friends. Always," I said, taking his hands in mine, and saw his poignant look of gratitude before he masked his feelings with a smile.

Utterly confused, thoroughly miserable and well-nigh beside myself with jealousy and rage I left him and drove to Oxmoon.

IX

"It's Mr. John, sir," said Bayliss, showing me into the library where my father was writing letters. To my relief there was no sign of Mrs. Straker.

My father looked up startled. Then he rose to greet me and we shook hands as Bayliss withdrew.

"Would you like a drink?" said my father, hospitable as ever, but he seemed relieved when I declined. No doubt I reeked of brandy.

Making a great effort to appear stone-cold sober, I said in a neutral voice, "I'm in a spot of trouble, Papa, and I've come to you for help."

"Delightful county, Cornwall, I believe," said my father, closing the blotter on his unfinished letter. "Wish I'd traveled more when I was younger, but Margaret never fancied it and we were always so busy at home."

"So Robert's been keeping you informed."

"No," said my father. "Mr. Armstrong telephoned to inquire where you were, and afterwards I telephoned your house and spoke to the children to make sure they were well. Marian said they were so pleased with all your postcards."

Unsure what to say next I sat down opposite him, and we faced each other across the writing table. My father, behaving like a model parent, made no attempt to pry or criticize but merely waited for me to confide.

"I'm supposed to be proposing to Armstrong's daughter," I said, "but after three weeks in Cornwall with another woman I don't see how I can."

"When in doubt, don't," said my father with what Robert would have described as Welsh hardheadedness and good sense.

"Yes. Quite." I was silent.

"Suppose that would put you in difficulties with Armstrong," said my father at last, helping me along.

"Not only me. Edmund."

"Edmund's old enough to fend for himself. And as far as Armstrong's concerned—"

"He's offering me such extraordinary prospects."

"Well, I've no doubt you can live with the prospects, John. But can you live with the woman?"

"Oh, she'd be a perfect wife, I'm certain of that."

"But if that's true then what were you doing in Cornwall with someone else?"

I was unable to reply. My father suddenly leaned across the table. "What good are extraordinary prospects if you can only get them by making yourself miserable?"

"I'm afraid I'd be even more miserable without them." Out of his sight, below the surface of the writing table, my fists were clenching. I stared down at them and said, "I'd give up my prospects in London tomorrow if I knew I had prospects here. But Robert tells me I have none." I raised my eyes to his. "I've come to find out whether that's true. I've got to find out, I must know—"

"I don't understand."

"Robert says he's going to use your old quarrel with him, whatever that was, to insist you leave Oxmoon to Kester. Is that true? Or is it just a story Robert's invented because he feels it's his duty to drive me back to London?"

My father's face was at once painfully fine-drawn. Several seconds passed before he was able to say: "Robert's said nothing to me."

"But would you make Kester your heir?"

"Ought to. Tradition. Eldest son to eldest son." He was now so white that his face had a grayish tinge.

"But that's rubbish. There's no entail. And there's not even a strict tradition of primogeniture. What about the eighteenth century when Robert Godwin the Renovator took over from the cousin who turned out to be an imbecile? You're under no obligation at all to leave Oxmoon to Kester!"

"But if that's what Robert wants," said my father, "then that's what Robert must have. That's only fair."

"*Not to me!*" I shouted, springing to my feet. Somehow I managed to get a grip on myself. Sinking down in my chair again I said in a level voice, "I'm sorry. Please do forgive me but the main reason I'm so distressed is because I find this quite impossible to understand. If you could only tell me what happened between you and Robert—"

"I can't," whispered my father. "I would if I could, but there are other people involved besides me and Robert, people I can't possibly betray."

I waited till I was sure I had myself well in control. Then I said, "Very well, I'll say no more." And leaving him abruptly I returned in desperation to Little Oxmoon.

X

"Do you understand, Robert?"

"Yes."

"Will you tell me?"

Silence.

"If I know," I said, "I'll be all right."

Another silence.

"You've got to tell me, Robert. You must. You owe it to me. Please—I beg of you—"

"Yes. Very well. Sit down."

I obeyed him. I was rigid with tension and so was he, but his face was expressionless and his voice was unemotional. When I was seated he said, "It concerns Ginevra," and the name he never used made his statement sound flat and impersonal. "He seduced her when she was sixteen."

Some seconds passed. I began to wonder if in my disturbed state I was hallucinating. "I'm sorry, Robert, but obviously you can't mean what you seem to be meaning. Perhaps if you could be a little more specific—"

"He fucked her."

That was certainly specific. Several more seconds trickled by. Finally I said, "I don't believe it."

"I found out in 1913 when I wanted to marry her. Naturally Mama made sure I knew the truth."

"My God. Oh my God, my God—"

"He wrecked Ginette's adolescence and in wrecking hers he wrecked mine. Of course after the seduction she was prepared to do anything to stay away from home, and so I lost her because of him—and even later when I got her back the past . . . soured everything. I wanted to forgive and forget but I never could. I used to look at him and hate him. Sometimes I still do. I came back to Gower because it suited me financially to do so, because I wanted Robin to grow up on the estate and because if one's going to spend a long time dying one may as well do it in the place one loves best, but that father of ours has been a continuing blight on the landscape. Fortunately he doesn't come here too often. He knows I prefer him to stay away."

"But Robert . . ." I searched for the words to express my revulsion, and when they eluded me I could only say in despair: "How *could* he have done such a thing?"

"Oh, he's so bloody muddled up he's capable of anything! Christ, what Mama must have suffered!"

"Don't." I covered my face with my hands. Then I said, "Right. That solves that. Of course there's nothing else that can possibly be said on the subject. Oxmoon goes to Kester to atone for what Papa did to Ginevra—and to you." I stood up to go.

"Promise me," said Robert, "promise me—"

"Oh, of course I'll never tell a soul. That goes without saying."

"—promise me you won't think any the worse of Ginette."

"How could I? For the first time I feel I've come within a thousand miles of understanding her." I stooped to cover his hands with mine and said, "I'm very grateful to you, Robert, for telling me. Forgive me for being such a bloody nuisance and putting you through hell."

All Robert said was "Make it up to me by proposing to Constance as soon as you arrive in London."

But I could not reply.

XI

I was in the library of Armstrong's house on Eaton Walk. Armstrong was shouting at me. He was a heavy man of medium height with silver hair, which gave him a look of spurious distinction, and a mouth like a steel trap. The scene was such a nightmare that I had ceased to be upset and was regarding him with detachment, as if he were a stranger who was determined to embarrass me by making an unpleasant exhibition of his bad manners.

". . . and sure I always knew you'd be the kind of guy who'd keep some woman or other on the side, but Jesus, what a way to behave, leading Constance on, leading me on and then vanishing without trace for three weeks in order to get an ex-mistress out of your system . . ."

I let him rant away for a while. When he finally paused for breath I said, "Look, sir, I still admire Constance very much but I'm in a great muddle and I speak with her best interests at heart when I say that I must have more time to consider whether or not I want to marry her."

"Your time's expired, sonny! Marry or quit! What kind of a man do you think I am? I don't let any man on earth mess me around like this and get away with it!"

"But—"

"You want more time? Okay, I'll give you more time. I'll give you ten minutes—ten minutes to remind yourself just what a mess you're proposing to make of your life if you don't wise up right away. I've got friends in this town now. I'll spread it around that you're not to be trusted, and then you'll never get another job that isn't a dead-end street. As far as Edmund goes, forget it. I can smash up that little romance if I put my mind to it, and Teddy will soon recover and fall in love with someone else. But Constance won't. Constance is a single-minded, serious girl who's one hundred percent devoted to you, and that's why if you jilt her now I'm going to blast you off the map—and don't think I'd be weak and sentimental just because I've been thinking of you as a son! The truth is I can only go on thinking of you as a son now if you marry my daughter, so make up your mind: do you want to be a success in the only way that matters a damn in this world or do you want to be washed up and plowed under before the year's out? Okay, let me leave you to think about that." He took out his watch, synchronized it with the clock on the chimneypiece and said, "You've got ten minutes starting from now."

XII

"Here I have my standards," said my mother, "and here I draw the line."

I thought: I'll be all right if I draw the line.

But I wasn't sure what line I was supposed to draw or where I was supposed to draw it. My head was throbbing. It was hard to think coherently. I felt as if I were on the brink of madness—but of course I wouldn't go mad, couldn't, because I'd draw the line and keep myself sane.

"You'll play your cards better than I ever have," said my father. "I know you will. I know it."

I shuddered as I remembered how my father had played his cards. No drawn lines there. I thought of him seducing Ginevra—I thought of blighted lives, of good people suffering—and suddenly as I heard my grandmother screaming and my father shouting about the wages of sin, the past smashed its way into the present again and tore my mind apart with glimpse after glimpse into hell.

Chaos, anarchy, madness and death—looking down at the cards in my hand I asked myself only how I could play them and survive.

Oxmoon had gone, I saw that at once. Oxmoon, Wales, a country life—all those cards had been wiped from the pack, and when I looked at the cards which remained I saw LONDON written on them all. Then I tried to imagine Bronwen in London but the possibility was unimaginable. She would be like a lark penned up in a cage. I pictured her cut off from her country, severed from her culture, blaming me for her misery, wishing we had never met. And was I seriously proposing to keep her in London as my mistress while I married Constance to secure my future? Not only was the idea ludicrous— Bronwen would never have debased herself in such a fashion—but it was also unworkable. If I had Bronwen in my life there would be no room for Constance. The marriage would be a sham which I would never be able to sustain.

Bronwen and Constance were both present in the hand of cards that I had been dealt and one of them would have to be discarded, I could see that, just as I could see that I favored discarding Constance, but if I discarded Constance I discarded London and this was a move I knew I could no longer make. I had to retain London. How else could I compensate myself for what had happened? Robert had said the life Armstrong was offering was the life that was owing to me, and now of course, having lost Oxmoon forever, I could so clearly see that he was right.

It was time to be honest with myself. To marry out of one's class was one of the quickest roads to marital misery available. I could instead keep

Bronwen discreetly as my mistress, but what sort of life would that be for her? The truth was that I would crucify her if I did marry her and crucify her if I didn't—and whether or not we were married, I'd crucify myself by terminating all my prospects in London. Bronwen was the most exceptional woman and I loved her but how could I choose any course of action that would ruin us both? To pursue a grand passion without regard for the consequences was the road to self-destruction and catastrophe, that was the truth of it—and that was the truth my grandmother had never been able to face.

But I was facing it. I was on the rack but I was facing it. I felt as if I were being beaten and brutalized, but I was facing it.

I drew the line.

XIII

That night I wrote to Bronwen. My final draft was completed at dawn.

I spent a long time trying to decide how to begin the letter. Any endearment, Welsh or English, seemed too cruel in view of what I had to say so in the end I merely plunged into the first sentence without addressing her. I wrote in English: *I can't think how to begin this except to tell you that I love you, but that will only seem a mockery when I tell you also, as I must, that I can't see you again. I know this will make you unhappy but all I can say is that if I continued to see you I would make you very much unhappier. I'm deeply sorry and wish I could undo all the unhappiness. I see now I was wrong to take you to Cornwall, wrong to treat you so selfishly and wrong to pretend we could have any kind of future together. I loved you so much I couldn't help myself. But it was wrong.*

I'm now doing what I believe is right and committing myself to my life in London. You'll realize what this means, so I shan't explain further. I don't ask you to understand and I certainly don't expect you to forgive me, so there's no need for you to reply to this letter, but I had to tell you my decision before you heard of it from someone else. I shouldn't close by telling you I love you but in fact that's all I have left to say.

I signed the letter JOHN to match both the English words on the paper and my decision to be an Englishman, and posted the letter at once before I could change my mind.

I did wonder if she would reply, despite my assurance that no reply was necessary, but she never wrote. Later when word reached me that she had returned to Cardiff I sent a check to the Home Farm to be forwarded, but the check found its way back, torn in two, and there was no covering letter.

My father wrote to me as soon as the engagement was announced. He usually wrote brief colloquial letters which said nothing of importance, but this time he had taken trouble. When I pictured him laboring over several drafts, as he undoubtedly had, and looking up every trying example of English spelling in the dictionary, I was touched—or at least in other circumstances I would have been touched. However after Robert's revelations I felt so angry that I could barely bring myself to open the envelope.

My dear John, my father had written. *Allow me to congratulate you on your engagement. I am delighted that you should be on the threshold of yet another match which by worldly standards must undoubtedly be judged as splendid. I have heard nothing but good of Miss Armstrong and I hope it will not be long before I can come up to town and have the honor of meeting her.*

However, mindful of your recent confidences to me on the subject of your future, I feel I must add that I have been very worried about you and that my worries are by no means allayed by your good news. I trust you are quite certain that you wish to marry this girl, because if you have any remaining doubts I would most strongly counsel you against marriage. It is the greatest possible mistake to marry in pursuit of worldly ambition alone—as my mother did. Perhaps you might be comforting yourself with the thought that I too married for worldly reasons, and indeed I did marry for money, but I liked your mother so much even before I began to love her. She was so jolly and sensible and I liked the way she made me laugh. Do you like Miss Armstrong? Love can come later but liking won't. And does she make you laugh? Marriage is often so difficult that one needs to laugh every now and then.

Please do not take offense at this letter. I am well aware that you are a mature man of thirty-one, and if you have no doubts about your decision I have absolute confidence that it is the right one. I remain ever your most devoted and affectionate father, R.G.

I thought of him putting my mother through hell by his abuse of Ginevra and setting in motion the chain of events that had deprived me of Oxmoon. In my opinion he was quite unfit to lecture anyone on the necessary ingredients of a happy marriage, and I tore up his letter without rereading it.

Just before the wedding Robert said uneasily, "Are you still in touch with Mrs. Morgan?"

"Good God, no," I said. "That's all over and I'm completely recovered."

I knew as I spoke that the words formed the biggest lie of my life, but I knew too that it was quite impossible for me to acknowledge it. My future, the future I had to have in order to be at peace with myself, depended on my ability to forget Bronwen, so I fought against her memory with every ounce of willpower I possessed and day by day, as I battled successfully against the truth, I moved deeper and deeper into my disastrous lie.

XIV

Armstrong gave his daughters a sumptuous double wedding on a mild sunny day in December at St. George's, Hanover Square. It was one of the biggest Society weddings of the year, and after the service the reception for five hundred at Claridges set the seal on the day's perfection. Guest after guest said what a romantic occasion it was, two ideal weddings between two ideal young couples with all parties blissfully in love.

"This is the most wonderful thing that's ever happened to me," confided Edmund misty-eyed over the champagne, and he was right: it was. I shook his hand and said how happy I was for him. Overshadowed by his brothers, brutalized by the war, bludgeoned for so many sad years by his melancholy, Edmund at the age of twenty-nine had emerged into the light of a dazzling good fortune. Falling in love had made him vivacious. He sparkled. He made Lion-like "naughty" remarks. Straight-backed, bright-eyed, glowing with health and happiness, he told me I was the best brother a man ever had and he would never forget all I had done for him.

". . . and I'll be grateful to you till my dying day, and I only hope you'll be as happy with Constance as I shall be with my wonderful, my divine, my celestial—"

"Isn't he gorgeous?" demanded Teddy, appearing from nowhere to gaze up at him in adoration.

I looked around for Constance but she was on the other side of the room. I felt tired. Acting is an exhausting profession and that day had required a gala performance. It was then that I realized how tired I was going to be in the future. I had told myself that everything would be well after the wedding; I had argued that once the deed was done and no further possibility of escape existed I would be able to relax, accept my situation and enjoy married life for I had become fond of Constance, fond enough to convince myself that I would love her once the strain of the engagement had given way to the relief of matrimony. But now at the reception it occurred to me that matrimony was not going to bring relief. The ordeal was going to go on but with the difference that escape was no longer possible. A door had been locked and I was trapped irrevocably behind it.

"Is everything all right, darling?" said Constance as we set off on our honeymoon to Paris and the Riviera.

"Everything's wonderful!" I said, kissing her warmly.

This was easier. This was a familiar role. I had traveled this road before. In fact so strong was the impression of the past repeating itself that it gave me a shock whenever Constance reminded me how different she was from Blanche. The reminders came with increasing frequency.

"Now, John, I don't want to be like some boring Victorian maiden—I want to be modern and enlightened, because I believe sex is healthy and right and I want to enjoy it and make you happy . . ."

The curious part was that as our lavish glamorous honeymoon progressed, I thought more and more of Blanche on our quiet little wartime honeymoon in Suffolk. Constance and I stayed at the most luxurious French hotels, but in my memory I was at the little inn in medieval Lavenham and Blanche was once more at my side.

On our first morning in Monte Carlo we breakfasted in our suite, and afterwards when the obligatory two dozen red roses had arrived in response to my order, Constance spent some time attending to them with her usual meticulous skill. She was full of theories about how flowers should look, but as I watched her I thought of Blanche, arranging flowers not with mathematical precision but with spontaneity and an unfailing eye for beauty.

"Darling, this is so romantic!" said Constance as the champagne arrived at noon, but in my memory Blanche and I were lunching at our country inn and Blanche was saying how fond she was of a glass of stone-ginger.

"Oh, they're playing 'The Blue Danube' again!" said Constance carelessly as we drank tea in the early evening. "What a bore—I think Strauss is so hackneyed!" And at once in my mind Blanche was playing "The Blue Danube" for Robert and Ginevra. It was their special tune.

"Darling, is anything the matter? You seem a little quiet."

"I'm merely savoring the glamour and the romance!" I said smiling, and suddenly I longed for someone gentle who never pestered me with questions, someone who knew when to be silent, someone who was sensitive and undemanding.

"You do love me, don't you, John?"

"You know I do!" I protested, and thought: I would have loved Blanche better now. Then I had a moment of sadness so deep that I feared Constance would notice, so to divert her I suggested we went shopping on the morrow. Constance loved shopping. The next morning I bought her a gold bracelet and the purchase made us both feel better; she stopped asking me if I loved her, and in the effort of pleasing her I stopped thinking about Blanche.

Later when we were back in England I was surprised to remember how Blanche had haunted me, but I knew why I had retreated into my first marriage. It was less painful to remember Blanche at Lavenham than Bronwen in Cornwall. In fact, I was unable to think of Bronwen. I was too frightened of where my thoughts might lead.

When we arrived home at the end of January, my father-in-law handed us the title deeds of our new mansion in Surrey, and presently we went down to Dorking to see it again. Built in the eighteenth century it was an architecturally superior Anglo-Saxon version of Oxmoon, and Constance declared with enthusiasm that after the necessary renovations by the right interior decorators it would be perfect for house parties. I walked through the empty rooms, which were devoid of all the memories that made Oxmoon precious to me, and said what a wonderful wedding present it was and how fortunate we were.

Constance had decided that my Kensington house was not smart enough for the home she had in mind, so we began our married life at a much larger house in Chester Square, not far from Eaton Walk. My father-in-law liked this because it meant he could call on us all the time, and Constance, who loved her father and perhaps loved him the more because she had never been the favorite daughter, basked in this constant paternal attention. I kept my thoughts on the subject to myself, but I found that Armstrong's brash personality, which I had once judged so refreshing, was becoming increasingly abrasive once it began to flood my private life. Fortunately we had a respite whenever he took himself off to visit Edmund and Teddy in their *pied-à-terre* in Chester Mews, but Edmund and Teddy were often absent from town. Shrewdly gauging Edmund's capabilities Armstrong had appointed him to run his estate in Kent, but as there was a manager in charge of the farms Edmund was not overworked. Armstrong himself used the Queen Anne mansion on weekends, but Edmund and Teddy were allocated the Regency dower house with its fine views over the Weald, and as far as Edmund was concerned he had been allocated paradise. I became weary of him telling me what bliss he was experiencing, and wearier still when Constance's demanding exuberance continued unabated.

"John, we must plan our trip to the States—Mother says she'll make sure we have a wonderful time. . . ."

Mrs. Armstrong, somehow conquering her nervous disorders, had crossed the Atlantic for her daughters' wedding and had spent much time being hysterical because they were settling down three thousand miles away from her. I had found her so tedious that I now searched for an excuse to postpone my American visit, but as matters turned out I hardly had to search hard. The excuse soon presented itself.

"Darling, there's something I want to tell you. . . . Oh, sweetheart, I think—I'm almost sure . . ."

She was pregnant. So was Teddy. Edmund was demented with delight. I managed to find the appropriate words to express pleasure and pride, but I barely heard myself utter them; I was too busy listening to the slam of the steel door as I found myself locked up in my new windowless cell.

"John, you *are* pleased, aren't you?"

Still I had to endure this quest for reassurance.

"John, you do love me, don't you?"

Still the futile questions droned on and on.

"John, I've asked the doctor and he says we can go on having sex for the time being . . ."

Constance liked sex and, just as I had anticipated, she was good at it. In fact my original estimate of her had proved accurate in every respect. She was an excellent wife. Although she was young she had just the right degree of authority with the servants; she was a first-class hostess, a splendid organizer of our social calendar and a superb administrator of my home. She took a conscientious and devoted interest in my children, and I had no doubt she would make a conscientious and devoted mother. She was already studying the subject of babies and working out how the perfect infant could be, as she put it in her American fashion, "raised."

". . . and the husband mustn't be overlooked—all the books say how important that is, darling, so you mustn't think I shall ever neglect you."

"My dear, after your ceaseless attentions during the past months I'm sure I could survive a little benign neglect!"

"What do you mean?" She was at once deeply wounded.

"Nothing. It was a joke, Constance, just a joke."

"I don't see it."

"No." I had married a girl who had no sense of humor. I could not imagine how I had once regarded her lack of humor as a charming seriousness, and in a terrible moment of truth I saw that although I respected her many excellent qualities, I was never going to love her and would often dislike her very much. That was when I first asked myself not how difficult it would be for me to sustain my marriage but how much longer I could continue with it. At first I thought marital breakdown would begin in the bedroom but ironically that was the one place where the marriage continued to flourish, the one place where Constance could be guaranteed to keep her mouth shut and I could be guaranteed the opportunity to do exactly as I liked. In the end the bedroom offered me my only compensation for my disastrous mistake but even there, as the months passed, my time ran out. Constance's pregnancy began to show. She was in good health but naturally I had to be careful, and this small attempt at restraint proved almost too much for me to bear. I found too that the visible signs of her pregnancy made me feel guilty. I felt guilty that I had fathered a child I did not want, guilty that I could not give Constance the love any pregnant woman needs and deserves, and guilty above all that I had wronged her by marrying her, by dragging her out onto the stage with me as I acted out my lies.

My marriage ended in the May of 1924, five months after our wedding day. I was breakfasting with Constance by the window of our bedroom, and outside the spring sunlight was shining on the new leaves of the trees in the square. My chauffeur was not due to bring the Rolls to the front door for another ten minutes, and I was just studying *The Times* before going to the nursery to have a word with the children. I remember that I had finished the cricket report and was steeling myself to face the parliamentary columns. The new Labour government had been horrifying and enthralling the country ever since they had failed to wear court dress at Buckingham Palace.

The butler entered the room and handed the morning's post to Constance.

She was wearing an emerald-green negligée which looked striking with her dark hair, and she had been reading the latest copy of *The Tatler*. On the table between us amidst the Royal Worcester breakfast set, two orchids wilted languidly in an exquisite silver vase.

"Here's a letter from Oxmoon," said Constance, sifting diligently through the post as usual in order that I might not be bothered by correspondence which would unnecessarily consume my time. She passed me the envelope bearing my father's handwriting. "We ought to go down there again soon, John—shall I arrange for the Manor to be prepared for us at the end of the month? I think we could fit in a weekend there before the Derby."

But I had now reached the stage where I was afraid to see those closest to me for fear I might break down and tell them the truth. Abandoning my newspaper I rose to my feet to make my escape and murmured, "But I have to go to Birmingham at the end of the month." Since my marriage I had been thrust deep into the dreariness of the Armstrong Canning Corporation.

"You surely don't have to go on a weekend, darling! Now, let me see: is there anything else here that you should look at before you go? Bills, receipts, invitations . . . oh, and what's this? Swansea postmark, cheap paper, probably a begging letter . . . Oh, my! It's in Welsh! Here, darling, for once I can't cope—over to you."

I had been halfway to the door. I looked back. Always I can remember looking back at the orchids dying in their silver vase while the spring sun shone beyond them on the brilliant green leaves of the square.

Returning to the table, I took the letter from her without a word.

Dear Mr. Godwin, Myfanwy Meredith had written on lined paper in a clear script. *I think you should do something about my sister. She'll never ask for help so I must. I write not to make trouble but because I believe you wouldn't want her to suffer. Please may I see you to explain?*

An hour later I was aboard the train to Swansea.

8

I

I SAW the pram immediately. It was parked in the shade of the tree that stood in front of the farmhouse. I had walked the short distance from the Manor but now I broke into a run. The sun shone sporadically from a sky dotted with small white clouds, and beyond the cart track the front meadow was gay with buttercups and clover.

The perambulator was little better than a wooden crate on wheels, but it had been painted a smart navy-blue and cleverly lined inside with white cotton. Beneath a blanket embroidered with yellow ducks the baby lay fast asleep. It had some fairish down on top of its head and very small, very new features. When I lifted the blanket, I found that the nappy was damp. Pulling the cloth to one side, I saw I had a son.

A light breeze fanned the delicate skin I had exposed, and he awoke. I rearranged him beneath the blanket, but he was inconsolable, and hardly knowing what I was doing, I picked him up. He whimpered against my chest. Twenty yards away the front door of the house slammed. As I looked up, rigid with misery, Bronwen stopped, rigid with anger, and we stared dumbly at each other for one long moment of all-consuming despair.

The baby began to cry again.

"Hush, Evan." She rushed forward, scooped him out of my arms and hugged him tightly. "Who told you?" she demanded, not looking at me. Her voice shook as she turned away. "Was it Huw? Was it Myfanwy? Was it some old gossip in the village? I thought no one doubted he was Gareth's—I didn't think anyone remembered exactly when Gareth died—" She broke off as the baby, sensing her distress, began to cry more loudly. "Shhh . . . there's a good boy . . . shhh." Her hair was loose, and as she bent her head over him, a long strand tickled his cheek. He stopped crying and peered at her. He was too young to smile, but I saw him focus his eyes as he gazed upward. Hugging him again she rocked him gently in her arms.

"Your sister wrote."

"How dare she! I'll never forgive her, never!"

"But why didn't you want me to be told?"

"Because I knew," she said, tears streaming down her face, "that we ought never to meet again."

We stood there side by side. Eventually she wiped her eyes with the back of her hand and said in a flat voice, "He's very wet. I must take him indoors to be changed."

Automatically I followed her but she turned on me in a rage. "Go away! I don't want your pity or your charity! Go back to your wife!"

"Never."

That silenced her. It silenced me. As her eyes filled with tears, I took her in my arms.

After a time she whispered, "You mustn't lie to me anymore. It's cruel. When you wrote and said Cornwall was wrong and marrying a girl you didn't love was right—"

"I'll get a divorce."

"Oh, damn you, what good would that do!" she shouted. "You'd only leave me later when you found another woman of your own class who suits you better than I ever could!"

"I'm never leaving you again."

That settled that. My arms tightened around her, she raised her tear-stained face to mine and the poor baby had to endure being crushed so hard between us that he screamed with rage. In consternation we sprang apart, and then as the sun blazed down upon us all our misery dissolved and once more we were smiling into each other's eyes.

II

It was late in the afternoon. The children were home from the village school but out playing somewhere in the fields. From the kitchen came the sound of Myfanwy's voice as she talked to a visiting neighbor, but after entering the house through the front door we avoided them by going straight upstairs to the room that Bronwen shared with the baby.

"I can't be with you yet," said Bronwen simply. "It's too soon after the birth."

"I understand. When was he born?"

We began to talk. I sat on the bed as she changed the nappy, and then she lay on the bed in my arms while she fed him. She told me that when she returned to Cardiff she had found domestic work again but had been dismissed by her employer when the pregnancy became obvious, and although she had tried to go on working she had begun to suffer from anemia, a misfortune that had made her afraid for the baby's health. Finally, unable to pay anything to her in-laws for her room and board, she had been obliged to return to the Merediths. Both of them had been horrified by her condition but had taken her in without hesitation.

"But I knew I couldn't go on living on their charity," said Bronwen, "and besides I was too afraid of you finding out, so I told Myfanwy I'd emigrate to Vancouver where we have cousins who would have lent me the fare. I suppose that was what drove her to write to you. She wanted you to pay for me to stay in Wales."

I told her that at some remote time in the future when we had been married so long that we had nothing better to do, I would take her on a visit to her Canadian cousins, and we laughed together. Meanwhile the baby had finished his feed and had to be held up and patted and encouraged to perform the rituals of digestion. As I stroked the down on the top of his head, I said abruptly, "You should have said something in Cornwall about the possibility of this happening. I assumed you couldn't have any more children."

"Why?"

I explained.

"Oh, I see," she said. "But Gareth was too drunk most of the time to be a husband to me." She wiped the baby's mouth carefully and smiled at him as if to negate the unhappy memories. Then a thought struck her. She looked up frightened. "Are you angry about the baby?"

"Of course I'm angry—but not with you or with him. I'm angry with myself for ignoring my responsibilities in Cornwall and leaving you alone to pay the price."

"That's silly," she said. "It takes two to make a baby. If I hadn't wanted him I would have said something."

I was interested to discover that I had not after all underestimated her practical streak. We discussed contraception idly for a time. Among the working classes, I learned, birth control consisted of *coitus interruptus*, sodomy and old wives' tales, although since the war French letters had provided a welcome relief for those who could afford them. Bronwen referred to sodomy as "what they did in the Bible," and as I laughed at this contraceptive vision which would have appalled all fundamentalists, she laughed with me. I tried to remember when I had last felt so happy and that was when I realized how miserable I had been ever since our holiday in Cornwall.

"But we'll both be happy again now," I said. "We'll live very quietly at the Manor—I'll engage a housekeeper so that you won't have to deal with the servants, and we needn't entertain so you won't have to meet a stream of people who would make you feel shy."

"I don't want to cut you off from—"

"I want to be cut off. My life requires surgery on the grand scale."

"But what about your father? Supposing he becomes angry and decides not to leave you Oxmoon?"

"Ah," I said. "It turned out that I wasn't destined for Oxmoon after all. But I don't care. Not anymore."

"You mean—"

"You were right. Love's the compensation I've always needed, and so long as I have you I know I can escape from the past and be free."

III

"But he's not free!" said Myfanwy to her sister. She was so stupefied by our news that she spoke in Welsh, forgetting I could understand her.

"He's going to get divorced."

"But you can't possibly marry him!" She was appalled. Her plump friendly little face was white and hostile. "How would you manage? He can't mean it! He's just making another of his false promises!"

"Oh no I'm not," I said.

Her hands flew to her mouth in the classic gesture of dismay. "Forgive me, sir, I quite forgot you'd know what I was saying—"

"I promise you I'll look after Bronwen now."

"But your wife . . ." She swung back to face her sister. "You can't have forgotten what's being said in the village. Both those American ladies are having babies in the autumn, both of them. How could you think of taking a man away from his pregnant wife? How could you think of building your happiness on someone else's misery?"

"Well, what about *my* misery?" screamed Bronwen, losing her temper. "And what about *my* baby?"

"You're not his wife, are you! You're just the girl who's fool enough to give him what he wants when he wants it!"

"I'm the girl who loves him and I'm the girl he loves and all else is falseness and wrong—for him, for me and for the American lady too! I shan't feel sorry for her having a deserting husband, indeed I shan't, no, not one bit, he'll be doing her a kindness by divorcing her—oh, I know all about the torture of being married to a husband who doesn't care so how dare you say he should stay chained to a loveless marriage for her sake, how dare you!"

There was a silence while Myfanwy passed the back of her hand across her forehead and leaned for support against the kitchen table, but at last she said unsteadily, "I'm sorry, Mr. Godwin, I mean no disrespect, but I'm just so worried about my sister."

"I understand. But I swear I'll put everything right."

"How can you?" she said in despair. "She'll never fit into your world—how can you bring her anything but misery?" And sinking down on the nearest chair, she covered her face with her hands and began to weep.

IV

"Well, John," said Robert, "what can I say? I've never before suffered from speechlessness, but this time I confess that the hitherto unimaginable has occurred and I'm at a loss for words. Let me try and collect my shattered thoughts. What should one brother say to another in such a truly catastrophic situation?"

" 'Good luck' would be a useful start."

"*Good luck?* My dear John, you're going to need far more than that to guarantee your survival! You're going to need the heroism of St. George, the hide of an elephant and the constitution of an ox—oh, and how about your fairy godmother, complete with magic wand? Since we're dealing with fantasy we may as well admit a little magical support to keep your dreams bowling merrily along, but may I be unbearably prosaic and ask how you're going to break the news to Papa? That would seem to be your most immediate problem."

"I was hoping you'd help me."

"My worst fears are now confirmed. Go on."

"I've been in rather a muddle about Papa for some time, and I'm afraid that if I break the news to him we'll generate some emotional scene which will only make the muddle worse. But you're so cool and levelheaded, Robert, and—"

"You want me to reduce Papa to order for you. John, you must surely realize you're asking the impossible; a raging love affair with a Welsh peasant is not a subject on which we can expect our father to be rational."

"But if you stress I'm going to marry her—"

"He'll be appalled, just like everyone else. The only way he could ever accept Mrs. Morgan's presence in your life would be if you were to keep her tucked discreetly away in Swansea."

"But if you could explain to him that Bronwen's good, decent and honest —and utterly different from that bloody villain Bryn-Davies—"

"Has it ever occurred to you," said Robert, "that we've only heard one highly prejudiced version of that story? It's quite possible that Grandmama too saw her lover as someone who was good, decent and honest."

"Oh, bloody hell, let's forget all that, I don't care about those horrors anymore, I've escaped from the past—"

"We never escape from the past," said Robert. "It's the biggest jail of all time. Very well, I'll tell Papa that although you're behaving like a lunatic, you're not automatically destined for incarceration in the Home of the Assumption. What else can I possibly say? Ah, here's Ginette. Come in, my dear, and mix yourself a very large pink gin. What do you think's happened? No, don't even try and guess—I'll tell you. John's leaving Constance and going to live at Penhale Manor with Mrs. Morgan and their new illegitimate infant. Intriguing, isn't it? Maybe country life's not so dull after all! Oh, and by the way, I nearly forgot to tell you—he's going to marry her once he can get his hands on a divorce."

Ginevra, who was wearing a tubelike navy dress with a very short skirt, stopped dead to gape at me. Her full feminine figure was so unsuited to the boyish style of her clothes that she was looking not only raffish but bizarre. I remembered the nightmare of her adolescence and tried to make allowances for her, but I was on the defensive by that time, and all my old antipathy towards her was rising to the surface of my mind. I knew she had never liked me. I knew she still privately judged me a prig, and I thought how entertained she would be to see me fall from grace. I pictured her savoring my discomfort behind my back and gossiping about me in amusement with her smart friends in London.

"Robert, you're joking. I don't believe a word of it."

"Don't worry," I said abruptly before Robert could reply. "I'm fully expecting you to share his view that this is a disaster of the highest order."

"Disaster?" said Ginevra. Then she laughed and cried, "Rubbish! I think it's absolutely wonderful and quite the most romantic thing I've ever heard in my life!" And she stretched out her hands to me—Ginevra whom I had always distrusted, Ginevra whom I had never liked—and as she kissed me on both cheeks she exclaimed with a sincerity I never forgot, "Darling Johnny, I didn't know you had it in you! Congratulations—well done—I'm with you all the way!"

V

"You're insane," said Constance dry-eyed, and set her mouth in a hard unyielding line.

"I'm sorry. I know this is an appalling shock for you, but I can't go on with this lie any longer."

"But you love me—you like me in bed, I know you do!"

"Constance—"

"What does she do that I don't? Whatever it is I can learn it."

"Constance, this has nothing to do with sex."

"What! *Nothing to do with sex?* Who do you think you're fooling!"

"Look, I know this is terrible for you. I know it is. And don't think it isn't terrible for me too. I feel riddled with guilt just standing here talking to you —guilty that I married you, guilty that I let you get pregnant, guilty, guilty

guilty, but I can't help it, Constance, I've got to leave and I think that once you've recovered from the shock you'll be glad—you'll realize, once I'm gone, that I could never have made you happy."

"You could. You have."

"But I've been acting, can't you see? I've been acting all the time—you've never known me as I really am! You're in love with someone who doesn't exist!"

"Sure you exist. You're tall, dark and handsome and wonderful in bed."

"What the devil's that got to do with what I'm talking about? A man's soul isn't located in his genitals!"

"Well, as far as you're concerned it's obviously no more than an inch away! Anyway, Freud says—"

"No, don't let's start on Freud. Freud's the biggest piece of intellectual claptrap you've ever bored me with, and my God, that's saying something!"

"Okay, I'll stick to the point. I love you. I want you to stay with me."

"Well, I suppose it's only natural that you should say that now when you're so shocked, but later the situation is bound to seem different to you. You'll meet someone else. You're clever and attractive, and I'm quite sure that in no time at all you'll have at least half a dozen suitors."

"I'm not interested in anyone else but you."

"All right. You're not interested. Not now. But later, when you've got the divorce—"

"What divorce?" said Constance, annihilating me.

VI

"Take it easy, sweetheart," said Armstrong as Constance finally broke down and wept against his chest. "That's my brave little girl—no divorce, no surrender. I'm very, very proud of you. Okay, now just you leave this to me. Run along to your room and dry your eyes and I'll be up to see you shortly."

Constance, who had indeed been very brave, now proved her courage afresh by controlling her tears and walking out of the room with her head held high. By this time I was feeling ill.

"You goddamned bastard," said Armstrong as soon as the door closed. "I'll see you goddamned ruined unless you pull yourself together in double-quick time."

"Go ahead. I don't give a damn."

Much shouting and abuse followed. Finally I tried to walk out but he grabbed me by the arm and shouted, "Okay, just you tell me this: how the fucking hell are you going to live with your conscience?"

"How the fucking hell are you going to live with yours? You flogged me into this mess! I accept that I've played the major role in the disaster, but don't try and pretend you haven't led a full supporting cast!"

He tried to hit me but I sidestepped him. He was just a fat stupid man on the far side of middle age. I walked out of the room but he blundered after me, and as I left the house I heard him shouting at the top of his voice that I was a cheater, a four-flusher and a goddamned son of a bitch.

VII

"Daphne?" I said rapidly to Lion's widow from the telephone kiosk at my nearest club. "Thank God, I wasn't sure whether you were in town. Has Ginevra been in touch with you?"

"Rather!" said Daphne, who was by no means as ingenuous as her hearty manner suggested. "My dear, I'm simply reeling! What can I do to help? Ginevra said you were worried stiff about the children."

I explained that Penhale Manor had been running on a skeleton staff since Edmund's departure for Kent, and this meant that I was unable to retire there immediately with two children, a nanny and a governess.

". . . and so I was wondering if—"

"Say no more. Toss them all over here to Cadogan Place—Elizabeth'll be thrilled! How soon can they come?"

I felt ready to collapse with relief. "Tomorrow morning?"

"Bring them tonight, if you like."

"No, that's very good of you, Daphne, and I can't thank you enough, but . . . well, I have to prepare the children for this and I'll need a little time to explain . . ."

VIII

"But Papa," said Marian, "how can you marry someone who's not a lady? In fact is such a thing even allowed? I seem to remember Nanny saying there's a law against it."

"No, there's no law against it, Marian. Mrs. Morgan's the woman I love, and love matters more than class."

"That's not what Nanny thinks," said Marian. "Nanny thinks nothing matters more than class, and I'll tell you this, Papa: Nanny will be *most put out* if we have to leave London, because how am I ever going to mix with girls of my own class in a provincial place like Wales? Nanny," said Marian, regarding me with baleful blue eyes, "will say it doesn't suit."

Nanny would have to go. A long vista of domestic difficulties stretched in front of me but I kept my face impassive. "I'll have a word with Nanny, Marian," I said.

"Yes, I think you'd better. And I warn you, Papa, she'll be terribly shocked that you and Mrs. Morgan have had a baby without being married, because Nanny believes babies don't happen unless there's a wedding first. By the way, will the baby be common like Mrs. Morgan or will he be a gentleman like you?"

Before I could reply to this question, which only a sociologist would have welcomed, Harry looked up from dismantling his best toy train and said sharply, "I don't think I want a brother, thank you very much."

"But brothers are fun, Harry! And think what fun it'll be to live at the Manor again!"

I saw his dark eyes, so like his mother's, glow with the animation her eyes had always lacked. Forgetting the engine in his hands he gazed enthralled at me. "Is there still a piano in the drawing room?"

"Silly baby," said Marian, "why should he have sold it since we were last there for a visit? Papa, I'm still worried about this. I realize you and Constance have to get unmarried and I don't mind that much, but I do wish you didn't have to marry Mrs. Morgan. Will there be any risk of me growing up common now? Because if there is—"

"The commonest thing you can do, Marian," I said strongly, "is to continue to talk in this vulgar fashion. Class is something true ladies never discuss."

Marian burst into tears and the next moment Nanny herself was bustling into the room to the rescue.

"There, there, my precious, my angel—"

Marian hurtled sobbing into her arms. "Oh Nanny, Papa's leaving Constance and marrying Mrs. Morgan and they already have a new baby even though they're not married and I'm so afraid of growing up common and Papa doesn't understand and he's being simply horrid to me . . ."

More terrible vistas opened up into the future. As Nanny became scarlet in the face with startling rapidity, I dredged up the dregs of my strength and once more prepared for battle.

IX

"What beats me," said Edmund that evening at Brooks's, "is how you can do this to your children—and I don't just mean Harry and Marian, although God knows how they'll turn out if you live openly with your working-class mistress. What about Constance's child? How are you going to face it in future when you walked out on it before it was born? No, I'm sorry but I think this decision of yours is absolutely disgusting and your behavior makes me sick."

"Edmund—"

"How could you be such a fool? I mean, I'm a jolly broad-minded chap, and God knows if I had your looks I'd be rolling in the hay with everything in sight, but at least even *I'd* have the brains to keep that sort of woman in the hay where she belongs. Why the devil can't you just keep her quietly somewhere and visit her now and then like any other decent civilized fellow?"

"Edmund, I don't want to quarrel. I know that in the circumstances this couldn't be more awkward for you, but please try and accept that there's nothing else I can do."

"No, I bloody well can't accept it! Can't you at least stay with poor Constance until after the baby's born?"

"It would be pointless. What sort of an atmosphere do you think there'd be if I stayed on now? It would be unendurable for us both, you must see that!"

"Well, don't expect me to stay on speaking terms with you. I've got my own wife to think about, and I don't want her to be more upset than she is already."

"I understand. But I hope later you'll feel differently."

"Good God, you don't think Teddy or I would ever receive that woman, do you?"

"I certainly hope that when she's my wife—"

"She'll never be your wife, John! I don't know why you keep behaving as if Constance doesn't mean what she says about a divorce!"

"She means it at the moment. But she's bound to change her mind."

"Don't you believe it! Hell hath no fury and all that. She'll hang on. And meanwhile you'll be in the biggest possible mess. Christ, how can you conceivably explain to those two children that you plan to live in sin with a woman who's barely fit to be their nursemaid?"

"That needn't concern you," I said, and walked out on him without another word.

X

"I told Papa," said Robert when I telephoned him later.

"What was the reaction?"

"Unmitigated horror. You'd better come down here first thing tomorrow morning, John."

"I can't! The children are safe with Daphne but I've got appointments with accountants and lawyers and bank managers—"

"They can wait. Papa can't. I mean that, John. I can't say any more on the telephone, but get that train tomorrow because I've got to talk to you without delay."

XI

The next morning I caught the earliest train to South Wales, and some hours later I was traveling around the great curve of Swansea Bay. The industrial approaches to the city seemed as grotesque as ever, but a stillness had fallen since the war on that ravaged landscape and the numbness of despair was paralyzing its people. Mining was a depressed industry. Brave buoyant Welsh Swansea, bunched on its hills above the sea, was limp with the dole queues and sodden with the misery of the unemployed.

I stepped off the train in my Savile Row suit, a visitor from a world those unemployed millions would never know, and found my caretaker waiting, his cap respectfully in his hand as if to exacerbate my guilt that I should be privileged. To negate it I reminded myself of the world I was rejecting, and as we drove beyond the outskirts of the city I thought of all the moneyed people I knew, dancing and drinking themselves to distraction to distance themselves from the war and its aftermath—and then it seemed to me that their lives were so far removed from reality that I wondered how I could ever have shared their futile illusions created by the two-faced glamour of affluence. We drove on into Gower, and when I saw the sunlit fields and the secret valleys and the sparkling sea flashing in the distance, I felt as if I were recovering from some illness which had nearly proved fatal.

At Little Oxmoon, I told my caretaker to drive on to the Manor with my luggage and then I joined Robert in the drawing room.

"Do you want a drink?" said Robert. "Or some food? There's a cold buffet laid out in the dining room."

"I don't think I could eat and I'm quite sure I shouldn't drink. Tell me the worst."

"I went to see him yesterday morning and said my piece, but he couldn't take it in—or, to be accurate, he took it in but couldn't face up to it. He became disconnected with reality again."

"Oh *God*. Robert, I think I will have a drink after all."

"A wise decision. Help yourself. You haven't heard the worst part yet. When it became obvious that I wasn't going to get a word of sense out of him, I yielded to the inevitable and summoned Straker. She was so competent that my suspicions were aroused. I thought to myself, Hullo, she's been here before, so after she'd led him off to rest I summoned Bayliss and cross-questioned him till he broke down, poor loyal old man, and confessed that the only reason why he was continuing to endure Straker's dictatorship was because he was so worried about 'The Master' that he couldn't bear to leave him. He hadn't planned to confide in me, since I was ill, but he had planned to write to you if things got worse—which they now have. In other words, John—"

"Papa's been deteriorating for some time but Straker's hushed it up."

"Exactly. And you can see why. If Papa has a complete mental breakdown we have a legitimate excuse to interfere in his affairs, and naturally the last thing Straker wants is an intervention which curtails her power."

I swallowed some whisky and said, "What do we do?"

"First we must help him over this present crisis. You must give him the reassurance he so obviously needs, and with luck that will restore his equilibrium."

"But what the devil's going on, Robert? Why's he like this? What's at the bottom of this instability?"

"That leads me on to what I was going to say next. As soon as he's rational we must coax him to see Gavin Warburton. We can't let him drift on like this without seeking medical help."

"But do you think—"

"No, I don't. There's no need for you to look as if we're all in the middle of your recurring nightmare. I'm convinced we're not dealing with hereditary madness here."

"What makes you so sure?"

"I'm sure because I don't think Grandmama was mad—at least, not in any sense that would be accepted today. It was Ginette who gave me that idea. She was mad as a hatter after Robin died, but that was just a temporary nervous breakdown and now she's her old self again."

I swallowed some more whisky. After a while, I heard myself say, "I can't cope with this crisis, Robert; I just can't face it, it's too much for me."

"That's exactly why I'm trying to drill it into your head that Papa's derangement, such as it is, has nothing whatsoever to do with Grandmama. I know perfectly well that you've got a bee in your bonnet about Grandmama, insanity and the Home of the Assumption."

"I can't talk about that." I got up and began to pace around the room. "I've nothing to say."

"Maybe not," said Robert, "but I have. It seems to me—after much speculation on the subject of this peculiarity of yours—that you've translated the past into some Gothic nightmare which has very little to do with reality." He paused to let that sink in before adding in his most soothing voice: "After all, what actually happened? Mama had an unusually awkward problem with her mother-in-law. With Papa's consent she took advantage of Grandmama's nervous breakdown to install her at the Home of the Assumption, a reputable asylum, where Grandmama was apparently well treated. Grandmama then submitted—perhaps out of some desire to be punished—to our parents' decision that she should remain there. The situation was tragic, I admit, but hardly worthy of a horrific poem by Poe."

"What can be more horrific than shutting up a sane woman in a lunatic asylum? No, I refuse to believe our parents would do anything so fiendish!"

"Those parents of ours were capable of anything."

"No!" I shouted. "Grandmama was insane and they were the innocent victims of her evil!"

"There you go again, translating a mere melancholy ditty into a raging grand opera! My dear John, you can't divide these unfortunate people neatly into heroes and villains—it's simply not that kind of story!"

"Oh yes it is," I said. "It's got to be. I've got to have it quite clear in my mind whom to hate and whom to love or the ambiguity will tear me apart and I'll go mad. In fact I feel I'm going mad now, just talking about it. I can't face it, can't cope, can't see Papa, can't be reminded of the past—"

"You've got to see him. There's no one else. Now look here, John. You're an intelligent man. It's inconceivable that you can go on being irrational about this—"

"Oh, shut up, you don't understand—"

But this was exactly the response Robert wanted. "Very well, then explain your feelings to me."

I made a great effort. At last I managed to say: "All I know is that I can't dismiss the past lightly as you can. I've suffered too much. I can't forgive and I can't forget, and because of this I have to blame someone for what I've had to endure, and I can't blame my parents because it was always so important that they should love me, and anyway I've always loved them—although God knows, when you told me about Papa and Ginevra—Christ, that was terrible, *terrible*, I was so shocked—and *so angry* too, angry with him for not behaving as I needed him to behave, it reminded me of how I used to feel as a child—I used to feel so *angry* with him . . . and with Mama . . . for being prejudiced against me just because . . . but I couldn't feel angry, of course I couldn't, not really, well, I mean how could I when I loved them and I knew they loved me, I knew they did, of course they did, but oh God, how upset I was when you told me about Papa and Ginevra . . . But there I was, being a hypocritical prig again. I've now treated Bronwen and Constance just as badly as he ever treated my mother, and I've no right to be angry with him anymore. I'm just as bad as he is, I'm just like him, and if he now goes mad— as Grandmama went mad—two people who committed murder—all that evil —hereditary madness—oh God, I'm so frightened, *so bloody frightened*, you don't know how frightened I am whenever I think what could happen to me in the future . . ." I had to stop. I could no longer go on. I rubbed my eyes furtively with the back of my hand and tried to drink some scotch.

Robert waited a moment before saying in his calmest voice: "I never used that word 'evil' when I was defending so-called evil people. It usually seemed more accurate to describe them as pathetic or unlucky or stupid. They weren't fiends in human guise. They tended to be almost boringly ordinary."

"What are you trying to say?"

"I'm suggesting that you should think of our parents—and of Grandmama and Bryn-Davies—as ordinary people trapped in a situation which was quite beyond them. I think that's a lot closer to the truth than your Gothic melodrama."

I was unable to speak.

"And try to see Grandmama," persisted Robert, "not as a fiend lapsing into a hereditary madness for her sins, but as a sexy woman who got in a mess and in consequence had a most understandable nervous breakdown."

I tried to consider this. A knot of tension seemed to be expanding in the pit of my stomach. "But if I see Grandmama as—as—"

"Forgivable," said Robert.

"—how do I see our parents?"

"As two children in their teens who had to grow up fast with disastrous results. They can be forgivable too, John."

"But if I forgive everyone, whom do I blame?"

" 'That Monster Fortune,' to quote Boethius. We're all locked to the Wheel of Fortune, John, and some of us have a rougher ride than others."

I thought about this. Then I said, "Are you saying we have no control over our fate?"

"No. I believe Fortune gives us choices and we have to choose. But think how hard it is, John, when one has choices, to draw the right lines in the right places."

There was no answer to that. I thought of the wrong line I had drawn when I had rejected Bronwen, and suddenly for one brief powerful moment I saw my grandmother as a pathetic old woman, cut off from those she loved by the wrong decisions which had ruined her.

I said, "If only I could believe there was no hereditary madness involved. But if Papa's now suffering from a severe mental disturbance again—"

"That need only indicate that he too is having some form of temporary mental collapse, but as far as I know nervous breakdowns aren't hereditary. I'm sorry, John, to deprive you of your melodrama, but the truth is real life just isn't grand opera. It's much more in the nature of *opéra bouffe*."

I looked at him, a man afflicted by tragedy, and at once despised myself for my cowardice. "Hold fast," I said aloud to myself. "Stand firm. Soldier on." And those phrases, so reminiscent of the simple world of John Buchan where the heroes never had any trouble being as brave as lions, were comforting to me as I struggled with the complexity of my emotions. "How weak I've been," I said ashamed to Robert, "and how very unheroic."

"Ah," said Robert, "but the real heroes of this world aren't the men who preen themselves on how well they're doing their moral duty. The real heroes are the men who somehow nerve themselves to face a crisis even when they want to shit with fright at the thought of where it's all going to end."

I took a deep breath. Then I said, "I shall be all right now," and I set off on the road to Oxmoon on the first stage of my journey into hell.

XII

"Good afternoon, Mr. John," said my enemy, emerging briskly into the hall as I was handing Bayliss my hat. "Would you care to come into the drawing room, sir?"

Thanking her with equal civility, I allowed myself to be led across the hall. Mrs. Straker was immaculate in dove-gray, not a hair out of place on her sleek head. Her black eyes were inscrutable.

We entered the drawing room. The door closed. We stripped off our masks.

"I understand my father's not well."

"Well, that's just it, dear, I'm afraid he's not well enough to see anyone at present."

"He'll see me. Go upstairs, please, and tell him I'm here."

"As a matter of fact, dear, he's not upstairs—I've coaxed him out into the garden to see if any of the strawberries are ripe yet. They won't be, but at least he'll have a breath of fresh air. He's been shut up in his room talking of you-know-who until I'm ready to scream. . . . By the way, you look a little peaky yourself, dear, you really do—would you like a whisky?"

"No, an explanation. When you say 'you-know-who'—"

"That mother of his, dear, and her ruddy lover. Why those two couldn't have managed their affair better I can't think. Pure selfishness, if you ask me. In fact she must have been a very stupid woman, letting her lover get out of hand like that—and why kill the poor old homo husband? Most homos are ever so sweet when you get to know them, and he probably only drank because she treated him like dirt. Still, never mind me, I'm prejudiced—I've never had any patience with women who do everything wrong from start to finish. Now, what are we going to do about you? Frankly I think if you see him you'll make him worse."

"Nevertheless—"

"You *have* put the cat among the pigeons, haven't you, dear! Not that I blame you. That girl's got something all right—I admire your taste, and I wouldn't say no to hers either! I'm sure you make very tuneful music together, and I hear there's ever such a lovely baby!"

"Mrs. Straker—"

"All right, I suppose it's no use hoping you'll take yourself off, but don't say I didn't warn you. Christ, there he is! Now, what's he doing by the summerhouse? He's supposed to be in the kitchen garden. Well, dear, do we toss for it? Who goes to the rescue, you or me?"

I made no reply but opened the door and stepped out onto the terrace. "Has Dr. Warburton been consulted?" I demanded over my shoulder.

"Don't be daft. Bobby's tough as old boots when it comes to keeping doctors at arm's length—he's too afraid of being carted off to the loony bin."

I closed the door in her face, crossed the terrace and ran down the steps to the lawn. My father, dressed casually in gray flannels and a tweed jacket, was standing motionless in front of the summerhouse with his back to me. I went on walking. Eventually Glendower saw me and gave a bark to warn my father of my approach, but my father, apparently absorbed in some private meditation, took no notice. Sweat prickled on my back. I was seized by the nightmarish fear that when I saw his face I would find it changed beyond recognition, and in an automatic attempt to steady my nerves, I called a greeting and broke into a run to cover the last yards which separated us.

My father glanced idly over his shoulder. To my profound relief he appeared to be normal.

"Hullo, John," he said. "I was just thinking that the summerhouse should be repainted. Looks a bit shabby."

He held out his hand. Controlling my rapid breathing I took the hand and shook it. We smiled at each other, and that was the moment when I realized his behavior was abnormal. He ought to have been distressed and angry. His casual affability indicated a mind that had deliberately disconnected itself from pain.

The sweat began to trickle down my spine. "How are you, Papa?"

"Wonderfully well," said my father. "I admit Robert did upset me yesterday, but I've quite recovered from that now."

"I'm sorry Robert upset you. It was I, in fact, who asked him to call."

"Robert's very cruel sometimes," said my father. "Like Margaret. They mean well—when they interfere, they call it 'sorting things out' and 'setting things straight'—but they don't understand how muddled life is, how confusing."

"I'm sure Robert didn't mean to be cruel, Papa. He just wanted to explain—"

"Don't worry, I didn't believe a word he said; I knew it wasn't true. You wouldn't do what he said you were going to do. You're a good decent boy. You'd draw the line."

"Ah. I can see he gave you a wrong impression." I wiped the sweat from my forehead and shoved back my hair in a quick movement of my hand. "Why don't we go and sit in the summerhouse? I'd like to talk to you and explain everything."

"Oh no," said my father, "not the summerhouse. Quite definitely not the summerhouse. They meet in the back room."

"Met. They're dead."

"Yes, I know. But everything's come a full circle and now it's all happening again."

"No, Papa, the past never happens twice. People play their cards differently, don't you remember?"

My father turned away and began to wander towards the bench by the tennis court. "My mother and Owain Bryn-Davies," he said, "used to meet in the back room of the summerhouse but that was a long time ago, and now we keep the tennis net there during the winter."

"That's right."

"Thomas will put up the tennis net," said my father, "when he comes home from school in July. Thomas plays tennis with the Bryn-Davies boys." He paused to survey the tennis lawn before adding carefully: "The Bryn-Davies boys are called Owen and Peter. Owen is spelled the English way, which I think is a pity, but their mother's English so what can you expect? Their father is Alun, who was at Harrow with Robert, and Alun's father is my friend Owain the Younger, and *his* father was my mother's lover who drowned on the Shipway at the Worm's Head. A little accident with the tide tables. Have you ever taken Harry and Marian out to the Worm for a picnic, John? It's such a beautiful spot. Blanche would enjoy it too."

We seated ourselves on the bench, and my father, crossing one leg over the other, whistled for Glendower.

"Papa," I said, "Blanche is dead. I'm married to Constance now, but it was all the most appalling mistake, and I've decided—"

"Did I say Blanche? Stupid of me! Old age. Awful. I'm sixty-two—no, wait a minute—am I? Yes. It's 1924, isn't it?"

"Yes, I've been married to Constance for five months. However I now realize—"

"Wonderful wedding that was, had the time of my life. Wonderful champagne too—Veuve Clicquot, wasn't it? I'm always very partial to Veuve Clicquot."

"Papa, I'm in love with this Welsh girl Bronwen Morgan, and I intend to marry her once I have my divorce from Constance. There's no question of living in sin indefinitely. Bronwen's an honest respectable woman, and I intend that she should remain so."

"Honest respectable women don't have bastards." He stood up again and moved restlessly back towards the summerhouse. "My mother had two miscarriages when she was living with Bryn-Davies," he said. "It was disgusting.

She was quite without shame. I was humiliated. She broke all the rules—and terrible things happen," said my father, tears suddenly streaming down his face, "as I well know, to people who fail to stick to the rules."

Far away Mrs. Straker had emerged from the house and was descending the steps of the terrace. The sight of her seemed to come as a relief to my father. He tried to wipe his eyes on the cuff of his jacket. "Ah, here's Milly—expect she wants to know if you're dining tonight. Wonderful woman, Milly, quite remarkable, don't know what I'd do without her. She wants to marry me, of course, but I won't because it's not the done thing for a man in my position to marry someone like that. Got to stick to the rules, you see—and then nothing very terrible can happen."

But it had happened. He saw my expression, knew I was thinking of my mother replaced by a whore and shouted, "You've no right to judge me!"

"And you've no right to judge *me!*" I shouted back before I could stop myself.

"I'll have to ask your mother to talk to you," said my father to me in despair. "Margaret will have to deal with it." He turned his back on me only to be confronted by the figure of Mrs. Straker, representing an intolerable present. He turned towards the summerhouse only to be confronted once more by the intolerable past. He rubbed his eyes and looked dazed. "Sorry," he muttered. "Not well."

Pity mingled with my guilt and drove me to make a final effort to communicate with him.

"Papa, you're under strain and I think you should see Warburton. There are modern drugs—"

"No!" said my father fiercely. "I'm not seeing a doctor!"

"But you've just admitted you're unwell!"

"Old age. Not so young as I used to be."

"But—"

"Nobody's going to shut me up anywhere!"

"That's all right, Bobby," said Mrs. Straker, covering the last few yards of lawn with the speed of lightning. "That's all right, my pet. Nobody gets shut up just because they get a bit upset now and then. The idea of it! If that were true we'd all be locked up, wouldn't we, John?"

Ignoring her I took my father's hands in mine. "Papa, I give you my word that I'll never let anyone take you to the Home of the Assumption—or indeed, to any other institution of that kind."

His eyes filled with tears once more. He whispered, "You're such a good kind boy, John—and that's why I can't bear to see you destroying yourself like this."

"Oh, come off it, Bobby!" said Mrs. Straker at once. "This one's not going to destroy himself in a hurry—just look at him! Smart as paint, smooth as glass and clever as the Indian rope trick! You mark my words, a man like that could keep a bloody harem in a church if he put his mind to it! Now, don't you worry, my poppet. You run along and look at those strawberry beds, just as you said you would, and John and I'll work out how he can live happily ever after at the Manor. He's not stupid and he's not interested in destroying himself and I'm sure we'll have everything settled in no time at all. Oh, and watch that dog in the kitchen garden. I hear he's a terror for digging holes in all the wrong places."

This demonstration of crude street-corner sanity was evidently just what my father needed. He wiped away his tears, kissed her briefly and trailed away across the lawn with Glendower at his heels. I watched him for some time but even before I had nerved myself to face Mrs. Straker, I knew she was poised to move in for the kill.

"Well, *Mr.* John!" she said with heavy irony. "Don't you think you should come down off your high horse before you fall flat on your face? Let's go and sit in that bloody love nest of a summerhouse for a moment. I think it's time you and I had a cozy little chat together."

XIII

Robert had implied that we might one day have to go to war with Mrs. Straker about her position at Oxmoon, but neither he nor I had anticipated that she might now seek to go to war with us. Horrified by my father's condition, I was no match for her at that moment. I could only follow her into the summerhouse, and when she sat down on one of the wicker chairs I saw no alternative but to sit down opposite her.

She had crossed her legs primly as if she were drinking tea in her native London suburb, and when she began to speak this illusion of respectability only made her words the more bizarre.

"I was thinking of having a word with you, Mr. Casanova," she said, "even before this trouble blew up over your gorgeous redhead. I'd decided it was time you and your brother Robert realized how bloody indispensable I am here nowadays. You're hoping, aren't you, that this little trouble of your father's will give you the excuse to step in and get rid of me. Well, think again, my friend! Just you think again! You can't afford to wipe me off the slate, and if you can somehow manage to keep that handsome mouth of yours shut for a moment, I'll tell you the way things really are at Oxmoon.

"That's better. I can see I've got your full attention. I knew you weren't stupid. Now just you listen to me.

"There are two sides to my job here, and I do each of them damn well. Let's take the formal side first. I run that house like God runs heaven—perfectly. And unlike God I don't have a lot of angels to help me, and from a domestic point of view Oxmoon's a long way from heaven. It's old-fashioned, inconvenient and hell to keep organized. How your mother stood it I don't know, but of course she had a full prewar indoor staff of ten, whereas I now count myself lucky if I can get five servants living in and a couple of dailies from the village—your father won't pay for anything more. Never mind, I manage. I rule with a rod of iron and stand no nonsense, and fortunately the unemployment situation helps—people want to hang on to their jobs so they'll stand for a lot, and my God, I make them stand for it. Yes, I hold this place together all right. But remove me and it would fall apart at the seams.

"All right, so that's one potent argument in favor of keeping me: I do the formal side of my job damn well. But it's on the informal side that I'm bloody well indispensable. You might replace me as a housekeeper—if you were lucky—but you'd never find anyone willing to replace me for long in your father's bed. Nor are you going to find anyone who can control him in the way I can. You think my control over him's a bad thing, don't you? Well, this is the moment when you change your mind, my friend, because neither you nor your brothers have any idea what would go on at Oxmoon if I packed my bags and walked out. Shall I continue? Or shall I give you a moment to digest that? You look as if you could do with a cigarette. That's right, take out your case. I'll have one too—here, give me the matches and I'll do the lighting. That's right. Ah . . . that's better, isn't it? Nothing like a good puff to steady the nerves, and my God, your nerves are going to need steadying when you hear what I'm going to say next."

She leaned forward in her chair. Her sharp pointed face was close to me, and I could see the mole on her chin and the powder in the pores of her sallow skin and the hard lines running from her nose to the corners of her mouth.

"Your father," she said, "isn't the man he used to be. The present deterioration set in after Robin died, but if you ask me he's never been right since his wife's death, and now it's got to the stage where it doesn't take much to upset him and trigger him off. The only reason why this incident is different from other more recent ones is that this time he has a genuine excuse for being upset. However let's leave Mrs. Morgan for the moment—we'll get to her later.

"The truth you've now got to face is that although your father still spends a lot of time being sound as a bell, he's getting to the point where he needs a keeper, because whenever he's upset like this his one remedy is sex. So long as I'm here he's not going to go around doing God-knows-what to the nearest scullery maid, but once I'm gone he'll do it and, what's worse, he won't even remember afterwards that he's done it, he'll shut it clean out of his mind. Now, I know what to do with him. I can keep him satisfied, but he's got some weird tastes, and while I don't mind that—the weirder the better, as far as I'm concerned—there aren't many women who'd stand for that kind of behavior. Except prostitutes, of course. And do you really want your father bringing the lowest form of street life into Oxmoon and turning the place into some kind of cross between a brothel and a lunatic asylum? Of course you don't. So look at me and be grateful because so long as I'm around you don't have to worry.

"Well, now that we've got all that straightened out, let's talk about the facts of life, otherwise known as pounds, shillings and pence. I'm worth my weight in gold, but Bobby only pays me a pittance as housekeeper. I filch a bit here and there, of course—why the hell shouldn't I, after all I do?—but Bobby's mean about money, and although he's a bit potty sometimes, he's still capable of being all too lucid when the subject of money comes up for discussion. The truth is he's so dependent on me that he gets a thrill out of saying no when I ask for things; it makes him feel more the master of his own home. Now I could go on filching—nothing easier—but why the hell should I have to scrape around like that? You're a rich man and it's in your best interests to pay me what I'm worth."

She stopped talking. I stubbed out my cigarette and stood up. Beyond the doorway, far away across the lawn, Oxmoon lay pallidly in the sunlight. I noticed that the creeper was beginning to die on the walls.

"I'll have to talk to my brother."

"Yes, I thought you'd say that, but think again, dear. For instance, why don't you and I come to a very private agreement, an agreement which will suit you as well as it'll suit me?"

"What do you mean?"

"Well, dear, before Bobby's really certifiable, why don't I whisper a little word in his ear about the will?"

"What will?"

"Oh, don't pretend you don't know about it! The will where he leaves everything to that little ninny Kester just because he wants to be kind to poor old Robert! What a lot of sentimental old balls—but don't you worry about it, my friend, because if you guarantee me five hundred a year, starting from now, I'll guarantee you Oxmoon when Bobby drops dead."

I knew it was vital that I never hesitated so the instant she stopped speaking I said, "I'll not cheat my dying brother. I draw the line." The most appalling part of this heroic statement was that I found myself wondering whether it was true.

"What's the matter, dear?" said the woman at my side. "Worried in case you wouldn't get away with it? But I'd keep my mouth shut, and anyway people can get away with anything if they put their minds to it. Look at your father! He got away with murder."

I turned to face her. "Did he?" I said.

We were silent. I thought of my ruined father, locked up in his private hell and shamed before the children he loved, but the thought was unendurable. Turning my back on the woman I walked out of the summerhouse.

"My God," said Milly Straker, "the man's incorruptible. That's the sexiest act I've seen in a month of Sundays." She followed me to the edge of the tennis lawn. "All right, dear, suit yourself, but let me know if you change your mind. And now—while we're still talking about sex—I think we'd better have a quick word about the luscious Mrs. Morgan. No, don't take offense! This is just a friendly word from a well-wisher. All I want to say, dear, is Don't live with her openly. I don't know whether you really intend to install her immediately in Penhale Manor as your mistress, but take it from me it just won't do."

"Mrs. Straker—"

"Oh, don't misunderstand! I'm not like your father—I'm not worried about *you*, I'm worried about *her!* You love her, don't you? All right, then if you're as decent as you've almost convinced me you are, take time off from your romantic dreams and imagine what hell life's going to be for her if you put her on public display nailed to a cross with a placard inscribed MISTRESS around her neck! If you've got to keep her at the Manor, let her call herself a housekeeper or a nanny or a tweeny or something—give her a title to hide behind when the inevitable happens and everyone realizes what's going on. Believe me, you'll have to fight tooth and nail to preserve that girl, and don't think I don't know what I'm talking about. My God, I've seen some crucifixions in my time! The bloody men get off scot-free and the girls end up in the bath with their wrists slashed—oh, I've seen it all! So take my advice for her sake and stop being so bloody selfish and naive."

After a pause I managed to say: "As I intend to marry Mrs. Morgan, I hardly think your advice is applicable."

"Why, yes, of course you intend to marry her, dear. A gentleman always intends to marry the girl at first, doesn't he? After all, he wouldn't be a gentleman if he didn't." She stepped past me and began to walk away across the lawn. "But Mrs. Morgan's a lucky girl," she added over her shoulder. "I can see that now. And maybe you really will be fool enough to marry her—if, of course, that new pregnant wife of yours is ever fool enough to agree to a divorce."

I watched her till she had disappeared from sight. Then I stumbled back into the summerhouse, sank down on the nearest chair and covered my face with my hands.

9

I

"SHE THEN SAID she would guarantee me Oxmoon if I guaranteed her an income," I said to Robert.

"How intriguing. What did you say?"

"I said I refused to cheat you."

"Oh, she'll never believe that," said Robert. "You should have reminded her instead that undue influence and unsoundness of mind can invalidate a will."

"No doubt I should. But I'm afraid I wasn't thinking too clearly at that stage."

"At that stage I'd have been dead of apoplexy. . . . Is that a car I hear outside?"

It was. Ginevra had arrived home from one of Esther Mowbray's smart bridge parties, and was looking overdressed in a shiny afternoon frock, an absurd hat like a semidestroyed Balaclava and a very, very long bead necklace.

"Are you going to tell her, Robert?"

"Of course. I always tell her everything."

This surprised me for Robert and Ginevra never gave an impression of marital intimacy and I had long since decided that their separate lives were linked by an enduring, genuine but not close affection. However when Robert now began to talk to her in the frankest possible manner, I found myself automatically trying to assess their marriage afresh. But it did not lend itself easily to assessment. The asexuality of the relationship struck odd notes; he made no effort to be charming or deferential to her, but was bossy and didactic as if she were a school chum who needed firm handling, while she in her turn made no effort to demonstrate her considerable feminine wiles but said exactly what she liked with varying degrees of rudeness. This meant they bickered frequently and energetically, but I had schooled myself to take no notice; I had realized that their two personalities, his so austere, hers so emotional, were locked in the harmony of opposites from which neither of them wished to escape.

When Robert finished speaking, she said to me, "How absolutely vile for you, Johnny," and suddenly as I realized she was genuinely upset I saw beyond her affectations to the sensitive woman I hardly knew.

She turned back to Robert. "What do we do?"

"I'm beginning to wonder. I'm afraid this is all much more hair-raising than I thought it was. How far did you believe Straker, John?"

"I hate to admit it but I believed every word."

Neither of them attempted to disagree with this verdict. Ginevra said, "So we daren't get rid of Straker. And he won't see a doctor. Is he legally certifiable, Robert?"

"Nowhere near. We've no evidence that he's not running the estate properly. Even Straker admits he spends most of the time being as sound as a bell."

"But he's deteriorating," I said. "He's going mad, Robert. This isn't just a nervous breakdown, it's hereditary insanity, I know it is, I know it—"

"Shut up. Pull yourself together. Christ, isn't it enough that Papa's sinking into this unspeakably sordid dotage? If you go round the bend as well I'll bloody well never forgive you!"

But Ginevra's hand slipped into mine and Ginevra's voice said gently, "Take no notice of him. He's only being awful because he's so upset."

"You bloody fool, stop pandering to him!" shouted Robert. "If he persists in clinging to this ridiculous obsession of his, he doesn't need kindness—he needs to be shaken till his bloody teeth rattle!"

Ginevra was furious. "My God, you are a bastard sometimes!"

"Oh, stop carping at me like a stupid bitch!"

"Shut up!" she screamed at him. "Just because you yourself can't stand any bloody emotion—"

"What I can't stand is everyone going to bloody pieces!"

"I'm sorry," I said hastily, jolted out of my fears by this searing marital squabble. "You're right to shout at me, I know I'm being useless—"

"Darling," said Ginevra, "after that scene at Oxmoon the miracle is that you're still conscious." She swung back to face Robert. "Since you're so bloody clever, you bastard," she said, "just you answer me this: if Bobby isn't going stark staring mad—and I agree with Johnny, I think he is—just what the hell do you think's going on?"

"I think the entire trouble's emotional. I suspect he's racked with shame because he's unable to stop himself sliding deeper and deeper into this appalling private life."

"My God, that's plausible," I said in spite of myself. "I hadn't thought of that."

"But why's he compelled to lead this ghastly private life in the first place?" demanded Ginevra. "Isn't that in itself evidence of derangement?"

"Possibly. But not necessarily. He told me once he regarded sex as an escape from facts he couldn't face. Straker now confirms this by saying he resorts to sex when he's upset. This nauseating private life may be evidence that he's disturbed, but it's not, repeat *not*, evidence of hereditary insanity."

"I think it is," I said.

"So do I," said Ginevra.

"If I don't quash this hereditary-insanity nonsense very soon," said Robert, "I swear I'll bloody well go mad myself. For God's sake let's get hold of Gavin Warburton and ask him for a rational, detached, qualified medical opinion on the subject. I think it's time we laid Grandmama's ghost once and for all."

II

"Without examining the patient," said Warburton, "it's impossible for me to give an opinion."

"All right, Gavin," said Robert. "We accept that's your official statement. Now let's talk unofficially. Could this mental disturbance result from a physical degeneration?"

"Yes, but I'd say that was unlikely. It's three years since I attended him after your mother died, but he struck me then as being in first-class health for a man of his age. He doesn't eat, drink or smoke to excess. He's not overweight. He moves well and there's nothing lifeless about his facial muscles so I think we can rule out a premature onset of senility—"

"What about syphilis?" said Robert as I shuddered in my chair.

"Most unlikely. There'd have been other symptoms, and besides the onset of syphilitic madness is somewhat different. There's usually a sort of—"

"Ginette, get John some brandy."

"I'm all right," I said. "I'm all right."

"Are you sure?" said Warburton in concern.

"Take no notice of him," said Robert. "He's merely incorrigibly squeamish about mental illness. Now, to return to my father—could he possibly be suffering from schizophrenia?"

"That's very hard to say," said Warburton evasively.

"Is that hereditary?" I said at once.

"No one knows."

"It's John's theory," said Robert to Warburton, "that my grandmother suffered from a form of hereditary madness with the result that all her descendants are doomed to be locked up one by one."

"Ah, I see." Warburton immediately looked more relaxed. "Well, that's much easier to ascertain. The Home of the Assumption would, of course, have a record of her medical history. I'll talk to de Vestris—he's the doctor in charge there, John—and arrange to see her file. What was your grandmother's first name, when did she go there and when did she die?"

I was unable to speak. Robert said: "Gwyneth. 1882. 1910."

Warburton wrote this information on a prescription pad and the conversation continued, but I did not hear it. I was still holding my glass of brandy but I could no longer drink. I sat motionless on the edge of my chair.

"Johnny?" said Ginevra suddenly.

"I'm all right," I said again. "I'm all right."

"John would like to see this doctor, Gavin," said Robert. "Can you make an appointment?"

"Yes, of course. When?"

"Now, if he's available."

"Let's find out," said Warburton, and headed for the telephone in the hall.

III

I listened to Warburton's side of the telephone call. I think I had some nightmarish fear that he and Dr. de Vestris would conspire to conceal the truth from me, but Warburton merely said the matter was of extreme urgency and asked if we could see him within the hour. De Vestris consented. Warburton then terminated the call, said to me, "Shall we go?" and drove me the fourteen miles to the Home of the Assumption at a brisk pace.

I had never been inside the gates. Only my father had ever visited my grandmother there, and when Ginevra had her nervous breakdown I had been with Bronwen in Cornwall. I had imagined hideous scenes being enacted daily behind that sinister Victorian facade, but as we were admitted by a cheerful nun I found the atmosphere was peaceful. I was hardly in a mood to perceive my surroundings clearly, but there was a not unpleasant smell of furniture polish emanating from the glowing wooden banisters of the staircase, and a tortoiseshell cat was washing its paws absentmindedly in a corner of the hall.

"Here I am again, Sister!" said Warburton. "No peace for the wicked!"

"Oh, Dr. Warburton, the things you say!"

This extraordinarily normal conversation was conducted in cheerful tones and even followed by laughter. I could not quite believe I was listening to it, and when the nun took us down the corridor to Dr. de Vestris' office I could not quite believe either that I was where I was.

I found a little old man with white hair in a pleasant civilized room overlooking a formal garden high above Swansea Bay. He had in his hand several sheets of paper, and he glanced now and then at the fine copperplate writing on the top page as Warburton talked briefly about a family crisis that had made a full knowledge of my grandmother's condition imperative.

"Quite so, quite so," said de Vestris soothingly. He had the air of a benign schoolmaster. "Do sit down, both of you. Yes, I looked up our records as soon as we'd finished speaking, Warburton, although of course I remember the case. Such a nice old lady she was, and always so devoted to her family."

"What was the original diagnosis?" said Warburton.

"An initial derangement caused by an acute nervous crisis followed by periodic bouts of melancholy."

Warburton turned to me. "Nowadays we would call that a nervous breakdown followed by recurring bouts of depression." He added to de Vestris: "Did you have any occasion to amend that diagnosis, sir?"

"Yes, I thought there was no real need for her to remain here. She was one of our very mildest cases, always a little inclined to melancholy, but such a normal old lady on her good days."

"Godwin feared her disorder might be hereditary."

"Good heavens, no!" said de Vestris. He seemed scandalized by the idea. "There was never any question of that."

Warburton stood up and said to me, "I'm going to leave you with Dr. de Vestris because I know you'd like to have a few words with him on your own. I'll be waiting outside in the motor."

I nodded, tried to thank him and failed. The door closed. I was alone with my bridge to the past in that tranquil room high above the bay.

"This is very singular," mused de Vestris, filling a pipe. "The relatives usually prefer to forget—what a pleasant change to find one who wants to remember! You should be encouraged! Now, let me see. I know you're one of the grandchildren, but which one? I can't recall all their names now, but I know there were a lot of them, and Mrs. Godwin liked to show me their photographs. She had a favorite—a very nice-looking little fellow—damn it, what was his name—something quite ordinary—oh yes, Johnny, that was it. He was the one who grew up speaking fluent Welsh. I remember she said none of the others had an ear for it. Yes, little Johnny was a great joy to her, but she swore me to secrecy because she didn't want her daughter-in-law to find out. That was one of her eccentricities, you understand. She was abnormally frightened of her daughter-in-law. One often finds these irrational streaks lingering on in a patient who might otherwise be considered fully recovered.

"When I first came here in 1901 I did suggest that Mrs. Godwin was fit enough to live at home with a nurse to look after her, but Mrs. Godwin at once became so terrified that I realized this wouldn't do, and unfortunately there were no other relatives willing to take her in. I had a conference with her son and daughter-in-law, but they both agreed that it was much better for Mrs. Godwin to remain where she was. They were the most charming couple, I remember, and the young Mrs. Godwin was such a pleasant motherly little figure and spoke so kindly of her mother-in-law that I saw at once how deeply irrational the older Mrs. Godwin was about her. And the son was such a delightful man—and most generous in his donations to the Order which runs the Home—yes, he was a devoted son; he came to see her regularly and always, every Christmas Eve, he would arrive to take her back to Oxmoon.

"Yet there was something odd about their relationship. I tried to coax Mrs. Godwin to talk to me about him because there was no doubt he used to disturb her—although since she always longed to see him and since he always behaved kindly to her when they met, I came to believe she was disturbed not by his visits themselves but by the fact that they reminded her of the past.

"When the melancholy was upon her she used to retreat into the past. She would tell me how happy she had been with—good God, I've forgotten his name—oh yes, Bryn-Davies, and sometimes she'd seem to forget he was dead —she'd talk of him as if he were still alive—but I don't think she really forgot. It was just part of a deliberate effort to blot out the pain-filled present by re-creating a past which was bearable. No matter how difficult the past might have been, it was at least finite and, in a peculiar way, safe. She knew where she was there; she couldn't get lost. But in contrast the present overwhelmed her with its potential for suffering; another of her little eccentricities, you see, was that she feared her daughter-in-law would cut her off entirely from her grandchildren and stop her son's visits. She was so afraid, poor woman, always so afraid of the younger Mrs. Godwin.

"I tried hard to get to the bottom of her trouble, but I'm afraid I never did. What I did find out, however, was that some huge guilt was constantly present in her mind—but the guilt, strangely enough, didn't center around Bryn-Davies. It centered around the husband. Yes, it was the guilt which had driven her beyond the edge of sanity, I'm sure of it, although the exact nature of her guilt was never disclosed to me; she took her secrets with her to the grave, and all I can tell you is that she seemed to believe she was responsible for her husband's death. She said her adultery had driven him to drink and ruined his health, but that couldn't have been the whole story because when I spoke to her son he said his father had been a drunkard long before the advent of Bryn-Davies. 'I was a bad wife,' she used to say, weeping and weeping, poor woman—I can see her now—'I was wicked,' she would say, 'I yielded to evil, I could have stopped but I went on and now I'm paying and paying forever.' She was very Welsh, you know, very emotional. . . . But of course, I was forgetting, you knew her, you're one of the grandsons.

"In the end I decided that the best way to exorcise this guilt over the adultery was to enlist the aid of her son—such a delightful fellow he was!— and I suggested that it might help her if he were to tell her clearly that he forgave her for her past wrongs. 'Yes, of course,' he said, charming as ever, but do you know, he never did. That was when I realized what a strange relationship they had. There was unquestionably love on both sides, but it was crippled by a mutual revulsion. I suspect he must have turned against

Bryn-Davies in the end . . . and of course it's always the children who suffer, isn't it, when the parents go off the rails.

"Well, I must stop rambling but the case interested me and stuck in my memory. After all, she was Mrs. Godwin of Oxmoon, wasn't she, and even though the great scandal took place twenty years before I met her, people still talked of it in Gower—well, look at us, talking of it today! The past doesn't die so easily sometimes, does it, and I can see your grandmother as if it were yesterday, such a nice ordinary old lady; I see her sticking those photographs of her grandchildren in her album and turning page after page after page. . . . Yes, she loved those grandchildren—but I keep forgetting, you're one of them, aren't you? Now, which one would you be? And exactly what can I tell you that will be of help?"

IV

It was almost ten by the time I reached Little Oxmoon again, but although Robert was in bed he was not asleep. Ginevra was sitting with him as they waited for me to return.

"It's all right," I said as I entered the room.

"Thank God," said Robert. "What did I tell you? I always knew it was rubbish to assume they were suffering from the same malaise!"

"You were wrong. The malaise was the same."

Both he and Ginevra boggled at me. I drew up a chair and sank down on it. I felt exhausted.

"But for God's sake!" said Robert, outraged by the possibility that he had drawn the wrong deductions from the facts. "What's the malaise?"

"Guilt."

They boggled at me again. "What the devil do you mean?" demanded Robert, but I saw that Ginevra had understood. I had noticed by that time that Robert's broad knowledge of human nature was essentially academic, whereas Ginevra's intuitive sensitivity gave her the power to comprehend complex emotional truths which lay beyond the reach of his rational analysis. Robert was capable of perceiving intellectually that I was unbalanced on the subject of my grandmother and that I had to be weaned from my melodramatic vision in order to be cured. But it was Ginevra who had the intuition to perceive the exact dimensions of my cure when it came.

"Guilt," she said. "Of course. They both committed murder."

Robert was still outraged by this solution which he saw as irrational. "But none of the murderers I ever knew ever went round the bend years after the event!"

"Darling," said Ginevra, "the murderers you knew were either hanged or locked up or allowed to vanish into the blue. You've had absolutely no experience of what happens to people when they've been carrying a huge burden of guilt for years."

"Obviously not all murderers react in this way, Robert," I said to pacify him. "But the point is that this mother and this son, who were no doubt emotionally similar, appear to break down in the same way when under stress."

"Exactly," said Ginevra. "It's not murder itself that's important here, Robert—any serious wrongdoing would have the same effect. It's the guilt they can't endure."

"So the thesis is that the malaise is guilt and that Papa inherited his mother's emotional inability to survive it—and now I suppose you'll say the madness is hereditary after all!" said Robert, more outraged than ever.

"I could say that, certainly," I said, "but the point is that this particular madness doesn't have to be inherited, Robert. What I have to do to ensure my sanity is to avoid the bad decisions which would later drive me out of my mind with guilt—and that means the choice between sanity and insanity will always be mine; it means I'm not at the mercy of an uncontrollable heredity, I'm not strapped to the Wheel of Fortune with no possibility of escape—"

"May I interrupt this emotional monologue," said Robert, "to inquire if our parents and our grandmother can now be regarded as forgivable?"

I looked at my grand opera but found the stage was in darkness.

"No more fiends?" said Robert. "No more villains busily generating evil?"

"No." I found myself looking at a different stage. "It's not that kind of story. You were right at least about that, Robert." I thought with love and pity of my sad lonely grandmother turning the pages of her photograph albums. I thought with love and pity of my young parents struggling to survive that tragedy which had haunted them. And I knew that the need to blame someone for my past unhappiness was no more. One could blame evil people for evil deeds but not tortured people for tragic decisions; tortured people deserved only compassion, and the compassion, long withheld, was now streaming through my mind. The weight of my old terror was lifted; the burden of my anger was destroyed, and it was at that moment, as I triumphed at last over the past which had so often and so fatally triumphed over me, that I was able to say simply in judgment: "They were just three ordinary people who failed to draw the line."

V

Later, after we had left Robert to sleep, I said, "Ginevra, there's something I want to ask you. Straker gave me some advice today and I have a terrible feeling that it may be sound; she says that while I'm waiting for my divorce I should pretend Bronwen's in my employment—for Bronwen's sake, of course, not for mine. She's right, isn't she?"

"Ghastly Straker!" said Ginevra. "I'm afraid she is. How mortifying!"

"I'm going to have to get rid of Nanny. I suppose I could say that Bronwen's taken her place."

"Oh, darling, what a good idea! That's the perfect solution!"

"Bronwen's not going to like it."

"Why not?"

"It's a lie. And we want to live in the truth."

"But darling, it won't be a lie! She'll be there at Penhale Manor looking after your children, just as a nanny should!"

"Yes," I said, "and Straker's there at Oxmoon, managing the house just as a housekeeper should."

"But that situation's utterly different!"

"Yes," I said, "of course. But it's the same lie, isn't it?" And leaving the hall, I went out into the night.

VI

"I'd rather live with you without pretense," said Bronwen.

"Yes. That's what I want too. But there are cogent reasons against it."

"The children?"

"The children, certainly. But my main concern is for you. I don't know how long it'll take to get this divorce. Obviously nothing can be done until after the child is born, but even then . . . Constance may be stubborn."

She looked away.

It was after midnight, and we were sitting in the little front parlor of the Home Farm on a small uncomfortable sofa. Bronwen's hair was loose. As I caressed her it shone fierily in the candlelight.

"Then there's my father," I said. "He's literally ill with worry. If he knew I was going to keep up appearances and behave according to his rules he'd feel better. I do want to live in the truth, you must believe that, but I don't want to hurt people."

She made up her mind. "No. Neither do I. Hurting people can never be right." She pushed back her hair and turned to face me again. "But we must be truthful with each other in private," she said. "You must never lie to me again."

I promised I never would. She was satisfied, and blowing out the candle I took her in my arms.

VII

"He's very poorly indeed today, dear," said Mrs. Straker. "He's searching the attics, although God knows what he's looking for. What did Robert say about my salary—or did you have second thoughts and decide to take advantage of my offer about the will?"

"I told him. We'll pay you. But I'll discuss that later," I said, detesting her, and headed for the attics in search of my father.

The top floor of Oxmoon consisted of a chain of rooms crammed with Godwin possessions which ranged from family treasures to junk. Early poverty had encouraged my parents to hoard anything of value, but the tradition of accumulation had preceded my father's rule and there were even tin trunks marked R. CLIFFORD, which had been the name of Robert Godwin the Renovator before he had prised his way into the inheritance of his cousin the imbecile. But my father was not wandering among the relics of the eighteenth century. I found him seated by a collection of old books in the room where my grandmother's portrait was kept under a dust sheet. When he saw me he rubbed his eyes as if making a desperate attempt to concentrate.

"Are you looking for something, Papa? Can I help you?"

He shook his head. I saw then that he was too afraid to speak in case he mixed up past and present, and I found his awareness of his condition far more terrible than any ignorance would have been. My last doubts about the pretense of employing Bronwen dissolved. Putting him out of his agony, I promised I would stick to his rules.

After he had shed a tear or two of relief he said, "Thank God you've come to your senses. I really thought you might marry her, and of course that would never do."

I was silent. The last thing I wanted was to upset him all over again. I told myself there would be time enough to face that crisis when I had my divorce.

My father began to stack the books nearby into a neat pile, and as he worked I saw they were not books at all but old photograph albums. I thought of my grandmother, and suddenly before I could stop myself, I pulled the dust sheet from her portrait.

"I suppose she called Bryn-Davies the bailiff," I said, "when he moved to Oxmoon."

"No, she never bothered. Awful. I was so ashamed."

I thought of Dr. de Vestris saying, "It's always the children who suffer, isn't it, when the parents go off the rails."

A coldness gripped me. Covering the portrait I turned away once more from my grandmother and in my mind drew the line which would separate me from her.

But the line seemed very fragile.

"Hope you won't be too bored living at the Manor," said my father unexpectedly, providing a more than welcome diversion, and when I faced him I saw that although he still looked ill with exhaustion, the lines of strain seemed less pronounced. His voice was normal. Sanity had apparently been regained.

"I shall be all right."

"Nothing much for you to do there." My father had been keeping an eye on the estate for me since Edmund's marriage. "It would be a full-time occupation for Edmund, of course, but not for someone like you."

"I'm not ambitious, not anymore."

My father gave a short laugh and said, "That's because all you can think about at the moment is the woman. But you'll feel differently later."

"Perhaps. But I do have my lands in Herefordshire. I'm sure I can keep myself busy."

"I can't change my mind about Oxmoon, John."

"I know. But I'm not interested in Oxmoon anymore. I just want to live quietly with Bronwen at Penhale Manor."

"The pond's too small, John. You're a big fish."

"Then I'll have to find a bigger pond eventually, won't I?"

"That's what I'm afraid of," said my father.

At once I turned to face him. "There's no need to treat me as a fanatic who would stop at nothing."

"No? You're behaving like one—walking out on your pregnant wife, smashing up your home, stopping at nothing to get that woman—"

"That's different."

"Is it? I don't see much difference. If you stop at nothing to get a woman, why shouldn't you stop at nothing to get an estate?"

"Because *you* stopped at nothing to get an estate, Papa, and I've seen what that's done to you. No, thank you! I'm not playing my cards as you played yours!"

He broke down again. There was a long and distressing interval during which he clung to my hand and said how glad he would be to have me living nearby but how frightened he was in case he became old and feeble and allowed me to persuade him to cheat Robert.

". . . and then I'll be damned utterly," he said, crying again. "This is my one chance for redemption, my one chance to right a terrible wrong."

"I understand. But you're safe, Papa—I'd never interfere with your affairs —I'd draw the line."

Or would I?

Yes, of course I would. I'd draw the line to stop myself ending up like my grandmother. But supposing . . . supposing I drew the line but the line became . . . eroded by circumstances beyond my control? Or supposing I drew the line but it became my moral duty to rub it out?

The nightmares burgeoned.

Chaos multiplied.

In terror I blotted the entire subject from my mind.

VIII

Meanwhile the chaos was streaming into my life as the result of the wrong line I had drawn when I had married Constance.

The moment I returned to London to resume the ordeal of winding up my life there, Marian's governess gave notice, and although I made no attempt to detain her, I was becoming very worried about Marian who had now lost her stepmother, her nanny and her governess in rapid succession. Nanny too had given notice as a gesture of protest, but she had expected me to beg her to stay, and my immediate acceptance coupled with the necessary glowing reference had shocked her to the core.

"How jolly awkward!" said Daphne unsurprised when I told her of the governess's decision. "Simply too diffy for words, my dear." She then told me that if Bronwen were to be the new nanny I would never find a governess who would stay. "Governesses can't bear being upstaged by nannies, John. It's one of the horrid facts of nursery life."

When I remained silent, forcing myself to face this unpalatable truth, Daphne said impulsively, "John, do let Marian stay here with Elizabeth! Harry'll be all right—he can share Kester's tutor, and so long as he has you perhaps he won't need a mother so much as Marian does, but Marian . . . Darling, don't be livid with me, you know I'm on your side, but what *is* it going to be like for Marian with your working-class mistress at Penhale Manor? Marian's nearly nine now, and she needs—"

"What Marian needs," I said, "is her father, working-class mistress or no working-class mistress, and I'm not going to abandon her by palming her off on you. She's coming to Penhale and that's my last word on the subject."

"I doubt if it'll be Marian's," said Daphne drily, and she was right. Marian, who was great friends with Elizabeth and who liked her cousin's nanny and governess, took a poor view of yet another upheaval in her small world and stormy scenes inevitably followed. These were exacerbated by the fact that Daphne, the nanny and the governess all secretly sympathized with Marian and thought I was behaving irresponsibly. At that point I knew Marian had to be removed as soon as possible, so after Ginevra had engaged the domestic staff I made a rapid visit to the Manor to install Bronwen and her children and then returned to London to tackle the nightmare of collecting my children from a home neither of them wanted to leave.

Marian became hysterical. Elizabeth became hysterical. Daphne was no use at all. I suddenly decided I disliked Daphne very much and could not imagine why Lion had married her. In my distress I needed someone to blame for this harrowing episode, and Daphne filled the role of scapegoat to perfection.

I had always thought with what I now classified as ignorant conceit that I was a good father, but at this point I found out that parenthood involved rather more than reading bedtime stories, patting little heads and distributing pocket money on Saturday mornings. I was alone with my children on the train to Swansea. There was neither a nanny nor a governess to cushion me from the realities of nursery life. Marian sobbed and screamed and sulked. Harry spent his time either picking fights with her or else misbehaving in some other way in order to gain my attention. Twice I restrained myself from spanking him but on the third occasion I did not, and afterwards I was as miserable as he was. I felt a complete failure as a parent.

My caretaker Willis, now restored to his former position as head gardener, met us in the car at Swansea, but at once the children were fighting again, this time for the honor of sitting on my lap. More tears and screams ensued. Willis looked shocked. I was exhausted. I had begun to think the journey would never end but at last we reached the Manor and Bronwen came out into the drive to meet us.

To this day I cannot recall what she said. But I can see the children looking at her, looking and remembering, and I knew she was reminding them of that other time when their mother had been alive. Their tearstained grubby little faces became smooth and still. Rhiannon and Dafydd were in the hall but I did not wait to see the reunion; I thought Bronwen could manage better without me, so I retired to my study and mixed myself a very dark whisky-and-soda.

A week later, just as I was thinking with relief that my home life was stable enough to permit me at least to attempt to find a new governess, I returned from a visit to Swansea to find that all my new domestic staff wanted to give notice.

IX

I made no effort to detain them. Employers do themselves no favor when they cringe and crawl before their servants, and I knew the only answer was to start afresh. The worst part of the disaster, however, was not the dislocation of life at the Manor but Bronwen's deep distress.

"It was because we shared the bedroom openly," she said. She was trying not to cry. "I overheard some remarks about it. I should have had my own room by the nurseries."

I had known that to preserve the proprieties fully, Bronwen should have had her own room, but the prospect of her position at the Manor being an exact mirror image of Milly Straker's position at Oxmoon was so repulsive to me that I had found this final hypocrisy intolerable. Now I realized that I had been stupid but at the same time I found myself unable to make more than a minor compromise.

"We'll set aside the room," I said, "but I'm damned if you're ever going to use it. We'll go to bed together in my room and wake up together in my room, just as if we were married, and I won't tolerate anything else."

"But no staff will stay—how will we manage . . ." She was crying, saying how frightened she was in case I already regretted my decision to live with her.

I stopped her tears. Then when I was sure she was convinced I had no regrets I told her not to worry, swallowed every ounce of my very considerable pride and went begging to Milly Straker.

X

She was very good about it. It would have been so easy for her to be smug, savoring my humiliation, but she was brisk and businesslike.

"Yes, I thought Mrs. Robert was making a mistake engaging good-quality servants," she said flatly. "I'm surprised they even stayed as long as a week. Never mind, dear, I'll talk to the agency I use in Swansea and get you a cook and a couple of maids—but what you really need is the right housekeeper, someone who'll flog everyone into shape and turn a blind eye to your sleeping arrangements. Let me telephone my friends in London and see what's going in the waifs-and-strays department. Whoever they suggest won't have references, but I'll make sure she's dead straight about money."

"I . . ." It was hard to find the right words. "She must be a decent woman. I couldn't possibly consider employing anyone who wasn't."

"Don't worry, dear, the victims of this world are usually a lot more decent than those who play their cards right. I'll see if I can find some able respectable woman whose employer asked her to be a bed warmer and then ended up with cold feet. After a dismissal with no references and a visit to the nearest back-street abortionist, a woman like that would think Penhale Manor was paradise and you were the Angel Gabriel."

I remained very worried but when Mrs. Wells arrived for her interview I found my worries were at an end. Good-looking but meticulously refined in her manner she had for the past five years been employed in a home where the wife was an invalid, and Mrs. Wells, having enjoyed a large amount of autonomy in consequence, was more than capable of taking sole charge of the household. This was exactly what I wanted. I engaged her.

"What did she do?" I said afterwards to Mrs. Straker. I despised myself for my curiosity, but I felt I ought to find out. "Was it the employer?"

"No, dear: his seventeen-year-old son, but keep Mabel away from hot-headed young men and you'll have no trouble at all; quite the reverse. I'm sure she'll suit very well."

For the next two weeks Mrs. Straker called daily at the Manor to make sure the new staff were behaving themselves. Bronwen said the servants used to tremble in their shoes, but I noticed the standard of my domestic comfort was rising. Mrs. Wells, established in her authority by Mrs. Straker, proved both capable and pleasant, treating Bronwen and me exactly as if we were married. Mrs. Straker had ruled that any servant who was rude to Bronwen was to be dismissed on the spot. Bronwen thought she was wonderful.

"She's been very kind to me, Johnny."

"She mistakenly thinks you need her compassion." I found I loathed Mrs. Straker all the more now that I was so absolutely in her debt, and I did not like being thwarted in my loathing by evidence that she could be kind.

However our bizarre alliance continued and was even strengthened when Thomas arrived home for the summer holidays and declared he had no intention of returning to Harrow in the autumn. This led to rows at Oxmoon, but my father, who always prided himself on his ability to manage children, evidently found himself unable to ask me for help. It was Mrs. Straker who cornered me during one of my visits and told me what was going on.

"Bobby's getting upset again," she said. "It's no good expecting him to cope with a boy of seventeen, he's too old and he hasn't the stamina to solve the problem—and Thomas *is* a problem, make no mistake about that. He might have a nice nature, but who can tell? He spends all his time being bloody-minded. I'm fed up with him."

I felt the last thing I needed at that moment in my life was a bloody-minded adolescent, but I said I would do what I could. Thomas was out at that time but I left a note asking him to call, and rather to my surprise he rode over to the Manor that same evening and tramped truculently into my study for his audience.

XI

"Of course I know why you want to see me," said Thomas, flinging himself down in the best armchair and swinging his feet insolently onto my desk.

"You've heard I'm refusing to go back for a final year at that bloody school and you want to give me some bloody lecture about the glories of education."

"Oh? Then let me set your mind at rest; I don't give lectures, bloody or otherwise. I say, would you mind very much if you took your feet off my desk? Try the fender; it's a far more comfortable height. . . . Thanks."

"I've had enough of school. I think education's a load of balls."

"I'm sure many people would agree with you. Too bad Papa isn't one of them. Cigarette?"

He grabbed the cigarette with such alacrity that he nearly pulled the case out of my hand. With compassion, I realized he was nervous, and in the knowledge that he was vulnerable I looked at him more closely. He was as tall as I was by that time but built differently. He was broader, heavier, more like my mother's side of the family than my father's, and he had a square, mulish jaw which reminded me suddenly of frightful Aunt Ethel in Staffordshire.

"Well," I said when our cigarettes were alight, "what do you plan to do now?"

"Raise hell, get drunk and fuck every woman in sight."

"Oh yes? Well, I agree that takes care of the nights. But what are you going to do during the day?"

Thomas immediately assumed his most belligerent expression. "Why do you want to know?"

"Sheer mindless curiosity."

"What are you after?"

"Why do I have to be 'after' anything?"

"Most people are," said Thomas, and I heard an echo of Milly Straker's cynicism in his pathetic attempt to appear worldly.

"I'm not most people, I'm your brother and I'm sorry that you and Papa should be at loggerheads. Is there anything I can do to help?"

"How about minding your own bloody business?"

"Certainly—if that's what you really want."

There was a silence while we smoked and eyed each other. Then in a gust of embarrassment Thomas stubbed out his cigarette. "Well, if that's all you want to say I'll be off. Unless you intend to offer me a drink."

"No. Just help."

"But what do you get out of helping me?"

"Abuse and bad language, apparently." I stood up and opened the door of the study. "Goodbye, Thomas."

He hesitated. He looked very young, and suddenly I was reminded of the scene in the summerhouse after my mother's death when he had been a frightened fourteen-year-old whose world had collapsed overnight.

I closed the door again. "What's it really like at Oxmoon," I said abruptly, "with Papa and Milly Straker? And how do you think you'll get on living there all the year round in their company?"

"Mind your own bloody business," said Thomas, and elbowed his way past me into the hall.

"Well, when you're ready to talk," I shouted after him, "remember that I'm always ready to listen!"

But the front door slammed in my face.

XII

Ten weeks later in October I received a letter from Constance, and as I ripped open the envelope at the breakfast table I found myself praying that after the news I expected, I would find the promise of a divorce.

My darling John, Constance had written, *our daughter was born yesterday at six o'clock in the morning and weighs exactly seven pounds. As we agreed earlier, she will be called Francesca Constance unless I hear from you to the contrary.*

Of course you may see her whenever you wish. Indeed you may see me whenever you wish, and perhaps when you see the baby, who is so lovely and so perfect, you will realize that divorce is not the answer for us, either now or at any other time.

Ever your loving and devoted wife, CONSTANCE.

I looked up. At the other end of the table, Bronwen was watching me. Around us the children were chattering, Marian and Rhiannon on one side, Harry and Dafydd on the other and the baby in his little portable cot by the window. It was a Saturday morning and the children, free from lessons, were in good spirits.

". . . and turtles live to be three hundred years old . . ."

". . . and it's called a six-shooter because . . ."

". . . although as I said to my governess, how do they know turtles live for hundreds of years when no one can live long enough to watch them? . . . What's the matter, Papa?"

Dafydd and Harry paused in their discussion of guns. All eyes were turned in my direction.

"Nothing," I said. I left the room. A second later I realized this had been the wrong thing to do, but I could not make myself go back. I was still hesitating when Bronwen slipped out of the room to join me.

"Is the baby all right?" she said rapidly.

"Yes." I handed her the letter. As she read it the color faded from her face until the freckles stood out starkly on the bridge of her nose. Handing the letter back she said, "Would you like me to tell the children?"

"No. I must."

We went back into the room. Bronwen picked up the baby, said briskly,

"Rhiannon—Dafydd—I want to talk to you" and led the way out again into the hall.

Her children trooped obediently after her, but although Marian tried to follow I held out my hand.

"Wait, Marian, I want to tell you about the baby."

"What baby? Oh, that one. Did it come?"

"Yes. It's a girl. She's going to be called Francesca."

"What a perfectly frightful name," said Marian, "but never mind; I shan't see her so what does it matter?"

She shook off my hand and headed for the door.

"Marian—"

The door slammed. I was reminded of Thomas. I thought again of Dr. de Vestris saying what happened when parents went off the rails, and for a second my blood ran cold.

"The baby won't make any difference, will it?" and Harry suspiciously. "I don't want to go back to London and live with Constance. I want to stay here with Bronwen and the piano." The thought of the piano cheered him. He wriggled off his chair and ran to the door. "I'm going to have my practice now," he said over his shoulder, and disappeared. I smiled, mercifully diverted from the memory of Dr. de Vestris, but then sighed at the thought of the music. Urged on by Bronwen I now allowed Harry to play the piano daily, though for no more than half an hour; I had no wish to spoil his fun but without a time limit he would have wasted all day at the keys.

I thought briefly of Blanche playing the piano, but Blanche seemed to have existed so long ago that I could not connect her with my present life. I thought of Constance and shuddered, though whether with rage, guilt, grief or shame I hardly knew. Leaving the table I went upstairs to Marian's room. Bronwen looked up as I came in.

"I was promising that of course you'll take her to visit Constance and the baby," she said, "but she tells me she doesn't want to go."

"I just want to forget it all," wept Marian as I sat down on the bed and put my arm around her. "If I remember it'll only make me miserable, and I can't bear being miserable anymore. . . ." Sobs overwhelmed her, and when I pressed her closer she clung to me. Bronwen began to tiptoe towards the door, but I motioned her to stay. "I want Mama," whispered Marian. "Every night I ask God to make her come back to life, like Lazarus, but He doesn't listen, I pray and pray but nothing happens."

"Marian . . ." I tried and failed to frame a response, but Bronwen said in the heavily accented English which sounded so soothing, "I was wondering if you thought of her often now that you're back in the house where she used to be. I think of her often too. She may not be here herself anymore, but the memory's here, isn't it, and memories are so precious, such a comfort, because no one can take them away from you, and although she's dead yet in a way she's still alive, alive in your mind, and that's how God can bring her back for you. And although that's not as good as having her here alive and well, it helps to look across at the past, doesn't it, to look at her and know that she'll be there always in your memory to be a comfort to you when you want to remember."

Marian rubbed her eyes and gave several little gasps as if the sobbing had left her out of breath. I found a handkerchief for her, and at last she whispered to Bronwen, "Do you really think of her?"

"Oh yes, she was such a lovely lady, and so kind to me. When she was alive I wished that there was something I could do to repay her for her kindness, and that's why I was so pleased when Papa suggested I should look after you and Harry. It was something I could do for her, a payment of the debt, and that made me happy."

Marian thought about this.

"We must talk about her," said Bronwen. "It's such a waste to shut away precious memories and never speak of them. We'll talk about her and by talking we'll bring her back to you and then you'll feel better."

Marian gave another little gasp and blew her nose before turning to me. "Is Bronwen here forever? Or might you fall in love with someone else, do you think, and leave her as you left Constance?"

"No, I could never leave Bronwen. Impossible. Out of the question."

I felt her relax in my arms. "I don't want anyone else going away," she whispered to me.

I kissed her and said, "Everything's going to be all right." But as I spoke I thought of Constance, alone with her stubborn pride in London, and I knew the happy ending I was promising Marian was still far beyond my reach.

XIII

Three days later I journeyed to London and bought a toy rabbit at Selfridges. At the Carlton Club I consumed a whisky-and-soda before telephoning Constance.

"It was thoughtful of you to call," she said, "but there's no need for you ever to make an appointment to come here. This is your home and you can come and go entirely as you please."

I consumed a second whisky, this time without soda, and took a taxi to Chester Square.

Constance should no doubt still have been in bed but she had put on the emerald-green negligée which she knew I liked and had arranged herself not unattractively on the drawing-room sofa. I found that this pathetic attempt to look her best made me feel angry. I was too angry to analyze the anger, but

I hated myself for giving way to it. Sheer misery overwhelmed me. I felt as if my consciousness were being hacked to pieces with a hatchet.

Giving her the carnations which I had forced myself to buy, I inquired formally after her health.

"I'm better now," she said, "but it was rough. I hope Teddy has an easier time."

"How is she?"

"Fine. But longing for it to be over." She sniffed the carnations. "Will you ring the bell? These ought to be put in water right away."

I did as she asked before departing for the nurseries.

It seemed a long way there but that was because I had to pause on the landing until I felt calmer. When I arrived the new nanny gave me a hostile stare but I got rid of her and moved to the cot.

The baby was so new that it still had a red face. Swathed in clouds of white linen and lace, it lay sound asleep, oblivious to luxury, in its expensive little resting place. Touching its small bald head with my index finger, I remembered Evan as I had first seen him in his wooden box on wheels, and I thought of my new daughter growing up to envy him. No money could ease emotional poverty. No material comfort could provide a substitute for an absent father.

I undid the toy rabbit from its gay wrapping, tucked it into the cot and turned away, but I was in such a state of grief and shame that I could not remember where I was. But when I looked back at the cot memory returned to me. I was on the far side of the line I had failed to draw when I had married Constance in the pursuit of avarice and ambition. I had wronged Bronwen, wronged Constance, and now I was wronging my child but there was no way back. The line could not be recrossed even in the event of a divorce. Constance and the child would still exist, and nothing could fully make amends to them for what I had done.

After a long while I reentered the drawing room and found Constance was still busy with the carnations; the arrangement was looking glacially formal.

"Isn't she lovely?"

I nodded. Constance offered me a drink but I declined. "I'm afraid I must be on my way."

"But you'll come again soon? Do bring Harry and Marian—I'd love to see them!"

"I'll have to write to you about it."

"Remember," she said, "that everything will always be waiting for you here. You can come back at any time."

"It's never going to happen, Constance."

" 'Never' is a long time, isn't it? I'm going to go on hoping."

There was nothing left to say.

I walked out.

XIV

"Was it awful?" said Bronwen.

"Yes. Bloody awful. I just want to go to bed and forget about it."

We went to bed and for a while I did forget, but even when I was physically exhausted I was unable to sleep. Eventually Bronwen lit a candle and said, "Talk to me."

"I can't."

"You must. You know what happens when you can't talk. You get all muddled and lie to yourself and end up doing something which makes you and everyone else miserable."

This was such an accurate description of my talent for making a mess of my life that I could only groan and bury my face in the pillow, but finally I managed to say, "I despise myself, how could I have married that woman, how could I have turned my back on you, how could I have fathered that child, I feel as if I'm split in two, half of me wants to lead a good decent life but the other half does these terrible things, and supposing the other half wins? It's not impossible. I've known from childhood, ever since I found out the truth about my grandmother and my parents, that absolutely anyone is capable of absolutely anything—"

"Yes," said Bronwen. "Absolutely anyone is capable of absolutely anything. *But not everyone has to do it.*"

"I know, I know, one draws the line, but supposing I draw the wrong line again, supposing I get in a muddle about what's right—I'm so weak, so contemptible, I've done such terrible things, how I can trust myself, I don't, I can't—"

"I trust you. I agree you've done dreadful things, but now you're trying to do what's right, you're being honest and truthful and brave, and so long as you're honest and truthful you can't get in a mess by living a lie, and so long as you're brave you can't despise yourself for cowardice, and so long as you're all those things you'll be strong enough to draw those lines, as the English say so strangely when all they mean is choosing the right circle to live in, and once the lines are drawn you'll be the man you want to be and the man I know you are, and you'll be safe."

I wanted to make love to her again, but I was too exhausted and I collapsed into her arms. After a long time I heard myself say, "My father thinks I still want Oxmoon. Probably Robert thinks I still want Oxmoon. Sometimes even *I* think I still want Oxmoon—oh, God, I'm in such a muddle still; I don't want Oxmoon anymore, I truly don't, I'm fully satisfied just to live here with you, but sometimes I can't help thinking—"

"Of course you covet it now and then. That's human. You covet it like I used to covet my lady in Cardiff's best teapot. But I wouldn't have stolen it. That would have been wrong."

"But supposing Robert thinks—"

"You don't lie to him, do you?"

"No, I told him how Straker tried to bribe me."

"Then you're safe. *Don't start lying to Robert.* So long as you're truthful with him you'll be safe."

"How can you be so sure?"

"Distrust grows out of lies. Wrongdoing grows out of distrust. Tragedy grows out of wrongdoing. But out of honesty grows love and love's so powerful, it'll be like a suit of armor, protecting Robert, protecting you."

"That ought to be true, but *is* it true? It all sounds vaguely religious but I can't believe in God, not after the war—"

"I never believed in God so long as I thought of Him as a person," said Bronwen. "To me He was like my father who'd gone away and couldn't help me. But then I stopped saying 'He' and said 'It,' and suddenly everything seemed simple. God's magic, that's all. It's all the things we can't see or explain. It's the rhythm of life. It's the circle of time."

"That reminds me of Robert talking about Boethius and the Wheel of Fortune," I said, and I began to tell her about that ancient theory of life which had become so popular in the Middle Ages. "I never studied Boethius," I said, "but when I was reading French and German up at Oxford I came across the work of Peter von Kastl and Jean de Meung who were both influenced by him . . ." And as I talked on about the Wheel of Fortune revolving in its endless cycle, I began at last to feel calmer.

"But that sounds as if people have no power to leave the wheel," said Bronwen, "and I think they have. I think there are many wheels, and if you have the will you can move from one to another."

"That's what I need to believe too but supposing free will is an illusion? For instance, take Robert's view: he says that although we're all strapped to the Wheel of Fortune, Fortune herself offers us choices to determine our fate. Now, that sounds fine but supposing those choices themselves are predetermined by forces beyond our control?"

"That's a horrible idea!"

"Horrible, yes—I've always detested and feared the concept of predestination. However I have a feeling Boethius solved the problem, although I can't remember how he did it."

This time I did manage to make love to her again. Then having proved that renewal could follow exhaustion on our own private wheel of fortune, I found my courage returning and knew I could discard my despair and struggle on.

XV

I had no respite. The chaos continued but by this time I had realized that a section of my life would be in chaos indefinitely, so I was becoming resigned to the hard core of misery in my mind. My father telephoned with the news that Edmund had a son. Letters started to arrive from Constance about the possibility of a double christening. The long aftermath of my disastrous marriage seemed about to overwhelm me again, but before I could give way a second time to despair I was diverted by a crisis at Oxmoon.

It was by that time early November, and when the news of the crisis reached me I had just returned from fetching Marian from her private school in Swansea. Once Daphne's opinion that no respectable governess would remain long at the Manor had been confirmed, I had had no difficulty convincing myself that it would be good for Marian to go to school, but as Bronwen had refused my offer that her children too should be privately educated, Rhiannon and Dafydd continued to attend school in the village. Marian, not unnaturally, wanted to go there too, and when I refused I found myself involved in inevitably distasteful explanations. There was no row, since Marian quickly accepted the fact that ladies never attended the village primary school, but I foresaw the class system pushing its long cruel bayonets deep into my home and in time impaling us all.

"We must give all the children the same education," I said to Bronwen stubbornly, but she was equally stubborn in disagreeing.

"I don't want my children given airs and graces and being taught to look down on their own class," she said. "It wouldn't make them happy. Dafydd wants to be a motor mechanic, not a gentleman, and if Rhiannon gets a lady's education she'll end up too good for the boys of her own class and not good enough for the boys who are better."

There was undoubtedly much truth in this observation, but I foresaw the situation deteriorating as the children became aware of their differences. Marian was too aware of them already. I had that very afternoon in the car been obliged to reprove her for making a snobbish criticism of Rhiannon.

On our arrival home Marian dashed off to the dining room where everyone was having tea and I went to the cloakroom to hang up my coat and hat. I had just returned to the hall when I was startled by a thunderous battering on the front door.

It was Thomas, wearing his best livid expression. I knew at once he was very upset.

"Hullo," I said swiftly. "What's the trouble?"

"It's the old bugger."

I steered him into my study, but just as I was opening my mouth to reprove him for referring to our father so disrespectfully he collapsed into the nearest armchair as if it were a sanctuary and I realized a reproof would be inappropriate. His mouth was trembling. He managed to tuck it down at the corners as usual, but when he spoke his voice was unsteady.

"Got a gasper, old boy?"

I gave him a cigarette. "What's happened?"

Thomas inhaled deeply and managed to say in a casual voice: "The old bugger's gone crazy. Well, of course he's been gaga off and on for ages, we all know that, but this is worse, this is the last straw, this is absolutely bloody . . ." He faltered to a halt.

"What happened?"

"We had a row about the estate. The old bugger won't let me do anything. Well, I didn't mind loafing around for a time while I recovered from bloody school, but I'm bored now and I want to do something so I asked him a month ago if he could teach me how to run the estate, and he said no, I was too young and I ought to be at school. So we had a row and I went off to Daxworth and learned about cows instead, but I got a bit bored because I don't think they're really my kind of animal, so I thought I'd get interested in estate management again, and this afternoon when Papa was out I sneaked into the library and had a look at the books—"

"—and he caught you red-handed."

"Yes. Christ, he was bloody angry."

"Well, I suppose he had a right to be angry since you were prying among his private papers, but on the other hand I'm surprised he wasn't glad to see how keen you are to learn." I tried to stop myself wondering why my father should be so abnormally sensitive about anyone seeing the accounts. "What happened next?"

Thomas did not answer immediately. His blue eyes reflected complex emotions; anger and resentment were mingling with some deep distress, and as I watched I saw the distress become uppermost in his mind.

"Out with it, Thomas. You'll feel better once you've told me."

But still he was silent, struggling with his feelings. At last he muttered, "Don't want to be disloyal."

I was touched by this because I saw how fond he was of his father, but I was also disturbed and to my dismay I realized I was in the middle of an interview that was far more crucial than I desired.

"There's no question of disloyalty, Thomas," I said quickly. "He's my father as well as yours and I know very well he's subject to mental disturbances. What did he do? Did he hit you?"

"No. God, I wish he had. I wouldn't have minded that. But he didn't. He yelled at me and then—suddenly—he went to pieces. He said, 'I can't manage you anymore,' and he went out into the hall and shouted for Mama."

There was a silence. Thomas bit his lip, pouted but finally tucked his mouth down at the corners again. "Silly old bugger," he muttered fiercely. "I felt so ashamed for him."

"I'd have been both shocked and frightened," I said at once, implying that shock and fear were permissible emotions in the circumstances. "What did you do next?"

"Nothing. I was too . . . well, I just stayed where I was. Then Milly came, but he said he wanted his wife, not the parlormaid."

"Christ. How did Milly cope?"

"She said, 'Very well, Mr. Godwin, but why don't you sit down for a minute while I fetch you a little glass of champagne.' Then there was an awful silence, and just when I thought I was going to be sick, Papa said, 'Milly' and burst into tears. Oh God, John, it was so absolutely *bloody*—"

"Bloody, yes. Did you manage to escape then?"

"No, Milly told me to help her take him upstairs. He was shaking and crying and could hardly stand, but we got him up to his room somehow without the servants seeing. Then Milly said to me, 'Go out of the house for an hour—*go right out.*' She was very fierce about it so I went downstairs but I was sick in the cloakroom and the vomit got over my shirt so I went upstairs to change and then I heard noises going on in the bedroom, awful noises, I couldn't stand it, I felt sick again—"

"Yes, all right, Thomas, you don't have to say anymore."

"It was hearing the noises—he was sort of screaming—"

"Sit down again and I'll get you some brandy."

Retrieving the decanter and two glasses from the dining room, I poured us each a stiff measure. Thomas drank his too fast and choked. Afterwards he whispered, "I don't want to go back there just yet."

"No, of course not, I wouldn't dream of suggesting it. You can stay here for as long as you like. I'll go over to Oxmoon, have a word with Milly and sort everything out."

Thomas was too overcome to speak but not too overcome to grab the decanter and pour himself another measure. When he had gulped it down he said, "You're the only one of all those bloody brothers that's ever cared more than a pail of pigshit for me. I'm sorry I was so bloody awful to you in the past. I suppose I was jealous. I didn't like it when the old bugger fawned over you, but I don't suppose you'd ever understand."

I began to tell him how jealous I had been of Robert when I had been his age, but he was too upset to listen.

"I hate Robert," he said interrupting me. "I hate everyone and everything except you—the world, the weather, women, politics, Ramsay MacDonald, Stanley Baldwin, Bolsheviks, the Prince of Wales, Harrow, the English, the Germans, clergymen, God, the Devil and bloody sex. I hate them all and I only like animals and you—animals are better than humans because they don't let you down, and you're as good as an animal. You're the only decent human being I know, and I don't care who you sleep with."

I casually removed the brandy decanter as his hand wavered towards it, but my feelings were very far from casual. I was thinking of Thomas pitchforked from the secure loving innocent world my mother had created for him into the world of Milly Straker, and I had a long chilling view of my father's moral debacle. Then suddenly I was contrasting Marian, racked by sobs, with the happy little girl who had said her prayers in the nursery with Blanche, and once more I had a glimpse of a wheel which terrified me.

I closed my mind against it. Struggling to my feet I said abruptly to Thomas, "I'll ask Mrs. Wells to prepare a room for you and I'll tell Bronwen you've come to stay."

An hour later, when Thomas had been safely settled at the Manor, I found myself once more on the road to Oxmoon at the beginning of a new journey into hell.

XVI

"Much better for Thomas to be with you, dear," said Milly. "I'll go and pack a couple of bags for him straightaway. As for your father, I put him in the library because he's always happy pottering around there with his papers, but don't be surprised if he's not entirely twenty shillings to the pound."

My father looked better than I had anticipated but not at all pleased to see me. He was seated at the library table in front of the estate books, and as I entered the room he looked up at me suspiciously over his spectacles.

I asked his permission to look after Thomas for a while. "I think he could be useful to me at the farm," I said, "and I'd enjoy his company."

"Yes, very well, you take care of him. I can't manage him anymore; he's too difficult."

I thought of the strong capable father of my early memories. When I could speak again I said, "Papa, there's a question I'd like to ask but if it upsets you too much then naturally I shan't expect an answer. Do you want Thomas out of the house because he's difficult or because you're afraid of his interest in the estate books?"

"I don't know what you mean," he said instantly, but he did. He looked furious.

Once again I had to pause before I could nerve myself to continue. "I was wondering if the estate's getting too much for you now that—by your own admission—you're not quite so young as you used to be. If I can be of any help—"

"Absolutely not," said my father. "You've got to be kept out."

There was another silence. I remember thinking, in the detached manner that sometimes accompanies harrowing circumstances, that an outsider would have thought our conversation bizarrely disjointed.

"Will you talk to Robert?" I said at last. "Perhaps he could arrange for a first-class agent to help you."

"I can manage. Go away and stop trying to interfere in my affairs."

But I stood my ground as I tried to work out how I could say what had to be said next, and finally I replied, "I quite understand why you don't wish me to be involved in the estate and of course I completely accept your decision. But can I help you at all with your private income? I could perhaps attend to the correspondence with your stockbrokers, your accountants, the Inland Revenue—"

"I don't use accountants. Waste of money. I'm good with money, always was. Head for figures."

"I know that. But I thought perhaps I might help you during those times when you're not well."

"No need. I've got Milly. She's got a head for figures too, wonderfully clever she is, thinks just like a man."

The conversation shattered into silence again. During the interval that followed I framed my next sentence several times in my head before I found the version that satisfied me.

"How fortunate," I said. "I didn't realize you'd given her a power of attorney."

My father immediately flew into a rage. "What power of attorney? I'm not giving anyone a power of attorney! How dare you imply I'm incapable of signing my name!"

"Oh, I see. Milly just prepares the checks."

"I refuse to be subjected to this cross-examination any longer! Go away and leave me in peace!"

I went away. Upstairs in Thomas's bedroom I found Milly completing the packing of his clothes.

"I want to warn you," I said, "that I know you've involved yourself in my father's financial affairs and that I'll go to court if I find any evidence—any evidence at all—that you're abusing your position here."

"Abusing my position, dear? But I do nothing without his written authorization! What kind of a fool do you think I am?"

"Written authorizations are meaningless when someone's not competent to conduct his own affairs."

"Well really, dear, what a nasty mind you've got! I'm quite shocked! Now look here, my friend. If you don't think your father's fit to conduct his affairs, then go to court and get an order but don't come whining to me about undue influence when he's not certified, not legally incompetent and still has a right to manage his affairs as he pleases!"

"I just wanted you to know that I don't intend to tolerate larceny."

"The day I go to jail for larceny, John Godwin, is the day you retire to a monastery and become a monk. Oh, don't be so silly, dear, really, I feel quite put out! I thought we were friends nowadays?"

I picked up the packed bags and walked out without another word.

XVII

I arrived at Little Oxmoon to find a marital row of earsplitting violence was being concluded, and although I had schooled myself to take no notice of these searing verbal battles, I found it hard this time to look the other way.

"Just another little disagreement, sir," said Bennett soothingly as he admitted me to the hall. I had jumped at the sound of breaking glass. The next moment Ginevra was screaming, "All right, die—and the sooner the better!" and there was another crash before she rushed sobbing into the hall. She saw me, screamed, "Hit him, kill him, I don't care!" and stumbled, weaving, down the passage to her bedroom. As Bennett and I approached the drawing room we were almost overcome with the reek of gin, and on crossing the threshold we found she had smashed both her glass and the bottle against the wall.

"Oh hullo, John," said Robert, unperturbed. "What's this? Two visits in one day? Don't start flagellating yourself again in the name of moral duty; my nerves couldn't stand it. Bennett, get me out of here before I die of alcohol fumes."

We retired to Robert's bedroom. As soon as Bennett had left I said in a voice that I hoped was laconic, "Has she been drinking too much again?"

"Yes, but it's nothing to be excited about, just another of her bouts. They come and go like the Cheshire Cat's smile."

"What happened to upset her?"

"I was bloody ill this morning. My sense of balance went haywire and my vision was affected. Gavin thought rest would help and gave me a sedative and sure enough when I awoke I was better."

"Thank God."

"No, don't waste your time. I've now made up my mind that I must die as soon as possible."

"But you may not suffer that sort of attack again for years—"

"I can tolerate a simple inconvenience like incontinence, but the thought of being blind and possibly deaf and dumb—"

"But surely—"

"Oh, *shut up!* I want to die and I'm going to will myself to do it. People will themselves to live, don't they? I know I did, on Ben Nevis after the accident. Well, now I'm going to will myself to die. Death wants me to continue for another twenty years as a vegetable, but I'm going to outwit him; I'm going to win."

Since speech was impossible, I busied myself in drawing up a chair.

"Think of the way I was, John. You wouldn't want me to live as a vegetable, would you?"

I shook my head. But I whispered, "I'll be so alone."

"We're all alone," said Robert. "We're born alone, we live alone and we die alone. Any companionship is transitory and for the most part meaningless. The human condition is essentially tragic. Ask anyone over eighty who's seen all their friends die one by one."

Unwilling to upset him by arguing I said nothing, and eventually he asked why I had returned to see him.

"Bad news," I said. "But it can wait."

"Don't be a fool, can't you see that any bad news would rank as light relief after all I've been through? Get hold of Ginette at once and bring her in here."

I was most reluctant to disturb Ginevra but when he insisted I went to fetch her. She was calm but looked exhausted and disheveled in a dirty dressing gown.

"Robert thought you might like to join us—there's another crisis at Oxmoon, and—"

"Oh good," said Ginevra. "How simply heavenly, I can't wait to hear all the divine details."

We returned to Robert.

"I hated to think of you missing the fun," he said to her.

"Sweet of you, darling, it's made my day. God knows it needed making." She sat down beside him and covered his hand with hers.

Marveling at their endurance, I began to talk about my father.

XVIII

"What can we do, Robert?"

"I'm afraid the answer's still damn all."

"But there must be something!" exclaimed Ginevra.

"So long as he's insisting that he's fine, we'd have a hard time proving in court that he's not. Can't you picture the judge, who would probably be over seventy, saying, 'There, there, Mr. Godwin, I suffer from a poor memory myself now and then, it happens to us all!' No, Papa would have to have a full breakdown before we could successfully claim he was incapable of managing his affairs."

"But I'm quite sure," I said, "that his financial affairs are getting in a mess."

"That may well be so," said Robert, "but it's not a crime under English law for a man to make a mess of his financial affairs and it's not evidence of insanity if he voluntarily signs checks prepared by his mistress."

"So we just stand by, do we," said Ginevra, "while Oxmoon goes down the drain?"

"We have to stand by at present, certainly, but if Oxmoon starts to go down the drain on a grand scale, I think we should be the first to know about it. Let's get in league with the lawyers."

We agreed that I would seek an interview with my father's solicitor Freddy Fairfax. Then I offered to call at the major farms and talk casually to the foremen to see if there was any imminent possibility of catastrophe.

"Although it's my guess," said Robert, "that the estate can muddle on well enough for some time. He'll probably delegate more and more responsibility to the foremen and that would be a good thing. At least Straker doesn't know enough about estate management to queer that particular pitch."

"And his private fortune?"

"Oh, hopeless! She'll get her paws on that all right—and legally, too. He'll simply give it away."

"If only he could break down now—"

"No such luck. Life isn't so tidy."

The three of us were silent, considering the untidiness of life.

"I can't quite see the bottom of the wheel of his fortune," said Robert, "but I'm beginning to think it's a very long way down."

"That reminds me, Robert: how did Boethius circumvent the horror of predestination?"

"Darling," said Ginevra, "what a frightful question! How you could!" She stood up, caught sight of herself in the glass and winced. "God, I look eighty! Johnny, come and have some coffee. Robert, you should be back in bed."

"The horror of a preordained future," said Robert, embracing the diversion with relief, "is circumvented by saying there *is* no future. God is outside time and therefore as far as God and his preordained plans are concerned, past, present and future are all happening simultaneously. This permits the exercise of the individual will and yet still permits God to remain omnipotent."

"Good heavens!"

"I agree it's weak," said Robert apologetically, "but the postclassical mind often left much to be desired."

"I think it's all rather heaven," said Ginevra idly, ringing for Bennett, and drifted away to the drawing room.

When I joined her later, she was drinking black coffee and reading the label on the bottle of aspirin in her hand. Pouring myself some coffee, I sat down beside her.

"Just warding off the inevitable hangover," she said, putting the bottle aside. "Sorry we were so awful when you arrived but this morning was a bad shock."

"Does he mean what he says about dying?"

"He does and he doesn't. He'll be all right so long as he can sit in a wheelchair and read and talk to people. He can accept that. But beyond that point . . . yes, he'd be better dead, and he knows it. I know it too, but I couldn't kill him; I've made that quite clear. I think Gavin might if things got quite beyond the pale, but of course doctors have to be so careful. Especially Gavin." She had been watching her cigarette as she spoke, but now she looked directly at me. "Has there been any gossip," she said, "about Gavin and me?"

"None."

"Good. Robert was worried in case Gavin couldn't cope and wound up being struck off the register, but Gavin can handle a dangerous situation without losing his head. He's tough—and I'm careful." She smoked thoughtfully for a time. "Gavin understands how I feel about Robert," she said at last. "None of the other men ever did. Gavin understands Robert too, and Robert likes him—Robert's glad I have someone he can trust and approve of, so you see, we're all very close, it's . . . but what word can possibly describe it? It's comforting—yes, that's it. Comforting—and not just for me but for all of us. We all benefit."

"I'm glad." I waited while she poured me some more coffee. Then I added: "I hadn't guessed. I suppose I've been far too preoccupied with my own affairs."

"Well, God knows they must be a full-time preoccupation, but all the same even though you don't have much time at present I do wish poor Bobby would let you help him with Oxmoon. Why won't he, do you think?"

I thought of Bronwen urging me to be truthful. "He doesn't trust me not to play the villain and cheat Robert."

"Don't be silly, darling, you mean he doesn't trust himself not to give Oxmoon to you and promptly die of remorse!" She smiled at me but her eyes were wary. "And that wouldn't be such a tragedy for you, would it?"

"Possibly not." I kept thinking of Bronwen. "I covet Oxmoon sometimes," I said. "Of course I do. But I couldn't take it by fraud or duress. I could only take it if I felt that was what Papa and Robert both wanted." I smiled at her suddenly and said, "I have to do what's right if I want to avoid the Home of the Assumption!"

"Darling Johnny!" said Ginevra, kissing me. "How thrilled your poor old grandmother would be if she knew what a fortifying influence she'd become!"

I was believed. As I held her hands I was aware of her trust. It made me want to believe too.

She escorted me outside to my car and when we opened the front door we saw that although there was no moon the stars were shining. It was cold.

"Thank you for telling me about Gavin," I said.

"I thought you might be worrying in case someone got hurt."

We embraced again.

"My God," said Ginevra, "what a life."

"What a life. Never mind. Hold fast, stand firm and soldier on."

"Darling, how divine—just like a poem by Kipling! It almost gives me the courage to say bugger Boethius and his ghastly Wheel!"

We laughed, drawing strength from each other. Then I left her, got into my car and drove on once more into the dark.

10

I

IT TOOK four years to complete my father's disintegration and all the while Bronwen and I moved deeper into a gathering chaos. Some of our early troubles were resolved: our domestic difficulties were eased after the advent of Mrs. Wells; Marian recovered from her initial misery; the children settled down tolerably well together. Most important of all Bronwen and I knew a deep personal contentment which created a happy atmosphere in the house, and by the end of 1924 it seemed we had evolved a pattern of life that transcended the differences between us.

That was the honeymoon. After that life became increasingly less easy.

At first Bronwen found life at the Manor so intimidating that she spent much time secluding herself in the nurseries and evading the servants, but gradually she adjusted to life in what was for her a large house, and she became less self-conscious. To help her I modified my own mundane daily habits; we did not dine at eight and on our own, as I would have done with Constance or Blanche, but instead ate an informal meal with all the children at seven o'clock. This was far past Harry's bedtime, but Bronwen's children seemed to stay up later without ill effect, so to my children's delight they found their day extended. By the time they were all in bed the evening was far advanced, but Bronwen and I were disinclined to spend much time on our own in Blanche's drawing room and we would retire to our bedroom, which had soon acquired armchairs and a table. It was here that Bronwen, shying away from the intimidating elegance of the downstairs receptions rooms, was able to relax and soon I too was drawn to the room's attractive informality. Needless to say it was not the bedroom I had shared with Blanche. There was another bedroom, equally large, on the other side of the house, and Blanche's room was now set aside for the guests who never came.

But I was at peace with Blanche. Bronwen, as she had proved to Marian, was not afraid of Blanche's memory and in her mystical acceptance of Blanche's past presence in the house I found my own release from past guilt. Once I did say to Bronwen, "You're sure you're not oppressed by her?" but she merely answered in surprise, "How could I be? She was a good person. All the memories are benign." And in these simple statements she brought harmony to a situation that might well have been too complex to endure with ease.

Unfortunately the atmosphere of harmony at the Manor did not extend to the world beyond the gates. No one cut me dead but I was aware that no one was rushing to invite me to dinner, and soon it became clear that I was being treated as a traitor to my class. This by itself did not disturb me since I was more than willing to embrace such treachery, but I was determined out of pride that I was not going to remain a social pariah, and after careful thought I joined a golf club in Swansea.

I then realized that what everyone had been craving was some sign that I could still be treated as a normal person, and when I played golf with modest competence and stood drinks in the bar afterwards people were soon prepared to turn a blind eye to my private life. I now realized how wise I had been not to live with Bronwen openly. Probably I would have been refused membership of the club in those circumstances, but as a man separated from his wife and keeping up appearances as he lived quietly with his children in Penhale I was, with an effort of will and a little imagination, acceptable.

I began to be invited out to dine. Later I even gave a dinner party at the Manor and asked Ginevra to act as hostess. Bronwen, who wholeheartedly approved of my determination not to be a social pariah, kept thankfully upstairs. In fact so pleased was I by my success in overcoming the disapproval of my own class that it took me some time to realize how absolutely Bronwen was overwhelmed by the disapproval of hers.

However as usual when Bronwen's welfare was at stake, her sister was only too ready to enlighten me once she judged that the time had come to take action. I was told that Bronwen was now so afraid to leave the Manor for fear of unpleasantness that Myfanwy herself had to escort her on her visits to the Home Farm. There had also been anonymous letters pointing out that Evan had been born eleven months after Gareth Morgan's death. The minister at the chapel was thundering regularly about the wages of sin, and even Anstey the vicar had abandoned his cozy comments on the weather and retreated into monosyllabism.

"Why the devil didn't you say something to me?" I said angrily to Bronwen. "I thought you prided yourself on being honest!"

"I didn't think I had to say anything. I thought you knew what it was like," she said flatly, and added in defiance: "I don't care."

But she cared when life became difficult for Rhiannon and Dafydd at the village school, and soon we were arguing painfully about education again.

"I'm not having them educated above their station!"

"But can't you see that's the kind of view which perpetuates the class system? If all children were educated in the same way—"

"All right, send *your* children to the village school! Why do my children have to be the ones to change?"

"Because private education is better."

"Not for them! Anyway you can't iron out class by treating everyone the same, everyone's not the same and never will be and to say otherwise is just dangerous socialist rubbish, giving people expectations which haven't a hope of coming true. I'm all for improving people's lot in life as Mr. Lloyd George did with his welfare schemes, but I'm not going to ruin my children's lives by making them misfits!"

"Well, what do we do about Evan? If you think—"

"Oh, I know I haven't a hope of doing what I want with Evan, I know he'll be sent to boarding school when he's eight even though I think it's wicked and cruel—"

"Jesus Christ!"

The quarrel deepened. The controversy raged. We stood on either side of the abyss of class which divided us and shouted at each other until finally I said, "Class is evil, evil, *evil*—I hope there's a bloody revolution to abolish it," and I went off to play golf. I had work to do on the estate but I felt a retreat was necessary into my own class, and when I returned I found that Bronwen had gone to see her sister as if she too had felt such a withdrawal was needed.

We made up the quarrel, but soon the problem reached its climax when Rhiannon became hysterical at the prospect of going to school and Dafydd was stoned in the playground. At that point I arranged for the children to be transferred to a primary school in the nearest suburb of Swansea. There was no difficulty about transport because either Willis or I had to drive Marian into Swansea each day to her private school.

Bronwen wept with relief; the children, continuing their working-class education, soon settled down, but I knew their dilemma had merely been alleviated. At home they led a solitary life, unable to mix with the hostile local children and uninvited to the houses where Harry and Marian regularly went to play and have tea.

"Dear me, it's all so diffy for them, isn't it?" confided Marian to me.

"Almost as diffy as it is for me not being able to invite any of my school friends here."

"I don't see your difficulty, Marian. Just say Bronwen's the nanny and that Rhiannon and Dafydd are her children."

"But how could I explain why they take their meals with us? They're both so common and it all looks so odd—"

"I'm sorry you should feel that's so important."

"Well, of course it's important!" stormed Marian, abandoning her precocious sophistication and becoming a tearful little girl of ten. "It's absolutely beastly, and I wish I could live with Aunt Daphne!"

Later I said to Bronwen, "That damned Daphne's a bad influence on Marian. I know she thinks it's monstrous that Marian should be brought up in these circumstances."

"Well, you can't stop Marian's visits to her. That would be disastrous."

"Everything I do with Marian's disastrous," I said. "Everything."

"It'll sort itself out once we're married."

"Ah yes. Of course," I said, but I knew that since Daphne would judge the marriage a hopeless *mésalliance*, Marian's embarrassment would continue.

Amidst all these difficulties I found it a welcome relief to teach Thomas as much as I could about estate management. I was in fact having a difficult time with my estate, and if my other troubles had not been so numerous I might well have become depressed by its ailing fortunes. My original plan to grow a surplus of cereals for sale with the aid of a motor lorry was sound enough, but a series of wet summers in the early Twenties had wreaked havoc with my adventurous schemes, and in addition the price of wheat had fallen from its postwar level of seventy-two and eleven a quarter to forty-nine and three in 1924, a year that turned out to be one of the wettest on record. I was considering a complete return to cattle breeding and growing cereals only for winter feed, but in the end I decided to wait, reasoning that both the weather and the price of wheat could only improve.

Meanwhile I thought I might try raising pigs. Thomas was keen on pigs and it occurred to me that the best way of keeping him out of mischief was to encourage an interest that gave him the chance to prove himself. Accordingly, to the Merediths' horror, I sanctioned the idea of a piggery and soothed them by promising to build it with an eye to the prevailing wind. Thomas was very excited, and as I listened to him expounding on the best methods of porcine castration I realized he was more of a farmer than I would ever be: I was interested not in farming for farming's sake but in farming as a business, and although I knew enough about farming to realize it could not be conducted in the same way as a manufacturing concern, I still tended to regard my estate solely from an accounting point of view. When my profits fell for reasons beyond my power to control I found myself growing impatient and restless, but I knew that a true farmer, while being equally disappointed, would have been able to console himself with the fact that he was still leading a life that satisfied him. No such consolation was available to me. I knew I was once more discontented with my career as a minor squire, and I began to wonder if I could carve out some business opportunities for myself in Swansea which as a large industrial port no doubt contained many attractive boardrooms. I resolved to cultivate the magnates of my acquaintance at the golf club.

However although I was privately dissatisfied with my situation Thomas was happy with his pigs, and fired by his enthusiasm I even began to share his interest in the brutes. They had a quick turnover. They bred frequently and in quantity. As far as I could see they stood a chance of being steadily profitable. I was intrigued.

I was also relieved that Thomas was enjoying his life at Penhale Manor. I gave him a certain freedom, as much as any young man of his age had a right to expect, but I drew up a set of rules which I insisted he should obey: he was to be civil to Bronwen; he was not to use bad language in front of the children; he was to be punctual at mealtimes; he was to drink wine or beer but on no account to touch spirits, and he was to report to my study for work at nine o'clock each morning. In exchange for obeying this elementary code of civilized behavior he received the instruction he wanted, a roof over his head and stability. This did not transform him instantly into an angel but he did improve.

I was interested to discover that he was by no means stupid despite his aversion to school, and although his strong opinionated humorless personality was not to everyone's taste, there was a childlike streak in him which I found touching. His devotion to me, once he had decided to bestow it, was so fierce that I sometimes felt in his presence as if I were accompanied by a large dog whose heart of gold lay beyond bared teeth. Bronwen, who was a little alarmed by him at first, soon found it easy to be friendly.

"I suppose you were sleeping with beautiful girls like that since you were younger than me," said Thomas gloomily, and recognizing this remark as a plea for guidance I said, "Not exactly" and told him of my protracted virginity, which had resulted in my rush to the altar while I was still emotionally immature. Thomas, who was obviously bothered by the subject of women, was so much cheered by this account of my youthful chastity that I took the opportunity to give him some useful information about sex. He was enthralled and gratified.

"I think you ought to be canonized as the patron saint of chaps my age," he said, and seemed surprised when I remarked drily that most people would consider me quite unfit to bring up an adolescent boy.

"Most people? I hate most people," said Thomas, closing the argument in his usual belligerent fashion, but although he talked truculently out of habit I never worried that he might get into trouble as the result of any violent behavior. I might have had acute anxieties in my private life, but they never centered around Thomas.

The anxieties deepened as time passed and Constance refused to change her mind about a divorce. In the end I gave up calling on her to discuss the situation. She made me too furious and Francesca made me feel too guilty. Photographs of Francesca arrived regularly but I could not bear to look at them and locked them away at once. Bronwen suggested it might be better if we looked at them together, but I found it impossible to agree and when she realized there was nothing she could do to help me the subject continued to lie between us like a lead weight.

Edmund sent me the occasional photograph of his children. His first son was followed by a second; he was blissfully happy. As he had soon regretted his decision not to remain on speaking terms with me, we did meet for a drink on my rare visits to town but he always made excuses not to visit Gower. No doubt Teddy found my father's domestic arrangements as objectionable as mine and had ruled that both Oxmoon and Penhale Manor were beyond the pale.

At first I thought that my father would be hurt by Edmund's desertion, but later I realized he was glad not to be obliged to entertain him. He had become more of a recluse. I suspected this was because he had come to distrust his ability to conduct a normal conversation, for Oswald Stourham, one of the few of his old friends who still saw him regularly, reported to me that "poor Bobby wasn't the man he used to be," and I realized he had been shocked by some new evidence of my father's decline. When I called at Oxmoon my father seemed pleased to see me, but he would not come to the Manor. He appeared to be withdrawing deeper and deeper into his home, and the house seemed to be withdrawing too, sinking in upon itself, the paint worn from the window frames, the walls stripped of the dead creeper, a slate or two missing from the roof. Once I had spoken to my father about the need for repairs, but he had only become angry so I learned to keep my conversations with him colorless. During my visits with my family he was always courteous to Bronwen but he never discussed her with me, and always, treating her as the nanny, he addressed her as Mrs. Morgan. With a cruelty that both enraged and staggered me, he took no notice of Evan at all.

"It's probably easier for him to pretend Evan isn't yours," said Bronwen, but I knew she was hurt. By that time Evan had fair hair, green eyes and a bright, intelligent little face. I thought any man would have been proud to have such a grandson, and I felt bitter.

When Evan was two, Bronwen said for the first time that she felt worried because he had no one to play with.

"He'll go to nursery school when he's older," I said.

"Yes—where everyone will know he's your bastard!" she cried and burst into tears.

The days were long since past when we could say to each other, "Everything will come right once we're married." I did start to say I would talk to Constance again, but Bronwen shouted, "You know bloody well that's useless!" and rushed upstairs to our room.

A very difficult conversation followed during which Bronwen admitted her unhappiness and said she thought I was unhappy too. I said I was unhappy only when I knew she was unhappy, and I offered to leave Gower to set up a home elsewhere.

"No, that would be disastrous." She spoke so promptly that I knew she had been dwelling on the idea for some time. "If we left it would mean that I'd cut you off entirely from your family and friends."

I no longer assured her that I wanted to be cut off. I merely said with truth: "I doubt that we can solve this problem by moving away because wherever we go people would eventually find out we weren't married, and then the trouble would begin all over again."

She said nothing. The silence deepened and suddenly I was so afraid that I could bear it no longer. Grabbing her to me so fiercely that she cried out with shock I shouted, "You mustn't go away, you mustn't leave, I won't let you go, I won't!"

She burst into tears again and said she couldn't. For a while we were silent, embracing each other, but still, as we both knew, nothing had been solved.

At last I said, "Tell me what I can do to make life more bearable for you. I'll do anything, anything at all."

"Do you truly mean that?"

"You know I do. I swear it."

She whispered, "I want another baby."

Conversation ceased again. As I released her and turned away, the silence was broken only by the rain drumming on the windowpane and the fire crackling in the grate.

"I wouldn't mind all the difficulties then," said Bronwen at last. "I'd have someone for Evan to play with, someone who would be there later when . . . when Evan goes away to school. Rhiannon and Dafydd will leave just as soon as they can, I know that now. They hate it here. I'm so worried about Dafydd that I'm even thinking of asking Gareth's family if he could board with them and finish his schooling in Cardiff. It would be better. He doesn't like you, he resents you because of the life we have to lead. . . . It's all so upsetting . . ." She paused but managed to check her tears. Presently she added: "Myfanwy's offered to have Rhiannon at the farm, and that might be better too. I'd hate it but I'd still see her every day and Rhiannon would be happier. . . . It's Marian, you see. Marian isn't always very kind."

"Oh, Marian's quite impossible," I said. "I'm well aware of that." I began to move around the room.

"You won't want another child, of course," she said, sensing my thoughts.

"Why should you? You don't need one. You have your work, your friends, your weekends at the golf club. You're not lonely, you're not isolated, you're not forced to watch your children growing away from you."

"No," I said, "I'm not. But if we have another baby that means we live openly together, and if you think we have difficulties now, all I can say is that they're nothing in comparison with the difficulties we'll have then."

"I shan't mind. If I have another baby I shan't mind anything, and anyway things couldn't be worse than they are now."

But I thought of Harry and Marian, no longer able to shelter behind the convention that Bronwen was their nanny. "I disagree," I said.

Bronwen lost her temper. A terrible interlude followed during which the full range of her misery and despair was finally revealed. She even said that although she was unable to imagine living without me, she was again tempted to emigrate to her cousins in Vancouver.

"Be quiet!" I shouted, overpowered by panic again as my worst suspicions were confirmed. "Don't you threaten me like that!"

"Then let me have a baby!"

"Oh, stop being so bloody selfish!"

We were a very long way now from those golden sunsets in St. Ives.

"You're the one who's being bloody selfish—all you can think of is what people will say if we live openly together—you're just a bloody upper-class snob after all!"

"Don't you talk of class to me and don't you call me a snob either! Have I ever complained that I can't dine at a civilized hour? Have I ever complained because you won't use the reception rooms and we have to spend all our time in this bloody bedroom which has come to look just like a bloody working-class parlor?"

She hit me. Then she screamed that she hated me.

I sank down on the bed. I was blind with pain but eventually I realized that she was sobbing, clinging to me, begging me to forgive her.

"For what? I'm the one to blame for your misery. It's all my fault." I opened the drawer of the bedside table, removed the contraceptives I kept there and walked to the door.

"Where are you going?" she said fearfully.

"To flush these down the lavatory."

Our second son was conceived less than a month later.

II

The hardest part to bear was the reaction of my family.

"Good God!" said Robert in disgust. "Is it too late for an abortion?"

I assume you don't want any congratulations, scrawled Edmund in reply to my letter, *so I won't offer any.*

Edmund tells me some truly appalling news, scribbled Celia from Heidelberg. *I am sorry—heavens above, just think what dearest Mama would have said. . . .*

"Well, we won't talk about it," said my father. "The less said the better. You'll be quite ruined now, of course, but we'll pretend I know nothing about it. I don't want to see Mrs. Morgan or her children anymore. Come to see me as usual on Sundays but only bring Harry and Marian with you."

"Christ, John," said Thomas, "imagine an old hand like you being caught out! What happened? Did the French letter break?"

There was only one answer I could make to all these comments and I made it. I said, "We wanted the child. It's not our fault we can't be married and now we've decided to live together without resorting to subterfuge."

After that my family somehow managed to preserve a tactful silence but Milly said to me, "You'll crucify that girl yet, dear. I'm surprised at you. I thought you had more sense."

I was so depressed by this comment that although Ginevra had just returned from a visit to London, I avoided Little Oxmoon because I felt unable to face yet another adverse reaction to the news of Bronwen's pregnancy. But the next morning Ginevra arrived to see us, her arms full of flowers, and Ginevra, brave Ginevra living always with death, cried radiantly, "Darlings—so exciting—another life coming into the world, I adore it!" and after she had kissed us both she looked me straight in the eyes and said, "Let me go back to London as soon as I can to talk to Constance. Let me see if there's anything I can do."

III

It was by that time the spring of 1927, and London was beginning to seem as remote to me as the moon. I no longer bothered myself with the parliamentary reports in *The Times.* I had lost interest after the General Strike the previous May. When that fizzled out I knew Britain would never change in my lifetime. There would be no revolution; class would be perpetuated—and this was obviously what the British wanted. People get the government they deserve, and now the Conservatives were firmly back in power.

I was a divided man again, "cleft in twain," visiting my estates in Herefordshire, playing the gentleman farmer restlessly at Penhale, writing to my stockbrokers about my investment portfolio—and living like a radical freethinker, defying the society in which I lived and hating its cruel conventions. Driven by the subtle but searing pressures of my divided life, I began to read as I had not read since leaving Oxford: voraciously and compulsively. To escape from the baffling and intractable nature of my problems, I trekked through history, I dabbled in philosophy, I even meddled futilely with religion, but all the time I knew there were no answers, and when Ginevra did go to London to see Constance I knew she had no hope of bringing unity to the two halves of my troubled life.

"That's an impossible woman, darling, truly awful," she said when she returned. "So dreary, no sense of humor and now she's gone all religious, saying God will punish you for breaking your sacred vows. Then she had the nerve to say: 'You're such a loyal and devoted wife—surely you must be on my side!' How I curbed my hysteria I can't imagine, but I did manage to point out soberly that loyalty and devotion can't flourish when the marriage is a prison, and when marriage is a prison it's no marriage at all. However that cut no ice, of course, and she just said it was her moral duty to be faithful to you until death. Julie says Constance is wallowing in religion in order to sublimate her sex drive—isn't that fun! Darling Freud, how did we all live without him in the old days . . ."

I thanked her for trying to help and then realized that she had more news, although she was uncertain how to impart it. "I saw Francesca—such a poppet though not much like either of you yet," she said tentatively at last. "But you should see Edmund's Richard! Such a look of Lion, really quite extraordinary . . . oh, and talking of Lion, darling, that reminds me: I saw Daphne in London."

"Oh yes?" I said, trying not to sound hostile. I knew Ginevra was fond of Daphne, and at once I could picture them having tea at the Ritz, discussing my situation and trying to work out what on earth could be done to save Marian.

"I told her," said Ginevra carefully, "that Harry would stop doing lessons with Kester and go off to prep school this autumn now that he's eight, and Daphne said she was going to send Elizabeth away this autumn too—to St. Astrith's in Surrey. Apparently it's such a good school and the girls have such a jolly time there and Daphne's sure Elizabeth will adore it—like me Daphne herself hated being educated at home with a governess, so she's just as keen as I am on boarding school for girls, and . . . well, suddenly, darling, we had this very exciting idea: why doesn't Marian go with Elizabeth to St. Astrith's? You know what friends they are, and it would be such fun for them . . . and let's be honest, Johnny, wouldn't it be better from your point of view as well as Marian's? I remember how I felt about Declan and Rory when I was first married to Robert. I adored them but whenever they appeared on the scene Robert and I were quite wrecked. I know school was a disaster for Declan, but Rory loved it in the end and it really was the best solution—for everyone."

"Yes," I said. I found I could say nothing else.

"You're in favor?"

"Yes."

"Shall I have a word with Marian for you?"

But I knew I had to tell Marian myself. I thought she might make a fuss, but after allowing herself one grand tantrum during which I was accused of wanting to get rid of her in order to wipe out her mother's memory, she was prepared to believe I did have her welfare in mind.

"How nice it'll be to mix with girls of my own sort at last!" she said satisfied. "All the girls I know at school at the moment are really rather middle-class, you know, Papa, but I'm sure things will be quite different at a lovely posh boarding school. I wonder how many titled girls there'll be in my form?"

"Probably none. They'll all be at home with their governesses."

"Divine for them," said Marian, borrowing as effortlessly from Ginevra's speech mannerisms as she did from Daphne's. "But then I don't suppose they come from homes where the nanny and the master of the house sleep in the same bedroom and have babies without being married."

She stood there, not yet twelve years old, blond, blue-eyed and outwardly the picture of innocence. My one thought, as I fought back the desire to strike her, was how horrified Blanche would have been if she could have seen us.

"I'm afraid I can't allow you to pass that sort of remark, Marian," I said politely at last, "and I'm only surprised that you should have seen fit to make it. I would have expected you to shun such vulgarity."

"Aunt Daphne thinks it's a wonder I'm not more vulgar, considering the example I've been set."

I did not seriously believe that Daphne had passed such a remark in Marian's presence, but I had no doubt I was hearing an accurate reflection of her sentiments.

"Marian, is it really your intention to make me very angry?" I said, but I knew it was. Marian was angry herself and wanted the chance to scream and shout at me. However it was not until the baby was born that she egged me into losing my temper.

The baby was healthy and good-looking for a newborn infant, pink-and-white with dark hair and a soft bloom on his cheeks. We both wanted a Welsh name so Bronwen chose Geraint. Marian said the name was quite ghastly and very common (that was when I lost my temper with her), and Harry said he hated it and would call the baby Gerry instead. We tried to persuade him to retain the hard Welsh G but he refused, and soon we found that our English-speaking acquaintances were following his example.

"Well, at least he won't be christened Gerry," said Bronwen. That was before she realized there would be no christening. Anstey the vicar had christened Evan without a murmur because he had believed him to be Gareth Morgan's son, but I knew he could not condone my union with Bronwen by christening its patently illegitimate offspring. I did talk to him but Anstey had a stubborn streak beneath his inoffensive manners, and he pointed out that if he were to perform the ceremony the entire population of Penhale would be outraged.

"Well, if that's Mr. Anstey's attitude," blazed Bronwen, "I don't want the baby christened at all!"

"Neither do I," I said strongly, but I knew she was upset, just as I knew that more upsetting events were sure to follow.

A stream of abusive anonymous letters was followed by an act of vandalism; someone daubed in red paint on the wall by the gates: BROTHEL—WHORES AND BASTARDS ONLY. Because of my private life I had not volunteered to be a magistrate, but I made sure the bench handed out a stiff sentence when the village constable and I succeeded in tracking down the vandals responsible for the outrage.

Two maids had to be sacked for insolence but Mrs. Wells stood by us and prevented a collapse within the household. Eventually the village quietened down but by this time the scandal had traveled to the far end of Gower and when I next entered the golf-club bar all conversation abruptly ceased.

I had become a pariah again. This made me feel particularly bitter because I had been on the point of being offered a directorship in a shipping firm and I knew now the offer would never be made. It made me realize too how much I had been looking forward to returning to the world of commerce. 1927 had turned into another disastrously wet year, and to make matters worse the spring months had been abnormally cold. I saw the ruin of my cereal crop again and I was thoroughly disillusioned with farming.

In an effort to divert myself from the knowledge that I was trapped in a way of life which was failing to satisfy me, I embarked on a restless search for occupations that would fill my hours of spare time. I arranged for electricity to be installed in the house. Then I studied the subject of electricity so that I would know what to do if the power failed. I read more voraciously than ever. But despite these diversions the time that meant most to me was the time I spent with Robert. I had always called on him every day but now I found myself staying longer because he alone could assuage the loneliness which for Bronwen's sake I struggled to keep concealed.

"I despise myself for caring what people think of me," I said when I told him I had become a pariah again, "but what I care about is not so much being cut off from the company of my own sort but being cut off from any hope of leading a more interesting life in my working hours."

"I'll have a word with Alun," said Robert. Alun Bryn-Davies had been a contemporary of his at Harrow. "He's on the board of Suez Petro-Chemicals as well as the Madog Collieries. Maybe he can help."

So I lunched with Bryn-Davies at the new Claremont Hotel, and after I had made sure the luncheon was a success, he asked me to play golf with him. Following the game we adjourned to the bar and this time no one cut me; in fact when Bryn-Davies bought me a drink the members realized it was still possible to treat me as normal, and later, when I was offered a directorship of Aswan Products, which was a subsidiary of Suez Petro-Chemicals, they even accepted that I was employable. Yet the directorship was modest, demanding my presence only on one afternoon a week at the company's headquarters in Swansea, and I still found myself wrestling too often with boredom and frustration.

"How naive I was," I said to Robert one day as I spooned up his food for him, "to imagine that Bronwen could solve all my problems. I'm beginning to realize my major problem is that I've never found my true *métier.*"

"Your *métier,*" said Robert, "is organization and making executive decisions. It probably doesn't matter much what business you wind up in so long as it's large and challenging."

In acknowledgment of the shrewdness of this observation I said depressed, "Well, you always said I was unsuited to a rural backwater, and how right you were."

"You're certainly unsuited for confinement in a rural backwater but that's not necessarily the same thing as saying you're unsuited to country life. Ideally, I suspect, you should be able to fuse your country background with your talent for executive management—maybe your true *métier* is indeed to be a farm manager, but on a large twentieth-century scale."

"You mean I should have about ten small estates and roam around supervising them all?"

"Ten small estates," said Robert, "or one big one."

We fell silent as the image of Oxmoon slipped between us. Food dribbled from his mouth but I quickly mopped it up with a napkin. When I had finished he said, "Can't you combine managing Penhale Manor with a more active management of your farms in Herefordshire?"

"Not without leaving Bronwen on her own frequently, and as things stand at present that's quite impossible." I tried to change the subject. "But don't let's talk of the present," I said. "Let's go back into the past." For we spent much time now talking of the times that were gone, not the near past of the war but the extreme past, the golden past, the fairy-tale past of Edwardian Oxmoon. We talked of the dances in the ballroom and the tennis parties on the lawn and the expeditions to the Downs and the sea and the village shop in Penhale, and although in the past the ten years' difference in our ages had separated us, we now found that time had encircled us so that his experiences could fuse with mine.

" 'In my beginning is my end,' " said Robert.

"Who said that?"

"It was the motto of Mary Queen of Scots. My motto would be to reverse those words and say, 'In my end is my beginning.' I feel so strongly that when there's no more future the present fades away and only the past is real."

We were silent, both thinking of Oxmoon again, and suddenly I knew that he was as aware as I was of that terrible ambiguity in my mind. I turned to him; I turned not merely to my brother but to my guide, my mentor and above all else my friend; I turned to him and I opened my mouth and I tried to say "Help me," but the words refused to be spoken. My ambiguity was so terrible to me that I feared I might never overcome it once I had formally acknowledged it in speech.

So I said nothing. But he knew. He could no longer reach out to take my hand in his, but I felt his mind flowing powerfully into mine.

After a moment he said, "In the beginning—my beginning—there was Oxmoon and it was a magic house. I tried to tell Kester that the other day. 'You're going to get this magic house,' I said, 'and you've got to put the magic back into it.' All my life I've wanted to do that, John, and now I never shall, but I can live with that knowledge—die with that knowledge—if I believe Kester will do it instead of me."

"I understand."

"I don't believe in a life after death," said Robert. "I don't believe human beings are capable of resurrection. But if Kester puts the magic back into my magic house then Oxmoon will *rise again* on the Wheel of Fortune, and *that* will be my resurrection; it'll be my redemption too because Kester will be so grateful to me for securing his inheritance for him and all my past neglect of him will be wiped out—and that means everything to me now, John, everything, I'm no longer extorting Oxmoon from Papa in revenge for the past, I'm extorting it to pass Kester the future which has been denied me and to give meaning to my death."

Robert was normally neither an emotional nor an imaginative man. Nor was he in the habit of baring his soul. Suddenly I realized that in an effort to demolish my ambiguity he had thrust the whole weight of his trust upon me, and I was dumb; I could only grope for his crippled hands to show that I wanted what he wanted, and for a moment his vision of Oxmoon united us, an Oxmoon radiant and restored, triumphing over the ravages of time.

"Well, so much for that," said Robert briskly with an alteration of mood so abrupt that I jumped. "Man cannot live on romantic sentimentality alone— thank God—and now that I've had my wallow I think I'd better get down to business. My dear John, how strong are you feeling? The truth is I'm in the devil of a mess and I'm afraid I'm going to have to ask you to rescue me."

IV

When I had recovered my equilibrium I said in great alarm, "What in God's name are you talking about? What kind of a mess?"

"A legal mess, naturally. Lawyers are notorious for making a cock-up of their legal affairs."

"But what on earth have you done?"

"It's not what I've done, it's what I've failed to do." Robert paused. Speech was no longer easy for him and the impairment, which gave his words a distorted staccato ring, was becoming more pronounced. I found myself leaning forward in my chair to make sure I heard him properly. "John, when Papa gave me Martinscombe back in 1919 there was no deed of gift. There were two reasons. First, it seemed unnecessary, since although I knew I was ill I had every intention of outliving Papa and inheriting Martinscombe along with the rest of Oxmoon when he died. And second, Papa was in a peculiar tax position at the time and needed Martinscombe for a year or two to set himself straight. So our arrangement was informal—always a fatal mistake."

"Fatal. But didn't you try to put matters right later?"

"Yes, but can't you imagine what happened? He couldn't face the increasingly obvious fact that I was going to die before he was, and he started talking about how he'd have to discuss the situation with Margaret. Having a pardonable horror of seeing him demented I then shied off. Time drifted by. However, goaded on quite rightly by Ginette, I nerved myself last month to dictate a letter to him on the subject. Back came a polite reply to the effect that he preferred to keep the estate together and that as Kester was the heir anyway, why not leave matters as they were. But you see the problem, don't you?"

"All too clearly. When you die Ginevra and Kester will have no legal right to remain here, and Papa may well be more unreliable than ever."

"Exactly. I detect the hand of Straker in this polite but profoundly unsatisfactory letter from Papa. She may not want the bungalow for her old age, but I can quite see her fancying the idea of letting it and pocketing the income."

"So can I. Very well, what's to be done?"

"Land Registration's been in force since the Act of '25. I want Martinscombe registered in my name, and I'll give you a power of attorney so that you can deal with the Land Registry on my behalf. Ginette's power of attorney is no use here; the Land Registry might look too closely at the matter if they knew they were dealing with a woman."

"Well, I'll certainly do all I can to help you, Robert, but how can you register something that's not legally yours?"

"That's the difficulty," said Robert, and beyond his speech impairment I heard the echo of a lawyer who was gliding with consummate skill around some very awkward facts. "We have two choices here. Either we involve Papa or we don't. If we involve him he'd have to sign a letter of authorization—at the very least; the Land Registry might well insist on seeing a formal deed of gift. However as Papa won't discuss the estate with you and has proved himself highly evasive with me, this doesn't seem to be a feasible course of action."

"What's the alternative?"

"We take matters into our own hands."

"I'm not sure I'm too keen on this, Robert."

"My dear John, to quote one of Mama's most notorious phrases, it's the right thing—indeed the only thing—to do. How else can I protect my wife and son from a predator like Straker?"

"All right, go on."

"I think I can see a solution based on the fact that Papa and I have the same name. We'll approach the Land Registry and ask for Martinscombe Farm to be registered in the name of Robert Charles Godwin. That'll include the bungalow, which is still legally on the Martinscombe lands."

"Yes, but—"

"I'll engage a London firm of solicitors whom I've never used before and ask them to attend to the formalities of the registration—the documents, fees and so on. Then when the Registry issues a certificate I can lodge it with my normal solicitors in Lincoln's Inn. Once that's done I ostensibly have a title which I can devise by will, and if I behave as if I'm the legal owner of Martinscombe by remaking my will to include it, no one in London will question the ownership when I die. My new will will be granted probate, the title will be reregistered and there's no reason why either Papa or Fairfax's firm in Swansea should ever find out about it—unless Papa goes completely insane, Straker tries to evict Ginette and the deed has to surface to prove Kester's title. And all that may never happen. This is purely a defensive measure, not an act of aggrandizement."

"If Papa does go completely insane, surely Ginevra would have a legal remedy?"

"His sanity would still be a debatable issue. No, I'm taking no chances—if there's even the faintest possibility that Ginette might lose her case in court, I don't want her involved with the law at all."

"Fair enough, but I still don't see how you're going to get around this without involving Papa. Surely the Land Registry will want proof of title?"

"That's not a problem. I'll simply ask Fairfax, who as the Oxmoon solicitor has the Oxmoon deeds in his safekeeping, to lend me the Martinscombe abstract of title—or whatever documents the Land Registry needs. I'll say there's a point I want to establish in relation to my son's inheritance, and

Fairfax isn't going to refuse me. In fact I may even improve on that story in order to keep the deeds in my possession. I'm sure that's well within my capabilities."

I ignored this chilling reference to the potential acrobatics of a legally trained mind. "And meanwhile," I said, working the scheme out, "the abstract of title will say the farm belongs to Robert Charles Godwin—"

"—and the Land Registry will innocently assume that's me and not Papa. Don't worry, John, this is nothing serious. It's just a little muddle over a name."

In such a manner might my mother have suggested my father's fatal juggling with the tide tables.

"My dear Robert, you appall me."

"I appall myself. But you answer me this: what the devil else can I do?"

I had no idea. I was silent, trying to consider the morality of the situation clearly. At last I said, "In my opinion it's unarguable that you have a moral right to that property—Papa intended in 1919 that it should be yours."

"Exactly. To square your conscience you can think of this as legalizing Papa's wishes."

"And since the estate will go to Kester anyway," I pursued, plowing doggedly on, "it doesn't matter whether he inherits Martinscombe from you soon or from Papa later. No one's being defrauded."

Robert hesitated. I looked at him sharply, but decided he was having trouble with his speech. His facial muscles were paralyzed so there was no expression for me to read. In the end he just said, "People will get what they deserve. Justice will be done."

" 'Fiat justitia!' " I quoted, smiling at him, but he was too exhausted to reply. Ringing the bell for Bennett I said, "Don't worry. I'll arrange everything" and heard him whisper back, "You're the best brother a man ever had."

I only hoped I could live up to his opinion of me. I had no doubt that I was doing the right thing by helping Robert protect Ginevra and Kester, but once I started manipulating the legal ownership of property I felt I was on dangerous ground indeed.

V

"That stupid sissyish baby Kester said such a silly thing to me today," said Harry, wandering up as I tinkered with the engine of my motor to distract myself from my worries. "He says he's going to inherit Oxmoon! Imagine!" And he laughed with scorn and took a large bite out of the apple in his hand.

I straightened my back to look at him. He was within days of his ninth birthday, and although he took after his mother in looks, he had a bold adventurous personality which reminded me of myself when I had been Johnny long ago, living dangerously with Lion at Oxmoon. After my own experiences as a child I strongly disapproved of parents who had favorites but secretly, in my unguarded moments, I felt Harry was quite perfect. He was very good-looking, very clever, very athletic, very well mannered and very personable, and I often felt sad that Blanche was not alive to share my joy in him.

"I told Kester quite frankly," he was saying as he munched his apple, "that he hadn't a hope of inheriting. 'Tough luck, old chap,' I said, not wanting to be too beastly, 'but that's one yarn you simply can't spin.' And do you know what he did, Papa? He laughed! He said 'I know something you don't know!' and he stuck out his tongue at me. Of course, never having been away to school he's just pampered and spoiled, and he can't help behaving like an idiot, I realize that. But all the same . . . I thought it was pretty peculiar behavior. Everyone knows Uncle Robert's dying, and everyone knows that when Uncle Robert's dead you'll be Grandfather's eldest surviving son. So that means you'll get Oxmoon eventually, doesn't it? And then I'll get it after you."

I glanced down at the complicated engine of my motor. I glanced at the damp cobbles of the stable yard, at the newly painted water butt, at the oil stains on my hands. I glanced everywhere except at Harry, shining perfect Harry who deserved everything a devoted father could give him. Several seconds ticked by. Then I picked up a nearby rag, wiped my hands and said, "Oxmoon passes from eldest son to eldest son, Harry, so Kester will inherit from Uncle Robert even though Uncle Robert may die before Grandfather."

Silence.

"You mean that's the done thing?" said Harry at last.

"Yes," I said. "It's the done thing. Grandfather has an absolute moral duty to leave Oxmoon to Kester."

"Oh, I see," said Harry. "I didn't realize." He stood looking at the apple in his hand. Then he threw the core away, said carelessly, "Well, never mind, I like the Manor much better than Oxmoon anyway" and skipped off across the cobbles.

I remember thinking with enormous relief that at least I had one child who never gave me a moment's anxiety.

VI

Christmas had become a bad time of the year for my father, and the Christmas of 1927 was no exception. When I arrived on Christmas afternoon with Thomas, Harry and Marian to pay our traditional call, we found he was in bed and seeing no one.

Against Milly's advice, I went up to his room.

"I'm not receiving you while you live openly with that woman and father bastards," he said when he saw me. "I don't suppose my disapproval will bring you to your senses, but I've made up my mind I must try and save you. I can't stand by passively while you ruin yourself."

Ironically this view reflected my own sentiments about him, but as there was no way the conversation could be prolonged I was obliged to leave.

In the new year Warburton said, "John, I think you ought to know I've been hearing rumors that your father's insane. Apparently there's a lot of discontent on the estate."

I had heard similar stories from Thomas, who mixed more with the local population than I could, but Warburton's words carried more weight with me. "I'll talk to Robert," I said automatically. "I'll see what he thinks I should do."

"No," said Warburton. "He mustn't be worried by your father's situation anymore—he's too ill. I'm sorry, John, but the moment's finally come: you're on your own."

The Wheel had become a rack, Fortune was tightening the screws and amidst all my grief I was aware of an overpowering fear that my courage would be insufficient to meet the ordeal that I could now so clearly see ahead.

But I had to conquer that fear. I could not allow myself to be defeated because too many people depended on me.

I struggled on.

VII

Again I saw Freddy Fairfax, the senior partner in the firm of Swansea solicitors who handled the Oxmoon estate. When I had seen him previously he had assured me he would let me know if ever he thought my father showed signs of being legally incompetent, but since then I had heard nothing from him.

Fairfax was in his late forties, a smooth sleek able and not unpleasant individual with whom I played golf occasionally at weekends. His reputation was good. Certainly I had never heard any story that reflected on either his honesty or his competence, and although he might have shunned me during my days as a pariah this was no reason why I should have distrusted his professional judgment.

"I'm worried about my father again," I said after we had exchanged preliminary greetings in his office. "Have you seen him lately?"

"I was over at Oxmoon the other day, old boy. Couple of new tenancy agreements needed. He seemed very much in the pink. Not quite the man he used to be, of course, but old age gets to us all in the end, what?"

"Have you heard rumors of trouble on the estate?"

"Rumors, old boy?"

"Well, you are the estate's solicitor, Fairfax! I assume you have your ear close to the ground!"

"Old boy, I hate to say this because I know you're well intentioned, but I really don't think I can discuss my client's affairs with you."

I persisted but got nowhere and eventually, profoundly skeptical, I left him and drove to Oxmoon.

VIII

"I won't receive you," said my father. "Please leave at once."

"I only want to help."

"I don't want your help. You're not to be trusted—you broke your word to me. You swore you wouldn't live openly with her."

"Surely despite my private life you can accept that my affection for you is genuine?"

"What if it is? My mother's affection for me was genuine too, but my God, what hell she put me through! Her spirit's possessed you, I can see that clearly now; you're her, you've come back to torment me, you've got to be kept out—"

"Papa—"

"Stay away from me!"

I left.

IX

"What can I do, Ginevra? Fairfax swears he's normal. He won't see Warburton, won't talk to me. Obviously he's mentally ill but how the devil do I get him certified?"

"My dear, what horrors, but I can't cope. I've got a mountain of horrors of my own."

"Oh, God, forgive me, I'm so sorry—"

"He can't bear being blind, he simply can't bear it. . . ."

She broke down, I took her in my arms and the darkness seemed to close over us as if we had been walled up alive in a tomb.

X

Five days later on Lady Day a band of tenants from the Oxmoon estate marched to see Robert to protest at the new steep increases in their rents. Treating my father as incompetent they had turned to his heir for justice, and when they found Robert was too ill to see anyone they refused to disperse. The telephone call came from Ginevra just as I returned to the Manor from the Home Farm, and taking Thomas with me I drove immediately to Little Oxmoon.

We found about thirty men encamped before the bungalow. They appeared peaceful enough at first glance, but as I halted the car they surged forward to surround it and I saw their mood was ugly.

"Keep your mouth shut," I said to Thomas, "and leave this entirely to me."

I noticed that the majority of the men were farm laborers who lived in my father's Penhale cottages, but when I saw that my father's foremen too were present, I knew the rise in rent was merely the straw which had broken the camel's back. Clearly this was the climax of years of increasing maladministration.

I got out of the car. The hostility seemed to thicken. I experienced a moment of acute uneasiness, but told myself their hostility could not be directed against me personally.

The next moment I was disillusioned.

"Here comes the adulterer!" said someone, and that was followed by the comment "We finally managed to get him out of bed!" There was contemptuous laughter. Someone spat at me. Flicking the spittle aside I pushed my way through the crowd, reached the doorstep and turned to address them. Cold sweat was inching down my spine.

"Good afternoon," I said strongly, projecting my voice to override the hostile mutterings. My mind, sharpened by shock, was darting in a dozen different directions at once. I was remembering the bullies at school and the necessity of displaying no fear which would heighten their pleasure, but I felt shattered, vulnerable and, most ambivalent of all, enraged that I should be judged in this fashion by men who should have been doffing their caps to me with respect. A second later, however, I saw that the class system could work in my favor and that this time all the bayonets would be on my side.

"If you want the justice you deserve," I said, "you'll treat me with the respect to which I'm entitled. I'm well intentioned but I refuse to negotiate with a rabble."

They stared at me. I saw their faces, young and old, still hostile but recog-

468

nizing an age-old authority which the twentieth century had so far been unable to destroy. Mentally congratulating myself on this successful assertion of my strength, I thought with a bitter humor, That's the spirit that built the Empire! And I was still savoring my restored confidence when someone threw a clod of mud which hit me in the chest.

That was undoubtedly the spirit which had led to the General Strike. It occurred to me that the age-old authority was wearing thin after all.

"Very well," I said calmly, heart thudding like a sledgehammer. "If you're determined to be a rabble I can't help you. Good day." I stepped down from the doorstep and tried to walk away, but Thornton, the foreman at Cherryvale, intervened.

"Wait, Mr. John." He turned to the others. "We must deal with him; there's no one else." And he thrust a list of grievances into my hand.

Immediately a confused babble broke out, during which I heard the words "extortion," "bare-faced robbery" and "that witch Milly Straker."

"We mean no disrespect to your father, Mr. John," said Thornton hurriedly, "but the old gentleman's well known now to be at the mercy of others, and One Other in particular."

I returned to the doorstep, and when everyone was quiet I said, "My brother's dying. I must ask you to leave him in peace. But if you can elect three men to come to Oxmoon at sunset, I'll examine these grievances one by one and see what can be done."

They were satisfied. Thornton, who was evidently one of nature's diplomats, pulled off his cap and thanked me with a humility which both appeased and nauseated me. Someone in the crowd said, "How's the wife in London?" but a dozen other voices said furiously, "Shhh!" and I pretended not to hear.

Seconds later I was driving away.

"My God, you were wonderful, John!" said Thomas, who was enjoying himself immensely. "As good as Jesus Christ!"

I said nothing. I was suffering from a nervous reaction, and I had to grip the wheel hard to stop my hands trembling. Nausea churned spasmodically in the pit of my stomach.

As soon as we reached Oxmoon I knew something was wrong, and when I saw the stigmata of violence I found I was bathed in a cold sweat again. Evidently the loutish sons of the disgruntled tenants had not been idle. The windows of the library had been smashed and a slogan had been daubed on the wall by the front door.

" 'WORKERS OF THE WORLD UNITE,' " mused Thomas. "Haven't I heard that before somewhere?"

I told myself that I had wanted class war and now I was getting it. In a detached manner which sprang from shock I realized that my primary emotion was again rage. I wanted to shoot every socialist in sight. So much for my intellectual radicalism. Apparently in a crisis reason and humanity counted for nothing and man's instinct was to return to the pack that had bred him. I knew then that at heart I was never going to change. I was what my class had made me; I was the victim of my education, the prisoner of my privileged life; all else was illusion and self-deception.

"My God!" cried Thomas, who had just seen the broken windows. "Look at that! Wait till I get my hands on whoever did it; I'll smash the bastards to pulp!"

I thought how pleasant it must be to have such a simple outlook, untroubled by any intellectual doubts or emotional complexities.

"Calm down, Thomas. We've got enough bulls in this particular china shop without you trying to join them." I was wondering if the mob was inside, wrecking everything in sight, but as we jumped out of the car the front door was opened by the village constable.

"Oh Mr. John, thank God you've come—"

"Where's my father?"

"I don't know, sir; he seems to have disappeared, but Mr. Bayliss summoned me half an hour ago when the windows were smashed—"

"Where is Bayliss?"

"He came over poorly, sir, and had to lie down. All the other servants have locked themselves in the kitchens and won't come out."

"And Mrs. Straker?"

"They say she's gone, sir—slipped out at first light. Maybe she knew there'd be trouble, sir, today being the quarter day and people so upset with the new rents."

"Very well, go with my brother, search the grounds and make sure all the vandals have gone."

I went into the house. The servants, cowering in the scullery, unlocked the door when they heard my voice. I asked if anyone had seen my father. No one had.

"Very well." I turned to the cook. "Make some tea." I swung round on the footman. "See how Bayliss is and if necessary telephone for Dr. Warburton." I faced the parlormaid. "Send word to the glazier. I want those windows replaced immediately." My glance fell on the daily housemaids. "Clear up the mess in the library at once." At the door I stopped to look back. "I authorize a finger of brandy for everyone," I said, "and once that's been taken and the tea drunk, I shall expect everyone to go about their business as usual."

Leaving them all bobbing and curtsying, I returned to the hall and ran upstairs. The bedrooms were all empty but as I reached the back stairs I suddenly knew where he was.

The attics were musty and still. I called, "Papa!" and waited but there was no answer. I walked down the corridor, my footsteps echoing on the floorboards, and found him where I had found him before. He was sitting by the covered portrait of his mother and this time the photograph albums were open in his hands.

He was crying quietly to himself. He barely looked up as I entered the room.

"Papa," I said, stooping to put an arm around his shoulders, "it's all right now, I'm here."

But my father only went on turning the pages of the first album, and in that flickering kaleidoscope of black-and-white I saw the past recaptured, the happy laughing children of long ago, the wife he had loved and the magic house he had resurrected from the grave.

"Papa . . ." As I slid my hand over his, the pages of the album stopped turning and he looked up at me at last. But his watery eyes remained bewildered and all he could say was "Who are you?"